S0-AJB-461

WITHDRAWN

World Cultures
AND
GEOGRAPHY

Western Hemisphere and Europe

McDOUGAL LITTELL

McDOUGAL LITTELL

World Cultures AND GEOGRAPHY

Western Hemisphere and Europe

Sarah Witham Bednarz

Inés M. Miyares

Mark C. Schug

Charles S. White

McDougal Littell

Evanston, Illinois • Boston • Dallas

CURR
LB
1584
W668
2003

Senior Consultants

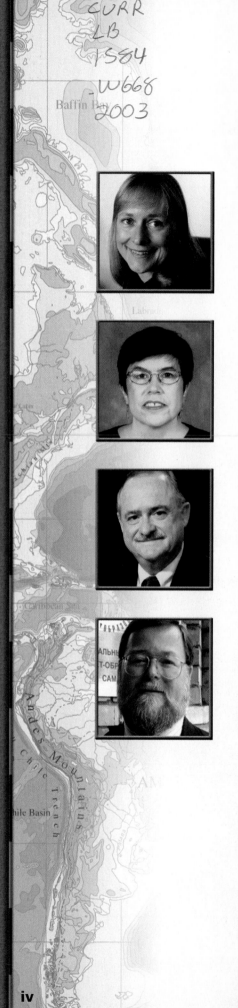

Sarah Witham Bednarz is associate professor of geography at Texas A&M University, where she has taught since 1988. She earned a Ph.D. in educational curriculum and instruction in 1992 from Texas A&M University and has written extensively about geography literacy and education. Dr. Bednarz was an author of *Geography for Life: National Geography Standards,* 1994. In 1997 she received the International Excellence Award from the Texas A&M University International Programs Office.

Inés M. Miyares is associate professor of geography at Hunter College–City University of New York. Born in Havana, Cuba, and fluent in Spanish, Dr. Miyares has focused much of her scholarship on Latin America, immigration and refugee policy, and urban ethnic geography. She holds a Ph.D. in geography from Arizona State University. In 1999 Dr. Miyares was the recipient of the Hunter College Performance Excellence Award for excellence in teaching, research, scholarly writing, and service.

Mark C. Schug is director of the University of Wisconsin–Milwaukee Center for Economic Education. A 30-year veteran of middle school, high school, and university classrooms, Dr. Schug has been cited for excellence in teaching by the University of Wisconsin–Milwaukee and the Minnesota Council on Economic Education. In addition to coauthoring eight national economics curriculum programs, Dr. Schug has spoken on economic issues to audiences throughout the world. Dr. Schug edited *The Senior Economist* for the National Council for Economics Education from 1986 to 1996.

Charles S. White is associate professor in the School of Education at Boston University, where he teaches methods of instruction in social studies. Dr. White has written and spoken extensively on the role of technology in social studies education. He has received numerous awards for his scholarship, including the 1995 Federal Design Achievement Award from the National Endowment for the Arts, for the Teaching with Historic Places project. In 1997, Dr. White taught his Models of Teaching doctoral course at the Universidad San Francisco de Quito, Ecuador.

Copyright © 2003 by McDougal Littell, a division of Houghton Mifflin Company. All rights reserved.

The USA TODAY® service mark has been licensed by USA TODAY® for use for certain purposes by McDougal Littell, a division of Houghton Mifflin Company. USA TODAY® charts and articles, incorporated in these reading materials are displayed for informational and promotional purposes only. The USA TODAY® charts, articles, and photographs incorporated herein are solely for private, personal, and noncommercial use. Any other use of the USA TODAY® charts, articles, and photographs incorporated herein, without prior express written permission of USA TODAY®, is strictly prohibited.

Maps on pages A1-A25 © Rand McNally & Company. All rights reserved.

No part of this work may be reproduced or transmitted in any form or by any means, electronic or mechanical, including photocopying and recording, or by any information storage or retrieval system without the prior written permission of McDougal Littell, a division of Houghton Mifflin Company, unless such copying is expressly permitted by federal copyright law. Send inquiries to Manager, Rights and Permissions, McDougal Littell, a division of Houghton Mifflin Company, P.O. Box 1667, Evanston, IL 60204.

Acknowledgments begin on page R31.

ISBN 0-618-20352-4

Printed in the United States of America
4 5 6 7 8 9 – VJM – 07 06 05 04 03

094903

Consultants and Reviewers

Content Consultants

Charmarie Blaisdell
Department of History
Northeastern University
Boston, Massachusetts

David Buck, Ph.D.
Department of History
University of Wisconsin–Milwaukee
Milwaukee, Wisconsin

Erich Gruen, Ph.D.
Departments of Classics and History
University of California, Berkeley
Berkeley, California

Charles Haynes, Ph.D.
Senior Scholar for Religious Freedom
The Freedom Forum First
    Amendment Center
Arlington, Virginia

Alusine Jalloh, Ph.D.
The Africa Program
University of Texas at Arlington
Arlington, Texas

Shabbir Mansuri
Council on Islamic Education
Fountain Valley, California

Michelle Maskiell, Ph.D.
Department of History
Montana State University
Bozeman, Montana

Vasudha Narayanan, Ph.D.
Department of Religion
University of Florida
Gainesville, Florida

Amanda Porterfield, Ph.D.
Department of Religious Studies
University of Wyoming
Laramie, Wyoming

Mark Wasserman, Ph.D.
Department of History
Rutgers University
New Brunswick, New Jersey

Multicultural Advisory Board

Dr. Munir Bashshur
Education Department
American University of Beirut
Beirut, Lebanon

Stephen Fugita
Ethnic Studies Program
Santa Clara University
Santa Clara, California

Sharon Harley
Afro-American Studies Program
University of Maryland at
    College Park
College Park, Maryland

Doug Monroy
Department of Southwest Studies
Colorado College
Colorado Springs, Colorado

Cliff Trafzer
Departments of History and
    Ethnic Studies
University of California, Riverside
Riverside, California

UNIT 1 Introduction to World Cultures and Geography

Asia
Europe
North America
PANGAEA
Africa
South America
Australia
Antarctica

UNIT 2 The United States and Canada

UNIT 4

Europe, Russia, and the Independent Republics

continued from page ix

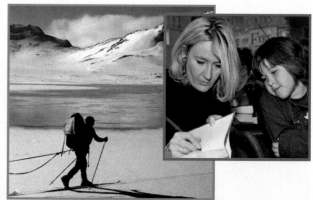

Features

SKILLBUILDER

Citizenship IN ACTION

Strange but TRUE

Connections To...

MAPS

CHARTS, DIAGRAMS, AND GRAPHS

This section will help you develop and practice the skills you need to study social studies and to take standardized tests. Part 1, **Strategies for Studying Social Studies,** shows you the features of this book. It also shows you how to improve your reading and study skills.

Part 2, **Test-Taking Strategies and Practice,** gives you strategies to help you answer the different kinds of questions that appear on standardized tests. Each strategy is followed by a set of questions you can use for practice.

CONTENTS

Part 1: Strategies for Studying Social Studies

Reading is important in the study of social studies or any other subject. You can improve your reading skills by practicing certain strategies. Good reading skills help you remember more when you read. The next four pages show how some of the features of *World Cultures and Geography: Western Hemisphere* can help you learn and understand social studies.

Preview Chapters Before You Read

Each chapter begins with a two-page chapter opener. Study these pages to help you get ready to read.

1 Read the chapter title. Read the section titles. These tell what topics will be covered in the chapter.

2 Look at the art and photographs. Use the illustrations to help you identify themes or messages of the chapter.

3 Study the **Focus on Geography** feature. Use the questions to help you think about the information you might find in the chapter.

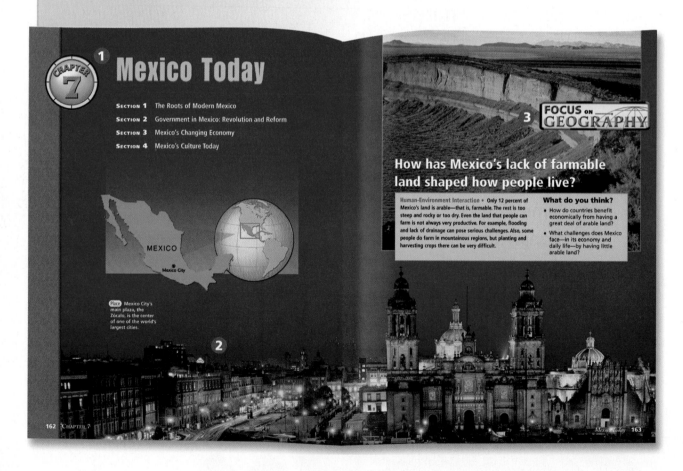

CHAPTER **1** **Mexico Today**

SECTION 1   The Roots of Modern Mexico
SECTION 2   Government in Mexico: Revolution and Reform
SECTION 3   Mexico's Changing Economy
SECTION 4   Mexico's Culture Today

MEXICO

Mexico City

Place Mexico City's main plaza, the Zócalo, is the center of one of the world's largest cities.

2

3 FOCUS ON GEOGRAPHY

How has Mexico's lack of farmable land shaped how people live?

Human-Environment Interaction • Only 12 percent of Mexico's land is arable—that is, farmable. The rest is too steep and rocky or too dry. Even the land that people can farm is not always very productive. For example, flooding and lack of drainage can pose serious challenges. Also, some people do farm in mountainous regions, but planting and harvesting crops there can be very difficult.

What do you think?

♦ How do countries benefit economically from having a great deal of arable land?

♦ What challenges does Mexico face—in its economy and daily life—by having little arable land?

162 CHAPTER 7

Mexico Today 163

Preview Sections Before You Read

Each chapter has three, four, or five sections. These sections cover shorter time periods or certain themes.

1 Study the sentences under the headings **Main Idea** and **Why It Matters Now.** These headings tell what's important in the material you're about to read.

2 Look at the **Terms & Names** list. This list tells you what people and issues will be covered in the section.

3 Read the feature titled **Dateline.** It tells about a historical event as if it were happening today.

4 Skim the pages to see how the section is organized. Red headings are major topics. Blue headings are smaller topics or subtopics. The headings provide an outline of the section.

5 Skim the pages of the section to find key words. These words will often be in **boldface** type. Use the **Vocabulary** notes in the margin to help you with unfamiliar terms.

TERMS & NAMES
peninsulares
criollos
mestizo
encomienda
Father Miguel Hidalgo
Treaty of Guadalupe Hidalgo
Gadsden Purchase

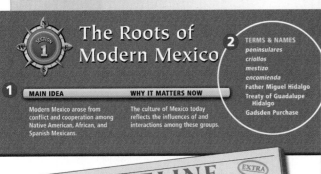

SECTION 1
The Roots of Modern Mexico

2 TERMS & NAMES
peninsulares
criollos
mestizo
encomienda
Father Miguel Hidalgo
Treaty of Guadalupe Hidalgo
Gadsden Purchase

1 | MAIN IDEA | WHY IT MATTERS NOW |

Modern Mexico arose from conflict and cooperation among Native American, African, and Spanish Mexicans.

The culture of Mexico today reflects the influences of and interactions among these groups.

3 DATELINE · EXTRA

TENOCHTITLÁN, AZTEC EMPIRE, 1519

Today, in the palace of the Aztec emperor Moctezuma, a Spanish explorer got a taste of something he is sure to remember. A treat enjoyed by both the Aztec and Maya, the drink, called *chocolatl*, is thick, smooth, and decisively bitter. With no sugar added to sweeten it, this unusual drink is spiced with flavors such as chili pepper and vanilla.

Always served in liquid form, the drink is consumed by the Native Americans at high rates. Moctezuma, the Aztec king, drinks up to 50 cups a day. The Spaniards hope to take the chocolate, as they call it, back to Europe—although they plan to add sugar to it to help ease the bitter taste.

Region · Cacao seeds grow inside pods like this. ▲

Human-Environment Interaction · The chocolate flavor comes from cacao seeds. ▲

The Arrival of the Spanish

The leader of the Spanish army that first landed on the shores of Mexico was Hernán Cortés. He hoped to win new lands for Spain, as well as gold and glory for himself.

Cortés reached the east coast of Mexico in 1519 with about 500 soldiers. He claimed the land for the king and queen of Spain. Quickly, however, he learned that the land was ruled by the powerful Aztec king Moctezuma.

Mexico Today **165**

---

4 ## A Clash of Cultures

Moctezuma ruled an empire of between 10 million and 25 million people. However, many of his Native American subjects wanted to be free. They helped the Spanish conquer the Aztec king. They did not expect that the Spanish would become their new rulers.

The First Encounter When Moctezuma heard about the arrival of the Spanish, he welcomed Cortés with gifts. He even allowed Cortés to stay in a royal palace in the Aztec capital, Tenochtitlán. Within a week, Cortés took Moctezuma prisoner—and took control of the Aztec Empire.

Connections to Science

Invisible Weapons Smallpox and other diseases from Europe killed millions of Native Americans between 1500 and 1900. Smallpox (germ cell shown below) had long been widespread in Europe, and most Europeans were at least partly immune. Native Americans, however, had no immunity to it because it had never before existed in the Americas.

Within months of the Spanish soldiers' arrival in Mexico, many thousands of Native Americans got sick with smallpox (shown below) and died from it—including Moctezuma's successor. Smallpox proved far more deadly to Native Americans than Spanish swords and cannons.

The Spanish Takeover Other Aztec leaders drove the Spanish from Tenochtitlán. However, during the fighting that followed, Moctezuma was killed. The Spanish then retook the city, greatly aided by their Native American allies. The Spanish also had an essential advantage over the Aztec: their weapons. The Aztec had only war clubs, spears, and arrows. The Spanish soldiers had steel swords, armor, guns, and cannons, as well as horses. The invading army destroyed Tenochtitlán street by street.

Culture · Aztec feather shields offered less protection than Spanish metal helmets and armor. ▲

Reading
Social Studies
A. Analyzing Motives Why did some Native Americans help the Spanish fight the Aztec?

The Founding of New Spain

The fall of Tenochtitlán in 1521 marked the end of the Aztec empire and the beginning of Spanish rule in Mexico. The Spanish called their empire "New Spain," just as the English called their territory in North America "New England." Where Tenochtitlán had stood, the Spanish established Mexico City as their capital. Spain ruled Mexico for the next 300 years.

A New Way of Life The Spanish victory caused more than a change of rulers in Mexico. The Spanish introduced a different way of life into the region. They brought new animals, such as horses, cattle, sheep, and pigs. They also brought new trades, such as ironsmithing and shipbuilding. They brought a new religion as well—Christianity.

Vocabulary **5**
ironsmithing: making items out of iron

166 CHAPTER 7

Use Active Reading Strategies As You Read

Now you're ready to read the chapter. Read one section at a time, from beginning to end.

1 Begin by looking at the **Reading Social Studies** page. Consider the questions under the **Before You Read** heading. Think about what you know already about the chapter topic and what you'd like to learn.

2 Review the suggestions in the **Read and Take Notes** section. These will help you understand and remember the information in the chapter.

3 Ask and answer questions as you read. Look for the **Reading Social Studies** questions in the margin. Answering these questions will show whether you understand what you've just read.

4 Study the **Background** notes in the margin for additional information on people, places, events, or ideas discussed in the chapter.

Reading Social Studies

B. Clarifying
What ideas from other parts of the world did Mexicans agree with?

CHAPTER 7

READING SOCIAL STUDIES

BEFORE YOU READ
▶▶ *What Do You Know?*

Before you read the chapter, think about what you already know about Mexico. You may have read about the Aztec in another class. Do you know about any aspects of Mexico's culture today? Think about what you've heard on the news about Mexico—do you know who the president of Mexico is?

▶▶ *What Do You Want to Know?*

Decide what else you want to know about Mexico. In your notebook, record what you hope to learn from this chapter.

Culture • The Aztec feather shields were no match against Spanish armor. ▲

READ AND TAKE NOTES
Reading Strategy: Organizing Information
One effective way to organize information is with a time line. Time lines show events in sequence, or the order in which they happened. Making a time line for the events in this chapter will help you better understand what happened when.

• Copy the time line in your notebook.
• As you read the chapter, note the key events discussed in the chapter.
• Write these events beside the appropriate dates on your time line.

Place • Mexico's Ballet Folklórico dancers are famous. ▲

| 1521 | | 1846 – 1848 | 1910 – 1920 | 1992 |

| 1500 | 1600 | 1700 | 1800 | 1900 | 2000 |

| 1853 | 1920 – 1940 | 2000 |

164 CHAPTER 7

Population of Mexico in 1810

- Native American
- Criollo
- Mestizo
- Peninsular
- African

0.3%
0.2%
12.8%
19.8%
66.9%

SKILLBUILDER: Reading a Graph
1. What percentage of the Mexican population in 1810 was Native American?
2. Were there more *peninsulares* or *criollos* in Mexico in 1810?

A fourth group of people arrived in Mexico unwillingly—the enslaved Africans brought by European slave ships. African farming techniques, musical traditions, and crafts soon blended into the Mexican culture.

Encomienda New Spain's largest group were Native Americans. They made up the bottom layer of society. The rulers of Spain established in Mexico a system called *encomienda* (en·coh·mee·AYN·duh). Under this system, Spanish men were each given a Native American village to oversee. The villagers had to pay tribute—in goods, money, or labor—to this Spaniard. They were essentially enslaved. The results of their labor helped to make Spain rich. However, the villagers lived in poverty and hardship.

Vocabulary
tribute:
a forced payment

The War of Independence

By 1800, political writers in Europe and the United States were saying that people should be free to choose their own governments. Many Mexican religious and political leaders agreed. They argued that Mexico should be independent from Spain. The demand for Mexican independence grew stronger after 1808, when France conquered Spain.

A Cry for Freedom Then, before dawn on September 16, 1810, the farmers in the mountain village of Dolores heard their church bells ringing. At the church their priest, **Father Miguel Hidalgo**, gave a fiery speech urging them to throw off Spanish rule. No one knows the exact text of the speech, but it is known as the *Grito de Dolores* (Cry of Dolores). Urged on by his words, a small army of Native Americans and *mestizos* marched with Father Hidalgo toward Mexico City. Along the way, thousands more joined them.

A Difficult Challenge Father Hidalgo's army had few weapons. Mostly, his men carried clubs and farm tools, such as sickles and axes. When they faced the government soldiers, the farmers were soon defeated. Father Hidalgo was captured and executed. But the revolution he had sparked did not die.

Reading Social Studies **3**
B. Clarifying
What ideas from other parts of the world did Mexicans agree with?

BACKGROUND **4**
Although *dolores* means "sorrow" in Spanish, here it is a reference to the town of Dolores.

Vocabulary
sickle:
a blade used for cutting tall grass or grain

168 CHAPTER 7

BACKGROUND

Although *dolores* means "sorrow" in Spanish, here it is a reference to the town of Dolores.

Review and Summarize What You Have Read

When you finish reading a section, review and summarize the information you have learned. Reread any information that is still unclear.

1 Look again at the red and blue headings for a quick summary of the section.

2 Study the photographs, maps, charts, graphs, and illustrated features in the section. Think about how these visuals relate to the information you've learned.

3 Answer the questions in the **Assessment** section. This will help you think critically about what you've just read.

---

1 ### The Influence of the Church

Because the Catholic Church was powerful in Spain, it soon became powerful in New Spain. Catholic priests set up churches, schools, and hospitals. Sometimes Native Americans accepted Christianity willingly. Sometimes, though, they were forced to become Christian against their will.

A Cultural Blend Even though the Native Americans had to accept many new ways of life, the old ways were not lost. For instance, an essential element of Native American cooking was the *tortilla*, a flat, round bread made from corn or flour. *Tortillas* are still made daily all over Mexico. As with food, many other aspects of the two cultures blended in the new Mexican culture.

Life in New Spain

A new multilayered society developed in Mexico. The ruling class were Spanish officials who were born in Spain. They were called **_peninsulares_** (pen·in·soo·LAR·ays) because they were from the Iberian Peninsula in Europe.

A second class were **_criollos_** (cree·OH·yohs), people who were born in Mexico but whose parents were born in Spain. *Criollos* were often wealthy and powerful, but they were not in the same social class as the *peninsulares*.

A **_mestizo_** (mess·TEE·zoe) is a person who is of mixed European and Native American ancestry. *Mestizos* formed the third layer of New Spain's society.

BACKGROUND
The Iberian Peninsula consists of two countries— Portugal and Spain. (See the map of Europe on page 252.)

Movement • Mexicans today celebrate Catholic holy days that the Spanish established. This festival honors Our Lady of Guadalupe. ▼

Mexico Today **167**

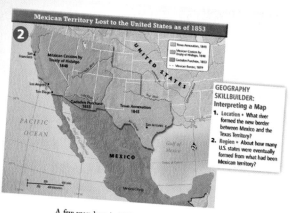

Mexican Territory Lost to the United States as of 1853

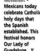

GEOGRAPHY SKILLBUILDER: Interpreting a Map

1. **Location** • What river formed the new border between Mexico and the Texas Territory?
2. **Region** • About how many U.S. states were eventually formed from what had been Mexican territory?

A few years later, in 1853, the **Gadsden Purchase** gave the United States more of Mexico's northern land. The two countries have since made slight adjustments to the border, but they have not fought a war again.

SECTION **1** ASSESSMENT

Terms & Names
1. Identify:
(a) peninsulares   (b) criollos   (c) mestizo   (d) encomienda
(e) Father Miguel Hidalgo   (f) Treaty of Guadalupe Hidalgo   (g) Gadsden Purchase

Taking Notes

2. Use a chart like this one to list the five social groups that made up New Spain and their characteristics.

Social Group	Characteristics

Main Ideas

3. (a) What advantages allowed Cortés's small army to conquer Mexico?

(b) In what ways did Spanish rule change life in Mexico?

(c) What were the results of the war between Mexico and the United States?

Critical Thinking

4. Analyzing Causes

Why did Mexicans decide to fight for independence from Spain?

Think About

• influential events around the world

• reasons for discontent among the criollos, mestizos, and Native Americans

ACTIVITY -OPTION-   Reread the information about the first meeting of the Spanish and Aztec. Write a short story describing the event from either the Spanish or Aztec viewpoint.

170 CHAPTER 7

Part 2: Test-Taking Strategies and Practice

Use the strategies in this section to improve your test-taking skills. First read the tips on the left page. Then use them to help you with the practice items on the right page.

Multiple Choice

A multiple-choice question is a question or incomplete sentence and a set of choices. One of the choices correctly answers the question or completes the sentence.

1 Read the question or incomplete sentence carefully. Try to answer the question before looking at the choices.

2 Read each choice with the question. Don't decide on your final answer until you have read all the choices.

3 Rule out any choices that you know are wrong.

4 Look for key words in the question. They may help you figure out the correct answer.

5 Sometimes the last choice is *All of the above*. Make sure that the other choices are all correct if you pick this answer.

6 Be careful with questions that include the word *not*.

1 1 Which of the following countries shares a border with the United States?

2 choices
- **A** Brazil
- **B** Canada
- **C** Cuba
- **D** Venezuela

3 Since Cuba is an island, you know that it cannot share a border with the United States.

2 Which language is spoken by (most) of the people who live in Latin America and the Caribbean?

- **A** English
- **B** French
- **C** Portuguese
- **D** Spanish

4 The word *most* is key here. All of the languages listed are spoken in Latin America and the Caribbean, but most people there speak Spanish.

3 The Andes mountains run through

- **A** Colombia.
- **B** Ecuador.
- **C** Peru.
- **D** All of the above

5 Before selecting *All of the above,* make sure that all of the choices are, indeed, correct.

4 Which of the following is (not) an island in the Caribbean?

- **A** Barbados
- **B** Cuba
- **C** Hawaii
- **D** Jamaica

6 First rule out all the choices that name islands in the Caribbean. The choice that remains is the correct answer.

answers: 1 (B); 2 (D); 3 (D); 4 (C)

Directions: Read each question carefully. Choose the *best* answer from the four choices.

1   Which of the following conquered the Inca?

   A Francisco Pizarro

   B Miguel Hidalgo

   C Hernán Cortés

   D Simón Bolívar

2   Until recent years, many Central American and Caribbean countries had single-product economies, depending on such crops as

   A bananas.

   B coffee.

   C sugar cane.

   D All of the above

3   Many Canadians are bilingual, which means that they speak

   A French at home and English at work.

   B English and their native language.

   C two languages.

   D several languages.

4   During the 1700s, England controlled which of the following?

   A the sugar trade

   B the Atlantic slave trade

   C the cotton trade

   D the coconut trade

Primary Sources

Sometimes you will need to look at a document to answer a question. Some documents are primary sources. Primary sources are written or made by people who either saw an event or were actually part of the event. A primary source can be a photograph, letter, diary, speech, or autobiography.

1 Look at the source line to learn about the document and its author. Consider how reliable the information might be.

2 Skim the article to get an idea of what it is about. As you read, look for the main idea. The main idea is the writer's most important point. Sometimes it is not directly stated.

3 Note any special punctuation. For example, ellipses (. . .) mean that words and sentences have been left out.

4 Ask yourself questions about the document as you read.

5 Review the questions. This will give your reading a purpose and also help you find the answers more easily. Then reread the document.

A Native American View of Nature

Plants are of different families. . . . It is the same with animals. . . . It is the same with human beings; there is some place which is best adapted to each. The seeds of the plants are blown about by the wind until they reach the place where they will grow best . . . and there they take root and grow. . . . In the early days the animals probably roamed over a very wide country until they found a proper place. An animal depends on the natural conditions around it. If the buffalo were here today, I think they would be different from the buffalo of the old days because all the natural conditions have changed. They would not find the same food, nor the same surroundings. We see the change in our ponies. . . . Now . . . they have less endurance and must have constant care [unlike in the past]. It is the same with the Indians; they have less freedom and they fall an easy prey to disease.

—Okute, a Teton Sioux (1911)

The Sioux were a Native American people who lived on the Great Plains of North America.

1 Okute thinks that horses and Indians now are different from those of the early days because

A the buffalo are gone.

B natural conditions have changed.

C they cannot roam to find the best place to live.

D there is no water.

2 Which sentence *best* expresses the main idea of this passage?

A "Animals and humans must always roam."

B "Each plant, animal, and human is different."

C "Each plant, animal, and human thrives in a particular place."

D "Plants and animals were created for humans to eat."

answers: 1 (B); 2 (C)

Directions: Read this passage from the English Bill of Rights. Use this document and your knowledge of social studies to answer the questions.

A Declaration of English Rights

The . . . Lords . . . and Commons, . . . being now assembled in a full and free representative of this nation, . . . declare:

1. That the pretended power of suspending of laws, or the execution of laws, by [the King], without consent of Parliament, is illegal. . . .

4. That [raising] money for or to the use of the [King], without grant of Parliament, . . . is illegal.

5. That it is the right of the subjects to petition the King, and all commitments and prosecutions for such petitioning are illegal.

6. That the raising or keeping a standing army within the kingdom in time of peace, unless it be with consent of parliament, is against the law. . . .

—*Declaration of Rights,* 1689
(English Bill of Rights)

1 Which of the articles of the *Declaration of Rights* is concerned with taxation?

A Article 1

B Article 4

C Article 5

D Article 6

2 The *Declaration of Rights* was aimed at limiting the power of the

A Parliament.

B nobles and clergy.

C rising middle class.

D King.

Secondary Sources

A secondary source is an account of events by a person who did not actually experience them. The author often uses information from several primary sources to write about a person or event. Biographies, many newspaper articles, and history books are examples of secondary sources.

1 Read the title to get an idea of what the passage is about. (The title here indicates that the passage is about a person named Malinche about whom people have different opinions.)

2 Skim the paragraphs to find the main idea of the passage.

3 Look for words that help you understand the order in which events happen.

4 Ask yourself questions as you read. (You might ask yourself: Why did people's opinions about Malinche change over time?)

5 Review the questions to see what information you will need to find. Then reread the passage.

1 **Malinche—Heroine or Traitor?**

No one knows much about Malinche's early life. People do know that in 1519 she met Hernán Cortés. The Spanish conquistador had landed in Mexico earlier that year. Malinche was only 15 years old. Even though she was very **2** young, Malinche helped Cortés conquer the Aztecs. She spoke the languages of the Aztec and the Maya. Over time, she learned Spanish. She translated for Cortés and advised him on Native American politics.

The Spanish conquistadors admired Malinche, calling **3** her Doña Marina. For many centuries, the Spanish people regarded her as a heroine. In the 1800s, however, Mexico won its independence from Spain. People rejected their Spanish rulers. Writers and artists started calling Malinche a traitor to her people. Today, however, she is seen as a heroine again. **4**

1 Which of the following statements about Malinche is an (opinion)?

> Remember that an opinion is a statement that cannot be proved. A fact is a statement that can be proved.

5

A She was very young when she met Cortés.

B She became a translator for Cortés.

C She was a traitor to her own people.

D She understood Native American politics.

2 Based on this source, which person or group would view Malinche as a heroine?

A a fighter for Mexican independence from Spain

B the soldiers and officers in Cortés's army

C the Aztec ruler and his court in Mexico

D a historian writing about Mexico in the 1800s

answers: 1 (C); 2 (B)

For more test practice online . . .

TEST PRACTICE
CLASSZONE.COM

Directions: Read this passage. Use the passage and your knowledge of social studies to answer the questions.

Before World War I

In 1892, France and Russia had become military allies. Later, Germany signed an agreement to protect Austria. If any nation attacked Austria, Germany would fight on its side. France and Russia had to support each other as well. For instance, if France got into a war with Germany, Russia had to fight Germany, too. This meant that in any war, Germany would have to fight on two fronts: France on the west and Russia on the east.

If a war broke out, what part would England play? No one knew. It might remain neutral, like Belgium. It might, if given a reason, fight against Germany.

1 If Russia and Germany went to war, which country had to help Russia?

  A England
  B Belgium
  C Austria
  D France

2 When World War I broke out, what part did England play?

  A It remained neutral, like Belgium.
  B It sided with Germany and Austria.
  C It joined France in fighting Germany.
  D It fought Russia after its revolution.

Political Cartoons

Cartoonists who draw political cartoons use both words and art to express opinions about political issues.

1 Try to figure out what the cartoon is about. Titles and captions may give clues.

2 Use labels to help identify the people, places, and events represented in the cartoon.

3 Note when and where the cartoon was published.

4 Look for symbols—that is, people, places, or objects that stand for something else.

5 The cartoonist often exaggerates the physical features of people and objects. This technique will give you clues as to how the cartoonist feels about the subject.

6 Try to figure out the cartoonist's message and summarize it in a sentence.

1 NEXT!

4 The cartoonist uses the swastika, a symbol used during World War II.

5 The swastika looks like a huge, frightening machine. It can easily crush Poland.

2 The label "Poland" tells which country is the subject of the cartoon's title.

Daniel Fitzpatrick / *St. Louis Post-Dispatch*, August 24, 1939.

3 The date is a clue that the cartoon refers to the beginning of World War II.

1 What does the swastika in the cartoon stand for?

A the Soviet Union
B Nazi Germany
C the Polish army
D the Austrian military

6 2 Which sentence *best* summarizes the cartoonist's message?

A Germany will attack Poland next.
B Poland should stop Germany.
C Germany will lose this battle.
D Poland will fight a civil war.

answers: 1 (B); 2 (A)

For more test practice online . . .

TEST PRACTICE
CLASSZONE.COM

STRATEGIES FOR TAKING STANDARDIZED TESTS

Directions: Study this cartoon. Use the cartoon and your knowledge of social studies to answer the questions.

The Granger Collection, New York

Benjamin Franklin (1754)

1 What do the sections of the snake in the cartoon represent?

   A army units

   B states

   C Native American groups

   D colonies

2 Which phrase best states the message of the cartoon?

   A "East is East, and West is West, and never the twain shall meet."

   B "Taxation without representation is tyranny."

   C "United we stand, divided we fall."

   D "Out of many, one."

Charts

Charts present facts in a visual form. History textbooks use several different types of charts. The chart that is most often found on standardized tests is the table. A table organizes information in columns and rows.

1 Read the title of the chart to find out what information is represented.

2 Read the headings at the top of each column. Then read the headings at the left of each row.

3 Notice how the information in the chart is organized.

4 Compare the information from column to column and row to row.

5 Try to draw conclusions from the information in the chart.

6 Read the questions and then study the chart again.

1 This chart is about the number of people who immigrated to different countries.

4 Notice that different years are used for different countries.

Immigration to Selected Countries

2 Country	Years	Number of Immigrants
Argentina	1856-1932	6,405,000
Australia	1861-1932	2,913,000
Brazil	1821-1932	4,431,000
British West Indies	1836-1932	1,587,000
Canada	1821-1932	5,206,000
Cuba	1901-1932	857,000
Mexico	1911-1931	226,000
New Zealand	1851-1932	594,000
South Africa	1881-1932	852,000
United States	1821-1932	34,244,000
Uruguay	1836-1932	713,000

Source: Alfred W. Crosby, Jr. *The Columbian Exchange: Biological and Cultural Consequences of 1492*

3 This chart lists countries in alphabetical order. Other charts organize information by years or by numbers.

5 Of all the countries listed, six received the most immigrants. Think about what these countries have in common.

1 The country that received the most immigrants was

A Canada.

B the British West Indies.

6 C the United States.

D Brazil.

2 Different countries received immigrants in different years. Which countries received immigrants the earliest?

A Argentina, New Zealand, and Canada

B Canada, Brazil, and United States

C Mexico, United States, and British West Indies

D Brazil, South Africa, and Cuba

answers: 1 (C); 2 (B)

Directions: Read the chart carefully. Use the chart and your knowledge of social studies to answer the questions.

Mexico and the Nations of Central America				
Country	Capital	Area (sq. miles)	Population	Per Capita Gross Domestic Product (in U.S. dollars)
Belize	Belmopan	8,900	249,183	3,000
Costa Rica	San José	19,700	3,710,558	6,700
El Salvador	San Salvador	8,100	6,122,515	3,000
Guatemala	Guatemala City	42,000	12,639,939	3,800
Honduras	Tegucigalpa	43,300	6,249,598	2,400
Mexico	Mexico City	761,600	100,349,766	8,300
Nicaragua	Managua	49,998	4,812,569	2,500
Panama	Panama City	32,200	2,808,268	7,300

Source: *World Almanac and Book of Facts* 2001

1 The largest country in terms of both area and population is

  A Guatemala.

  B Honduras.

  C Mexico.

  D Nicaragua.

2 Which correctly states the countries' rank from high to low in terms of per capita gross domestic product?

  A Honduras, Nicaragua, Belize, Guatemala

  B Mexico, Panama, El Salvador, Honduras

  C Panama, Costa Rica, Mexico, Belize

  D Mexico, Costa Rica, Panama, Guatemala

Line and Bar Graphs

Graphs are often used to show numbers. Line graphs often show changes over time. Bar graphs make it easy to compare numbers.

1 Read the title of the graph to find out what information is represented.

2 Study the labels on the graph.

3 Look at the source line that tells where the graph is from. Decide whether you can depend on the source to provide reliable information.

4 See if you can make any generalizations about the information in the graph. Note whether the numbers change over time.

5 Read the questions carefully and then study the graph again.

1 **Exports of English Manufactured Goods, 1699–1774**

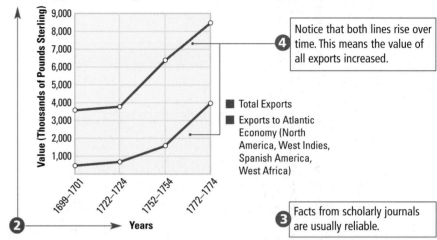

4 Notice that both lines rise over time. This means the value of all exports increased.

■ Total Exports
■ Exports to Atlantic Economy (North America, West Indies, Spanish America, West Africa)

3 Facts from scholarly journals are usually reliable.

Source: R. Davis, "English Foreign Trade, 1700–1774," *Economic History Review* (1962)

5 **1** Which of the following is a true statement?

A Exports to the New World declined over time.
B Total exports stayed the same over time.
C Total exports rose sharply after 1724.
D Exports to the New World fell sharply after 1754.

1 **Nations with High Foreign Debt, 1998**

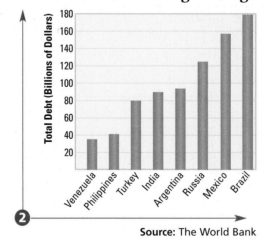

3 Facts from major organizations, such as the World Bank, usually are reliable.

Source: The World Bank

5 **2** The nation with the largest foreign debt is

A Brazil.
B Argentina.
C Mexico.
D Venezuela.

answers: 1 (C); 2 (A)

Line graph adapted from "Exports of English Manufactured Goods, 1700–1774," from *A History of World Societies, Fifth Edition* by John P. McKay, Bennett D. Hill, John Buckler, and Patricia Buckley Ebrey. Copyright © 2000 by Houghton Mifflin Company. All rights reserved. Used by permission.

Directions: Read the graphs carefully. Use the graphs and your knowledge of social studies to answer the questions.

Canada: Imports and Exports, 1995–2000

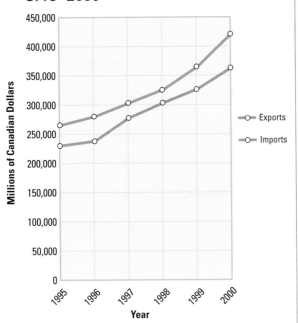

Source: *Statistics Canada*

Unemployment Rates for Selected Countries, 2000

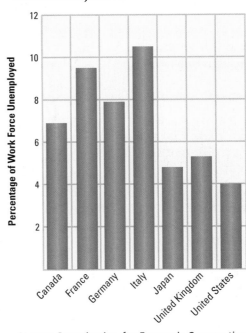

Source: Organization for Economic Cooperation and Development

1 In which year was the difference in the value of imports and exports the greatest?

A 1995

B 1996

C 1999

D 2000

2 Which country had the lowest unemployment rate in 2000?

A Canada

B Japan

C United Kingdom

D United States

Pie Graphs

A pie, or circle, graph shows the relationship among parts of a whole. These parts look like slices of a pie. Each slice is shown as a percentage of the whole pie.

1 Read the title of the chart to find out what information is represented.

2 The graph may provide a legend, or key, that tells you what different slices represent.

3 The size of the slice is related to the percentage. The larger the percentage, the larger the slice.

4 Look at the source line that tells where the graph is from. Ask yourself if you can depend on this source to provide reliable information.

5 Read the questions carefully, and study the graph again.

1 **World Population by Region, 2000**

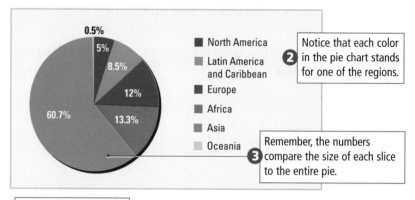

- ■ North America
- ■ Latin America and Caribbean
- ■ Europe
- ■ Africa
- ■ Asia
- ■ Oceania

2 Notice that each color in the pie chart stands for one of the regions.

3 Remember, the numbers compare the size of each slice to the entire pie.

The Population Reference Bureau studies population data for the United States and other countries.

4 **Source:** Population Reference Bureau

1 Which region accounts for nearly 5 percent of the world's population?

A Africa

B North America

C Europe

D Asia

2 About one-twelfth of the world's population lives in

A Africa.

B Europe.

C Latin America and Caribbean.

D North America.

answers: 1 (B); 2 (C)

S18

Directions: Read the pie graph. Use the graph and your knowledge of social studies to answer the questions.

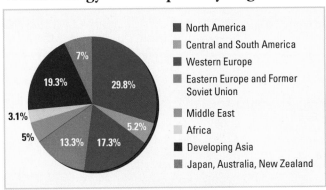

World Energy Consumption by Region

- North America
- Central and South America
- Western Europe
- Eastern Europe and Former Soviet Union
- Middle East
- Africa
- Developing Asia
- Japan, Australia, New Zealand

Source: "Earth Pulse," *National Geographic* (March 2001)

1 Which region uses the most energy?

A Western Europe

B Developing Asia

C North America

D Eastern Europe and Former Soviet Union

2 Two regions consumed nearly the same amount of the world's energy. They are Central and South America and

A Middle East.

B Western Europe.

C Developing Asia.

D North America.

Political Maps

Political maps show the divisions within countries. A country may be divided into states, provinces, etc. The maps also show where major cities are. They may also show mountains, oceans, seas, lakes, and rivers.

1 Read the title of the map. This will give you the subject and purpose of the map.

2 Read the labels on the map. They also give information about the map's subject and purpose.

3 Study the key or legend to help you understand the symbols in the map.

4 Use the scale to estimate distances between places shown on the map. Maps usually show the distance in both miles and kilometers.

5 Use the North arrow to figure out the direction of places on the map.

6 Read the questions. Carefully study the map to find the answers.

1 Canada and Its Provinces

3 The legend gives symbols for Canada's boundaries and major cities.

2 The labels identify Canada's provinces.

1 Which province or territory is the furthest west?

A Northwest Territories

B Yukon Territory

C British Columbia

D Alberta

2 About how many miles is the United States-Canada border from the Great Lakes west to Vancouver on the Pacific Ocean?

A 1,000

B 1,500

C 2,000

D 2,500

answers: 1 (B); 2 (B)

Directions: Study the map carefully. Use the map and your knowledge of social studies to answer the questions.

The Roman Empire, A.D. 400

1 Which area was part of the Eastern Roman Empire?

   A Spain

   B Gaul

   C Anatolia

   D All of the above

2 The most northern country in the Western Roman Empire was

   A Syria.

   B Gaul.

   C Spain.

   D Britain.

Thematic Maps

Thematic maps focus on special topics. For example, a thematic map might show a country's natural resources or major battles in a war.

1 Read the title of the map. This will give you the subject and purpose of the map.

2 Read the labels on the map. They give information about the map's subject and purpose. (The labels identify the three European empires.)

3 Study the key or legend to help you understand the symbols and/or colors on the map. (The legend shows the colors that indicate the three European Empires.)

4 Try to make generalizations about information shown on the map.

5 Read the questions. Carefully study the map to find the answers.

1 European Empires in North America, 1700

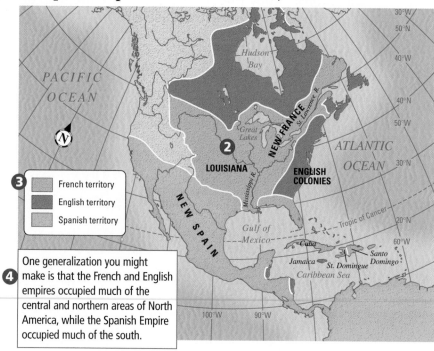

3
French territory
English territory
Spanish territory

4 One generalization you might make is that the French and English empires occupied much of the central and northern areas of North America, while the Spanish Empire occupied much of the south.

1 The land around the Great Lakes was controlled by

A England.

B France.

C Spain.

D All of the above.

2 Which of the following statements about the English colonial empire in North America is *not* true?

A English lands shared borders with both French and Spanish lands.

B English lands did not stretch as far west as those held by Spain.

C England held no land on the Pacific Coast of North America.

D England held no lands east of 60° W longitude.

answers: 1 (B); 2 (D)

For more test practice online . . .

TEST PRACTICE
CLASSZONE.COM

Directions: Read the map carefully. Use the map and your knowledge of social studies to answer the questions.

The Christian Conquest of Muslim Spain

Bay of Biscay

FRANCE

Santiago

Leon

Saragossa

Barcelona

N

40°N

Toledo

Valencia

Lisbon

Córdoba

Mediterranean Sea

Seville

Granada

ATLANTIC OCEAN

- City
- Conquered before 914
- Conquered 915–1080
- Conquered 1081–1130
- Conquered 1131–1210
- Conquered 1211–1250
- Conquered 1251–1480
- Conquered after 1481

0   100   200 miles
0   100   200 kilometers

1 By A.D. 1250, how much of Spain did Christians control?

   A Only a small portion

   B About one third

   C About one half

   D Almost all the land

2 When did Spain recover Granada?

   A 1000

   B 1150

   C 1450

   D 1492

Time Lines

A time line is a chart that lists events in the order in which they occurred. Time lines can be vertical or horizontal.

1 Read the title to learn what subject the time line covers.

2 Note the dates when the time line begins and ends.

3 Read the events in the order they occurred.

4 Think about what else was going on in the world on these dates. Try to make connections.

5 Read the questions. Then carefully study the time line to find the answers.

1 The Struggle for Mexican Independence

1810

Father Miguel Hidalgo issues the "Cry of Dolores," launching the Mexican independence movement.

1811
Spanish forces capture Hidalgo and execute him. Father José María Morelos takes over leadership of the revolt.

2 Vertical time lines show the earliest date at the top. Horizontal time lines show the earliest date on the far left.

1813
Morelos calls a congress of representatives from all of Mexico's provinces. The congress writes a constitution for a Mexican republic.

1815
Spanish forces capture and execute Morelos.

4 Note that Mexico, like other Latin American countries, was deeply influenced by the revolutions in the United States and France.

1820
Spain sends large force, under the command of Agustín de Iturbide, to round up guerilla bands. Iturbide throws his support to the rebellion.

1815 to 1820
Vicente Guerrero, with a small band of followers, continues the rebellion against Spain.

1821
Iturbide and rebel leaders declare Mexico's independence.

5

1 In which year did Father José María Morelos become the leader of the Mexican independence movement?

A 1810

B 1811

C 1813

D 1815

2 Which of the following switched sides during the struggle for Mexican independence?

A Vicente Guerrero

B Father Miguel Hidalgo

C Augustín de Iturbide

D José María Morelos

answers: 1 (B); 2 (C)

Directions: Read the time line. Use the information shown and your knowledge of social studies to answer the questions.

The Breakup of the Soviet Union

1991
Boris Yeltsin is elected president of Russia.

Communist and army hard-liners seize power; Yeltsin leads resistance that defeats them.

Soviet Union ceases to exist.

1985
Mikhail Gorbachev becomes leader of Soviet Union.

1989
In Soviet elections many Communist candidates are defeated.

1986
Gorbachev starts economic and political reforms.

1988
New Soviet constitution allows for open elections.

1990
Lithuania declares independence; over the next several months 13 other republics become independent.

1 What happened after Lithuania became independent?

A Gorbachev started economic and political reforms.

B Many other republics became independent.

C A new constitution allowed for open elections.

D Gorbachev defeated Yeltsin in a new election.

2 In which year did Communist and army hard-liners try to seize power?

A 1985

B 1988

C 1990

D 1991

Constructed Response

Constructed-response questions focus on a document, such as a photograph, cartoon, chart, graph, or time line. Instead of picking one answer from a set of choices, you write a short response. Sometimes, you can find the answer in the document. Other times, you will use what you already know about a subject to answer the question.

1 Read the title of the document to get an idea of what it is about.

2 Study the document.

3 Read the questions carefully. Study the document again to find the answers.

4 Write your answers. You don't need to use complete sentences unless the directions say so.

1 The Temple of Inscriptions, Palenque, Mexico

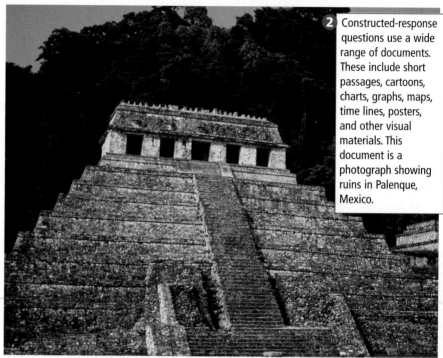

2 Constructed-response questions use a wide range of documents. These include short passages, cartoons, charts, graphs, maps, time lines, posters, and other visual materials. This document is a photograph showing ruins in Palenque, Mexico.

Copyright © Kevin Shafer/Corbis

The Temple of Inscriptions stands over the tomb of Pakal, a great Maya king. The Maya used the temple for religious purposes. Such flat-topped, pyramid-like buildings are typical of Maya architecture.

3 1 Palenque, with its massive pyramid structures, was one of the city-states of what civilization?

4 _Maya_

2 For what purpose was this building used?

religious purposes

3 This civilization went into decline around A.D. 900. Which great civilization arose in its place?

Aztec civilization

Directions: Read the following passage from *Zlata's Diary.* Use the passage and your knowledge of social studies to answer the questions. You do not need to use complete sentences.

Saturday, May 2, 1992

Dear Mimmy,

Today was truly, absolutely the worst day ever in Sarajevo. The shooting started around noon. Mommy and I moved into the hall. Daddy was in his office, under our apartment, at the time. We told him on the intercom to run quickly to the downstairs lobby where we'd meet him. . . . The gunfire was getting worse, and we couldn't get over the wall to the Bobars', so we ran down to our own cellar.

The cellar is ugly, dark, smelly. Mommy, who's terrified of mice, had two fears to cope with. The three of us were in the same corner as the other day. We listened to the pounding shells, the shooting, the thundering noise overhead. We even heard planes. At one moment I realized that this awful cellar was the only place that could save our lives. Suddenly, it started to look almost warm and nice. It was the only way we could defend ourselves against all this terrible shooting. We heard glass shattering in our street. Horrible. I put my fingers in my ears to block out the terrible sounds. I was worried about Cicko. We had left him behind in the lobby. Would he catch cold there? Would something hit him? I was terribly hungry and thirsty. We had left our half-cooked lunch in the kitchen.

—Zlata Filipovic, *Zlata's Diary: A Child's Life in Sarajevo* (1994)

1   In the early 1990s, war broke out in the Balkans. Why were people fighting in Bosnia and Herzegovina?

2   What does Zlata say is happening in the city of Sarajevo?

3   How does the war affect Zlata and her family?

Excerpt from *Zlata's Diary* by Zlata Filipovic. Copyright © 1994 Editions Robert Laffont/Fixot.
Used by permission of Viking Penguin, a division of Penguin Putnam Inc.

Extended Response

Extended-response questions, like constructed-response questions, focus on a document of some kind. However, they are more complicated and require more time to complete. Some extended-response questions ask you to present the information in the document in a different form. You might be asked to present the information in a chart in graph form, for example. Other questions ask you to complete a document such as a chart or graph. Still others require you to apply your knowledge to information in the document to write an essay.

1 Read the title of the document to get an idea of what it is about.

2 Carefully read directions and questions.

3 Study the document.

4 Sometimes the question may give you part of the answer. (The answer given tells how inventions were used and what effects they had on society. Your answers should have the same kind of information.)

5 The question may require you to write an essay. Write down some ideas to use in an outline. Then use your outline to write the essay. (A good essay will contain the ideas shown in the rubric to the right.)

3 Read the column heads carefully. They offer important clues about the subject of the chart. For instance, the column head "Impact" is a clue about why these inventions were so important.

1 Inventions of the Industrial Revolution

Invention	Impact
Flying shuttle, spinning jenny, water frame, spinning mule, power loom	Spun thread and wove cloth faster; more factories were built and more people were hired **4**
Cotton gin	Cleaned seeds faster from cotton; companies produced more cotton
Macadam road, steamboat, locomotive	Made travel over land and water faster; could carry larger, heavier loads; railroads needed more coal and iron
Mechanical reaper	Made harvesting easier; increased wheat production

2 1 Read the list of inventions in the left-hand column. Then in the right-hand column briefly state what the inventions meant to industry. The first item has been filled in for you.

2 The chart shows how some inventions helped create the Industrial Revolution. Write a short essay describing how the Industrial Revolution changed people's lives.

5 **Sample Response** The best essays will point out that progress in agriculture meant that fewer people were needed to work the farms. As a result, many farm workers went to the city looking for work in factories. As cities grew, poor sanitation and poor housing made them unhealthy and dangerous places to live. Life for factory workers was hard. They worked long hours under very bad conditions. At first, the Industrial Revolution produced three classes of people: an upper class of landowners and aristocrats; a middle class of merchants and factory owners; and a large lower class of poor people. Over the long term, though, working and living conditions improved, even for the lower class. This was partly because factory goods could be sold at a lower cost. In time, even lower classes could afford to buy many goods and services.

Directions: Use the drawing and passage below and your knowledge of social studies to answer the following question.

Smallpox Spreads Among the Aztecs

The Granger Collection, New York.

European diseases were like a second "army" of conquerors. Native people had no way to treat diseases like smallpox, typhoid fever, or measles. This "army" was more deadly than swords or guns.
— Based on P. M. Ashburn, *The Ranks of Death* (1947)

1 What role did disease play in the Spanish conquest of the Aztecs and Inca?

Document-Based Questions

To answer a document-based question, you have to study more than one document. First you answer questions about each document. Then you use those answers and information from the documents as well as your own knowledge of history to write an essay.

1 Read the "Context" section. It will give you an idea of the topic that will be covered in the question.

2 Read the "Task" section carefully. It tells you what you will need to write about in your essay.

3 Study each document. Think about the connection the documents have to the topic in the "Task" section.

4 Read and answer the questions about each document. Think about how your answers connect to the "Task" section.

Introduction

1 **Context:** South America is made up of 12 very different countries. However, these countries have many features in common. The ways of living in these countries are quite similar. The challenges they face are similar, too.

Task: Identify and discuss the common features that make the countries of South America a culture region.

2 **Part 1: Short Answers**

Study each document carefully. Answer the questions that follow.

3 **Document 1: The Countries of South America**

Country	Main Language	Major Religion	Colonized by	Date Became Independent
Argentina	Spanish	Catholic	Spain	1816
Bolivia	Spanish	Catholic	Spain	1825
Brazil	Portuguese	Catholic	Portugal	1822
Chile	Spanish	Catholic	Spain	1818
Colombia	Spanish	Catholic	Spain	1819
Ecuador	Spanish	Catholic	Spain	1830
Guyana	English	Christian	Great Britain	1966
Paraguay	Spanish, Guarani	Catholic	Spain	1811
Peru	Spanish	Catholic	Spain	1821
Suriname	Dutch	Christian	Netherlands	1975
Uruguay	Spanish	Catholic	Spain	1828
Venezuela	Spanish	Catholic	Spain	1830

4 **What are the dominant language and religion in South America?**

Spanish, Catholicism

Document 2: Government in South America

Oligarchy (government by the few) and military rule have characterized the governments of many of the countries of South America since they won their independence . . .

Although many South American nations gained freedom in the 1800s, hundreds of years of colonialism had its effects. Strong militaries, underdeveloped economies, and social class divisions still exist in the region today.

—Daniel D. Arreola, et al., *World Geography*

What kinds of governments have ruled in South America for much of the time since independence?

Oligarchies and military governments

Document 3: Crowded São Paulo

Over the last 60 years, many South Americans have moved to the cities. Today, nearly 80 percent of the people live in cities. Close to 18 million people live in the Brazilian city of São Paulo.

What is one of the major challenges facing the countries of South America today?

rapid urbanization and overcrowding of cities

❺ Part 2: Essay

Using information from the documents, your answers to the questions in Part 1, and your knowledge of social studies, write an essay identifying and discussing the features that make South America a culture region. ❻

❺ Read the essay question carefully. Then write a brief outline for your essay.

❻ Write your essay. The first paragraph should introduce your topic. The middle paragraphs should explain it. The closing paragraph should restate the topic and your conclusion. Support your ideas with quotations or details from the documents. Add other supporting facts or details from your knowledge of world history.

❼ A good essay will contain the ideas in the sample response below.

Sample Response The best essays will begin by noting that a culture region is a large geographic area marked by a common culture. Essays will go on to discuss the common historical and cultural background of the countries of South America (Document 1). Essays also will note that most South American countries share similar experiences in political and economic development (Document 2). Finally, essays will point out that the major challenges that South American countries face today are alike (Document 3).

Introduction

Historical Context: For many centuries, kings and queens ruled the countries of Europe. Their power was supported by nobles and armies. European society began to change. In the late 1700s, those changes produced a violent revolution in France.

Task: Discuss how social conflict and new ideas contributed to the French Revolution and why the Revolution turned radical.

Part 1: Short Answers

Study each document carefully. Answer the questions that follow.

Document 1: Social Classes in Pre-Revolutionary France

LE GRAND ABUS

This cartoon shows a peasant woman carrying women of nobility and the Church. What does the cartoon say about the lives of the poor before the revolution?

 Engraving: *Le Grand Abus*. Engraving of a cartoon held in the collection of M. de baron de Vinck d'Orp of Brussels/Mary Evans Picture Library, London.

Document 2: A Declaration of Rights

1. Men are born and remain free and equal in rights. . . .

2. The aim of all political association is the preservation of the natural and [unlimited] rights of man. These rights are liberty, property, security, and resistance to oppression. . . .

— *Declaration of the Rights of Man and of the Citizen* (1789)

According to this document, which rights belong to all people?

Document 3: The French Revolution — Major Events

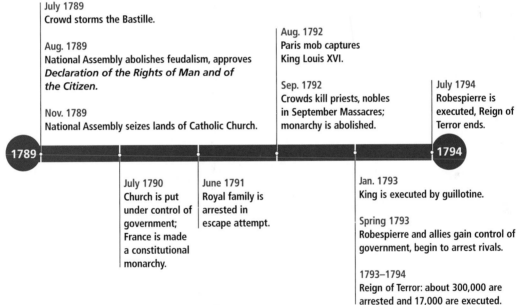

July 1789
Crowd storms the Bastille.

Aug. 1789
National Assembly abolishes feudalism, approves *Declaration of the Rights of Man and of the Citizen.*

Nov. 1789
National Assembly seizes lands of Catholic Church.

Aug. 1792
Paris mob captures King Louis XVI.

Sep. 1792
Crowds kill priests, nobles in September Massacres; monarchy is abolished.

July 1794
Robespierre is executed, Reign of Terror ends.

July 1790
Church is put under control of government; France is made a constitutional monarchy.

June 1791
Royal family is arrested in escape attempt.

Jan. 1793
King is executed by guillotine.

Spring 1793
Robespierre and allies gain control of government, begin to arrest rivals.

1793–1794
Reign of Terror: about 300,000 are arrested and 17,000 are executed.

1789   1794

Over time, the revolution became more violent. How does the information in the timeline show this?

Part 2: Essay

Write an essay discussing how social conflict and new ideas led to the French Revolution and why it became so violent. Use information from the documents, your short answers, and your knowledge of social studies to write your essay.

RAND McNALLY
World Atlas

Contents

Complete Legend for Physical and Political Maps

Symbols

 Lake

 Salt Lake

 Seasonal Lake

 River

\ Waterfall

—— Canal

△ Mountain Peak

▲ Highest Mountain Peak

Cities

■ **Los Angeles**   City over 1,000,000 population

▣ **Calgary**   City of 250,000 to 1,000,000 population

• Haifa   City under 250,000 population

✪ *Paris*   National Capital

★ **Vancouver**   Secondary Capital (State, Province, or Territory)

Type Styles Used to Name Features

CHINA   Country

O N T A R I O   State, Province, or Territory

PUERTO RICO (U.S.)   Possession

A T L A N T I C O C E A N   Ocean or Sea

A l p s   Physical Feature

Borneo   Island

Boundaries

 International Boundary

 Secondary Boundary

Land Elevation and Water Depths

Land Elevation

Meters		Feet
3,000 and over --		-- 9,840 and over
2,000 - 3,000 --		-- 6,560 - 9,840
500 - 2,000 --		-- 1,640 - 6,560
200 - 500 --		-- 656 - 1,640
0 - 200 --		-- 0 - 656

Water Depth

Less than 200 --		-- Less than 656
200 - 2,000 --		-- 656 - 6,560
Over 2,000 --		-- Over 6,560

ATLAS

ARCTIC OCEAN

Greenland

Baffin
Bay

Baffin
Island

Jan Mayen

Arctic Circle

Iceland

Faroe Is.

Yukon

Mt. McKinley △
20,320 Ft.
6,194m

Mackenzie

NORTH

Canadian Shield

Hudson
Bay

British
Isles

Newfoundland

London

Aleutian Islands

Vancouver

Rocky Mountains

AMERICA

St. Lawrence

Appalachian Mts.

Great Plains

Azores

Iberian
Peninsula

Midway Is.

Los Angeles

Colorado

Mississippi

Washington D.C.

Cape Hatteras

ATLANTIC

Atlas
Mts.

Tropic of Cancer

Baja
California

Gulf of Mexico

Yucatan
Peninsula

Cuba

Hispaniola

Canary
Islands

Hawaiian
Islands

Puerto Rico

Jamaica

Caribbean
Sea

Cape Verde
Islands

Cape Verde

PACIFIC

Trinidad

Orinoco

OCEAN

Niger

Palmyra

Galapagos Islands

Amazon

Amazon
Basin

SOUTH

St. Helena

Equator

Kiribati

Marquesas Is.

AMERICA

Samoa
Islands

Andes

Mato Grosso
Plateau

Tonga
Is.

Cook
Islands

Tahiti

Rio de Janeiro

Tropic of Capricorn

Easter Island

Paraná

Archipiélago
Juan Fernández

△ Mt. Aconcagua
22,831 Ft.
6,959m

Buenos Aires

Chatham Is.

Patagonia

Falkland Is.

South
Georgia

0   1000   2000 Miles

0   1000   2000   3000 Kilometers

Copyright by Rand McNally & Co.
Robinson Projection

Tierra del Fuego

Cape Horn

South
Sandwich Is.

South
Orkney Is.

Antarctic Circle

South
Shetland Is.

Antarctic
Peninsula

Weddell
Sea

Ross
Sea

Marie
Byrd
Land

△ Vinson Massif
16,066 Ft.
4,897m

N

ARCTIC OCEAN

Spitsbergen
North Cape
Franz Josef Land
Novaya Zemlya
Scandinavian Peninsula
North Sea
EUROPE
Moscow
Volga
Don
Alps
Balkan Peninsula
Black Sea
Caucasus
Mt. Elbrus 18,510 Ft. 5,642m
Sardinia
Sicily
Crete
Cyprus
Mediterranean Sea
Cairo
Zagros Mts.

Siberia
Yenisey
Ob'
Ural Mts.
Lena
Altai Mts.
ASIA
Aral
Pamir
Gobi Desert
Beijing
Huang
Plateau of Tibet
Himalayas
Mt. Everest 29,035 Ft. 8,850m
Ganges
Yangtze
Bering Sea
Sea of Okhotsk
Kamchatka Peninsula
Sakhalin
Hokkaidō
Sea of Japan
Honshū
Kyūshū
East China Sea
Taiwan
Hainan Island
South China Sea
Amur

PACIFIC
OCEAN
Tropic of Cancer
Mariana Islands
Guam
Wake Island
Caroline Islands
Marshall Islands

Sahara Desert
AFRICA
Sahel
Nile
Red Sea
Arabian Peninsula
Arabian Sea
Mumbai (Bombay)
Deccan Plateau
Socotra
Lakshadweep
Sri Lanka
Bay of Bengal
Mekong
Malay Peninsula
Mindanao
Luzon
Palau Islands
Gulf of Guinea
Congo
Congo Basin
Kasai
Ubangi
Kilimanjaro 19,340 Ft. 5,895m
Maldive Islands
Seychelles
Ethiopian Plateau
Sumatra
Borneo
Celebes
Java
Timor
New Guinea
Solomon Islands
Equator
Zambezi
Madagascar
Mauritius
Reunion
INDIAN
Cocos Island
Kalahari Desert
OCEAN
AUSTRALIA
Great Sandy Desert
New Hebrides
New Caledonia
Fiji Is.
Coral Sea
Darling
Great Dividing Range
Sydney
North Island
Tropic of Capricorn
Cape Town
Cape of Good Hope
Cape Leeuwin
Aoraki (Mt. Cook) 12,316 Ft. 3,754m
Tasmania
South Island
Kerguelen Islands
Queen Maud Land
Enderby Land
Wilkes Land
Victoria Land
Antarctic Circle
ANTARCTICA

Land Elevation		
Meters		Feet
3,000		9,840
2,000		6,560
500		1,640
200		656
0		0

Water Depth		
0		0
200		656
2,000		6,560

RAND McNALLY

RAND McNALLY

A4

ATLAS

National Capital
Major Cities

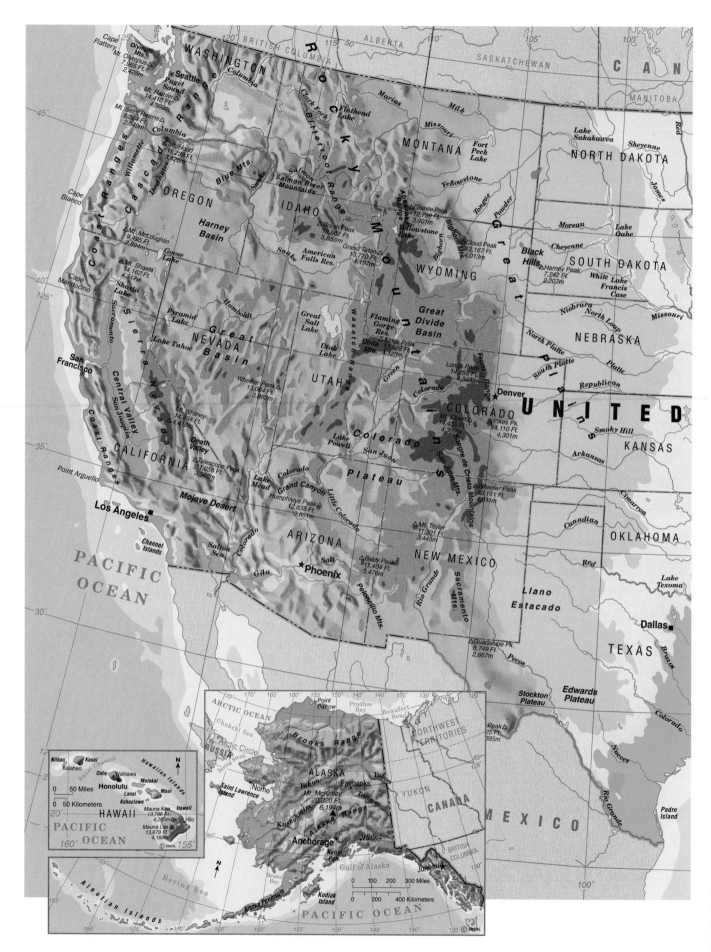

PACIFIC
OCEAN

ARCTIC OCEAN

HAWAII

PACIFIC OCEAN

MEXICO

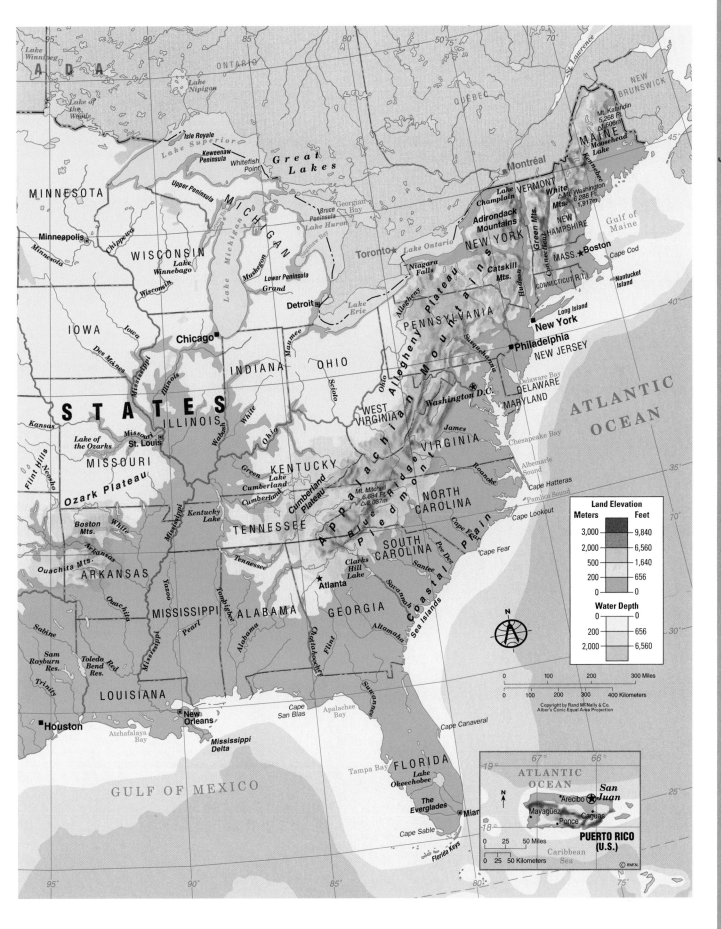

Land Elevation

Meters		Feet
3,000		9,840
2,000		6,560
500		1,640
200		656
0		0

Water Depth

0		0
200		656
2,000		6,560

0   100   200   300 Miles

0 100 200 300 400 Kilometers

Copyright by Rand M°Nally & Co.
Alber's Conic Equal Area Projection

PUERTO RICO (U.S.)

0   25   50 Miles

0 25 50 Kilometers

RAND M°NALLY

RAND M℃NALLY

ATLAS

RAND M^cNALLY

A9

ASIA

RUSSIA

Arctic Circle

ARCTIC OCEAN

North Pole

Bering Strait

Point Hope

Point Barrow

Prudhoe Bay

Beaufort Sea

Cape Bathurst

Queen Elizabeth Islands

Banks Island

Victoria Island

Devon Island

Ellesmere Island

Baffin Bay

Cape Adair

GREENLAND (Denmark)

Ice Cap

Arctic Circle

ICELAND

Norwegian Sea

Bering Sea

Aleutian Islands

Brooks Range

U.S.

Yukon

Kuskokwim

Mt. McKinley 20,320 ft.

Alaska Range

Anchorage

Mt. Logan 19,551 ft.

Alaska Peninsula

Gulf of Alaska

Mackenzie

Great Bear Lake

Great Slave Lake

Baffin Island

Cape Mercy

Foxe Basin

Cape Farvel

PACIFIC OCEAN

Queen Charlotte Islands

Vancouver Island

Vancouver

Coast Mountains

Whitehorse

Columbia

Rocky Mountains

Peace

Lake Athabasca

Churchill

Nelson

Saskatchewan

Edmonton

CANADA

Lake Winnipeg

Hudson Bay

James Bay

Canadian Shield

Péninsule d'Ungava

Newfoundland

Gulf of St. Lawrence

Cape Blanco

Cape Mendocino

Cascade Range

Coast Ranges

Sierra Nevada

Snake

Great Salt Lake

Great Basin

Los Angeles

Mt. Whitney 14,494 Ft.

Colorado Plateau

Death Valley -282ft.

Denver

Colorado

Arkansas

Red

Great Plains

Missouri

Mississippi

UNITED STATES

Chicago

Lake Superior

Lake Michigan

Lake Huron

Lake Erie

Lake Ontario

Niagara Falls

Ottawa

Montréal

St. Lawrence

Cape Cod

New York

Washington D.C.

Appalachian Mts.

Ozark Plateau

Ohio

Coastal Plain

Cape Hatteras

ATLANTIC OCEAN

BERMUDA (U.K.)

Tropic of Cancer

Gulf of California

Cabo San Lucas

Sierra Madre Occidental

Rio Grande

MEXICO

Houston

Cape Canaveral

The Everglades

Miami

BAHAMAS

Tropic of Cancer

Sierra Madre Oriental

GULF OF MEXICO

Havana

CUBA

DOMINICAN REPUBLIC

HAITI

PUERTO RICO (U.S.)

Mexico City

Gulf of Campeche

Yucatán Peninsula

JAMAICA

CARIBBEAN SEA

BELIZE

GUATEMALA

HONDURAS

EL SALVADOR

NICARAGUA

Lago de Nicaragua

VENEZUELA

PACIFIC OCEAN

COSTA RICA

PANAMA

Golfo de Panamá

COLOMBIA

Equator

SOUTH AMERICA

BRAZIL

Land Elevation

Meters		Feet
3,000		9,840
2,000		6,560
500		1,640
200		656
0		0

Water Depth

0		0
200		656
2,000		6,560

N

0 200 400 600 800 1000 Miles

0 300 600 900 1200 1500 Kilometers

Copyright by Rand McNally & Co.
Lambert Azimuthal Equal Area Projection

ATLAS

RAND McNALLY

National Capital

★ Secondary Capital
(State, Province, or Territory)

■ City over 1,000,000 population

◉ City of 250,000 to 1,000,000 population

· City under 250,000 population

```
0    200   400   600   800   1000 Miles
0  300  600  900  1200  1500 Kilometers
```

Copyright by Rand McNally & Co.
Lambert Azimuthal Equal Area Projection

A11

GULF OF MEXICO

NORTH AMERICA

CUBA
Greater Antilles

HAITI

DOMINICAN REPUBLIC

JAMAICA

PUERTO RICO (U.S.)

BELIZE

MEXICO

Gulf of Honduras

GUATEMALA
HONDURAS

EL SALVADOR

NICARAGUA

CARIBBEAN SEA

Lesser Antilles

ATLANTIC OCEAN

COSTA RICA

PANAMA
Gulf of Panama

Cristóbal Colón Peak △ 18,948 Ft. 5,775m

Caracas

TRINIDAD AND TOBAGO

Llanos

Orinoco

VENEZUELA

GUYANA

Magdalena

Bogotá ✪

SURINAME

FRENCH GUIANA

Cape Orange

COLOMBIA

Galapagos Islands (Ec.)

ECUADOR

△ Chimborazo 20,703 Ft. 6,310m

Putumayo

Japurá

Negro

Amazon

Manaus

Ilha de Marajó

Belém

Equator

Amazon

Amazon Basin

Tocantins

Tapajós

Juruá

B R A Z I L

P E R U

Selvas

Madeira

Ucayali

Mt. Huascarán △ 22,133 Ft. 6,746m

Recife

A n d e s

Lima

Mt. Illampu △ 21,066 Ft. 6,421m

Mato Grosso Plateau

São Francisco

Lake Titicaca

Cordillera Oriental

BOLIVIA

Brasília ✪

Serra do Espinhaço

△ Mt. Sajama 21,463 Ft. 6,542m

Gran Chaco

Atacama Desert

PARAGUAY

Paraná

Tropic of Capricorn

Tropic of Capricorn

Isla San Ambrosio (Chile)

São Paulo

Rio de Janeiro

Mt. Ojos del Salado 22,615 Ft. 6,893m

Isla San Felix (Chile)

A n d e s

Paraná

PACIFIC OCEAN

Archipiélago Juan Fernández (Chile)

URUGUAY

C H I L E

△ Mt. Aconcagua 22,831 Ft. 6,959m

A R G E N T I N A

Santiago ✪

Buenos Aires ✪

Rio de la Plata

Pampas

N

Chiloé

San Matías Gulf

Península Valdés

P a t a g o n i a

San Jorge Gulf

Point Medanoso

ATLANTIC OCEAN

Land Elevation

Meters		Feet
3,000		9,840
2,000		6,560
500		1,640
200		656
0		0

Water Depth

0		0
200		656
2,000		6,560

Grand Bay

FALKLAND ISLANDS (U.K.)

West Falkland

East Falkland

Strait of Magellan

Tierra del Fuego

Cape Horn

South Georgia (U.K.)

| 0 | 200 | 400 | 600 | 800 | 1000 Miles |

| 0 | 300 | 600 | 900 | 1200 | 1500 Kilometers |

Copyright by Rand McNally & Co.
Lambert Azimuthal Equal Area Projection

Drake Passage

South Shetland Islands (U.K.)

South Orkney Islands (U.K.)

South Sandwich Islands (U.K.)

RAND MCNALLY

ATLAS

National Capital

★ Secondary Capital
(State, Province, or Territory)

■ City over 1,000,000 population

▣ City of 250,000 to 1,000,000 population

· City under 250,000 population

0   200   400   600   800   1000 Miles

0   300   600   900   1200   1500 Kilometers

Copyright by Rand McNally & Co.
Lambert Azimuthal Equal Area Projection

RAND McNALLY

A13

ICELAND

Horn

Fontur

Surtsey

ATLANTIC

OCEAN

Arctic Circle

NORWEGIAN
SEA

Lofoten Islands

Kebnekaise
6,926 Ft.
2,111m

Lap

Torneälven

Lulealven

FAROE ISLANDS
(Den.)

Scandinavian
Peninsula

NORWAY SWEDEN

Galdhøpiggen △
8,100 Ft.
2,469m

Umeälven

Gulf of Bothnia

Hebrides

Orkney
Islands

Klaralven

Dalälven

Grampian
Mts.

UNITED

KINGDOM

NORTH
SEA

Skagerrak

DENMARK

Stockholm ✪

Vänern

Vättern

Öland

BALTIC SEA

Land Elevation

Meters	Feet
3,000	9,840
2,000	6,560
500	1,640
200	656
0	0

Water Depth

0	0
200	656
2,000	6,560

N

IRELAND

Irish
Sea

Cheviot
Hills

Great
Britain

St. George's Channel

Thames

London ✪

Bornholm
(Den.)

RUSSIA

NETHERLANDS

Elbe

Oder

Northern Europ

Berlin ✪

GERMANY

POLAND

Wisla

0	100	200	300	400 Miles
0	200	400		600 Kilometers

Copyright by Rand McNally & Co.
Lambert Conformal Conic Projection

English Channel

Strait of Dover

BELGIUM

Rhine

LUX.

Paris ✪

Paris
Basin

Seine

Loire

FRANCE

Bay of Biscay

Dordogne

Saone

Jura

SWITZERLAND

LIECH.

Black
Forest

Danube

CZECH
REPUBLIC

Bohemian
Forest

AUSTRIA

SLOVAKIA

HUNGARY

Great Hungarian
Plain

Cantabrian Mts.

Douro

Duero

Iberian Mts.

Ebro

Pyrenees

ANDORRA

Massif
Central

Mt. Blanc
15,771 Ft.
4,808m

Rhone

A l p s

SLOVENIA

Po

Drava

CROATIA

Dinaric Alps

BOSNIA AND
HERZEGOVINA

Balkan

ADRIATIC SEA

PORTUGAL

Lisbon ✪

Tagus

Iberian
Peninsula

SPAIN

Sierra Morena

Balearic Islands

Minorca

Ibiza

Majorca

MONACO

Corsica
(Fr.)

Rome ✪

Apennines

SAN
MARINO

ITALY

YUGOSLAVIA

ALBANIA

MACE-
DONIA

Pindus Mts.

Strait of Gibraltar

GIBRALTAR
(U.K.)

Algiers

△Vesuvius
4,190 Ft.
1,277m

Sardinia
(It.)

TYRRHENIAN
SEA

IONIAN
SEA

MOROCCO

AFRICA

ALGERIA

TUNISIA

Mt. Etna
10,902 Ft.
3,323m △

Sicily

MALTA

M E D I T E R R A N E

Murmansk

Kola
Peninsula
Ponoy

WHITE
SEA

Timan Ridge

Pechora

Mezen

Northern Dvina

Ob'

Irtysh

FINLAND

Onega

Lake
Onega

Sukhona

Northern Uvals
(Uplands)

Kama

Ural Mountains

ASIA

Lake
Ladoga

Rybinsk
Res.

RUSSIA

Helsinki

Gulf of Finland

ESTONIA

Lake
Peipus

Valdai
Hills

Moscow

Oka

Khopë

50°

70

LATVIA

LITHUANIA

e a-n Plain

Central
Russian
Upland

Don

Ural

KAZAKHSTAN

Neman

Caspian Depression

Syr Darya

BELARUS

Pripyat

Dnieper

Lowland

Donets Basin

Volga

Aral Sea

Kiev

UKRAINE

Dnieper

UZBEKISTAN

Dniester

Amu Darya

60°

Carpathian Mts.

MOLDOVA

Sea of Azov

CASPIAN

40°

TURKMENISTAN

ROMANIA

Transylvanian Alps

Crimean
Peninsula

Caucasus

Mt. Elbrus
18,510 Ft.
5,642m

GEORGIA

Baku

SEA

Danube

BLACK SEA

ARMENIA

AZERBAIJAN

Peninsula

AZER.

BULGARIA

Istanbul

Tehran

IRAN

Mt. Olympus
9,570 Ft.
2,917m

TURKEY

GREECE

AEGEAN SEA

IRAQ

N

S E A

30°

Rhodes

NORTH
CYPRUS

Crete

CYPRUS

SYRIA

LEBANON

Euphrates

Tigris

30°

40°

50°

RAND McNALLY

A15

ICELAND
Reykjavík

ATLANTIC OCEAN

Arctic Circle

NORWEGIAN SEA

FAROE ISLANDS (Den.)

Trondheim

NORWAY   SWEDEN

Umeå

Bergen

Tampere

Aberdeen

SCOTLAND

Glasgow

Edinburgh

UNITED

NORTH SEA

Oslo

Vänern

Stockholm

Vättern

Göteborg

DENMARK

Copenhagen

Skagerrak

Gulf of Bothnia

BALTIC SEA

LITHUANIA

Kaliningrad   RUSSIA

Gdańsk

Szczecin   POLAND

Wisła

Warsaw

KINGDOM

NORTHERN IRELAND

Belfast

Irish Sea

Dublin

IRELAND

Cork

Liverpool   Manchester

WALES

Birmingham   ENGLAND

Cardiff

Thames

NETHERLANDS

Amsterdam

The Hague

London

Hamburg

Elbe

Berlin

Oder

GERMANY

Dresden

Wrocław

Kraków

Plymouth

St. George's Channel

English Channel

Strait of Dover

Le Havre

Brussels   BELGIUM

Cologne

Bonn

LUX.

Frankfurt

Luxembourg

Paris

Rhine

CZECH REPUBLIC

Prague

SLOVAKIA

National Capital

Secondary Capital
(State, Province, or Territory)

■ City over 1,000,000 population

▣ City of 250,000 to 1,000,000 population

• City under 250,000 population

0   100   200   300   400 Miles

0   200   400   600 Kilometers

Copyright by Rand McNally & Co.
Lambert Conformal Conic Projection

Nantes

Loire

Seine

Strasbourg

Stuttgart

Danube

Vienna

Bratislava

AUSTRIA

Munich

FRANCE

Bay of Biscay

Bordeaux

Zürich

Bern

SWITZERLAND

Geneva

Lyon

LIECH.

Rhône

SLOVENIA

Ljubljana

Budapest

HUNGARY

A Coruña

Gijón

Bilbao

Valladolid

Ebro

Zaragoza

ANDORRA

Toulouse

Marseille

MONACO

Turin

Milan

Venice

Po

Zagreb

CROATIA

Belgrade

Porto

Genoa

Nice

SAN MARINO

BOSNIA AND HERZEGOVINA

Sarajevo

Lisbon

Tagus

Madrid

PORTUGAL

SPAIN

Barcelona

Florence

YUGOSLAVIA

ADRIATIC SEA

Valencia

Córdoba

Corsica (Fr.)

Rome

VATICAN CITY

ITALY

Skopje

MACE-DONIA

ALBANIA

Tiranë

Seville

Palma

Sardinia (It.)

Naples

Bari

Málaga

GIBRALTAR (U.K.)

Strait of Gibraltar

Cagliari

TYRRHENIAN SEA

Rabat

Algiers

AFRICA

MOROCCO

ALGERIA

Tunis

TUNISIA

Palermo

Sicily

Catania

IONIAN SEA

MEDITERRANEAN SEA

Valletta   MALTA

Hammerfest

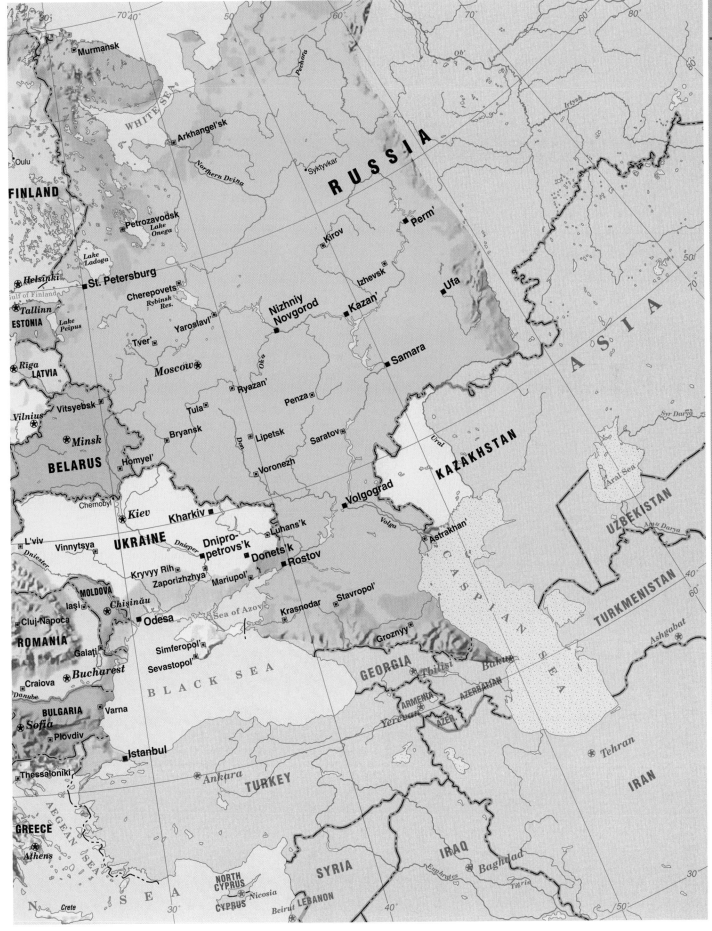

Murmansk

WHITE SEA

Oulu

FINLAND

Arkhangel'sk

Northern Dvina

Pechora

RUSSIA

Syktyvkar

Petrozavodsk
Lake
Onega

Helsinki

Lake
Ladoga

St. Petersburg

Kirov

Perm'

Tallinn

Gulf of Finland

ESTONIA

Lake
Peipus

Cherepovets
Rybinsk
Res.

Izhevsk

Ufa

Riga

Tver'

Yaroslavl'

Nizhniy
Novgorod

Kazan'

LATVIA

Oka

ASIA

Vilnius

Vitsyebsk

Moscow

Samara

Volga

Minsk

Ryazan'

Tula

Penza

BELARUS

Homyel'

Bryansk

Don

Lipetsk

Saratov

Ural

KAZAKHSTAN

Aral Sea

Chernobyl

Voronezh

Kiev

Kharkiv

Volgograd

UZBEKISTAN

Amu Darya

Syr Darya

L'viv

Vinnytsya

UKRAINE

Dnieper

Dnipro-
petrovs'k

Luhans'k

Astrakhan'

Dniester

Kryvyy Rih

Donets'k

Rostov

CASPIAN

TURKMENISTAN

MOLDOVA

Iaşi

Chişinău

Zaporizhzhya

Mariupol'

Krasnodar

Stavropol'

SEA

Cluj-Napoca

Odesa

Sea of Azov

Ashgabat

ROMANIA

Galaţi

Simferopol'

Groznyy

Baku

Craiova

Danube

Sevastopol'

BLACK   SEA

GEORGIA

Tbilisi

AZERBAIJAN

Tehran

BULGARIA

Varna

ARMENIA

AZER.

Sofia

Plovdiv

Yerevan

IRAN

Thessaloniki

Istanbul

Ankara

TURKEY

IRAQ

Baghdad

GREECE

Athens

AEGEAN SEA

Euphrates

Tigris

N

Crete

NORTH
CYPRUS

Nicosia

CYPRUS

SYRIA

Beirut LEBANON

ATLANTIC

OCEAN

EUROPE

ASIA

FRANCE · AUS. · HUNG. · ROMANIA · UKRAINE · RUSSIA · KAZ.

Aral Sea · UZBEKISTAN

PORTUGAL · ITALY · BOS · YUGO · BUL. · Black Sea · GEORGIA · ARM. · AZER. · TURKMENISTAN

Azores (Port.) · SPAIN · ALB. · GREECE · TURKEY · IRAQ · IRAN

Madeira Islands (Port.) · Strait of Gibraltar · Mediterranean Sea · MALTA · CYPRUS · SYRIA · LEBANON · ISRAEL · JORDAN · KUWAIT

Algiers · Gulf of Sidra · Cairo · SAUDI ARABIA · U.A.E. · QATAR

Canary Islands (Spain) · MOROCCO · TUNISIA · Qattara Depression · Red Sea · OMAN

Atlas Mountains · Great Western Desert · Great Eastern Desert · ALGERIA · LIBYA · EGYPT · Libyan Desert · Lake Nasser · Nubian Desert · YEMEN

WESTERN SAHARA (MOROCCO)

Tropic of Cancer · Ijafene · Sahara · Desert · Tahat 9,541 Ft. 2,908m · Ahaggar Mts. · Tibesti Massif · Mt. Koussi 11,204 Ft. 3,415m · Ennedi · Khartoum · Blue Nile · White Nile · ERITREA · DJIBOUTI · Gulf of Aden · Cape Gwardafuy · Socotra (Yem.)

MAURITANIA · MALI · Aïr (Mts.) · NIGER · CHAD · SUDAN · Lake Tana · Ethiopian Plateau

CAPE VERDE · Sénégal · Sahel · Lake Chad · As Sudd · Great Rift Valley · ETHIOPIA · SOMALIA

Cape Verde · Dakar · SENEGAL · Niger · BURKINA FASO · NIGERIA · Jos Plateau · Benue · CENTRAL AFRICAN REPUBLIC · Mountain Nile · Uele · Lake Turkana

GAMBIA · GUINEA-BISSAU · GUINEA · BENIN · GHANA · TOGO · Lake Volta

SIERRA LEONE · COTE D'IVOIRE · Lagos · CAMEROON · Mt. Cameroon 13,451 Ft. 4,100m · UGANDA · KENYA · Mt. Kenya 17,058 Ft. 5,199m

LIBERIA · Gulf of Guinea · Bioko · EQUATORIAL GUINEA · Congo · REP. OF CONGO · Ubangi · Congo · Lake Victoria · RWANDA · Nairobi · Kilimanjaro 19,340 Ft. 5,895m

Equator · SAO TOME AND PRINCIPE · GABON · Congo Basin · DEM. REP. OF CONGO · BURUNDI · Serengeti Plain · Masai Steppe

Ascension (St. Helena) · Kinshasa · Kwango · Kasai · Lake Tanganyika · TANZANIA · Zanzibar · INDIAN OCEAN

SEYCHELLES

Cuango · Cuanza · ANGOLA · Lake Nyasa · COMOROS · Cape Ambre

ATLANTIC · St. Helena (U.K.) · MALAWI · Mayotte (Fr.)

Cunene · ZAMBIA · Zambezi · MOZAMBIQUE · MADAGASCAR · MAURITIUS

OCEAN · Cuando · Okavango · Victoria Falls · Lake Kariba · Reunion (Fr.)

NAMIBIA · Namib Desert · BOTSWANA · Kalahari Desert · ZIMBABWE · Limpopo · Barra Point

Tropic of Capricorn · Johannesburg · SWAZILAND · Cape Sainte-Marie

Vaal · LESOTHO · Drakensberg · Orange · SOUTH AFRICA

Cape of Good Hope · Cape Agulhas

Tristan da Cunha Group (St. Helena)

Prince Edward Islands (S. Af.) · Crozet Islands (Fr.)

Land Elevation

Meters		Feet
3,000		9,840
2,000		6,560
500		1,640
200		656
0		0

Water Depth

0		0
200		656
2,000		6,560

0 200 400 600 800 1000 Miles

0 300 600 900 1200 1500 Kilometers

Copyright by Rand McNally & Co.
Lambert Azimuthal Equal Area Projection

RAND M\cNALLY

A18

ATLAS

ATLANTIC
OCEAN

ICELAND

Arctic Circle

ARCTIC OCEAN

Barents
Sea

IRELAND

UNITED
KINGDOM

FAROE
ISLANDS
(Den.)

Severnaya
Zemlya

London

NORWAY

North Sea

DENMARK

SWEDEN

FINLAND

Novaya
Zemlya

Kara Sea

Yamal
Pen.

PORTUGAL

SPAIN

FRANCE

GERMANY

POLAND

BELARUS

ESTONIA
LATVIA
LITH.

Ural Mountains

Ob

West

Siberian

MOROCCO

ANDORRA

MONACO

AUSTRIA HUNGARY

SLOVAKIA

Moscow

Lowland

Yenisey

ALGERIA

ITALY

CROAT.

YUGO.

ROMANIA

UKRAINE

Volga

Ob

Irtysh

Novosibirsk

TUNISIA

ALB.

BULGARIA

Ishim

Irtysh

GREECE

Black Sea

Caspian Depression

Astana

KAZAKHSTAN

LIBYA

Ankara

GEORGIA

Caucasus

Aral
Sea

Syr Darya

Lake
Balkhash

TURKEY

N. CYPRUS

ARM.

AZER.

Mount Ararat
16,940 Ft.
5,165m

Ust-Urt
Plateau

UZBEKISTAN

Tian Shan

CYPRUS

LEBANON

SYRIA

Caspian
Sea

Kara Kum
(Desert)

Amu Darya

KYRGYZSTAN

ISRAEL

Tigris

TURKMENISTAN

TAJIKISTAN

Tarim Basin

Cairo

Sinai
Pen.

JORDAN

IRAQ

Euphrates

Tehran

Dasht-e Kavir

Pamirs

K2 (Qogir Feng)
28,250 Ft.
8,611m

Altun Shan

Nile

Zagros Mts.

IRAN

Hindu Kush

Kunlun Mts.

An-Nafud

KUWAIT

AFGHANISTAN

EGYPT

Persian Gulf

SAUDI
ARABIA

BAHRAIN

QATAR

PAKISTAN

HIMALAYA MTS.

CHAD

SUDAN

Red Sea

Arabian
Peninsula

U.A.E.

Gulf of
Oman

Indus

New
Delhi

Great
Indian
Desert

Ganges

NEPAL

Mt. Everest
29,035 Ft.
8,850m

ERITREA

Rub Al-Khali

OMAN

INDIA

YEMEN

DJIBOUTI

Gulf of
Aden

Godavari

Mumbai
(Bombay)

Western Ghats

Deccan
Plateau

Eastern Ghats

ETHIOPIA

Socotra
(Yem.)

Arabian Sea

Bay of
Bengal

DEM. REP.
OF THE CONGO
(ZAIRE)

UGANDA

KENYA

SOMALIA

N

RWANDA

Lakshadweep
(India)

SRI LANKA

BURUNDI

MALDIVES

TANZANIA

INDIAN OCEAN

ZAMBIA

0   200   400   600   800 Miles

MALAWI

0   200   400   600   800   1000 Kilometers

Copyright by Rand McNally & Co.
Lambert Azimuthal Equal Area Projection

MOZAMBIQUE

ATLAS

Land Elevation

Meters		Feet
3,000		9,840
2,000		6,560
500		1,640
200		656
0		0

Water Depth

0		0
200		656
2,000		6,560

RUSSIA

Taymyr Peninsula

Laptev Sea

New Siberian Islands

East Siberian Sea

Central Siberian Uplands

Kolyma

Indigirka

Arctic Circle

Bering Sea

Aleutian Islands (U.S.)

Sayan Mountains

Angara

Siberia

Lake Baikal

Verkhoyansk Mts.

Lena

Stanovoy Range

Amur

Stanovoy Range

Greater Khingan Range

Sikhote-Alin Mts.

Tatar Strait

Sea of Okhotsk

Kamchatka Peninsula

Sakhalin

Kuril Islands

Sea of Japan

Hokkaido

Honshu

PACIFIC OCEAN

Tropic of Cancer

Altai Mts.

MONGOLIA

Gobi Desert

Beijing

NORTH KOREA

SOUTH KOREA

Yellow Sea

Shanghai

East China Sea

Tokyo

Mt. Fuji 12,388 ft. 3,776m

JAPAN

Shikoku

Kyushu

Qilian Shan

Huang

Qinling Shandi

Chang (Yangtze)

CHINA

NORTHERN MARIANA ISLANDS (U.S.)

GUAM (U.S.)

FEDERATED STATES OF MICRONESIA

BHUTAN

Brahmaputra

Irrawaddy

Salween

Xi

TAIWAN

Luzon Strait

Luzon

Hainan Island

Gulf of Tonkin

Philippine Sea

BNGL.

MYANMAR

LAOS

Mekong

Red

South China Sea

Manila

PHILIPPINES

PALAU

Equator

THAILAND

Bangkok

CAMBODIA

VIETNAM

Mindanao

Sulu Sea

Andaman Islands (India)

Andaman Sea

Gulf of Thailand

Celebes Sea

Moluccas

New Guinea

PAPUA NEW GUINEA

Nicobar Islands (India)

MALAY PENINSULA

MALAYSIA

BRUNEI

MALAYSIA

Celebes

Ceram

Str. of Malacca

Singapore

Borneo

Greater Sunda Islands

Banda Sea

Arafura Sea

Gulf of Carpentaria

Coral Sea

Sumatra

INDONESIA

EAST TIMOR

Timor

Timor Sea

AUSTRALIA

Jakarta

Java

Java Sea

RAND McNALLY

A21

ATLANTIC
OCEAN

ARCTIC OCEAN

ICELAND

Arctic Circle

FARØE
ISLANDS
(Den.)

SVALBARD
(Nor.)

Spitsbergen

Franz Josef
Land

Severnaya
Zemlya

80°

Novaya
Zemlya

Norwegian Sea

Barents
Sea

Kara Sea

Noril'sk

20°

IRELAND

UNITED
KINGDOM

London

NORWAY

SWEDEN

FINLAND

Pechora

Ob'

Yenisey

PORTUGAL

10°

SPAIN

France

Paris

DENMARK

North Sea

ESTONIA

LATVIA

LITH.

Moscow

R U S

Yekaterinburg

Chelyabinsk

MOROCCO

GIBRALTAR

ALGERIA

TUNISIA

MONACO

ANDORRA

ITALY

Adriatic Sea

GERMANY

POLAND

BELARUS

Ishim

Irtysh

Ob'

Novosibirsk

Omsk

Barnaul

30°

AUSTRIA

HUNGARY

BOS.
CRO.
YUGO.
ALB.
MAC.

ROMANIA

BULGARIA

Kiev

UKRAINE

Danube

Volga

Astana

KAZAKHSTAN

Karaganda

Semipalatinsk

Öskemen

Mediterranean Sea

GREECE

Black Sea

Istanbul

Izmir

Ankara

TURKEY

GEORGIA

Tbilisi

ARM.

Yerevan

AZER.

Baku

Caspian Sea

Aral
Sea

Syr Darya

Lake
Balkhash

Almaty

Ürümqi

LIBYA

20°

EGYPT

Nile

Cairo

N. CYPRUS
CYPRUS
LEBANON
ISRAEL

Damascus

SYRIA

Amman

JORDAN

Euphrates

Tigris

Tabriz

Tehran

Mashhad

UZBEKISTAN

Ashgabat

TURKMENISTAN

Tashkent

Bishkek

KYRGYZSTAN

Dushanbe

TAJIKISTAN

CHAD

IRAQ

Baghdad

IRAN

Eşfahān

Kuwait

KUWAIT

Persian Gulf

SAUDI
ARABIA

Riyadh

Jiddah

Red Sea

SUDAN

10°

Nile

Blue Nile

ERITREA

DJIBOUTI

ETHIOPIA

BAHRAIN
QATAR

Abu Dhabi

U.A.E.

Gulf of Oman

Muscat

OMAN

YEMEN

Sanaa

Gulf of Aden

Socotra
(Yem.)

Kabul

AFGHANISTAN

Islāmābād

Lahore

Amritsar

PAKISTAN

Indus

Delhi
New
Delhi

Karachi

Hyderābād

Ahmadābād

Brahmaputra

NEPAL

Kathmāndu

Ganges

Kānpur

Ganges

INDIA

Nāgpur

Godāvari

Kolkata
(Calcutta)

Hyderābād

DEM. REP.
OF THE CONGO
(ZAIRE)

UGANDA

RWANDA

BURUNDI

KENYA

SOMALIA

Arabian
Sea

Mumbai
(Bombay)

Bangalore

Lakshadweep
(India)

Chennai
(Madras)

Bay of
Bengal

TANZANIA

N

0°

0°

Colombo

SRI LANKA

MALDIVES

INDIAN OCEAN

ZAMBIA

MALAWI

MOZAMBIQUE

0   200   400   600   800 Miles

0   200 400 600 800 1000 Kilometers

Copyright by Rand McNally & Co.
Lambert Azimuthal Equal Area Projection

RAND McNALLY

A22

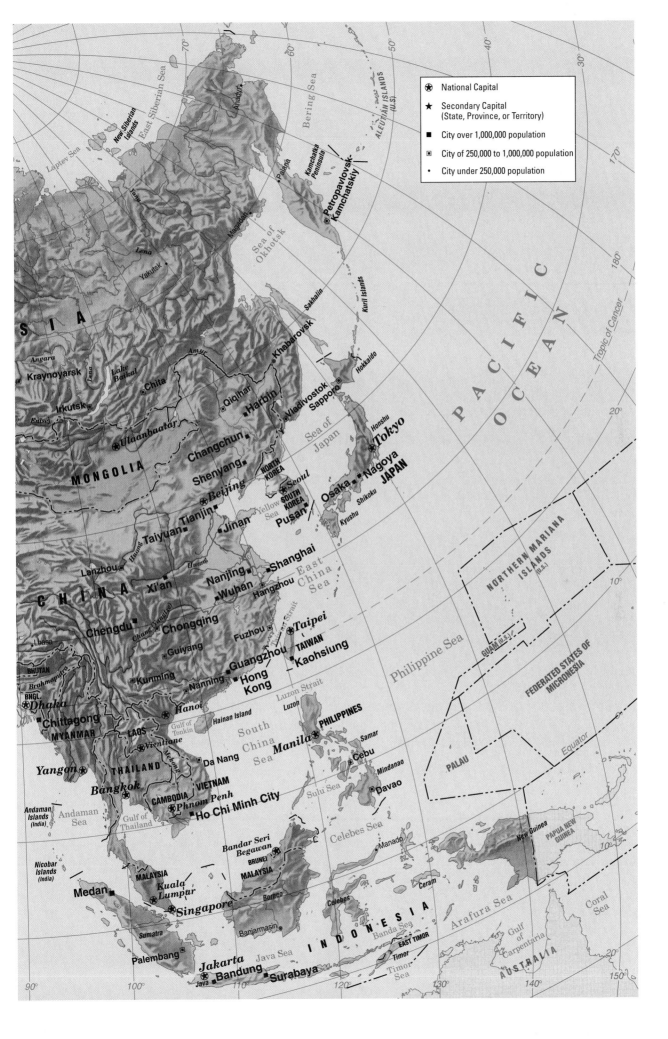

✪	National Capital	
★	Secondary Capital (State, Province, or Territory)	
■	City over 1,000,000 population	
▣	City of 250,000 to 1,000,000 population	
•	City under 250,000 population	

ATLAS

RAND McNALLY

A23

RAND M^cNALLY

A24

North Pole

ALASKA
(U.S.)
Chukchi
Sea
Wrangell I.
Barrow
Point Barrow
Srednekolymsk
East Siberian
Sea
CANADA
Norman Wells
Great Bear
Lake
Amundsen
Gulf
Banks
Beaufort
Sea
New
Siberian I.
New Siberian
Islands
Kotelny I.
Tiksi
RUSSIA
Verkhoyansk
Lena
Laptev Sea
ARCTIC OCEAN
Queen Elizabeth Islands
Prince Patrick
Island
Melville
VICTORIA I.
Kalukiutiak
Prince of Wales
Somerset
Gulf of
Boothia
Devon I.
ELLESMERE I.
Bylot I.
Etah
Thule
Peary
Land
BAFFIN
Baffin
Bay
Godhavn
Disko
Davis Strait
GREENLAND
(Den.)
Elleh
Ringnes I.
Axel
Heiberg I.
North Magnetic
Pole
North Pole
Alert
Taymyr
Peninsula
Severnaya
Zemlya
Kotuj
Lake
Taymyr
Khatanga
Dikson
Kara
Sea
Franz
Josef
Land
Novaya
Zemlya
SVALBARD
(Nor.)
SPITSBERGEN
Greenland Sea
Jan Mayen
(Nor.)
Gunnbjorn Fjeld
12,139 ft.
3,700m
Angmagssalik
Vorkuta
Barents
Sea
North Cape
Hammerfest
Murmansk
Kola
Peninsula
NORWAY FINLAND
Arhangel'sk

0   200   400   600 Miles
0 200 400 600 800 1000 Kilometers
Copyright by Rand McNally & Co.
Azimuthal Equidistant Projection

Land Elevation		
Meters		Feet
3,000		9,840
2,000		6,560
500		1,640
200		656
0		0
Water Depth		
0		0
200		656
2,000		6,560

South Pole

FALKLAND ISLANDS
(U.K.)
Strait of
Magellan
Cape Horn
Drake Passage
PACIFIC OCEAN
Antarctic Circle
Thurston I.
Amundsen
Sea
Bellingshausen
Sea
South Shetland
Islands (U.K.)
Graham
Land
Adelaide I.
Alexander I.
Antarctic Peninsula
Larsen Ice
Shelf
South Orkney
Islands (U.K.)
Scotia Sea
South Georgia
(U.K.)
South Sandwich
Islands (U.K.)
ATLANTIC OCEAN
Ellsworth
Land
Mt. Sidley
13,717 Ft.
4,181m
Marie
Byrd
Land
Rockefeller
Plateau
Roosevelt I.
Ross
Sea
Ross Ice
Shelf
Cape
Adare
Mt. Erebus
12,451 Ft.
3,795m
Victoria Land
Transantarctic Mountains
Mt. Kirkpatrick
14,856 Ft.
4,528m
Ellsworth Mts.
Vinson Massif
16,066 Ft.
4,897m
Ronne Ice
Shelf
Berkner I.
Filchner Ice
Shelf
Pensacola
Mts.
Weddell Sea
Coats
Land
Cape Norvegia
South
Pole
ANTARCTICA
Queen Maud
Land
Mülig
Hofmann
Mts.
Ser Rondane
Mts.
Antarctic Circle
Macquarie Island
(Austl.)
South
Magnetic
Pole
George V Coast
Wilkes Land
American
Highland
Lambert Glacier
Amery Ice
Shelf
Enderby
Land
Napier
Mts.
Cape
Ann
Cape
Darnley
Prince
Edward Is.
(S. Afr.)
Cape
Poinsett
INDIAN OCEAN
Crozet
Archipelago
(Fr.)

0   200   400   600   800   1000 Miles
0 300 600 900 1200 1500 Kilometres
Copyright by Rand McNally & Co.
Polar Stereographic Projection

RAND McNALLY

A25

Human-Environment Interaction
An orbiting satellite took these photographs of Earth after dark. They have been combined into one image. The glow of electric lights shows the locations of cities and towns.

INTRODUCTION TO WORLD CULTURES AND GEOGRAPHY

Map Basics

Maps are an important tool for studying the use of space on Earth. This handbook covers the basic map skills and information that geographers rely on as they investigate the world—and the skills you will need as you study geography.

Mapmaking depends on surveying, or measuring and recording the features of Earth's surface. Until recently, this could be undertaken only on land or sea. Today, aerial photography and satellite imaging are the most popular ways to gather data.

Location • Magnetic compasses, introduced by the Chinese in the 1100s, help people accurately determine directions. ▲

Location • Determining a ship's location at sea was the purpose of this 1750 instrument, called a sextant. ▶

Location • An early example of a three-dimensional geographic grid. ▼

Human-Environment Interaction • Nigerian surveyors use a theodolite, which measures angles and distances on Earth. ▲

South America's Economic Activity

►► Reading a Map
Most maps have these parts, which help you to read and understand the information presented.

TITLE The title indicates the subject of the map and tells you what information it contains.

SYMBOLS Symbols may stand for capital cities, economic activities, or natural resources. Check the map legend for more details.

COLORS Colors show a variety of information on a map. The map legend tells what the colors mean.

LABELS Labels are words or phrases that name features on the map.

LINES OF LONGITUDE These are imaginary lines that show distances east or west of the prime meridian.

LINES OF LATITUDE These are imaginary lines that show distances north or south of the equator.

LEGEND A legend or key lists and explains the symbols and colors used on the map.

COMPASS ROSE The compass rose shows you north (N), south (S), east (E), and west (W) on the map. Sometimes only north is shown.

SCALE A scale compares a unit of length on the map and a unit of distance on Earth.

ATLANTIC OCEAN

PACIFIC OCEAN

Orinoco River

AMAZON BASIN

Amazon River

BRAZILIAN HIGHLANDS

Paraguay River

Recife

La Paz

Lima

Santiago

Buenos Aires

ANDES MOUNTAINS

20°S
30°S
40°S
50°S

Legend
- Commercial fishing
- Farming
- Hunting and gathering
- Livestock ranching
- Limited economic activity
- Gold
- Hydroelectric power
- Natural gas
- Petroleum
- Silver
- Timber

0   250   500 miles
0   250   500 kilometers

Map Basics, cont.

Longitude Lines (Meridians)

Latitude Lines (Parallels)

▶▶ Longitude and Latitude Lines

Longitude and latitude lines appear together on a map and allow you to pinpoint the absolute locations of cities and other geographic features. You express these locations as coordinates of intersecting lines. These are measured in degrees.

Longitude lines are imaginary lines that run north and south; they are also known as meridians. They show distances in degrees east or west of the prime meridian. The prime meridian is a longitude line that runs from the North Pole to the South Pole through Greenwich, England. It marks 0° longitude.

Latitude lines are imaginary lines that run east to west around the globe; they are also known as parallels. They show distances in degrees north or south of the equator. The equator is a latitude line that circles Earth halfway between the north and south poles. It marks 0° latitude. The tropics of Cancer and Capricorn are parallels that form the boundaries of the tropical zone, a region that stays warm all year.

▶▶ Hemisphere

Hemisphere is a term for half the globe. The globe can be divided into northern and southern hemispheres (separated by the equator) or into eastern and western hemispheres. The United States is located in the northern and western hemispheres.

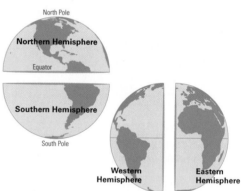

▶▶ Scale

A geographer decides what scale to use by determining how much detail to show. If many details are needed, a large scale is used. If fewer details are needed, a small scale is used.

Small scale used, without a lot of detail. ▼

WASHINGTON, D.C., METRO AREA
Scale: 1:4,500,000
1 inch = 70 miles

Larger scale used, with a lot of detail. ▼

WASHINGTON, D.C.
Scale: 1:88,700
1 inch = 1.4 miles

▶▶ Projections

A projection is a way of showing the curved surface of Earth on a flat map. Flat maps cannot show sizes, shapes, and directions with total accuracy. As a result, all projections distort some aspect of Earth's surface. Below are four projections.

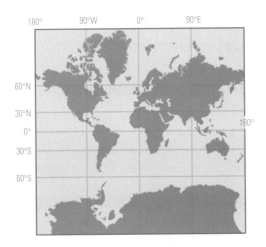

Mercator Projection • The Mercator projection shows most of the continents as they look on a globe. However, the projection stretches out the lands near the north and south poles. The Mercator projection is used for all kinds of navigation. ▲

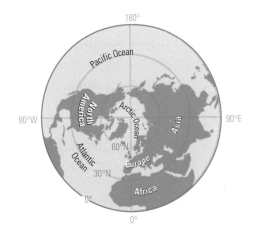

Azimuthal Projection • An azimuthal projection shows Earth so that a straight line from the central point to any other point on the map corresponds to the shortest distance between the two points. Sizes and shapes of the continents are distorted. ▲

Homolosine Projection • This projection shows landmasses' shapes and sizes accurately, but distances are not correct. ▲

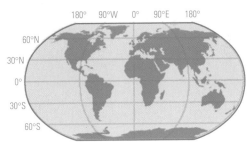

Robinson Projection • For textbook maps, the Robinson projection is commonly used. It shows the entire Earth, with continents and oceans having nearly their true sizes and shapes. However, the landmasses near the poles appear flattened. ▲

MAP PRACTICE

MAIN IDEAS

1. (a) What are the longitude and latitude of your city or town?

(b) What information is provided by the legend in the map on page 5?

(c) What is a projection? Compare and contrast the depictions of Antarctica in the Mercator and Robinson projections.

CRITICAL THINKING

2. **Making Inferences** Why do you think latitude and longitude are important to sailors?

Think About

• the landmarks you use to find your way around

• the landmarks available to sailors on the ocean

Different Types of Maps

▶▶ Physical Maps

Physical maps help you see the landforms and bodies of water in specific areas. By studying a physical map, you can learn the relative locations and characteristics of places in a region.

On a physical map, color, shading, or contour lines are used to show elevations or altitudes, also called relief.

Ask these questions about the physical features shown on a physical map:

- ◆ Where on Earth's surface is this area located?
- ◆ What is its relative location?
- ◆ What is the shape of the region?
- ◆ In which directions do the rivers flow? How might the directions of flow affect travel and transportation in the region?
- ◆ Are there mountains or deserts? How might they affect the people living in the area?

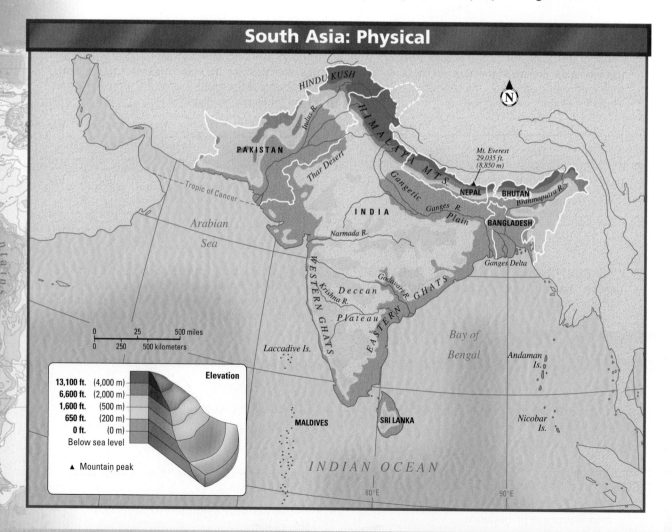

South Asia: Physical

▶▶ Political Maps

Political maps show features that humans have created on Earth's surface. Included on a political map may be cities, states, provinces, territories, and countries.

Ask these questions about the political features shown on a political map:

- ◆ Where on Earth's surface is this area located?
- ◆ What is its relative location? How might a country's location affect its economy and its relationships with other countries?
- ◆ What is the shape and size of the country? How might its shape and size affect the people living in the country?
- ◆ Who are the region's, country's, state's, or city's neighbors?
- ◆ How populated does the area seem to be? How might that affect activities there?

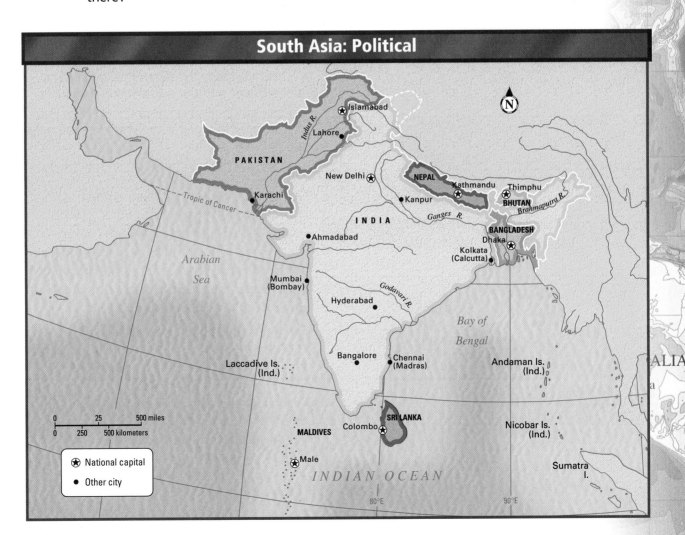

▶▶ Thematic Maps

Geographers also rely on thematic maps, which focus on specific ideas. For example, in this textbook you will see thematic maps that show climates, types of vegetation, natural resources, population densities, and economic activities. Some thematic maps show historical trends; others may focus on movements of people or ideas. Thematic maps may be presented in a variety of ways.

Cultural Legacy of the Roman Empire

Christian areas around A.D. 500

Romance language spoken, present day

Boundary of Roman Empire, A.D. 395

North Sea
ATLANTIC OCEAN
Rhine R.
Rome
Danube R.
Black Sea
40°N
Mediterranean Sea
30°N
Red Sea
20°N

0   500   1,000 miles
0   500   1,000 kilometers
Azimuthal Equidistant Projection

Qualitative Maps On a qualitative map, colors, symbols, dots, or lines are used to help you see patterns related to a specific idea. The map shown here depicts the influence of the Roman Empire on Europe, North Africa, and Southwest Asia.

Use the suggestions below to help you interpret the map.

♦ Check the title to identify the theme and the data being presented.

♦ Carefully study the legend to understand the theme and the information presented.

♦ Look at the physical or political features of the area. How might the theme of the map affect them?

♦ What are the relationships among the data?

Oil Reserves Cartogram

1. KAZAKHSTAN
2. AZERBAIJAN

NORWAY
CANADA
UNITED KINGDOM
ROMANIA
RUSSIA
CHINA   MALAYSIA
UNITED STATES
SYRIA   IRAN   INDIA   BRUNEI
MEXICO   IRAQ   INDONESIA
AUSTRALIA
COLOMBIA   KUWAIT
ECUADOR   VENEZUELA   ALGERIA   EGYPT
ARGENTINA   LIBYA   QATAR
SAUDI ARABIA
NIGERIA   GABON   U.A.E.
BRAZIL   REP. OF CONGO   ANGOLA
YEMEN   OMAN

1–10 billion barrels   40–100 billion barrels
10–40 billion barrels   100+ billion barrels
▪ Each square equals 1 billion barrels

Cartograms A cartogram presents information about countries other than their shapes and sizes. The size of each country is determined by the data being presented, and not by its actual land size. On the cartogram shown here, the countries' sizes show the amounts of their oil reserves.

Use the suggestions below to help you interpret the map.

♦ Check the title and the legend to identify the data being presented.

♦ Look at the relative sizes of the countries shown. Which is the largest?

♦ Which countries are smallest?

♦ How do the sizes of these countries on a physical map differ from their sizes in the cartogram?

♦ What are the relationships among the data?

Flow-Line Maps Flow-line maps illustrate movements of people, goods, or ideas. The movements are usually shown by a series of arrows. Locations, directions, and scopes of movement can be seen. The width of an arrow may show how extensive a flow is. Often the information is related to a period of time. The map shown here portrays the movement of the Bantu peoples in Africa.

Use the suggestions below to help you interpret the map.

♦ Check the title and the legend to identify the data being presented.

♦ Over what period of time did the movement occur?

♦ In what directions did the movement occur?

♦ How extensive was the movement?

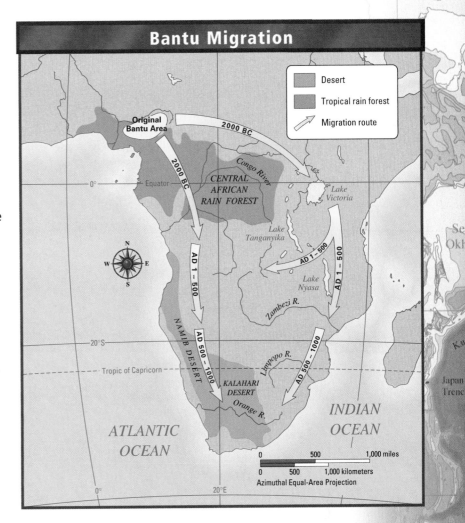

MAP PRACTICE

Use pages 8–11 to help you answer these questions. Use the maps on pages 8–9 to answer questions 1–3.

1. In what direction does the Ganges River flow?

2. Kathmandu is the capital of which South Asian nation?

3. Which city is closer to the Thar Desert— Lahore, Pakistan, or New Delhi, India?

4. Why are only a few nations shown in the cartogram?

5. Which kind of thematic map would be best for showing the locations of climate zones?

Exploring Local Geography Obtain a physical-political map of your state. Use the data on it to create **two separate maps.** One should show physical features only, and the other should show political features only.

Geographic Dictionary

SEA LEVEL
the level of the ocean's surface, used as a reference point when measuring heights and depths on Earth's surface

VOLCANO
an opening in Earth's surface through which gases and lava escape from Earth's interior

BAY
part of an ocean or a lake partially enclosed by land

(RIVER) MOUTH
the place where a river flows into a lake or an ocean

CAPE
a pointed piece of land extending into an ocean or a lake

HARBOR
a sheltered area of water, deep enough for docking ships

STRAIT
a narrow strip of water connecting two large bodies of water

MARSH
a soft, wet, low-lying, grassy area located between water and dry land

ISLAND
a body of land surrounded by water

DELTA
a triangular area of land formed from deposits at the mouth of a river

FLOOD PLAIN
flat land alongside a river, formed by mud and silt deposited by floods

SWAMP
an area of land that is saturated by water

DESERT
a dry area where few plants grow

OASIS
a spot of fertile land in a desert, supplied with water by a well or spring

BUTTE
a raised, flat area of land with steep sides, smaller than a mesa

MOUNTAIN
a natural elevation of Earth's surface
with steep sides, higher than a hill

STEPPE
a wide, treeless plain

PRAIRIE
a large, level area
of grassland with
few or no trees

VALLEY
low land
between hills
or mountains

GLACIER
a large ice mass that
moves slowly down a
mountain or over land

CATARACT
a large, powerful
waterfall

MESA
a wide, flat-topped
mountain with steep sides,
larger than a butte

CANYON
a deep, narrow valley
with steep sides

CLIFF
the steep, almost
vertical edge of a hill,
mountain, or plain

PLATEAU
a broad, flat area of land higher
than the surrounding land

Welcome to the World

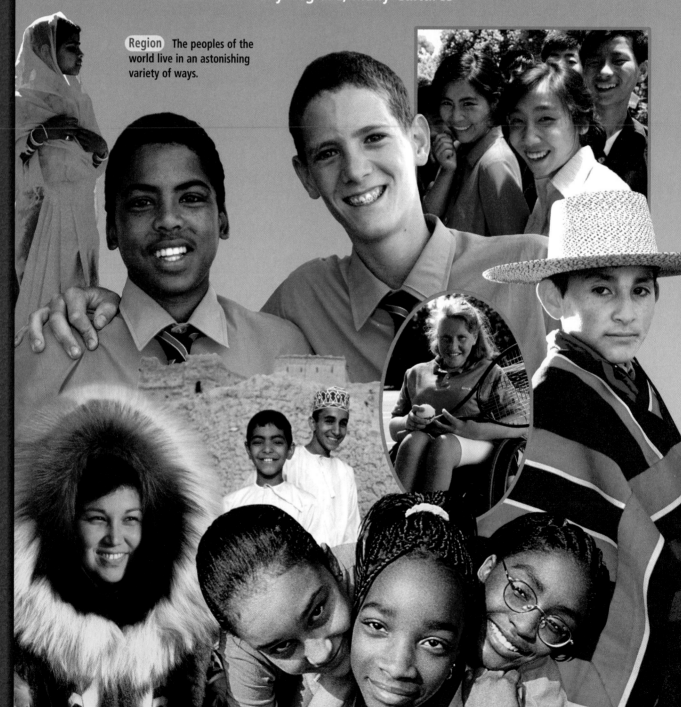

SECTION 1 The World at Your Fingertips

SECTION 2 Many Regions, Many Cultures

Region The peoples of the world live in an astonishing variety of ways.

How have geographic features influenced settlement patterns?

Movement • People settle where they can most easily and comfortably meet their needs for clean water, food, work, communication, trade, and transportation. Before there were good roads, boats were the easiest way to travel or send and receive goods. As a result, people often settled near rivers, lakes, and oceans. They also often settled where the land was suitable for cultivation and the climate was comfortable. You will not find many cities in the frozen wastelands of Siberia.

What do you think?

♦ Why are there few settlements in the desert?

♦ Why is there often a city where two rivers meet?

BEFORE YOU READ

▶▶ *What Do You Know?*

You live in the world, but how much do you know about it? The best way to find out is through social studies. *Social studies* is an umbrella term. It covers history, geography, economics, government, and culture. History, as you probably know, is the study of the past. How clearly can you define the other terms? How do you think they can help you to learn about the world?

▶▶ *What Do You Want to Know?*

Think about what else you need to know before you can come up with clear, complete, and accurate definitions. Record any questions you have in a notebook before you read this chapter.

Region • Citizens have more rights under some governments than others. ▼

READ AND TAKE NOTES

Reading Strategy: Categorizing One way to make sense of information is to organize it in a chart. Writing your notes in a chart with categories can help you remember the most important parts of what you have read.

- Copy the chart below into your notebook.
- As you read the chapter, note the definition of each term listed on the chart.
- Write these definitions next to the appropriate heading.

Region •
Prepared for a flood,
this house was built to suit its environment. ▲

Term	Definition
history	
geography	
economics	
government	
culture	

The World at Your Fingertips

TERMS & NAMES
history
geography
government
citizen
economics
scarcity
culture
culture trait

MAIN IDEA

Social studies includes information from five fields of learning to provide a well-rounded picture of the world and its peoples.

WHY IT MATTERS NOW

Understanding your world is essential if you are to be an informed citizen of a global society.

DATELINE

EXTRA

SAN FRANCISCO, USA, JUNE 26, 1945

Fifty nations signed a charter today to establish a new organization called the United Nations. The organization will go into effect October 24.

The United Nations is a successor to the old League of Nations, founded after World War I to prevent another world war, which it failed to do.

The purpose of the new organization is to maintain peace and develop friendly relations among nations.

The member nations hope to cooperate to solve economic, social, cultural, and humanitarian problems and to promote respect for human rights and freedom.

Region • Flags of member countries fly in front of the United Nations headquarters in New York City. ▲

The Peoples of the World

For centuries, people in different parts of the world have been trying to get along with one another, not always with success. Part of the problem is a lack of understanding of other people's ways of life. Certain advances in communication and transportation, such as the Internet and high-speed planes, have brought people closer together. So have increased international trade and immigration. Knowledge of other societies can be a key to understanding them.

Learning About the World

Social studies is a way to learn about the world. It draws on information from five fields of learning—geography, history, economics, government, and culture. Each field looks at the world from a different angle. Consider the approaches you might use if you were starting at a new school. Figuring out how to get around would be learning your school's geography. Asking other students where they come from is learning their history. Making choices about which school supplies you can afford to buy is economics. Learning the school rules is learning about its government. Clubs, teams, styles of clothing, holidays, and even ways of saying things are part of the school's culture.

Place • The five fields of learning in social studies are well represented in daily life. ▲

Connections to Science

Digging into the Past
Archaeologists are scientists who study artifacts to learn about people's culture and history. Artifacts include pots, tools, artworks, and even food remains. Using special techniques and tools, archaeologists carefully remove artifacts from underground or underwater. They use their knowledge about the place and people they are studying to figure out how the artifact was used.

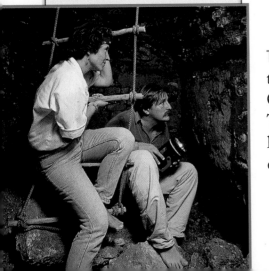

History and Geography

Knowing history and geography helps orient you in time and space. **History** is a record of the past. The people and events of the past shaped the world as it is today. Historians search for primary sources, such as newspapers, letters, journals, and other documents, to find out about past events.

> ### A VOICE FROM TODAY
>
> How can we know who we are and where we are going if we don't know anything about where we have come from and what we have been through, the courage shown, the costs paid, to be where we are?
>
> **David McCullough, Historian**

The Five Themes of Geography **Geography** is the study of people, places, and the environment. Geography deals with the world in spatial terms. The study of geography focuses on five themes: location, region, place, movement, and human-environment interaction.

Vocabulary

orient: to become familiar with a situation

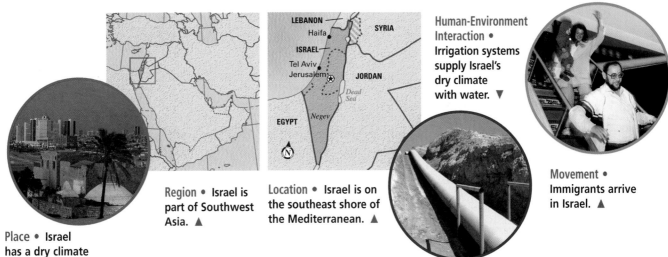

Region • Israel is part of Southwest Asia. ▲

Location • Israel is on the southeast shore of the Mediterranean. ▲

Human-Environment Interaction • Irrigation systems supply Israel's dry climate with water. ▼

Movement • Immigrants arrive in Israel. ▲

Place • Israel has a dry climate in the south, and a wetter climate in the north, with prosperous farms and thriving cities. ▲

Location tells where a place is. Several countries that have features in common form a region. Place considers an area's distinguishing characteristics. Movement is a study of the migrations of people, animals, and even plants. Human-environment interaction considers how people change and are changed by the natural features of Earth.

Government

Every country has laws and a way to govern itself. Laws are the rules by which people live. **Government** is the people and groups within a society that have the authority to make laws, to make sure they are carried out, and to settle disagreements about them. The kind of government determines who has the authority to make the laws and see that they are carried out.

Limited and Unlimited Governments In a limited government, everyone, including those in charge, must obey the laws. Some of the laws tell the government what it cannot do. Democracies and republics are two forms of limited government. In a democracy, the people have the authority to make laws directly. In a republic, the people make laws through elected representatives. The governments of the United States, Mexico, and India are examples of republics.

Rulers in an unlimited government can do whatever they want without regard to the law. Totalitarianism is a form of unlimited government. In a totalitarian government the people have no say. Rulers have total control.

BACKGROUND

Local, state, and national governments provide needed services, such as schools, parks, electricity, and roads.

Vocabulary

totalitarian government: a government in which the rulers have total control

Citizenship A **citizen** is a legal member of a country. Citizens have rights, such as the right to vote in elections, and duties, such as paying taxes. Being born in a country can make you a citizen. Another way is to move to a country, complete certain requirements, and take part in a naturalization ceremony.

Vocabulary
naturalization: the process of becoming a citizen

Movement •
One way people become American citizens is by participating in a naturalization ceremony. ▲

Economics

Looking at the long list of flavors at the ice cream store, you have a decision to make. You have only enough money for one cone. Will it be mint chip or bubble gum flavor? You will have to choose. **Economics** is the study of how people manage their resources by producing, exchanging, and using goods and services. Economics is about choice.

Some economists claim that people's desires are unlimited. Resources to satisfy these desires, however, are limited. These economists refer to the conflict between people's desires and their limited resources as **scarcity**.

Resources Economists identify three types of resources: natural, human, and capital. Natural resources are gifts of nature, such as forests, fertile soil, and water. Human resources are skills people have to produce goods and services. Capital resources are the things people make, such as machines and equipment, to produce goods and services.

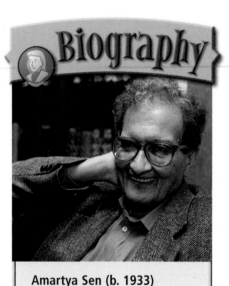

Amartya Sen (b. 1933)
Amartya Sen (ah•MART•yah sen) was born in India. As a professor at Trinity College in Cambridge, England, he taught and studied economics. An important part of his research was to look at catastrophes, such as famine, that happen to the world's poorest people. By showing governments that food shortages are often caused by social and economic conditions, he hoped to prevent famines in the future. In 1998, Sen won the Nobel Prize in Economic Sciences for his research in welfare economics.

Kinds of Economies

Blue jeans are a product. Who decides whether to make them and how many to make and what price to charge? In a command economy, the government decides. In a market economy, individual businesses decide, based on what they think consumers want.

Levels of Development Different countries and regions have different levels of economic development. In a country with a high level of development, most people are well educated, have good health, and earn decent salaries. Services such as clean running water, electricity, and transportation are plentiful. Technology is advanced, and businesses flourish.

Reading
Social Studies

A. Contrasting How does a market economy differ from a command economy?

Vocabulary

literacy:
ability to read and write

life expectancy:
average number of years people live

Reading
Social Studies

B. Recognizing Important Details
What are three characteristics that can define a culture?

A country with a low level of development is marked by few jobs in industry, poor services, and low literacy rates. Life expectancy is low. These countries are often called developing countries.

Culture

Some people wear saris. Others wear T-shirts. Some people eat cereal and milk for breakfast. Others eat pickled fish. Some people go to church on Sunday morning. Others kneel and pray to Allah five times a day. All these differences are expressions of **culture.** Culture consists of the beliefs, customs, laws, art, and ways of living that a group of people share.

Religion is part of most cultures; so is a shared language. The ways people express themselves through music, dance, literature, and the visual arts are important parts of every culture; so are the technology and tools they use to accomplish various tasks. Each kind of food, clothing, or technology, each belief, language, or tool shared by a culture is called a **culture trait.** Taken together, the culture traits of a people shape their way of life.

High Tech for the Developing World Mae Jemison, below, is a former astronaut and the first African-American woman to orbit Earth. In 1993, she left the space program and set up the Jemison Institute for Advancing Technology in Developing Countries. This organization uses space program technology to help developing countries.

One project uses a satellite-based telecommunication system to improve health care in West Africa. Another project is an international science camp for students aged 12 to 16.

SECTION 1 ASSESSMENT

Terms & Names

1. **Identify:**
   (a) history
   (b) geography
   (c) government
   (d) citizen
   (e) economics
   (f) scarcity
   (g) culture
   (h) culture trait

Taking Notes

2. Use a chart like this one to list the five themes of geography and their characteristics.

Theme	Characteristics

Main Ideas

3. (a) What five areas of learning does social studies include?

   (b) What are the three main kinds of resources, and how is each one defined?

   (c) What is the difference between limited and unlimited government?

Critical Thinking

4. **Making Inferences**

   Does the United States have a shared, or common, culture?

   Think About
   - what you eat and wear, where you live, how you spend your free time
   - who else shares these activities with you

ACTIVITY -OPTION- Reread the section on citizenship. Make a **poster** showing the rights and responsibilities of a citizen.

Investigate Your World

Suppose that someone has given you a globe as a gift. What a great present! Unlike a flat map, your globe gives you a more accurate view of the world. Best of all, this new globe is programmable. You can input new information about different features and places on Earth. In fact, the manufacturer has set up a contest—the Global Game—giving prizes for the best and most creative approaches to programming the globe. Good luck!

COOPERATIVE LEARNING On these pages are challenges you will meet in trying to win the Global Game. Working with a small group, choose which one you want to solve. Divide the work among group members. Look for helpful information in the Data File. Keep in mind that you will present your solution to the class.

STATE CAPITOL

Austin

HISTORY/ECONOMICS CHALLENGE

". . . you want to know more about the world closer to home."

Now that your globe has shown you the worldwide picture, you want to know more about the world closer to home. How has geography influenced the history of your community? What features or resources brought settlers there? Choose one of these options. Look in the Data File for information.

ACTIVITIES

1. Make a time line of major events in the growth of your community. If possible, begin with the Native Americans who originally inhabited the area. Include the arrival of immigrants from various places.
2. Draw or trace an outline of your state. Then make a thematic map of its major products and industries. Use words or symbols (such as a cow, a factory, a computer) and create a map key to identify each product.

Ft. Worth • • Dallas

T E X A S

⭐ Austin

• San Antonio

Rio Grande

Gulf of Mexico

LANGUAGE ARTS CHALLENGE

". . . you are taken on an audio journey to new places."

Your new globe has built-in sensors activated by a laser wand. When you point the wand at a spot on the globe, you are taken on an audio journey to new places. The sound clip introduces you to a place's culture—the things that make it unique.

As part of the Global Game, the manufacturer is looking for new ways to present this information. What will you include in your approach? How can you add to the globe's popular appeal? Choose one of these options. Look in the Data File for help.

ACTIVITIES

1. Choose one continent and write a script about it for a seven-minute "audio journey." Remember to include information about geographic features as well as aspects of culture.
2. Design another geography game that the manufacturer can use to market its globe. The game should appeal to students of your age. Write a brief description of the game and its rules.

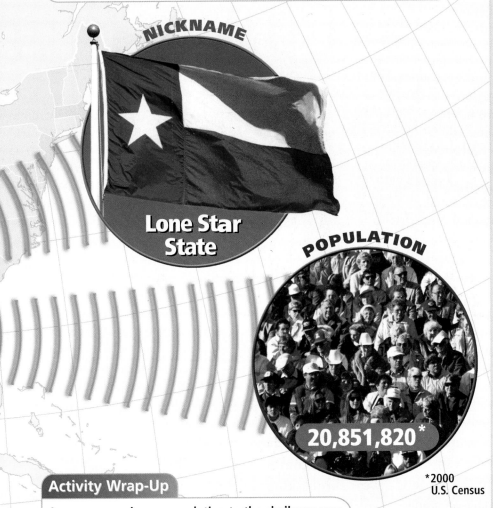

NICKNAME

Lone Star State

POPULATION

20,851,820*

*2000 U.S. Census

WORLD STATISTICS

- **Circumference** at Equator: 24,902 mi.
- **Earth's speed** of orbit: 18.5 mi./sec.
- **Total area:** 197,000,000 sq. mi.; land area: 57,900,000 sq. mi.
- **Highest point:** 29,035 ft.— Mt. Everest.
- **Lowest point:** 35,800 ft. below sea level—Marianas Trench, Pacific Ocean.
- **Lowest point on land:** 1,312 ft. below sea level, Dead Sea, Israel, and Jordan.

HIGHEST ELEVATIONS BY CONTINENT

- **Asia:** Mt. Everest, Nepal–Tibet, 29,035 ft.
- **South America:** Mt. Aconcagua, Argentina–Chile, 22,834 ft.
- **North America:** Mt. McKinley (Denali), Alaska, 20,320 ft.
- **Africa:** Mt. Kilimanjaro, Tanzania, 19,340 ft.
- **Europe:** Mt. Elbrus, Russia, 18,510 ft.
- **Antarctica:** Vinson Massif, 16,066 ft.
- **Western Europe:** Mont Blanc, France, 15,771 ft.
- **Australia:** Mt. Kosciusko, 7,310 ft.

SOME MAJOR RIVER SYSTEMS

- **Nile,** Africa: 4,160 mi.
- **Amazon,** South America: 4,080 mi.
- **Mississippi**–Missouri, North America (U.S.): 3,740 mi.
- **Chang Jiang** (Yangtze), China: 3,915 mi.
- **Yenisey,** Russia: 2,566 mi.
- **Plata,** South America: 3,030 mi.
- **Huang He** (Yellow), China: 3,010 mi.
- **Congo** (Zaire), Africa: 2,880 mi.

To learn more about Earth's geography, go to

RESEARCH LINKS
CLASSZONE.COM

Activity Wrap-Up

As a group, review your solution to the challenge you selected. Then present your solution to the class.

Many Regions, Many Cultures

MAIN IDEA	**WHY IT MATTERS NOW**
The world can be divided into regions according to culture.	Understanding other cultures can help you understand how people in other regions live and think.

DATELINE

MEERUT, INDIA, MAY 10, 1857— Indian troops serving in the army of the British East India Company rebelled today. Reasons given for the revolt include anger at the way the company has been taking over Indian lands and a lack of respect for Indian customs. The immediate cause was the new Enfield rifles issued to the troops. To load them, soldiers have to bite off the ends of the cartridges.

Word quickly spread that the cartridges were greased with cow and pig fat. This was an insult to both Hindu and Muslim soldiers.

Hindus hold cows sacred and never kill them. Muslims believe the meat of pigs is unclean.

Place • The rebellion in Meerut spread to the city of Lucknow and left the Chutter Munzil Palace in ruins. ▲

Different Places, Different Cultures

Indian soldiers and British officials belonged to cultures with different beliefs. The British came from a region of the world where most people ate the meat of pigs and cows. The Indians lived in a region where most people did not. A **culture region** is an area of the world in which many people share similar beliefs, history, and languages. The people in a culture region may have religion, technology, and ways of earning a living in common as well. They may grow and eat similar foods, wear similar kinds of clothes, and build houses in similar styles.

Culture • Cows are sacred to Hindus in India. ▲

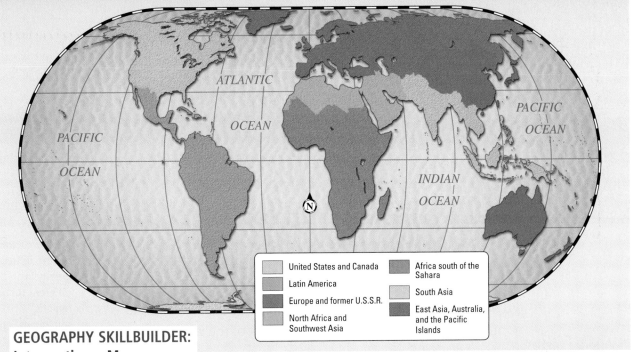

GEOGRAPHY SKILLBUILDER:
Interpreting a Map

1. **Region** • How many culture regions are shown on this map?
2. **Location** • Name three culture regions in the Eastern Hemisphere.

Map Legend:
- United States and Canada
- Latin America
- Europe and former U.S.S.R.
- North Africa and Southwest Asia
- Africa south of the Sahara
- South Asia
- East Asia, Australia, and the Pacific Islands

The World's Culture Regions

The map above shows the major culture regions of the world. Latin America is one culture region. The Spanish and Portuguese languages help to tie its people together. So does its common history. Southwest Asia and North Africa is another culture region. Most countries in this region share a common desert climate and landscape. People have adapted to the desert in similar ways, thus creating a common culture. Islam, which is the major religion in this region, also helps shape a common culture.

Usually, not every person in a region belongs to the dominant, or mainstream, culture. Some regions are multicultural. For example, the United States and Canada contain other cultures besides the dominant one. Although most people in this region speak English, many people in eastern Canada speak French. Many people in the United States speak Spanish, especially in the Southwest. In both countries, Catholics, Protestants, Jews, Muslims, Buddhists, and members of other religions are free to worship.

Reading Social Studies

A. Recognizing Important Details Name two characteristics that make the United States multicultural.

Strange but TRUE

Children Invent Language In the late 1700s, most people in Hawaii spoke English or native Hawaiian. As people began immigrating to Hawaii to work on the sugar cane plantations, they brought their native languages with them: Japanese, Chinese, Korean, Spanish, and Portuguese.

At school, the children of these immigrants began speaking a form of English that was a blend of native Hawaiian, Pidgin English, Pidgin Hawaiian, and their native languages, especially Portuguese. Eventually, children began to learn this form of English as their native language. This was the beginning of Hawaii Creole English, and it soon became the language of the majority of Hawaiians.

Da kaet ste in da haus.

Culture Regions Change For thousands of years, culture regions have changed and evolved as they have borrowed culture traits from one another. They have also come to depend upon each other economically. Decisions and events in one part of the world affect other parts. Advances in transportation and communication have increased this **interdependence.** When oil-producing nations in the Middle East raise the price of oil, for example, the price of gasoline at the neighborhood gas station is likely to rise. If there is an especially abundant banana crop in parts of Latin America, the price of bananas may drop at the local grocery store. More and more, people of different countries are becoming part of one world.

Region • Home life can differ greatly in different culture regions, sometimes depending on a region's climate or natural resources. ▲

SECTION 2 ASSESSMENT

Terms & Names

1. Identify: (a) culture region   (b) interdependence

Taking Notes

2. Use a chart to list the major culture regions of the world.

Major Culture Regions of the World
1.
2.
3.
4.
5.
6.
7.

Main Ideas

3. (a) List at least three things people in a culture region may have in common.

(b) Which continents have more than one culture region?

(c) What is one cause of cultural change?

Critical Thinking

4. Clarifying

Why might Brazilian coffee at your local supermarket suddenly cost more?

Think About

- price setting
- coffee supplies

ACTIVITY -OPTION-   Write a **dialogue** between you and a visitor from another country in which you explain what makes the culture in your region different from others.

Reading a Time Zone Map

▶▶ Defining the Skill

A time zone map shows the 24 time zones of the world. The prime meridian runs through Greenwich (GREHN•ich), England. Each zone east of Greenwich is one hour later than the zone before. Each zone west of Greenwich is one hour earlier. The International Date Line runs through the Pacific Ocean. It is the location where each day begins. If it is Saturday to the east of the International Date Line, then it is Sunday to the west of it.

▶▶ Applying the Skill

Use the strategies listed below to help you find times and time differences on a time zone map.

How to Read a Time Zone Map

Strategy ❶ Read the title. It tells you what the map is intended to show.

Strategy ❷ Read the labels at the top of the map. They show the hours across the world when it is noon in Greenwich. The labels at the bottom show the number of hours earlier or later than the time in Greenwich.

Strategy ❸ Locate a place whose time you know. Locate the place where you want to know the time. Count the number of time zones between them. Then add or subtract that number of hours.

For example, if it is noon time on the west coast of Africa, you can see that it is 7:00 A.M. on the east coast of the United States. That is a difference of five hours.

❶ **WORLD TIME ZONES**

▶▶ Practicing the Skill

Practice determining the difference in hours between various time zones. For example, if you select the yellow zone in western Asia and you live in Texas, you will have a time difference of 11 hours. Now select one time zone in Africa, one in Europe, and one in Australia. For each location, determine the number of hours' difference with the time zone in which you live.

The Giant Kuafu Chases the Sun

FROM THE EARLIEST TIMES, people have created myths and legends to explain the natural world. Some stories explain why earthquakes occur or lightning strikes. Others tell how rivers, deserts, canyons, and other landforms came to be. This ancient Chinese myth, dating back at least 2,500 years, comes from the area of northern China where Chinese civilization first began. The myth explains how the province of Shaanxi got its mountains.

Shaanxi, also known as Shensi, is in northern China. The southern part of the province contains the high and rugged Qinling Range, also called the Tsinling Mountains, where the average peak is 8,000 feet high and some are over 12,000 feet high.

Long ago, soon after time began, giants roamed the flat and fertile Earth. One of the largest, bravest, and fastest of them all was named Kuafu—and his strength knew no bounds.

Every day, Kuafu watched the sun rise in the east and set in the west. When night came, he became greatly saddened. He thought, "I do not like the darkness. All life falls into a silent slumber. If I could catch the sun, then I could keep night as bright as day. The plants could grow forever, and it would always be warm. I would never have to sleep again."

The next day, Kuafu stretched his legs and started to race after the sun. He ran like the wind over several thousand miles without rest. Finally, he chased the sun to the Yu Valley where it came to rest every day but Kuafu was thirsty and very, very tired. His thirst grew, and soon it became overwhelming. He had never known a thirst like this, and his body seemed to be drying up like mud bricks in an oven.

Kuafu found the nearest stream and drank it dry. It was not enough. With a giant's stride, he quickly reached the mighty Yellow River. He drank it dry, but again, it was not enough. He continued toward the Great Sea—surely it held water enough to quench his thirst.

On his journey, he drank dry every well and every stream and every lake he came across. His thirst became overpowering, and Kuafu fell to the ground before he reached the Sea. In a fit of anger, with a branch of a peach tree, he made a final swing at the sun. But before the branch reached the sun, Kuafu died of thirst.

The sun set in the Yu Valley, and night came. When the sun rose again, Kuafu's body had been transformed into a mountain range. The peach tree branch extended from his side and formed a peach tree grove. To this day, the peaches in this grove are sweet and moist, always ready to relieve the thirst of those who would choose to chase the sun.

Reading
THE LITERATURE

Before you read, examine the title. Why might the title character want to chase the sun? What abilities will he or she need to catch it?

Thinking About
THE LITERATURE

Contests involving the sun, as well as efforts to reach the sun, are common in the myths and legends of many societies. Why do you think stories about the sun are told in so many cultures?

Writing About
THE LITERATURE

Although Kuafu was not a real person, his myth has survived for thousands of years. Why? What does it teach about human behavior?

Further Reading

Legends of Landforms by Carole G. Vogel explores Native American legends about the origins of many places in the United States.

Why Snails Have Shells by Carolyn Han retells the folk tales of the Han people and other Chinese ethnic groups.

TERMS & NAMES

Explain the significance of each of the following:

1. history
2. geography
3. government
4. citizen
5. economics
6. scarcity
7. culture
8. culture trait
9. culture region
10. interdependence

REVIEW QUESTIONS

The World at Your Fingertips (pages 17–21)

1. What are the five themes of geography?
2. What are the main differences between a limited and an unlimited government?
3. How can someone become a citizen of a country?
4. What is the difference between a command economy and a market economy?
5. What are some characteristics of a culture?

Many Regions, Many Cultures (pages 24–26)

6. How can decisions made in one part of the world affect people in another part of the world?
7. What aspects of daily life might people in the same culture region share?
8. What makes the United States and Canada a multicultural region?

CRITICAL THINKING

Remembering Definitions

1. Using your completed chart from Reading Social Studies, p. 16, tell how understanding the culture could help you make friends in a new country.

Making Inferences

2. Why might someone's life expectancy be low in a region with a low level of development?

Identifying Problems

3. If countries in the Middle East stopped producing oil, how might that affect the economy of the United States?

Visual Summary

1 The World at Your Fingertips

- History, geography, government, economics, and culture are five ways to understand Earth and its peoples.

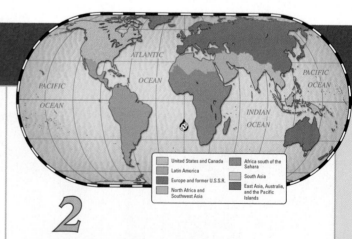

United States and Canada	Africa south of the Sahara
Latin America	South Asia
Europe and former U.S.S.R.	East Asia, Australia, and the Pacific Islands
North Africa and Southwest Asia	

2 Many Regions, Many Cultures

- People live, dress, and think differently in each of the world's culture regions.

SOCIAL STUDIES SKILLBUILDER

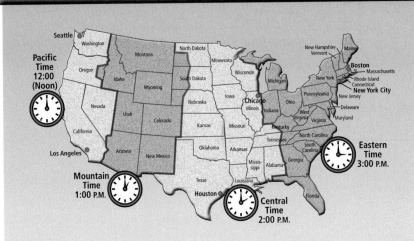

SKILLBUILDER: Reading a Time Zone Map

1. If it is 2 P.M. in Houston, what time is it in Chicago?
2. What is the time difference between Los Angeles and New York City?

FOCUS ON GEOGRAPHY

1. **Human-Environment Interaction** • What needs determine where people settle?
2. **Place** • What geographic features made the location of this town a good place to settle?

CHAPTER PROJECTS

Interdisciplinary Activity: Art
Making a Poster Research what kinds of clothing people wear in other parts of the world. Create a poster that shows the clothing, both modern and traditional, that different groups of people wear. Use photographs or drawings with captions that illustrate the types of clothes.

Cooperative Learning Activity
Setting Up a Peace Conference
With a group of three to five students, set up a peace conference to help two warring groups make peace. Choose two specific groups and a specific issue that caused the hostility, such as harming a cow in a Hindu society.
• Take on the roles of intermediary and spokesperson for each group.
• See how understanding the other group's perspective helps you agree.
• Present your conference to the class as a skit.

INTERNET ACTIVITY

Use the Internet to research a culture, such as the people of Lebanon or Hong Kong. Find out what most people value, what jobs they have, what foods they eat, what governments they live under, and what difficulties they face.

Writing About Geography Write a report of your findings. List the Web sites you used to prepare your report.

For Internet links to support this activity, go to

CLASSZONE.COM

CHAPTER 2

The Geographer's World

SECTION 1   The Five Themes of Geography

SECTION 2   The Geographer's Tools

Place "Viewed from the distance of the moon," said scientist and writer Lewis Thomas, "the astonishing thing about the Earth . . . is that it is alive."

How has new technology increased our knowledge of Earth?

Human-Environment Interaction • *Terra,* the Earth Observing System (EOS) satellite launched in 1999, helps scientists understand how Earth's lands, oceans, air, ice, and plant and animal life work together as a system. Scientists at the National Aeronautics and Space Administration (NASA) use sensors mounted on satellites to study Earth's air, land, and water.

Terra helps to answer such questions as: Which environmental changes result from natural causes? Which are caused by humans? Satellites like *Terra* also help scientists study natural disasters such as hurricanes, volcanic eruptions, and floods. Today, several countries are working together in the Earth Observing System program to gather information about climate and environmental change on Earth.

What do you think?

♦ How can *Terra* benefit people?

♦ Why do countries work together to study climate and environmental change?

READING SOCIAL STUDIES

BEFORE YOU READ

▶▶ *What Do You Know?*

Do you know how to find important places in your town? Have you visited cities, towns, or rural areas and noticed what made these places special? Do you ever use terms like "up north" or "back east"? Have you ever moved from one neighborhood, town, or country to another? Do you know about the harmful effects of pollution on wildlife habitats? If you answered yes, then you know something about each of geography's five big themes—location, place, region, movement, and human-environment interaction.

▶▶ *What Do You Want to Know?*

Decide what more you want to learn about geography's five themes. Write your ideas, and any questions you may have, in your notebook before you read this chapter.

READ AND TAKE NOTES

Reading Strategy: Identifying Main Ideas One way to make sense of what you read is to look for main ideas and supporting details. Each paragraph, topic heading, and section in a chapter usually has a main idea. Supporting details help to explain the main idea. Use this spider map to write a main idea and its supporting details from this chapter.

- Copy the spider map in your notebook.
- As you read, look for information about the five themes of geography.
- Write a main idea in the center circle.
- Write details supporting the main idea in the other circles.

Place • **Physical and human characteristics reveal patterns in places.** ▲

The Five Themes of Geography

The Five Themes of Geography

SECTION 1

TERMS & NAMES
continent
absolute location
latitude
longitude
relative location
migrate

MAIN IDEA

The five themes of geography are location, place, region, movement, and human-environment interaction.

WHY IT MATTERS NOW

The five themes enable you to discuss and explain people, places, and environments of the past and present.

DATELINE

EXTRA

FRANKFURT, GERMANY, JANUARY 6, 1912

Scientist Alfred Wegener sent out shock waves today when he proposed a radical new hypothesis. The continents were once joined together as one huge landmass. In time, he suggests, pieces of this landmass broke away and drifted apart.

Wegener calls this supercontinent *Pangaea*. To support his theory, Wegener points out that the continents seem to fit together.

He notes, for example, that the east coast of South America fits snugly against the west coast of Africa. Mountain ranges continue across both continents as smoothly as the lines of print across torn pieces of a newspaper.

Other scientists reject Wegener's claim. They say that they know of no force strong enough to cause continents to move.

Movement • Seven continents were once one continent. A <u>continent</u> is a landmass above water on earth. ▲

Region • Alfred Wegener was born in Germany in 1880. ▲

The Five Themes

Eventually, the scientific community accepted Alfred Wegener's theory. Scientists discovered that giant slabs of Earth's surface, called tectonic plates, move, causing the continents to drift. This creates earthquakes, volcanoes, and mountains. Geographers study the processes that cause changes like these. To help you understand how geographers think about the world, consider geography's five themes—location, place, region, movement, and human-environment interaction.

Vocabulary

tectonic plates: huge slabs of Earth's surface

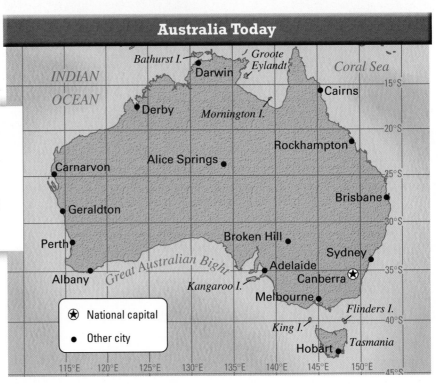

GEOGRAPHY SKILLBUILDER:
Interpreting a Map

1. **Location** • What is the latitude of Adelaide?
2. **Location** • What island is almost entirely enclosed by the lines 40° and 45° south latitude and 145° and 150° east longitude?

The Galápagos Islands The Galápagos Islands are an archipelago, or group of islands, 600 miles off the coast of South America. These islands, which contain many forms of plant and animal life found nowhere else in the world, are a unique "living museum."

Scientists and tourists are fascinated by the islands' creatures, such as Galápagos hawks, land iguanas, waved albatrosses, and blue-footed boobies. The islands are also home to giant tortoises, which can weigh up to 650 pounds and can live to be 200 years old. One of the 11 subspecies of giant tortoises has only one member left. Lonesome George, shown below, is about 80 years old.

Location

Often, the first thing you want to know about a place is where it is located in space. Geography helps you think about things spatially—where they are located and how they got there. Location allows you to discuss places in the world in terms everyone can understand.

Absolute Location If someone asks you where your school is, you might say, "At the corner of Fifth Street and Second Avenue." Ask a geographer where Melbourne, Australia, is located, and you may get the answer "38° south latitude, 145° east longitude." This is the absolute location of the city of Melbourne. **Absolute location** is the exact spot on Earth where a place can be found.

Using a system of imaginary lines drawn on its surface, geographers can locate any place on Earth. Lines that run parallel to the equator are called **latitude** lines. They show distance north and south of the equator. Lines that run between the North and South Poles are called **longitude** lines. They show distance east and west of the prime meridian.

Reading
Social Studies

A. Contrasting
Contrast absolute
location with
relative location.

Relative Location Another way to define the location of a place is to describe its relation to other places. You might say your school is "near the fire station" or "two blocks west of the pet store." If someone asks you where Canada is, you might say, "North of the United States." The location of one place in relation to other places is called its **relative location**.

Place • Thousands of years ago, this part of Southwest Asia, then called Mesopotamia, was green and fertile. Today, as you can see, this area is mostly desert. ▲

Place

Another useful theme of geography is place. If you go to a new place, the first thing you want to know is what it is like. Is it crowded or is there a lot of open space? How is the climate? What language do people speak? Every place on Earth has a distinct group of physical features, such as its climate, landforms and bodies of water, and plant and animal life. Places can also have human characteristics, or features that human beings have created, such as cities and towns, governments, and cultural traditions.

Places Change If you could go back to the days when dinosaurs roamed Earth, you would see a world much different from the one you know. Much of Earth had a moist, warm climate, and the continents were not located where they are today. Rivers, forests, wetlands, glaciers, oceans—the physical features of Earth—continue to change. Some changes are dramatic, caused by erupting volcanoes, earthquakes, and hurricanes. Others happen slowly, such as the movement of glaciers or the formation of a delta.

Place • This satellite photo shows the Ganges River delta. It was formed from sediment and mud carried by the river to its mouth. ▼

Region

Geographers group places into regions. A region is a group of places that have physical features or human characteristics, or both, in common. A geographer interested in languages, for example, might divide the world into language regions. All the countries where Spanish is the major language would form one Spanish-speaking language region. Geographers compare regions to understand the differences and similarities among them.

Natural Regions of the World

Region	Climate	Plant Life
Tropical Rain Forest	Hot and wet all year	Thick trees, broad leaves Trees stay green all year
Tropical Grassland	Hot all year Wet and dry seasons	Tall grasses Some trees
Mediterranean	Hot, dry summers Cool-to-mild winters	Open forests Some clumps of trees Many shrubs, herbs, grasses
Temperate Forest	Warm summers Cold-to-cool winters	Mixed forests; some trees lose leaves in winter, others stay green all year
Cool Forest	Cool-to-mild summers Long, cold winters	Mostly trees with needles; stay green all year; some trees lose leaves in winter
Cool Grassland	Warm summers Cool winters Drier than forest regions	Prairies: Tall, thick grass Higher lands: Shorter grass
Desert	Hot all year Very little rain	Sand or bare soil, few plants May have cactus, some grass and bushes
Tundra	Short, cool summers Long, cold winters Little rain or snow	Rolling plains: No trees Some patches of moss, short grass, flowering plants
Arctic	Very cold Covered in ice all year	None
High Mountain	Varies, depending on altitude	Varies, depending on altitude

SKILLBUILDER: Interpreting a Chart

1. **Region** • How are desert regions and tropical grasslands alike and how are they different?
2. **Region** • In which type of climate are trees most likely to stay green all year?

Natural Regions The world can be divided into ten natural regions. A natural region has its own unique combination of plant and animal life and climate. Tropical rain forest regions are in Central and South America, Africa south of the Sahara, Southeast Asia, Australia, and the Pacific Islands. Where are desert regions located?

Region • The tundra is one of the ten natural regions of the world. ▲

Movement

People, goods, and ideas move from one place to another. So do animals, plants, and other physical features of Earth. Movement is the fourth geographic theme. The Internet is a good tool for the movement of ideas. Sometimes people move within a country. For example, vast numbers of people have migrated from farms to cities. **Migrate** means to move from one area to settle in another. You may have ancestors who immigrated to the United States—perhaps from Africa, Europe, Latin America, or Asia. When people emigrate, they take their ideas and customs with them. They may also adopt new ideas from their new home.

Vocabulary

immigrate:
to move to an area

emigrate:
to move away from an area

Reasons for Moving Migration is a result of push and pull factors. Problems in one place push people out. Advantages in another place pull people in. Poverty, overcrowding, lack of jobs and schooling, prejudice, war, and political oppression are push factors. Pull factors include a higher standard of living, employment and educational opportunities, rights, freedom, peace, and safety.

Reading
Social Studies

B. Synthesizing
How do push and pull factors work together?

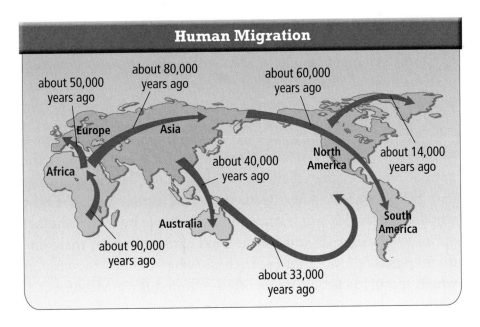

Human Migration

about 50,000 years ago

about 80,000 years ago

about 60,000 years ago

Europe

Asia

Africa

North America

about 40,000 years ago

about 14,000 years ago

Australia

South America

about 90,000 years ago

about 33,000 years ago

Movement •
As you can see, people have been on the move for at least 90,000 years. ◄

Vocabulary

navigable: deep and wide enough for boats to travel on

Barriers to Movement Natural barriers, such as mountain ranges, canyons, and raging rivers, can make migration difficult. Oceans, lakes, navigable rivers, and flat land can make it easier. Modern forms of transportation have made it easier than ever for people to move back and forth between countries.

Human-Environment Interaction

Interaction between human beings and their environment is the fifth theme of geography. Human-environment interaction occurs because humans depend on, adapt to, and modify the world around them. Human society and the environment cannot be separated. Each shapes and is shaped by the other. Earth is a unified system.

Some places are the way they are because people have changed them. For example, if an area has a lot of open meadows, this may be because early settlers cleared the land for farming.

Saving Special Places Many of the most wonderful and special places on Earth may be destroyed or ruined over time unless they are protected. To prevent this, UNESCO (the United Nations Educational, Scientific, and Cultural Organization) set up the World Heritage Committee in 1972. This group identifies human-made and natural wonders all over the world and looks for ways to protect them for the benefit of the world community. So far, the list of World Heritage Sites numbers more than 690. The Grand Canyon (see photograph at right), the Galápagos Islands, the Roman Colosseum, and the Pyramids of Giza are just a few of the places protected for future generations.

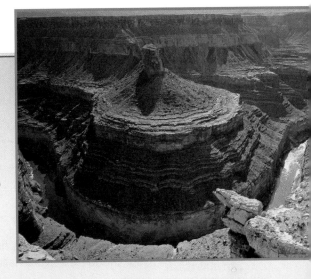

Human changes may help or hurt the environment. Pollution is an example of a harmful effect. The environment can also harm people. For example, hurricanes wash away beaches and houses along the shore; earthquakes cause fire and destruction.

Adaptation Humans have often adapted their way of life to the natural resources that their local environment provided. In the past, people who lived near teeming oceans learned to fish. Those who lived near rich soil learned to farm. People built their homes out of local materials and ate the food easily grown in their surroundings. Cultural choices, such as what clothes to wear or which sports to participate in, often reflected the environment.

Because of technology, this close adaptation to the environment is not as common as it once was. Airplanes, for example, can quickly fly frozen fish from the coast to towns far inland. Even so, there are many more ice skaters in Canada and surfers in California than the other way around.

Interaction People and the environment continually interact. For example, when thousands of people in a city choose to use public transportation or ride bicycles rather than drive, less gasoline is burned. When less gasoline is burned, there is less air pollution. In other words, when the environment is healthy, the people who live in it are able to lead healthier lives.

SECTION 1 ASSESSMENT

Terms & Names

1. Identify: (a) continent   (b) absolute location   (c) latitude   (d) longitude   (e) relative location
(f) migrate

Taking Notes

2. Use a chart like this one to list and explain the five themes of geography.

Theme	Explanation

Main Ideas

3. (a) What physical processes can cause places to change over time?

(b) How do push and pull factors cause migration?

(c) What are some ways people have adapted to their environment?

Critical Thinking

4. Making Inferences

What factors make your part of the United States a region?

Think About

◆ similar human geography

◆ similar physical geography

ACTIVITY -OPTION- Write and illustrate a **magazine advertisement** to persuade people to move to a new place. Include several pull factors for the place you are advertising.

Reading Latitude and Longitude

▶▶ Defining the Skill

To locate places, geographers use a global grid system (see the chart directly below). Imaginary lines of latitude, called parallels, circle the globe. The equator circles the middle of the globe at 0°. Parallels measure distance in degrees north and south of the equator.

Lines of longitude, called meridians, circle the globe from pole to pole. Meridians measure distance in degrees east and west of the prime meridian. The prime meridian is at 0°. It passes through Greenwich, England.

▶▶ Applying the Skill

The world map below shows lines of latitude and longitude. Use the strategies listed directly below to help you locate places on Earth.

How to Read Latitude and Longitude

Strategy ❶ Place a finger on the place you want to locate. With a finger from your other hand, find the nearest parallel. Write down its number. Be sure to include north or south. (You may have to guesstimate the actual number.)

Strategy ❷ Keep your finger on the place you want to locate. Now find the nearest meridian. Write down its number. Be sure to include east or west. (You may have to guesstimate the actual number.)

Strategy ❸ If you know the longitude and latitude of a place and want to find it on a map, put one finger on the line of longitude and another on the line of latitude. Bring your fingers together until they meet.

Write a Summary

Writing a summary will help you understand latitude and longitude. The paragraph below and to the right summarizes the information you have learned.

▶▶ Practicing the Skill

Turn to page 36 in Chapter 2, Section 1, "The Five Themes of Geography." Look at the map of Australia and write a paragraph summarizing how you located the city of Adelaide.

> Use latitude and longitude to locate a place on a globe or map. Lines of latitude circle Earth. Lines of longitude run through the poles. The numbers of the lines at the place where two lines cross is the location of that place.

The Legacy of World Exploration

Early Pacific Navigation

More than 2,000 years ago, Polynesian sailors were among the first people to sail the Pacific Ocean. Without charts or instruments to help them find their way, these ancient navigators made sea charts from palm sticks tied together with coconut threads, using small shells to represent islands.

Magnetic Compass

In the 1100s, mariners of China and Europe independently discovered the magnetic compass. They discovered that an iron or steel needle touched by a lodestone, or piece of magnetic ore, tends to point roughly in a north-south direction. Today, surveyors and navigators consider the magnetic compass an essential tool for determining direction.

Portolan Charts

Portolan charts were first made in the 1300s in Italy and Spain. *Portolan* comes from an Italian word meaning "navigation instructions." These charts, which were actually rough maps, were based on accounts of medieval Europeans who sailed the Mediterranean and Black seas. Drawn on sheepskin, portolan charts show coastal features and main ports. The straight lines crisscrossing the charts represent the 32 directions of the mariner's compass.

Modern Electronic Navigation

In the 1970s, the U.S. Department of Defense developed the Global Positioning System (GPS). GPS allows people on land, at sea, or in the air to pinpoint their location or to track moving objects in any weather. A network of 24 satellites that orbit Earth beam down data to palm-sized receivers, aiding the military in maneuvers. Civilians use them for hiking or finding shorter travel routes.

Astrolabe

The astrolabe was first used in the 1400s in Europe and the Islamic world. It is a flat, circular piece of either metal or wood. The edge of the circle is marked to show 360 degrees. Sailors used the astrolabe to measure the sun's and stars' angles above the horizon in order to determine their ships' positions at sea.

Chronometer

John Harrison worked for nearly half a century before he perfected, in 1762, a ship's clock that would revolutionize navigation. This tool, called a chronometer, enabled sailors for the first time to determine accurately a ship's longitude, or east-west position. The modern chronometer, which looks like a large, heavy watch, continues to help sailors find their ships' longitude.

Sextant

In the 1730s, the sextant replaced the astrolabe. This device measures the angle between the horizon and the sun, the moon, or a star and is used to calculate latitude, or north-south position. The sextant continues to be a basic navigational tool today.

Find Out More About It!

Study the text and photos on these pages to learn about world exploration. Then choose the item that interests you the most and research it in the library or on the Internet to learn more about it. Use the information you gather to write a short play that you and your classmates can perform.

RESEARCH LINKS
CLASSZONE.COM

A Map of Earth in 3-D

On February 11, 2000, the space shuttle *Endeavour* was launched into space on an 11-day mission to complete the most in-depth mapping project in history. The Shuttle Radar Topography Mission (SRTM) collected data on 80 percent of Earth's surface. This information was gathered by beaming radar waves at Earth and converting the echoes into images through a process known as interferometry (IHN•tuhr•fuh•RAHM•ih•tree).

With the aid of computers, the resulting information can be used to produce almost limitless numbers of three-dimensional (3-D) maps. These maps show the topography—rivers, forests, mountains, and valleys—of Earth's surface. It took one year to process the data into 3-D maps. These maps, the most accurate topographical maps ever, will help scientists to better study Earth's surface. The data will also be useful to the general public; for example, it can be used to find new locations for cellular-phone towers and to create maps for hikers.

The data collected on the 11-day SRTM mission can be used by many people—such as the military, the science community, and civic groups—and can be tailored to their needs.

The 200-foot mast is the longest structure used in space today.

Radar interferometry uses radar images taken from two different angles to produce a single 3-D image.

THINKING *Critically*

1. Drawing Conclusions
How will new, sophisticated tools such as radar interferometry and computers change the study of Earth and the environment?

2. Making Predictions How will these topographical maps help the world?

The Geographer's Tools

TERMS & NAMES
cartographer
thematic map
map projection

MAIN IDEA

Geographers use maps, globes, charts, graphs, and new technology to learn about and display the features of Earth.

WHY IT MATTERS NOW

Knowing how to use the tools of geography adds to your ability to understand the world.

DATELINE

BABYLONIA, ABOUT 600 B.C.— Palace officials today released the first map of the world seen in this area. As suspected, Babylon lies at the center of the world. The star-shaped map is drawn on a clay tablet disk about four inches high.

It shows the world surrounded by the Earthly Ocean, which we call the Bitter River. Seven outer regions are also shown as equal triangles rising up out of the oceans. One side of the tablet gives the names of the countries and cities in cuneiform. The other side describes the seven islands. Officials say the map will enable viewers to see the relation of these foreign places to Babylon.

Location • The Babylonian world map was drawn on a clay tablet. ▲

Location • This diagram shows the Babylonian world map translated into English. ▲

Maps and Globes

People have been drawing maps of their world for thousands of years. Geographers today have many tools, such as remote sensing and the Global Positioning System, to help them represent Earth. Increased knowledge and technology allows a **cartographer,** or mapmaker, to construct maps that give a much more detailed and accurate picture of the world. The "Linking Past and Present" and "Technology: 2000" features on pages 42–44 provide more information on modern mapmaking technology.

Location • Draw a picture on the entire surface of an orange and then peel the orange in one continuous piece. After you lay the peel flat, your image will be distorted. ◄

Differences Between Maps and Globes Both maps and globes represent Earth and its features. A globe is an accurate model of the world because it has three dimensions and can show its actual shape. Globes are difficult to carry around, however. Maps are more practical. They can be folded, carried, hung on a wall, or printed in a book or magazine. However, because maps show the world in only two dimensions, they are not perfectly accurate. Look at the pictures above to see why. When the orange peel is flattened out, the picture on the orange is distorted, or twisted out of shape. Cartographers have the same problem with maps.

Reading Social Studies

A. Clarifying Why does a globe represent Earth better than a map?

Three Kinds of Maps General reference maps, which show natural and human-made features, are used to locate a place. **Thematic maps** focus on one specific idea or theme. The population map on page 48 is an example of a thematic map. Pilots and sailors use nautical maps to find their way through air and over water. A nautical map is sometimes called a chart.

Location • A road map is a reference map that shows how to get from one place to another. ▼

Connections to Math

Measuring Earth In 230 B.C., the Greek scientist Eratosthenes used basic geometry to measure the circumference of Earth. Eratosthenes knew that at noon on June 21, the sun cast no shadow in the Egyptian city of Syene (now Aswan). (See the diagram below.) At the same time, the sun cast a shadow of 7°12′ in Alexandria, about 500 miles from Syene.

The circumference of a circle is 360°; 7°12′ is about 2 percent, or 1/50, of 360°. Therefore, he concluded, 500 miles must be about 2 percent of the distance around Earth, which at the equator would be about 25,000 miles.

7°12′ = 1/50 circumference

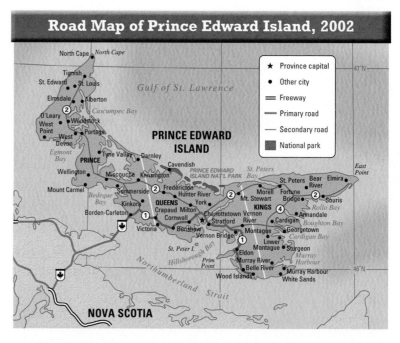

Road Map of Prince Edward Island, 2002

Mercator Projection

NORTH AMERICA
EUROPE
ASIA
AFRICA
SOUTH AMERICA
AUSTRALIA
ANTARCTICA

Robinson Projection

NORTH AMERICA
EUROPE
ASIA
AFRICA
SOUTH AMERICA
AUSTRALIA
ANTARCTICA

GEOGRAPHY SKILLBUILDER: Interpreting a Map

1. **Location** • Compare the size of Africa in relation to other continents on the two projections. How do they differ?
2. **Location** • What other differences do you notice between the Mercator projection and the Robinson projection?

Reading Social Studies

B. Identifying Problems What are the main problems faced by cartographers?

Map Projections The different ways of showing Earth's curved surface on a flat map are called **map projections**. All projections distort Earth, but different projections distort it in different ways. Some make places look bigger or smaller than they really are in relation to other places. Other projections distort shapes. For more than 400 years, the Mercator projection was most often shown on maps of the world. Recently, the Robinson projection has come into common use because it gives a fairer and more accurate picture of the world.

 Spotlight on CULTURE

Mercator Map This map of the Arctic was drawn in 1595 by Gerardus Mercator (1512–1594), the famous mapmaker for whom the map projection was named. It is one of many old maps that are rare, beautiful, and important historical artifacts.

THINKING CRITICALLY

1. **Recognizing Important Details** Does Mercator's map show more land or more water?

2. **Identifying Problems** What types of problems might Mercator have faced when he created this map?

World Population and Life Expectancy, 2000

Population

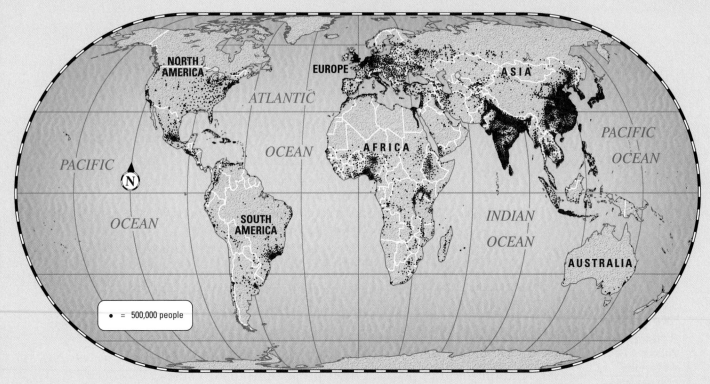

NORTH AMERICA
EUROPE
ASIA
ATLANTIC
OCEAN
PACIFIC
OCEAN
AFRICA
PACIFIC
OCEAN
INDIAN
OCEAN
SOUTH AMERICA
AUSTRALIA

• = 500,000 people

Life Expectancy

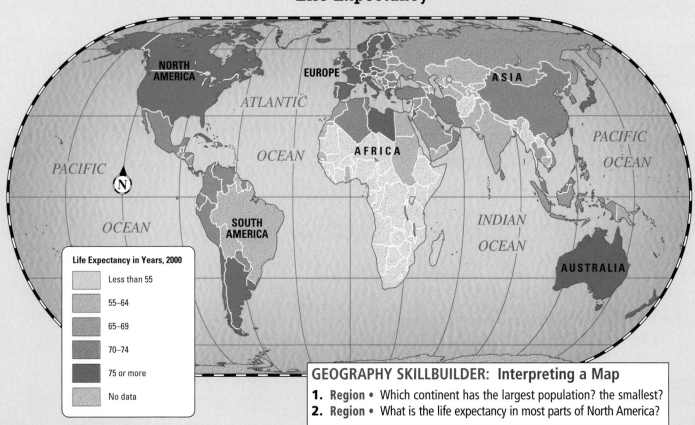

NORTH AMERICA
EUROPE
ASIA
ATLANTIC
OCEAN
PACIFIC
OCEAN
AFRICA
PACIFIC
OCEAN
INDIAN
OCEAN
SOUTH AMERICA
AUSTRALIA

Life Expectancy in Years, 2000

- Less than 55
- 55–64
- 65–69
- 70–74
- 75 or more
- No data

GEOGRAPHY SKILLBUILDER: Interpreting a Map

1. Region • Which continent has the largest population? the smallest?

2. Region • What is the life expectancy in most parts of North America?

Comparing Maps, Charts, and Graphs

Along with maps, geographers use charts and graphs to display and compare information. The graphs on this page and the maps on page 48 contain related information about the world's population. Notice how each quickly and clearly presents facts that would otherwise take up many paragraphs of text.

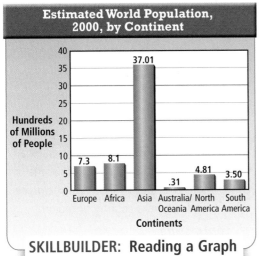

Estimated World Population, 2000, by Continent

SKILLBUILDER: Reading a Graph

1. How many people live in Europe?
2. Which continent has the smallest population?

World Population Growth, 1600–Present

SKILLBUILDER: Reading a Graph

1. How many people lived in the world in 1900?
2. How much did the world's population increase between 1600 and 1900? between 1900 and 2000?

SECTION 2 ASSESSMENT

Terms & Names

1. Identify: (a) cartographer (b) thematic map (c) map projection

Taking Notes

2. Use a chart like the one below to compare the advantages and disadvantages of maps and globes.

	Maps	Globes
Advantages		
Disadvantages		

Main Ideas

3. (a) What are the differences among the three main kinds of maps?
   (b) How have new tools and knowledge helped cartographers?
   (c) What kinds of information can be displayed in maps and graphs?

Critical Thinking

4. **Using Maps**

   What kind of map would show how many students are in each school in your district?

   Think About
   - the three kinds of maps
   - what information different kinds of population maps show

ACTIVITY -OPTION- Draw a **map** of the route you take to and from school or some other familiar destination. Include the names of streets, landmarks such as shops and other buildings, and any other useful information.

TERMS & NAMES

Explain the significance of each of the following:

1. absolute location
2. latitude
3. longitude
4. relative location
5. cartographer
6. thematic map
7. map projection
8. migrate
9. continent

REVIEW QUESTIONS

The Five Themes of Geography *(pages 35–40)*

1. What system do geographers use to determine absolute location?
2. How is relative location different from absolute location?
3. What are some of the natural barriers that made migration difficult in the past?
4. How has technology changed the way humans adapt to their environment?

The Geographer's Tools *(pages 45–49)*

5. Why is a globe an accurate representation of the world?
6. Why would a pilot use a nautical map?
7. How has modern technology helped cartography?
8. Why do most modern cartographers prefer the Robinson projection to the Mercator projection?

CRITICAL THINKING

Drawing Conclusions

1. Using your completed spider map from Reading Social Studies, p. 34, draw a conclusion about which theme of geography is most useful in familiarizing you with an area of the world. Which details in your chart help you understand a country or region?

Contrasting

2. Maps and globes both represent Earth and its features. Contrast the advantages of a map with the advantages of a globe.

Clarifying

3. Why would the leaders of a country find a population density map of their country useful?

Visual Summary

The Five Themes of Geography *1*

- The five themes of geography are location, place, region, movement, and human-environment interaction.
- These themes are the keys to understanding the geography of the world.

The Geographer's Tools *2*

- Maps, globes, charts, graphs, and other tools are available to geographers to help them understand the features of Earth.
- Geographers use these tools to organize and explain Earth's features.

SKILLBUILDER: Reading Longitude and Latitude

A hurricane is expected to touch land briefly at latitude 34°N and longitude 79°W. It will move over the water and touch land again at latitude 30°N and longitude 82°W. Then it will move out over the sea.

1. Which state will feel the effects of the hurricane first?
2. Which state will be touched by the hurricane next?

FOCUS ON GEOGRAPHY

1. Location • What is special about a satellite view of Earth?
2. Location • How might scientists use satellite images such as this to help people?

CHAPTER PROJECTS

Interdisciplinary Activity: Language Arts

Writing a Description Most people use relative location when they are giving directions. Write a paragraph describing the relative location of your home.

Cooperative Learning Activity

Describing Geography In a group of three to five students, choose a country and use the five themes of geography to describe it. Assign the themes to members of the group:

• Where is your country located?
• What are the physical and human characteristics of the place?
• How can you classify the region?
• What movement has occurred in the country?
• How have the people who live there adapted to the environment?

Gather your findings and present them to the class in the form of a book or on a poster board.

INTERNET ACTIVITY

Use the Internet to research how technology can be used to study natural events. Focus on one natural event, like tropical rainfall or global warming, and look into how technology is helping us understand it.

Writing About Geography Write a report of your findings. Include information about the technology and how it is used. Make a prediction about the future uses of technology.

For Internet links to support this activity, go to

RESEARCH LINKS
CLASSZONE.COM

Place Mount Rushmore is a monument located in the Black Hills of South Dakota. The 60-foot likenesses of (from left to right) George Washington, Thomas Jefferson, Theodore Roosevelt, and Abraham Lincoln took 14 years to carve into the granite cliff.

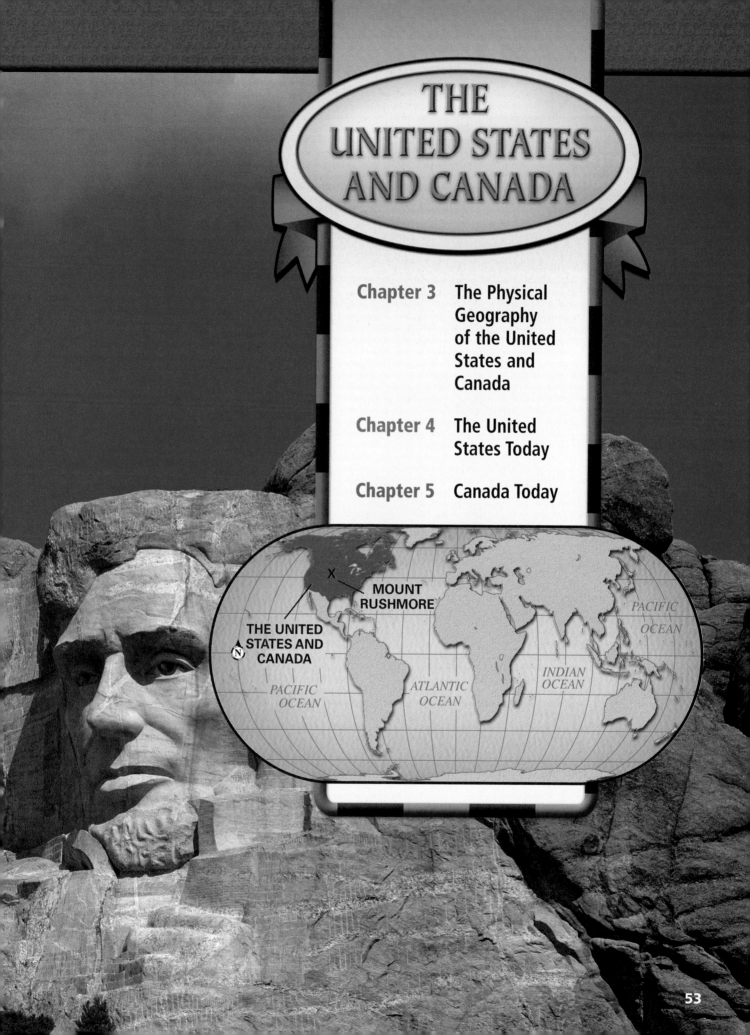

THE UNITED STATES AND CANADA

MOUNT RUSHMORE

THE UNITED STATES AND CANADA

N

PACIFIC OCEAN

PACIFIC OCEAN

ATLANTIC OCEAN

INDIAN OCEAN

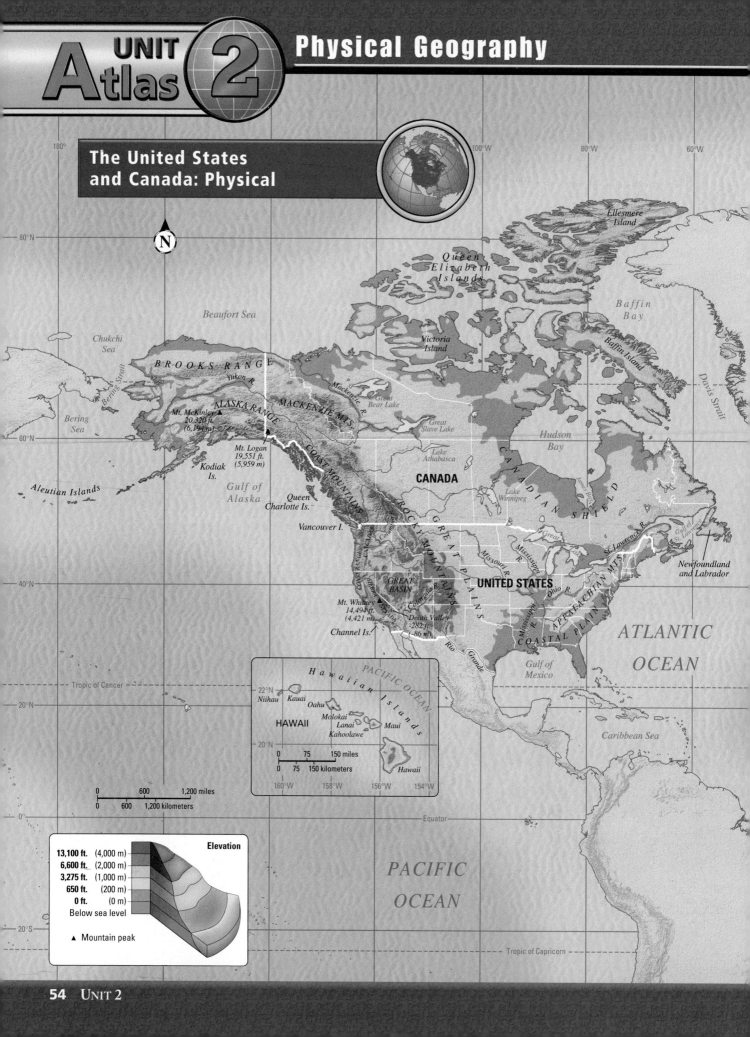

The United States and Canada: Physical

180°
100°W
80°W
60°W

80°N

Beaufort Sea

Chukchi Sea

Ellesmere Island

Queen Elizabeth Islands

Baffin Bay

BROOKS RANGE

Yukon R.

ALASKA RANGE

Mt. McKinley ▲
20,320 ft.
(6,194 m)

Bering Strait

Bering Sea

MACKENZIE MTS.

Mackenzie R.

Great Bear Lake

Victoria Island

Baffin Island

Davis Strait

60°N

Mt. Logan
19,551 ft.
(5,959 m)

Kodiak Is.

COAST MOUNTAINS

Great Slave Lake

Lake Athabasca

Hudson Bay

Aleutian Islands

Gulf of Alaska

Queen Charlotte Is.

CANADA

Lake Winnipeg

CANADIAN SHIELD

Vancouver I.

ROCKY MOUNTAINS

Columbia R.

GREAT PLAINS

Missouri R.

Great Lakes

St. Lawrence R.

Gulf of St. Lawrence

Newfoundland and Labrador

40°N

COAST RANGES

CASCADE RANGE

SIERRA NEVADA

GREAT BASIN

Mt. Whitney
14,494 ft.
(4,421 m)

Colorado R.

Death Valley
-282 ft.
(-86 m)

UNITED STATES

Mississippi R.

Ohio R.

APPALACHIAN MTS.

Channel Is.

Rio Grande

COASTAL PLAIN

ATLANTIC OCEAN

Gulf of Mexico

Tropic of Cancer

20°N

PACIFIC OCEAN

Hawaiian Islands

22°N
Niihau *Kauai* *Oahu*
HAWAII
Molokai
Lanai
Kahoolawe
Maui
20°N
Hawaii

Caribbean Sea

| 0 | 75 | 150 miles |
| 0 | 75 | 150 kilometers |

160°W   158°W   156°W   154°W

| 0 | 600 | 1,200 miles |
| 0 | 600 | 1,200 kilometers |

0°
Equator

PACIFIC OCEAN

Elevation

13,100 ft.	(4,000 m)
6,600 ft.	(2,000 m)
3,275 ft.	(1,000 m)
650 ft.	(200 m)
0 ft.	(0 m)
Below sea level	

▲ Mountain peak

20°S

Tropic of Capricorn

Natural Hazards of the United States and Canada

□ Earthquakes in the 20th century
▲ Volcanoes in the 20th century
〜 Tsunamis
◄•• Tropical storm track
▨ Areas at high risk for tornadoes
〜 Selected rivers subject to flooding
▨ Areas subject to desertification

Canada–United States: Landmass and Population

Canada

United States

LANDMASS

Canada
▬▬▬▬▬▬▬▬
3,851,809 square miles

Continental United States
▬▬▬▬▬▬
3,165,630 square miles

POPULATION

Canada
30,750,100

United States
281,421,906

👤 = 50,000,000

FAST FACTS

HIGHEST TIDE:
The Bay of Fundy, between New Brunswick and Nova Scotia in Canada, has the highest tides in the world, sometimes running as high as 70 feet.

HIGHEST MOUNTAIN:
Mt. McKinley, 20,320 ft.

LONGEST RIVER:
Mississippi River, 2,357 mi.

HIGHEST RECORDED TEMPERATURE:
134°F, Death Valley, California, July 10, 1913

LOWEST RECORDED TEMPERATURE:
–81.4°F, Snag, Yukon, February 3, 1947

GEOGRAPHY SKILLBUILDER: Interpreting Maps and Visuals

1. **Location** • What is the elevation of the land along the Gulf of Mexico and Hudson Bay?
2. **Place** • Where are most of the volcanoes in the United States and Canada?

The United States and Canada: Political

N

180°   100°W   80°W   60°W

80°N

60°N

40°N

Tropic of Cancer

20°N

Chukchi Sea

Beaufort Sea

Bering Strait

Yukon R.

AK (U.S.)

Anchorage

Bering Sea

Gulf of Alaska

YUKON TERRITORY

NORTHWEST TERRITORIES

Mackenzie R.

Great Bear Lake

Great Slave Lake

NUNAVUT

Baffin Bay

Davis Strait

BRITISH COLUMBIA

Edmonton

Calgary

Vancouver

ALBERTA

SASKATCHEWAN

Lake Athabasca

MANITOBA

CANADA

Lake Winnipeg

Winnipeg

Hudson Bay

James Bay

ONTARIO

QUEBEC

NEWFOUNDLAND AND LABRADOR

Gulf of St. Lawrence

St. Lawrence R.

Montreal

Ottawa

NEW BRUNSWICK

PRINCE EDWARD ISLAND

NOVA SCOTIA

ME

NH

Boston

VT

MA

RI

CT

NY

New York

Philadelphia

DE

Washington, D.C.

WA

Seattle

Columbia R.

OR

ID

MT

ND

Minneapolis

SD

WY

NE

Salt Lake City

UT

Great

WI

MN

MI

Detroit

Toronto

Chicago

IA

IL

IN

OH

PA

NJ

MD

WV

VA

Mississippi R.

Missouri R.

NV

San Francisco

Los Angeles

San Diego

CA

AZ

Phoenix

CO

Colorado R.

KS

Kansas City

St. Louis

MO

Ohio R.

KY

TN

NC

SC

NM

OK

AR

Dallas

TX

Houston

UNITED STATES

Rio Grande

LA

MS

New Orleans

AL

GA

Atlanta

FL

Miami

ATLANTIC OCEAN

Gulf of Mexico

Caribbean Sea

PACIFIC OCEAN

Hawaiian Islands

22°N

Niihau

Kauai

Oahu

Honolulu

Molokai

Lanai

Maui

Kahoolawe

HAWAII

20°N

Hawaii

0   75   150 miles

0   75   150 kilometers

160°W   158°W   156°W   154°W

20°N

Tropic of Cancer

0°   Equator

0   600   1,200 miles

0   600   1,200 kilometers

⭐ National capital

• Other city

PACIFIC OCEAN

20°S   Tropic of Capricorn

Population Density of the United States and Canada, 2001

0 500 1,000 miles
0 500 1,000 kilometers

Persons per sq. mi.	Persons per sq. km
Over 520	Over 200
260–520	100–200
130–259	50–99
25–129	10–49
1–24	1–9
0	0

⊙ Metropolitan area greater than 2 million

• Other major metropolitan area

The United States and Canada: Selected Native Peoples, c. 1600

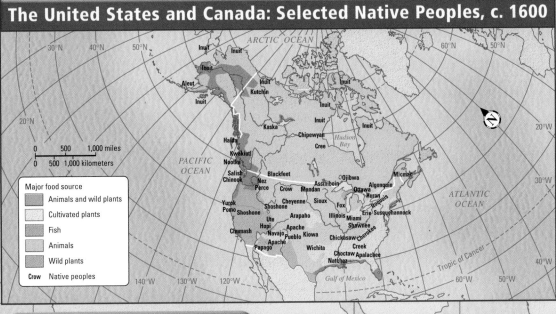

0 500 1,000 miles
0 500 1,000 kilometers

Major food source

- Animals and wild plants
- Cultivated plants
- Fish
- Animals
- Wild plants

Crow Native peoples

FAST FACTS

✓ **WORLD'S HIGHEST IMMIGRATION RATE:** Canada, with about 240,000 immigrants per year.

✓ **LOWEST POPULATION DENSITY:** Canada has only about 3.4 people per square kilometer. Nearly 90 percent of Canada's population lives within about 100 miles of the Canada–U.S. border.

✓ **LARGEST CITY:** New York City, 16,640,000 (2000)

GEOGRAPHY SKILLBUILDER: Interpreting Maps and Visuals

1. **Location** • Name the Canadian provinces and the U.S. states that lie along the border between the two countries.
2. **Location** • Which native peoples lived along the Pacific Coast circa 1600?

State Flag	State/ Capital	Population (2000)	Population Rank (2000)	Infant Mortality (per 1,000 live births) (1998)	Doctors (per 100,000 pop.) (1998–1999)
	Alabama (AL) Montgomery	4,447,100	23	10.2	198
	Alaska (AK) Juneau	626,900	48	5.9	167
	Arizona (AZ) Phoenix	5,130,600	20	7.5	202
	Arkansas (AR) Little Rock	2,673,400	33	8.9	190
	California (CA) Sacramento	33,871,600	1	5.8	247
	Colorado (CO) Denver	4,301,300	24	6.7	238
	Connecticut (CT) Hartford	3,405,600	29	7.0	354
	Delaware (DE) Dover	783,600	45	9.6	234
	*District of Columbia (DC)	572,100	—	12.5	737
	Florida (FL) Tallahassee	15,982,400	4	7.2	238
	Georgia (GA) Atlanta	8,186,500	10	8.5	211
	Hawaii (HI) Honolulu	1,211,500	42	6.9	265
	Idaho (ID) Boise	1,294,000	39	7.2	154
	Illinois (IL) Springfield	12,419,300	5	8.4	260
	Indiana (IN) Indianapolis	6,080,500	14	7.6	195
	Iowa (IA) Des Moines	2,926,300	30	6.6	173
	Kansas (KS) Topeka	2,688,400	32	7.0	203

*The federal district of Washington, D.C., is the capital city of the United States.

DATA FILE

Population Density (per square mile)	Per Capita Income ($) (1999)	High School Graduates (%) (1998)	Area Rank (2000)	Total Area (square miles)	Map (not to scale)
85.1	21,941	78.8	30	52,237	
1.0	27,274	90.6	1	615,230	
45.0	24,199	81.9	6	114,006	
50.3	21,146	76.8	28	53,182	
213.2	28,513	80.1	3	158,869	
41.3	30,291	89.6	8	104,100	
614.3	37,452	83.7	48	5,544	
327.0	29,341	85.2	49	2,396	
8,412.6	36,554	83.8	51	68	
266.7	26,796	81.9	23	59,928	
138.8	26,007	80.0	24	58,977	
187.6	26,623	84.6	47	6,459	
15.5	22,418	82.7	14	83,574	
214.4	29,908	84.2	25	57,918	
167.0	24,949	83.5	38	36,420	
51.9	24,600	87.7	26	56,276	
32.7	25,467	89.2	15	82,282	

State Flag	State/Capital	Population (2000)	Population Rank (2000)	Infant Mortality (per 1,000 live births) (1998)	Doctors (per 100,000 pop.) (1998–1999)	
	Kentucky (KY) Frankfort	4,041,800	25	7.5	209	
	Louisiana (LA) Baton Rouge	4,469,000	22	9.1	246	
	Maine (ME) Augusta	1,274,900	40	6.3	223	
	Maryland (MD) Annapolis	5,296,500	19	8.6	374	
	Massachusetts (MA) Boston	6,349,100	13	5.1	412	
	Michigan (MI) Lansing	9,938,400	8	8.2	224	
	Minnesota (MN) St. Paul	4,919,500	21	5.9	249	
	Mississippi (MS) Jackson	2,844,700	31	10.1	163	
	Missouri (MO) Jefferson City	5,595,200	17	7.7	230	
	Montana (MT) Helena	902,200	44	7.4	190	
	Nebraska (NE) Lincoln	1,711,300	38	7.3	218	
	Nevada (NV) Carson City	1,998,300	35	7.0	173	
	New Hampshire (NH) Concord	1,235,800	41	4.4	237	
	New Jersey (NJ) Trenton	8,414,400	9	6.4	295	
	New Mexico (NM) Santa Fe	1,819,000	36	7.2	212	
	New York (NY) Albany	18,976,500	3	6.3	387	
	North Carolina (NC) Raleigh	8,049,300	11	9.3	232	

DATA FILE

Population Density (per square mile)	Per Capita Income ($) (1999)	High School Graduates (%) (1998)	Area Rank (2000)	Total Area (square miles)	Map (not to scale)
100.0	22,147	77.9	37	40,411	
90.0	21,794	78.6	31	49,651	
37.8	23,867	86.7	39	33,741	
430.7	30,757	84.7	42	12,297	
687.1	34,168	85.6	45	9,241	
102.8	26,625	85.4	11	96,705	
56.6	29,281	89.4	12	86,943	
58.9	19,608	77.3	32	48,286	
80.3	25,040	82.9	21	69,709	
6.1	21,337	89.1	4	147,046	
22.1	26,235	87.7	16	77,358	
18.1	29,022	89.1	7	110,567	
133.1	29,552	84.0	44	9,283	
1,024.3	34,525	86.5	46	8,215	
15.0	21,097	79.6	5	121,598	
351.5	32,459	81.5	27	53,989	
153.0	25,072	81.4	29	52,672	

State Flag	State/ Capital	Population (2000)	Population Rank (2000)	Infant Mortality (per 1,000 live births) (1998)	Doctors (per 100,000 pop.) (1998–1999)
	North Dakota (ND) Bismarck	642,200	47	8.6	222
	Ohio (OH) Columbus	11,353,100	7	8.0	235
	Oklahoma (OK) Oklahoma City	3,450,700	27	8.5	169
	Oregon (OR) Salem	3,421,400	28	5.4	225
	Pennsylvania (PA) Harrisburg	12,281,100	6	7.1	291
	Rhode Island (RI) Providence	1,048,300	43	7.0	338
	South Carolina (SC) Columbia	4,012,000	26	9.6	207
	South Dakota (SD) Pierre	754,800	46	9.1	184
	Tennessee (TN) Nashville	5,689,300	16	8.2	246
	Texas (TX) Austin	20,851,800	2	6.4	203
	Utah (UT) Salt Lake City	2,233,200	34	5.6	200
	Vermont (VT) Montpelier	608,800	49	7.0	305
	Virginia (VA) Richmond	7,078,500	12	7.7	241
	Washington (WA) Olympia	5,894,100	15	5.7	235
	West Virginia (WV) Charleston	1,808,300	37	8.0	215
	Wisconsin (WI) Madison	5,363,700	18	7.2	227
	Wyoming (WY) Cheyenne	493,800	50	7.2	171
	United States Washington, D.C.	281,422,000	3	7.0	251

DATA FILE

Population Density (per square mile)	Per Capita Income ($) (1999)	High School Graduates (%) (1998)	Area Rank (2000)	Total Area (square miles)	Map (not to scale)
9.1	22,488	84.3	18	70,704	
253.3	25,895	86.2	34	44,828	
49.4	21,802	84.6	20	69,903	
35.2	25,947	85.5	10	97,132	
266.6	27,420	84.1	33	46,058	
851.6	24,418	80.7	50	1,231	
128.6	22,467	78.6	40	31,189	
9.8	24,007	86.3	17	77,121	
135.0	24,461	76.9	36	42,146	
78.0	25,363	78.3	2	267,277	
26.3	22,333	89.3	13	84,904	
63.3	24,758	86.7	43	9,615	
167.2	28,193	82.6	35	42,326	
83.4	28,968	92.0	19	70,637	
74.6	19,973	76.4	41	24,231	
82.0	26,212	88.0	22	65,499	
5.0	24,864	90.0	9	97,818	
74.3	33,900	83.0	4	3,787,319	

Province or Territory Flag	Province or Territory/ Capital	Population (2000)	Population Rank (2000)	Infant Mortality (per 1,000 live births) (1998)	Doctors (per 100,000 pop.) (1998–1999)
	Alberta (AB) Edmonton	2,997,200	4	4.8	162
	British Columbia (BC) Victoria	4,063,800	3	4.7	193
	Manitoba (MB) Winnipeg	1,147,900	5	7.5	177
	New Brunswick (NB) Fredericton	756,600	8	5.7	153
	Newfoundland and Labrador (NF) St. John's	538,800	9	5.2	171
	Northwest Territories (NT) Yellowknife	42,100	11	10.9	92
	Nova Scotia (NS) Halifax	941,000	7	4.4	196
	Nunavut (NU) Iqaluit	27,700	13	N/A	N/A
	Ontario (ON) Toronto	11,669,300	1	5.5	178
	Prince Edward Island (PE) Charlottetown	138,900	10	4.4	128
	Quebec (QC) Quebec City	7,372,400	2	5.6	211
	Saskatchewan (SK) Regina	1,023,600	6	8.9	149
	Yukon Territory (YT) Whitehorse	30,700	12	8.4	149
	Canada Ottawa, Ontario	30,750,000	36	5.5	185

DATA FILE

Population Density (per square mile)	Per Capita Income ($) (1999)	High School Graduates (%) (1998)	Area Rank (2000)	Total Area (square miles)	Map (not to scale)
11.7	30,038	86	6	255,285	
11.1	31,592	87	5	366,255	
4.6	26,829	79	8	250,934	
26.7	26,607	78	11	28,345	
3.4	27,692	71	10	156,649	
0.08	33,738 (1994)	64 (1996)	3	503,951	
44.0	25,712	78	12	21,425	
0.03	27,421 (1994)	N/A	1	818,959	
28.3	32,537	84	4	412,582	
49.4	25,534	74	13	2,814	
12.4	28,826	78	2	594,860	
4.1	26,463	82	7	251,700	
0.2	36,130	67 (1996)	9	186,661	
8.0	23,000	82	3	3,850,420	

GEOGRAPHY SKILLBUILDER: Interpreting a Chart

1. **Place** • Which province or territory in Canada has the fewest people? How is it ranked in area? How do these two facts explain the population density?
2. **Place** • What is the highest percentage of high school graduates in a state? What is the lowest percentage?

CHAPTER 3

The Physical Geography of the United States and Canada

THE UNITED STATES AND CANADA

ATLANTIC

PACIFIC OCEAN

OCEAN

INDIAN OCEAN

PACIFIC OCEAN

Place The aurora borealis, or northern lights, is a natural phenomenon most commonly seen in the winter skies over Alaska and northern Canada.

How do Canada and the U.S. benefit from the variety of natural features?

Place • North America is a vast area with varied physical features and climates. A mountain range runs parallel to each coastline. Grasslands cover much of the land between the mountain ranges. One of the world's longest rivers runs from north to south through the east central portion of the United States. Oceans and seas almost completely surround the continent. In northern Canada, the ground is always frozen. In the southeastern United States, plants grow year round.

What do you think?

♦ How does the variety of types of land benefit the people of North America?

♦ How are some places in North America better to live in than others?

♦ Describe the landforms, climate, and vegetation where you live.

BEFORE YOU READ

▶▶ What Do You Know?

Before you read the chapter, reflect on what you already know about the United States and Canada. On which continent will you find these countries? Remember what you have read, seen, or learned in other classes about their physical features and natural resources. They are two of the wealthiest and most powerful countries in the modern world. What makes nations powerful in today's world?

▶▶ What Do You Want to Know?

Decide what you want to know about the United States and Canada. In your notebook, record what you hope to learn from this chapter.

Region • Water resources, such as the Mississippi River, contribute to the wealth of the United States and Canada and to their positions of leadership in the world. ▲

READ AND TAKE NOTES

Reading Strategy: Drawing Conclusions

As you read Chapter 3, think about how geographic factors support the strong economies of the United States and Canada. Use this chart to show how natural features have assisted in creating a strong economy. Notice that several geographic features may contribute to the same economic strength.

- Copy the chart into your notebook.
- On the chart, read the characteristics of the strong economies of the United States and Canada.
- As you read the chapter, identify the geographic features that contribute to each group of economic strengths. Note them on the chart.

Human-Environment Interaction • Rich soil and a moderate climate support a productive agricultural industry. ▲

Geographic Features	Contribute to	Economic Strengths/Benefits
	→	productive farmland, agricultural exports
	→	natural routes for travel to and trade with Canada and the United States, easy-to-defend location, fishing industry, recreation and tourism
	→	transportation by water for people and goods within North America, fishing industry, power source, recreation
	→	raw materials, sources of fuel and power for transportation, industry, and new technologies
	→	good trade and regulatory relations between Canada and the United States, tourism

From Coast to Coast

TERMS & NAMES
Sacagawea
landform
glacier
erosion
river system

MAIN IDEA

North America has varied regions and landforms.

WHY IT MATTERS NOW

North America's geography contributes to the prosperity of the people who live there.

DATELINE

EXTRA

MOUNT ST. HELENS, WASHINGTON, MAY 18, 1980

Mount St. Helens, an ancient volcano in Washington's Cascade Mountains, erupted this morning, killing 60 people and thousands of animals. An earthquake caused the mountain's north face to fall away. The debris from this landslide filled Spirit Lake. Hot air blasts traveling at 300 miles per hour threw both gas and volcanic ash 12 miles high and destroyed 10 million trees.

The avalanche and the mudslide that followed buried parts of the Toutle River Valley to a depth of almost 500 feet. The hot ash and rock started forest fires, ruined crops, and covered cities. Fortunately, the land around the volcano has begun to recover from the eruptions.

Place • Gas and volcanic ash from the eruption of Mount St. Helens vaporized trees and caused widespread devastation as far as 19 miles from the volcano. ▲

Region •
More than 200 square miles of forest were destroyed by the eruption and its aftermath. ▲

North America

Earth's geography changes continually. Sometimes change happens violently, as in the eruption of a volcano such as Mount St. Helens, or the jolt of an earthquake. At other times, change occurs very slowly, as when rain washes away soil, or weather wears down a mountain. All these natural processes affect the physical geography of North America.

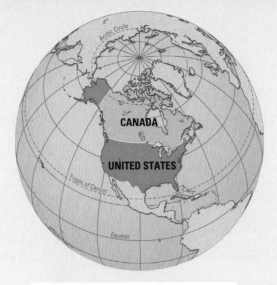

GEOGRAPHY SKILLBUILDER:
Interpreting a Map

1. **Region** • Do you think Canada or the United States has the colder climate? Why?
2. **Location** • Where in Canada would you expect to find the most people living? Explain.

Countries on the Continent
North America's huge landmass is home to several large countries and many smaller ones. Find Canada and the United States on the Unit Atlas map on page 56. Canada is the second largest country in area in the world. The United States is almost as great in area. North America also includes the Danish dependency Greenland, which is the world's largest island.

Mexico, the Central American countries, and the Caribbean island nations, such as Cuba, the Dominican Republic, and Haiti, are part of the continent of North America. These countries, along with the South American nations, make up what is considered Latin America. Find these countries on the Unit 3 Atlas map on page 144. Their heritage differs from that of the United States and Canada. Historically, Latin America owes much of its culture to Spain and Portugal. The United States and Canada were greatly influenced by the British and French. Because of these different cultural heritages, geographers study the United States and Canada separately from Latin America.

Human-Environment Interaction • Crops raised in the United States and Canada feed the people of these countries and are exported to other countries all over the world. ▼

Middle Latitudes Most of the United States and Canada is located in the middle latitudes of the northern hemisphere of Earth. This area between the Arctic Circle and the Tropic of Cancer has a temperate climate. It is not as hot as land closer to the Equator. It is not as cold as regions near the North or South Poles. Many plants and animals thrive in this climate. Productive farming enables countries in the middle latitudes to feed large populations.

Reading
Social Studies

A. Analyzing Effects Why do the middle latitudes have a moderate climate?

An Isolated Continent

North America is almost completely surrounded by water. Its landmass stretches from the Arctic Ocean to the Gulf of Mexico and from the Pacific Ocean to the Atlantic Ocean. Find these bodies of water on page 54 of the Unit Atlas.

At one time, these waters isolated North America, or kept it separate from the rest of the world. Unique plants, such as the giant sequoia and the saguaro cactus, and animals, such as the bald eagle and the American alligator, developed in North America.

Region • The bald eagle has been the national bird of the United States since 1782. ▲

The oceans and seas were also a barrier to people. The earliest settlers arrived 12,000 to 35,000 years ago. No other people reached this continent until thousands of years later.

Crossing the Barriers

As people learned more about shipbuilding and navigation, the oceans became a hazardous but passable travel route. Settlers arrived in North America with plants and animals from their home countries. Many of these plants and animals were new to the continent. In some places, these replaced the native plants and animals.

In the 20th century, the distance from other countries helped protect Canada and the United States mainland from attack during the two World Wars. Today, satellites, the Internet, modern transportation, and other technologies link people everywhere.

BACKGROUND

Hawaii, the 50th state of the United States, is a group of volcanic islands in the central Pacific Ocean.

Place • Sailors have used the sextant to navigate their ships since its invention in 1731. ▲

Sacagawea **Sacagawea** (SAK•uh•guh•WEE•uh) was a Shoshone woman who had a vital role in the exploration of what is now the northwestern United States. She guided explorers Meriwether Lewis and William Clark from what is now North Dakota into the Pacific Northwest. They had been sent to explore the newly purchased Louisiana Territory. Sacagawea's husband, French Canadian trapper Toussaint Charbonneau, and their baby son were also on the journey, which lasted from 1804 to 1806.

Sacagawea identified fruits and vegetables for the group to eat and helped the explorers communicate with the Native Americans whom they met along the trail. Historians believe that she was born around 1786 and probably died in 1812.

Regions of the United States and Canada

The United States and Canada share many geographic regions. Find these regions on the Unit Atlas map on page 54.

Atlantic Coastal Plain This region runs along the Gulf of Mexico and the east coast of North America. The region has much rich farmland and some swamps and wetlands.

Appalachian Mountains This 400-million-year-old mountain range lies west of the Atlantic Coastal Plain. These forest-covered mountains have weathered, or worn down, over time.

Central Lowlands West of the Appalachians are the Central Lowlands. They extend west to the Great Plains and are generally flat. The soil is rich, and many farms are located here.

Great Plains The Great Plains have grasslands and few trees. The land gradually rises from the Central Lowlands to the Rocky Mountains. Farmers grow crops and ranchers raise cattle in some areas.

The Rocky Mountains and Coastal Ranges North America's highest mountain ranges lie in the west. They include the Rocky Mountains, the Sierra Nevada and the Cascade ranges of the United States, and the Coast Mountains of Canada. These high, rugged, and heavily forested mountain ranges run along the western part of the continent from Mexico to Alaska.

Region • The Canadian Rocky Mountains are part of the rugged range that reaches from Mexico to Alaska in western North America. ▼

Intermountain Region Located between the Rocky Mountains and the western coastal mountains, this region is dry and contains plateaus, basins, and deserts. Ranchers raise cattle and sheep in some areas. The Grand Canyon is found here.

Region • The Grand Canyon in Arizona is one of the natural wonders of the world. ▼

Reading
Social Studies

B. Clarifying
Which regions of Canada and the United States have productive farmland?

Canadian Shield or Laurentian Plateau The Canadian Shield covers most of Greenland, curves around the Hudson Bay, and reaches into the United States along the Great Lakes. The central and northwestern part of this huge rocky region has flat plains with hills and lakes. The northeast has high mountains and the south is covered with forests. The shield is rich in minerals, such as iron, gold, copper, and uranium. Most of the land is not farmable and is sparsely populated.

Physical Processes That Shaped the Land

Natural processes have shaped North America. Some of the continent's most dramatic landforms were created by the action of wind, water, ice, and moving slabs of Earth's crust. **Landforms** are features of Earth's surface, such as mountains, valleys, and plateaus.

A **glacier** is a thick sheet of ice that moves slowly across land. Thousands of years ago, when Earth was much colder, glaciers covered much of North America. As they flowed across the land, they smoothed out rough surfaces, carved depressions and deep trenches, and piled up rock and dirt. When the ice melted, North America had new valleys, lakes, and hills.

Quakes Shake Central U.S. Lands Usually, earthquakes shake up California and other parts of the western United States. But from December 1811 to February 1812, Mississippi River Valley residents were shocked by several powerful quakes.

The earthquakes changed the Mississippi River's path. Islands disappeared, riverbanks collapsed, and waves capsized boats and drowned people. Farmland was flooded, new lakes appeared, and forests were destroyed. Trees such as this one were uprooted.

Eyewitnesses saw "houses, gardens, and fields . . . swallowed up" in New Madrid, Missouri, in the final quake.

Formation of the Rocky Mountains

Plates collide over millions of years

Main Ranges

Collision causes uplifting of rock layers

Front Ranges

Movement of plate under Pacific Ocean

Movement of North American plate

Region •
The Rocky Mountains were formed 40 to 70 million years ago as a result of a collision between the tectonic plate under the Pacific Ocean and the North American plate. ◄

The WORLD'S HERITAGE

The St. Lawrence Seaway This seaway, completed in 1959 by Canada and the United States, is one of the largest civil engineering projects ever built. It enables ships to travel 2,340 miles inland from the Atlantic Ocean through locks such as this one, to the Great Lakes. As a result, trade between the United States and Canada and between North America and other continents has improved. Grain, iron ore, and coal are three vital goods shipped on the seaway.

Wind, rivers, and rain wear away soil and stone in a process called **erosion.** Erosion can create magnificent landforms. The Grand Canyon is at least partly the result of millions of years of erosion by the Colorado River. Volcanoes, such as Mount St. Helens, and earthquakes are other natural forces that change the land. All these mighty forces have created landforms across North America.

Waterways

North America has an extensive **river system**, or network of major rivers and their tributaries. The longest rivers are the Mississippi and Missouri rivers in the United States and the Mackenzie River in Canada. Find these rivers on the Unit Atlas map on page 54. When snow melts and rain falls, the water runs down into creeks that collect more water, becoming rivers. North America's rivers empty into bays, oceans, seas, gulfs, lakes, and other rivers.

Vocabulary

gulf: large area of a sea or ocean partially enclosed by land

---

SECTION 1 ASSESSMENT

Terms & Names

1. **Identify:**   (a) Sacagawea   (b) landform   (c) glacier
                    (d) erosion   (e) river system

Taking Notes

2. Use a Venn diagram like the one shown, to compare two geographic regions of North America.

   Region 1   Both   Region 2

Main Ideas

3. (a) Describe North America's location on Earth and tell how this affects its climate and plant and animal life.

   (b) What barriers prevented plants, animals, and people from reaching North America? How were the barriers overcome?

   (c) What processes of nature help to shape the land?

Critical Thinking

4. **Making Inferences**

   What natural features of North America attracted people from other lands? Support your conclusion with details from the text.

   Think About
   - the natural resources
   - the climate

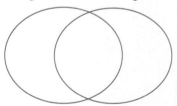
ACTIVITY -OPTION-   **List** two regions of North America. Describe in a few words the kinds of plants, animals, and jobs that are found in each.

A Rich Diversity in Climate and Resources

TERMS & NAMES

weather
precipitation
climate
vegetation
economy

MAIN IDEA	WHY IT MATTERS NOW
A region's climate, vegetation, and natural resources are contributing factors to economic activities.	The prosperity of people living in the United States and Canada affects the prosperity of the modern global economy.

DATELINE

St. Louis, Missouri, U.S.A., October 7, 1993—The worst flood in United States history is finally over. Heavy, almost continuous rain fell on much of the upper Midwest. In St. Louis, where the Mississippi and Missouri rivers meet, the flooding began in April and continued for six months.

The disaster affected nine states. Tens of thousands of people had to leave their homes. More than 10,000 homes were destroyed, and 50 people lost their lives.

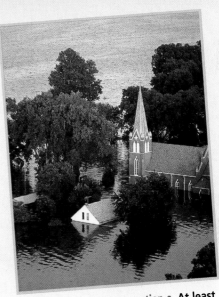

Human-Environment Interaction • At least 75 towns are under water as a result of the flooding. ▲

Climate and Vegetation

The flood of 1993 was caused by unusual **weather.** Weather is the state of the atmosphere near Earth at a given time and place. It includes temperature, wind, and **precipitation,** or moisture such as rain or snow that falls to Earth. **Climate** is the typical weather in a region over a long period of time. A region's climate helps determine what types of **vegetation**—trees, shrubs, grasses, and other plants—will grow there.

The Dust Bowl Disaster From 1931 to 1939, the southern Great Plains suffered one of the worst droughts in U.S. history. In the 1920s, farmers used up the soil's natural nutrients, and cattle and sheep ranchers destroyed native grasses by over-grazing. When the drought began, crops died, and there were no plant root systems to hold the soil.

The southern Great Plains became known as the Dust Bowl. By 1934, dust storms of topsoil were causing serious damage in 27 states. Ships 300 miles off the Atlantic Coast were covered by blowing dirt. Thousands of people, like this boy, had to leave their farms.

Vegetation Zones

North America's vegetation zones are determined by the climate and physical geography of each area. It is usually warmer in the south and colder in the north, but physical features such as mountains and oceans also affect the climate. Find these vegetation zones on the map on page 77.

Polar and Tundra Northern Canada and Alaska have cool summers and very cold winters. It is usually above freezing (32°F/0°C) there for only two months each year. Precipitation varies from 4 to 20 inches a year. Much of the ground is frozen all year except for the surface, which thaws in summer.

Forest Forests of conifer (evergreen) and broadleaf trees cover much of Canada and the northwest, northeast, and southeast United States. Precipitation averages between 10 and 80 inches annually. Temperatures vary from mild to cold in different forested areas.

Rain Forest Along the Pacific Coast, precipitation can reach 167 inches each year. Rain forests with trees 300 feet tall grow in these areas. The ground is covered in bushes, small trees, and other plants. Moss and lichen are the smallest vegetation. One acre of rain forest might have 6,000 pounds of these tiny plants. The temperature is moderate even in the north, seldom falling below 32°F in winter.

Vocabulary
lichen (LY•kuhn): organism that grows with algae on rocks or tree trunks

Grassland The center of North America is covered by grasslands. The prairie in the Mississippi Valley may get 30 inches or more of precipitation each year. Grasses are tall and thick. Farther west, the land gets less rainfall—as little as 15 inches in Alberta, Canada—and the grass is shorter. People grow grain and raise cattle in these areas.

Desert The deserts of the American Southwest get less than 10 inches of precipitation a year. Plants in the deserts must be able to endure harsh sun, high temperatures, and little rain. Only the hardiest bushes, shrubs, a few small trees, and cacti survive there.

Reading Social Studies

A. Recognizing Effects How do climate and geography influence the attraction of people to an area?

Vegetation Zones of Canada and the United States

ARCTIC OCEAN

ALASKA (U.S.)

Baffin Bay

180°W
60°N
40°W
50°N
160°W
40°N
50°N
PACIFIC OCEAN
Hudson Bay
CANADA
40°N
40°N
30°N
UNITED STATES
ATLANTIC OCEAN
30°N
Gulf of Mexico
Tropic of Cancer
20°N
MEXICO
Caribbean Sea
120°W
100°W

HAWAII (U.S.)

0 50 150 miles
0 50 150 kilometers

160°W   158°W   156°W   154°W
22°N
20°N

PACIFIC OCEAN

GEOGRAPHY SKILLBUILDER: Interpreting a Map

1. **Region •** What kind of vegetation zone covers most of Canada?
2. **Region •** What part of the United States is covered by temperate grassland?

Legend
- Temperate rain forest
- Tropical rain forest
- Tropical grassland
- Desert and dry shrub
- Temperate grassland
- Mediterranean shrub
- Deciduous and mixed forest
- Coniferous forest
- Tundra
- Icecap

0   250   500 miles
0   250   500 kilometers

Natural Wealth

The United States and Canada are rich in natural resources. This wealth has influenced their economic development.

Land and Power Resources The farmlands of the midwestern United States and the prairies in the central provinces of Canada have rich soil. Forests are found in western Canada and the northwestern, northeastern, and southeastern United States. There are oil fields in Alberta, Canada; in Texas, California, Louisiana, Oklahoma, and Alaska; and in the Gulf of Mexico. Coal is in Canada's western provinces; in the Appalachian Mountains; and in Illinois, Indiana, and Wyoming.

Water Resources Water routes affect where people and industry are located. Settlers in North America followed rivers to areas where fresh water and good soil permitted farming and raising cattle. Businesses grew in new communities. People still use rivers to ship natural resources, such as timber and coal, and as trade and travel routes. Fishing is a food source and an industry. Rivers and lakes supply water and power, and offer recreational activities.

Region • The Mississippi River has been an important commercial shipping route for more than a century. ▼

BACKGROUND

The Mississippi River is the largest river in North America. From its source, Lake Itasca in Minnesota, to its mouth in the Gulf of Mexico, it flows for 2,350 miles. The name *Mississippi* is from the Native American Algonquian language and means "Big River."

Spotlight on CULTURE

The Cajuns: Americans with Canadian Roots The French settled in Acadia, which is now Nova Scotia, Canada, in 1604. The British gained control of much of Nova Scotia, and in 1755, they expelled most French Acadians. Many of the displaced settlers relocated to southern Louisiana, which was under the rule of France at that time.

Known as Cajuns, the descendants of those French Canadians share a special cultural heritage. Their language has French, English, Spanish, German, and Native American influences. Their music is played with fiddles, accordions, and guitars and has a unique sound. The man shown at left plays the accordion at a Cajun music festival in Louisiana.

THINKING CRITICALLY

1. **Recognizing Effects** What effect did Britain's rule over Nova Scotia have on the French in Acadia?

2. **Recognizing Important Details** What are some features of the Cajun culture?

Neighbors and Leaders

More than 200 million people cross the U.S.-Canadian border every year. Trade between the two countries exceeds $1 billion a day. They cooperate on issues as diverse as national security and defense, the environment, air traffic, and fishing regulations. A United States president described the relationship between these countries.

> ### A VOICE FROM THE UNITED STATES
>
> Geography has made us neighbors, history has made us friends, economics has made us partners, and necessity has made us allies.
>
> **John F. Kennedy**

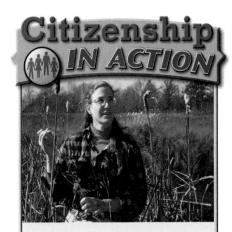

Citizenship IN ACTION

The Nature Conservancy The Conservancy works with communities to protect natural areas, plants, and animals. It has safeguarded 12 million acres and 1,400 land preserves, such as this one, in the United States. In its Great Lakes Program, and in Minnesota, the Conservancy is working with Canadian and U.S. groups to protect wildlife and 10,000 acres of the last tallgrass prairie on the U.S.-Canadian border.

Reading
Social Studies

B. Finding Causes
What common interests make the United States and Canada allies and partners?

Both countries have strong economies and are leaders in world trade. An **economy** is the way that business owners use resources to provide the goods and services that people want.

SECTION 2 ASSESSMENT

Terms & Names
1. Identify: (a) weather   (b) precipitation   (c) climate
              (d) vegetation   (e) economy

Taking Notes
2. Make a chart such as this one to list details about vegetation zones of the United States and Canada.

Polar and Tundra	Forest	Rain Forest	Grassland	Desert

Main Ideas
3. (a) How do climate and geography affect vegetation?

   (b) What natural resources are found in North America?

   (c) How have waterways affected settlement and development in the United States and Canada?

Critical Thinking
4. **Drawing Conclusions**

   How does the variety of vegetation zones affect the economies of the United States and Canada?

   Think About
   - crops and resources found in each vegetation zone
   - world economy

ACTIVITY -OPTION-   Choose one of the vegetation zones discussed in the section. Draw a **picture** showing what the land looks like.

Reading a Physical Map

▶▶ Defining the Skill

Physical maps show the natural features of Earth's surface. These include landforms such as mountains, hills, and plains; and bodies of water such as rivers, lakes, bays, and oceans. Land elevation may be shown in a map key. National boundaries and major cities may also be included.

▶▶ Applying the Skill

The physical map below shows the natural features of Canada. Use these strategies to identify the information shown on the map.

How to Read a Physical Map

Strategy ❶ Read the title. It tells you which region's physical features are being represented.

Strategy ❷ Read the key. It tells you the elevation of land each color represents. A map key may also show boundaries between nations, national capitals, and other cities.

Strategy ❸ Read the scale. It tells you how many miles or kilometers each inch on the map represents.

Make a Chart

A chart can help you organize information given on maps. The chart below organizes information from the map on this page.

Canada	
Bodies of Water	Atlantic Ocean, Pacific Ocean, Arctic Ocean, Hudson Bay, Davis Strait, Baffin Bay, Labrador Sea, Beaufort Sea, Mackenzie River, Lake Winnipeg, Saskatchewan River, Lake Superior, Lake Huron, Lake Erie, Lake Ontario, St. Lawrence River, Gulf of St. Lawrence
Landforms	Rocky Mountains, Coast Ranges, Mackenzie Mountains, Canadian Shield, Interior Plains, Laurentian Highlands

▶▶ Practicing the Skill

Turn to page 54 in the Unit 2 Atlas. Study the physical map of North America. Make a chart listing major physical landforms of North America that you see on the map. You may also include a section in your chart labeled "Countries."

Technology: 1971

IMAX

Although the IMAX system was first successfully demonstrated during Expo '70 (a world's fair) in Osaka, Japan, it has its roots in Expo '67 in Montreal, Canada. There people flocked to special motion-picture theaters, where they stood in the middle of circular auditoriums to watch images projected on the surrounding walls. What they saw was incredible. Hockey players seemed to skate right through them, and cars seemed to drive over them!

The first permanent IMAX theater was built in Toronto in 1971. Two years later, the first IMAX Dome (also called OMNIMAX) was built in San Diego. Since then, IMAX has developed three-dimensional and high-definition systems and incorporated the technology into amusement-park rides. Because of the size of its frames, an IMAX movie generally has a shorter running time than a standard movie. However, IMAX movies require more film. A typical 45-minute IMAX feature requires nearly 16,000 feet of film!

① Dome Early IMAX theaters had flat screens up to eight stories high, but most are now domes up to 100 feet in diameter. When large images are projected, they extend beyond normal peripheral vision—what a person can see without moving his or her eyes—and create the sensation of being in the middle of the action.

② Film IMAX movies use what is called the 15/70 format, in which the film has 15 perforations—little holes along the side—per frame and is 70 millimeters wide. This makes each frame ten times larger than conventional 35-millimeter film and accounts for the exceptional size and sharpness of IMAX images.

③ Projector Because of its size, IMAX film is fed through the projector horizontally in a wavelike motion, or "rolling loop" movement. The newest IMAX systems project film at 48 frames per second, twice the rate of standard movie film, which results in even sharper images.

THINKING *Critically*

1. Recognizing Effects
How does IMAX make images appear three-dimensional?

2. Drawing Conclusions
Despite the system's technical advantages, IMAX theaters have not been as financially successful as standard movie theaters. Why do you think this is so?

CHAPTER 3

TERMS & NAMES

Explain the significance of each of the following:

1. Sacagawea
2. landform
3. glacier
4. erosion
5. river system
6. weather
7. precipitation
8. climate
9. vegetation
10. economy

REVIEW QUESTIONS

From Coast to Coast *(pages 69–74)*

1. Describe the location of North America.
2. What effect did the oceans have on the settlement of North America?
3. What regions are best for farming and ranching? for mining? for lumber?
4. What natural processes have changed the geography of North America?

A Rich Diversity in Climate and Resources *(pages 75–79)*

5. Why are there different vegetation zones?
6. Which vegetation zones permit farming and ranching?
7. How do natural resources affect the economies of the United States and Canada?
8. How have waterways helped people in the past, and how do they help people today?

CRITICAL THINKING

Synthesizing

1. Using your completed chart from Reading Social Studies p. 68, list the geographic features that contribute to productive farmland and agricultural exports.

Drawing Conclusions

2. Choose one of the regions of the United States and Canada. Think about what you know about the region's natural resources and economics. What do you think are the economic advantages and disadvantages of the region?

Making Inferences

3. What industries that depend on natural resources might flourish in the United States and Canada? Why?

Visual Summary

From Coast to Coast

- North America is located in the middle latitudes and is surrounded on most sides by oceans.
- Various regions, each with its own characteristics, make up the United States and Canada.

A Rich Diversity in Climate and Resources

- The vegetation of North America is affected by both climate and geography.
- Natural resources contribute to the prosperous economies of the United States and Canada.

SOCIAL STUDIES SKILLBUILDER

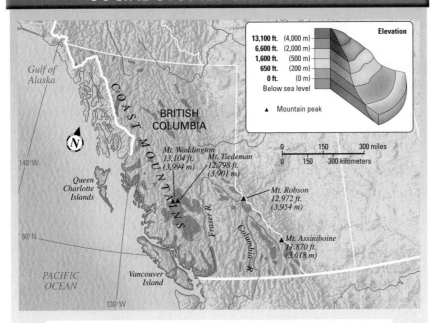

SKILLBUILDER: Reading a Physical Map

1. **Place** • What is the highest mountain in British Columbia? How tall is it?
2. **Place** • Near what island does the Fraser River empty into the Pacific Ocean?

FOCUS ON GEOGRAPHY

1. **Region** • Name four major tributaries of the Mississippi River.
2. **Region** • Into what body of water does the Mississippi River flow?

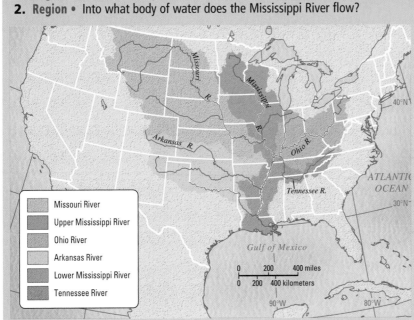

Missouri River
Upper Mississippi River
Ohio River
Arkansas River
Lower Mississippi River
Tennessee River

CHAPTER PROJECTS

Interdisciplinary Activity: Art

Drawing a Map Research fur traders, such as Jedediah Smith, John Jacob Astor, Alexander Mackenzie, or James McGill, who first traveled across the United States and Canada. Draw a map that one of them might have created to illustrate one of the major trade routes. Show important landmarks along the way.

Cooperative Learning Activity

Presenting a Television News Report In a group of two or three classmates, prepare and present a television news report on the Lewis and Clark Expedition.

- One of you should be the news anchor. Others will be reporters, Lewis, Clark, Sacagawea, Native Americans, or other members of the group.
- Make a list of interview questions.
- Do research to learn answers to the questions.
- Present your news broadcast to your class.

INTERNET ACTIVITY

Use the Internet to learn more about the climate and vegetation of one region of North America. Focus on how climate and vegetation affect people's lives, the economy, or history in the region.

Writing About Geography Write a report of your findings. If possible, include photographs that you find on the Internet. Create a map or chart to present information. Include a list of the Web sites you used.

For Internet links to support this activity, go to

RESEARCH LINKS
CLASSZONE.COM

The United States Today

Movement Between 1892 and 1943, 17 million immigrants arrived in the United States through Ellis Island in New York Harbor. Today, ferries bring tourists to the Ellis Island Immigration Museum, which commemorates the stories of these immigrants.

How do immigrants contribute to a country's culture?

Hakeem Olajuwon

Itzhak Perlman

Midori

Isabel Allende

Andy Garcia

FOCUS on **GEOGRAPHY**

I. M. Pei

Madeleine Albright

Movement • In 1998, about 675,000 people immigrated to the United States from around the world. Of these immigrants, 33 percent came from Asia and 20 percent came from Mexico.

This country has been a land of immigrants from its earliest days. People have contributed customs, art, music, languages, foods, and ideas from their homelands to enrich U.S. culture. Violinist Itzhak Perlman, writer Isabel Allende, violinist Midori, actor Andy Garcia, architect I. M. Pei, basketball player Hakeem Olajuwon, and former Secretary of State Madeleine Albright are just a few famous U.S. immigrants.

What do you think?

♦ How do immigrants change and benefit the United States?

♦ What contributions by immigrants have influenced your life?

BEFORE YOU READ

▶▶ *What Do You Know?*

Before you read the chapter, think about how you would describe the United States to a person from another country. What do you and your classmates do for fun? What information could you give about U.S. history, government, economy, and culture? Reflect on your experience and what you have already read or learned about these aspects of the United States. How accurate and complete do you think your knowledge is?

▶▶ *What Do You Want to Know?*

Decide what you want to know about the characteristics of history, government, economy, and culture that make the United States unique. In your notebook, record what you hope to learn from this chapter.

Place • After years of campaigning, women won the right to vote in 1920 when the 19th Amendment to the Constitution was adopted. ▲

READ AND TAKE NOTES

Reading Strategy: Identifying Main Ideas Look for main ideas as you read to help you identify and remember important information. Record the main ideas of this chapter in the chart below.

- Copy the chart into your notebook.

- Notice that each section of Chapter 4 covers a different topic: history, government, economy, and culture.

- As you read each section, look for the main ideas. Use section titles and headings, and find the main idea of each paragraph.

- After you read each section, record what you think are the main ideas about aspects of the United States.

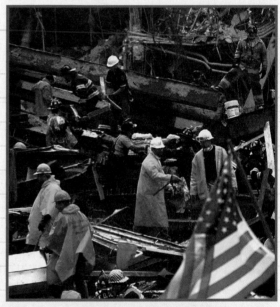

Place • Firefighters and rescue personnel rushed to the scene of the terrorist attacks on New York City's World Trade Center, on September 11, 2001. ▲

The United States Today	
History	
Government	
Economy	
Culture	

We the People

TERMS & NAMES
immigrant
Anasazi
equal opportunity
citizenship
democracy
republic
political process
patriotism

MAIN IDEA

Citizens of the United States come from many cultures and share the same rights and responsibilities.

WHY IT MATTERS NOW

The ideas and values of U.S. immigrants have helped shape the success of the country in the world today.

DATELINE

EXTRA

NEW YORK CITY, 1849

Ships docked today, bringing more people from their Irish homeland to live in the United States. These immigrants have suffered through four years of a deadly potato famine. A blight, or disease, has almost completely destroyed the potato crop every year since 1845. The Irish, especially those who are poor, depend on this crop to survive.

The failure of the potato crop has resulted in the deaths of more than 1 million people—12% of the population of Ireland—from starvation and disease. Today's arrivals join more than 1 million Irish people who are already in the United States.

Movement • Irish immigrants wait to board a ship that will bring them to the United States. ▲

One Country, Many Cultures

Immigrants, such as the Irish, have brought unique contributions to the United States from their homelands all over the world. The United States is sometimes called a "melting pot," a "salad bowl," or a "patchwork quilt" to illustrate how U.S. society combines aspects of many cultures. Some features may blend into the culture of the United States, while others retain their original characteristics.

BACKGROUND

The motto *E Pluribus Unum,* Latin for "out of many, one," is on the Great Seal of the United States and many U.S. coins.

For example, settlers from Great Britain brought English, the most widely spoken language in the United States. Spanish is often spoken in the Southeast and the Southwest, where people from Spain and Mexico settled. French is heard in Louisiana, which was once held by France. People in the United States enjoy the influence of different groups on their foods, music, sports, and other areas of their lives.

Why People Immigrate An **immigrant** is someone who chooses to move to a new country. They come to the United States for different reasons. Some are escaping from discrimination, persecution, or war. Others leave their homelands because of drought, earthquake, or other natural disasters. Often, people come hoping to improve their economic or educational opportunities.

People from Many Lands

Over the past 500 years, millions of immigrants have come to the land that is now the United States and Canada. However, this land was inhabited long before they arrived. In fact, people have lived in North America for thousands of years.

The First Americans Native Americans were the first people to inhabit the Western Hemisphere. They came to North America from Eastern Asia, 12,000 to 35,000 years ago. Some groups, such as the Mississippians and **Anasazi** (Navajo for "Ancient Ones"), developed complex civilizations.

The Anasazi civilization developed around A.D. 100 and reached its height in the 11th to 13th centuries. The Anasazi were experts at irrigation. They built homes called cliff dwellings that had from 20 to 1,000 rooms. Remains of these structures survive in the Mesa Verde National Park in Colorado and in other places in the Southwestern United States.

Reading
Social Studies

A. Summarizing Why have people immigrated to the United States?

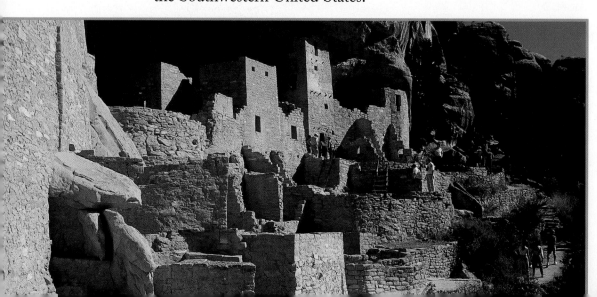

Human-Environment Interaction • The remains of Anasazi cliff dwellings, such as Cliff Palace in Mesa Verde National Park, are found in the Southwestern United States. ◀

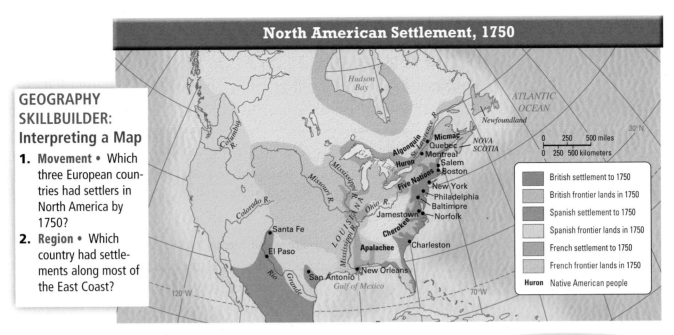

North American Settlement, 1750

GEOGRAPHY SKILLBUILDER: Interpreting a Map

1. **Movement** • Which three European countries had settlers in North America by 1750?
2. **Region** • Which country had settlements along most of the East Coast?

Map labels: Hudson Bay, ATLANTIC OCEAN, Newfoundland, 30°N, Columbia R., Micmac, NOVA SCOTIA, Algonquin, Quebec, Huron, Montreal, Salem, Boston, Five Nations, New York, Philadelphia, Baltimore, Norfolk, Jamestown, Cherokee, Santa Fe, Apalachee, Charleston, El Paso, San Antonio, New Orleans, Gulf of Mexico, Missouri R., Mississippi R., Ohio R., Colorado R., LOUISIANA, Rio Grande, 120°W, 70°W

Legend:
- British settlement to 1750
- British frontier lands in 1750
- Spanish settlement to 1750
- Spanish frontier lands in 1750
- French settlement to 1750
- French frontier lands in 1750
- **Huron** Native American people

Scale: 0 250 500 miles / 0 250 500 kilometers

The Europeans Arrive European exploration of the Americas began in the late 1400s. Colonists soon followed the explorers. The British settled along the Atlantic coast, in what is now southeastern Canada and the Northeastern United States. Spaniards settled in Florida and came north from Mexico to build towns in the Southwest. Often, the settlers' ways of life and needs for resources conflicted with those of the Native Americans. As the European population grew, competition for land intensified. Europeans often took land from Native Americans. Cultural differences and land disputes led to distrust and war.

Slaves in the Colonies European settlers began to plant and harvest crops and started businesses and towns. This created a demand for cheap labor, so Europeans forced some people to migrate to America.

They had been buying people from slave traders in Africa since the 1500s. Beginning in 1619, enslaved Africans were shipped to the American colonies under such harsh conditions that many died during the journey. Those who survived were bought and sold as property and forced to work for free all their lives. Their children were born into slavery. Although these Africans did not arrive by choice, their labor helped build the country, and their influence is seen in our culture today.

Connections to History

Indentured Servants Indentured servants were immigrants who agreed to work in the colonies for a certain number of years in exchange for passage to America. Their indentures, or contracts, could be bought and sold by employers.

Indentured servants were often forced to work long hours and were sometimes treated very badly. Many did not live long enough to gain their freedom. Most, however, settled in the colonies after completing their contracts.

From Far and Near In the second half of the 1800s, many Chinese immigrants entered the United States. Some worked in mines, while others helped build the transcontinental railroad. In the 1880s and the 1920s, new laws limited the number of U.S. immigrants from various countries. In 1952, legislation again allowed immigrants of all nationalities to become citizens.

Rights of Citizens

Although the United States is among the world's leaders in protecting individual freedom, many U.S. citizens have struggled for their rights. Even after African Americans were freed from slavery in 1865 by the 13th Amendment to the Constitution, they were denied their rights. Women could not vote in the United States until 1920. Native Americans, as well as Hispanics, Asians, the Irish, and other immigrants, have fought against discrimination.

The guarantee of **equal opportunity** in education, employment, and other areas of life has expanded over the years. Today, it is illegal for the government or private institutions to discriminate because of race, gender, religion, age, or disability.

Reading
Social Studies

B. Making Inferences Do you think citizens of a democracy have greater responsibilities because they have more rights? Explain.

Responsibilities of Citizenship

U.S. citizens' rights come with responsibilities. Citizens should help decide who will run their government and what actions it will take.

Citizenship IN ACTION

Americans Join Together On September 11, 2001, terrorists hijacked four U.S. planes. They flew two into the twin towers of the World Trade Center in New York City and one into the Pentagon in Washington, D.C. Both towers collapsed, and one wing of the Pentagon was damaged. Thousands of people were killed, and hundreds more were injured or trapped under debris. The fourth plane crashed in Pennsylvania after passengers struggled with the hijackers.

During the crisis, Americans like these rescue workers showed their patriotism and heroism. Hundreds of firefighters, police officers, and medical personnel worked tirelessly, risking their own lives to save others. Citizens and companies across the country donated time, blood, supplies, and millions of dollars to the victims and their families through organizations such as the Red Cross and the United Way. Americans came together in response to the attack on their nation.

90 CHAPTER 4

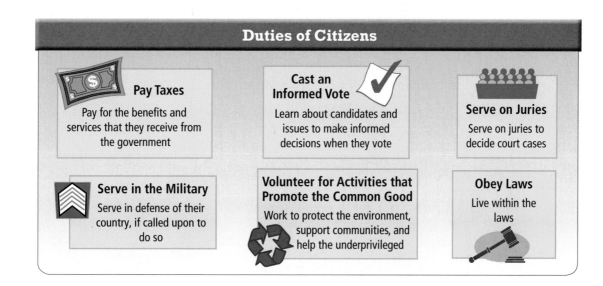

Duties of Citizens

Pay Taxes
Pay for the benefits and services that they receive from the government

Cast an Informed Vote
Learn about candidates and issues to make informed decisions when they vote

Serve on Juries
Serve on juries to decide court cases

Serve in the Military
Serve in defense of their country, if called upon to do so

Volunteer for Activities that Promote the Common Good
Work to protect the environment, support communities, and help the underprivileged

Obey Laws
Live within the laws

Citizenship is a combination of the duties and rights of a citizen. Good citizenship means doing more than the minimum required by law to secure the good of the people.

The Political Process in a Democracy and a Republic In a democracy, government receives its power from the people. **Democracy** is a Greek word that means "rule of the people." In a **republic**, the people also hold power, but they rule through elected representatives. The United States is a republic. The citizens of a democracy or a republic have the responsibility to take part in the political process. The **political process** refers to those legal activities through which citizens can change public policy. By becoming involved, citizens demonstrate their **patriotism,** or love for their country.

Vocabulary

public policy: Actions that a government takes to carry out its responsibilities, such as making laws and creating rules and regulations.

SECTION 1 ASSESSMENT

Terms & Names

1. **Identify:**
   (a) immigrant
   (b) Anasazi
   (c) equal opportunity
   (d) citizenship
   (e) democracy
   (f) republic
   (g) political process
   (h) patriotism

Taking Notes

2. Use a chart like this one to list five groups that immigrated to America. List the approximate date they began arriving.

Group	First Arrived

Main Ideas

3. (a) Why do people immigrate to the United States?

   (b) What are some of the rights guaranteed to U.S. citizens by the Constitution?

   (c) What are some responsibilities of U.S. citizens?

Critical Thinking

4. **Draw Conclusions**

   In what ways do the rights and duties of U.S. citizens reflect the ideas of the writers of the Constitution?

   Think About

   • reasons people immigrated to the colonies

   • the way a democracy works

ACTIVITY -OPTION-

Think about one of the immigrant populations described. Write and illustrate a **magazine article** about the contributions this group has made to the culture of the United States.

Plan an Earth-Surveying Satellite Mission

You and your team of scientists are getting ready to launch a new satellite. Satellites supply scientists with a great deal of information, such as data on Earth's surface, the atmosphere, and even the ocean floor. They carry sensitive instruments to analyze weather conditions and survey the ozone layer. They relay phone conversations and TV programs. Satellites measure heat radiation, plant growth, ocean conditions, tropical rainfall, and other features of our environment. Your job is to plan a new Earth-surveying satellite mission.

COOPERATIVE LEARNING On these pages are challenges you will encounter as you plan a satellite mission. Working with a small group, choose one of these challenges to meet. Divide the work among group members. You will find helpful information in the Data File. Keep in mind that you will present your solution to the class.

LANGUAGE ARTS CHALLENGE

"How can you find these talented people?"

As your planning continues, you find that you need new team members for a variety of jobs. You need computer scientists and software engineers. Other engineers will design instruments to measure data. Experts in forestry, geology, weather, and other fields will help interpret the satellite data. How can you find these talented people? Use one of these options to present information. Look in the Data File for help.

ACTIVITIES

1. As part of the satellite team, you give recruitment speeches to science students. Write and deliver a speech explaining what you do, what background and education you needed, and why your job is interesting.

2. Write help-wanted ads for three different positions on the satellite team. Describe the education, technical background, and personality traits needed for each position.

Engineers working on the satellite. ▲

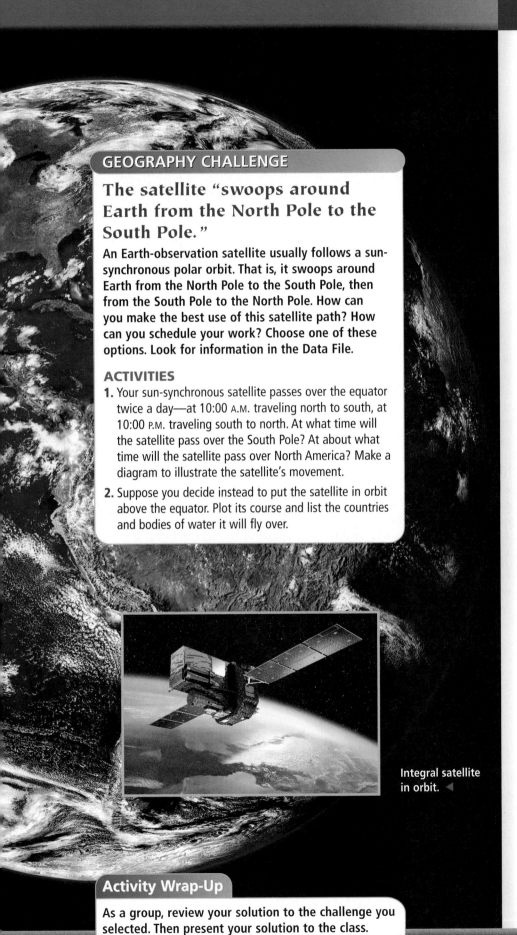

GEOGRAPHY CHALLENGE

The satellite "swoops around Earth from the North Pole to the South Pole."

An Earth-observation satellite usually follows a sun-synchronous polar orbit. That is, it swoops around Earth from the North Pole to the South Pole, then from the South Pole to the North Pole. How can you make the best use of this satellite path? How can you schedule your work? Choose one of these options. Look for information in the Data File.

ACTIVITIES

1. Your sun-synchronous satellite passes over the equator twice a day—at 10:00 A.M. traveling north to south, at 10:00 P.M. traveling south to north. At what time will the satellite pass over the South Pole? At about what time will the satellite pass over North America? Make a diagram to illustrate the satellite's movement.

2. Suppose you decide instead to put the satellite in orbit above the equator. Plot its course and list the countries and bodies of water it will fly over.

Integral satellite in orbit. ◄

DATA FILE

SATELLITE ORBITS

- **High-altitude geosynchronous orbit:** The satellite travels above the equator at a height of about 22,300 miles. It moves at the same speed and in the same direction as Earth is turning. Because the satellite's orbit coordinates with Earth's movement, to an observer on the ground it seems to hover overhead at the same place in the sky.

- **Sun-synchronous polar orbit:** The satellite passes over the north and south poles, circling the globe north to south and south to north in a 24-hour day. As a result, the satellite always crosses the equator at the same local times—say, 2:00 A.M. and 2:00 P.M. As it circles Earth, it makes observations of lands at every latitude.

- **Low-altitude orbit:** The satellite travels within Earth's atmosphere, but in the highest layer, where friction is less because the air is thin.

TYPES OF ARTIFICIAL SATELLITES

- **Earth observation:** map and monitor physical changes on Earth.

- **Scientific research:** gather data for scientists to analyze.

- **Weather:** make local or worldwide observations, depending on orbit; measure cloud patterns, air pressure, air pollution, and air chemistry.

- **Communications:** relay radio, TV, and telephone signals.

- **Navigation:** provide location information.

- **Military:** gather information for military use.

To learn more about Earth-surveying satellites, go to

RESEARCH LINKS
CLASSZONE.COM

Activity Wrap-Up

As a group, review your solution to the challenge you selected. Then present your solution to the class.

A Constitutional Democracy

TERMS & NAMES

United States
Constitution

limited
government

unlimited
government

constitutional
amendment

Bill of Rights

federal
government

MAIN IDEA	**WHY IT MATTERS NOW**
The founders of the United States drafted a constitution that protected the rights of citizens.	After more than 200 years, the Constitution continues to protect the freedoms of U.S. citizens.

DATELINE

U.S. SUPREME COURT, MAY 17, 1954—Oliver Brown, an African American, wanted his daughter to attend a nearby all-white school. When the Board of Education in Topeka, Kansas, refused to admit her, Brown went to court. Today, the U.S. Supreme Court ruled that separate schools for different races violate the equal protection guaranteed by the 14th Amendment to the U.S. Constitution.

In 1896, the Supreme Court had allowed states to provide "separate but equal" facilities for blacks and whites. The words in the Constitution remain the same, but changes in society have led to a new interpretation of those words.

Place • Soldiers and police escort students into a formerly all-white school following this Supreme Court ruling. ▲

The Law of the Land

The basis for U.S. law is the **United States Constitution,** written by the country's first leaders. Amazingly, this document remains the foundation for all laws and the framework for the U.S. government more than 200 years after its creation. The Supreme Court decides whether the actions of states, businesses, and individuals are in accordance with the ideas in the Constitution, as it did in this 1954 case.

Forming a New Government American colonists living under British rule did not have the rights and the protections they wanted. After gaining independence from Great Britain in 1783, they established a nation called the United States of America. The writers of the Constitution designed a government that received its power from the people.

Reading
Social Studies

Making Inferences
What were two goals that the writers of the Constitution wanted to achieve?

The founders, or early American leaders, wanted to protect people's individual rights and freedoms from government interference. They also knew that a society needs strong laws and a stable government to ensure the common good. They wrote a constitution that achieved both goals. The U.S. Constitution describes and limits the power of the government and its leaders. It also defines the rights of citizens and their role in governing their country. In 1902, President Theodore Roosevelt explained the relationship between U.S. citizens and their government.

A VOICE FROM THE UNITED STATES

The government is us; we are the government, you and I.

Theodore Roosevelt

Limited and Unlimited Governments

The constitutional republic of the United States is one example of a **limited government.** In other types of government, called **unlimited governments,** the leaders have almost total power. For instance, dictators control their countries' laws and people.

The United States Constitution The U.S. Constitution is the oldest national constitution still in use. It was written in 1787 at the Constitutional Convention in Philadelphia and ratified in 1789. Ideas that shaped the U.S. Constitution came from many places and times, including Great Britain, France, and ancient Rome. Native American nations, such as the Iroquois Confederacy, may also have influenced political ideas at the time that the Constitution was drafted. This painting, *Scene at the Signing of the Constitution of the United States* by H. C. Christy, hangs in the Capitol in Washington, D.C.

Place • Women began the fight for suffrage, or the right to vote, in the early 1800s and continued until they succeeded in 1920. ▲

The Constitution Grows and Changes

The Constitution went into effect in 1789. A condition of ratifying, or approving, it in many states was the promise of a bill of rights. In 1791, the states adopted ten constitutional amendments proposed by Congress. A **constitutional amendment** is a change or addition to the Constitution. This **Bill of Rights** lists specific freedoms guaranteed to every U.S. citizen. Among them are freedom of speech and religion, the right to a fair trial, and the right to gather peaceably. In all, 27 amendments have adapted the Constitution to the country's changing needs. Some amendments passed after the Bill of Rights include ones that ended slavery, gave women the right to vote, and limited a president's terms to two.

Limiting Powers of Government

Leaders of the new country wanted to limit government power and to preserve each state's right to govern itself. To accomplish these goals, they created a federal system in which power is divided between the **federal government,** or national government, and the state governments. The federal government is a republic headed by the President.

Biography

Martin Luther King, Jr. (1929–1968) Reverend King was a civil rights leader in the 1950s and 1960s. A gifted speaker, he argued for voting rights, equal opportunities in education and jobs, and justice not based on the color of people's skin. He expressed these hopes in a famous 1963 speech in Washington, D.C., shown at right.

Influenced by his study of Christianity and his admiration for India's civil rights leader Mahatma Gandhi, Reverend King used nonviolent protest. He received the Nobel Peace Prize in 1964.

On April 4, 1968, he was assassinated. Since 1986, a U.S. holiday has been observed in January to honor him, and he is remembered around the country for his leadership in the civil rights movement.

Places of Interest in Washington, D.C.

GEOGRAPHY SKILLBUILDER: Interpreting a Map

1. **Location** • On what river is Washington, D.C., located?
2. **Location** • What is the distance between the Capitol, where Congress meets, and the Supreme Court Building?

Federal and State Government The Constitution gives the federal government specific powers, including establishing an army, waging war, raising money through taxes, and making laws to carry out its duties. All other powers are held by the states. The Constitution does not refer to local government, so each state determines the form of town or county rule.

Checks and Balances Three branches share the powers of the U.S. government. Each branch checks the power of the other branches. The process by which a bill, or a proposal for a new law, becomes a law shows how this balance of power works.

How a Bill Becomes a Law

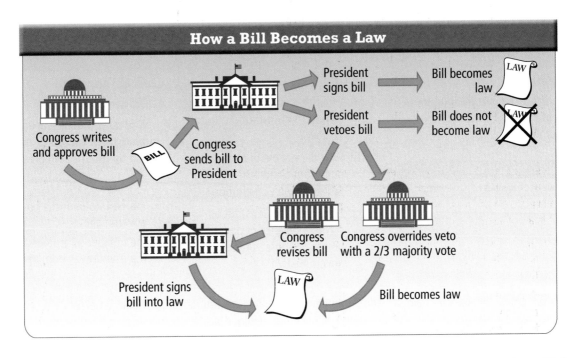

Three Branches of Government

The Constitution separates powers of government into the executive, legislative, and judicial branches. Each branch has its own job. All are located in the U.S. capital, Washington, D.C.

Executive Branch
Enforces the laws

The Executive Branch The President is elected to head the executive branch. He enforces the laws, serves as commander in chief of the armed forces, and conducts foreign affairs. The Vice-President is elected with the President. The President's cabinet includes the secretaries of the 14 executive departments and other key members of the executive branch.

Legislative Branch
Makes the laws and controls taxes and spending

The Legislative Branch Congress is made up of two houses—the Senate and the House of Representatives—and makes national laws. Two senators are elected from each of the 50 states. The House of Representatives has 435 members, elected from each state according to its population. The two houses have some shared responsibilities and some separate ones.

Judicial Branch
Decides if laws agree with the U.S. Constitution

The Judicial Branch The judicial branch is the system of federal courts that makes sure all laws and treaties are constitutional, or agree with the U.S. Constitution. The highest federal court, the Supreme Court, has nine justices, or judges, nominated by the President and approved by the Senate.

SECTION 2 ASSESSMENT

Terms & Names

1. Identify: (a) United States Constitution   (b) limited government   (c) unlimited government
              (d) constitutional amendment   (e) Bill of Rights   (f) federal government

Taking Notes

2. Use a diagram like this one to record the organization of the government.

Branches of Government		
Executive	Legislative	Judicial

Main Ideas

3. (a) What two goals did the writers of the U.S. Constitution try to achieve?

   (b) Why did people think it was important to add the Bill of Rights to the Constitution?

   (c) Why does the Constitution create a balance of powers among the three branches of government?

Critical Thinking

4. **Drawing Inferences**

   Why do you think Congress is made up of two parts, the Senate and the House of Representatives?

   Think About

   • the wish to limit the power of government

   • the number of senators and representatives from each state

---

ACTIVITY -OPTION- If you were going to add an amendment to the Constitution, what would it be? Write a **proposal** for it. Tell what the law would do, whom it would affect, and why people should support it.

Sequencing Events

▶▶ Defining the Skill

Sequence is the order in which events follow one another. If you learn to follow the sequence of events through history, you can better understand how events relate to each other.

▶▶ Applying the Skill

This passage at the right describes the sequence of events that improved the transportation of natural resources and goods in the United States. Use the strategies listed below to understand how transportation has improved.

How to Sequence Events

Strategy ❶ Look for time periods of events or discoveries. Some dates may be exact, and others may be indicated only by decades or centuries. Words such as *day, month, year,* or *century* may help you to sequence the events or discoveries.

Strategy ❷ Look for clues about time that allow you to order events according to sequence. Words such as *first, next, later,* and *finally* may help you order events that are not dated.

RESOURCES, GOODS, AND PEOPLE

The United States could not have developed without new ways of transporting natural resources and ❶ goods. In the early 19th century, water provided the fastest way to transport goods. Canals linked some lakes and rivers, so places became more ❷ accessible. A little later, steamboats allowed river traffic to go upstream and downstream easily.

❶ By the middle of the century, steam-powered railroads had replaced steamboats because they could reach more places and carry larger loads. At the ❶ beginning of the 20th century, people and goods in many cities and towns were linked by railroad.

❶ In the early 1900s, automobiles and trucks began to move raw materials and goods. Airplanes ❶ began to transport goods in the 1930s. By the ❶ 1950s, paved roads connected much of the country. ❷ Today, fast jets also bring goods and people to many parts of the United States.

Make a Time Line

Making a time line can help you sequence events. This time line shows the sequence of events in the passage you just read.

Methods of Transporting Goods

| Water routes: rivers, lakes, canals | Steam-powered railroads | Wide use of railroads, automobiles, and trucks | Paved roads throughout U.S. | Jet airplanes |

1800s — 1850s — 1900s — 1950s — 2000s

1810s — Steamboats

1930s — Airplanes

▶▶ Practicing the Skill

Turn to Chapter 4, Section 1, "We the People." Read about the different groups of people who settled the land that became the United States. Make a list showing the sequence of the arrival of different immigrant groups.

WITH A LAND AREA of over 3.7 million square miles and a population of more than 285 million, the United States is an amazingly varied country. From small towns, forests, and farmland to big cities like San Francisco and New York, the United States has a wealth of both human-made and natural features. The poems here celebrate this variety.

CONEY

By Virginia Schonborg

There's hot corn
And franks.
There's the boardwalk
With lots of games,
With chances
To win or lose.
There's the sun.
Underneath the boardwalk
It's cool,
And the sand is salty.
The beach is
Like a fruitstand of people,
Big and little,
Red and white,
Brown and yellow.
There's the sea
With high green waves.
And after,
There's hot corn
And franks.

KNOXVILLE, TENNESSEE

By Nikki Giovanni

I always like summer
best
you can eat fresh corn
from daddy's garden
and okra
and greens
and cabbage
and lots of
barbecue
and buttermilk
and homemade ice-cream
at the church picnic
and listen to
gospel music
outside
at the church
homecoming
and go to the mountains with
your grandmother
and go barefooted
and be warm
all the time
not only when you go to bed
and sleep

SCENIC ★

By John Updike

O when in San Francisco do
As natives do: they sit and stare
And smile and stare again. The view
Is visible from anywhere.

Here hills are white with houses whence,
Across a multitude of sills,
The owners, lucky residents,
See other houses, other hills.

The meanest[1] San Franciscan knows,
No matter what his past has been,
There are a thousand patios
Whose view he is included in.

The Golden Gate, the cable cars,
Twin Peaks, the Spreckles habitat,[2]
The local ocean, sun, and stars—
When fog falls, one admires *that*.

Here homes are stacked in such a way
That every picture window has
An unmarred prospect of the Bay
And, in its center, Alcatraz.[3]

1. Poorest.
2. In the late 1950s, Twin Peaks was a well-to-do residential neighborhood where a very wealthy family, the Spreckles, lived.
3. An island in San Francisco Bay, site of a former federal prison.

Reading
THE LITERATURE

Pick out the words each poet uses to give a sense of place. How can you tell that some places are rural, some urban? What aspects of geography has each poet highlighted?

Thinking About
THE LITERATURE

Imagine that you live in one of these places. What kinds of jobs might people have there? What might they do for fun? How does the place where you live influence your daily activities?

Writing About
THE LITERATURE

Which of the poems creates the strongest image in your mind? Using examples from that poem, write a short paragraph explaining why.

About the Authors

Virginia Schonborg (b. 1913) was born in Rhode Island and is the author of *The Salt Marsh* and *Subway Swinger.*

Nikki Giovanni (b. 1943) was born in Tennessee and became well-known as a poet in the 1960s.

John Updike (b. 1932), born in Shillington, Pennsylvania, is the author of many short stories, novels, and poems.

Further Reading For more outstanding poems about the United States, read *My America: A Poetry Atlas of the United States*, edited by Lee Bennett Hopkins.

The United States Economy

TERMS & NAMES
factors of production
GDP
free enterprise/ market economy
consumer
profit
competition

MAIN IDEA

The United States has an economy based on free enterprise. Consumers and business owners decide what goods and services to produce.

WHY IT MATTERS NOW

This economic system has made it possible for the United States to become a leader in the worldwide economy.

DATELINE

JUNE 2001, THE UNITED STATES—The collapse of many dot-coms has shaken consumer confidence. Internet-based companies, nicknamed "dot-coms" for the last part of their Web addresses, have been failing by the hundreds.

In the mid-1990s, investors backed dot-com companies in hopes of making a huge return on their investments. This ready money encouraged people with limited management experience, untested technologies, and experimental Web sales strategies to start companies. In 1999, more than 1,700 Internet start-ups were born.

When investors realized that many start-ups were losing money, they began to withdraw their support. Between January 2000 and May 2001, 435 Internet companies shut down. Over 31,000 people have lost their jobs.

Place • When companies fail, employees are often left without jobs and office equipment is sold. ▲

The Study of Economics

Business start-ups and shutdowns, the rise and fall of investor and consumer confidence, the increase and decrease in the number of people without jobs—all of these changes are part of the market economy of the United States. Investors, service providers, manufacturers, and consumers make choices each day, and these choices affect the state of the economy.

Vocabulary
investor: one who commits money or capital in order to earn a financial return

102 CHAPTER 4

Goods and Services Suppose you want a CD recording just released by your favorite music group. To earn the money to pay for it, you might rake your neighbor's leaves or care for his or her child for a few hours. The CD is a good. A good is any object you can buy to satisfy a want. Raking leaves or baby-sitting is a service you provide. A service is an action that meets a want. Your neighbor buys your service to meet his or her want.

What to Buy People constantly decide which goods and services to buy. They usually satisfy basic needs such as food, clothing, housing, transportation, childcare, and medical treatment first. If there is money left over, they might choose to spend it on music CDs, in-line skates, a computer game, or a vacation.

A government must also make decisions. Tax dollars must be set aside to pay for police and fire protection, schools, roads, and military forces. Once these expenses have been determined, other choices can be made.

Reading
Social Studies

A. Synthesizing
After a government has set aside money for basic wants, what additional goods or services might it pay for?

A Growing Economy

A nation must produce goods and provide services to support a growing economy. In an expanding economy, citizens have better-paying jobs, so the government collects more tax money. Then people and the government can satisfy more wants.

To sustain a growing economy, business owners must keep production at a high level. Production is the making of goods and services. The four **factors of production** are the ingredients, or elements, needed for production to occur.

Culture • Christina Aguilera's critical contribution in the production of a CD is as one of the labor resources. ▼

Factors of Production for a Music CD

Entrepreneur
(owner of recording studio and factory)

Labor Resources
(musicians, sound technician, producer, factory manager, factory workers)

Natural Resources
(materials to manufacture CDs)

Capital Resources
(recording equipment, studio, factory and manufacturing equipment)

MUSIC CD

Natural Resources Raw materials are used to make goods. Examples include land, water, forests, minerals, soil, and climate.

Labor Resources Workers are needed with the appropriate knowledge, skills, and experience to make goods or provide services.

Capital Resources Machines, factories, and supplies are needed.

Entrepreneurs These are the people who bring natural resources, labor resources, and capital resources together to produce goods and services.

Strange but TRUE

The Value of Money The U.S. Department of the Treasury first issued paper money in 1861. During the Civil War, people hoarded coins. This caused a severe shortage of coins in circulation.

The Bureau of Engraving and Printing printed "fractional currency" bills of 3 cents, 5 cents, 10 cents, 25 cents, and 50 cents. These were the smallest bills ever printed in this country. The largest note was the $100,000 Gold Certificate printed in 1934 and 1935. These notes were used for bank transactions and were not available for the public to use.

The United States Economy

The U.S. economy is one of the wealthiest in the world. One way to measure a country's economy is to look at its **GDP**, or gross domestic product. This tells the total value of the goods and services that a country produces each year. The GDP is also a way to compare the economies of different countries.

U.S. industries include services, such as health care and legal services; communications, such as publishing, television and radio, telephone, and mail delivery; finance, such as banks and stock markets; manufacturing, such as food products, automobiles, and clothing; and electronics, such as televisions, computers, and sound equipment. The success of these industries helps make many Americans wealthier than people in other parts of the world.

BACKGROUND

In 2000, 2.8 billion of the world's 6 billion people lived on less than $2 a day.

Estimated 2000 Per Capita* GDP	
Country	**U.S. Dollars**
United States	36,200
China	3,600
India	2,200
Saudi Arabia	10,500
France	24,400
Zimbabwe	2,500

Per capita means for each person.
Source: *CIA World Factbook*

The Free Enterprise or Market Economy U.S. citizens and businesses make most economic decisions. Business owners control the factors of production. The government plays a limited role. It does not decide which or how many goods are produced. It does not set prices or tell people where to work. These are the qualities of a **free enterprise/market economy**. A market is a setting for exchanging goods and services. In a free enterprise economy, business owners compete in the market with little government interference. Other nations, such as Canada, many countries in Western Europe, Japan, and some Latin American countries, also have market economies.

Culture • The machines that make CDs are a capital resource, one of the four factors of production. ▲

Supply and Demand In a free enterprise or market economy, **consumers**—the people who use goods and services—help decide what will be produced. Prices affect how products are distributed to consumers. For example, suppose a music company produces 1,000 CDs priced at $16.95 each, but 1,100 people want to buy them. There are not enough CDs to satisfy the wants of these consumers. Because demand for the good is greater than the supply, the seller can increase the price to $17.95. He or she sells all the CDs and makes an extra $1.00 profit on each. The seller, like all entrepreneurs, wants to increase profit. **Profit** is the money that remains after all the costs of producing a product have been paid.

Now suppose the seller offers 1,000 more CDs at the original $16.95 price. One hundred sell right away, leaving 900 CDs that no one wants at this price. The seller then reduces the price to $15.95. Consumers who didn't want the CD at $16.95 may want it at this lower price. Because the supply of the good is greater than the demand, the seller must reduce the price.

Supply and Demand

1. Price is high.
2. Producer wants to increase supply.
3. More goods push price down.
4. Demand increases.
5. Producer increases supply.
6. Price decreases again.
7. Producer supplies fewer goods.
8. Price increases and demand falls.

Supply and demand explain how price and availability are affected by how much consumers are willing to pay for an item and how much the seller decides to charge for it. The number of CDs offered at each price is the supply. The number of CDs that people will buy at each price is the demand.

Competition In a free enterprise or market economy, many businesses produce similar goods or services. There is competition to attract consumers. **Competition** is the rivalry among businesses to sell goods to consumers and make the greatest profit. To achieve these goals, a company may offer an improved product, manufacture it more cheaply, or sell it at a better price.

Culture • Stores compete in malls and online to attract consumers. They use advertising and appealing store displays to catch the attention of potential customers. ▲

Other Economic Systems

Most countries combine features from three types of economic systems: market, command, and traditional economies.

Command Economy In this system, the government decides how many of which goods are produced and sets the prices. Countries, such as North Korea and Cuba with Communist governments, have command economies. China has elements of market and command economies.

Traditional Economy In this system, social roles and culture determine how goods and services are produced, what prices and individual incomes are, and which consumers are allowed to buy certain goods. For instance, a family's status may determine whether they can own a tractor. Farmers may give much of their produce to community leaders. India has features of both market and traditional economies.

Reading
Social Studies

B. Making Inferences Why might countries combine features of different economic systems?

The Global Economy

Today, more countries than ever before have market economies. Communication and transportation are fast and dependable, making trade easier among countries. The movement of people, goods, and ideas around the world has helped build a global, or worldwide, economy in which the United States is a leader. Expanding trade can open new markets and keep prices low and quality high for consumers. U.S. citizens buy many cars and clothes from other countries that take part in the global economy.

World Trade Partners of the United States, 2000

NAFTA – 32.9%

East Asia NICs* – 19.8%

European Union – 19.3%

Japan – 10.6%

Latin America – 7.8%

Middle East – 2.9%

Africa – 1.9%

East Europe and Former Soviet Union – 1.1%

India – 0.4%

* Newly industrialized countries: China, Hong Kong, Indonesia, Malaysia, Singapore, South Korea, Taiwan, Thailand

Source: *U.S. Dept. of Commerce, International Trade Summary, 1998–2001*

0   3,000 miles
0   3,000 kilometers

GEOGRAPHY SKILLBUILDER: Interpreting a Map

1. **Movement** • Who are the largest U.S. trade partners?
2. **Movement** • With which countries or regions does the United States trade least?

Trade Barriers Sometimes countries establish barriers to restrict trade because they prefer to produce their own goods or services. Tariffs, or taxes on imported goods, raise the price to the consumer and make it more difficult for other countries to compete.

In 1994, NAFTA, the North American Free Trade Agreement, reduced trade barriers among the United States, Canada, and Mexico. There was concern that companies would move factories to Mexico, where workers earn less, and U.S. workers would lose jobs. However, many economists believe free trade benefits all three countries.

SECTION 3 ASSESSMENT

Terms & Names

1. Identify:
   (a) factors of production
   (b) GDP
   (c) free enterprise/market economy
   (d) consumer
   (e) profit
   (f) competition

Taking Notes

2. Use a chart like this one to take notes on the characteristics of free enterprise/market, command, and traditional economies.

Free Enterprise/ Market Economy	Command Economy	Traditional Economy

Main Ideas

3. (a) How is the price of goods decided in the U.S. economic system?

   (b) What are the four factors of production?

   (c) What role does government have in the U.S. market economy?

Critical Thinking

4. **Making Inferences**

   What effect will reducing trade barriers between countries have on the price of goods? Explain.

   Think About

   • the characteristics of a free enterprise/market economy

   • competition

ACTIVITY -OPTION- Write an **advertisement** for a new business showing the goods or services it will produce. Make a chart showing the type of materials, labor, and capital you will need to produce the product.

The Legacy of North America

Telephones

In 1876, the Scottish-born American Alexander Graham Bell (1847–1922) invented the telephone. Telephones have come a long way since Bell's day. Today, caller identification, automatic redialing, and call waiting are common telephone services. Cordless phones, mobile phones, and the Internet allow people throughout the world to communicate over great distances.

Lacrosse

Native peoples of North America played an early version of lacrosse long before Columbus landed. Players used a racket, now known as a crosse, to throw a hard ball down the field and into the opposing team's goal. Today, lacrosse is a popular sport not only in North America but also in Ireland, Australia, and South Africa. Men's teams play for the ILF World Championship, and women's teams compete for the World Cup.

Airplanes

In 1903, Wilbur (1867–1912) and Orville (1871–1948) Wright achieved the first powered, sustained flight near Kitty Hawk, N.C. The flight lasted 12 seconds and reached a height of 120 feet. By the 1920s, aviation had become a booming industry. Today, jumbo and supersonic jets allow people to travel around the world in just a day or two. More than 1.5 billion passengers land and take off at the world's 50 busiest airports every year.

Find Out More About It!

Study the text and photos on these pages to learn about inventions, creations, and contributions that have come from North America. Then choose the item that interests you the most and do research in the library or on the Internet to learn more about it. Use the information you gather to construct a model of the item you choose.

RESEARCH LINKS
CLASSZONE.COM

Skyscrapers

In the late 1800s, U.S. architects and engineers worked together to build the first skyscrapers in Chicago and New York City. Today, these enormous structures rise in cities all over the world. The tallest skyscrapers in the world are the Petronas Towers in Kuala Lumpur, Malaysia, which reach a height of 1,483 feet.

Snowmobiles

In the winter of 1922, 15-year-old Joseph-Armand Bombardier of Canada invented the first crude snow-mobile by attaching a car engine to sleigh runners and adding a wooden propeller to the back. In 1935, he refined his invention after his young son died from appendicitis because they couldn't make it through the snow to the hospital in time. Today, people around the world use snowmobiles for winter fun, and people in the remote north depend on them for transportation when the snows are deep.

United States Culture: Crossing Borders

MAIN IDEA	WHY IT MATTERS NOW
The American way of life reflects the cultures of people from many countries around the world.	People around the world are more closely connected than ever before.

DATELINE

NEW YORK CITY, 1905—Visit Gennaro Lombardi's pizzeria—the first in the United States—to try a pizza. This baked, flat pie has a bread crust covered with cheese, tomato sauce, and seasonings.

Lombardi's pizzas are not exactly like the pizzas made in Naples, Italy, because different seasonings, flour, and cheese are available here. Also, instead of using sliced tomatoes like those put on Italian pizzas, Lombardi adds a spicy homemade tomato sauce. Customers say this pizza is as good as any from Naples. Judging by the warm reception it has received so far, pizza may become a popular U.S. food.

Place • **Pizza, brought here by Italian immigrants, is becoming a popular food.** ▲

American Way of Life

People in the United States have brought diverse customs, traditions, and foods, like pizza, from their homelands, but they share many of the same values. **Values** are the principles and ideals by which people live. U.S. citizens care about individual freedoms; equal opportunities for jobs and education; fair treatment of people regardless of race, religion, or gender; and private ownership of property. Many of these values are part of the U.S. Constitution and help define American culture.

Education U.S. citizens believe they can improve their lives through education. In 1647, Massachusetts established the first colonial public school system. Today, state laws require that all children attend school or be taught at home until they are at least 16. More than 99 percent of U.S. children finish elementary school, and more than 85 percent complete high school.

Reading
Social Studies

Drawing Conclusions
Why do you think values such as freedom of religion were written into the U.S. Constitution?

U.S. Religions About 70 percent of all U.S. citizens are members of religious groups. Many colonists, such as British Protestants and Catholics, settled in America so that they could worship as they wished. Since then, people with many different religious beliefs have come to the United States. Most Spanish, French, and Italian immigrants were Catholic. In the 1900s, many European Jews settled in the United States. Asian immigrants practice Buddhism and Hinduism. North Africans and Southwest Asians brought Islam. Many Native Americans continue to practice their ancestors' religions.

The Arts and Entertainment

Leisure activities in the United States reflect the influence of other cultures. For example, sports such as tennis, golf, soccer, and even baseball originated in other countries. Tennis came from France, golf from Scotland, and soccer from England. Baseball is probably based on rounders, a game played in Great Britain in the late 1700s. Basketball was invented in the United States by a Canadian and later spread to other countries. Football is played chiefly in the United States and Canada.

Place •
Americans eat foods from the traditions of many countries, such as Japanese sushi and sashimi. ▼

Culture • Baseball, often called America's national pastime, was probably adapted from a British game played in the 1700s. ▲

The movie and television industries and certain musical forms, such as rock 'n' roll, developed in the United States, although they were affected by other cultures. Jazz was greatly influenced by the blues, which is rooted in spirituals once sung by enslaved Africans. Today, artists and audiences around the world enjoy these American musical styles.

Globalization of Culture The international popularity of U.S. music is an example of the globalization of culture. **Globalization** means spreading around the world. Today, cultural influences often cross national boundaries. People around the world enjoy blue jeans, sodas, and fast food from the United States. McDonald's serves about 45 million people a day in 121 countries.

U.S. citizens eat Japanese sushi, listen to Italian operas, and drive South Korean cars. Literature from many nations is translated into different languages. Print and electronic communication, television, movies, and the Internet provide speedy ways to share the products and creations of different cultures.

U.S. Science and Technology

U.S. scientists are mapping DNA, discovering treatments and cures for diseases, and finding new energy sources for industry and homes. Once discoveries are made, inventors create **technology**, such as tools or equipment, to apply the new knowledge in practical ways. Modern technology enables U.S. scientists to work with other scientists from around the world.

Science and Technology Change the World Discoveries by U.S. scientists help people throughout the world. Polio, a disease that usually affects children, was widespread in the 1940s and 1950s.

BACKGROUND

DNA is the molecule that carries the information that determines the characteristics of every living thing. It was first identified by Francis Crick, James Watson, and others in 1953.

Skyscrapers The skyscraper originated in the United States in the 1870s and has caught on in other countries. Limited space in cities, plus materials and technology, such as steel and elevators, have inspired architects to design taller buildings.

The height of each building is measured from the ground-level main entrance to the structural top, including spires but not antennas or flagpoles. Today, many of the tallest buildings are located outside the United States in places such as Kuala Lumpur, Malaysia, and Hong Kong and Shanghai in China.

World's Tallest Skyscrapers

Height in Feet

Name	Petronas Towers	Sears Tower	Jin Mao Building	Plaza Rakyat	Empire State Building	Central Plaza	Bank of China
City	Kuala Lumpur	Chicago	Shanghai	Kuala Lumpur	New York	Hong Kong	Hong Kong
Year Built	1998	1974	1998	1999	1931	1992	1989

THINKING CRITICALLY

1. **Finding Causes**
   What were two factors that led architects to design skyscrapers?

2. **Recognizing Important Details**
   How is building height measured?

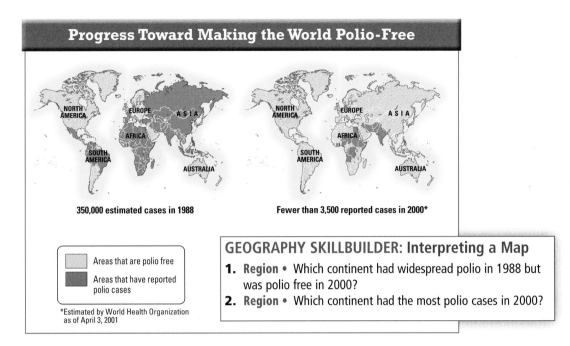

Progress Toward Making the World Polio-Free

350,000 estimated cases in 1988

Fewer than 3,500 reported cases in 2000*

☐ Areas that are polio free

■ Areas that have reported polio cases

*Estimated by World Health Organization as of April 3, 2001

GEOGRAPHY SKILLBUILDER: Interpreting a Map

1. **Region** • Which continent had widespread polio in 1988 but was polio free in 2000?
2. **Region** • Which continent had the most polio cases in 2000?

Then, U.S. doctors Jonas Salk and Albert Sabin each developed a different vaccine. As a result, great progress has been made toward making the world free of polio.

Negative effects of technology include increased pollution of the environment and the loss of unique cultural features as countries share languages, foods, and customs. Poorer nations may lack the money and skilled labor needed to benefit from new applications of science.

SECTION 4 ASSESSMENT

Terms & Names

1. Identify: (a) value (b) globalization (c) technology

Taking Notes

2. Make a chart like the one below to show features of U.S. culture and science that have spread to other parts of the world.

| U.S. Culture and Science Around the World ||
Culture	Science and Technology

Main Ideas

3. (a) What are some values shared by people in the United States?

   (b) What are some examples of contributions from other cultures to the American way of life?

   (c) In what ways does American culture influence people in other countries?

Critical Thinking

4. **Forming and Supporting Opinions**

   Do you think globalization has a positive or a negative effect on the world? Support your opinion.

   Think About

   - the effects of globalization
   - the changes caused by international trade and communication
   - the effects of scientific discoveries worldwide

ACTIVITY -OPTION-

Reread "The Arts and Entertainment" on page 111. Think about the sports, music, and movies you enjoy. Write an **essay** describing how the cultures of other countries influence your activities.

TERMS & NAMES

Explain the significance of each of the following:

1. immigrant
2. citizenship
3. democracy
4. political process
5. United States Constitution
6. Bill of Rights
7. factors of production
8. free enterprise/ market economy
9. value
10. globalization

REVIEW QUESTIONS

We the People *(pages 87–91)*

1. What are some reasons that people have immigrated to the United States?
2. What are some responsibilities of citizens of the United States?

A Constitutional Democracy *(pages 94–98)*

3. What were the goals of the early leaders when they wrote the United States Constitution?
4. What were the leaders attempting to do when they set up a system of checks and balances within the federal government?

The United States Economy *(pages 102–107)*

5. What are examples of wants that a government must fund?
6. How does each factor of production contribute to the making of a product?

United States Culture: Crossing Borders *(pages 110–113)*

7. What can you conclude from the fact that cultural values were directly stated in the U.S. Constitution?
8. If globalization continues, how will it affect the cultures of the world?

CRITICAL THINKING

Synthesizing

1. Using your completed chart from Reading Social Studies, p. 86, explain why the economy, form of government, and cultural values of the United States continue to attract so many immigrants each year.

Forming and Supporting Opinions

2. Martin Luther King, Jr., fought against laws he thought were unjust. How was this good citizenship? Explain.

Making Inferences

3. What were the major concerns of the leaders who wrote the U.S. Constitution and how did they address them?

Visual Summary

1 We the People

- The United States is made up of immigrants from many countries.
- U.S. citizens share many rights and responsibilities.

A Constitutional Democracy 2

- After the American colonists gained independence, they wrote a Constitution that created a limited government and protected their rights and freedoms.

The United States Economy 3

- The United States has a free enterprise/market economy.
- Because more countries have market economies, a global economy is developing with expanded trade among nations.

United States Culture: Crossing Borders 4

- Americans believe in strong values, many of which are protected by the U.S. Constitution.
- American culture has been shaped by many groups and now influences the cultures of other nations.

SOCIAL STUDIES SKILLBUILDER

Civil Rights Movement in the U.S.

| 1865: Abolition of slavery |
| 1870: Right to vote for African-American men |
| 1920: Right to vote for American women |
| 1954: End of school segregation |
| 1964: Civil Rights Act |

SKILLBUILDER: Sequencing Events

1. What information does this sequence chart show?
2. When did segregation in schools end?
3. Did school segregation end before or after women received the right to vote?

FOCUS ON GEOGRAPHY

1. **Place** • Which states have the highest percentage of foreign-born people?
2. **Place** • Name three states where less than 5 percent of the population is foreign-born.
3. **Region** • Why do you think most states with a high percentage of foreign-born people are on the coasts or borders of the United States?

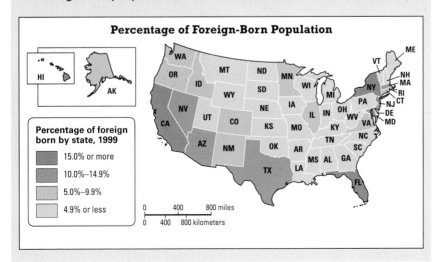

Percentage of Foreign-Born Population

Percentage of foreign born by state, 1999

- 15.0% or more
- 10.0%–14.9%
- 5.0%–9.9%
- 4.9% or less

CHAPTER PROJECTS

Interdisciplinary Activity: Music

Writing a Magazine Article Research a favorite musician of today or from the past. Learn what musical influences shaped this performer's work. Were some of the influences from other cultures or times? Include illustrations with captions for your article.

Cooperative Learning Activity

Creating a Display In a group of four to six classmates, think of a natural event, such as a flood, drought, or storm, that affected your community or your region of the country. Working in pairs, research the event in the library or interview people. Together with your group, create a display about the event, explaining its causes and exploring how it affected the area.

- Create drawings or models. Prepare labels to identify and explain them.
- Consider using audio recordings of eyewitness accounts or interviews.
- Use before-and-after photographs or diagrams, if appropriate.

INTERNET ACTIVITY

Use the Internet to learn about the Constitutional Convention. What were the concerns of the large and small states? Explore how a compromise was reached that allowed the Convention to draft the Constitution.

Writing About Government Write a report of your findings. If possible, use a chart or graph to present information about the different proposals and the final compromise. In your report, include a list of the Internet sites you used to gather information.

For Internet links to support this activity, go to

RESEARCH LINKS
CLASSZONE.COM

CHAPTER 5

Canada Today

CANADA

ATLANTIC

PACIFIC
OCEAN

PACIFIC

OCEAN

INDIAN
OCEAN

OCEAN

How does a country's geography influence its culture?

Region • In 1989, the Canadian Museum of Civilization opened in Hull, Quebec, on the banks of the Ottawa River. The museum celebrates the geographic and cultural diversity of Canada. Douglas Cardinal, an architect from Calgary, Alberta, and a descendant of the Canadian Blackfoot people, designed the two distinct buildings. He wanted them to reflect Canada's landforms.

The structures evoke the glaciers and rocky formations of the western Canadian Shield. The limestone from which the walls are made comes from the province of Manitoba. Totem poles carved from red cedar trees by First Nations people of British Columbia line the museum entrance.

What do you think?

♦ How are the varied landforms and resources of Canada represented in the museum?

♦ Describe some geographic features in the area where you live. Explain how they affect the traditions and activities of people in your community.

Region Hudson Bay, a huge body of water in northeast Canada, is home to ice floes nine months of the year. Nevertheless, the bay is open to shipping throughout the year.

BEFORE YOU READ

▶▶ *What Do You Know?*

Before you read this chapter, consider what you know about Canada. Have you ever read that Canada has the world's longest coastline? Did you know that Canada is an independent democracy with a constitution, yet it pledges loyalty to the British monarch? Perhaps you know that 60 percent of the National Hockey League's players are Canadian? Recall what you have learned about Canada from personal experience, television, and other classes. Think about how Canada is similar to the United States and how it is different.

▶▶ *What Do You Want to Know?*

Decide what you would like to know about Canada's history, government, economy, and culture. In your notebook, record what you hope to learn from this chapter.

Culture • The art of totem pole carving almost disappeared in the mid-1800s. Museums began to preserve totem poles in the 1850s. ▼

READ AND TAKE NOTES

Reading Strategy: Analyzing Causes and Effects To help you understand how geographic, historical, and cultural factors have influenced Canada's development, pay attention to causes and effects as you read Chapter 5. Notice that several factors may cause the same effect. Use the chart below to make connections between statements about geography, history, and culture and statements describing Canada today.

• Copy the chart into your notebook.
• On the chart, read statements describing issues and conditions in Canada today (effects).
• As you read the chapter, identify the effects of the listed causes and note them on the chart.

Culture • The 1893 Montreal Amateur Athletic Association was the first hockey team to win the Stanley Cup. ▲

Causes		Effects
Early settlers were from France and Britain, two nations that had conflicts. French-speaking Canadians have kept their own language and culture separate from the rest of the nation. The people of First Nations and other culture groups want to preserve their traditions.	→	
Cold climate, geographic barriers, and poor soil exist in northern parts of Canada.	→	
The Arctic Ocean and Hudson Bay are frozen for most of the year. Landforms such as the Rocky Mountains create transportation barriers.	→	

O Canada! Immigrant Roots

TERMS & NAMES
First Nation
multiculturalism
refugee

MAIN IDEA

Canada's population includes many groups of people from different lands who retain their cultural identities.

WHY IT MATTERS NOW

Knowing the history of the people of Canada helps in understanding Canada's policy of multiculturalism.

DATELINE

EXTRA

QUEBEC, NEW FRANCE, JUNE 1609

New colonists have just arrived to join the first settlers of Quebec. Only French explorer Samuel de Champlain and 8 of the 32 men he led here survived their first winter in the new colony. Champlain chose this location that the Algonquins call Quebec, or the Narrows, after much searching.

After arriving last July, he and his men built houses, planted grain, and worked to encourage fur trading and friendly relations with the native people. Champlain has spent years traveling around New France and mapping and recording information about the seacoast and rivers.

Place • Champlain has great hopes for the future of Quebec. ▲

Champlain used an astrolabe, such as this one, to navigate during his travels. ▲

Who Are the Canadians?

The people of Canada come from many countries—not just France. More than 50 ethnic groups make up the population. More than two-thirds of Canadians have European ancestry. About 40 percent have British roots and 27 percent share a French heritage. Other Canadians trace their families back to Germany, Italy, and Ukraine, as well as to nations in Africa and Asia. Less than 5 percent of all Canadians are people of the First Nations.

The First Nations

People have lived in North America for at least 12,000 years. At times in the past, the levels of the oceans were as much as 300 feet lower than they are today. Then the narrow water passage between Asia and North America—the Bering Strait—became dry land. Small bands of people crossed this land bridge into North America and settled throughout North America and South America.

The Canadians of the **First Nations** are descendants of those first settlers from Asia. In the Arctic north, Inuit and other native people make up more than half the population. Large numbers of First Nations people, including Cree, Micmac, Abenaki, and Ojibwa, live in southern Canada near the United States border.

European Immigrants

The first major wave of European settlement began in the 1600s. Both Britain and France established colonies in what is now Canada. These two countries had a long history of conflict, and they continued their rivalry on the North American continent. Between 1754 and 1763, they fought the French and Indian War for control of North America.

BACKGROUND

The name *Canada* comes from *Kanata,* a First Nations Huron-Iroquois word that means "village."

Spotlight on CULTURE

Totem Poles—Carving History The Haida people in Canada's Queen Charlotte Islands and the Kwakiutl in central British Columbia have been skilled totem carvers for centuries. Early craftspeople believed that red cedar was a gift from the Great Spirit. They used simple tools to carve beautiful, detailed totem poles from these trees.

Totem poles, such as these in Stanley Park, Vancouver, display brightly painted animal figures, or totems. These include eagles, whales, grizzly bears, wolves, ravens, frogs, and halibut. Totems are symbols that tell stories, celebrate important events, and preserve the history of native clans. Totem poles have also been used as grave markers and monuments.

THINKING CRITICALLY

1. Making Inferences
What do the totem poles tell you about the First Nations people's relationship with nature?

2. Drawing Conclusions
What roles do totem poles play in native culture?

France lost the war and surrendered most of its Canadian territory to Great Britain. However, many French settlers remained, and disputes continued between them and the fast-growing population of British settlers.

Culture • British General James Wolfe's troops defeated the French and captured Quebec in 1759 during the French and Indian War. Benjamin West's painting *The Death of General Wolfe* shows Wolfe's death at the end of the battle. ▲

Canada and the United Kingdom

In 1791, the British government established itself in two areas in Canada. Upper Canada, now Ontario, had mostly British settlers. Lower Canada, now Quebec, remained largely French. Although hostilities continued between the two populations, in 1867 they were united as the Dominion of Canada, along with Nova Scotia and New Brunswick. Canada became a self-governing nation, although the British monarch remained its head of state.

In 1869, the Hudson's Bay Company sold land to Canada that later became the provinces of Manitoba, Alberta, and Saskatchewan. In 1871, British Columbia joined the Dominion, and Canada now reached to the Pacific Ocean. In 1931, with the enactment of the Statute of Westminster, Canada gained equal status with the United Kingdom and joined the Commonwealth of Nations. In 1982, the last legal connection between Canada and the British Parliament ended, although Canada remains a member of the Commonwealth.

Later Immigrants

Most of Canada's early immigrants were English, Scottish, Irish, and French. After World War I, other Europeans arrived from countries such as Italy, Poland, and Ukraine. Most Italian immigrants settled in Toronto and Montreal. Most Ukrainians moved to the prairies of central Canada. After World War II, Germans and Dutch entered the country, settling primarily in Ontario and British Columbia. In the 1960s, new immigration laws allowed people to migrate from Africa, Latin America, Asia, and the Pacific Islands.

Canadian Citizens and Citizenship

Reading **Social Studies**

A. Drawing Inferences How might Canada's policy of multiculturalism lead to increased immigration?

As Canadian citizens, those of English or French descent have retained their separate languages and identities. Other groups have also kept the traditions of their homelands after settling in Canada. To support these citizen groups, Canada has adopted an official policy of **multiculturalism**—an acceptance of many cultures instead of just one.

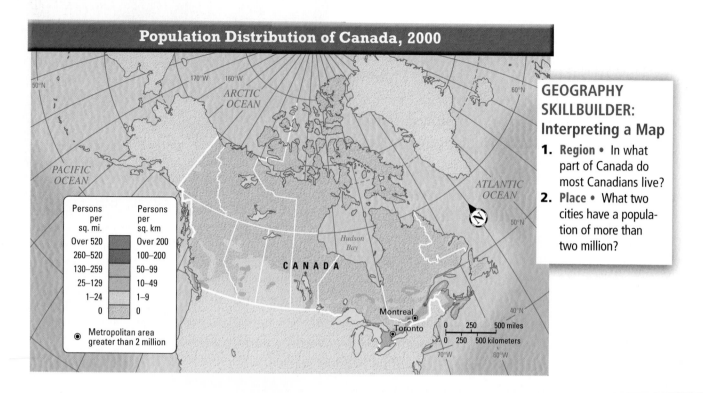

Population Distribution of Canada, 2000

Persons per sq. mi.
- Over 520
- 260–520
- 130–259
- 25–129
- 1–24
- 0

Persons per sq. km
- Over 200
- 100–200
- 50–99
- 10–49
- 1–9
- 0

⊙ Metropolitan area greater than 2 million

Montreal
Toronto

0   250   500 miles
0   250   500 kilometers

GEOGRAPHY SKILLBUILDER:
Interpreting a Map

1. **Region** • In what part of Canada do most Canadians live?
2. **Place** • What two cities have a population of more than two million?

Canadian citizens have many of the same rights and responsibilities as U.S. citizens. They must obey Canada's laws. They have the option of voting and participating in the political system. They are guaranteed freedom of religion, speech, and assembly, as well as equal protection and treatment for all under Canadian law.

Where Do Most Canadians Live?

While Canada's land area is second only to Russia's, its population is a relatively small 31 million people. Canadians often live where they find a favorable combination of geographic features and economic opportunities. Three-fourths of the population live in the cities and towns of southern Canada. In this region, the Great Lakes, the St. Lawrence Seaway, numerous rivers, and an excellent railway system provide convenient transportation for people and goods. Some Canadians live on farms in the central prairies and in port cities along the coasts. The northern regions of Canada are rugged and very cold. Few people live in those remote areas.

Vancouver, Gateway to the Pacific Vancouver, British Columbia, is called Canada's "Gateway to the Pacific." As Canada's largest port, it trades heavily with Asian countries.

Thousands of Chinese from Hong Kong and many Japanese arrived in Canada at the end of the 20th century. Recent refugees have come from Vietnam, Laos, and Cambodia. **Refugees** are people who flee a country because of war, disaster, or persecution.

Reading
Social Studies

B. Analyzing Motives What geographic and economic features attract people to settle in some parts of Canada?

Toronto, City of Immigrants Toronto, Ontario's capital, is home to one-twelfth of Canada's population but contains one-fourth of its immigrants. More than 70,000 immigrants arrive each year from more than 100 countries in Asia, Europe, the West Indies, and North America. More than 40 percent of Toronto's population is foreign-born, and 10 percent arrived after 1991. Toronto's location, with access to the Atlantic Ocean and the United States, has helped it become a center of industry and international trade.

Place • Toronto is on the shore of Lake Ontario, the easternmost Great Lake. Toronto's skyline is highlighted by the CN Tower. ▲

SECTION 1 ASSESSMENT

Terms & Names
1. Identify: (a) First Nation   (b) multiculturalism   (c) refugee

---

Taking Notes

2. Make a spider map like this one to record details about the people who settled in Canada.

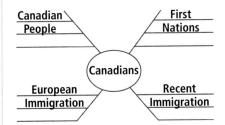

Canadian People   First Nations

Canadians

European Immigration   Recent Immigration

Main Ideas

3. (a) How did the first people reach North America? Who are their descendants?

(b) Describe the relationship between the British and Canada in the 1700s and the 1800s.

(c) What are some of the rights and responsibilities of Canadian citizens?

Critical Thinking

4. Synthesizing

How has the policy of multiculturalism benefited recent immigrants to Canada?

Think About

◆ the historic relations between the French and the English

◆ the many groups of immigrants and refugees in Canada

ACTIVITY -OPTION-   Choose one place in Canada where you might like to live. Look at the information in the Unit Atlas and in this section. Write and illustrate a **magazine article** about this location.

A Constitutional Monarchy

TERMS & NAMES

constitutional monarchy
Parliament
prime minister
Pierre Trudeau
separatist

MAIN IDEA

Canada is a democracy that protects the rights of individuals and of different cultures.

WHY IT MATTERS NOW

Canada's form of government has enabled the country to remain united despite conflicts among different groups of citizens.

DATELINE

NUNAVUT, CANADA, APRIL 1, 1999—The Inuit, the native people of Arctic Canada, have today been granted a separate territory in northern Canada. This historic day comes as a result of almost 25 years of negotiations with Canada's government. The Inuit argued that as a First Nations people, they have lived here for at least 4,000 years and have the right to govern their own land.

Today the Canadian government turned over 733,600 square miles of land that had been the eastern part of the Northwest Territories. Nunavut (NOO•nuh•voot)—which means "our land" in Inuktitut, the language of the Inuit—becomes the third territory of Canada. The capital is Iqaluit on Baffin Island.

Place • The Inuit build igloos out of blocks of snow to use as temporary winter homes. ▲

A Nation of Provinces and Territories

Other First Nations people also seek the self-government that the Inuit won. At this time, Canada remains a nation of ten provinces and three territories. The responsibilities of the central government include national defense, trade and banking, immigration, criminal law, and postal service. The provincial governments administer education, property rights, local government, hospitals, and provincial taxes. Territorial governments have fewer responsibilities but still enjoy limited self-government.

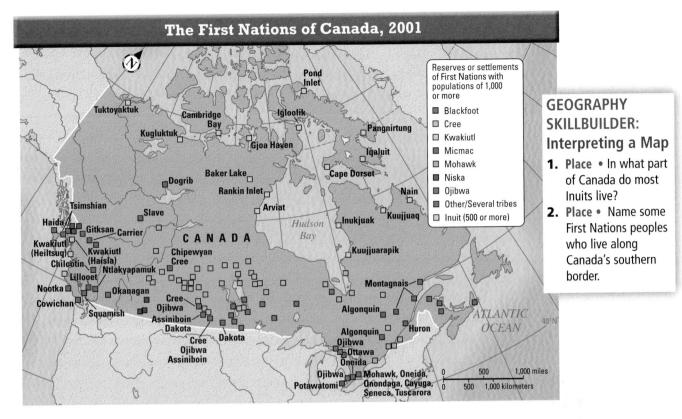

The First Nations of Canada, 2001

Reserves or settlements of First Nations with populations of 1,000 or more
- Blackfoot
- Cree
- Kwakiutl
- Micmac
- Mohawk
- Niska
- Ojibwa
- Other/Several tribes
- Inuit (500 or more)

GEOGRAPHY SKILLBUILDER:
Interpreting a Map

1. **Place** • In what part of Canada do most Inuits live?
2. **Place** • Name some First Nations peoples who live along Canada's southern border.

Organization of Canada's Government

BACKGROUND

The prime minister and his cabinet are accountable to the members of the House of Commons. If they lose the support of the majority of members, they must resign, or ask the governor-general to dissolve Parliament and call an election.

Canada is a **constitutional monarchy**. It has a constitution to explain the powers of the government and owes allegiance to a monarch, a king or a queen. The Canadian government consists of the legislative and the judicial branches. Executive duties are within the legislature.

Head of State The British monarch is Canada's head of state. Since the queen or king does not live in Canada, she or he selects a governor-general as a representative. The monarch and the governor-general have little genuine power in Canadian government. They represent the historical traditions of Canada.

Legislature Canada's legislature, called **Parliament,** has two bodies, the House of Commons and the Senate. Together they determine Canadian laws and policies. Citizens elect members of the House of Commons. The leader of the party with the most members becomes the head of government, or **prime minister,** who runs the executive branch within the legislature. Senators are chosen by the prime minister from each of the ten provinces and three territories.

Reading Social Studies

A. Comparing What are some of the powers of the prime minister, and how do these differ from those of the U.S. president?

Location • The Parliament Buildings in Ottawa, Canada's capital, house the legislature of the central government. ▼

Comparing the Canadian and U.S. Governments

Aspects of Government	Canada	United States
Type	Constitutional Monarchy (limited power)	Constitutional Republic (limited power)
Head of State	Monarch	President
Head of Government	Prime Minister	President
Legislature	Parliament	Congress
System	Federal (central and provinces)	Federal (central and states)

SKILLBUILDER:
Reading a Chart

1. **Place** • Name three ways in which the government of Canada differs from that of the United States.
2. **Place** • How are the governments of Canada and the United States alike?

Judiciary Canada has both federal and provincial courts. The highest court is the federal Supreme Court. It is made up of the chief justice of Canada and eight other judges.

Pierre Elliott Trudeau (1919–2000) From 1968 to 1979 and from 1980 to 1984, Pierre Trudeau was Canada's prime minister. Born in Montreal, Quebec, of French and Scottish ancestry, he grew up speaking both French and English. Despite his French-Canadian background, Trudeau successfully opposed Quebec's attempts to separate from Canada. He considered keeping Quebec a part of Canada one of his great achievements.

In 1982, Trudeau also helped enact a new Canadian constitution. At right, British Queen Elizabeth II signs a proclamation in 1982, making the new Canadian Constitution law, while Trudeau, seated, looks on. He worked to establish diplomatic relations with China and achieved Canada's complete independence from the British Parliament.

Equality and Justice

Canada is a democracy. Its government is responsible for protecting people's rights.

Civil Rights Prime Minister **Pierre Trudeau** led an effort to add a Charter of Rights and Freedoms to the Canadian Constitution in 1982. The Charter is similar to the U.S. Constitution's Bill of Rights. Among other rights, the Charter guarantees freedom of speech and freedom of religion. It protects every citizen's right to vote and to be assisted by a lawyer if arrested. It says that Canadians are free to live and work anywhere in Canada. The Charter also says that people have equal rights regardless of their race, religion, gender, age, or national origin.

Vocabulary

judiciary: the judicial branch of government, the court system

Reading **Social Studies**

B. Analyzing Motives Why did Prime Minister Trudeau want a special document stating the rights of all Canadians?

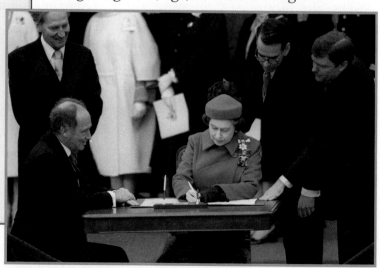

Many Cultures, Many Needs

Canada's people come from different cultures, and many wish to safeguard their special language and customs. Some French-speaking Canadians are **separatists,** or people who want the province of Quebec to become an independent country. In 1980 and in 1995, separatists asked for a vote on whether Quebec should become independent. Both times the issue was defeated, but the separatists promised to try again.

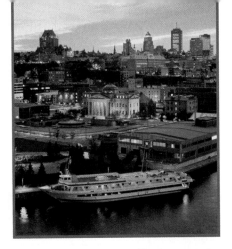

Place • Quebec City, overlooking the St. Lawrence River, is the capital of the province of Quebec and the center of French-Canadian culture. ▲

Quebec's Importance The federal government wants Quebec to remain part of Canada. Quebec is a major contributor to Canada's economy. Quebec is responsible for half of Canada's aerospace production, half of its information technology, and 38 percent of its high-tech industry. French culture is important in Canada's history and modern-day identity.

Laws Protecting Multiculturalism The Quebec provincial government has passed laws to preserve its citizens' French heritage. In an attempt to satisfy the separatists, Canada's federal government passed the Canadian Multicultural Act in 1988. This act guarantees the right of all Canadians to preserve their cultural heritage. Finding ways to maintain a unified country remains a critical issue in Canada today.

Reading
Social Studies

C. Finding Causes
What led to the passage of the Multicultural Act of 1988?

SECTION 2 ASSESSMENT

Terms & Names

1. **Identify:**   (a) constitutional monarchy   (b) Parliament   (c) prime minister   (d) Pierre Trudeau
   (e) separatist

Taking Notes

2. Make a diagram like the one shown below. Add details to show how the Canadian government is organized.

Canada's Government	
Head of state	
Legislature	
Judiciary	

Main Ideas

3. (a) What are some similarities and differences between Canadian and U.S. governments?

   (b) Describe some of the rights guaranteed in the Charter of Rights and Freedoms.

   (c) What is the purpose of the Multicultural Act?

Critical Thinking

4. **Predict**

   What might happen if Quebec became a separate country?

   Think About
   - Quebec's location
   - Canada's multiculturalism
   - economic impacts on Quebec and Canada

ACTIVITY
-OPTION-

Conduct research and create a **travel poster** to attract tourists to French-speaking Canada. Highlight the culture of Quebec.

Canada's Economy

TERMS & NAMES
industry
export
import
transportation corridor
transportation barrier

MAIN IDEA

Canada has a strong economy built on natural resources, a variety of industries, and good transportation.

WHY IT MATTERS NOW

Canada is a leader in the global economy.

DATELINE

DAWSON, YUKON TERRITORY, AUGUST 1898— Gold! That's the cry on the street here in Dawson. Just two years ago, this was a small, unknown town of 5,000 people. Then gold was discovered nearby on a branch of the Klondike River. The Klondike Gold Rush was on. People came here from all over the world hoping to strike it rich.

Now Dawson has more than 30,000 people crowding its streets. Most live in tents. Every day, thousands head up the creeks looking for gold. Most of these people haven't found any yet and never will. However, a few lucky prospectors have already made their fortunes.

Human-Environment Interaction •
Prospectors use gold dust to pay for merchandise in a store in the Yukon Territory. ▲

Contributors to the Economy

Canada is rich in natural resources, including gold. Europeans were first drawn to Canada by the abundant fishing and fur trading. In the 1800s, gold and other minerals were discovered. Today, most Canadians work in the service and manufacturing industries. Canada's skilled labor force, natural resources, and international trade all contribute to the country's economy.

Land Use and Resources of Canada

GEOGRAPHY SKILLBUILDER: Interpreting a Map

1. **Human-Environment Interaction** • For what is most of Canada's land used?
2. **Region** • Where is most of Canada's commercial farming located?

Legend (resources):
- Coal
- Copper
- Fish
- Hydroelectric power
- Iron ore
- Lead
- Natural gas
- Nickel
- Petroleum
- Timber
- Uranium
- Zinc

ARCTIC OCEAN

CANADA

Hudson Bay

ATLANTIC OCEAN

0   500   1,000 miles
0   500   1,000 kilometers

Legend (land use):
- Manufacturing and trade
- Commercial farming
- Livestock raising
- Subsistence farming
- Nomadic herding
- Forestry
- Commercial fishing
- Hunting, fishing, and forestry
- Little or no economic activity

Industry Based on Natural Resources A nation's resources are a source of wealth. The prairie provinces of central Canada have extensive grasslands and good soil, making this area an ideal place to raise beef cattle and grow wheat. On the rich farmlands along the St. Lawrence River, farmers harvest grains, vegetables, and fruit. People plant potatoes and raise dairy cattle on the east coast. The Grand Banks, located off the coast of Newfoundland, is one of the world's most abundant fisheries. The salmon caught off Canada's Pacific coast enrich that area's economy.

Much of Canada is covered in forests, making the timber industry important, especially in British Columbia. **Industry** refers to any area of economic activity. Mining in the northern territories yields iron ore, gold, silver, copper, and other metals.

Trade Canada's openness to trade has contributed to the growth of its economy. Today almost 80 percent of Canada's raw materials are shipped as exports. **Exports** are goods traded to other countries. Canada's main exports are wood and paper products, fuel, minerals, aluminum, wheat, and oil. These and manufactured goods are sold around the world.

BACKGROUND

The Grand Banks, first noted by explorer John Cabot in 1498, extends 350 miles north to south and 420 miles east to west.

Reading **Social Studies**

A. Recognizing Important Details What are Canada's main exports?

Canada and the United States share a valuable trade partnership. Most of Canada's exports go to the United States. Most of its **imports**, or goods brought into the country, are from the United States. In 1994, Canada, the United States, and Mexico signed the North American Free Trade Agreement, or NAFTA, which lowered trade barriers among the three countries.

Industry and the Economy

Canada's well-educated work force is important to its economy. Canadians work in all four types of industry seen in the chart shown below. Since World War II, Canada has shifted from a mostly rural economy to a major industrial and urban economy.

Types of Industry		
Primary Industries	Prepare and process raw materials, such as timber, wheat, and iron ore, so other companies or consumers can use them *Examples:* **farms; mining companies; logging companies**	
Secondary Industries	Manufacturing—turn raw materials into products that consumers or other businesses can use *Examples:* **bakeries; car manufacturers; furniture makers**	
Tertiary Industries	Service industries—do not make goods or consume goods; distributors—move goods from the manufacturer to another business or to consumers *Examples:* **wholesalers; transportation companies (truck, train, airplane, or ship); retailers of food, clothing, and other goods; health care; education; recreation; banking**	
Quaternary Industries	Pass on information *Examples:* **communication companies, such as Internet service providers and cable companies; financial, research, and other companies that gather and pass on information**	

Tertiary, or service, industries, such as health care, recreation, education, transportation, banking, and the government, occupy about two-thirds of Canada's work force. About 30 percent of Canadians work in secondary, or manufacturing, industries. One of Canada's main products is transportation equipment, including automobiles, trucks, subway cars, and airplanes. Food processing, especially meat and poultry processing, is an important industry in Canada as well. Canada also makes chemicals, medicines, machinery, metal products, steel, and paper.

Transportation

Transportation is a major Canadian industry. The ability to import and export goods and move them from place to place across Canada's vast land area affects many consumers and businesses.

Reading
Social Studies

B. Analyzing
Effects Why are
transportation
corridors
important to the
development of
industry?

Vocabulary

transcontinental:
spanning or crossing
a continent

Canada's geography both helps and hinders transportation. Canada has natural **transportation corridors**, or paths that make transportation easier. Rivers and coastal waters, sometimes combined with human-made canals and locks, provide convenient travel routes. The St. Lawrence Seaway, for example, allows oceangoing ships to travel between the Atlantic Ocean and the Great Lakes. Another important route is Canada's transcontinental railway system, which crosses the continent from coast to coast.

Canada also has **transportation barriers**, or geographic features that prevent or slow down transportation. In much of the north, snow and ice block travel by land or water. The Rocky Mountains in the west are another major obstacle. Industry develops slowly in regions where transportation is difficult.

Region • The Canadian Pacific Railway Company completed a transcontinental line from Montreal to a Vancouver suburb in 1885. ▲

SECTION 3 ASSESSMENT

Terms & Names

1. Identify:
   (a) industry
   (b) export
   (c) import
   (d) transportation corridor
   (e) transportation barrier

Taking Notes

2. Make a chart like the one shown below to list goods that might be produced in each area.

Prairie Provinces	St. Lawrence River Valley	East Coast	British Columbia	Northern Territories

Main Ideas

3. (a) What important factors have helped build Canada's economy?

   (b) Give an example of a primary, a secondary, a tertiary, and a quaternary industry.

   (c) What are some transportation corridors and barriers in Canada?

Critical Thinking

4. **Drawing Conclusions**

   Why do you think Canada and the United States have become such good trade partners?

   Think About

   - geographic location
   - their languages
   - their governments

ACTIVITY -OPTION- Imagine that you are prospecting for gold in Dawson during the Klondike Gold Rush. Write a **newspaper article** describing what you have brought with you, how you traveled there, and what the town is like.

A Multicultural Society

MAIN IDEA

Many immigrant groups have contributed to Canadian culture while preserving their own identities.

WHY IT MATTERS NOW

Canada's desire to safeguard its cultural diversity is one of its most serious challenges.

DATELINE

MONTREAL, CANADA, 1893—Score! The Montreal Amateur Athletic Association team is the best hockey team in Canada, and it has a silver trophy cup to prove it. Canada's governor-general, Sir Frederick Arthur, Lord Stanley of Preston, presented the award to "the championship hockey club of the Dominion of Canada."

Many Canadians love this sport. First played by the Micmac, a First Nations people in Nova Scotia, ice hockey has spread across Canada and south to the United States. Competition for Stanley's Cup will make the sport even more exciting.

Culture • The winning team poses with Lord Stanley's Cup, which was purchased for about $50. ▲

Canadian Identity

Hockey is one of many good things about living in Canada. From 1994 to 2000, the United Nations rated Canada the best of 175 countries in a survey that examines the health, education, and wealth of each country's citizens. Yet, Canadians still seek a **national identity,** or sense of belonging to a nation, to unite its many immigrant cultures.

Distribution of Bilingual Speakers, 2001

ARCTIC OCEAN

ATLANTIC OCEAN

Hudson Bay

CANADA

Percentage of population who speak English and French

- 50.0–70.3
- 35.0–49.9
- 20.0–34.9
- 10.0–19.9
- 5.0–9.9
- 0–4.9

0   250   500 miles
0   250   500 kilometers

GEOGRAPHY SKILLBUILDER: Interpreting a Map

1. **Culture** • What part of Canada has the highest percentage of people who speak both English and French?
2. **Culture** • Where in Canada do less than five percent of the people speak both English and French?

Languages Many Canadians are **bilingual,** which means they speak two languages. Look at this map to see where bilingual Canadians live. Canada has two official languages, English and French. Literature, official documents, road signs, newspapers, and television broadcasts are in both languages. The two languages are not exactly like those spoken in England, the United States, and France. **Francophones** are French-speaking people. Canadian French, based on the French of the 1800s, is pronounced differently from the French spoken in modern France.

Culture •
Business signs on a street in Quebec City reflect the strong influence of French culture. ▶

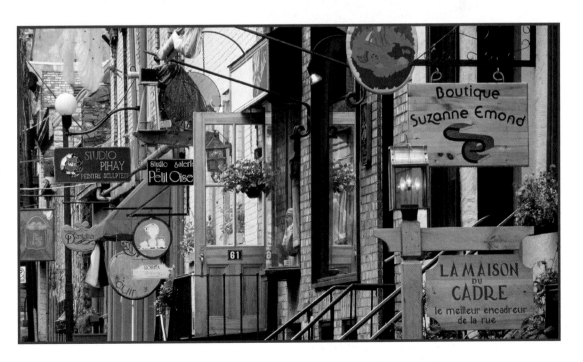

Canadian English uses some words, pronunciations, and spellings that differ from those used in the United States. For example, Canadians say *taps* and *serviettes* when people in the United States say *faucets* and *napkins*. For *about* and *house*, Canadians might say *aboot* and *hoos*. Many Canadians write *colour* for *color*, *theatre* for *theater*, and *cheque* for *check*. The nation's first prime minister, Sir John A. Macdonald, ordered that all official Canadian documents be written using standards set by dictionaries written in England.

Reading
Social Studies

A. Synthesizing
Why does Canada have two official languages?

Arts and Entertainment

Canada has rich traditions in the arts, actively supported by government funding. For example, the Canada Council for the Arts gives money to more than 8,400 artists and art organizations each year. Provincial governments also support regional arts programs.

Vocabulary

provincial:
of, or relating to, a province

Canadians read many of the same newspapers and magazines, and watch many of the same television shows and movies as do people in the United States. Canadian musicians, such as Neil Young, Joni Mitchell, Buffy Ste. Marie, Céline Dion, and Shania Twain, are popular in both countries. Comedian-actors Dan Aykroyd and Jim Carrey are also from Canada.

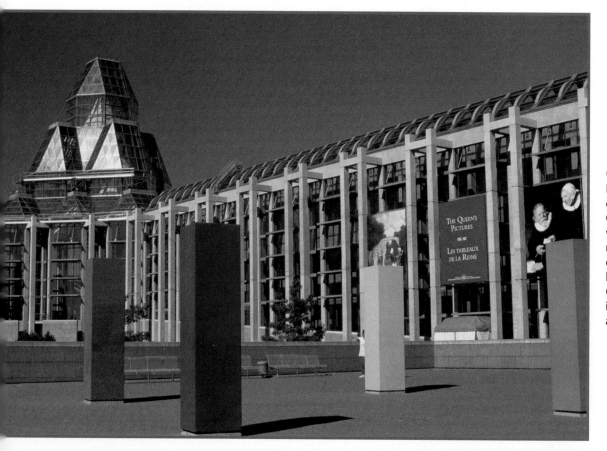

Culture • The National Gallery of Canada in Ottawa is a visual arts museum that exhibits works by both Canadian and international artists. ◄

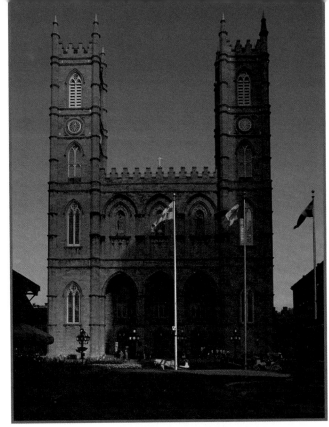

Culture • Notre-Dame was built in Montreal between 1824 and 1829. The architecture of the church—as well as the paintings, sculptures, and stained-glass windows inside—attracts many thousands of visitors each year. ◀

Religion

Christianity is widely practiced in Canada, but many other religions are followed as well, including Buddhism, Hinduism, Islam, and Judaism. Some religions are grounded in a spirituality based on respect for Earth and all forms of life. People of every cultural group are free to worship as they choose.

Culture Regions

BACKGROUND

Inuit culture has been greatly affected by contact with the modern world. However, some Inuit traditions have been preserved in their arts and crafts, dialects, and ways of living in Arctic Canada.

Most Canadian immigrants during the 1600s, 1700s, and 1800s were European. Recently, more people have arrived from Asia and South America. People who share the same language and background often settle in the same area. As a result, Canada has various culture regions, or areas where many people belonging to one cultural group live together.

Culture regions exist in different parts of Canada. Quebec is home to many French-speaking Canadians. In Nunavut more than 50 percent of the people are Inuit. Almost 16 percent of the population of Vancouver are Chinese, mostly from Hong Kong.

Connections to History

Raising the Maple Leaf A country's flag is an important national symbol. After 1763, when the United Kingdom won the French and Indian War, the British Royal Union Flag, or Union Jack, became Canada's flag. Efforts to design a new flag for Canada began in 1925. The Red Ensign, which had the Union Jack in its upper left corner and the Canadian coat of arms on its right side, was raised 20 years later.

In 1965, the Houses of Parliament adopted the Maple Leaf, which remains the flag of Canada today. The red background is a connection to the Red Ensign, and the maple leaf is Canada's national symbol.

Maple Leaf

Red Ensign

Union Jack

Getting different culture regions to agree on national issues is sometimes difficult. The adoption of the Maple Leaf as Canada's flag in 1965 was one successful effort to unite all Canadians.

A VOICE FROM CANADA

The flag is the symbol of the nation's unity, for it, beyond any doubt, represents all the citizens of Canada without distinction of race, language, belief or opinion.

—Speaker of the Senate Maurice Bourget

Conflict and Cooperation Languages, customs, and lifestyles differ among the cultural groups of Canada. Sometimes these differences lead to conflict. For example, in the second half of the 20th century, some Canadians thought that the thousands of Chinese immigrants settling in the Vancouver area would change Canadian culture through their language and customs.

In 1975, the government began reviewing immigration policy. Chinese groups in Vancouver organized a Chinese-Canadian conference. They asked for continued support of multiculturalism and that immigration laws remain open for all people. The concerned groups solved the problem through human rights laws.

Reading
Social Studies

B. Analyzing Causes How do cultural differences cause conflicts among people?

SECTION 4 ASSESSMENT

Terms & Names

1. Identify: (a) national identity   (b) bilingual   (c) Francophone

Taking Notes

2. Make a spider map like the one shown below to illustrate how various groups contribute to making a unique Canadian culture.

Main Ideas

3. (a) What are the two main languages spoken in Canada?

   (b) How does Canada support its own arts and entertainment?

   (c) What do people living in culture regions have in common?

Critical Thinking

4. **Forming and Supporting Opinions**

   Do culture regions create more benefits or more disadvantages for Canada as a whole?

   Think About

   • existing and future conflicts

   • how different groups contribute to Canadian culture

ACTIVITY -OPTION-   With a partner, choose a culture region of Canada. Create a **mural** or **collage** to show characteristics of the culture.

Identifying Cause and Effect

▶▶ Defining the Skill

A cause is an event, a person, or an idea that brings about a result, or an effect. An effect is something that results from a cause. Understanding the relationship between cause and effect is key to understanding the world and its cultures.

▶▶ Applying the Skill

The following paragraph describes where most Canadians live. Use the strategies listed below to help you identify why Canadians live there.

How to Identify a Cause-and-Effect Relationship

Strategy 1 Look for the cause of, or reason for, the cause-and-effect relationship. It might be suggested in the title and topic sentence. Ask yourself what happened and why it happened. Writers may indicate a cause-and-effect relationship by using words such as *thus, therefore, so,* and *as a result.* Use those words as clues.

Strategy 2 Look for the results of the event or action. Ask yourself what happened as a result of the action. You have found the effect.

Strategy 3 Remember that several causes can combine to create one event. Also remember that one cause can have several effects. Ask yourself if anything else helped to bring about the event. Ask yourself if there are any other results.

1 WHERE CANADIANS LIVE
2 Most of Canada's people live within 100 miles of the United States border. This heavily populated area covers only about 10 percent of the country. **1** The mild climate in that part of the country makes living there more pleasant than living in the colder northern regions. **3** People can find jobs more easily in the large cities located near the border. **3** Many Americans who live in Canada can cross the border easily to visit family and friends.

Make a Diagram

Using a diagram can help you understand causes and effects. The diagram to the right shows what causes people in Canada to live close to the U.S. border and what effect is created.

| Mild climate |
| Better economic opportunities | → | A majority of Canada's population live close to the U.S. border. |
| Closeness to U.S. friends and family |

▶▶ Practicing the Skill

Turn to Chapter 5, "Canada Today," Section 3, "Canada's Economy," and make a diagram of the causes that have resulted in Canada's strong economy.

Explain the significance of each of the following:

1. multiculturalism
2. refugee
3. Parliament
4. prime minister
5. export
6. import
7. transportation corridor
8. transportation barrier
9. bilingual
10. Francophone

REVIEW QUESTIONS

O Canada! Immigrant Roots *(pages 119–123)*

1. How did the United Kingdom gain control of Canada?
2. What effects does the policy of multiculturalism have on Canada?

A Constitutional Monarchy *(pages 124–127)*

3. How is Canada's federal government organized?
4. How has Canada tried to satisfy the needs of its many culture groups?

Canada's Economy *(pages 128–131)*

5. How does Canada's wealth of natural resources contribute to its economy?
6. What are Canada's chief transportation corridors and barriers?

A Multicultural Society *(pages 132–136)*

7. How have the native languages of England and France changed in Canada?
8. What are some major culture groups of Canada?

CRITICAL THINKING

Analyzing Causes and Effects

1. Using your completed chart from Reading Social Studies, p. 118, describe some factors that influence where people settle in Canada.

Drawing Conclusions

2. Many people in Quebec wanted the province to separate from the rest of Canada. What in Prime Minister Pierre Trudeau's background made him effective in keeping Quebec part of Canada?

Making Inferences

3. How do you think the policy of multiculturalism affects the way Canadians of different cultures respond to one another?

Visual Summary

1 O Canada! Immigrant Roots

- The Canadian people have come from many countries.
- Canada is a very large country with a small population; most people settled in the southern part of the country.

2 A Constitutional Monarchy

- The Canadian government is a constitutional monarchy that is made up of two main branches: a legislative branch and a judicial branch.
- Canada has passed laws to protect the civil rights of its people and to support multiculturalism.

Canada's Economy 3

- Canada has many natural resources that contribute to its economy.
- Canada's most important trade partner is the United States.

A Multicultural Society 4

- Many cultural groups have helped to build the unique Canadian culture of today.

- The diverse cultures of the population create challenges in unifying Canada.

First Migration to North America

Climate became colder.

⌐ CAUSE ⌐

EFFECT
More of Earth's water froze.

⌐ CAUSE ⌐

EFFECT
Ocean water level was as much as 125 feet below its current level.

⌐ CAUSE ⌐

EFFECT
Land between Asia and North America became dry.

⌐ CAUSE ⌐

EFFECT
People could walk from Asia to North America.

SKILLBUILDER: Identifying Cause and Effect

1. What information does this cause-and-effect chart show?
2. What happened because the ocean level fell to 125 feet below its current level?

FOCUS ON GEOGRAPHY

1. **Movement •** About how many miles would you have to travel to transport limestone from Manitoba to Quebec?
2. **Region •** Which provinces are along the Atlantic Coast? the Pacific Coast?
3. **Place •** In which province is Canada's capital city, Ottawa, located?

CHAPTER PROJECTS

Interdisciplinary Activity: Art
Writing an Editorial Research the Canadian government's support of the arts. Decide whether government support is necessary. Should it be increased or decreased? Write an editorial stating your views.

Cooperative Learning Activity
Presenting a Television-News Interview In a group of four or five classmates, prepare an interview for a public television broadcast. Your topic will be self-government for cultural groups.

- One of you should take the role of news moderator. Each of the others will represent a cultural group.
- Brainstorm a list of cultural groups. Then prepare questions.
- Do research to learn what your group thinks about self-government.
- Present your discussion to the class.

INTERNET ACTIVITY

Use the Internet to learn more about the geography of Canada. Choose a region, such as the Yukon Territory or the Maritime Provinces. Research what it is like to live there. What kind of weather and plants are there? What kinds of jobs do residents have? How would you travel around the area?

Writing About Geography Write a report of your findings. If possible, include photographs or your own illustrations. Include a list of Internet sites you used.

For Internet links to support this activity, go to

RESEARCH LINKS
CLASSZONE.COM

LATIN AMERICA

ATLANTIC

PACIFIC OCEAN

PACIFIC OCEAN

OCEAN

INDIAN OCEAN

N

X

MACHU PICCHU

LATIN AMERICA

Place Machu Picchu is a complex of Inca ruins perched high in the Andes Mountains of Peru. The remains of the impressive granite structures were designated a UNESCO World Heritage Site in 1983.

Latin America: Physical

Sierra Madre Occidental
Baja California
Gulf of California
MEXICO
Rio Grande
Sierra Madre Oriental
Gulf of Mexico
BAHAMAS
Tropic of Cancer
Orizaba 18,854 ft. (5,747 m)
Yucatán Peninsula
Greater Antilles
CUBA
DOMINICAN REPUBLIC
HAITI
WEST INDIES
Lesser Antilles
ATLANTIC OCEAN
Popocatépetl 17,930 ft. (5,465 m)
CENTRAL AMERICA
BELIZE
JAMAICA
HONDURAS
Caribbean Sea
Netherlands Antilles
Tajumulco 13,844 ft. (4,220 m)
NICARAGUA
Panama Canal
GUATEMALA
EL SALVADOR
COSTA RICA
Isthmus of Panama
PANAMA
VENEZUELA
GUYANA
SURINAME
French Guiana (Fr.)
Barú 11,400 ft. (3,475 m)
Llanos
Orinoco R.
Guiana Highlands
COLOMBIA
Equator
ECUADOR
AMAZON BASIN
Negro R.
Amazon R.
SOUTH AMERICA
PERU
Madeira R.
BRAZIL
Xingu R.
Araguaia R.
São Francisco R.
ANDES
PACIFIC OCEAN
Lake Titicaca
Mato Grosso Plateau
BOLIVIA
BRAZILIAN HIGHLANDS
PARAGUAY
Parand R.
Atacama Desert
Gran Chaco
Paraguay R.
Tropic of Capricorn
Mt. Aconcagua 22,831 ft. (6,959 m)
ARGENTINA
Uruguay R.
URUGUAY
Pampas
Plata R.
CHILE
Patagonia
ATLANTIC OCEAN
Tierra del Fuego
Falkland Is.
South Georgia I.
Cape Horn

Elevation

13,100 ft.	(4,000 m)	
6,600 ft.	(2,000 m)	
3,275 ft.	(1,000 m)	
650 ft.	(200 m)	
0 ft.	(0 m)	
Below sea level		

▲ Mountain peak

N

0   500   1,000 miles
0   500   1,000 kilometers

100°W   80°W   60°W   40°W

20°N   0°   20°S   40°S

Elevation Profile: South America

21,000 ft.
ANDES MOUNTAINS
18,000 ft.
15,000 ft.
12,000 ft.
COASTAL LOWLANDS OF BRAZIL
9,000 ft.
6,000 ft.
BRAZILIAN PLATEAU
3,000 ft.
AMAZON RIVER BASIN
1,200 ft.
sea level
PACIFIC
OCEAN
−12,000 ft.
PERU-CHILE TRENCH
ATLANTIC
OCEAN
−24,000 ft.

Latin America–United States Landmass and Population

Latin America

United States

LANDMASS

Latin America

7,981,950 square miles

Continental United States

3,165,630 square miles

POPULATION

Latin America
514,662,785

United States
281,421,906

= 50,000,000

Fast Facts

✔ **HIGHEST MOUNTAIN:**
Mt. Anconcagua, 22,831 ft.

✔ **LONGEST RIVER:**
Amazon River, 3,900 mi. long

✔ **HIGHEST RECORDED TEMPERATURE:**
120°F, Rivadavia, Argentina,
December 11, 1905

✔ **LOWEST RECORDED TEMPERATURE:**
-27°F, Sarmiento, Argentina,
June 1, 1907

✔ **HIGHEST AVERAGE ANNUAL PRECIPITATION IN THE WORLD:**
Lloro, Colombia, 523.6 in.

✔ **LOWEST AVERAGE ANNUAL PRECIPITATION IN THE WORLD:**
Arica, Chile, 0.03 in.

GEOGRAPHY SKILLBUILDER: Interpreting Maps and Visuals

1. **Location** • The Isthmus of Panama separates what two bodies of water?
2. **Place** • What is the depth of the Peru-Chile Trench?

Latin America: Political

Turks & Caicos (U.K.)
DOMINICAN REPUBLIC
Virgin Is. (U.S. & U.K.)
Anguilla (U.K.)
ST. KITTS & NEVIS
ANTIGUA & BARBUDA
San Juan
Santo Domingo
Puerto Rico (U.S.)
Guadeloupe (Fr.)
Montserrat (U.K.)
Martinique (Fr.)
DOMINICA
BARBADOS
ST. LUCIA
ST. VINCENT & THE GRENADINES
GRENADA
TRINIDAD & TOBAGO
ATLANTIC OCEAN
Caribbean Sea

Tijuana
Ciudad Juárez
Chihuahua
Monterrey
MEXICO
Guadalajara
Gulf of California
Gulf of Mexico
Tropic of Cancer
Havana
BAHAMAS
CUBA
México City
Córdoba
Puebla
Acapulco
Cayman Is. (U.K.)
BELIZE
Belmopan
JAMAICA
Kingston
HAITI
Port-au-Prince
GUATEMALA
Guatemala City
HONDURAS
Tegucigalpa
San Salvador
NICARAGUA
EL SALVADOR
Managua
Netherlands Antilles (Neth.)
Aruba (Neth.)
Caracas
Caribbean Sea
Panama City
San José
PANAMA
COSTA RICA
Maracaibo
Mérida
Medellín
Bogotá
Cali
COLOMBIA
VENEZUELA
GUYANA
Georgetown
SURINAME
Paramaribo
Cayenne
French Guiana (Fr.)
Quito
ECUADOR
Galápagos Is. (Ec.)
Guayaquil
Equator
Manaus
Belém
Fortaleza
Recife
PACIFIC OCEAN
PERU
Lima
BRAZIL
Salvador
BOLIVIA
La Paz
Sucre
Santa Cruz
Brasília
Goiânia
Belo Horizonte
Rio de Janeiro
PARAGUAY
Asunción
São Paulo
Curitiba
Pôrto Alegre
Juan Fernández Is. (Chile)
Santiago
ARGENTINA
Rosario
URUGUAY
Montevideo
Buenos Aires
CHILE
Falkland Is. (U.K.)
ATLANTIC OCEAN
South Georgia I. (U.K.)

20°N
0° Equator
20°S
40°S

100°W   80°W   60°W   40°W

National boundary
National capital
Other city

0   500   1,000 miles
0   500   1,000 kilometers

N

City Populations of Latin America

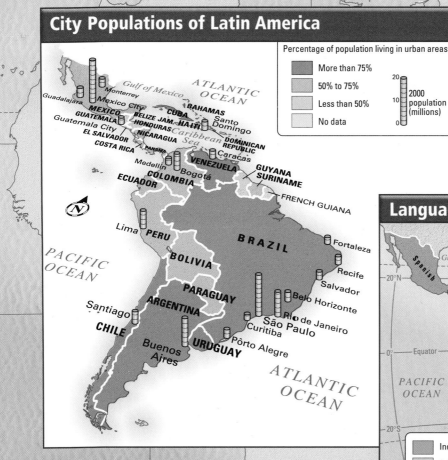

Percentage of population living in urban areas

- More than 75%
- 50% to 75%
- Less than 50%
- No data

2000 population (millions)

Languages of Latin America

- Indo-European
- Other languages
- French — Spoken language

0   500   1,000 miles
0 500 1,000 kilometers

FAST FACTS

✔ **LARGEST COUNTRY (in land area):** Brazil, 3,300,171 sq. mi.

✔ **SMALLEST COUNTRY (in land area):** Grenada, 120 sq. mi.

✔ **LARGEST CITY (population):** Mexico City, 18,131,000 (2000)

✔ **HIGHEST POPULATION DENSITY:** Barbados, 1,612 people per sq. mi.

✔ **LOWEST POPULATION DENSITY:** French Guiana, 5 people per sq. mi.

GEOGRAPHY SKILLBUILDER: Interpreting Maps and Visuals

1. **Location** • Which countries have no coastline?
2. **Region** • What language do most people in Brazil speak?

Data File

Country Flag	Country/Capital	Currency	Population (2001 estimate)	Life Expectancy (years)	Birthrate (per 1,000 pop.) (2000)
	Antigua and Barbuda St. John's	East Caribbean Dollar	67,000	70	20
	Argentina Buenos Aires	Peso	37,385,000	75	19
	Bahamas Nassau	Bahamian Dollar	298,000	71	20
	Barbados Bridgetown	Barbadian Dollar	275,000	73	14
	Belize Belmopan	Belizean Dollar	256,000	71	32
	Bolivia La Paz, Sucre	Boliviano	8,300,000	64	28
	Brazil Brasília	Real	174,469,000	63	19
	Chile Santiago	Chilean Peso	15,328,000	76	17
	Colombia Bogotá	Colombian Peso	40,349,000	70	23
	Costa Rica San José	Costa Rican Colon	3,773,000	76	21
	Cuba Havana	Peso	11,184,000	76	13
	Dominica Roseau	East Caribbean Dollar	71,000	73	18
	Dominican Republic Santo Domingo	Dominican Peso	8,581,000	73	25
	Ecuador Quito	U.S. Dollar and Sucre	13,184,000	71	27
	El Salvador San Salvador	Salvadoran Colon	6,238,000	70	29
	Grenada St. George's	East Caribbean Dollar	89,000	65	23
	Guatemala Guatemala City	Quetzal	12,974,000	66	35
	Guyana Georgetown	Guyanese Dollar	697,000	64	18

DATA FILE

Infant Mortality (per 1,000 live births) (2000)	Doctors (per 100,000 pop.) (1997–1998)	Literacy Rate (percentage) (1996–1998)	Passenger Cars (per 1,000 pop.) (1991–1998)	Total Area (square miles)	Map (not to scale)
20.0	114	90	207	171	
17.8	268	96	136	1,073,399	
17.8	152	98	245	5,386	
16.2	125	97	167	166	
30.8	55	93	10	8,867	
60.2	130	83	26	424,164	
33.8	127	85	84	3,300,171	
9.6	110	95	62	292,135	
23.2	116	91	31	440,831	
12.7	141	95	14	19,730	
7.7	530	96	2	42,804	
8.5	49	90	104	290	
40.8	216	82	14	18,704	
29.3	170	90	22	103,930	
27.2	107	71	6	8,124	
10.9	50	96	94	120	
45.0	93	56	9	42,042	
48.6	18	98	34	83,000	

Data File

Country Flag	Country/Capital	Currency	Population (2000 estimate)	Life Expectancy (years)	Birthrate (per 1,000 pop.) (2000)
	Haiti Port-au-Prince	Gourde	6,965,000	49	32
	Honduras Tegucigalpa	Lempira	6,406,000	70	33
	Jamaica Kingston	Jamaican Dollar	2,666,000	75	19
	Mexico Mexico City	New Peso	101,879,000	71	23
	Nicaragua Managua	Gold Cordoba	4,918,000	69	28
	Panama Panama City	Balboa	2,846,000	75	20
	Paraguay Asunción	Guarani	5,734,000	74	31
	Peru Lima	New Sol	27,484,000	70	24
	St. Kitts and Nevis Basseterre	East Caribbean Dollar	39,000	71	19
	St. Lucia Castries	East Caribbean Dollar	158,000	72	22
	St. Vincent and the Grenadines Kingstown	East Caribbean Dollar	116,000	72	18
	Suriname Paramaribo	Surinamese Guilder	434,000	71	21
	Trinidad and Tobago Port of Spain	Trinidad and Tobago Dollar	1,170,000	68	14
	Uruguay Montevideo	Uruguayan Peso	3,360,000	75	17
	Venezuela Caracas	Bolivar	23,917,000	73	21
	United States Washington, D.C.	Dollar	281,422,000	77	15

DATA FILE

Infant Mortality (per 1,000 live births) (2000)	Doctors (per 100,000 pop.) (1997–1998)	Literacy Rate (percentage) (1996–1998)	Passenger Cars (per 1,000 pop.) (1991–1998)	Total Area (square miles)	Map (not to scale)
96.3	8	45	5	10,714	
39.8	83	73	14	43,277	
13.4	140	85	17	4,244	
23.4	186	90	87	756,066	
38.7	86	66	16	50,464	
22.7	167	91	54	29,157	
35.3	110	92	14	157,048	
37.1	93	89	20	496,225	
16.9	117	90	130	104	
16.2	47	80	68	238	
14.6	88	82	44	150	
25.6	25	93	111	63,251	
18.3	79	98	107	1,978	
12.9	370	97	147	68,498	
25.5	236	91	68	352,144	
7.0	251	97	489	3,787,319	

GEOGRAPHY SKILLBUILDER: Interpreting a Chart
(Do not give United States as an answer.)
1. **Place** • Which countries have the highest life expectancy?
2. **Place** • Which country has the most cars per person?

Latin America: Its Land and History

SECTION 1   Physical Geography

SECTION 2   Ancient Latin America

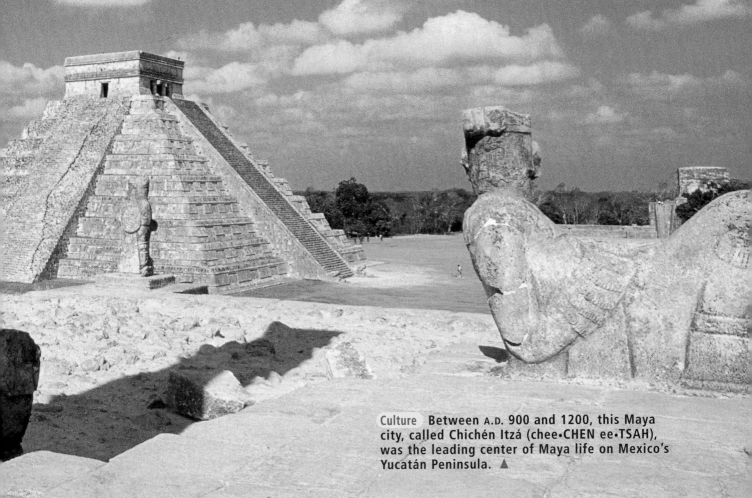

What conflicts arise when there is competition for a natural resource?

Human-Environment Interaction • About 50 percent of the world's rain forests are in Latin America, with 30 percent in Brazil alone. In Latin America, the rain forest is a natural resource that plays many different roles. It serves as a habitat for exotic plants and animals and a home to Native Americans. It is a moderator of the world climate and a destination for tourists. It also acts as a source of land that can be cleared and put to other uses, such as cattle ranching or logging.

What do you think?

♦ How might different groups want to use a rain forest as a resource? Think about the rain forest's inhabitants, tourists, environmentalists, and businesses.

♦ How might these different uses conflict with one another?

Culture Between A.D. 900 and 1200, this Maya city, called Chichén Itzá (chee•CHEN ee•TSAH), was the leading center of Maya life on Mexico's Yucatán Peninsula. ▲

151

BEFORE YOU READ

▶▶ What Do You Know?

Before you read the chapter, consider what you already know about the history and geography of Latin America. What countries make up Latin America? Does the region have well-known geographic features, such as mountains or rivers? You may have read folk tales from the ancient Maya, Aztec, and Inca civilizations. Think about what happened to these cultures and their people. Have you heard of the Aztec ruler Montezuma II?

▶▶ What Do You Want to Know?

Decide what else you want to know about Latin America. In your notebook, record what you hope to learn from this chapter.

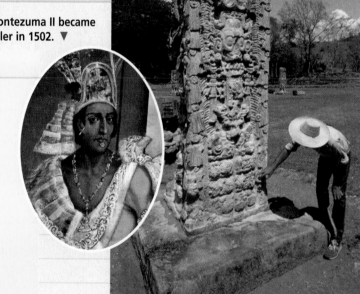

Culture • The Maya carved many stone monuments. ▼

Culture • Montezuma II became the Aztec ruler in 1502. ▼

READ AND TAKE NOTES

Reading Strategy: Comparing and Contrasting Comparing and contrasting can be a useful strategy for studying cultures. When you compare, you look for similarities. When you contrast, you look for differences. Use the chart shown here to compare and contrast the ancient civilizations of Latin America.

- Copy the chart into your notebook.
- As you read Section 2, take notes on the Maya, Aztec, and Inca.
- Write your notes under the appropriate headings.

	Maya	Aztec	Inca
Location			
Dates			
Achievements			
Reasons for Decline			

Latin America: Physical Geography

MAIN IDEA

Latin America's landforms, bodies of water, and climate offer a wide range of environments and resources.

WHY IT MATTERS NOW

Physical geography influences Latin America's cultures, offering them both resources and obstacles.

DATELINE

EXTRA

PUEBLA, MEXICO, DECEMBER 19, 2000

Yesterday, Mount Popocatépetl erupted, spewing out glowing five-foot-long rocks for miles in one of its largest eruptions in a thousand years. More than 30 million people live within sight of the volcano, and tens of thousands live close enough to be at risk when it erupts.

Government trucks drove through villages sounding warnings on speakers while church bells rang out the danger. In spite of the resulting damage, no one has been killed. However, authorities warn, a larger eruption could occur at any time.

Place • The Aztec named the volcano Popocatépetl, which means "smoking mountain." ▲

Defining Latin America

Latin America includes Mexico, Central America, the Caribbean, and South America. Because the languages of most of its colonizers—Spanish and Portuguese—are derived from Latin, Europeans later referred to the region's colonies as *Latin America*. Because the region is defined by a cultural connection, in this case language, it is called a culture region.

Mexico

Look at the map on page 155. Mexico is the farthest north of the Latin American countries. You can see that Mexico's major physical features include mountains, plateaus, and plains.

A Varied Landscape Mexico's two major mountain ranges share the name Sierra Madre (see·EHR·uh MAH·dray). Notice that in between the two ranges—the Sierra Madre Occidental and the Sierra Madre Oriental—sits Mexico's large central plateau. The vast northern stretches of the central plateau are desert.

Vocabulary

occidental: western

oriental: eastern

Now look just south of the central plateau. There you will see Mexico's two highest mountain peaks, Orizaba (or·ih·ZAH·buh) and Popocatépetl (POH·puh·KAT·uh·PEHT·uhl). Both are volcanoes. Volcanic activity and earthquakes frequently plague Mexico—and many other parts of Latin America too. They are caused by the movement of five tectonic plates.

A Problem of Place At the southern end of the central plateau sits Mexico City, the world's second most populated city. Air pollution is severe there, and the city's location has contributed to this problem. The mountains surrounding the city to the east, south, and west trap automobile exhaust and other pollutants that the city's huge population generates.

An added problem of location for Mexico City is the ground on which it was built—a drained lakebed. The vibrations that earthquakes send through Earth grow much stronger and more damaging when they pass through the soft, loose soils of a lakebed, thus making Mexico City highly vulnerable to the effects of earthquakes.

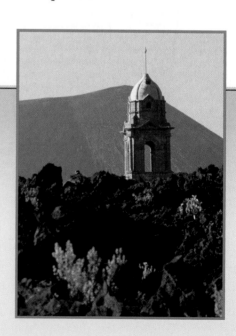

Eruption Disruption On February 20, 1943, something very strange happened in a cornfield in west-central Mexico. Before the eyes of a startled farmer, the land violently split open. Within 24 hours, a small, smoking cone had appeared—the tiny beginning of a mighty volcano called Paricutín (pah·REE·koo·TEEN). Scientists rushed to the area to watch the volcano being born. Within a year, a mountain stood in place of what had been farmland and a village.

While it was active, Paricutín rose to 10,400 feet above sea level. It poured lava over about a 10-square-mile area, burying streets and buildings, such as this nearby church. In 1952, it stopped erupting completely and became dormant. But the volcano that sprouted in a cornfield had given scientists a rare opportunity to study the life cycle of one of nature's most dramatic and dangerous features.

UNITED STATES

GEOGRAPHY SKILLBUILDER:
Interpreting a Map
1. **Location** • What is the tallest mountain in Central America?
2. **Region** • Which area of Mexico is almost entirely at sea level?

ATLANTIC OCEAN

Gulf of California

Sierra Madre Occidental

Central Plateau

Sierra Madre Oriental

Gulf Coastal Plain

Gulf of Mexico

Popocatépetl 17,802 ft. (5,426 m.)

Havana

Tropic of Cancer

Pico de Orizaba 18,854 ft. (5,747 m.)

Yucatán Peninsula

Pico Duarte 10,417 ft. (3,175 m.)

20°N

Paricutín 9,210 ft. (2,808 m.)

Mexico City

Pico Turquino 6,561 ft. (2,000 m.)

Santo Domingo

Sierra Madre del Sur

Belmopan

Port-au-Prince

Tacaná 13,428 ft. (4,093 m.)

Tegucigalpa

Caribbean Sea

Tajumulco 13,845 ft. (4,220 m.)

Guatemala City

San Salvador

Managua

San José

Chirripó Grande 12,530 ft. (3,819 m.)

Barú 11,400 ft. (3,475 m.)

Panama City

Elevation

13,100 ft.	(4,000 m)
6,600 ft.	(2,000 m)
1,600 ft.	(500 m)
650 ft.	(200 m)
0 ft.	(0 m)

Below sea level

▲ Mountain peak

⊛ National capital

N

0   250   500 miles
0   250   500 kilometers

Equator

SOUTH AMERICA

PACIFIC OCEAN

110°W   100°W   90°W   80°W

10°N

0°

10°S

Place • Seven islands make up the Caribbean island group that is called Guadeloupe (GWAHD•uhl•OOP). ▲

Central America and the Caribbean

Look at the physical map in the Unit Atlas. Central America is the mountainous landmass that forms a bridge between Mexico and South America. Now look to the east, and you will see island nations scattered throughout the Caribbean Sea.

Central America About 80 percent of Central America is hilly or mountainous, and most of it is covered with forests. Rain forests cover much of the lowlands. In the higher regions, deciduous trees cloak many of the slopes.

A string of more than 40 volcanoes lines 900 miles of Central America's Pacific coast, where two tectonic plates crash against each other. This is the most active group of volcanoes in North or South America. Earthquakes also occur frequently. They can completely destroy buildings, towns, and cities. They can also set landslides and mudslides in motion, sending land, houses, and people hurtling down the slopes.

The Caribbean Islands As you can see on the map (page 155), the Caribbean Islands lie to the east of Central America. Some of these islands, such as St. Kitts and Grenada, are actually the peaks of volcanic mountains rising from the ocean floor. Over thousands of years, the volcanoes erupted, spewing lava that cooled, hardened, and added to the mountains' height.

Other islands, such as the Bahamas, began as coral reefs. Coral is made of organisms that shed hard skeletons when they die. The skeletons pile up, and a reef, or ridge, develops. A coral reef that becomes an island usually encircles a volcanic island and then grows over it.

Vocabulary

deciduous:
a tree that loses its leaves each year

Reading
Social Studies

A. Clarifying
What causes so many volcanoes and earthquakes in this region?

Place • Coral reefs form in lots of different colors. ▼

South America

Look at the map on page 142 of the Unit Atlas. You can see that the equator runs through Ecuador, Colombia, and Brazil. You can also see that only the Isthmus of Panama links South America to North America.

Look at the map on page 142 of the Unit Atlas.

Vocabulary

isthmus:
a narrow strip of land that connects two landmasses

The Andes On the map, you can see the Andes mountain range, which stretches over 5,000 miles along South America's west coast. It is the longest continuous mountain range on Earth's surface. Mount Aconcagua (AK·uhn·KAH·gwuh) in Argentina is the highest peak in the Western Hemisphere.

Beyond the Andes Notice the central plains east of the Andes. The plains in southern South America are called the *Pampas*. South America's largest rivers begin in the Andes, drain the central plains, and then flow into the Atlantic Ocean. They include the Orinoco (AWR·uh·NOH·koh), the Paraná-Paraguay-Plata (PAR·uh· NAH-PAR·uh·gwy-PLAH·tuh), and the Amazon.

BACKGROUND

The word *pampa*, meaning "flat surface," comes from the language of an Andean group of Native Americans called the Quechua (KEHCH•wuh).

The Amazon In 2000, 22 people explored the Andes's rivers to confirm the source of the Amazon River, which had been discovered in 1971. The mighty river begins in the Peruvian Andes as a trickle of water. It then flows for nearly 4,000 miles to the Atlantic Ocean. No other river carries as much water to the sea. Along with more than 1,000 **tributaries**, which are rivers or streams that flow into a larger body of water, the Amazon drains water from Peru, Ecuador, Colombia, Bolivia, Venezuela, and Brazil.

The Amazon at Risk **Deforestation,** or the process of cutting and clearing away trees from a forest, has greatly affected the Amazon rain forest. In recent years, Amazon deforestation has provided timber and cleared land for cattle ranches.

Vocabulary

timber:
wood used as building material

Place • The Andes make a good home for animals like the *llama.* ▼

Most plants release oxygen into the air and absorb carbon dioxide. By reducing the number of trees and plants, deforestation increases the amount of carbon dioxide in the air. Some scientists think the increase in carbon dioxide contributes to global warming because carbon dioxide traps warm air at Earth's surface.

Others worry that animals who find food in the rain forest may need to move—or may die out—when large areas of forest are cut down. The Native American tribes that inhabit the rain forest are also at risk of being squeezed out of the land they live on.

Climate

Latin America's climate varies greatly from area to area. It is influenced by elevation, location, wind patterns, and ocean currents.

The Tropical Zone A large portion of Latin America lies in the **Tropical Zone,** which, as you can see on the map below, is between the latitudes 23°27' north and 23°27' south. The Tropical Zone may be rainy or dry, but it is typically hot. Also, temperature is always lower at higher elevations, but in the Tropical Zone, all elevations are warmer than they are elsewhere.

Wind and Water The waters in the Caribbean Sea stay warm most of the year and heat the air over them. A warm wind then blows across the islands, keeping the climate warm even in the winter.

Reading
Social Studies

B. Drawing Conclusions
What aspect of the Tropical Zone's location on Earth causes it to be warmer than the other areas?

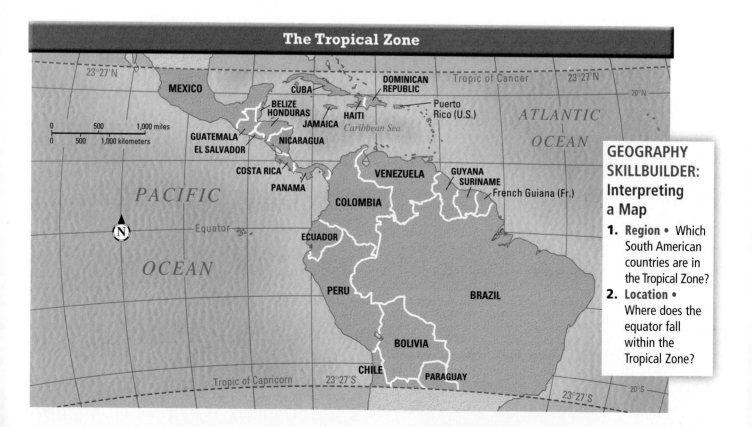

The Tropical Zone

GEOGRAPHY SKILLBUILDER: Interpreting a Map

1. **Region •** Which South American countries are in the Tropical Zone?
2. **Location •** Where does the equator fall within the Tropical Zone?

Normal Year	El Niño Year

Westerly trade winds

Warm surface water

Westerly trade winds die out

Warm surface water, warm air, and storms

SKILLBUILDER:
Interpreting a Diagram

1. What effect does the increased air pressure of *El Niño* have on the warm surface water of the Pacific?
2. What are the patterns of wind and water in a normal year?

El Niño At times, unusually high air pressure in the south Pacific causes certain winds over the ocean, called trade winds, to die out. Without the trade winds, the ocean's sun-warmed surface water flows eastward, toward North and South America. Because this typically occurs around Christmastime, people call the current **El Niño** (ehl NEE·nyaw). This term is Spanish for "the Christ child" because Christmas celebrates the birth of Jesus.

The warmer water of *El Niño* warms the air. Warmer air holds more water and so releases more rain when it cools. This added precipitation often causes heavy rains and flooding in Latin America and other parts of the eastern Pacific. At the same time, areas in the western Pacific, such as Indonesia, may have less rain than usual.

SECTION 1 ASSESSMENT

Terms & Names
1. **Identify:** (a) tributary   (b) deforestation   (c) Tropical Zone   (d) *El Niño*

Taking Notes

2. Use a chart like the one below to list the key physical features of each country or region.

Key Physical Features			
Mexico	Central America	The Caribbean Islands	South America

Main Ideas

3. (a) Name two types of natural disasters that occur frequently in Latin America.

(b) Describe two ways in which the Caribbean Islands formed.

(c) What happens when increased air pressure causes trade winds to lessen?

Critical Thinking

4. **Forming and Supporting Opinions**
   Do you favor limiting the deforestation of the Amazon rain forest? Why? Why not?

   Think About
   - the economic benefits of timber production and cattle ranching
   - the destruction of habitats
   - the effects on the global environment

ACTIVITY
-OPTION-

Look at the map on page 158 that shows the Tropical Zone. Make a **list** of all the Latin American countries that are wholly or partly in the Tropical Zone.

Ancient Latin America

TERMS & NAMES
hieroglyph
chinampa
Machu Picchu
Hernán Cortés
Montezuma II
Francisco Pizarro
Atahualpa
Columbian Exchange

MAIN IDEA

The ancient cultures of Latin America established civilizations in challenging geographic settings.

WHY IT MATTERS NOW

These cultures serve as models for how successful civilizations develop.

DATELINE

EL MIRADOR, GUATEMALA, 200 B.C.—In El Mirador today, a council of the city's leaders made a major announcement. Next month, construction will begin on a massive building complex for the city's center.

The plans include an enormous pyramid made of three smaller pyramids sitting atop a large stepped platform. The council expects to employ thousands of people to cut and carry the stone slabs that will be used to build the structure. The project is expected to take many months to complete.

Place • An artist made this drawing to show what El Mirador's three-part pyramid will look like. ▼

Place • The building complex will be made of cut slabs of limestone. ▲

Ancient Civilizations of Latin America

Many ancient civilizations, such as the Egyptian, developed in river valleys and thrived there. The rivers provided water for both irrigation and transportation. In Latin America, however, some ancient civilizations flourished far from rivers. For example, the Maya of Mexico and Central America built cities in dense jungles. The Aztec of Mexico constructed their capital on a swampy island. The Inca of South America built cities high up in the Andes.

The Maya

In the areas that are today southern and eastern Mexico, western Honduras, Guatemala, El Salvador, and Belize, the ancient Maya built a widespread civilization. Small Maya communities existed as early as 1600 B.C. From A.D. 250 to A.D. 900, the Maya established one of Latin America's most important civilizations.

Maya Intellectual Advances The ancient Maya studied math and astronomy extensively. The Maya were among the first civilizations in the world known to understand the advanced mathematical concept of zero. They also had an intricate calendar system that included a 260-day calendar of sacred days, a 365-day calendar based on the sun's movement, and a calendar that measured the number of days that had passed since a fixed starting point.

The Maya established the best-developed written language in ancient Latin America. The basic units of the writing system were symbols called

BACKGROUND

Many of the Maya hieroglyphs have now been deciphered.

hieroglyphs, or glyphs. Each glyph represented a word or a syllable. The U.S. lawyer John Lloyd Stephens, while traveling through the Maya area in the 1800s, described his awe at seeing the glyphs and not being able to read them because no one had yet deciphered them.

Culture • **The Maya often carved hieroglyphs on stone monuments.** ▲

A VOICE FROM LATIN AMERICA

These structures . . . these stones . . . standing as they do in the depths of a tropical forest, silent and solemn, strange in design, excellent in sculpture, rich in ornament . . . their whole history so entirely unknown, with hieroglyphics explaining all, but perfectly unintelligible.

John Lloyd Stephens

Reading
Social Studies

A. Drawing Conclusions How does having a system of writing help a civilization survive?

Maya Agriculture Farming was essential to Maya life. Using a method called slash-and-burn agriculture, the Maya cut down and burned trees, planting crops in their place. After a few years, they let the forest grow back, so the soil could regain its nutrients. Later the area could again be cut, burned, and farmed. The Maya also built up ridges of farming land on floodplains. The floodplains were rich with nutrients, and the ridges kept the crops from getting too wet.

Colossal Olmec Heads Mexico's oldest known civilization is called the Olmec, which flourished from about 1200 to 600 B.C. The Olmec are famous for the colossal heads (like the one shown below) that they carved from a type of stone called basalt.

Thought to be portraits of Olmec rulers, some of these heads stand over nine feet tall. Each weighs thousands of pounds. All of Mexico's later Native American cultures were influenced by the Olmec. However, only the Olmec produced these giant stone monuments.

Decline of Maya Civilization Around A.D. 900, the Maya way of life began to change. For unknown reasons, the construction of massive temples and stone monuments stopped. Cities were abandoned. However, the Maya people did not disappear—they just spread out. More than 6 million Maya people still live in Guatemala, Belize, and southern Mexico and speak dialects based on the languages of their Maya ancestors.

The Aztec

Where modern Mexico City now stands, the waters of Lake Texcoco once lapped the shores of an island city called Tenochtitlán (teh·NOHCH·tee·TLAHN). With as many as 200,000 inhabitants, Tenochtitlán served as the capital of the Aztec Empire.

Aztec Origins The Aztec were composed of a number of tribes of wandering warriors. Of these, the Mexica (MEH·hee·KAH) were dominant. Mexico took its name from the Mexica. During the 1200s, the Aztec gradually grew in numbers and military strength until they controlled the region. They dominated until the early 1500s, when the Spanish conquered them.

Aztec Warfare and Religion The Aztec Empire centered on warfare. All able men, including priests, were expected to join the Aztec army, for two reasons. The first was to maintain a powerful empire, but the second was religious. The Aztec believed that anyone who died in battle had the great honor of dying for Huitzilopochtli (WEE·tsuh·loh·POHCH·tlee), the Aztec god of war.

Culture • This stone carving honors the Aztec sun god, whose face is shown in the center. ▼

Aztec Agriculture The Aztec held great power over their empire. One reason for their success was that the island location of their capital protected them from attack. However, much of the island was marsh, posing a major challenge to farming. The resourceful Aztec built floating gardens, called *chinampas* (chee·NAHM·pahs), on which they grew crops. First, they piled up plants from the water. Then they anchored these rafts between trunks of willow trees.

Willows

Crops

Mud

Plants

Human-Environment Interaction • **This infographic shows how the Aztec built and farmed the** *chinampas.* ▲

Finally, they heaped the lake's fertile mud on the piles to create plots for farming. The Aztec grew many crops, such as maize, beans, squash, avocados, tomatoes, peppers, and flowers. They also raised turkeys, ducks, geese, and dogs for food.

The Inca

Around 1400, high in the Andes of Peru, a group of people called the Inca rose up to conquer the people of the surrounding areas. From their capital, Cuzco, the Inca soon ruled a huge empire that included parts of what are now Colombia, Ecuador, Bolivia, northern Chile, and northwestern Argentina.

Inca Agriculture To farm on the steep mountainsides, the Inca built stone terraces. These gave the Inca large areas of flat land to farm. The terraces also helped prevent erosion of the soil. In the desert lands to the west, the Inca built irrigation canals to water their crops. Some of these canals spanned entire valleys. Because of terracing and irrigation, Inca farmers were able to grow crops such as potatoes, maize, and a grain called *quinoa.*

Andean Agriculture

Long before the rise of the Inca Empire, people living in the Andes had learned to farm the steep valley walls by building terraces into the sides of the mountains. They had also learned to build canals, many of them lined with stone, to carry water to their crops. The Inca improved and expanded the existing terraces and canals until they could feed 15 million people, with enough food left over to put away stores for three to seven years.

In the Andes, valley walls rise as high as 10,000 feet and temperatures can span a 55-degree range.

Inca canals stretched for miles. They were often lined and covered with stones. Some were cut through solid rock.

The Inca grew maize, hundreds of kinds of potatoes, and many other crops. Farmers had to plant crops adapted to many different climates because of the great variations in altitude and temperature.

The Inca had few farm tools. The most widely used was the *taclla,* or digging stick. It consisted of a pointed hardwood pole with a footrest for pushing the tool into the ground. Some *tacllas* had metal tips. The other main tools were hoes and clubs.

Workers directed by royal architects built stone retaining walls. Inside the walls, they placed layers of stone, clay, gravel, and topsoil. This combination allowed water to slowly work its way to lower terraces.

THINKING Critically

1. Analyzing Motives
Why did people living in the Andes need to build terraces and canals?

2. Recognizing Effects
What role did agriculture play in the building and maintenance of the Inca Empire?

Communicating Across the Inca Empire Stone roads were a major technological feat of the Inca. These roads are still in use today. Having no written language or knowledge of the wheel, Inca rulers ordered roads built on which runners carried verbal messages to distant places. The runners worked in relay teams stationed along the roads. One runner told the message to the next. Messages could travel 150 miles a day along the stone roads. This system of communication was important to the Inca because their empire spread out over thousands of miles.

Reading
Social Studies

B. Recognizing Effects How did building stone roads improve the ability of the Inca rulers to control a large region?

Culture •
The Inca kept records by tying knots in a series of strings called *quipu* (KEE•poo). ◄

Inca Stonework The Inca are known for their stonework. They erected many massive buildings, some with stones weighing as much as 200 tons. Wooden rollers were used to move these heavy stone blocks. The most remarkable of Inca stonework is the city of **Machu Picchu** (MAH•choo PEEK•choo), which still stands almost 8,000 feet above sea level. The walls of Machu Picchu were constructed so that they appear to emerge from the mountainsides. Around them, terraces connected by stairways run down the steep slopes. (See photograph on pages 140–141.)

Spotlight on CULTURE

Inca Weaving The Inca had no formal written language, but they used weaving as a means of representing ideas. Using wool sheared from llamas and alpacas, as well as many colorful plant dyes, the Inca wove images into the fabrics they wore and traded. Concepts related to the passing of seasons, agricultural practices, and history were all represented in the weavings. In Peru today, Edwin Sulca Lagos is famous for his Inca-inspired weavings. This one is covered in designs from the Inca calendar.

THINKING CRITICALLY

1. **Hypothesizing**
   What sorts of images might the Inca have used to convey concepts such as time or seasons?

2. **Identifying Problems**
   What risks did the Inca face by recording ideas only on fabric?

Culture •
Montezuma II
was a great
warrior who
was feared
throughout the
Aztec Empire. ▲

The Spanish in Latin America

Until about 500 years ago, Latin America was populated solely by Native Americans. In the 1500s, the Spanish arrived in the region. One famous Spanish soldier, **Hernán Cortés** (ehr·NAHN kawr·TEHS), captured the Aztec ruler, **Montezuma II** (MAHN·tih·ZOO·muh), in 1519. He claimed the Aztec Empire for Spain in 1521 and renamed it New Spain. A decade later, another Spanish soldier, **Francisco Pizarro,** defeated the Inca ruler, **Atahualpa** (AH·tuh·WAHL·puh), and claimed Atahualpa's empire for Spain.

Time of Change Once in control of Latin America, the Spanish enslaved many Native Americans and forced them to do labor, such as mining silver. The Spanish also worked hard to convert the Native Americans to Christianity.

Latin America and Spain also exchanged culture. Ships carrying Latin American goods sailed to Spain. The Spanish soon began growing corn, peppers, and tomatoes—crops they had never seen before. Manufactured products from Spain, especially textiles, were also shipped to Latin America. So were foods and animals, such as peaches and pigs. This trade was part of the **Columbian Exchange,** or the exchange of goods and ideas between European countries and their colonies in North and South America.

SECTION 2 ASSESSMENT

Terms & Names

1. **Identify:**
   (a) hieroglyph
   (b) *chinampa*
   (c) Machu Picchu
   (d) Hernán Cortés
   (e) Montezuma II
   (f) Francisco Pizarro
   (g) Atahualpa
   (h) Columbian Exchange

Taking Notes

2. Use a chart like the one below to list effects of the Spanish arriving in Latin America.

Effects of Spanish Arrival in Latin America	
1.	
2.	
3.	
4.	

Main Ideas

3. (a) Describe the writing system that the Maya developed.

   (b) How did the Inca pass important messages across great distances?

   (c) What was the Columbian Exchange and how did it work?

Critical Thinking

4. **Recognizing Effects**

   How did the Maya, Aztec, and Inca develop agricultural methods that responded to the environments in which they each lived?

   Think About

   ◆ physical surroundings
   ◆ available resources

ACTIVITY -OPTION-

Imagine you live in Tenochtitlán and have spent the day constructing *chinampas*. Write a **letter** to a friend describing the process.

Finding and Summarizing the Main Idea

▶▶ Defining the Skill

When you find and summarize the main idea, you restate the subject of a written passage in fewer words. You include only the main idea and the most important details. It is important to use your own words when summarizing.

▶▶ Applying the Skill

The passage to the right tells about the climate in Latin America. Use the strategies listed below to help you find the main idea and summarize a passage.

How to Summarize

Strategy ❶ Look for a topic sentence stating the main idea. This is often at the beginning of a section or paragraph. Briefly restate the main idea in your own words.

Strategy ❷ Include key facts, numbers, dates, amounts, or percentages from the text.

Strategy ❸ After writing your summary, review it to see that you have included the main idea and the most important details.

The Tropical Zone

❶ A large portion of Latin America lies within the Tropical Zone, ❷ which is the region between the latitudes 23°27' north and 23°27' south. ❷ The Tropical Zone may be rainy or dry, but it is typically hot. ❷ Also, temperature is always lower at higher elevations, but in the Tropical Zone, all elevations are warmer than they are elsewhere.

Write a Summary

You can write your summary in a paragraph. The paragraph below summarizes the passage you just read.

> ❸ Much of Latin America is in the Tropical Zone. This zone is between latitudes 23°27' north and 23°27' south. Usually, the Tropical Zone is hot. Also, the elevations in the Tropical Zone are warmer than the same elevations in other places.

▶▶ Practicing the Skill

Turn to page 161 in Chapter 6, Section 2, "Ancient Latin America." Read "Maya Agriculture," find the main idea, and write a paragraph summarizing the passage.

TERMS & NAMES

Explain the significance of each of the following:

1. tributary
2. deforestation
3. Tropical Zone
4. *El Niño*
5. hieroglyph
6. *chinampa*
7. Machu Picchu
8. Hernán Cortés
9. Montezuma II
10. Columbian Exchange

REVIEW QUESTIONS

Physical Geography *(pages 153–159)*

1. Describe two problems that Mexico City faces because of its location.
2. What two types of islands are found in the Caribbean?
3. Describe the climate in the Tropical Zone.
4. How have tectonic plates affected Latin America's physical geography? Give two examples.

Ancient Latin America *(pages 160–166)*

5. Explain the use of each of the three Maya calendars.
6. Why was warfare so important to the Aztec?
7. Describe two means of communication used by the Inca.
8. What types of changes took place in Latin America once the Spanish took control?

CRITICAL THINKING

Comparing

1. Using your completed chart from Reading Social Studies, p. 152, compare two ancient Latin American civilizations. List the similarities in the locations, dates, characteristics, achievements, and declines of the two civilizations.

Synthesizing

2. How are the farming methods of the Maya, the Aztec, and the Inca examples of people adapting to their environment?

Hypothesizing

3. Around A.D. 900, the Maya civilization—though not the people— began to disappear. What might have contributed to this decline?

Visual Summary

1 Physical Geography

- A variety of physical features, such as mountains and rivers, have impacted life in Latin America. Also, natural disasters, such as earthquakes and volcanic eruptions, occur frequently because of the region's location on five tectonic plates.
- The variations in Latin America's climate are caused by factors such as elevation, location, wind, and water.

2 Ancient Latin America

- The Maya, the Aztec, and the Inca all built major civilizations in Latin America.
- Each civilization developed creative solutions to problems presented by the physical geography around them.

Inca Stone Roads Stone roads were a major technological feat of the Inca. These roads are still in use today. Having no written language or knowledge of the wheel, Inca rulers ordered roads built on which runners carried verbal messages to distant places. The runners worked in relay teams stationed along the roads. One runner told the message to the next. Messages could travel 150 miles a day along the stone roads. This system of communication was important to the Inca because their empire spread out over thousands of miles.

SKILLBUILDER: Finding and Summarizing the Main Idea

1. What is the main idea of the paragraph?
2. What details support the main idea?

FOCUS ON GEOGRAPHY

1. **Region** • In 2000, was South America's rain forest larger or smaller than the original forest?
2. **Region** • Was there any rain forest in the southern parts of South America in 2000?
3. **Location** • In what region of South America did the largest area of rain forest still exist in 2000?

ATLANTIC OCEAN

Equator

PACIFIC OCEAN

Original rain forest

Rain forest as of 2000

0   500   1,000 miles
0   500   1,000 kilometers

CHAPTER PROJECTS

Interdisciplinary Activity: Language Arts

Writing a Magazine Article Research the Columbian Exchange. Find out what crops, goods, and animals were sent in each direction across the Atlantic Ocean. Write a magazine article that explains which trade items came from Latin America and which came from Europe. Also include information about how the new items were used in each region.

Cooperative Learning Activity

Creating a Calendar Like the Maya, the Aztec used both a calendar with 260 days and a calendar with 365 days. Working in a small group, research one of the Maya or Aztec calendars. Find out how many months were in a year and how many days were in a month. Also find out the names of months or days. Then create a calendar that shows what your group found, and display it in your classroom.

 INTERNET ACTIVITY

Use the Internet to do research about daily life in the Aztec, Maya, or Inca culture. Focus on one part of daily life, such as religion, trade, or warfare.

Writing About Culture Write a report of your findings. Include any illustrations you found or make your own drawings. List the Web sites you used to prepare your report. Then create a calendar that shows what your group found, and display it in your classroom.

For Internet links to support this activity, go to

RESEARCH LINKS
CLASSZONE.COM

Mexico Today

MEXICO

ATLANTIC

PACIFIC

PACIFIC
OCEAN

OCEAN

INDIAN
OCEAN

OCEAN

Place Mexico City's
main plaza, the
Zócalo, is the center
of one of the world's
largest cities.

How has Mexico's lack of farmable land shaped how people live?

Human-Environment Interaction • Only 12 percent of Mexico's land is arable—that is, farmable. The rest is too steep and rocky or too dry. Even the land that people can farm is not always very productive. Inconsistent rainfall, erosion, and pollution problems can pose serious challenges to farming. Also, some people do farm in mountainous regions, but planting and harvesting crops there can be very difficult.

What do you think?

♦ How do countries benefit economically from having a great deal of arable land?

♦ What challenges does Mexico face—in its economy and daily life—as a result of having little arable land?

BEFORE YOU READ

▶▶ *What Do You Know?*

Before you read the chapter, think about what you already know about Mexico. You may have read about the Aztec in another class. Do you know about any aspects of Mexico's culture today? Think about what you've heard on the news about Mexico—do you know who the president of Mexico is?

Culture • **The Aztec feather shields were no match for Spanish armor.** ▲

▶▶ *What Do You Want to Know?*

Decide what else you want to know about Mexico. In your notebook, record what you hope to learn from this chapter.

READ AND TAKE NOTES

Reading Strategy: Organizing Information
One effective way to organize information is with a time line. Time lines show events in sequence, or the order in which they happened. Making a time line for the events in this chapter will help you better understand what happened when.

• Copy the time line in your notebook.
• As you read the chapter, note the key events discussed in it.
• Write these events beside the appropriate dates on your time line.

Place • **At the Ballet Folklórico, the culture of Mexico takes center stage.** ▲

| 1521 | | 1846–1848 | 1910–1920 | 1992 |

| 1500 | 1600 | 1700 | 1800 | 1900 | 2000 |

| 1853 | 1920–1940 | 2000 |

The Roots of Modern Mexico

TERMS & NAMES
peninsular
criollo
mestizo
encomienda
Father Miguel Hidalgo
Treaty of Guadalupe Hidalgo
Gadsden Purchase

MAIN IDEA

Modern Mexico arose from conflict and cooperation among Native American, African, and Spanish Mexicans.

WHY IT MATTERS NOW

The culture of Mexico today reflects the influences of and interactions among these groups.

DATELINE

EXTRA

TENOCHTITLÁN, AZTEC EMPIRE, 1519

Today, in the palace of the Aztec emperor Montezuma II, a Spanish explorer got a taste of something he is sure to remember. A treat enjoyed by both the Aztec and Maya, the drink, called *chocolatl*, is thick, smooth, and decidedly bitter. With no sugar added to sweeten it, this unusual drink is spiced with flavors such as chili pepper and vanilla.

Always served in liquid form, the drink is consumed by the Native Americans at a high rate. Emperor Montezuma II drinks up to 50 cups a day. The Spaniards hope to take the chocolate, as they call it, back to Europe—although they plan to find some way to help ease the bitter taste.

Region • Cacao seeds grow inside pods like this. ▲

Human-Environment Interaction • The chocolate flavor comes from cacao seeds. ▲

The Arrival of the Spanish

The leader of the Spanish army that first landed on the shores of Mexico was Hernán Cortés. He hoped to win new lands for Spain, as well as gold and glory for himself.

Cortés reached the east coast of Mexico in 1519 with about 500 soldiers. He claimed the land for the king and queen of Spain. Quickly, however, he learned that the land was ruled by the powerful Aztec emperor Montezuma II.

A Clash of Cultures

Montezuma II ruled an empire of between 5 and 6 million people. However, many of his Native American subjects wanted to be free. They helped the Spanish conquer the Aztec king. They did not expect that the Spanish would become their new rulers.

The First Encounter Montezuma II heard about the arrival of the Spanish, and soon he welcomed Cortés with gifts. He even allowed Cortés to stay in a royal palace in the Aztec capital, Tenochtitlán. Within a week, Cortés took Montezuma II prisoner—and took control of the Aztec Empire.

The Spanish Takeover Other Aztec leaders drove the Spanish from Tenochtitlán. However, during the fighting that followed, Montezuma II was killed. The Spanish then retook the city, greatly aided by their Native American allies. The Spanish also had an essential advantage over the Aztec: their weapons. The Aztec had only war clubs, spears, and arrows. The Spanish soldiers had steel swords, armor, guns, and cannons, as well as horses. The invading army destroyed Tenochtitlán street by street.

The Founding of New Spain

The fall of Tenochtitlán in 1521 marked the end of the Aztec Empire and the beginning of Spanish rule in Mexico. The Spanish called their empire "New Spain," just as the English called their territory in North America "New England." Where Tenochtitlán had stood, the Spanish established Mexico City as their capital. Spain ruled Mexico for the next 300 years.

A New Way of Life The Spanish victory caused more than a change of rulers in Mexico. The Spanish introduced a different way of life to the region. They brought new animals, such as horses, cattle, sheep, and pigs. They also brought new trades, such as ironsmithing and shipbuilding. They brought a new religion as well—Christianity.

> Culture • Aztec feather shields offered less protection than Spanish metal helmets and armor. ▲

> **Reading Social Studies**
>
> **A. Analyzing Motives** Why did some Native Americans help the Spanish fight the Aztec?

> **Vocabulary**
>
> **ironsmithing:** making items out of iron

Connections to Science

Invisible Weapons Smallpox and other diseases from Europe killed millions of Native Americans between 1500 and 1900. Smallpox (germ cell shown below right) had long been widespread in Europe, and most Europeans were at least partly immune. Native Americans, however, had no immunity to it because it had never before existed in the Americas.

Within months of the Spanish soldiers' arrival in Mexico, many thousands of Native Americans got sick with smallpox (shown below) and died from it—including Montezuma II's successor. Smallpox proved far more deadly to Native Americans than Spanish swords and cannons.

The Influence of the Church

Because the Catholic Church was powerful in Spain, it soon became powerful in New Spain. Catholic priests set up churches, schools, and hospitals. Sometimes Native Americans accepted Christianity willingly. Sometimes, though, they were forced to become Christian against their will.

A Cultural Blend Even though the Native Americans had to accept many new ways of life, the old ways were not lost entirely. For instance, an essential element of Native American cooking was the tortilla, a flat, round bread made from corn or flour. Tortillas are still made daily all over Mexico. As with food, many other aspects of the two cultures blended in the new Mexican culture.

Life in New Spain

BACKGROUND

The Iberian Peninsula consists of two countries—Portugal and Spain. (See the map of Europe on page 262.)

A new multilayered society developed in Mexico. The ruling class were Spanish officials who were born in Spain. They were called _peninsulares_ (peh·neen·soo·LAH·rehs) because they were from the Iberian Peninsula in Europe.

A second class were _criollos_ (kree·AW·yaws), people who were born in Mexico but whose parents were born in Spain. _Criollos_ were often wealthy and powerful, but they were not in as high a social class as the _peninsulares._

A _mestizo_ (mehs·TEE·saw) is a person who is of Spanish and Native American ancestry. _Mestizos_ formed the third layer of New Spain's society.

Movement •
Mexicans today celebrate Catholic holy days that the Spanish established. This festival honors Our Lady of Guadalupe. ▼

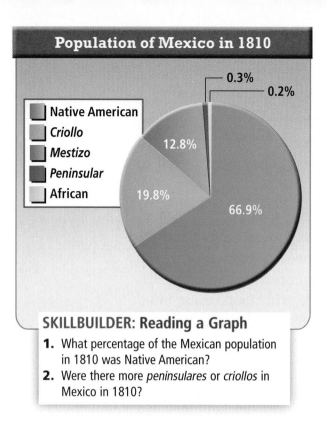

Population of Mexico in 1810

- Native American
- Criollo
- Mestizo
- Peninsular
- African

0.3%
0.2%
12.8%
19.8%
66.9%

SKILLBUILDER: Reading a Graph

1. What percentage of the Mexican population in 1810 was Native American?
2. Were there more *peninsulares* or *criollos* in Mexico in 1810?

A fourth group of people arrived in Mexico unwillingly—the enslaved Africans brought by European slave ships. African farming techniques, musical traditions, and crafts soon blended into the Mexican culture.

Encomienda New Spain's largest group was the Native Americans. They made up the bottom layer of society. The rulers of Spain set up in Mexico a system called ***encomienda*** (ehn·kaw·MYEHN·dah). Under this system, Spanish men were each given a Native American village to oversee. The villagers had to pay tribute—in goods, money, or labor—to this Spaniard. They were essentially enslaved. The results of their labor helped to make Spain rich. However, the villagers lived in poverty and hardship.

Vocabulary

tribute:
a forced payment

The War of Independence

Based on earlier European and American political writers, many Mexican religious and political leaders in the early 1800s were saying that Mexicans should be free to choose their own government. They argued that Mexico should be independent from Spain. The demand for Mexican independence grew stronger after 1808, when France conquered Spain.

A Cry for Freedom Then, before dawn on September 16, 1810, the farmers in the mountain village of Dolores heard their church bells ringing. At the church, their priest, **Father Miguel Hidalgo,** gave a fiery speech urging them to throw off Spanish rule. No one knows the exact text of the speech, but it is known as the *Grito de Dolores* (Cry of Dolores). Urged on by his words, a small army of Native Americans and *mestizos* marched with Father Hidalgo toward Mexico City. Along the way, thousands more joined them.

A Difficult Challenge Father Hidalgo's army had few weapons. Mostly, his men carried clubs and farm tools, such as sickles and axes. When they faced the government soldiers, the farmers were soon defeated. Father Hidalgo was captured and executed, but the revolution he had sparked did not die.

Reading
Social Studies

B. Clarifying
What ideas from other parts of the world did Mexicans agree with?

Vocabulary

sickle:
a blade used for cutting tall grass or grain

Biography

BACKGROUND

Mexico's independence was based on "three guarantees": that it would be independent from Spain, that it would be Catholic, and that *criollos* and *peninsulares* would be equal.

Independence at Last New leaders took Father Hidalgo's place. A few wealthy Spanish nobles and many *criollos* joined the fight for independence. The struggle lasted for 11 years. In 1821, the rebels finally overthrew the Spanish government, and Mexico became independent. However, the *peninsulares* and *criollos* still ruled the country. Native Americans and *mestizos* benefited little from independence from Spain.

War with the United States

In 1821, the new nation of Mexico was far larger than it is today. You can see on the map on page 178 that northern Mexico included much of what is now the Southwestern United States. Spanish explorers claimed this entire region in the 1500s and 1600s. Spanish and Mexican priests built missions there in the 1600s.

Desert and Distance Much of this land was desert. Travel was slow and communication difficult. Mexico was at war with Native Americans in this region, such as the Apache and the Comanche tribes. For all these reasons, few Mexicans settled there.

Father Hidalgo Father Miguel Hidalgo y Costilla, shown in the center of the illustration above, was born in 1753. He was a *criollo* who felt great sympathy for the Native Americans and *mestizos*. As a priest in the small village of Dolores, Father Hidalgo joined a secret group that fought for Mexico's independence.

Father Hidalgo is known as the Father of Mexican Independence. Every September 16, Mexicans shout slogans from the *Grito de Dolores* in celebration of their independence and Father Hidalgo.

To encourage settlement, the Mexican government invited foreigners to move into these northern lands. Most of the newcomers were from the United States and still felt some loyalty to that country. By the 1830s, settlers in Texas from the United States greatly outnumbered those from Mexico.

Texas Independence In 1835, many settlers in Texas decided to break away from Mexico and rose in revolt. After several fierce battles, the Texans won their independence. They set up the Republic of Texas in 1836.

Most Texans wanted to become part of the United States. In 1845, the United States agreed, but Mexico and the United States could not agree where the boundary between Texas and Mexico should be. Each side claimed land that the other wanted.

The Mexican War In 1846, the dispute grew into a war. During the next two years, U.S. forces won control of northern Mexico; it was made official when Mexico was forced to sign the **Treaty of Guadalupe Hidalgo.**

Place • **You can still see this mission, built in 1700, in Arizona today.** ▼

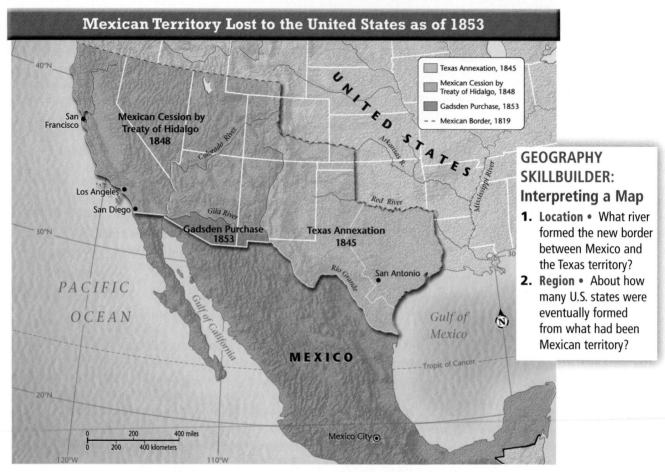

Mexican Territory Lost to the United States as of 1853

Legend:
- Texas Annexation, 1845
- Mexican Cession by Treaty of Hidalgo, 1848
- Gadsden Purchase, 1853
- – – Mexican Border, 1819

GEOGRAPHY SKILLBUILDER: Interpreting a Map

1. **Location** • What river formed the new border between Mexico and the Texas territory?
2. **Region** • About how many U.S. states were eventually formed from what had been Mexican territory?

A few years later, in 1853, the **Gadsden Purchase** gave the United States more of Mexico's northern land. The two countries have since made slight adjustments to the border, but they have not fought a war again.

SECTION 1 ASSESSMENT

Terms & Names

1. **Identify:** (a) *peninsular*   (b) *criollo*   (c) *mestizo*   (d) *encomienda*
   (e) Father Miguel Hidalgo   (f) Treaty of Guadalupe Hidalgo   (g) Gadsden Purchase

Taking Notes

2. Use a chart like this one to list the five social groups that made up New Spain and their characteristics.

Social Group	Characteristics

Main Ideas

3. (a) What advantages allowed Cortés's small army to conquer Mexico?

(b) In what ways did Spanish rule change life in Mexico?

(c) What were the results of the war between Mexico and the United States?

Critical Thinking

4. **Analyzing Causes**

Why did Mexicans decide to fight for independence from Spain?

Think About

- influential events around the world
- reasons for discontent among the *criollos, mestizos,* and Native Americans

ACTIVITY -OPTION-   Reread the information about the first meeting of the Spanish and the Aztec. Write a **short story** describing the event from either the Spanish or Aztec viewpoint.

Government in Mexico: Revolution and Reform

TERMS & NAMES
Benito Juárez
Francisco Madero
hacienda
Emiliano Zapata
ejido
Institutional
  Revolutionary Party
Vicente Fox

MAIN IDEA

Through periods of reform and revolution, Mexico struggled to establish a strong democratic national government.

WHY IT MATTERS NOW

Other countries, such as the United States, are more willing to work as partners with Mexico because its government is democratic.

DATELINE

QUERÉTARO, MEXICO, 1917—Amid the battles of the Mexican Revolution, politicians today took a step toward reforming the nation. After many weeks of discussion and debate, they produced a new constitution for Mexico. The document presents new approaches to issues such as education, landownership, and religion.

Perhaps this constitution will become a basis for a new and stable Mexican government. For now, though, the constant fighting among sides continues. The potential power of the constitution will be revealed only in time, as the government puts the document into action.

Location • President Venustiano Carranza organized the meetings that resulted in the 1917 constitution. ▲

A Struggle for Power

The constitution of 1917 was written as a response to the struggles of the previous century. During that time, Mexico spent many years fighting wars. In 1821, Mexico won its war for independence from Spain. Two decades later, Mexicans entered into and then lost a war with the United States over Texas, California, and other lands. During all these years, still another struggle was going on—a struggle for power within Mexico.

In the years after independence, army leaders often took over Mexico's government. In some parts of the country, bandits attacked travelers. Elsewhere, Mexicans fought with Spanish landowners. Everywhere, a few people enjoyed great wealth, while many suffered in poverty.

Benito Juárez Brings Reform

By the 1850s, many Mexicans were eager for reform. They found a leader in **Benito Juárez,** a man who rose from poverty to become president of Mexico and a hero to his people. He became minister of justice in 1855, and he later became chief justice of the Supreme Court. In 1858, he gained the presidency, giving control of the Mexican government to the reformers.

Response to Reform The reformers wrote a new constitution for Mexico in 1857. For the first time, Mexicans had a bill of rights, promising them freedom of speech and equality under the law. The constitution of 1857 also ended slavery and forced labor. However, the new constitution did not promise freedom of religion. Nor did it make Catholicism Mexico's official religion, as many church leaders had hoped it would. The reformers also cut back the army's power in the government.

These reforms stirred up a storm of controversy. Church leaders, army leaders, and wealthy landowners were outraged. From 1858 to 1860, the War of Reform raged between the reformers and their opponents.

Foreign Intervention in Mexico The War of Reform left Mexico so weak—because of death, debt, and unemployment—that the country was an easy target for foreign takeover. Spain, Britain, and France sent troops into Mexico. In 1863, after more than a year of fighting, the French marched into Mexico City and established themselves in control of the country. They made a European nobleman named Maximilian emperor. Maximilian did not reign long. The Mexicans overthrew Maximilian and executed him in 1867.

Culture • Benito Juárez was a Zapotec, one of the many Native American groups in Mexico. He grew up in a mountain village, studied law, and then went into politics. ▲

Culture • Mexican forces fight their way to victory in an early battle against the French in 1862. ▼

An End to Reform That same year, Benito Juárez and the reformers returned to power. Juárez remained president until his death in 1872. Unfortunately, his successors cared about reform less than he had. Poverty and lack of education remained problems. A few rich families held most of the political and economic power. Not until the 20th century did a new wave of reform begin.

The Mexican Revolution

By 1910, the divisions between rich and poor in Mexico were huge. Just 800 families owned more than 90 percent of the farmland. Of Mexico's 15 million people, 10 million owned no land at all.

A Decade of War Once again, many Mexicans decided to fight for reforms. And once again, the struggle turned bloody. From 1910 to 1920, Mexico endured the Mexican Revolution.

The Revolution was a fight among many armies. Almost every part of Mexico had an army of rebels and reformers with particular goals. One of the first revolutionary leaders was a wealthy rancher named **Francisco Madero,** who became president in 1911. For Madero and his supporters, the key issue was free, honest elections. For others, however, the most important problem was landownership.

The Problem of Land Poor farmers wanted land of their own. They believed the government should give each farm family a few acres by breaking up the giant *haciendas*. A ***hacienda*** is a big farm or ranch, often as large as 40,000 or 50,000 acres. Much of the *hacienda* land had once belonged to village farmers. But a law passed in 1883 allowed some of the wealthiest ranch owners to easily take away land from the village farmers. During the 1880s and 1890s, the ranch owners took over millions of acres of land owned by village farmers, and that land became part of their *haciendas.*

Region • During the Revolution, Francisco "Pancho" Villa was a famous leader in the north of Mexico. ▼

Reading Social Studies

A. Analyzing Issues What sorts of concerns led Mexicans to fight in the Mexican Revolution?

Region • Like this one, many of Mexico's *haciendas* were situated on huge pieces of land. ▶

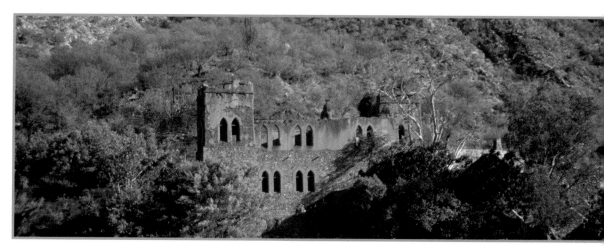

Emiliano Zapata was a legendary fighter for farmers' rights. With his famous motto—"Land and Liberty!"—Zapata gathered an army in the south of Mexico and urged farmers to join him.

A VOICE FROM MEXICO

Join me. . . . We want a much better president. Rise up with us because we don't like what the rich men pay us. It is not enough for us to eat and dress ourselves. I also want for everyone to have his piece of land so that he can plant and harvest corn, beans, and other crops. What do you say? Are you going to join us?

Emiliano Zapata

Connections to Citizenship

The Mexican Flag In the middle of Mexico's flag sits an eagle holding a snake in its mouth— a symbol from an Aztec legend about the founding of their capital, Tenochtitlán. The legend says that in the 1100s, the Aztec sun god told the Aztec to build a city on the spot where they saw an eagle with a snake in its mouth. When they saw just such an eagle in the middle of Lake Texcoco, they knew where to build their capital.

Each of the flag's red, white, and green stripes represents one of the "three guarantees" of the Mexican War of Independence. By flying a flag that combines a symbol from Aztec times with one from the period of independence, Mexico shows how important its roots are to its modern identity.

A Continuing Revolution

Over the course of a decade, dozens of large and small armies fought with one another. In 1913, Madero was murdered. The same fate befell Zapata in 1919. Between 1910 and 1920, more than 1 million Mexicans died in the battles of the Revolution. In 1920, a new government managed to make peace among the many armies. The fighting was over, but the Revolution—the effort to reform Mexico's government and economy— went on.

Answering Demands for Land In 1917, a new constitution was written, and one of its promises was to distribute land more equally among the people. Between 1920 and 1940, the government broke up many of the giant *haciendas*. Millions of acres were divided among small farmers or given to *ejidos*. An ***ejido*** (eh·HEE·daw) is a community farm owned by all the villagers together. Farmers were proud and happy to have their own land once again.

Reading Social Studies

B. Summarizing How did the 1917 constitution respond to concerns about landownership?

The Revolution in Politics The idea of the Revolution was so important and popular among new Mexicans that the most powerful political party called itself the party of the Revolution. Its name changed several times, but the word *revolution* was always part of it. Today, it is called the **Institutional Revolutionary Party** (Partido Revolucionario Institucional, or PRI). This party won every presidential election in Mexico from 1929 until 2000, with power passing peacefully from one president to the next.

Mexico's Government Today

December 1, 2000, was a historic occasion in Mexico. On that day, **Vicente Fox** became Mexico's new president. Fox was the first president in more than 70 years who did not belong to the PRI. Instead, he belonged to the National Action Party (Partido Acción Nacional, or PAN). The election of a president from a party other than the PRI confirmed that Mexico was entering a time of new political possibilities.

National Government Mexico's official name is Estados Unidos Mexicanos, or the United Mexican States. Thirty-one states make up the nation. Mexico is a democracy and a republic. All Mexicans who are 18 or older have the right to vote. The Mexican government has three branches. As in the United States, these branches are the executive, legislative, and judicial.

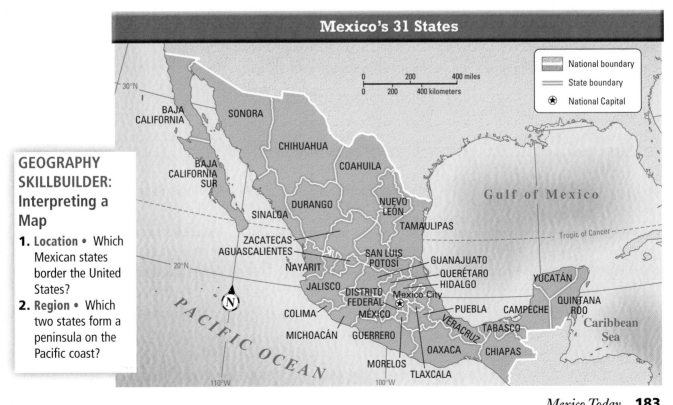

GEOGRAPHY SKILLBUILDER: Interpreting a Map

1. **Location** • Which Mexican states border the United States?
2. **Region** • Which two states form a peninsula on the Pacific coast?

Mexico's 31 States

National boundary
State boundary
National Capital

State Government Like the United States, Mexico has a federal system of government, in which power is shared between the national government and state governments. Voters in each state elect a governor. Each state also has its own legislature that makes laws. However, the national government has some control over the state governments. For example, the president and the national Senate together can remove a state governor from office.

Local Government Most towns and villages depend on money from the national government. Therefore, a local government has less say in its town's affairs than the national government does. However, local governments do provide essential public services, such as maintaining sewer systems and public safety.

Region •
The Mexican government issues stamps that celebrate its people and achievements. ▶

SECTION 2 ASSESSMENT

Terms & Names

1. Identify:
(a) Benito Juárez
(b) Francisco Madero
(c) *hacienda*
(d) Emiliano Zapata
(e) *ejido*
(f) Institutional Revolutionary Party
(g) Vicente Fox

Taking Notes

2. Use a chart like this one to record details about each level of Mexico's government.

National	State	Local

Main Ideas

3. (a) What changes did reformers such as Benito Juárez help bring about in Mexico?

(b) Why was the Mexican Revolution fought among many armies?

(c) How did the Mexican government help farmers gain land of their own?

Critical Thinking

4. Analyzing Points of View

How did different groups view the need for reform and change in Mexico during the years from 1850 to 1940?

Think About

• Juárez and the reformers
• Madero and his supporters
• the owners of the *haciendas*
• Zapata and the small farmers

ACTIVITY -OPTION- Think about a constitution's bill of rights. Write a **speech** explaining why a bill of rights is important to citizens.

Mexico's Changing Economy

SECTION 3

TERMS & NAMES

Carlos Salinas
de Gortari

privatization

distribution

maquiladora

nationalize

PEMEX

tourism

MAIN IDEA

In the mid-1900s, the basis of Mexico's economy changed from farming to industry and tourism.

WHY IT MATTERS NOW

Mexico's successful expansion of its economy has helped the nation to prosper.

DATELINE

EXTRA

MEXICO CITY, MEXICO, MARCH 18, 1938

President Lázaro Cárdenas's radio address today established a new course for Mexico's economy. Speaking to the nation, the president announced that foreigners will no longer be allowed to control petroleum companies in Mexico.

The oil industry will now be run by the Mexican government itself. It is hoped that this change will boost both Mexico's economy and its national identity.

Human-Environment Interaction • The Mexican government will now own all oil-producing equipment, such as these oil wells in Veracruz. ▶

Farming in a Time of Change

The 1938 decision that the government would own Mexico's oil industry was made in an effort to expand Mexico's economy. The expansion was necessary because, from ancient times until the mid-1900s, most Mexicans worked in just one industry—farming. Since the 1950s, great numbers of Mexicans have left farming for other kinds of work. However, farming is still important to Mexico's economy.

The Problems of Farming About one-fourth of Mexican workers are farmers. Many small farmers still work on the *ejidos,* or community farms, that were set up after the Revolution.

Although the *ejido* system gave land to many poor villagers, it did not lift them out of poverty. Farmers could not use the land as security for a bank loan because they did not really own their land—the *ejido* did. Without much money, they could not buy tractors, plows, or fertilizer. They had to continue to farm in the old ways, with hand tools on worn-out soil.

A New System In 1991, Mexican president **Carlos Salinas de Gortari** decided it was time to change the *ejido* system. Under Salinas's new laws, farmers could vote to divide their *ejido* into individual farms. Each farm family would have its own piece of land. The family could sell, rent, or trade its land. This process of replacing community ownership with individual, or private, ownership is called **privatization.**

The supporters of privatization hope that private farms will be able to grow more crops. Many of these farms are run like big businesses. Banks lend them money so they can afford to buy and use modern machinery. They can then grow the crops that Mexico sells to other countries, such as cotton, coffee, sugar cane, and strawberries.

Ejidos still make up about half the farmland in Mexico. This is partly because some farmers do not want to divide their *ejidos* into private farms. They worry that privatization might once again put most of the country's land into the hands of a few wealthy people.

Reading
Social Studies

A. Clarifying How does using land on an *ejido* differ from owning one's own land?

Region • **In this Mexican factory, workers make car parts.** ▲

The Growth of Business and Industry

During the mid-1900s, industry became a larger part of Mexico's economy because the Mexican government took steps to encourage its growth. For example, the government built new power plants to supply energy for factories. It also constructed homes for factory workers.

The Mexican government also helped new companies get started by lending them money from the national bank. Sometimes the government lowered taxes on businesses or helped companies pay back money they had borrowed.

Effects of Government Aid The new policies encouraged production. As a result, new factories sprang up that made products such as steel, chemicals, paper, soft drinks, and textiles. The Mexican government also promoted the building of highways, railroads, and airports to aid manufacturers in the distribution of goods. **Distribution** is the process of moving products to their markets.

Privatization of Business In the same way that it was privatizing farms, the Mexican government during the 1990s began to privatize businesses. It raised millions of dollars by selling businesses, such as banks, mines, and steel mills, to private companies. By 2000, only a few key industries—such as the oil industry—were still in government hands.

Foreign-Owned Businesses in Mexico During the 1990s, many of Mexico's fastest-growing factories were situated along its border with the United States. These factories are called *maquiladoras*. In Mexico, a **_maquiladora_** (mah·kee·lah·DAW·rah) is a factory that imports duty-free parts from the United States to make products that it then exports back across the border. The lack of a tax on the parts helps keep operating costs low. Also, most of Mexico's *maquiladoras* are owned by foreigners, who save money because wages are lower in Mexico than in countries such as the United States. Although the wages are not great, *maquiladoras* have provided hundreds of thousands of jobs in Mexico.

Vocabulary

duty-free: free of government-imposed taxes

Citizenship IN ACTION

Na Bolom Since 1951, an organization called Na Bolom (headquarters shown below) has tried to help maintain Mexico's national heritage. Na Bolom works with the Maya living in the southeastern part of Mexico to uphold their traditional ways of life while also developing their economic opportunities. The group also tries to protect the often-threatened resources of the surrounding environment, such as the rain forest.

NAFTA Giving tax breaks on trade items is also a goal of the North American Free Trade Agreement (NAFTA). NAFTA has reduced taxes on items traded among Mexico, the United States, and Canada. However, some Mexicans are not sure NAFTA is a good idea—they worry that having such close ties to the United States and Canada gives those countries too much influence over Mexico. Despite these concerns, Mexico has nearly doubled its trade with the United States and with Canada since NAFTA was approved in 1992.

Mexico's Rich Resources

Just as gold and silver drew the Spanish to Mexico in the 1500s, other minerals that are found there attract worldwide interest today. While Mexico produces more silver than any other country in the world, it also mines lead, zinc, graphite, sulfur, and copper.

The Booming Oil Industry By far the most important of Mexico's natural resources is petroleum, or oil. In 1938, the Mexican government decided to **nationalize,** or establish government control of, the oil industry. Today, when many other businesses have been privatized, the oil industry is still government owned. An agency called **PEMEX** (which stands for Petróleos Mexicanos, or Mexican Petroleum) runs the industry. PEMEX is Mexico's largest and most important company. Oil is Mexico's biggest export, and the United States is its largest buyer.

Reading
Social Studies

B. Contrasting
How does nationalization differ from privatization?

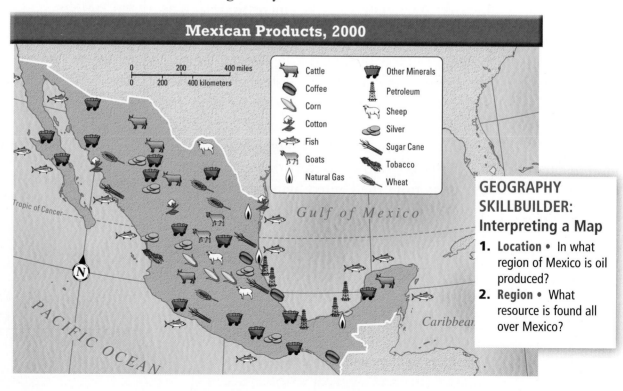

Mexican Products, 2000

Cattle		Other Minerals	
Coffee		Petroleum	
Corn		Sheep	
Cotton		Silver	
Fish		Sugar Cane	
Goats		Tobacco	
Natural Gas		Wheat	

GEOGRAPHY SKILLBUILDER: Interpreting a Map

1. **Location** • In what region of Mexico is oil produced?
2. **Region** • What resource is found all over Mexico?

Tourism Is Big Business

Mexico's second-largest business is tourism. **Tourism** is the business of helping people travel on vacations. Tourists come to Mexico to enjoy its warm weather and its sunny beaches. Many people also visit the ancient Native American ruins. Visitors admire art in Mexico City's spectacular museums. They also shop for fine silver jewelry, weavings, wood carvings, and other handicrafts.

Place •
Tourists who travel to Santa Catalina Island, off western Mexico, can see rattleless rattlesnakes, which live nowhere else on Earth. ▲

Economic Effects of Tourism A popular tourist place in Mexico is Cancún, on the country's southeastern coast. The story of Cancún shows the effect tourism has had on Mexico's economy.

Until 1970, Cancún was a small Maya village of about 100 people. Its shoreline had white sand beaches and palm trees. The weather was sunny almost every day. In 1970, the Mexican government decided Cancún was an ideal place for a holiday resort. Working together, the government and private businesses built an airport, new roads, and skyscraper hotels.

Today, more than 2.5 million people from all over the world visit Cancún's resorts each year. Because of the tourism boom, the once tiny village has become a city with about 500,000 people.

SECTION 3 ASSESSMENT

Terms & Names
1. Identify:
   (a) Carlos Salinas de Gortari
   (b) privatization
   (c) distribution
   (d) *maquiladora*
   (e) nationalize
   (f) PEMEX
   (g) tourism

Taking Notes
2. Use a chart like this one to take notes on four important parts of Mexico's economy.

Mexico's Economy	
Farming	
Industry	
Mining	
Tourism	

Main Ideas
3. (a) How has privatization changed the *ejido* system?

   (b) What part has Mexico's government played in the growth of industry?

   (c) How does tourism contribute to Mexico's economy?

Critical Thinking
4. **Forming and Supporting Opinions**

   Do you think the privatization of farmland in Mexico has been a positive step for Mexico's farmers? Why or why not?

   Think About
   • the concerns of some *ejido* farmers
   • farmers' need to modernize
   • Mexico's history of land reform

ACTIVITY -OPTION- Draw a **flow chart** that shows the process by which goods are produced and distributed by a *maquiladora.*

Mexico's Culture Today

TERMS & NAMES
Diego Rivera
Frida Kahlo
Octavio Paz
rural
urban
Day of the Dead
fiesta

MAIN IDEA

Modern Mexican culture reflects a blending of Native American and Spanish heritages, as well as many new elements.

WHY IT MATTERS NOW

Cultures change over time, but understanding their histories can help you better understand their characteristics today.

DATELINE

GUADALAJARA, MEXICO, NOVEMBER 2, 2000—The streets of Guadalajara today buzzed with activity. Families strolled into cemeteries with armfuls of brightly colored flowers to lay on the gravesites of their relatives.

While eating picnics of spicy meat dishes, egg bread, and sugary desserts, family members shared favorite stories about their departed loved ones. In performing these and other customs, which mix Christian and Aztec traditions, they celebrated the Day of the Dead in typical Mexican fashion.

Culture • This gravesite is decorated for the Day of the Dead. ▲

Culture • Marigolds are the most popular flowers left on graves on the Day of the Dead. ▲

Mexico's Blend of Cultures

Mexican culture today reflects the same pattern seen in the Day of the Dead celebrations—a mixing of traditions. This mix includes three main cultures. The first two, Native American and Spanish, have long histories. The third, modern Mexican, results from the natural changes Mexicans have gone through over time.

Culture in Architecture A plaza near the center of Mexico City symbolizes the traditions that have come together in Mexico. At the center of this Plaza of Three Cultures stand the stone ruins of the Aztec marketplace. Nearby, a Spanish Catholic church borders the plaza. Beyond the plaza, skyscrapers rise against the sky and stand as landmarks of modern Mexico.

Culture in Other Forms of Art Just as Mexico's architecture reveals the multiple layers of its culture, so do other art forms. A series of historical murals decorates the walkways of the National Palace in Mexico City. Painted by **Diego Rivera,** one of Mexico's most celebrated 20th-century artists, these murals depict scenes from the Aztec Empire, New Spain, and the Mexican Revolution. Rivera's wife, **Frida Kahlo** (FREE·duh KAH·loh), is another favorite Mexican painter. After being injured badly in a bus accident, Kahlo painted many famous self-portraits from her bed.

BACKGROUND

Each year, a foundation in Sweden gives a Nobel Prize to a world leader in a particular field, such as literature.

Mexican literature also echoes the country's three cultural traditions. **Octavio Paz,** who won the Nobel Prize in literature in 1990, often writes about the connections between elements of Mexico's past.

Life in the City

About one of every five Mexicans lives in Mexico City. Thousands of people move there each year, hoping to work in factories or attend one of the city's universities or colleges. While Mexico City is by far the largest city in the country, many other cities and towns are growing quickly. Like Mexico City, they offer a blend of opportunities and problems.

Place • Aztec ruins, Spanish colonial architecture, and modern high-rises share space in the Plaza of Three Cultures. ▼

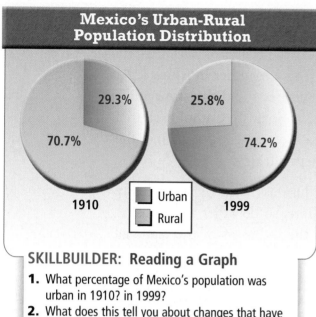

Mexico's Urban-Rural Population Distribution

1910
29.3%
70.7%

1999
25.8%
74.2%

Urban
Rural

SKILLBUILDER: Reading a Graph

1. What percentage of Mexico's population was urban in 1910? in 1999?
2. What does this tell you about changes that have taken place in Mexican society?

A Lively Capital With more than 18 million inhabitants, Mexico City is the second-largest city in the world, after Tokyo, Japan. It is also the cultural center of Mexico. The great marble Palace of Fine Arts houses the national opera, theater, and symphony. It is also home to the famous Ballet Folklórico, a group that performs spectacular dances based on Mexican traditions.

The Cost of Growth Growth has, however, created problems. Streets are jammed with traffic. Car exhaust creates a blanket of smog over the city. The government has responded to the pollution problem in a number of ways. One solution was to free taxi drivers from paying taxes on their vehicles if they drive cars that pollute less.

Culture • The dancers in Ballet Folklórico wear detailed, bright costumes. ▶

As is true in most large cities, a noticeable gap exists between the lives of Mexico City's rich and poor citizens. While luxurious homes and fine shopping centers line some streets, many people also live in poverty.

Life in the Countryside

In the smaller villages and farming towns, much of Mexico's older way of life still goes on. At the center of each village is a plaza, where people gather to talk and visit with neighbors. Most people speak Spanish, but many also speak Native American languages, such as those of the Aztec and Maya.

Each village sets aside one day a week as market day. People gather in the plaza to buy, sell, or trade food, clothing, and other goods. Farmers come in from surrounding areas, bringing vegetables and handicrafts. The scent of freshly baked *tortillas* and *frijoles,* or beans, fills the air.

Poverty in the Countryside Mexico's **rural** areas—those in the countryside—face the serious problem of poverty. Some homes have only one room and a dirt floor. Farmhouses may lack electricity and running water. These hardships have driven many rural Mexicans to seek jobs in **urban,** or city, settings.

Education is also more limited in the rural areas than in the urban ones. Without education, it is especially hard for people to escape poverty.

Mexican Muralist After the Mexican Revolution, artist Diego Rivera (1886–1957) painted a series of famous murals on the walls of the National Palace in Mexico City. Rivera wanted to use his art to remind Mexicans of the important events in their country's past. This mural shows a typical day in the Aztec capital, Tenochtitlán—now Mexico City.

THINKING CRITICALLY

1. **Synthesizing**
   What aspects of Aztec society was Rivera celebrating in this mural?

2. **Recognizing Details**
   Identify three activities depicted in the mural.

Our Lady of Guadalupe In 1531, many Mexicans believe, Mary, the mother of Jesus, appeared to Juan Diego, a Native American man, in the Villa de Guadalupe Hidalgo. Mary asked Juan Diego to carry some roses in his cloak to the local bishop. Amazingly, Juan Diego found that roses were blooming even in winter on a harsh, rocky hillside. More astonishingly, when he opened his cloak, Juan Diego saw on it an image of Mary.

Many Mexicans saw these events as miraculous. They began calling Mary "Our Lady of Guadalupe" (shown at right). She was so loved that Father Hidalgo carried a banner with her image to rally support for independence. Mexicans still regard her as their protector.

Holidays

September 16 is Mexico's Independence Day. To celebrate, Mexicans reenact Father Hidalgo's call in 1810 to rise up against Spanish rule. Then people watch fireworks, dance, and play music in the streets late into the night.

Another major holiday has a somber name— the **Day of the Dead**. Nevertheless, Mexicans see it as a joyful time. They set aside November 1 and 2 to remember and honor their loved ones who have died. They decorate the graves with candles and flowers. Bakeries sell loaves of bread shaped like bones, and many stores sell small candy skulls. Relatives gather for meals at the cemeteries.

At least once a year, each village or town celebrates a **fiesta**. A fiesta is a holiday with parades, games, and feasts. It usually takes place on a saint's day—a day set aside by the Catholic Church to honor the memory of a holy person. While these days have religious origins, they are also celebrated as big neighborhood parties.

SECTION 4 ASSESSMENT

Terms & Names

1. Identify:
   (a) Diego Rivera
   (b) Frida Kahlo
   (c) Octavio Paz
   (d) rural
   (e) urban
   (f) Day of the Dead
   (g) fiesta

Taking Notes

2. Use a chart like this one to list the positive and negative features of living in urban or in rural Mexico.

	Positive Features	Negative Features
Rural Mexico		
Urban Mexico		

Main Ideas

3. (a) What three traditions mix in Mexico's culture today?

   (b) Why is Mexico City growing so rapidly? What are the effects of that growth?

   (c) Describe some of Mexico's holidays.

Critical Thinking

4. Comparing

   Do you see any similarities between the mix of cultural traditions in Mexico and the mix in the United States? What are they?

   Think About

   • forms of art, music, dance, and architecture
   • languages spoken
   • holidays celebrated

ACTIVITY -OPTION- Imagine that you are traveling through Mexico. Write a **journal entry** describing what you saw and did in its cities and towns.

Reading a Graph

▶▶ Defining the Skill

Graphs use pictures and symbols, along with words, to show information. There are many different kinds of graphs. Bar graphs, line graphs, and pie graphs are the most common. Bar graphs compare numbers or sets of numbers. The length or height of each bar shows a quantity. It is easy to compare different categories using a bar graph.

▶▶ Applying the Skill

The bar graph to the right shows the number of Mexican state governors who belong to each political party. Use the strategies listed below to help you interpret the graph.

How to Read a Graph

Strategy 1 Read the title to identify the main idea of the graph.

Strategy 2 Read the vertical axis (the one that goes up and down) on the left side of the graph. This one shows the number of state governors. Each bar represents the number of Mexican state governors who were members of a particular political party.

Strategy 3 Read the horizontal axis (the one that runs across the bottom of the graph). This one shows the three political parties of Mexico's governors in 2000.

Strategy 4 Summarize the information given in each part of the graph. Use the title to help you focus on what information the graph is presenting.

Write a Summary

Writing a summary will help you understand the information in the graph. The paragraph to the right summarizes the information from the bar graph.

1 Political Parties of Mexico's State Governors in 2000

2 Number of State Governors

3 Political Party: National Action Party, Democratic Revolutionary Party, Institutional Revolutionary Party

4 In the year 2000, the state governors in Mexico belonged to three different political parties. The majority belonged to the Institutional Revolutionary Party. The next largest group was the National Action Party, and the smallest number of governors belonged to the Democratic Revolutionary Party. This shows that the Institutional Revolutionary Party was probably the most powerful party in Mexico.

▶▶ Practicing the Skill

Turn to page 176 in Chapter 7, Section 1, "The Roots of Modern Mexico." Look at the graph entitled "Population of Mexico in 1810," and write a paragraph summarizing what you learned from it.

How Quetzalcoatl Brought Music to the World

THIS MEXICAN FOLK TALE was first written down as a poem in Nahuatl (NAH•WAHT•uhl), the language of the Aztec, in the 1500s. The myth on which it is based may be a thousand years older. It was passed by word of mouth from one storyteller to another for centuries.

1. A name of Tezcatlipoca (tehs•KAH•tlee•POH•kah), a powerful Aztec god.

2. The quetzal is a bird that lives in the rain forests of southern Mexico and Central America. *Coatl* means "serpent" in Nahuatl.

W hen time began, Earth had no music. Brooks did not babble, and birds did not sing. This, however, does not mean that music did not exist. High in the heavens in the Palace of the Sun, musicians of every sort filled the air with dazzling notes.

The god Smoking Mirror[1] envied this music, and he knew that the Sun would never share his prized possession with Earth. Therefore, Smoking Mirror lifted his voice to the air and shouted in every valley and cave for his friend Quetzalcoatl,[2] the feathered serpent who was also Lord of the Winds.

At a distance just beyond the horizon, Quetzalcoatl slumbered in silence. At the sound of Smoking Mirror's call, Quetzalcoatl slowly opened one eye and muttered with a sigh, "What does Smoking Mirror want now? Just as I find a dream, he finds a problem." With that being said, he whirled his serpent body 'round and stormed toward Smoking Mirror's ringing voice.

When Quetzalcoatl reached Smoking Mirror, he asked, "What is the matter now?" Smoking Mirror replied, "This morning, as I walked upon the bright and brilliant Earth that the two of us created, I realized that it is incomplete."

Quetzalcoatl responded doubtfully, "That is not so! There are beautiful creeks and colorful birds in the world! Don't you smell the fragrance of the rose or feel the soft grass beneath your feet?"

"I do," responded Smoking Mirror, "but there is no music! Earth cannot sing its joy when there is no music. That is why I must ask you to go to the Palace of the Sun and return with musicians who are able to spread music across Earth."

"The musicians are faithful servants of the Sun," replied Quetzalcoatl. "They will never leave him." Smoking Mirror remained silent. After a while, the silence began to bother Quetzalcoatl, and he realized the importance of music. So up he went, through the blue smoke of the sky, to the Palace of the Sun.

The Sun saw the Lord of the Winds coming and told his musicians that they must be very quiet, or the feathered serpent would carry them away to the dark and silent Earth. As Quetzalcoatl reached the palace, the glorious music stopped, and the musicians turned their instruments away from the feathered serpent.

But with his command over the wind, Quetzalcoatl brought forth fierce storm clouds that blocked the radiance of the Sun. He then produced his own light as a guide for the frightened musicians. Mistaking the serpent's light for the light of the Sun, the musicians stepped into Quetzalcoatl's embrace. The feathered serpent gently floated the musicians to Earth.

When the musicians saw Smoking Mirror, they knew instantly that they had been tricked. What they saw, however, was not the horrible place described by the Sun. Instead, Earth was full of wondrous colors and activity. It was still within reach of the Sun's warming rays. The musicians then embarked on journeys throughout the world. On their way, they taught the birds to sing, the brooks to babble, the leaves to rustle, and the people to make music of their very own.

Reading THE LITERATURE

What words and phrases give the reader a sense of Quetzalcoatl's personality? How does the author convey Quetzalcoatl's attitude toward the task Smoking Mirror gives him?

Thinking About THE LITERATURE

What does this folk tale suggest about the role of music in Aztec society? Why might this folk tale be popular in Mexico today?

Writing About THE LITERATURE

Write a dialogue involving the musicians, Quetzalcoatl, and the Sun, in which Quetzalcoatl tries to persuade the musicians to come with him to Earth and the Sun urges them to stay. As a class, compare and contrast the arguments each side makes.

Further Reading To learn about more Mexican stories, read *The Tree Is Older Than You Are*, edited by Naomi Shihab Nye.

TERMS & NAMES

Explain the significance of each of the following:

1. *criollo*
2. *mestizo*
3. Father Miguel Hidalgo
4. Treaty of Guadalupe Hidalgo
5. Benito Juárez
6. *hacienda*
7. *maquiladora*
8. PEMEX
9. Diego Rivera
10. fiesta

REVIEW QUESTIONS

The Roots of Modern Mexico *(pages 173–178)*

1. Why did Cortés need the help of some Native Americans to defeat Montezuma II?
2. How was Mexico's War of Independence connected to events elsewhere in the world at that time?

Government in Mexico: Revolution and Reform
(pages 179–184)

3. What concerns did Mexicans in the 1800s and 1900s have about land ownership?
4. What was unique about Mexico's presidential election in 2000?

Mexico's Changing Economy *(pages 185–189)*

5. Why has the *ejido* system been unsuccessful at ending poverty for many villagers?
6. What is the role of oil in Mexico's economy?

Mexico's Culture Today *(pages 190–194)*

7. What are some of the problems caused by Mexico City's rapid growth?
8. What event do Mexicans celebrate every September 16?

CRITICAL THINKING

Sequencing Events

1. Using your completed time line from Reading Social Studies, p. 172, list the points in Mexico's history when the nation's government changed drastically.

Forming and Supporting Opinions

2. Do you think the Mexican government's decision in the 1990s to privatize farming and business was a good one? Explain.

Hypothesizing

3. Modern artists, such as Diego Rivera and Octavio Paz, have used images from both Mexico's past and its present in their works. What do you think this says about the way Mexicans today view their nation's history?

Visual Summary

The Roots of Modern Mexico

1

- From 1810 to 1821, Mexico fought for and gained independence from Spain.

Government in Mexico: Revolution and Reform

2

- The Mexican Revolution (1910–1920) established a new government.
- Today, the government of Mexico is a federal republic.

Mexico's Changing Economy

3

- Farming is still an important part of Mexico's economy, but today its top businesses are oil production and tourism.

Mexico's Culture Today

4

- Mexico's culture combines its Native American and Spanish pasts with new elements.
- Mexico's holidays and arts show the influence of its history.

SOCIAL STUDIES SKILLBUILDER

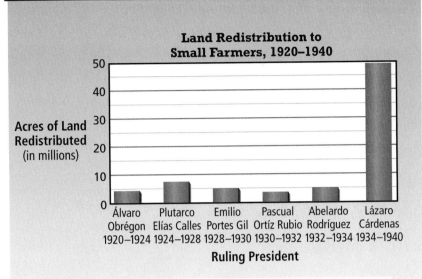

Land Redistribution to Small Farmers, 1920–1940

Acres of Land Redistributed (in millions)

Álvaro Obrégon 1920–1924
Plutarco Elías Calles 1924–1928
Emilio Portes Gil 1928–1930
Pascual Ortíz Rubio 1930–1932
Abelardo Rodríguez 1932–1934
Lázaro Cárdenas 1934–1940

Ruling President

SKILLBUILDER: Reading a Graph

1. What information does the bar graph present?

2. About how much land did President Cárdenas give to small farmers?

FOCUS ON GEOGRAPHY

1. Region • Where does more farming occur, in the north or south of Mexico?

2. Human-Environment Interaction • What are the most common uses of land in the north of Mexico?

3. Location • From looking at this map, why do you think Mexico City is located where it is?

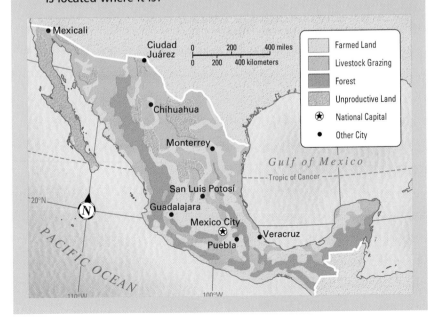

Mexicali

Ciudad Juárez

0   200   400 miles
0   200   400 kilometers

Chihuahua

Monterrey

San Luis Potosí

Guadalajara

Mexico City

Puebla

Veracruz

Gulf of Mexico

- - - Tropic of Cancer - - -

20°N

N

PACIFIC OCEAN

110°W   100°W

Legend:
- Farmed Land
- Livestock Grazing
- Forest
- Unproductive Land
- ⭐ National Capital
- • Other City

CHAPTER PROJECTS

Interdisciplinary Activity: Art

Making a Poster Research one of Mexico's holidays. Create a poster that explains the focus of the holiday and how it is celebrated. Include photographs or drawings with captions that illustrate various aspects of the holiday.

Cooperative Learning Activity

Creating a News Broadcast With a group of three to five students, create a news show about the experience of Mexicans during the Mexican Revolution. Choose a specific year between 1910 and 1920 and a specific location, such as the National Palace in Mexico City or a battlefront.

- Take on the role of anchor, reporter, or interviewee.
- Write a script for your role.
- Conduct your "broadcast" in front of the class.

INTERNET ACTIVITY

Use the Internet to do research about climate in Mexico. Focus on one region in Mexico, such as the southern mountains, and how that region's climate affects its people's way of life.

Writing About Geography Write a report of your findings. Include a map or a bar graph that visually presents information on Mexico's climate. List the Web sites you used to prepare your report.

For Internet links to support this activity, go to

RESEARCH LINKS
CLASSZONE.COM

CHAPTER

8

Central America and the Caribbean Islands

PACIFIC OCEAN

ATLANTIC OCEAN

PACIFIC OCEAN

OCEAN

INDIAN OCEAN

CENTRAL AMERICA AND THE CARIBBEAN ISLANDS

N

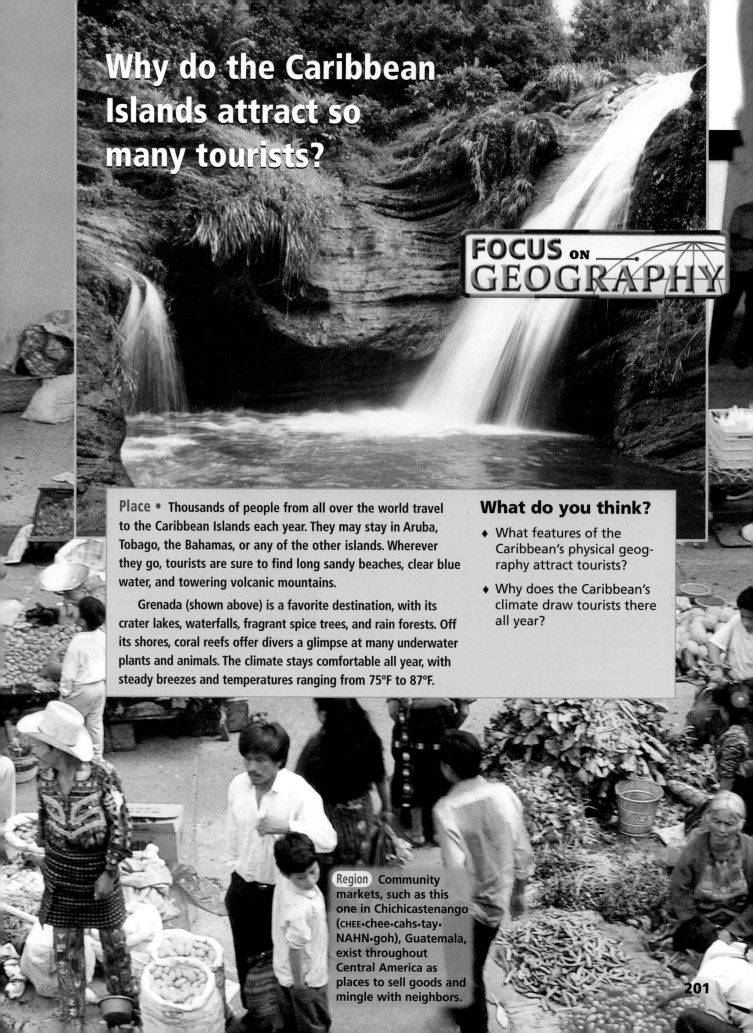

Why do the Caribbean Islands attract so many tourists?

FOCUS ON
GEOGRAPHY

Place • Thousands of people from all over the world travel to the Caribbean Islands each year. They may stay in Aruba, Tobago, the Bahamas, or any of the other islands. Wherever they go, tourists are sure to find long sandy beaches, clear blue water, and towering volcanic mountains.

Grenada (shown above) is a favorite destination, with its crater lakes, waterfalls, fragrant spice trees, and rain forests. Off its shores, coral reefs offer divers a glimpse at many underwater plants and animals. The climate stays comfortable all year, with steady breezes and temperatures ranging from 75°F to 87°F.

What do you think?

♦ What features of the Caribbean's physical geography attract tourists?

♦ Why does the Caribbean's climate draw tourists there all year?

Region Community markets, such as this one in Chichicastenango (CHEE·chee·cahs·tay·NAHN·goh), Guatemala, exist throughout Central America as places to sell goods and mingle with neighbors.

201

BEFORE YOU READ

▶▶ *What Do You Know?*

Before you read the chapter, think about what you already know about Central America and the Caribbean Islands. You may have heard Caribbean music like reggae. Perhaps you have seen colorful woven cloth from Central America. Do you know where the Panama Canal is? Have you heard of Fidel Castro?

▶▶ *What Do You Want to Know?*

Decide what else you want to know about Central America and the Caribbean Islands. In your notebook, record what you hope to learn from this chapter.

Place • This painting shows people working on a Caribbean sugar cane plantation. ▲

READ AND TAKE NOTES

Reading Strategy: Identifying Problems and Solutions Identifying problems and solutions is a useful strategy for increasing your understanding of what you read. You can make a chart that lists issues. In the chart, identify the problems with those issues and the solutions to the problems to better understand the issues.

- Copy the chart into your notebook.
- As you read the chapter, look for issues related to government and economy.
- Record the problems and solutions involved in each issue on your chart.

Culture • Cubans celebrate a holiday called Carnival. ◀

Issues	Problems	Solutions
Colonization (1492–1800s)		
The Panama Canal (1903–1914)		
Spanish-American War (1898)		
Dictatorships		
Economic Development		
U.S./Cuba Relations		
Civil War in Guatemala		

W N E S

Establishing Independence

TERMS & NAMES
West Indies
dependency
mulatto
ladino
dictator

MAIN IDEA

Central America and the Caribbean Islands have struggled to become independent nations with democratic governments.

WHY IT MATTERS NOW

The quest for democracy continues in Central America and the Caribbean, as it does elsewhere in the world today.

DATELINE

EXTRA

ST. DOMINGUE, CARIBBEAN ISLANDS, 1803

Word has arrived from France that François Dominique Toussaint L'Ouverture died there recently. He was taken to France last year to be imprisoned after leading the slave rebellion here in St. Domingue. The rebellion was so successful that St. Domingue seems just days away from declaring its independence once and for all.

Toussaint was given the nickname L'Ouverture, which means "opening" in French, because he always found an opening in enemy lines. His success in leading the rebellion is staggering when one realizes that his army of former slaves, mostly uneducated, defeated, in turn, the French, the British, and the Spanish.

Culture • Toussaint has become a hero to many. ▲

Central America and the Caribbean

Central America includes seven nations—Belize, Guatemala, Honduras, El Salvador, Nicaragua, Costa Rica, and Panama. Its neighbors—St. Domingue, now called Haiti, and the other islands of the Caribbean—are known as the **West Indies.** They include 13 nations and 11 dependencies. A **dependency** is a place that is governed by or closely connected with another country. For example, Puerto Rico is a dependency of the United States.

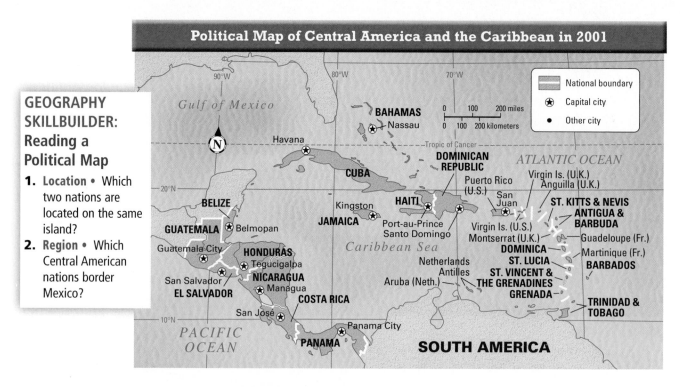

Political Map of Central America and the Caribbean in 2001

GEOGRAPHY SKILLBUILDER: Reading a Political Map

1. **Location** • Which two nations are located on the same island?
2. **Region** • Which Central American nations border Mexico?

Peoples of the Caribbean When Christopher Columbus reached the West Indies in 1492, about 750,000 Native Americans lived there. The Europeans who took over forced Native Americans to work on plantations and in mines. The harsh labor, plus European diseases unknown in the Americas, killed many Native Americans. Others died in battles with the Europeans. Within a few years, nearly all the Native Americans on the islands had died.

Without Native Americans to use for labor, European rulers looked for a new source of workers. By the 1520s, the Spanish began bringing shiploads of enslaved Africans to the West Indies. Other European nations joined in the slave trade. From the 1500s to the mid-1800s, about 10 million enslaved Africans arrived in the West Indies. As a result, many people in the Caribbean today are **mulattos** (mu·LAT·ohz), or people who have African and European ancestry. Few Caribbean people have Native American ancestry.

BACKGROUND

About 75 million people live in Central America and the Caribbean today.

Region • Like this man, many Caribbean people are of African descent. ▼

Central American People In Central America, the situation for the Native Americans was different. When the Spanish arrived in 1501, many Native Americans withdrew to the inland mountains and thus survived what proved to be a deadly encounter with the Spanish elsewhere. Today, one-fifth of Central Americans are Native Americans.

Reading
Social Studies

A. Finding Causes How did geography help the Native Americans in Central America survive the arrival of Europeans?

The slave ships also arrived in Central America, bringing Africans to the region. Africans from the Caribbean also migrated to the area. As the years passed, the Spanish, Native Americans, and Africans intermarried. Those people with mixed European and Native American ancestry are called *ladinos* (luh·DEE·naws), and they make up about two-thirds of Central America's population today.

From Colonies to Independence

From the 1500s to the 1800s, European nations ruled Central America and the West Indies as colonies. These differed from the dependencies of today. Usually, a dependency is free to break off its connection to the other country, but a colony must either win its independence or be granted it.

The Lure of Gold and Sugar Spain was the first European country to colonize this region. Soon, however, the French, Dutch, and English set up their own colonies in the islands. While they found the gold they were looking for, they also found another source of wealth—sugar. Soon many of the islands were home to sugar plantations. Most of the workers who grew and cut the sugar cane were enslaved.

Becoming Independent By the 1800s, the people of Central America and the Caribbean Islands began to demand their independence. In 1804, the French colony of St. Domingue became the first nation in the region to win independence.

Other nations soon followed St. Domingue's example. In 1821, Guatemala, Honduras, Costa Rica, and Nicaragua declared independence from Spain. At first they united, but since 1839, they have existed as separate nations.

Relations with the United States

The United States of America is the largest neighbor of Central America and the West Indies. U.S. policies have long played a part in shaping the region's history.

Region • Central Americans today reflect the region's rich mix of cultures and people. ▲

BACKGROUND

After independence, St. Domingue took a new name—Haiti (HAY·tee).

The WORLD'S HERITAGE

Reggae After the Caribbean island of Jamaica gained independence from Britain in 1962, musicians such as Bob Marley (shown below) developed a new style of music called reggae (REHG·ay). Today, reggae is popular around the world. It is known for its political messages.

With their lyrics, the early reggae singers commented on social and economic problems. Reggae is enjoyed both for pleasure and for its ability to let the poor and the oppressed make their voices heard. Music has played a similar role in many cultures throughout history.

Central America and the Caribbean Islands **205**

The Panama Canal Until the early 1900s, people who wanted to travel from one side of North or South America to the other had two choices. They could make the long, dangerous trip by land or sail all the way around South America. Because the Isthmus of Panama is about 40 miles wide, by 1900, first France, then the United States were eager to build a canal across it to connect the two oceans.

At that time, Panama was part of the South American nation of Colombia. The United States tried to buy from Colombia a strip of land on the isthmus. Colombia refused, and so the United States urged the people of Panama to break away. Soon, Panama did revolt. After establishing its own country in 1903, Panama agreed to lease the United States land to build a canal. The canal opened in 1914 and soon became one of the most important transportation routes in the world. Now ships only had to sail the 50 miles from one end of the canal to the other.

Human-Environment Interaction • **By using the Panama Canal, ships save 2,000 to 8,000 miles, depending on where they start and end their trips.** ▲

The Spanish-American War Long after Central America broke free of Spanish rule, Spain continued to control Cuba and Puerto Rico. During the late 1800s, the islanders there rebelled many times but were not able to gain independence.

In 1898, the United States declared war on Spain. It did so partly because it wanted to help the people of Cuba and Puerto Rico gain freedom from Spain. However, the United States also wanted to protect the many sugar cane plantations that U.S. businesses owned on the islands. By the end of the war, which lasted less than a year, Spain had lost its last colonies in the Americas. Puerto Rico became a U.S. dependency, a territory under the control of another nation. Cuba became an independent country, but the U.S. military set up bases there and kept tight control over the country.

Reading
Social Studies

B. Recognizing Effects How did world affairs in the late 1800s affect the Caribbean?

Place • **The United States controlled the Panama Canal and the land around it until December 31, 1999, when control passed to Panama.** ▶

Dictatorships and Democracy

Independence did not necessarily bring freedom to the people of Central America and the West Indies. Only Costa Rica has been a democracy since the beginning of the 20th century.

Dictatorships Nearly all the other countries have spent many years under the rule of dictators. A **dictator** is a person who has complete control over a country's government. At times, dictators ruled Guatemala, Honduras, Panama, El Salvador, Haiti, and the Dominican Republic. Dictators often used violence to grab and keep power.

Hopes for Democracy Most countries in Central America and the West Indies now have democratically elected governments. The people of these countries removed most of their dictators, one by one. For example, in 1990, Nicaraguans replaced dictatorial rule by electing Violetta Barrios de Chamorro (vee·oh·LE·tuh BA·ree·ohs day chah·MOH·roh) as president. However, elected leaders sometimes refuse to give up power, thus becoming dictators. Sometimes, elections are not run fairly. Nevertheless, freedom is more widespread than it was 50 years ago.

Culture •
Nicaragua's first female president, Violetta Barrios de Chamorro, governed from 1990 to 1996. ▲

SECTION 1 ASSESSMENT

Terms & Names

1. **Identify:**
   (a) West Indies
   (b) dependency
   (c) mulatto
   (d) *ladino*
   (e) dictator

Taking Notes

2. Use a chart like this one to note the effects Europeans had on the Native American populations in Central America and the Caribbean.

In Central America	In the Caribbean

Main Ideas

3. (a) Why are there more Native Americans in Central America today than in the Caribbean?

   (b) Describe the difference between dependencies and colonies.

   (c) List two reasons why the United States declared war on Spain.

Critical Thinking

4. **Identifying Problems**

   Why have some countries in Central America and the Caribbean had trouble establishing democracies?

   Think About

   • the region's history of being controlled by other countries and dictatorship

   • the powers and resources of dictators

ACTIVITY -OPTION- Imagine you lived on the island that became Haiti in 1804. Write a short **biography** of your island's hero, François Dominique Toussaint L'Ouverture.

Building Economies and Cultures

TERMS & NAMES
sugar cane
single-product economy
diversify

MAIN IDEA

The economies and cultures of this region reflect both the colonial past and efforts to modernize.

WHY IT MATTERS NOW

Though small in size, the region exports its culture and products to the United States and beyond.

◁ ▷ ✕ ⇄ ⌂
Back Forward Stop Refresh Home

Address: ▸ go

DATELINE

TEGUCIGALPA, HONDURAS, 1998—
A devastating hurricane hit Central America this week, reminding people that live here of the dangers of having an economy based mainly on agriculture. In addition to about 10,000 deaths, Honduras faces the loss of 70 percent of its crops to the hurricane's ferocious winds.

For example, the banana industry, which brings in $200 million for Hondurans each year, was nearly wiped out. Honduran president Carlos Roberto Flores Facusse described the horrific results of Hurricane Mitch: "In 72 hours, we saw what took as much as 50 years to build… destroyed."

Human-Environment Interaction • Many houses have been destroyed by Hurricane Mitch. ▲

The Economies of the Caribbean Islands

In the Caribbean, the economies of most islands have depended on growing one or two crops to sell to other countries. However, the islanders have also worked hard to create new businesses as well as new industries.

Human-
Environment
Interaction •
**Many Caribbean
islanders spent
their days
planting and
then harvesting
sugar cane.** ▲

The Colonial Period For most of the colonial period, the Caribbean Islands focused mainly on one industry—growing **sugar cane**. From the 1600s to the 1800s, most islanders worked on sugar cane plantations. In the early years, the majority of these workers were enslaved. Even after slavery ended by the late 1800s, most workers owned no land of their own. Instead, they planted, tended, and cut sugar cane on plantations owned by the wealthy.

During the colonial period, most of the islands traded only with their ruling countries. Cuba, for example, sold its sugar to Spain and bought goods from Spain in return. But after the colonial period ended, many of the islands traded mostly with the United States.

Single-Product Economies Sugar was so valuable that plantation owners raised few other crops. Most did not even grow food. Many of the islands had to buy almost all their food from other countries. A country that depends on just one product for almost all its jobs and income has a **single-product economy**.

Economies Must Change A single-product economy can be unstable—if something happens to that single product, the country's economy will be ruined. By the late 1800s, the sugar business in the West Indies was in trouble. People raising sugar cane in other parts of the world offered the West Indies fierce competition. Steam-powered machines allowed these foreigners to process sugar cane at lower prices. The people of the West Indies had to find new ways to make a living.

Reading
Social Studies

A. Analyzing Issues Why did production of sugar elsewhere in the world affect the economies of the Caribbean?

The islanders found they needed to diversify their economies. To **diversify** an economy means to invest in a variety of industries. People began to raise other crops, such as pineapples and bananas. Industries, such as textiles, medical supplies, and electronic equipment, also developed in the Caribbean.

Percentage of Tourism in GDP, 1997–1999

BAHAMAS

ANTIGUA AND BARBUDA

CUBA

ST. KITTS AND NEVIS

BELIZE

GUATEMALA

HAITI

DOMINICAN REPUBLIC

DOMINICA

HONDURAS

JAMAICA

EL SALVADOR

NICARAGUA

ST. LUCIA

COSTA RICA

ST. VINCENT & THE GRENADINES

BARBADOS

PANAMA

GRENADA

TRINIDAD AND TOBAGO

■ Each square equals 1 percent contribution of tourism to the GDP

GEOGRAPHY SKILLBUILDER: Interpreting a Map

Human-Environment Interaction • In this cartogram, countries with a greater percentage of GDP coming from tourism are larger than countries with a smaller percentage. In which country does tourism make up the greatest percentage of GDP?

Citizenship IN ACTION

María Elena Cuadra Movement
In Central America, poverty and unemployment are widespread. In Nicaragua, many women take jobs in factories, like the one shown here, under poor conditions and for low wages.

Since 1994, the María Elena Cuadra Movement of Working and Unemployed Women (MEC) has been working to improve the position of women at work and in the home. MEC protects workers' rights, trains women in new skills, and lends money to women to start their own small businesses.

Tourism Takes Hold One of the most important industries in the Caribbean Islands is tourism. With warm weather and beautiful beaches, the islands attract tourists from around the world. About 8 million tourists flock there each year. On some of the smaller islands, such as Antigua, tourism is now the major industry.

The Economies of Central America

After the Spanish Central American countries became independent in the 1820s, they wanted to increase their trade with other nations. To do so, they needed to develop exports. During the 1800s, several Central American countries began to produce coffee. Soon it became an important export crop for Costa Rica, Guatemala, Honduras, El Salvador, and Nicaragua. In exchange for their exports, Central American countries purchased imports from other parts of the world.

The United States Steps In In the late 1800s, a major new export business got started in Central America. U.S.-based United Fruit Company (UFCO) set up huge banana plantations in the hot, wet lowlands of Central America.

UFCO did a huge amount of business, and bananas became another important Central American product.

Two Crops Are Not Enough The Central American economies grew to depend on bananas and coffee. Whenever the price of these items on the world market fell, Central Americans faced hardship. Like the Caribbean islanders, Central Americans wanted to diversify their economies.

B. Making Inferences
What are some factors that would cause the price of a product on the world market to fall?

Central American countries have worked to build more factories. Costa Rica, for example, has factories that make machinery, furniture, cloth, and medicine. The countries of the region have also developed tourism as an industry. Visitors arrive by the thousands in Guatemala to see the spectacular ruins of Maya temples. As different businesses grow, Central Americans will not be as dependent on agriculture as they were in the past.

Region •
Coffee grows well in the cool highlands of Central America. ▲

Caribbean Cultures

Each country in the Caribbean has its own particular way of life. Native American, African, and European influences blend differently from place to place.

Languages In the Caribbean, people speak a variety of languages. These reflect the area's history. Look at page 145 of the Unit Atlas to see which languages are spoken in which areas.

Religions Roman Catholicism is the most widespread religion in the West Indies. However, many islanders practice religions that have African influences. In Haiti, elements of Catholic and African religious practices combine in the religion known as voodoo.

Strange but TRUE

A Language Lives On When Europeans arrived on the Caribbean island of St. Vincent in 1635, they encountered a startling mystery. The women of St. Vincent spoke one language, and the men spoke another.

Originally, they all spoke the Arawak language. However, when speakers of the Carib language attacked the Arawak-speaking islands, most of the Arawak-speaking men were killed. Only the female Arawak speakers survived.

The Arawakan women continued to speak their language, while the conquering men spoke the Carib language. Today, the language inherited from the Arawakan women is called Garífuna. Like the woman at the right, 30,000 people living on the Caribbean coast of Central America still speak it.

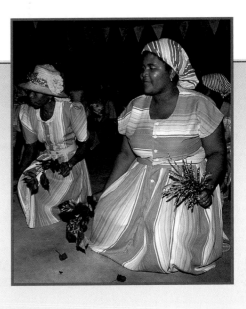

In Cuba, Yoruba beliefs from Africa combine with Catholic beliefs in the religion called Santeria. In Trinidad, the Shango religion blends Catholic, Baptist, and West African beliefs.

Music Music, too, shows a blending of cultures. From Cuban salsa to Jamaican reggae, much Caribbean music combines African and European styles to make something completely new. The rap music that is popular in the United States also has Caribbean roots. Some of the first rappers to perform in the United States introduced to this country the Jamaican technique of mixing together tracks from different songs.

Central American Cultures

The countries of Central America share a common history. In their cultures, the Native American and Spanish heritages blend.

Languages Look again at the map on page 145. You can see that in most of Central America, people speak Spanish. Central Americans also speak about 80 Native American languages, nearly half of which are Maya languages.

Spotlight on CULTURE

Merengue Dancing is a popular pastime in Latin America. One of the favorite dances (and the national dance of the Dominican Republic) is the merengue (*shown below*). This dance form originated in the neighboring nations of Haiti and the Dominican Republic. It is known for its unique dance step, called a sliding step, in which the dancer always rests his or her weight on the same foot. People commonly explain this step with one of two legends. One legend says that enslaved people developed the step while chained to one another at the leg. Another legend has it that a Dominican war hero, wounded in the leg during a revolt, designed the step. Whatever the true story behind the dance, the merengue did arise as a folk dance in rural areas. Later it became a favorite of ballroom dancers.

THINKING CRITICALLY

1. **Drawing Conclusions**
   What do the two legends about the origins of the merengue's sliding step tell you about the significance of dancing in Latin American culture?

2. **Synthesizing**
   What different roles do you think dancing can play in a culture?

Religions Catholicism is the most widespread religion in Central America. In recent years, however, millions of Central Americans have become Protestants and Mormons. Also, some ancient Maya religious beliefs still thrive. An example is the companion spirit. Maya people today believe that when a person is born, so is an animal. That animal, the companion spirit, lives through the same experiences as the person does. A person usually learns about his or her companion spirit in dreams.

Crafts Many Central American towns are known for their crafts, such as weaving, embroidery, pottery, silversmithing, and basketmaking. Many of the styles and methods used originated with ancient Native Americans. For example, many weavers use a backstrap loom—a 2,000-year-old device consisting of threads that are attached to a fixed post or tree on one end and a belt on the other end.

Culture • **By wearing the belt around her waist, the weaver stretches the threads tight to weave on them.** ▲

SECTION 2 ASSESSMENT

Terms & Names

1. Identify: (a) sugar cane (b) single-product economy (c) diversify

Taking Notes

2. Use a chart like this one to check off the languages spoken in each region, country, or island mentioned in the text.

	Guatemala	Haiti
Native American		
Spanish		
French		
English		

Main Ideas

3. (a) List some ways in which sugar production affected the lives of Caribbean people.

(b) How have Central American countries diversified their economies?

(c) How do the religions in Central America and the Caribbean reflect the regions' histories?

Critical Thinking

4. Forming and Supporting Opinions
How do you think the success of a foreign-owned company affects a country?

Think About

- the importance of UFCO's product to Central American economies
- the jobs created by a successful company
- who receives the company's profits

ACTIVITY -OPTION- A country with a single-product economy risks losing a great deal if that product fails. Make a **chart** of the factors that put the country in this risky position but that it cannot control.

Reading a Political Map

▶▶ Defining the Skill

Political maps show the boundaries of nations and other political areas, such as dependencies. Lines show these boundaries. Often political maps also show capitals and other cities.

▶▶ Applying the Skill

The political map at right shows the nations of Central America. Use the strategies listed below to identify the information shown on the map.

How to Read a Political Map

Strategy ❶ Read the title. It tells you which region's political areas are being represented.

Strategy ❷ Read the key. It tells you what each symbol stands for. This key shows boundaries between nations, national capitals, and other cities.

Strategy ❸ Read the scale. It tells you how many miles or kilometers each inch represents.

Make a Chart

A chart can help you organize information given on maps. The chart below organizes information about the map you just studied.

▶▶ Practicing the Skill

Turn to Chapter 8, Section 1, "Establishing Independence." Study the political map of Central America and the Caribbean on page 204. Make a chart listing the nations of the Caribbean and the capitals that are shown on the map.

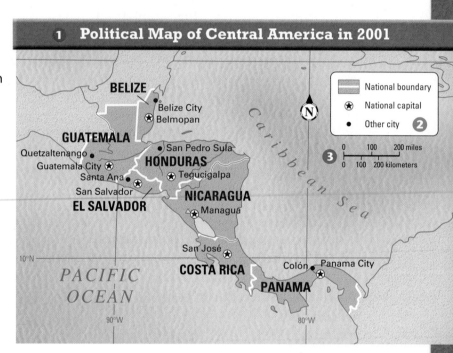

❶ Political Map of Central America in 2001

Key:
National boundary
⊛ National capital
● Other city ❷

❸ 0 100 200 miles / 0 100 200 kilometers

BELIZE — Belize City, Belmopan
GUATEMALA — Quetzaltenango, Guatemala City, San Pedro Sula, HONDURAS, Santa Ana, San Salvador, Tegucigalpa, EL SALVADOR, NICARAGUA, Managua
San José, COSTA RICA, Colón, Panama City, PANAMA
Caribbean Sea
PACIFIC OCEAN
10°N, 90°W, 80°W

Central America		
Countries	Capitals	Other Cities
Guatemala	Guatemala City	Quetzaltenango
Belize	Belmopan	Belize City
Honduras	Tegucigalpa	San Pedro Sula
El Salvador	San Salvador	Santa Ana
Nicaragua	Managua	
Costa Rica	San José	
Panama	Panama City	Colón

Cuba Today

TERMS & NAMES
José Martí
Fidel Castro
Communism
malnutrition
Carnival

MAIN IDEA

After Cuba became independent, the country was ruled by a series of dictators. Since 1959, revolutionary leader Fidel Castro has ruled the nation.

WHY IT MATTERS NOW

At the turn of the century, Cuba was the only Communist country in the Western Hemisphere.

DATELINE

SIERRA MAESTRA, CUBA, 1956—Word has leaked out that revolutionary leader Fidel Castro has returned to Cuba. Three years ago, he received a 15-year prison sentence for leading an attack on the government. He was released early, a year ago, at which time he fled to Mexico to organize a group of revolutionaries.

Sources say that he and about 80 of his followers have returned to Cuba, though many of them were killed or captured upon arrival. The rest are hiding out in the Sierra Maestra, mountains in southeastern Cuba. People have been speculating about what kind of revolution may develop now that Castro is back in Cuba.

Place • While hiding deep in the Sierra Maestra, Castro is organizing his followers for revolution. ▲

Independence and Revolution

Long after Mexico and Central America gained independence, Cuba, the largest island in the Caribbean, still suffered Spanish rule. In 1895, Cubans led by **José Martí** continued fighting for the nation's independence. Three years later, the Spanish-American War reached the island. By the end of the war, Cuba had gained its independence from Spain. However, the United States maintained great influence over the nation.

Connections to Science

Partners Against Disease

A partnership between the United States and Cuba helped save Cubans from serious diseases, especially malaria and yellow fever. These illnesses killed or weakened many people each year.

In 1900, Dr. Carlos Finlay from Cuba and Dr. Walter Reed from the United States worked together to find the cause of yellow fever. They learned that mosquitoes like the one shown below spread the disease, just as they do malaria. To help put an end to these diseases, the U.S. Army sprayed chemicals that killed off the mosquitoes.

U.S. Ties to Cuba Before the Spanish-American War, the United States wanted to add Cuba to the nation. After the Spanish-American War ended, the United States appointed a military governor for Cuba. From 1899 to 1902, the U.S. Army stayed in Cuba to keep peace and help set up a new government. Most Cubans resented the U.S. presence. However, during these years, Cubans and U.S. soldiers did build many needed roads, bridges, and public schools.

In 1902, the U.S. Army withdrew from Cuba, which then became independent. However, the United States insisted that it still had the right to send soldiers to Cuba any time. The U.S. Navy also kept a large base for its ships at Guantánamo Bay.

Time of Dictatorship After independence, Cuba had a series of leaders. Some were elected, and some took power by force. Most governed as dictators. Cuba's dictators were careful to stay friendly with the United States. They welcomed U.S. businesses and tourists. Havana, Cuba's capital, offered tourists luxury hotels and casinos. Most Cubans, however, remained poor.

Revolution Takes Hold Time and again, Cubans protested against the dictators. In the 1950s, Cubans who were angry at the government found a leader for their cause. He was a young lawyer named **Fidel Castro.** Born in 1927 to a wealthy family, Castro was known for being a dynamic speaker. In college, he developed a deep interest in politics. By late 1956, Castro and a few followers had established headquarters for their revolution in the mountains of southeastern Cuba.

Reading Social Studies

A. Drawing Conclusions If Cubans resented the U.S. presence in Cuba, why did their dictators stay friendly with the United States?

Culture • The two extremes of life in Cuba are apparent in this contrast of one of Havana's fancy hotels with one Cuban's simple dwelling. ▼

A few at a time, Cubans began to join Castro's small army. The rebel army won several battles against government troops. As the revolution grew stronger, Cuba's dictator, Fulgencio Batista (fool·HEHN·see·oh buh·TEES·tuh), fled the country on January 1, 1959. On January 8, 1959, Castro and his followers marched triumphantly into Havana. More than half a million Cubans greeted them joyfully. In a speech to the crowds, Castro promised that Cuba would have no more dictators.

The revolution had succeeded. Castro became the new commander-in-chief of Cuba's army. By July 1959, he had taken full control of Cuba's government.

A VOICE FROM CUBA

We cannot ever become dictators. Those who do not have the people with them must resort to being dictators. We have the love of the people, and because of that love, we will never turn away from our principles.

Fidel Castro

Cuba in the Cold War Castro took power in Cuba during the Cold War—a period of conflict between the United States and the Soviet Union. Castro needed the friendship of a powerful country. The Soviet Union was eager to have Cuba as an ally. It proved its interest in the smaller country by engaging in large-scale trade with Cuba as well as providing Cuba with weapons. This attention helped Castro choose to side with the Soviet Union in the Cold War.

Human-Environment Interaction • One of Castro's Communist policies was to take government control of farms, such as this one. ▼

Cuba Becomes a Communist Country The Soviet Union practiced an economic and political system known as **Communism.** Under this system, the government plans and controls a country's economy—in effect, the government owns the country's farms, factories, and businesses. Soon, Castro began to adopt Communist policies for Cuba's economy. His government took over the big sugar cane plantations, many of which had been owned by U.S. companies. His government then took over U.S. banks, oil refineries, and other businesses on the island.

In return, the United States cut off all trade with Cuba. Cubans could no longer sell their huge sugar crop to the United States. Instead, the Soviet Union bought Cuba's sugar. The Soviet government also sent weapons, farm machinery, food, and money to Cuba. In 1961, Castro declared that he and Cuba were Communist.

Castro as Dictator While the poor usually supported Castro's policies, many wealthier Cubans did not. They were particularly upset when he redistributed land so that no family or farm owned more than a certain amount. Castro also imprisoned people who spoke out against him. As a result, Cubans who opposed Castro began to flee to the United States and other countries. Over the years, hundreds of thousands of people left Cuba.

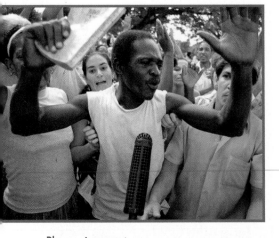

Castro has kept a tight hold on power for more than 40 years. Without ever being elected, he has remained head of state. His government has controlled all newspapers and radio and television stations. No one has been allowed to criticize his actions or the government. Despite his 1959 promise, Castro became a dictator.

Place • **In recent years, Cubans like these have continued to protest Castro's policies.** ▲

Reading
Social Studies

B. Clarifying
What actions did Castro take that went against his 1959 promise?

Cuba's Economy

Since the Cuban revolution, the Cuban economy has changed in many ways. Since the collapse of the Soviet Union in 1991, Cuba has struggled to maintain its Communist way of life without Soviet aid.

Sugar and the Economy Sugar is Cuba's most important product in the world economy. The yearly sugar cane harvest is a key event for Cuba's economy. Once, workers with machetes cut the tough canes by hand. Then, with Soviet help, Castro's government bought huge machines to cut most of the cane. The cane harvest grew to record size.

While the Soviet Union was powerful, it traded oil, grain, and machinery with Cuba for sugar. Most of these products were worth more than sugar, so the Soviet Union was, in large part, supporting Cuba's economy.

Vocabulary
machete: large, wide-bladed knife

Living in Cuba

As with the economy, ways of life in Cuba have been greatly affected by Communism. Both education and health care reflect these changes.

Culture • These Cuban children sing their national anthem together at school. ▲

Education After the revolution, Cuba's government set up many new schools. In the 1960s, teachers and even school-children went into small villages to teach those who could not read or write. Many older people who had never had the chance to go to school learned to read for the first time.

Today, Cuban children must go to public school from ages 6 to 12. They can choose whether to continue their education after that. All schools are free, including college. Besides their academic subjects, students must take classes that teach Communist beliefs.

Health Care Like education, all health care in Cuba is paid for by the government. Cuba's health care system is probably the largest in Latin America. Every small village has a clinic.

However, Cuba had economic problems in the 1990s that affected both education and health care. Lack of fuel for buses and cars prevented some children from getting to school.

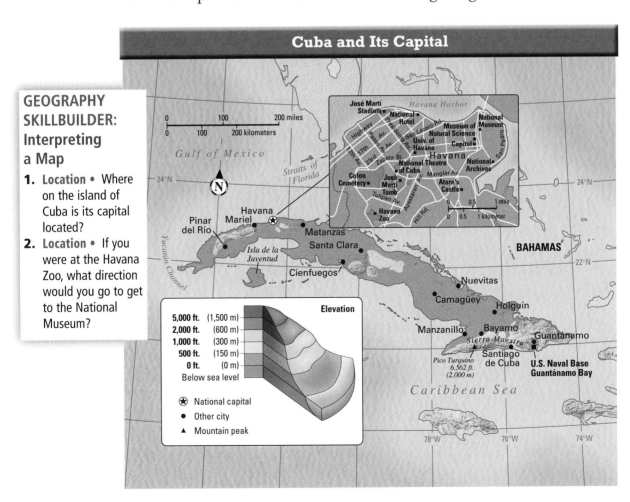

GEOGRAPHY SKILLBUILDER: Interpreting a Map

1. **Location** • Where on the island of Cuba is its capital located?

2. **Location** • If you were at the Havana Zoo, what direction would you go to get to the National Museum?

Food shortages caused malnutrition. **Malnutrition** is poor health due to a lack of eating the right kinds of food. It often causes sickness. From the 1960s to the 1980s, Cuba had almost wiped out malnutrition. Since 1990, malnutrition has again become a problem in Cuba.

Arts, Sports, and Holidays

Both Castro's government and earlier dictators have placed strict limits on what artists, writers, and filmmakers may say in their work. As a result, some Cubans have fled to other countries in search of greater freedom of expression.

However, some art forms thrive in Cuba. Music is part of everyday life there. The unique sound of Cuban music combines African drums and Spanish guitars. Each different style and rhythm has its own name—son, mambo, cha-cha, rumba, salsa.

Sports are also popular in Cuba. The nation's favorite sport is baseball. Cuba's baseball team won a gold medal at the Olympics in 1996.

A favorite Cuban holiday, **Carnival,** takes place each year at the end of July. Cities and villages celebrate the end of the sugar harvest with festivals filled with music and dancing.

Culture • During Carnival, the air fills with the lively music played by musicians such as these drummers. ▲

SECTION 3 ASSESSMENT

Terms & Names

1. Identify: (a) José Martí   (b) Fidel Castro   (c) Communism   (d) malnutrition   (e) Carnival

Taking Notes

2. Use a diagram like this one to show the stages Cuba's government has gone through.

```
┌──────────────┐   ┌──────┐   ┌──────┐
│ Fight for    │ → │      │ → │      │ →
│ independence │   │      │   │      │
└──────────────┘   └──────┘   └──────┘
```

Main Ideas

3. (a) What U.S. actions caused Cubans to resent the United States?

(b) Describe how Fidel Castro instituted Communism in Cuba.

(c) How was the Cuban economy once dependent on the Soviet Union?

Critical Thinking

4. **Drawing Conclusions**

Why might some Cubans think Castro has helped their nation and others think he has hurt it?

Think About

  ◆ Cuba's possible trade partners
  ◆ Cuba's health care system
  ◆ Cuba's education policies

ACTIVITY -OPTION-   Reread the sections about the U.S. ties to Cuba. Then make a **poster** displaying information about the relationship.

Guatemala Today

TERMS & NAMES
Rafael Carrera
Jacobo Arbenz Guzmán
departamento

MAIN IDEA

The establishment of a stable government in Guatemala has been a struggle, causing much suffering along the way.

WHY IT MATTERS NOW

Guatemala's increased stability has improved its relationship with its neighbors, such as the United States.

Back   Forward   Stop   Refresh   Home

Address: ▶ go

DATELINE

GUATEMALA CITY, GUATEMALA, DECEMBER 28, 1996
Tonight, Guatemala City is celebrating. However, the festivities don't mark a holiday or a party. They are, instead, signs of the historic action that will take place here tomorrow.

Guatemala's leaders will join their opponents in signing a peace agreement that will end a civil war that killed more than 100,000 Guatemalans over the past four decades. Finally, hopes for peace have arrived in the country that has suffered through Latin America's longest-lasting and most deadly civil war.

Place • Many Guatemalans expressed relief and appreciation when they heard about the peace agreement. ▶

History of Government

In 1821, along with three other Central American states, Guatemala gained independence from Spain. It broke from the other states in 1839 to become the nation we know today. Between 1821 and 1839, peasants in the mountains had staged revolts against the government. In 1837, an uneducated farmer, **Rafael Carrera** (rah·fy·EHL kuh·REHR·uh), led a revolt and emerged as a new leader for Guatemala. In 1854, he took over the presidency, which he held until his death in 1865.

From Dictatorial Rule to Reforms After Carrera died, a steady flow of dictators filled Guatemala's presidency. In 1944, a set of military officers revolted and won control of the nation. One of these officers, **Jacobo Arbenz Guzmán** (YAH·koh·boh AHR·bayns gooz·MAHN), saw the need for social reforms in Guatemala. When he became president in 1951, Guzmán decided to develop a market economy and raise Guatemala's standard of living. Guzmán also redistributed 1.5 million acres of land to 100,000 families. As in Mexico, the goal of redistributing land was to give many more people access to land that they could farm.

Place • Born in 1913, Jacobo Arbenz Guzmán was president of Guatemala from 1951 to 1954. ▲

U.S. Ties to Guatemala Serious opposition to Guzmán's redistribution program arose in the United States. Both United Fruit Company and the U.S. government owned much land in Guatemala. Guzmán established a policy of giving farmers any land that was not already being used. Eighty-five percent of UFCO's land in Guatemala was unused. Thus, UFCO was at great risk of losing that land.

The United States Steps In The United States took action in 1954. Accusing Guzmán of supporting Communism—a political system that the United States believed threatened national safety—the U.S. Central Intelligence Agency (CIA) supported an invasion of Guatemala's capital, Guatemala City. A Guatemalan colonel, Carlos Castillo Armas (CAR·lohs kah·STEE·yoh AR·mahs), led the attack. A frightened Guzmán quickly gave in. A new government, backed by the United States, took control of Guatemala.

Place • Rebel forces in Guatemala have included thousands of *ladinos* and Maya people. ▼

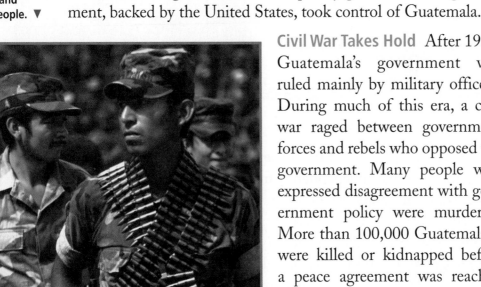

Civil War Takes Hold After 1954, Guatemala's government was ruled mainly by military officers. During much of this era, a civil war raged between government forces and rebels who opposed the government. Many people who expressed disagreement with government policy were murdered. More than 100,000 Guatemalans were killed or kidnapped before a peace agreement was reached in 1996.

Reading
Social Studies

A. Synthesizing Given the opposition to the new government after Guzmán's overthrow, do you think it continued social reforms?

Guatemala's Government Today

Guatemala's current constitution was written in 1985. It established the nation's government as a democratic republic with three branches. They are executive, legislative, and judicial.

Government's Three Branches A president heads Guatemala's executive branch. He or she is elected by the people every four years and may not be reelected. The president appoints a cabinet, or a group of advisers, to carry out the government's work.

Location •
Since the 1930s, Guatemala City's National Palace has housed the government's offices. ▲

Guatemala's legislative branch is called Congress. It has 113 members who are elected to four-year terms. Guatemala's Congress is unicameral, or has one chamber. Members of Congress may be reelected.

Guatemala's judicial branch has different levels of courts, somewhat like the United States. Unlike U.S. Supreme Court justices, whom the President appoints to serve for as long as they choose, Guatemala's Supreme Court judges are elected to five-year terms.

State and Local Governments Guatemala is a federal republic, so the national government shares power with state and local governments. Governors head Guatemala's 22 states, called _departamentos_ (deh·pahr·tah·MEHN·taws). The president appoints each of the governors. Mayors elected by popular vote oversee the city governments.

Guatemala's Economy

At the turn of the century, Guatemala had the largest gross domestic product (GDP) in Central America. It also had the fastest growing GDP in the region.

Agriculture Guatemala's dominant industry is agriculture, which employs more than half of its work force. The nation's economy largely relies on the export of agricultural products. Since 1870, coffee has been Guatemala's leading export. Other agricultural exports include sugar, a spice called cardamom, and bananas.

Banana production began in the early 1900s, when U.S. companies built banana plantations in Guatemala. These fruit companies also developed railroads, ports, and communication systems in order to transport the bananas to foreign markets.

Other Parts of the Economy Guatemala also relies on manufacturing to bring in money. Food, beverages, and clothing are among its manufactured goods. These goods are sold both within Guatemala and as exports to other countries. While other Central American nations purchase many of Guatemala's manufactured goods, the United States purchases more of Guatemala's exports than any other country does.

In past years, Guatemala's economy has boomed with the sale of both textiles and clothing. Also, new nontraditional agricultural products, such as cut flowers and winter fruits, are selling quite well on the international market. Tourism is also a strong industry in Guatemala, which is home to many ancient Maya ruins.

Human-Environment Interaction • Bananas are produced in mass quantity on Guatemala's many banana plantations. ▲

Living in Guatemala

More than half of Guatemala's people are Maya. The rest are *ladinos*. In Guatemala, *ladinos* are either of mixed Maya and Spanish ancestry, or they are of Maya ancestry but no longer practice Maya ways or speak Maya languages. Like the ancient Maya, most of Guatemala's Maya today work in agriculture and live in small rural villages. They speak Maya languages, though many of them also speak Spanish. They wear traditional clothing, much of which they weave by hand.

Education Guatemalan children are required to attend school from the age of 7 through 13. However, about one-third do not. Most of these children live in rural areas that have no schools. Only 15 percent of Guatemalans attend high school.

Reading
Social Studies

B. Clarifying
Does Guatemala have a single-product economy? Why or why not?

Place •
Standing nearly 150 feet high, this Maya temple at Tikal is one of Guatemala's major tourist attractions. ▼

Culture • This Guatemalan woman sells many traditional Maya handwoven cloths. ▲

Two Sides of Guatemala Daily life in Guatemala is a matter of extremes. On the one hand, rural Guatemalans have few of the comforts that North Americans take for granted, such as indoor bathrooms, running water, and electricity. Outside the cities, most homes are very small, and many have dirt floors.

On the other hand, urban Guatemalans live in modern homes, attend schools and universities, and go to theaters, museums, and restaurants. Many of the cultural influences in the cities, such as movies, restaurant chains, clothing styles, magazines, cars, and television programs, come from foreign countries. The cultural influences in the rural areas are much more local in origin.

SECTION 4 ASSESSMENT

Terms & Names
1. Identify: (a) Rafael Carrera   (b) Jacobo Arbenz Guzmán   (c) *departamento*

Taking Notes
2. Use a table like this one to keep track of the sequence of events in Guatemala's history.

Year	Event
1837	
1839	
1944	
1951	
1954	
1985	
1996	

Main Ideas
3. (a) Why did the United States feel threatened when Jacobo Arbenz Guzmán established his policy of land redistribution?

(b) After 1954, how did the Guatemalan government treat people who expressed disagreement with its policies?

(c) What is Guatemala's leading export?

Critical Thinking
4. Synthesizing

What is the impact of having a powerful nation, such as the United States, be the largest purchaser of Guatemala's exports?

Think About

◆ the role of exports in Guatemala's economy

◆ U.S. interventions in Guatemala

ACTIVITY -OPTION-   Write a **paragraph** explaining three facts about Guatemala that you did not know before you read this section.

TERMS & NAMES

Explain the significance of each of the following:

1. West Indies
2. dependency
3. mulatto
4. *ladino*
5. dictator
6. single-product economy
7. diversify
8. Fidel Castro
9. Communism
10. Rafael Carrera

REVIEW QUESTIONS

Establishing Independence *(pages 203–207)*

1. Why did the United States want to build the Panama Canal?
2. What event freed the Caribbean Islands from Spanish rule?

Building Economies and Cultures *(pages 208–213)*

3. What risk did Caribbean islanders face by having single-product economies?
4. What two crops did Central American economies depend on before the countries diversified their economies?

Cuba Today *(pages 215–220)*

5. Why did hundreds of thousands of people flee from Cuba to the United States after Castro took over?
6. How did Cuba's relationship with the Soviet Union affect Cuba?

Guatemala Today *(pages 221–225)*

7. Why did Jacobo Arbenz Guzmán's program of land redistribution upset people in the United States?
8. What are the cultural backgrounds of Guatemala's *ladinos?*

CRITICAL THINKING

Identifying Problems and Solutions

1. Using your completed chart from Reading Social Studies, p. 202, choose one issue, such as dictatorship or colonization, and summarize the problems with it. Then summarize the solutions to the problems.

Drawing Conclusions

2. How do you think Fidel Castro's control of newspapers and television and radio stations has helped keep him in power?

Contrasting

3. Contrast the fates of Native Americans in the Caribbean Islands and in Central America after Europeans took over.

Visual Summary

1 Establishing Independence

- People in Central America and the Caribbean fought first for independence and then for democracy.
  - Central America's people are mostly *ladinos* and Native Americans, while the Caribbean's are largely of African or European descent.

2 Building Economies and Cultures

- The countries of the region had to diversify their economies so they would be more stable.
- The region's languages, religions, and music were influenced by the cultures of the colonizers, the enslaved Africans, and the Native Americans.

3 Cuba Today

- In 1959, Fidel Castro led a revolution and took over Cuba's government. He has ruled ever since.
- Throughout the 1900s, both the United States and the Soviet Union influenced events in Cuba.

4 Guatemala Today

- After decades of struggle, Guatemala's government has become more stable.
- Guatemala's economy relies heavily on agriculture, especially coffee production.
- More than half of Guatemala's people are Maya. The rest are *ladinos.*

SKILLBUILDER: Reading a Political Map

1. What political region is represented on the map?
2. What city is the capital of this country?
3. List two other cities shown on the map.

FOCUS ON GEOGRAPHY

1. **Place** • Look at the map. What physical features do you think would attract tourists to Belize?
2. **Human-Environment Interaction** • What human-made features might tourists like to see in Belize?

CHAPTER PROJECTS

Interdisciplinary Activity: Language Arts

Writing a Letter Choose one of the Caribbean Islands, such as Grenada or Cuba, to research. Then imagine that you traveled to that island. Write a letter to a friend describing what you saw when you got there. Include photographs or drawings to show your friend what you saw.

Cooperative Learning Activity

Creating a Bulletin Board In a group of three to five students, create a bulletin board about one of the countries in the Caribbean or Central America. Include maps, charts, and pictures to provide different kinds of information about the country.

- Describe the climate of the country.
- List the natural resources that are found there.
- Provide information about the cities.
- Include information about politics and the economy.

INTERNET ACTIVITY

Use the Internet to do research about cultural heritage in Central America and the Caribbean. Focus on one country, such as Jamaica or Belize, and how its people have preserved cultural traditions from the past.

Writing About Culture Write a report of your findings. Include any illustrations you found, or make your own drawings. List the Web sites you used to prepare your report.

For Internet links to support this activity, go to

RESEARCH LINKS
CLASSZONE.COM

CHAPTER 9

South America

ATLANTIC
OCEAN

PACIFIC
OCEAN

PACIFIC
OCEAN

INDIAN
OCEAN

SOUTH
AMERICA

Location The Amazon
River winds eastward
from the Andes through
South America for
nearly 4,000 miles.

How has movement from rural to urban areas affected South America?

Movement • Some of the largest and fastest-growing cities in the world are in South America—for example, São Paulo, Brazil, and Buenos Aires, Argentina. Since the mid-1900s, people have been moving from rural to urban areas. Today, three-quarters of all South Americans live in cities.

Although cities often offer more jobs, they also have serious drawbacks. For example, not everyone in South America's cities can find jobs. Others cannot find housing. In some cities, such as Rio de Janeiro, Brazil, some people live in extreme poverty. Because of problems like these, many people, including professionals such as teachers and doctors, have left South America for the United States and other countries that may offer better opportunities.

What do you think?

◆ Why do South Americans leave the countryside and move to cities?

◆ How might South America change when skilled professionals, such as doctors, move to other countries?

BEFORE YOU READ

▶▶ *What Do You Know?*

Before you read the chapter, consider what you already know about South America. What do you know about the region's history? What do you know about its role in the world's economy and culture? In particular, what do you know about Brazil and Peru? You may know that Brazil is famous for its successes in soccer. Think about what else you have read or seen on the news or in sports reports. Also consider connections to your own life: Have you ever heard music from South America, such as salsa?

▶▶ *What Do You Want to Know?*

Decide what else you want to know about South America. In your notebook, record what you hope to learn from this chapter.

Region • **This Andean girl plays the region's music, called *huayno*.** ▲

READ AND TAKE NOTES

Reading Strategy: Making Generalizations
Making generalizations is a useful strategy for understanding themes in social studies. A generalization is a conclusion supported by facts. Use the chart of generalizations below to better understand events and situations in South America.

- Copy the chart into your notebook.
- As you read the chapter, look for facts that support each generalization. Examples may be found in more than one section of the chapter.
- Beside each generalization, record the facts that support it.

Place • **People crowd the streets of São Paulo in Brazil.** ▲

Generalizations	Facts
Independence led to different types of governments in South America.	
South American countries are trying to cooperate with one another and with the United States.	
Geography and politics affect the economies of South America.	
Urban growth presents serious problems for some South American countries.	
South America's different cultures contribute to world culture.	

Establishing Independence

TERMS & NAMES
Simón Bolívar
José de San Martín
Pan-American
Organization of
American States

MAIN IDEA	**WHY IT MATTERS NOW**
After 300 years of rule by Spain and Portugal, South Americans won independence and established their own nations.	Because the United States has close economic and political ties with South America, it is important to understand the history of the region.

DATELINE

EXTRA

CAJAMARCA, THE ANDES, 1533

Word has just arrived that the Inca ruler, Atahualpa, was executed by a small group of Spanish adventurers. A few weeks ago, Atahualpa's messengers informed him that the Spanish were coming. Atahualpa commanded 30,000 warriors and saw no reason to worry. However, the Spanish, with cannons and guns, killed around 4,000 of Atahualpa's guards and then captured the Inca king. Atahualpa tried to buy his freedom, offering the Spanish a stack of gold 9 feet high in a room measuring 17 feet by 22 feet. The Spanish accepted the gold—and then executed Atahualpa anyway. Now many fear for the future of the Inca Empire.

Culture • The portrait on the left shows Atahualpa, while the one on the right shows Pizarro. ▲

Europeans Arrive in South America

In 1531, Spanish explorer Francisco Pizarro landed on the coast of what is now the South American country of Peru. He had with him horses, guns, cannons, and about 200 soldiers. His forces began the long climb up into the Andes Mountains, following the Inca road that led to the city of Cajamarca (KAH·hah·MAHR·kah).

Europeans Establish Control When Pizarro first encountered the Inca, he found a kingdom weakened by a bitter civil war. Pizarro quickly captured and executed the Inca ruler, Atahualpa. The Inca Empire soon fell under Spanish control.

Meanwhile, Portugal had claimed what is now Brazil, and so the Portuguese began to settle the region. However, dense rain forests prevented much exploration of the region's interior. The Portuguese therefore built most of their settlements along the Atlantic Coast.

Colonial South America Many Spanish and Portuguese settlers soon made their way to South America. As happened throughout the New World, the arrival of the Europeans led to the deaths of many Native Americans. Millions died from disease or overwork. As the Native American population shrank, the Europeans imported enslaved Africans to work mainly on the large sugar cane plantations in Brazil.

European Colonizers of South America, 1500s

GUYANA
VENEZUELA
SURINAME
FRENCH GUIANA
COLOMBIA
ATLANTIC OCEAN
ECUADOR
PERU
BRAZIL
BOLIVIA
N
PARAGUAY
Tropic of Capricorn
PACIFIC OCEAN
ARGENTINA
URUGUAY
CHILE

Portugal
Great Britain
France
Netherlands
Spain

0   500   1,000 miles
0   500   1,000 kilometers

GEOGRAPHY SKILLBUILDER: Interpreting a Map

1. **Region** • What countries, other than Spain and Portugal, established colonies in South America?
2. **Place** • Which country controlled the smallest area of South America?

For nearly 300 years, Europeans ruled much of South America. Spain and Portugal between them claimed most of the land. Ships loaded with South American silver, gold, and sugar regularly sailed to these two countries. Both, especially Spain, grew enormously wealthy from their South American colonies.

Independence

In the early 1800s, Spain and Portugal were still taking most of the wealth out of the South American colonies. People of Spanish or Portuguese descent born in South America wanted to share in the political and economic power. They were encouraged by the American Revolution in 1776 and the French Revolution

Key Independence Days in South America

| Feb.12, 1818 Chile | July 28, 1821 Peru | Sept. 7, 1822 Brazil |

1815 — 1820 — 1825 — 1830

Dec. 17, 1819 Gran Colombia

Aug. 6, 1825 Bolivia

SKILLBUILDER: Reading a Time Line

1. For each country on the time line, what event occurred on the date given?
2. On what day did Brazil achieve independence?

in 1789. At the same time, the *mestizos* and mulattos wanted to bring about change because they were often treated no better than slaves. South Americans soon decided to fight for independence.

Gaining Independence Beginning in 1810, two generals led a series of wars for independence. One was **Simón Bolívar** (see·MOHN boh·LEE·var), whose leadership freed the northern parts of South America. The other was **José de San Martín** (san mahr·TEEN). He was responsible for defeating Spanish forces in the south. By 1825, nearly all of Spanish South America was independent.

Meanwhile, Brazil gained its independence without a major war. When the French general Napoleon Bonaparte invaded Portugal in 1807, the Portuguese royal family fled to Brazil. After Napoleon's later defeat, the Portuguese king returned to Portugal in 1821. He left his son Pedro to be regent of Brazil. When the Brazilians demanded their freedom in 1822, Pedro agreed. Brazil then named Pedro its emperor.

Reading
Social Studies

A. Recognizing Important Details How did Brazil gain its independence differently from other South American countries?

Biography

Simón Bolívar Simón Bolívar (shown at right) was born in Caracas, Venezuela, in 1783. As a teenager, Bolívar lived in Spain. He was influenced by the European Enlightenment and the philosophers Voltaire and Rousseau. A dream of freedom and independence for Hispanic America stirred Bolívar's soul, and he returned to South America.

Bolívar became a leader of the revolution in Venezuela in 1810. His clever military tactics led to victory over the Spanish and the creation of the republic of Gran Colombia, which included what are now Colombia, Panama, Venezuela, and Ecuador. Bolívar became president of Gran Colombia and continued fighting farther south. Victorious there, he soon became the president of Peru and Bolivia, which was named for him. Because of his role in gaining South American independence from Spain, Bolívar is often called "the Liberator." He died in Colombia in 1830.

Governments of South America

However, South America's new independence did not lead to a stable, fair society, as revolutionary leaders had hoped. These leaders had little experience in government. Many of them wanted to establish constitutions that set limits on the powers of government. Doing this would allow citizens to participate in government.

Unlimited Governments However, wealthy citizens and former Spanish officials in South America wanted to keep their property and power. They did not want all citizens to have a say in government. To maintain order and to protect their interests, the powerful often gave control of the government to the military. This frequently resulted in unlimited governments, in which one person or one group held total power. In other cases, military leaders used their armies to take over limited governments in South America. By the 1990s, however, the majority of governments in South America were democratic.

BACKGROUND

A small group of people, usually military, who join together to seize government power is called a *junta* (HUN·tuh).

Place • **General Augusto Pinochet** (pee·noh·CHEHT) ruled Chile as a military dictator from 1974 to 1990. ▲

Region • **An OAS official and a U.S. government official are shown here using a map of South America to discuss Pan-American issues.** ▼

South American Cooperation Simón Bolívar tried to create a united South America—a nation of states like the United States. Although he was not successful, in the late 1800s the U.S. government began encouraging Pan-American unity. *Pan* means "all," so **Pan-American** means "all of the Americas."

In 1948, Latin American nations joined with the United States to form the **Organization of American States** (OAS). The OAS promotes economic cooperation, social justice, and the equality of all people. It encourages democracy within its member nations. For example, OAS officials observe elections to make sure they are run fairly. The organization also helps settle conflicts among its members. In 1979, the OAS established a special court to protect human rights in its member countries.

The countries of South America will probably never join together in the way that Simón Bolívar envisioned. They are, however, working together to achieve justice and a better life for all their people.

Reading
Social Studies

B. Analyzing Motives Why do you think the United States wanted to establish Pan-American ties?

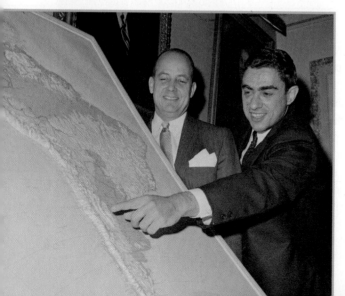

The People of South America

Until the 1800s, immigrants to South America came mostly from Spain and Portugal. During the 1880s, South America attracted many more European immigrants.

Region • Welsh settlers started sheep ranches in South America, while Swiss immigrants in Brazil developed the cheese industry. ▼

Immigrants Influence Society The new immigrants helped build South America's economy by establishing a variety of industries. Also, as all immigrants do, they brought their own customs to their new home. For example, the British introduced the game of football (which people in the United States call soccer), and it quickly became a popular sport across South America.

South America's Population Today There are many ethnic groups within South America's population—Native Americans, descendants of Europeans or of enslaved Africans, and people of mixed ancestry. Some of these groups live in particular regions, while others are more widespread. For example, many Africans live in the tropical lowlands where their enslaved ancestors worked. Native Americans make up a large part of the population in the Andean nations of Peru, Bolivia, and Ecuador. The majority of South Americans, however, are either *mestizos* or mulattos.

SECTION 1 ASSESSMENT

Terms & Names

1. Identify:
   (a) Simón Bolívar
   (b) José de San Martín
   (c) Pan-American
   (d) Organization of American States

Taking Notes

2. Use a chart like this one to list the contributions to South America's history made by the four main groups from which the people of South America are descended.

Group	Contributions
Native Americans	
European Colonists	
Enslaved Africans	
Other Immigrants	

Main Ideas

3. (a) From what South American products did European nations profit?

   (b) How has South America's population changed since the 1500s?

   (c) What challenges have many South American governments faced in recent years?

Critical Thinking

4. **Synthesizing**

   What challenges do you think South Americans faced in their fights for independence?

   Think About

   • differences in wealth between the colonial rulers and the general population

   • who held political power

   • living conditions

ACTIVITY -OPTION- Imagine you work for the OAS. Make a **poster** that highlights the benefits the organization offers its members.

Explore the Mysteries of Chichén Itzá

You are a movie director making a documentary film called *Mysteries of the Maya*. You are shooting your film at the ruins of Chichén Itzá, a city of stone deep in the jungle of Mexico's Yucatán Peninsula. Many things about the Maya culture are still a mystery. You want to inform your audience about Chichén Itzá, but you also want to make them feel the mood of the place—awesome and mysterious.

COOPERATIVE LEARNING On these pages you will find challenges that you and your crew will face in making the documentary. Working with your crew, decide which one of these problems you will solve. Divide the work among crew members. Look for helpful information in the Data File. Keep in mind that you will present your solution to the class.

LANGUAGE ARTS CHALLENGE

"As darkness falls, colored lights play on the buildings . . ."

While your film crew visits Chichén Itzá, you are awed by the nighttime "light and sound show." As darkness falls, colored lights play on the buildings, and a narrator tells the Maya's story. How can you include this scene in your film? How can you convey the mood of this site to a TV audience? Choose one of these options. Use the Data File for help.

ACTIVITIES

1. Write a brief (60-second) promotional advertisement to be shown during TV station breaks. Include sketches or descriptions of photographs or art you will use in the commercial. If possible, think of background music, too.
2. As a member of the film crew, write a journal entry describing your experiences at the light and sound show.

CHICHÉN ITZÁ

- **City was founded by Maya** about sixth century A.D.

- The name, which means **"mouth of the wells of Itzá,"** refers to the site's two deep natural wells, or cenotes. The Itzá were a Maya group.

- One **cenote** supplied water. The other, about 200 feet across, was sacred to the rain god. Human sacrifices, mostly young people, were thrown into it, along with gold and jade ornaments.

- The Maya had many gods. **Chac** was the rain god. Kukulcan was pictured as a feathered serpent.

- Major buildings—**Pyramid of Kukulcan** (El Castillo), **Temple of the Warriors, Great Ball Court**— were built about A.D. 900–1200.

- City was abandoned about A.D. 1450.

TEMPLE OF KUKULCAN/ EL CASTILLO ("THE CASTLE")

- Four-sided pyramid represents the **Maya calendar** in several ways.

- Four steep stairways, with 91 steps each, climb each side of the pyramid. Including the top platform, the **steps total 365.** There are 18 flat platforms—the number of months in the Maya calendar.

- At the **spring and fall equinoxes,** sunlight falls on one staircase in a pattern that looks like a serpent creeping down the pyramid.

SCIENCE CHALLENGE

"El Castillo, the pyramid of the serpent god"

From the top of El Castillo, the pyramid of the serpent god Kukulcan, you can see the stone ruins and the jungle surrounding them. This great temple-pyramid is the heart of Chichén Itzá. Maya priests, who were also scientists, studied the skies and made an accurate calendar. This pyramid reflects their knowledge of astronomy. How will your film explain this knowledge? Use one of these options to present information. Look in the Data File for help.

ACTIVITIES

1. Draw a diagram of El Castillo. Write a speech in which the film's narrator uses the diagram to explain the significance of the pyramid's structure and location.
2. Draw a storyboard to show what happens at El Castillo during the spring equinox.

To learn more about Chichén Itzá, visit

RESEARCH LINKS
CLASSZONE.COM

Activity Wrap-Up

As a group, review the way you solved the challenge you chose. Organize your solution and present it to the class.

Building Economies and Cultures

TERMS & NAMES
free-trade zone
economic indicator
urbanization

MAIN IDEA

While South America's countries work to overcome challenges to their economies, their cultures flourish.

WHY IT MATTERS NOW

Cultural elements from South America, such as music, literature, and dance, are popular around the world.

DATELINE

BOGOTÁ, COLOMBIA, SEPTEMBER 9, 2000— All over Bogotá, people are talking about last week's meeting in Brazil's capital, Brasília. It marked the first-ever meeting of the presidents of South America's 12 nations.

Many people here say that holding this meeting in Brazil's capital indicates that Brazil is going to take a leadership role in the region. As one Colombian official in Bogotá said: "We have

Region • Brazil's president, Fernando Henrique Cardoso, sponsored the 12-nation meeting. ▲

serious economic and political problems here. Brazil, the biggest and richest nation in South

America, needs to exercise leadership." Indeed, it seems that Brazil has decided to do just that.

Geography and Trade in South America

Many South American nations have found that working together results in greater economic opportunity. Partly this is because they face similar challenges and possibilities. A common factor influencing many of the region's economies is geography. South America's physical geography presents the region with both transportation barriers and transportation corridors.

Barriers South America's transportation barriers have interfered with trade and contacts with other cultures. For example, Portuguese explorers had trouble penetrating the dense Amazon rain forest. Because of this, they built their settlements along the coastline. Today, rain forests and rugged regions such as the Andes still prevent easy travel across the continent.

Corridors South America also has transportation corridors, such as the Amazon River system. Before the Europeans arrived, Native Americans canoed along the Amazon and its tributaries. Today, oceangoing vessels enter the Amazon system on Brazil's north coast. They carry goods such as food, clothing, and tools. They bring back lumber, rubber, animal skins, Brazil nuts, and other raw materials for shipment overseas.

Movement • Ships like this one can carry goods inland on the Amazon for more than 2,000 miles. ▲

Spotlight on CULTURE

Gabriela Mistral Chilean poet Gabriela Mistral (1889–1957; shown at right) used poetry to express her deep feelings for the people and land of South America, as in this poem, "Chilean Earth." She particularly loved children, and their rhymes and lullabies influenced her writing.

South Americans and people around the world greatly admire Mistral's work. As the first South American to win the Nobel Prize in Literature, she became a symbol of the hopes and dreams of a whole continent.

THINKING CRITICALLY

1. **Drawing Conclusions**
   What about Chile does Mistral celebrate in this poem?

2. **Forming and Supporting Opinions**
   Why do you think Mistral's poetry inspired South Americans?

Chilean Earth

We dance on Chilean earth
more beautiful than Lia and Raquel:
the earth that kneads men,
their lips and hearts without bitterness.

The land most green with orchards,
the land most blond with grain,
the land most red with grapevines,
how sweetly it brushes our feet!

Its dust molded our cheeks,
Its rivers, our laughter,
and it kisses our feet with a melody
that makes my mother sigh.
For the sake of its beauty,
we want to light up the fields with song.
It is free,
and for freedom we want
to bathe its face in music.

Tomorrow we will open its rocks;
we will create vineyards and orchards;
tomorrow we will exalt its people.
Today we need only to dance!

South America **239**

South American Agriculture, 2001

ATLANTIC OCEAN

PACIFIC OCEAN

Tropic of Capricorn

Legend:
- Cassava
- Cattle
- Cacao
- Coffee
- Corn
- Fruit
- Sheep
- Grain
- Sugar Cane
- Timber
- Tobacco
- Wheat

GEOGRAPHY SKILLBUILDER: Interpreting a Map

1. **Place** • Name an agricultural product from southern South America.
2. **Region** • Name an agricultural product that is produced in many parts of South America.

Products and Industries of South America

The rich natural resources of South America include abundant minerals and fertile land. However, few South American countries have fully developed their natural resources.

Mineral Resources Under the surface of South America's land lie many precious minerals—including gold, iron ore, lead, petroleum, tin, and copper. Many South American countries mine these minerals for export. For example, Chile mostly mines copper, Bolivia has a great amount of tin, and Colombia supplies the world with emeralds.

Agricultural Products South America is not only rich in mineral resources, but it also boasts some of the largest farms in the world. These farms produce goods for export, such as beef, grain, sugar, wool, bananas, and coffee. However, most of South America's farms are small. On these farms, individual farmers struggle to grow even enough food to feed their families. Many poor farmers have given up and moved to cities, hoping to find jobs there.

Manufacturing The most important South American industrial countries are Venezuela, Chile, Argentina, and Brazil. In fact, Brazil is one of the most important industrial nations in the world. It manufactures enough cars and trucks to supply the entire continent. Brazil also manufactures computers, televisions, and airplanes. In other South American countries, manufactured goods include shoes, furniture, beverages, and textiles.

Economic Cooperation Lack of funding prevents many South American countries from developing manufacturing. To improve their economies, countries may cooperate economically. For example, in 1994, the heads of 34 North and South American countries met in Miami, Florida, at the first Summit of the Americas.

Reading **Social Studies**

A. Contrasting How do South America's small farms and large farms differ?

BACKGROUND

The countries continued to develop the idea of a Free-Trade Zone of the Americas at additional Summit of the Americas meetings in 1998 and in 2001.

There, they agreed to create the huge Free-Trade Zone of the Americas, which would include almost every country in North and South America by the year 2005. In a **free-trade zone,** people and goods move across borders without being taxed. Many South Americans are confident that the Free-Trade Zone of the Americas will lead to greater prosperity in the region.

Economic Indicators Economic cooperation among nations can be challenging if some economies are strong and others are weak. Differences can be measured by **economic indicators,** statistics that show how a country's economy is doing. The literacy rate shows the percentage of a country's people who can read and write at an elementary school level. Life expectancy, or the average age to which people in a country live, gives clues about a country's health care and nutrition.

Country	Literacy Rate	Life Expectancy
Argentina	96%	75 years
Bolivia	83%	64 years
Brazil	85%	63 years
Chile	95%	76 years
Colombia	91%	70 years
Ecuador	90%	71 years
Guyana	98%	64 years
Paraguay	92%	74 years
Peru	89%	70 years
Suriname	93%	71 years
Uruguay	97%	75 years
Venezuela	91%	73 years

SKILLBUILDER: Interpreting a Chart

1. Which nation has the highest literacy rate? Which has the lowest?
2. What is the life expectancy in Brazil?

Reading Social Studies

B. Making Inferences How do you think a high literacy rate can help boost a country's economy?

Daily Life in South America

As with all regions, South America is home to both urban and rural areas. Many of the urban areas are enormous. City populations include some very wealthy people and many middle-class people who work in government or business. Millions more, however, live in extreme poverty. Nevertheless, South Americans enjoy a proud tradition of music and literature.

The Urban Setting For the past 50 years or so, South America has experienced major **urbanization,** meaning that many people have moved from the countryside to cities. Multiple factors caused this movement to occur. For example, the growth of manufacturing created more jobs in cities. At the same time, many rural people lived in poverty, without enough land to support their families. The promise of jobs, schools, and health services drew them to cities.

Today, several South American cities rank among the largest in the world. In 2000, São Paulo (sown POW·loh) in Brazil was home to nearly 18 million people, and Buenos Aires (BWAY·nos AIR·ays) in Argentina had nearly 13 million people.

Region •
Peruvians play
huayno on
flutes like the
one this girl is
using. ▲

Houses cannot be built quickly enough to keep up with the growing number of people. Large slums surround South America's biggest cities. In these areas, people live in shacks of cardboard, wood scraps, or tin. They often have no electricity or running water.

The Arts Despite the terrible poverty of millions, the arts in South America have thrived. The region's literature is admired throughout the world. The Nobel Prize in Literature has been given to three South Americans—Chilean poets Gabriela Mistral (mih·STRAHL) and Pablo Neruda (neh·ROO·duh), and Colombian novelist Gabriel García Márquez (gar·SEE·uh MAR·kez). Many South American poets and writers express their unique cultural heritage in their work. South American novelists also founded a literary style, magical realism, in which everyday reality mixes with fantasy.

Music, too, is an important part of the culture of South America. The traditional music of the Andean regions, called *huayno,* is played on flutes and drums. Some forms of music, such as salsa, have African roots. As more and more South Americans move to urban areas, musicians there are combining the traditional musical styles with rock and other popular types of music from Europe and North America.

SECTION 2 ASSESSMENT

Terms & Names

1. Identify:　(a) free-trade zone　　(b) economic indicator　　(c) urbanization

Taking Notes

2. Use a spider map like this one to show six factors that have influenced South America's economic progress.

South America's Economic Progress

Main Ideas

3. (a) Name one geographic feature that is a transportation barrier and one that is a transportation corridor.

(b) List five of South America's important natural resources.

(c) Name the three South Americans who have won the Nobel Prize in Literature.

Critical Thinking

4. **Identifying Problems**

What challenges do South American countries face in building strong economies?

Think About

- physical geography
- the needs of a rapidly growing population
- the effects of urbanization

ACTIVITY -OPTION-　Look at the physical map of South America on page 142. Write a short **description** of a way to overcome one of South America's transportation barriers.

Brazil Today

TERMS & NAMES
inflation
São Paulo
Rio de Janeiro
Brasília
Carnival

MAIN IDEA

As the largest country in South America, Brazil has achieved economic success while facing challenges such as unemployment.

WHY IT MATTERS NOW

Brazil's huge land area, population, and economic success enable it to influence its neighbors in South America and North America.

DATELINE

RIO DE JANEIRO, BRAZIL, DECEMBER 30, 2001—Preparations are almost complete for the New Year's Eve celebration tomorrow. Shop owners are sold out of the small blue and white boats that worshipers of the sea goddess Iemanjá will set adrift on the sea. They will fill the boats with offerings to the goddess in hopes that she will bless them with a good fishing season.

Millions of people will also throw flowers into the water. If the flowers drift back to shore, Iemanjá is not happy with the offering. If the flowers drift out to sea, the people can expect to have a good year.

Culture • These residents of Rio de Janeiro get ready to set their boat off to greet Iemanjá. ▲

Brazil: Regional Leader

Almost anything that happens in Brazil is newsworthy—because Brazil is the largest country in South America, covering almost half the continent. Its population of 172 million is close in size to the combined population of all the other South American countries. Brazil's gross domestic product is larger than that of any other South American country.

The Government of Brazil

After gaining independence from Portugal in 1822, Brazil was ruled by a series of emperors. In 1889, Brazil became a constitutional republic. Beginning in 1930, a series of dictators and military leaders ruled Brazil. Democratic government was restored in 1985. Power today is shared by a president, an elected congress, and a court system.

The Economy of Brazil

Brazil has the largest economy in South America. The country's gross domestic product is nearly twice that of Argentina, which is the next largest economy in South America.

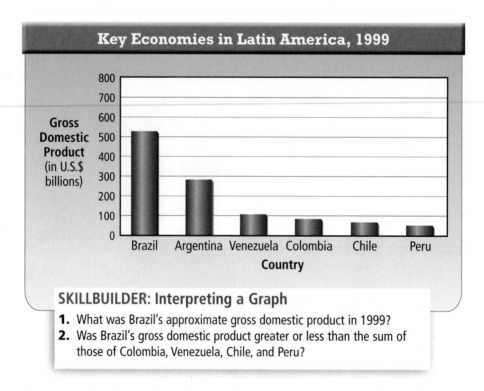

Key Economies in Latin America, 1999

SKILLBUILDER: Interpreting a Graph

1. What was Brazil's approximate gross domestic product in 1999?
2. Was Brazil's gross domestic product greater or less than the sum of those of Colombia, Venezuela, Chile, and Peru?

The Growth of Industry In Brazil, the government controls or influences certain industries to help the economy grow. For example, in the 1950s, the government promoted the building of automobile factories to cut down on the number of cars imported into Brazil. By the late 1980s, Brazil was building more than 1 million vehicles a year, enough to export some to other countries.

Agricultural Production In the world, Brazil is second only to the United States in exporting crops. When it comes to coffee, Brazil produces more than any other country in the world. Brazil is also a leading producer of oranges, bananas, and corn.

Unemployment and Inflation Even though Brazil's economy is the strongest in Latin America, many Brazilians are unemployed. Unemployment results when not enough businesses hire workers, or when workers do not have the education or training they need for the jobs available. Even those who have jobs may face hard times, especially due to inflation. **Inflation** is a general increase in the price of goods or services. It occurs when goods or services are in great demand, allowing producers to charge higher prices for them. The combination of unemployment and inflation has led to much poverty in Brazil.

Place • Automobile plants supply Brazil with many cars, like these parked in a plant lot, for export each year. ▲

Reading
Social Studies

A. Synthesizing How would inflation pose challenges even to people who do have jobs?

The People of Brazil

When explorers from Portugal arrived in Brazil in 1500, as many as 5 million Native Americans lived there. During the 1500s, the Portuguese established large sugar cane plantations in northeastern Brazil. At first they enslaved Native Americans to work on the plantations. Soon, however, many Native Americans died of disease. The plantation owners then turned to Africa for labor. Eventually, Brazil brought over more enslaved Africans than any other North or South American country.

Today, Native Americans make up less than 1 percent of Brazil's population. In northeastern Brazil, most people have African ancestors, while many people in Brazil have both European and African ancestors.

BACKGROUND

Of the 10 million to 15 million enslaved Africans brought to North and South America, more than 3.5 million ended up in Brazil.

Strange but TRUE

Can Cars Run on Sugar? Brazil's first major export was sugar made from sugar cane (shown at right). However, the plentiful sugar cane isn't just used to make sugar. Today, Brazilians use sugar cane to produce ethanol. Like gasoline, ethanol is a fuel used to run cars.

Nearly half of the cars sold in Brazil run on a gasoline-ethanol mix. Thousands run on ethanol alone. Producing ethanol from sugar cane makes good use of an abundant resource and creates more jobs in the sugar cane industry. Also, its production is less harmful to the environment than is gasoline's.

Population Density of Brazil, 2000

Persons per sq. mi.	Persons per sq. km	
Over 520	Over 200	
130–520	50–200	
65–129	25–49	
13–64	5–24	
2.6–12	1–4	
Fewer than 2.6	Fewer than 1	

⊙ Metropolitan area greater than 5 million

• Metropolitan area greater than 1 million

GEOGRAPHY SKILLBUILDER:
Interpreting a Map

1. **Place** • How many cities in Brazil have populations greater than 5 million?
2. **Region** • Which parts of Brazil are nearly unpopulated?

Place • The overcrowding of Brazil's cities, such as São Paulo, has put many stresses on the nation. ▲

City Populations Today, four out of five Brazilians live in cities. Brazil's two largest cities, **São Paulo** and **Rio de Janeiro,** are growing quickly. In 2000, São Paulo's population was close to 18 million. At the rate it is growing, the population will be more than 20 million in 2015. The national population is also increasing rapidly. In 1999, Brazil's population was almost 172 million. If current trends continue, by 2025 it could reach 210 million.

Because of much crowding along Brazil's Atlantic coast, the government wanted people to move into Brazil's vast interior. In 1956, it decided to create a new capital, **Brasília,** 600 miles inland. Now, like every other city in Brazil, Brasília has problems with overcrowding.

Reading
Social Studies

B. Hypothesizing What problems can rapid population growth cause?

The Culture of Brazil

Brazil's lively culture is a blend of influences from the many cultural groups that have come to Brazil over the centuries. Brazil's music, foods, and religious practices reflect that blend.

A Rich Mix Brazilian languages, religions, and musical traditions all reflect the multiple roots of Brazil's culture. For example, Brazil's official language is Portuguese. Included in Brazilian Portuguese, however, are many words from Tupi-Guarani (TOO·pee·GWAH·ruh·NEE), the language of Native Americans from the interior of northern Brazil.

As for religion, most Brazilians are Catholic, the religion brought to Brazil by the Portuguese. However, the number of non-Catholics is increasing. In 1940, only 5 percent of Brazilians were not Catholic. In 2000, non-Catholics had risen to 20 percent of the population because immigrants and missionaries had brought other religions to Brazil. Even so, more Catholics live in Brazil than in any other country in the world.

In addition, African religions still thrive in Brazil. For example, many people worship the African sea goddess Iemanjá. African influences can also be heard in Brazilian music, such as samba, which is based on African rhythms.

Holidays A Brazilian holiday called <u>Carnival</u> highlights the country's cultural diversity. This famous festival occurs during the four days before Lent. Carnival includes huge parades and street parties. In Rio de Janeiro, groups of African Brazilians perform samba dances. The dancers wear elaborate costumes of feathers and brightly colored, sparkling cloth.

BACKGROUND

In Christianity, Lent is the 40-day period before Easter.

Sports Brazilian football, called soccer in the United States, is a sport that most of the country gets excited about. Brazil is often a finalist in the World Cup, the sport's world championship competition. Brazilians enjoy watching professional football; millions of them also enjoy playing the game.

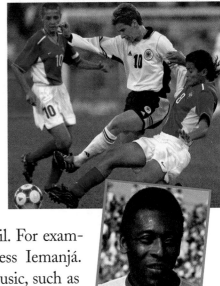

Culture • Top: Players on Brazil's women's soccer team move in for the win. Bottom: Brazilian soccer hero Pelé (PAY•lay) smiles for the crowd. ▲

SECTION ③ ASSESSMENT

Terms & Names

1. Identify: (a) inflation (b) São Paulo (c) Rio de Janeiro
              (d) Brasília   (e) Carnival

Taking Notes

2. Use a chart like this one to record key facts about Brazil's geography, history, government, economy, and culture.

Geography	History	Government	Economy	Culture

Main Ideas

3. (a) Why can Brazil be described as an "economic giant"?

   (b) Where do most people in Brazil live today?

   (c) Why did the Brazilian government move the capital inland to Brasília?

Critical Thinking

4. **Drawing Conclusions**

   Why do you think Brazil's economy is the most successful in South America?

   Think About

   • the government's role in the economy

   • natural resources

   • population size

ACTIVITY -OPTION-   Write a **speech** about the different groups that have influenced Brazilian culture. Include descriptions of each group's contributions.

900 1910 1920 1930 1940 1950 1960 1970   1700 1710 1720 1730 1740 1750 1760 1780
990 2000   1800 1810 1820 1830 1840 1850 1860 1870
                                           1890 1900 1910 1920 1930 1940 1950 1960
                                           1980 1990 2000

Linking Past and Present

The Legacy of Latin America

Food

People the world over have developed a taste for foods that originated in Latin America. Chile peppers, tomatoes, sweet potatoes, corn, and chocolate are just a few of the Latin American foods regularly found in kitchens and restaurants around the globe.

Natural Rubber

Ancient Latin Americans were the first to make use of natural rubber. Harvested from trees of the genus *Hevea,* native to Brazil, natural rubber is used around the world for everything from erasers to tires for racecars, airplanes, and trucks. The Maya invented chewing gum more than 1,000 years ago. They chewed a rubberlike substance called chicle (CHIHK•uhl), which is made from the sap of the sapodilla tree. Natural chicle was used to make chewing gum in the United States until the 1940s, when it was replaced with artificial ingredients.

Cowboys

Pioneers in the southwestern United States first learned many of the skills of cattle ranching from *vaqueros* (vah•KEH•rohs), Mexican cowboys working on Texas cattle ranches. The *vaqueros* showed the newcomers how to use lariats, saddles, spurs, and branding irons.

Language

Some of the words we use every day come from Spanish or from Native American languages. Examples are *coyote, patio, tomato, cocoa, cafeteria, canyon, corral, chile, lariat, lasso, rodeo,* and *stampede.*

stam·pede (stăm-pēd´) *n.* **1.** A sudden frenzied rush of panic-stricken animals. **2.** A sudden headlong rush or flight of a crowd of people. **3.** A mass impulsive action: *a stampede of support for the candidate. v.* **-ped·ed, -ped·ing, -pedes** —*tr.* **1.** To cause (a herd of animals) to flee in panic. **2.** To cause (a crowd of people) to act on mass impulse. —*intr.* **1.** To flee in a headlong rush. **2.** To act on mass impulse. [Spanish *estampida,* uproar, stampede, from Provençal, from *estampir,* to stamp, of Germanic origin.] —**stam·ped´er** *n.*

Life-Saving Medicines

Native peoples in Latin America, especially in the Amazon rain forest, have been sharing their knowledge of medicinal plants for centuries—to the world's benefit. Two important contributions to modern medicine have been quinine, used to cure malaria, and curare, used to fight serious nerve diseases, such as multiple sclerosis.

Quinine ▲

Find Out More About It!

Study the text and photos on these pages to learn about inventions, creations, and contributions that have come from Latin America. Then choose the item that interests you the most and do research in the library or on the Internet to learn more about it. Use the information you gather to create a poster that celebrates the contribution.

RESEARCH LINKS
CLASSZONE.COM

Peru Today

MAIN IDEA	WHY IT MATTERS NOW
Peru's physical features and its unstable governments have posed challenges to the development of its economy and its people.	Peru's economic problems also affect its trading partners, including the United States.

DATELINE

CHINCHA ISLANDS, PERU, 1842— Officials recently announced a major new source of prosperity for Peru. Dried sea-bird droppings, called guano, are now being exported around the world to be used as plant fertilizer.

The idea of using guano as fertilizer came from ancient Inca farmers. Recently, scientific research has confirmed that guano is rich in phosphates and nitrates, which help plants to grow. Fertilizer companies in Britain and other countries are now paying huge sums of money for the right to dig guano from Peru.

Human-Environment Interaction • Guano comes from a number of sea birds, including cormorants like this one. ▲

The Land of Peru

Though Peru is rich in resources, such as guano, variations in its physical geography also present problems. Three types of landforms exist in Peru: mountains, rain forest, and desert. Each type has its own special characteristics, but all three are transportation barriers rather than transportation corridors. Traveling from one part of Peru to another is not easy.

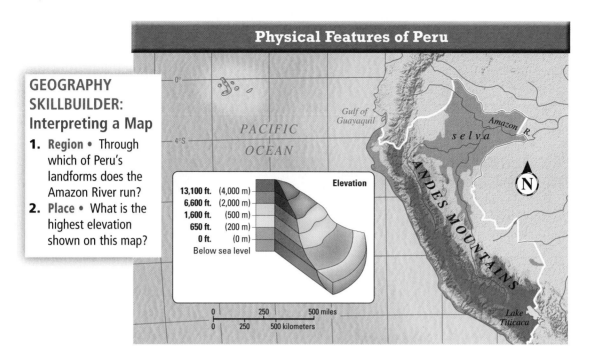

Physical Features of Peru

GEOGRAPHY SKILLBUILDER: Interpreting a Map

1. **Region** • Through which of Peru's landforms does the Amazon River run?
2. **Place** • What is the highest elevation shown on this map?

Elevation

13,100 ft.	(4,000 m)
6,600 ft.	(2,000 m)
1,600 ft.	(500 m)
650 ft.	(200 m)
0 ft.	(0 m)
Below sea level	

Three Types of Landforms Look at the map above. You can see that the Andes Mountains run the entire length of Peru, dividing the country in two. In places, the mountains are so steep that they are practically impassable. Notice that off the eastern slopes of the Andes stretches rain forest, which is called selva in Spanish. Now look to the west of the Andes, along the Pacific coast. Here the northern stretches of Chile's Atacama Desert reach into Peru. Most of Peru's cities, large farms, and factories are located in the desert, in or near oases. An **oasis** is a fertile region in a desert that formed around a river or spring.

The Economy of Peru

Reading Social Studies

A. Clarifying Why do you think Peru's cities are located in the desert rather than in other environments?

Peru has many resources, but it also has many problems. The country's harsh geography affects its economy. For example, the cold, rocky highlands and the cool, dry desert cover so much area that there is not enough arable land to feed the growing population.

Place • Because of cold currents in the Pacific Ocean, Peru's desert has an average summer temperature of only 73°F. ▶

Place • At left, a freight train transports copper ingots through Peru. At center, cotton plants grow in Ica, Peru. ▲

Place • Many crates of anchovies are sold in Peru each year. ▲

Agriculture Like many other countries, Peru must import certain foods. These include grains, vegetable oils, and some meats, many of which come from the United States. However, Peruvians do grow sugar cane, cotton, and coffee for export. Also, southern Peru has a large dairy industry that serves markets both in Peru and beyond. Meats from cattle, sheep, alpaca, and goats are also processed and distributed within the country.

Fishing The cold waters along the Pacific Coast are fine fishing grounds. Sardines and anchovies are the most important fish in the Peruvian catch. They are dried and made into fishmeal, which is sold as feed for livestock throughout the world.

Mining Peru is an important supplier of metals such as silver, copper, and bismuth. It also contains oil and gold deposits. However, the richest deposits of minerals in the country exist in dense rain forests and at elevations of over 12,000 feet. Because it is difficult to mine in these locations, Peru's mineral resources have not brought the country the great wealth that they could.

The Government of Peru

Peru declared itself independent of Spain in 1821. The nation was not completely free, however, until December of 1824, when Simón Bolívar finally drove out the Spanish. Following independence, Peru's military leaders began fighting one another. Struggles between military and civilian leaders continued until late in the 20th century.

Guerrilla Warfare Perhaps the greatest struggle in Peru's modern history arose in the early 1980s. At that time, Communist groups rose up to fight against the democracy that they felt was failing Peru. The most powerful of these groups was Sendero Luminoso (sen·DAIR·oh loo·mih·NOH·soh), or Shining Path.

BACKGROUND

Although in Spanish *guerrilla* is pronounced geh-REE-yuh, in English it is pronounced like the word *gorilla*. The word is Spanish for "small-scale war."

Sendero Luminoso fought for changes using **guerrilla warfare,** or nontraditional military tactics characterized by small groups using surprise attacks. The military responded, and many citizens died in the crossfire. Until Sendero Luminoso's leader, Abimael Guzmán Reynoso (ah·bee·mah·EHL gooz·MAHN ray·NAW·saw), was imprisoned in 1992, the civil war continued.

Government in Crisis The 1990s did not bring better times to Peru. From 1990 to 2000, **Alberto Fujimori,** the son of Japanese immigrants, was president. At first, many of Peru's poor rural people supported him. By May 2000, however, he and his officials were accused of corruption. Many resignations followed, and in November, Fujimori abandoned the presidency and fled to Japan. The new president, Alejandro Toledo (al·eh·HAHN·droh toh·LAY·doh), faced the challenge of trying to win back the trust of Peruvians after the government scandals.

Peruvian People and Culture

Today, more Native Americans live in Peru than in any other South American country. Forty-five percent of Peru's people are Native Americans— the descendants of the Inca. Many of these people are **Quechua** (KEHCH·wuh), people who live in the Andes highlands and speak the Inca language Quechua. Along with Spanish, Quechua is one of Peru's official languages. Many people in the highlands speak the language of another Native American group, the Aymara (EYE·mah·RAH). The Inca conquered the Aymara in the 15th century, but the language lived on.

After Native Americans, *mestizos* are Peru's next largest group. Peru's population also includes people with European, African, and Asian ancestors.

Urban and Rural Life Most of Peru's people live in cities or towns. Lima is Peru's capital and its biggest city, with about 7 million people. Lima has grown very quickly, which poses some severe problems. At the dawn of the 21st century, many neighborhoods lacked basic city services, such as electricity, running water, and public transportation.

B. Drawing Conclusions How do you think the violence and corruption in government affected people's daily lives in Peru?

Committee to Protect Journalists In a democracy, freedom of the press helps to prevent wrongdoing by the government. In Peru, for example, many administrators resigned in disgrace after journalists exposed widespread corruption in Alberto Fujimori's administration. Elsewhere, however, many governments have jailed journalists like the one shown below for their reports.

The Committee to Protect Journalists (CPJ) was formed in 1981 to promote freedom of the press. CPJ tracks abuses against the press all over the world, makes the abuses public, and organizes protests.

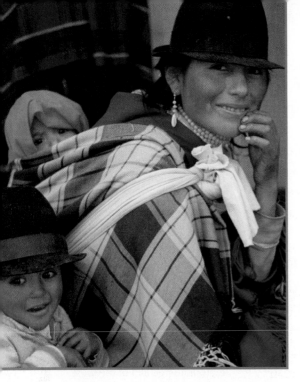

Many of Peru's rural farmers are very poor. They farm such small plots of land that often they cannot grow enough to feed their families. These rural people, who are mainly Native Americans, often move to the cities in search of a better life. However, many have little education and cannot speak Spanish, making it hard to find work.

Religion Peru's religions reflect multiple cultural traditions. Catholicism is the national religion of Peru, and more than 90 percent of Peruvians are Catholic. However, many Inca religious practices also still exist. At times, the Inca and Catholic customs mix. For example, some villages honor Catholic saints with traditional Inca festivals.

Region • Like this mother and daughter, many Quechua live in the Andes of Ecuador, Peru, and Bolivia. ▲

Literature The literature of Peru reveals modern themes as well as traditional ones. Peru's most famous living novelist, Mario Vargas Llosa (MAHR·yoh VAHR·guhs YOH·suh), is known for his belief that a novel should represent life to the fullest. César Vallejo (SAY·sar vuh·YAY·hoh), a *mestizo,* is Peru's most famous poet and is considered one of the world's best Spanish-language poets. His poetry describes what life is like for Peru's Native Americans and tells about suffering and struggles that all people may face.

SECTION 4 ASSESSMENT

Terms & Names

1. **Identify:**   (a) oasis   (b) guerrilla warfare   (c) Alberto Fujimori   (d) Quechua

Taking Notes

2. Use a chart like this one to list the products generated by each of Peru's industries.

Industry	Products
Agriculture	
Fishing	
Mining	

Main Ideas

3. (a) Describe the three types of landforms in Peru.

   (b) Describe the challenges facing Peru's economy.

   (c) Which group makes up the largest part of Peru's population?

Critical Thinking

4. **Forming and Supporting Opinions**

   Why did Peru's guerrillas use violence to bring about change? Were they right to do so? Explain.

   Think About

   • reasons for discontent in Peru
   • the history of democracy in Peru
   • other possible methods of demanding change

ACTIVITY -OPTION-   Imagine you live in Peru. Write a **short story** describing your daily life, including what you do for work and for recreation.

Reading a Time Line

▶▶ Defining the Skill

A time line is a visual list of dates and events shown in the order in which they occurred. Time lines can be horizontal or vertical. On horizontal time lines, the earliest date is on the left. On vertical time lines, the earliest date is usually at the top.

▶▶ Applying the Skill

The time line below shows the dates of expeditions to explore the Amazon River. Use the strategies listed below to help you read the time line.

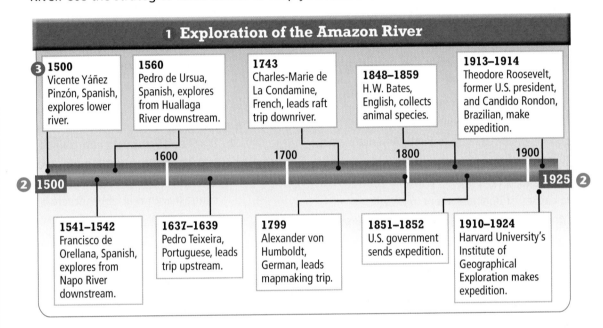

1 Exploration of the Amazon River

3 1500
Vicente Yáñez Pinzón, Spanish, explores lower river.

1560
Pedro de Ursua, Spanish, explores from Huallaga River downstream.

1743
Charles-Marie de La Condamine, French, leads raft trip downriver.

1848–1859
H.W. Bates, English, collects animal species.

1913–1914
Theodore Roosevelt, former U.S. president, and Candido Rondon, Brazilian, make expedition.

2 1500   1600   1700   1800   1900   **1925 2**

1541–1542
Francisco de Orellana, Spanish, explores from Napo River downstream.

1637–1639
Pedro Teixeira, Portuguese, leads trip upstream.

1799
Alexander von Humboldt, German, leads mapmaking trip.

1851–1852
U.S. government sends expedition.

1910–1924
Harvard University's Institute of Geographical Exploration makes expedition.

How to Read a Time Line

Strategy ❶ Read the title. It will tell you the main idea of the time line.

Strategy ❷ Read the dates at the beginning and the end of the time line. These will show the period of time that the time line covers.

Strategy ❸ Read the dates and events in order, beginning with the earliest one. Think about how each event may have influenced later events. Take note of which nations were involved in each expedition.

Strategy ❹ Summarize the main idea of the time line. Remember that the title will help you focus on the main idea.

Write a Summary

Writing a summary can help you understand the information shown on a time line. The summary to the right states the time period covered and the main idea of the time line.

> ❹ The time line covers the period between 1500 and 1925. During that period of time, people from Europe and the United States explored the Amazon River. The time line shows that on their expeditions, people explored the river, made maps, and collected animal species.

▶▶ Practicing the Skill

Turn to page 233 in Chapter 9, Section 1. Look at the time line entitled "Key Independence Days in South America," and write a paragraph summarizing what you learned from it.

TERMS & NAMES

Explain the significance of each of the following:

1. Simón Bolívar
2. Pan-American
3. free-trade zone
4. urbanization
5. São Paulo
6. Brasília
7. Carnival
8. oasis
9. guerrilla warfare
10. Quechua

REVIEW QUESTIONS

Establishing Independence *(pages 231–235)*

1. What caused the death of so many Native Americans after the arrival of the Europeans in South America?
2. How did many South American nations end up with unlimited governments after independence?

Building Economies and Cultures *(pages 238–242)*

3. List three of South America's major natural resources.
4. Why have so many people moved to South America's cities in the past 50 years?

Brazil Today *(pages 243–247)*

5. What are two causes of unemployment in Brazil?
6. Why did the government of Brazil build the city of Brasília?

Peru Today *(pages 250–254)*

7. Describe the three types of landforms that make up Peru.
8. How does the Native American population in Peru compare in size with the Native American populations elsewhere in South America?

CRITICAL THINKING

Making Generalizations

1. Using your completed chart from Reading Social Studies, p. 230, write a paragraph explaining the facts that support one generalization about South America.

Contrasting

2. Brazil and Venezuela both gained independence from European countries. How did the road to freedom for Brazil contrast with that of Venezuela?

Synthesizing

3. When South American nations form trade blocs, how is that different from uniting politically?

Visual Summary

Establishing Independence

1

- After 300 years of colonial rule, the countries of South America gained independence.
- South America's population today reflects the arrival of immigrants from Europe, Africa, and Asia.

Building Economies and Cultures

2

- Geographic features and growing populations have challenged economic progress in South America.
- The countries of the region work together to benefit all of their economies.

Brazil Today

3

- Brazil is South America's largest and most economically successful country.
- Despite economic success, Brazil still faces unemployment and inflation.

Peru Today

4

- Peru's physical geography hinders the development of its economy.
- Peru has suffered many political problems, such as guerrilla warfare and corrupt government.

SOCIAL STUDIES SKILLBUILDER

1822
Brazil declares independence.

1942
Brazil enters World War II.

1960
Brazil moves its capital to Brasília.

1917
Brazil enters World War I.

1985
Civilian rule is restored.

1820 1850 1880 1910 1940 1970 **2000**

1888
Slavery is abolished.

1930
Getúlio Vargas becomes president.

1964
Military leaders take control.

1945
Brazil joins the United Nations.

SKILLBUILDER: Reading a Time Line

1. What period is covered in the time line?
2. What events has Brazil participated in with other countries of the world?
3. Use the time line to write a brief summary of events in Brazil since independence.

FOCUS ON GEOGRAPHY

1. **Region** • How many South American cities had populations over 1 million in 1950?
2. **Movement** • How many more South American cities had populations over 1 million in 2000 than in 1950?
3. **Location** • Are more of South America's cities located on the coast or inland?

1900

1950

2000

 City with population greater than 1 million

CHAPTER PROJECTS

Interdisciplinary Activity: Language Arts

Describing Geography Imagine that you are on an expedition flying over Peru. Record your observations about the long coastline, the mountains, and the jungles you see below you. Write two or three paragraphs describing what you see.

Cooperative Learning Activity

Planning a City In a group of three to five students, plan a new city. Decide on a problem that your country faces, such as overcrowding. Use this city's development to help solve the problem, as was done with Brasília. Describe how the city is organized, what services are provided for the people, and where parks, homes, and businesses are.

- Explain why the new city needed to be built.
- Provide a map of the new city.
- Draw illustrations of important buildings.
- List key services that the city provides.

INTERNET ACTIVITY

Use the Internet to research at least three useful products that come from the Amazon rain forest. Focus on one product, such as medicinal plants, and describe how it is used in different parts of the world.

Writing About Geography Write a report of your findings. Include a map or a chart that shows products from the rain forest and what they are used for. List the Web sites you used to prepare your report.

For Internet links to support this activity, go to

RESEARCH LINKS
CLASSZONE.COM

UNIT 4

Place Completed in A.D. 80, the Colosseum in Rome, Italy, held 50,000 spectators. There they watched battles between gladiators, among other contests. The Colosseum is the largest structure that survives from the Roman Empire.

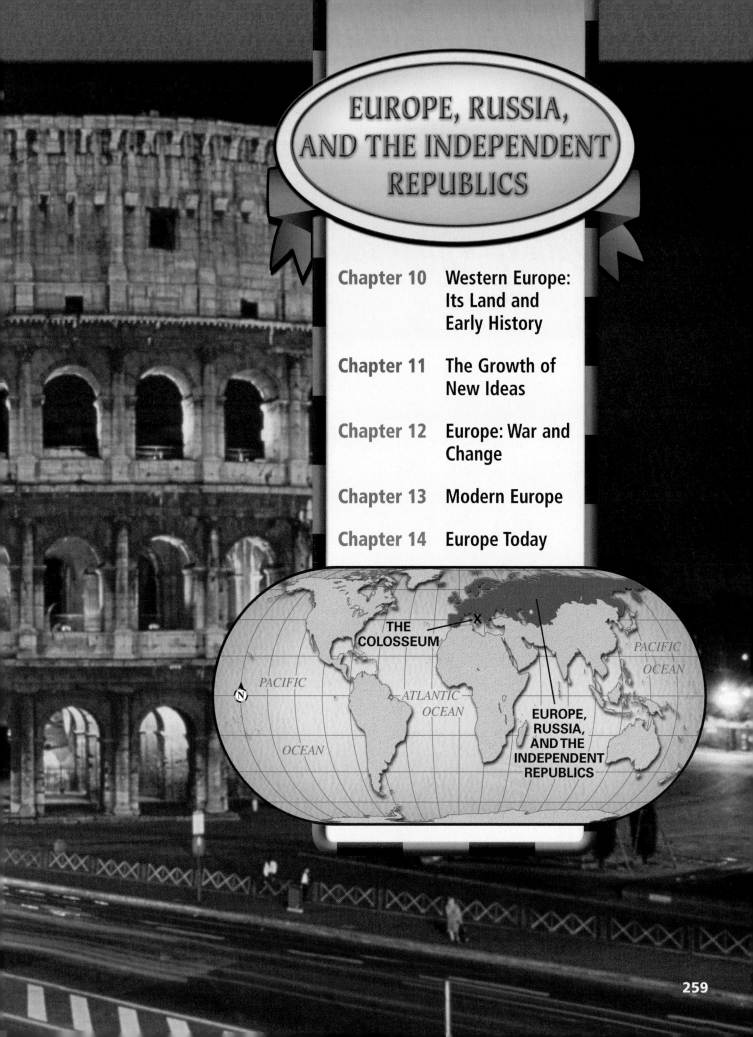

EUROPE, RUSSIA, AND THE INDEPENDENT REPUBLICS

THE COLOSSEUM

X

PACIFIC OCEAN

PACIFIC OCEAN

N

ATLANTIC OCEAN

EUROPE, RUSSIA, AND THE INDEPENDENT REPUBLICS

OCEAN

UNIT 4 Physical Geography

ARCTIC OCEAN

N

| 0 | 500 | 1,000 miles |
| 0 | 500 | 1,000 kilometers |

Svalbard

Franz Josef Land

Novaya Zemlya

Kara Sea

Barents Sea

Norwegian Sea

Arctic Circle

Central Siberian Plateau

West Siberian Plain

ICELAND

SWEDEN

FINLAND

60°N

NORWAY

ESTONIA

Yenisey R.

Angara R.

RUSSIA

Dvina R.

LATVIA

LITHUANIA

Ob R.

Ob R.

Irtysh R.

Jutland

North Sea

DENMARK

Baltic Sea

RUS.

Volga R.

Kama R.

U
R
A
L

M
O
U
N
T
A
I
N
S

Sayan Mts.

IRELAND

UNITED KINGDOM

NETH.

GERMANY

POLAND

BELARUS

Central Russian Upland

BEL.

Rhine R.

LUX.

CZECH R.

Carpathian Mts.

UKRAINE

Dnieper R.

Don R.

KAZAKHSTAN

ATLANTIC OCEAN

FRANCE

SWITZ.

SLOVAKIA

AUS. HUNGARY

SLO. CRO.

ROMANIA

MOLDOVA

Aral Sea

UZBEKISTAN

KYRGYZSTAN

Mt. Blanc 15,771 ft. (4,807 m)

ALPS

BOS. & H.

Danube R.

Mt. Elbrus 18,510 ft. (5,642 m)

Caspian Sea

TURKMENISTAN

TAJIKISTAN

Douro R.

Pyrenees

Corsica

ITALY

YUGO.

MAC.

BULGARIA

Black Sea

Caucasus

GEORGIA

Iberian Peninsula

Sardinia

Mt. Etna 10,902 ft. (3,323 m)

ALB.

GREECE

ARMENIA

AZERBAIJAN

PORTUGAL

SPAIN

Sicily

Crete

Mediterranean Sea

40°N

20°N

20°W   0°   20°E   40°E   60°E   80°E   100°E

Climates of Europe, Russia, and the Independent Republics

N

ARCTIC OCEAN

ARCTIC OCEAN

Arctic Circle

80°N

60°N

ATLANTIC OCEAN

Black Sea

PACIFIC OCEAN

40°N

Mediterranean Sea

0°   40°E   60°E   80°E   120°E   140°E   160°E   180°E

| 0 | 1,000 | 2,000 miles |
| 0 | 1,000 | 2,000 kilometers |

Desert	Humid continental
Semiarid	Subarctic
Mediterranean	Tundra
Marine west coast	Highland
Humid subtropical	

Europe, Russia, and the Independent Republics: Physical

120°E

ARCTIC OCEAN

80°N

New Siberian Islands

Laptev Sea

Wrangel Island

East Siberian Sea

Verkhoyansk Range

Chersky Range

Kolyma R.

Chukchi Peninsula

Lena R.

RUSSIA

Kolyma Mts.

Lena R.

60°N

Stanovoy Range

Sea of Okhotsk

Kamchatka Peninsula

Bering Sea

Sakhalin Island

PACIFIC OCEAN

Tropic of Cancer

Elevation

13,100 ft.	(4,000 m)
6,600 ft.	(2,000 m)
3,275 ft.	(1,000 m)
650 ft.	(200 m)
0 ft.	(0 m)
Below sea level	

▲ Mountain peak

FAST FACTS

✔ **LONG COASTLINE:**
The coastline of Europe alone is 24,000 miles long. Earth measures 24,902 miles around at the Equator.

✔ **BELOW SEA LEVEL:**
Almost a third of the Netherlands and a large portion of the land by the Caspian Sea are below sea level.

✔ **HIGHEST MOUNTAIN:**
Mt. Elbrus in Russia, 18,510 ft.

✔ **DEEPEST LAKE:**
Lake Baikal, 5,714 ft. deep

✔ **LARGEST INLAND SEA:**
Caspian Sea, 149,200 sq. mi.

✔ **LONGEST RIVER:**
Volga River, 2,193 mi.

GEOGRAPHY SKILLBUILDER: Interpreting Maps and Visuals

1. **Location** • Which countries have mountains at their borders?
2. **Place** • About how many times larger is the population of Europe, Russia, and the Independent Republics than that of the United States?

Europe, Russia, and the Independent Republics– United States Landmass and Population

120°E

Europe, Russia, and the Independent Republics

United States

LANDMASS

Europe, Russia, and the Independent Republics

10,489,029 square miles

Continental United States

3,165,630 square miles

POPULATION

Europe, Russia, and the Independent Republics
654,628,000

United States
281,421,906

👤 = 50,000,000

ARCTIC OCEAN

Franz Josef
Land

Svalbard
(Nor.)

Severnaya
Zemlya

Norwegian Sea

Kara Sea

Barents Sea

Novaya Zemlya

Murmansk

Norilsk

Arctic Circle

ICELAND
Reykjavik

SWEDEN

FINLAND

Arkhangelsk

R U S S I A

Dvina R.

Ob R.

Yenisey R.

Trondheim

Tampere

NORWAY

Bergen
Oslo

Stockholm

Helsinki

St. Petersburg

Perm

Yekaterinburg

Omsk

Novosibirsk

Krasnoyarsk

Göteborg

ESTONIA

Moscow
Nizhniy
Novgorod

Kazan

Kama R.

Chelyabinsk

Glasgow Edinburgh

North
Sea

DENMARK

LATVIA

LITHUANIA

Volga R.

Ufa

Semey

Irkutsk

Belfast

BEL.

Copenhagen

Minsk

Togliatti

Samara

Astana

Dublin
IRELAND

UNITED
KINGDOM

Berlin

NETH.

Amsterdam

BELARUS

Kiev

Don R.

Volgograd

KAZAKHSTAN

Angara R.

London

Brussels

GERMANY

Warsaw

POLAND

Dnieper R.

Kharkiv

ATLANTIC
OCEAN

Paris

LUX.

Rhine R.

CZECH R.

SLOVAKIA

UKRAINE

Donetsk

Rostov

Astrakhan

Nantes

SWITZ.

Bern

AUS. HUNGARY

MOLDOVA

Krasnodar

Caspian Sea

Bishkek

Almaty

FRANCE

SLO.

CRO.

ROMANIA

Odessa

Aral
Sea

UZBEKISTAN

KYRGYZSTAN

Bordeaux

Milan

ITALY

BOS. & H.

Belgrade

Bucharest

Black Sea

GEORGIA

Tbilisi

Tashkent

Douro R.

Marseille

Corsica

Sarajevo

YUGO.

Sofia

BULGARIA

Baku

TAJIKISTAN

Rome

MAC.

ARMENIA

TURKMENISTAN

Dushanbe

PORTUGAL

Madrid

Barcelona

Tirane

ALB.

GREECE

Yerevan

Ashgabat

Lisbon

SPAIN

Sardinia

Naples

AZERBAIJAN

Seville

Sicily

Athens

Crete

Mediterranean Sea

Population Density of Europe, Russia, and the Independent Republics

ARCTIC OCEAN

ARCTIC OCEAN

Arctic Circle

ATLANTIC
OCEAN

Black Sea

PACIFIC OCEAN

Mediterranean Sea

ATLANTIC
OCEAN

Equator

ATLANTIC
OCEAN

Persons per sq. mi.	Persons per sq. km
Over 520	Over 200
260–520	100–200
130–259	50–99
25–129	10–49
1–24	1–9
0	0

1,000   2,000 miles

1,000   2,000 kilometers

Europe, Russia, and the Independent Republics: Political

120°E 140°E 160°E 180°E

New Siberian Islands

Laptev Sea

East Siberian Sea

Wrangel Island

Lena R.

Kolyma R.

R U S S I A

Yakutsk

Lena R.

60°N

Sea of Okhotsk

Bering Sea

Petropavlovsk-Kamchatskiy

Sakhalin Island

Khabarovsk

PACIFIC OCEAN

40°N

Vladivostok

Tropic of Cancer

120°E 140°E 160°E 180°E

National boundary

★ National capital

• Other city

0   500   1,000 miles

0   500   1,000 kilometers

FAST FACTS

✓ **SMALLEST COUNTRY IN THE WORLD:**
Vatican City, less than 0.2 sq. mi.

✓ **LARGEST COUNTRY IN THE WORLD:**
Russia, 6,592,800 sq. mi.

✓ **LONGEST ROAD TUNNEL:**
Oslo, Norway, 15.3 mi. long

✓ **OLDEST PAINTINGS:**
Cave paintings near Verona, Italy, at 32,000 to 37,000 years of age

GEOGRAPHY SKILLBUILDER: Interpreting Maps and Visuals

1. **Location** • Name two countries that do not have seaports.
2. **Movement** • What route would you take to drive from Paris to Bern?

Road Map of Selected European Countries

A4   A4

★ Paris

N104

A10   A5   Troyes   A31   GERMANY

A11   A35   A5

Orléans

A10   A6   A31   A3

A38   Dijon   A36

FRANCE

A71   A1   A2

A5

A39   Bern   SWITZERLAND

A6   A12   Lausanne

A1   Geneva   Lausanne

A40

Lyon   Chambéry   ITALY

A72

0   25   50 miles

0   25   50 kilometers

★ National capital

• Other city

— Major road

Country Flag	Country/Capital	Currency	Population (2001 estimate)	Life Expectancy (years)	Birthrate (per 1,000 pop.) (2000)
	Albania Tiranë	Lek	3,510,000	71	19
	Andorra Andorra la Vella	French Franc	68,000	83	11
	Armenia Yerevan	Dram	3,336,000	75	10
	Austria Vienna	Euro*	8,151,000	78	10
	Azerbaijan Baku	Manat	7,771,000	70	15
	Belarus Minsk	Ruble	10,350,000	68	9
	Belgium Brussels	Euro*	10,259,000	78	11
	Bosnia-Herzegovina Sarajevo	Conv. Mark	3,922,000	73	13
	Bulgaria Sofia	Lev	7,707,000	71	8
	Croatia Zagreb	Kuna	4,334,000	73	11
	Czech Republic Prague	Koruna	10,264,000	75	9
	Denmark Copenhagen	Danish Krone	5,353,000	77	12
	Estonia Tallinn	Kroon	1,423,000	70	8
	Finland Helsinki	Euro*	5,176,000	78	11
	France Paris	Euro*	59,551,000	79	13
	Georgia Tbilisi	Lavi	4,989,000	73	9
	Germany Berlin	Euro*	83,029,000	77	9

*On January 1, 2002, the euro became the common currency for 12 of the member nations of the European Union.

DATA FILE

Infant Mortality (per 1,000 live births) (2000)	Doctors (per 100,000 pop.) (1990–1998)	Literacy Rate (percentage) (1991–1998)	Passenger Cars (per 1,000 pop.) (1996–1997)	Total Area (square miles)	Map (not to scale)
41.3	129	83	10 (1990)	11,100	
6.4	253	100	552	174	
41.0	316	98	2	11,506	
4.9	302	100	468	32,378	
83.0	360	99	36	33,436	
15.0	443	100	111	80,154	
5.6	395	99	434	11,787	
25.2	143	86	23	19,741	
14.9	345	98	202	42,822	
8.2	229	98	160	21,830	
4.6	303	99	428	30,448	
4.7	290	100	339	16,637	
13.0	297	99	294	17,413	
4.2	299	100	378	130,560	
4.8	303	99	437	212,934	
53.0	436	99	80	26,911	
4.7	350	100	504	137,830	

Country Flag	Country/Capital	Currency	Population (2001 estimate)	Life Expectancy (years)	Birthrate (per 1,000 pop.) (2000)
	Greece Athens	Euro*	10,624,000	78	10
	Hungary Budapest	Forint	10,106,000	71	9
	Iceland Reykjavik	Krona	278,000	80	15
	Ireland Dublin	Euro*	3,841,000	76	15
	Italy Rome	Euro*	57,680,000	78	9
	Kazakhstan Astana	Tenge	16,731,000	65	14
	Kyrgyzstan Bishkek	Som	4,753,000	67	22
	Latvia Riga	Lat	2,385,000	70	8
	Liechtenstein Vaduz	Swiss Franc	33,000	73	14
	Lithuania Vilnius	Litas	3,611,000	72	10
	Luxembourg Luxembourg	Euro*	443,000	77	13
	Macedonia Skopje	Denar	2,046,000	73	15
	Malta Valletta	Lira	395,000	77	12
	Moldova Chisinau	Leu	4,432,000	67	11
	Monaco Monaco	French Franc	32,000	79	20
	Netherlands Amsterdam	Euro*	15,981,000	78	13
	Norway Oslo	Krone	4,503,000	79	13
	Poland Warsaw	Zloty	38,634,000	74	10

*On January 1, 2002, the euro became the common currency for 12 of the member nations of the European Union.

DATA FILE

Infant Mortality (per 1,000 live births) (2000)	Doctors (per 100,000 pop.) (1990–1998)	Literacy Rate (percentage) (1991–1998)	Passenger Cars (per 1,000 pop.) (1996–1997)	Total Area (square miles)	Map (not to scale)
6.7	392	97	223	50,950	
8.9	357	99	222	35,919	
4.0	326	100	489	39,768	
6.2	219	100	292	27,135	
5.5	554	98	540	116,320	
59.0	353	99	61	1,048,300	
77.0	301	97	32	76,641	
16.0	282	100	174	24,595	
5.1	100	100	592 (1993)	62	
15.0	395	100	242	25,174	
5.0	272	100	515	999	
16.3	204	89	132	9,927	
5.3	261	91	321	124	
43.0	400 (1995)	99	46	13,012	
5.9	664	100	548	0.6	
5.0	251	100	372	16,033	
4.0	413	100	399	125,050	
8.9	236	99	195	124,807	

Country Flag	Country/Capital	Currency	Population (2001 estimate)	Life Expectancy (years)	Birthrate (per 1,000 pop.) (2000)	
	Portugal Lisbon	Euro*	10,066,000	76	11	
	Romania Bucharest	Leu	22,364,000	70	11	
	Russia Moscow	Ruble	145,470,000	67	8	
	San Marino San Marino	Italian Lira	27,000	80	11	
	Slovakia Bratislava	Koruna	5,415,000	73	11	
	Slovenia Ljubljana	Tolar	1,930,000	75	9	
	Spain Madrid	Euro*	40,038,000	78	9	
	Sweden Stockholm	Krona	8,875,000	80	10	
	Switzerland Bern	Franc	7,283,000	80	11	
	Tajikistan Dushanbe	Ruble	6,579,000	68	21	
	Turkmenistan Ashgabat	Manat	4,603,000	66	21	
	Ukraine Kiev	Hryvnya	48,760,000	68	8	
	United Kingdom London	Pound	59,648,000	77	12	
	Uzbekistan Tashkent	Som	25,155,000	69	23	
	Vatican City Vatican City	Vatican Lira/Italian Lira	870 (2000)	N/A	N/A	
	Yugoslavia Belgrade	New Dinar	10,677,000	73	11	
	United States Washington, D.C.	Dollar	281,422,000	77	15	

*On January 1, 2002, the euro became the common currency for 12 of the member nations of the European Union.

DATA FILE

Infant Mortality (per 1,000 live births) (2000)	Doctors (per 100,000 pop.) (1990–1998)	Literacy Rate (percentage) (1991–1998)	Passenger Cars (per 1,000 pop.) (1996–1997)	Total Area (square miles)	Map (not to scale)
6.0	312	91	295	35,514	
20.5	184	98	106	92,042	
20.0	421	100	120	6,592,812	
8.8	252	99	955	23	
8.8	353	100	185	18,923	
5.2	228	99	343	7,819	
5.7	424	97	384	195,363	
3.5	311	100	417	173,730	
4.8	323	100	460	15,942	
117.0	201	99	31	55,251	
73.0	300 (1997)	98	N/A	188,455	
22.0	299	100	97	233,089	
5.7	164	100	434	94,548	
72.0	309	88	37	173,591	
N/A	N/A	100	N/A	0.17	
10.4	203	98	173	39,448	
7.0	251	97	489	3,787,319	

GEOGRAPHY SKILLBUILDER: Interpreting a Chart

1. **Place** • Which country in the region has the highest life expectancy?
2. **Place** • How many fewer cars per thousand people does Greece have than Germany?

CHAPTER 10

Western Europe: Its Land and Early History

EUROPE

ATLANTIC

PACIFIC

OCEAN

PACIFIC

OCEAN

OCEAN

INDIAN
OCEAN

OCEAN

Region Many European cities show their history in their architecture. In Segovia, Spain, an ancient Roman aqueduct lies below the walls of a castle built in the Middle Ages.

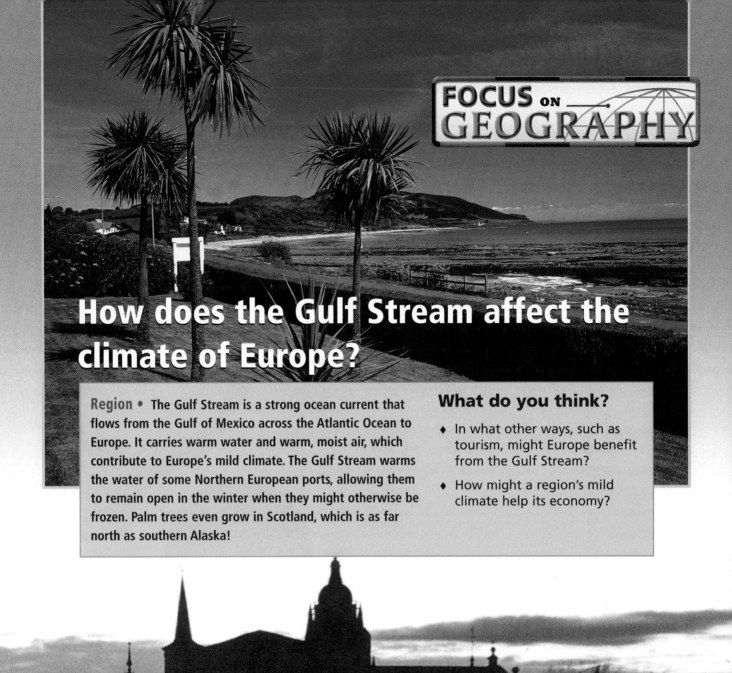

How does the Gulf Stream affect the climate of Europe?

Region • The Gulf Stream is a strong ocean current that flows from the Gulf of Mexico across the Atlantic Ocean to Europe. It carries warm water and warm, moist air, which contribute to Europe's mild climate. The Gulf Stream warms the water of some Northern European ports, allowing them to remain open in the winter when they might otherwise be frozen. Palm trees even grow in Scotland, which is as far north as southern Alaska!

What do you think?

♦ In what other ways, such as tourism, might Europe benefit from the Gulf Stream?

♦ How might a region's mild climate help its economy?

READING SOCIAL STUDIES

READING SOCIAL STUDIES

BEFORE YOU READ

▶▶ *What Do You Know?*

Before you read the chapter, think about what you already know about Europe. What are some of its geographical features? What do you know about its early history? Have you ever read myths from ancient Greece or ancient Rome? Have you ever heard of Julius Caesar or Hercules? What do you know about knights and castles from the Middle Ages?

▶▶ *What Do You Want to Know?*

Decide what you want to know about these early periods of European history. Record your questions in your notebook before you read this chapter.

Region • Ancient Greece made important contributions in literature, philosophy, and architecture. ▼

READ AND TAKE NOTES

Reading Strategy: Categorizing One way to make sense of what you read is to categorize, or sort, information. Making a chart to categorize the information in this chapter will help you to understand the contributions made by early European cultures.

- Copy the chart below into your notebook.
- As you read, look for information relating to the categories of social structure, architecture, religion, and arts and sciences.
- Write your notes under the appropriate headings.

Region • The Middle Ages saw the rise of the Catholic Church and the growth of a middle class. ▲

Region • Ancient Rome made its mark in government, law, and engineering. ▲

Time Period	Social Structure	Architecture	Religion	Arts and Sciences
Ancient Greece				
Ancient Rome				
Middle Ages				

A Land of Varied Riches

TERMS & NAMES
Mediterranean Sea
peninsula
fjord
Ural Mountains
plain

MAIN IDEA

Europe is a continent with varied geographic features, abundant natural resources, and a climate that can support agriculture.

WHY IT MATTERS NOW

The development of Europe's diverse cultures has been shaped by the continent's diverse geography.

DATELINE

EXTRA

LONDON, ENGLAND, MAY 6, 1994

Rough waters have always made the English Channel, which separates England and France, difficult to cross. Now, however, you can make the trip under the water! Today, a tunnel nicknamed "the Chunnel" opens, allowing high-speed trains to travel between London and Paris in about three hours. The Chunnel—short for Channel Tunnel—was carved through chalky earth under the sea floor and took seven years to build. It is the largest European construction project of the 20th century.

Movement • Eurostar trains make the 31-mile trip under the English Channel in only 20 minutes. ▲

Location • The Channel Tunnel connects England and France. ▲

The Geography of Europe

Today, cars, airplanes, and trains are common forms of high-speed transportation across Europe. Before the 19th century, however, the fastest form of transportation was to travel by water—on top of it, rather than under it.

Waterways Look at the map of Europe on page 277. Water surrounds the continent to the north, south, and west. The southern coast of Europe borders the warm waters of the **Mediterranean Sea.** Europe also has many rivers. The highly traveled Rhine and Danube rivers are two of the most important. The Volga, which flows nearly 2,200 miles through western Russia, is the continent's longest. For hundreds of years, these and other waterways have been home to boats and barges carrying people and goods inland across great distances.

Landforms Several large **peninsulas,** or bodies of land surrounded by water on three sides, form the European continent. In Northern Europe, the Scandinavian Peninsula is home to Norway and Sweden. Along the jagged shoreline of this peninsula are beautiful fjords (fyawrdz). A **fjord** is a long, narrow, deep inlet of the sea located between steep cliffs. In Western Europe, the Iberian Peninsula includes Portugal and Spain. The Iberian Peninsula is separated from the rest of the continent by a mountain range called the Pyrenees (PEER·uh·NEEZ). The entire continent of Europe, itself surrounded by water on three sides, is a giant peninsula.

Reading
Social Studies

A. Clarifying Why were waterways important for the movement of people and goods?

BACKGROUND

Europe can be divided into four areas: Western Europe, Northern Europe, Eastern Europe, and Russia and its neighboring countries.

Place • **The Scandinavian Peninsula is the location of many spectacular fjords, such as this one in Norway.** ▶

Reading
Social Studies

B. Clarifying
What natural
landform separates
Europe from Asia?

Mountain ranges, including the towering Alps, also stretch across much of the continent. Along Europe's eastern border, the **Ural Mountains** (YUR·uhl) divide the continent from Asia. The many mountain ranges of Europe separated groups of people from one another as they settled the land thousands of years ago. This is one of the reasons why different cultures developed across the continent.

The Great European Plain Not all of Europe is mountainous. A vast region called the Great European Plain stretches from the coast of France to the Ural Mountains. A **plain** is a large, flat area of land, usually without many trees. The Great European Plain is the location of some of the world's richest farmland. Ancient trading centers attracted many people to this area, which today includes some of the largest cities in Europe—Paris, Berlin, Warsaw, and Moscow.

Climate

Although the Gulf Stream brings warm air and water to Europe, the winters are still severe in the mountains and in the far north. In some of these areas, cold winds blow southward from the Arctic Circle and make the average temperature fall below 0°F in January. The Alps and the Pyrenees, however, protect the European countries along the Mediterranean Sea from these chilling winds. In these warmer parts of southern Europe, the average temperature in January stays above 50°F.

The summers in the south are usually hot and dry, with an average July temperature around 80°F. This makes the Mediterranean coast a popular vacation spot. Elsewhere in Europe, in all but the coldest areas of the mountains and the far north, the average July temperature ranges from 50°F to 70°F.

Natural Resources

Europe has a large variety of natural resources, including minerals. The rich coal deposits of Germany's Ruhr (rur) Valley region have helped to make that area one of the world's major industrial centers. Russia and Ukraine have large deposits of iron ore, which is used to make iron for automobiles and countless other products.

Region • Western Europe benefits from a varied landscape rich in natural resources. ▼

Land Use in Europe Today

Legend:
- Forest
- Orchards and vineyards
- Dairy land and fodder crops
- Rye and potatoes
- Wheat
- Upland grazing
- Unused land
- Urban and industrial

0 250 500 miles
0 250 500 kilometers

ATLANTIC OCEAN
Arctic Circle
North Sea
Baltic Sea
Bay of Biscay
Black Sea
Adriatic Sea
Mediterranean Sea
40°N
30°N
10°W   0°   10°E   20°E   30°E   40°E

GEOGRAPHY SKILLBUILDER: Interpreting a Map

1. Place • What are the three most common uses of land in Europe?

2. Location • Where is the majority of unused land?

Vocabulary

precipitation: moisture, including rain, snow, and hail, that falls to the ground

Europe also has rich soil and plentiful rainfall. The average precipitation for the Great European Plain, for example, is between 20 and 40 inches per year. The map above shows the agricultural uses of the land, highlighting the major crops. Notice that few parts of the continent are too cold or too hot and dry to support some form of agriculture. These characteristics have made Europe a world leader in crop production.

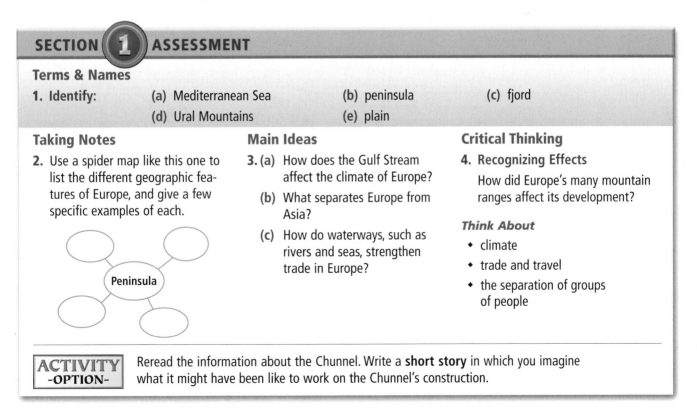

SECTION 1 ASSESSMENT

Terms & Names

1. Identify:
(a) Mediterranean Sea
(b) peninsula
(c) fjord
(d) Ural Mountains
(e) plain

Taking Notes

2. Use a spider map like this one to list the different geographic features of Europe, and give a few specific examples of each.

Peninsula

Main Ideas

3. (a) How does the Gulf Stream affect the climate of Europe?

(b) What separates Europe from Asia?

(c) How do waterways, such as rivers and seas, strengthen trade in Europe?

Critical Thinking

4. **Recognizing Effects**

How did Europe's many mountain ranges affect its development?

Think About

- climate
- trade and travel
- the separation of groups of people

ACTIVITY -OPTION- Reread the information about the Chunnel. Write a **short story** in which you imagine what it might have been like to work on the Chunnel's construction.

Ancient Greece

TERMS & NAMES
city-state
polis
Aegean Sea
oligarchy
Athens
philosopher
Aristotle
Alexander the Great

MAIN IDEA

The ancient Greeks developed a complex society, with remarkable achievements in the arts, sciences, and government.

WHY IT MATTERS NOW

The achievements of the ancient Greeks continue to influence culture, science, and politics in the world today.

DATELINE

ATHENS, GREECE, FEBRUARY 2, 1997— Five years after construction workers began building the new Athens subway, artifacts from ancient Greek civilization are still being discovered. When completed, the new subway will reduce traffic and air pollution in the capital. Historians and archaeologists, however, have been the first to benefit from this massive public works project.

Workers have discovered statues, coins, jewelry, and gravesites from ancient Greece. Recently, workers digging the foundation for a downtown Athens station found an ancient dog collar decorated with gemstones. Local officials have promised to create

Place • Building the subway in Athens led to spectacular discoveries of ancient artifacts. ▲

permanent displays of some artifacts in stations throughout the new subway system.

The Land and Early History of Greece

The Greek Peninsula is mountainous, which made travel by land difficult for early settlers. Most of the rocky land also contains poor soil and few large trees, but settlers were able to cultivate the soil to grow olives and grapes. The greatest natural resource of the peninsula is the water that surrounds it. The ancient Greeks depended on these seas for fishing and trade, and they became excellent sailors.

Vocabulary

cultivate: to prepare land for growing crops

The Formation of City-States As the ancient Greek population grew, people created city-states. A **city-state** included a central city, called a **polis,** and surrounding villages. Each ancient Greek city-state had its own laws and form of government. The city-states were united by a common language, shared religious beliefs, and a similar way of life.

The Growth of Colonies By the mid-eighth century B.C., the Greeks were leaving the peninsula in search of better land and greater opportunities for trade. During the next 200 years, they built dozens of communities on the islands and coastline of the **Aegean Sea** (ih·JEE·uhn). Some Greeks settled as far away as modern-day Spain and North Africa.

Once established, these distant Greek communities traded with each other and with those communities on the Greek Peninsula. This made a great variety of goods available to the ancient Greeks, including wheat for bread, timber for building boats, and iron ore for making strong tools and weapons.

Connections to Language

Metropolis When ancient Greeks moved away from a large polis to a distant community, they referred to their former city-state as their metropolis. In Greek, this means "mother-city." Today, we use the word *metropolis* to mean any large urban area, such as Los Angeles, London, Tokyo, or Athens *(shown below).*

Greek Colonization, 800 B.C.

GEOGRAPHY SKILLBUILDER: Interpreting a Map

1. **Place** • What was the value to the Greeks of controlling Byzantium?

2. **Location** • What was the southernmost Greek territory at this time?

Ionia Historic city name

Sparta Historic and current city name

Greek colonization

Spartan Soldiers Sparta was the only city-state with a permanent army. At age seven, Spartan boys were sent by their families for military training. They had to remain in the army until they were 30 years old.

Individual Forms of Government Some ancient Greek city-states were oligarchies (AHL·ih·GAHR·kees). An **oligarchy** is a system in which a few powerful, wealthy individuals rule. The word *oligarchy* comes from an ancient Greek word meaning "rule by the few." Other city-states were ruled by a tyrant, a single person who took control of the government against the wishes of the community. Still other ancient Greek city-states developed an early form of democracy. The word *democracy* comes from an ancient Greek word meaning "rule by the people." In a democracy citizens, take part in the government.

Athens and Sparta

<u>Athens,</u> centrally located on the Greek Peninsula, was one of the largest and most important ancient Greek city-states. By the end of the sixth century B.C., Athens had developed a democratic form of government. Athenian citizens took part in political debates and voted on laws, but not everyone who lived in Athens enjoyed these rights. Participation in government was limited to free, adult males whose fathers had been citizens of Athens. Women, slaves, and foreign residents could not take part in government.

Athens's chief rival among the other Greek city-states was Sparta. Located in the southernmost part of the Greek Peninsula, Sparta was an oligarchy. It was ruled by two kings, who were supported by other officials. Sparta, like Athens, had a powerful army. Each city-state's army helped protect it from slave rebellions, guard against attack by rival city-states, and defend it from possible foreign invaders.

Learning and the Arts

In 480 B.C., the Persians, who controlled a large empire to the east, tried to conquer the Greek Peninsula. Several Greek city-states, including Athens and Sparta, joined forces to defeat the Persians. In the years following this victory, the ancient Greeks made remarkable achievements in literature, learning, and architecture.

Reading
Social Studies

A. Comparing Compare the three forms of government most common in ancient Greek city-states.

BACKGROUND

After the defeat of Persia, Athens became the most powerful Greek city-state. The most important Athenian leader of the time was Pericles (PEHR·ih·KLEEZ), who lived from c. 495 to 429 B.C.

Literature To honor their gods and goddesses, the ancient Greeks created myths and wrote poems and plays. Some of the greatest Greek plays were written during the fifth century B.C. During that time, the playwrights Aeschylus (EHS·kuh·luhs), Sophocles (SAHF·uh·KLEEZ), and Euripides (yu·RIHP·ih·DEEZ) wrote tragedies, which are serious plays that end unhappily. Many of these stories have been the basis for modern films and operas.

In addition to using the gods as characters, ancient Greek playwrights sometimes poked fun at important citizens, including generals and politicians. Aristophanes (ar·ih·STAHF·uh·NEEZ) was a popular writer of comedies of this type.

Philosophy Ancient Greece was the birthplace of some of the finest thinkers of the ancient world. Socrates (SAHK·ruh·TEEZ) was an important philosopher of the fifth century B.C. A **philosopher** studies and thinks about why the world is the way it is. Socrates studied and taught about friendship, knowledge, and justice. Another great philosopher, Plato (PLAY·toh), was a student of Socrates who studied and taught about human behavior, government, mathematics, and astronomy.

The ancient Greek philosopher Heraclitus (hehr·uh·KLY·tuhs) wrote the following lines.

Reading
Social Studies

B. Making Inferences Why do you think philosophers felt the need to teach?

> **A VOICE FROM ANCIENT GREECE**
>
> One cannot step twice into the same river, for the water into which you first stepped has flowed on.
>
> **Heraclitus**

Many people continue to study and write about the same philosophical questions that these, and other, ancient Greek philosophers explored.

The WORLD'S HERITAGE

Ancient Greek Architecture Ancient Greek builders created some of the world's most impressive works of architecture. They built several beautiful temples atop the Acropolis (uh·KRAHP·uh·lihs) in Athens, shown at right. The most famous of the temples is the Parthenon (PAHR·thuh·nahn).

In the United States and elsewhere, government buildings, such as courthouses and post offices, have been built similar in style to the Parthenon. This use of ancient architecture echoes the democratic ideals of ancient Greece.

Biography

Aristotle At the age of 17, Aristotle (384–322 B.C.) began studying philosophy with Plato. After Plato died, Aristotle received his most important assignment—to teach Alexander, the teenage son of King Philip II of Macedonia.

After teaching Alexander, Aristotle returned to Athens. There he taught and wrote about poetry, government, and astronomy. He started a famous school called the Lyceum (ly•SEE•uhm). Aristotle also collected and studied plants and animals. The work of this brilliant philosopher continues to greatly influence scientists and philosophers today.

The Spread of Greek Culture The city-states of ancient Greece were constantly at war with one another. By the fourth century B.C., this fighting had weakened their ability to defend themselves against foreign invaders. In 338 B.C., King Philip II of Macedonia conquered the land. After Philip died, his son, Alexander—who had been taught by **Aristotle**—took control.

Alexander the Great was an excellent military leader, and his armies conquered vast new territories. As Alexander's empire expanded, Greek culture, language, and ideas were spread throughout the Mediterranean region and as far east as modern-day India. Upon Alexander's death, however, his leading generals fought for control of his territory and divided it among themselves. This marked the end of one of the great empires of the ancient world.

Region • In this mosaic Alexander the Great is shown riding into battle on his beloved horse, Bucephalus (byoo•SEHF•ah•luhs). ▲

SECTION 2 ASSESSMENT

Terms & Names

1. **Identify:**
   (a) city-state
   (b) polis
   (c) Aegean Sea
   (d) oligarchy
   (e) Athens
   (f) philosopher
   (g) Aristotle
   (h) Alexander the Great

Taking Notes

2. Use a chart like this one to list and describe the ancient Greek achievements in government, literature, and architecture.

Government	Literature	Architecture

Main Ideas

3. (a) Why were the surrounding areas of water an important natural resource of the Greek Peninsula?

   (b) Which people were allowed to participate in the government of ancient Athens?

   (c) How did Alexander the Great help to spread Greek culture?

Critical Thinking

4. **Summarizing**

   Why was the fifth century B.C. a remarkable time in ancient Greek history?

   Think About
   - warfare
   - leaders
   - literature and philosophy

ACTIVITY -OPTION- Reread the information about the individual forms of government common in ancient Greece. Present an **oral report** to the class that compares and contrasts two of the forms.

Making a Generalization

▶▶ Defining the Skill

To make generalizations means to make broad judgments based on information. When you make generalizations, you should gather information from several sources.

▶▶ Applying the Skill

The following three passages contain different information on the government of ancient Athens. Use the strategies listed below to make a generalization about Athenian government based on the passages.

How to Make a Generalization

Strategy ① Look for all the information that the sources have in common. These three sources all explain about Athenian government.

Strategy ② Form a generalization that describes ancient Athenian government in a way that all three sources would support. State your generalization in a sentence.

Make a Chart

Using a chart can help you make generalizations. The chart below shows how the information you just read can be used to generalize about the government of ancient Athens.

① Athenian citizens took part in political debates and voted on laws, but not everyone who lived in Athens enjoyed these rights. Participation in government was limited to free, adult males whose fathers had been citizens in Athens.

—*World Cultures and Geography*

In return for playing their parts as soldiers or sailors, ① ordinary Athenians insisted on controlling the government.

—*Encyclopaedia Britannica*

Unlike representative democracies or republics, in which one man is elected to speak for many, Athens was a true ① democracy: every citizen spoke for himself.

—*Classical Greece*

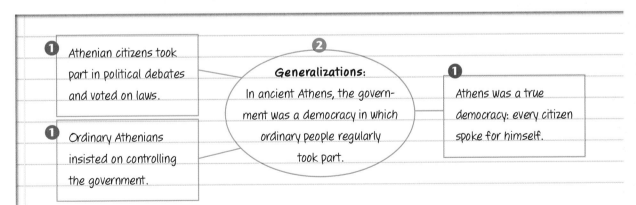

▶▶ Practicing the Skill

Turn to Chapter 10, Section 2, "Ancient Greece." Read the sections on literature and philosophy. Also read about ancient Greek writings in an encyclopedia, a library book, or on the Internet. Then make a chart like the one above to form a generalization about the importance of knowledge and learning to the ancient Greeks.

Ancient Rome

TERMS & NAMES
republic
Senate
patrician
plebeian
Julius Caesar
empire
Augustus
Constantine

MAIN IDEA

The ancient Romans made important contributions to government, law, and engineering.

WHY IT MATTERS NOW

The cultural achievements of the Romans continue to influence the art, architecture, and literature of today.

DATELINE EXTRA

ROME, 295 B.C.

Yet another Roman road was completed today! Rome is famous for its vast network of roadways. Repairing old roads and adding new ones keeps Roman engineers busy. Construction is time-consuming because the lengthy roads, which are paved with large stones, must be carefully planned. However, the benefits are worth the effort.

The roads connect the great city to distant lands under Roman rule. These roadways also enable the army to move quickly. These days, it seems that almost all roads lead to Rome. In fact, when this massive undertaking is finished, Roman roads will stretch for tens of thousands of miles across the land.

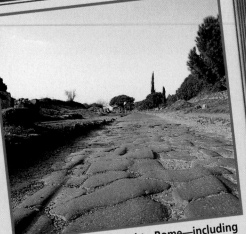

Location • All roads lead to Rome—including the Via Appia (VEE•uh APP•ee•uh) shown here. ▲

The Beginnings of Ancient Rome

Ancient Rome began as a group of villages located along the banks of the Tiber River in what is now Italy. There, early settlers herded sheep and grew wheat, olives, and grapes. Around 750 B.C., these villages united to form the city of Rome.

The Formation of the Roman Republic For more than 200 years, kings ruled Rome. Then, in 509 B.C., Rome became a republic. A **republic** is a nation in which power belongs to the citizens, who govern themselves through elected representatives.

The Senate The Roman **Senate** was an assembly of elected representatives. It was the single most powerful ruling body of the Roman Republic. Each year, the Senate selected two leaders, called consuls, to head the government and the military.

BACKGROUND

In ancient Rome, a senator held his position for life.

Patricians At first, most of the people elected to the Senate were patricians (puh·TRIHSH·uhns). In ancient Rome, a **patrician** was a member of a wealthy, landowning family who claimed to be able to trace its roots back to the founding of Rome. The patricians also controlled the law, since they were the only citizens who were allowed to be judges.

Plebeians An ordinary, working male citizen of ancient Rome—such as a farmer or craftsperson—was called a **plebeian** (plih·BEE·uhn). Plebeians had the right to vote, but they could not hold public office until 287 B.C., when they gained equality with patricians.

The Expansion of the Roman World

Over hundreds of years, Rome grew into a mighty city. By the third century B.C., Rome ruled most of the Italian Peninsula. This gave Rome control of the central Mediterranean.

The city-state of Carthage, which ruled North Africa and southern Spain, controlled the western Mediterranean. To take control over this area as well, Rome fought Carthage and eventually won.

As Rome's population grew, its army also expanded in size and strength. Under the leadership of ambitious generals, Rome's highly trained soldiers set out to conquer new territories one by one.

Roman Law It may be hard to believe, but in the early Roman Republic, laws were not written down. Only the patrician judges knew what the laws were. This meant that judges usually ruled in favor of fellow patricians and against plebeians.

The plebeians grew tired of unfair treatment and demanded that the judges create a written code of laws that applied to all Roman citizens. This code, called the Law of the Twelve Tables, was written around 450 B.C. It formed the foundation of Roman law.

Extent of Roman Control, 509 B.C. to 146 B.C.

- 509 B.C.
- 241 B.C.
- 146 B.C.
- • Major city

ATLANTIC OCEAN

GAUL

SPAIN

ITALY

Rome

Adriatic Sea

Black Sea

SICILY

Carthage

GREECE

AFRICA

Mediterranean Sea

EGYPT

0 250 500 miles
0 250 500 kilometers

GEOGRAPHY SKILLBUILDER: Interpreting a Map

1. **Location** • Around which body of water was Roman control located in 146 B.C.?
2. **Region** • When was Roman control at its greatest?

As Rome's control over its neighbors expanded, its culture and language continued to spread into Spain and Greece. By the end of the second century B.C., the Romans ruled most of the land surrounding the Mediterranean Sea. The ancient Romans even called the Mediterranean *mare nostrum* (MAH•ray NOH•struhm), which means "our sea."

Region • Once in power, Julius Caesar had his likeness stamped on coins such as this one. ▼

From Republic to Empire

As the Roman Republic grew, its citizens became a more and more diverse group of people. Many Romans practiced different religions and followed different customs, but they were united by a common system of government and law. In the middle of the first century B.C., however, Rome's form of government changed.

The End of the Roman Republic **Julius Caesar,** a successful Roman general and famous speaker, was the governor of the territory called Gaul. By conquering nearby territories to expand the land under his control, he increased both his power and his reputation. The Roman Senate feared that Caesar might become too powerful, and they ordered him to resign. Caesar, however, had other ideas.

BACKGROUND

Ancient Gaul included the lands that are modern-day France, Belgium, and parts of northern Italy.

Rather than resign, Caesar fought a long, fierce battle for control of the Roman Republic. In 45 B.C., he finally triumphed and returned to Rome. Caesar eventually became dictator of the Roman world. A dictator is a person who holds total control over a government. Caesar's rule marked the end of the Roman Republic.

The Beginning of the Roman Empire Julius Caesar had great plans to reorganize the way ancient Rome was governed, but his rule was cut short. On March 15, 44 B.C., a group of senators, angered by Caesar's plans and power, stabbed him to death on the floor of the Roman Senate. A civil war then erupted that lasted for several years.

Reading
Social Studies

A. Recognizing Important Details How many years separated the rules of Julius Caesar and Augustus?

In 27 B.C., Caesar's adopted son, Octavian, was named the first emperor of Rome. This marks the official beginning of the Roman Empire. An **empire** is a nation or group of territories ruled by a single, powerful leader, or emperor. As emperor, Octavian took the name **Augustus.**

Region • Sculptures of Augustus were sent all over the Roman Empire to let people know what their leader looked like. ▲

The Augustan Age Augustus ruled the Roman Empire for more than 40 years. During this time, called the Augustan Age, the empire continued to expand. To help protect the enormous amount of land under his control, Augustus sent military forces along its borders, which now extended northward to the Rhine and Danube rivers.

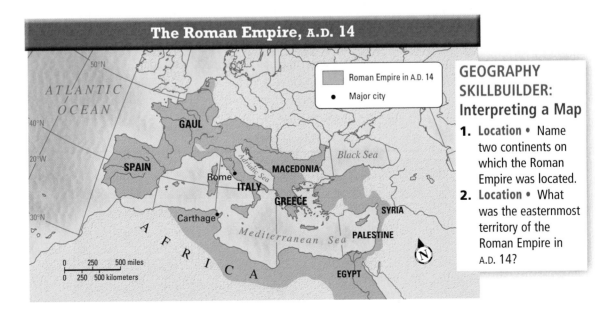

The Roman Empire, A.D. 14

ATLANTIC OCEAN

GAUL

SPAIN

Rome
ITALY
Carthage

Adriatic Sea

MACEDONIA
Black Sea

GREECE

Mediterranean Sea

SYRIA

PALESTINE

AFRICA

EGYPT

0   250   500 miles
0   250   500 kilometers

Roman Empire in A.D. 14
• Major city

GEOGRAPHY SKILLBUILDER: Interpreting a Map

1. **Location** • Name two continents on which the Roman Empire was located.

2. **Location** • What was the easternmost territory of the Roman Empire in A.D. 14?

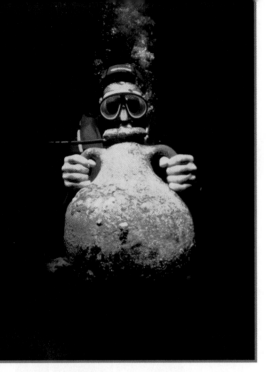

While the Roman army kept peace, architects and engineers built many new public buildings. Trade increased, with olive oil, wine, pottery, marble, and grain being shipped all across the Mediterranean. Lighthouses were constructed, too, to help ships find their way into port.

Vocabulary

marble:
a hard, smooth stone, often white in color

The Augustan Age was also a time of great Roman literature. One of the most famous works of the age is the *Aeneid* (ih·NEE·ud). This long poem tells the story of Rome's founding. Augustus himself asked the famous poet Virgil to write it. This period of peace and cultural growth that Augustus created in the Roman Empire was called the "Pax Romana" (pahks roh·MAH·nah). The Pax Romana, or Roman Peace, lasted for 200 years.

Region • A diver holds an artifact from an ancient Roman shipwreck in the Mediterranean Sea. ▲

Spotlight on CULTURE

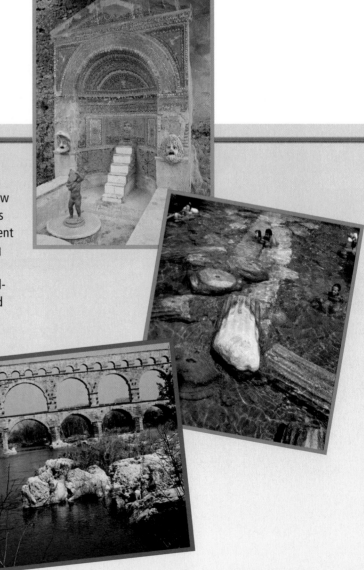

Architecture Various inventions helped the Roman Empire grow and prosper. In addition to buildings and roads, Roman architects and engineers constructed water systems called aqueducts. Ancient aqueducts were raised tunnels that carried fresh water over long distances.

Built throughout the empire, aqueducts poured millions of gallons of water into Rome and other cities every day. They supplied clean water to private homes, fountains, and public baths. Today, some ancient Roman aqueducts still stand in France, Spain, and even on the outskirts of Rome itself.

THINKING CRITICALLY

1. **Analyzing Motives**
   Why did Romans want a way to transport water?

2. **Hypothesizing**
   Do you think the Roman Empire would have grown so large and prosperous without the aqueducts?

The Rise of Christianity

Reading
Social Studies

B. Making Inferences How do you think the Roman Empire indirectly helped the spread of Christianity?

In the years following the death of Augustus in A.D. 14, a new religion from the Middle East began to take hold in the rest of the Mediterranean world: Christianity. At first, this religion became popular mainly in the eastern half of the Roman Empire. Many followers there preached about its teachings. Christianity spread along the transportation network constructed by the Romans. By the third century A.D., this religion had spread throughout the empire.

Most earlier Roman leaders had tolerated the different religions practiced throughout the empire. Christians, however, were viewed with suspicion and suffered persecution as early as A.D. 64. Roman leaders and people of other religions even blamed the Christians for natural disasters. Many Christians during this time were punished or killed for their beliefs.

Region • Constantine (died A.D. 337) was the first Christian emperor of Rome. ▼

The First Christian Emperor

Things changed when **Constantine** became emperor of Rome in A.D. 306. In A.D. 312, before a battle, Constantine claimed to have had a vision of a cross in the sky. The emperor promised that if he won the battle, he would become a Christian. Constantine was victorious, and the next year he fulfilled his promise. Christianity became the official religion of the Roman Empire. Today, Christianity has nearly two billion followers worldwide.

SECTION 3 ASSESSMENT

Terms & Names

1. **Identify:**
   (a) republic
   (b) Senate
   (c) patrician
   (d) plebeian
   (e) Julius Caesar
   (f) empire
   (g) Augustus
   (h) Constantine

Taking Notes

2. Use a chart like this one to outline the achievements of ancient Rome's Augustan Age.

Achievement	Effects

Main Ideas

3. (a) On what waterway is the city of Rome located?
   (b) What helped to unite the many different citizens of the Roman Republic?
   (c) How did Christianity spread throughout the Roman Empire?

Critical Thinking

4. **Drawing Conclusions**

   Why was ancient Rome able to control most of the land surrounding the Mediterranean Sea?

   Think About
   * the location of the Italian Peninsula
   * Rome's army
   * Rome's wars with Carthage

ACTIVITY
-OPTION-

Review the information about the beginnings of ancient Rome. Create a **chart** that compares the two important classes of Roman society: patricians and plebeians.

Time of Change: The Middle Ages

TERMS & NAMES
medieval
Charlemagne
feudalism
manorialism
guild
Magna Carta

MAIN IDEA

The Middle Ages was a time of great change in Western Europe.

WHY IT MATTERS NOW

Some developments that occurred during the Middle Ages continue to affect life in Europe today.

DATELINE

ROME, A.D. 476—A Germanic tribe called the Visigoths has attacked our city of Rome and overthrown the emperor, Romulus Augustulus. The Roman army—no longer as large or as well organized as it was during the height of the empire—was unable to fight off the invaders.

After looting the great city, fierce bands of warriors and bandits have continued raiding towns and villages throughout Western Europe. They are stealing jewels and money, killing both people and animals, and even seizing control of entire territories. The Roman Empire seems to have breathed its last breath.

Region • Visigoth artifacts, like these saddle buckles, were found near Rome. ▲

Western Europe in Collapse

As the Roman Empire collapsed in the fifth century, more and more people fled to the countryside to escape invaders from the north and east. Eventually, there was no central government to maintain roads, public buildings, or water systems. Most towns and cities in Western Europe shrank or were totally abandoned. Long-distance travel became unsafe, and trade less common.

The Beginning of the Medieval Era The period of history between the fall of the Roman Empire and the beginning of the modern world is called the Middle Ages, or **medieval** (MEE·dee·EE·vuhl) era. During this time, many of the advances and inventions of the ancient world were lost. Without a strong central government, many Europeans turned to military leaders and the Roman Catholic Church for leadership and support.

Charlemagne and the Christian Church

Among the most famous military leaders was the Germanic King Charlemagne (SHAHR·luh·mayn). In the late 700s, **Charlemagne,** or Charles the Great, worked to bring political order to the northwestern fringes of what had been the Roman Empire. This great warrior not only fought to increase the size of his kingdom, he also worked to improve life for those who lived there.

A New Roman Emperor Eventually, news of Charlemagne's accomplishments spread to Rome. Although the old empire was gone, Rome was now the center of the Catholic Church. The Pope recognized that joining forces with Charlemagne might bring greater power to the Church.

In 800, the Pope crowned Charlemagne as the new Holy Roman Emperor. During Charlemagne's rule, education improved, the government became stronger, and Catholicism spread. But after Charlemagne's death, Western Europe was once again without a strong political leader.

Region •
Charlemagne established order and supported education and culture for a brief period in the early Middle Ages. ▲

The Role of the Church

Throughout Western Europe in medieval times, each community was centered around a church. The church offered religious services, established orphanages, and helped care for the poor, sick, and elderly. They also hosted feasts, festivals, and other celebrations. As communities grew, their members often donated money and labor to build new and larger churches.

Monks and Nuns Some people chose to dedicate their lives to serving God and the Church. These religious people were called monks and nuns. Monks were men who devoted their time to praying, studying, and copying and decorating holy books by hand. Monks lived in communities called monasteries. Many monasteries became important centers of learning in medieval society.

Location •
Convents and
monasteries
often were
located in
hard-to-reach
areas. ▲

Women who served the Church were called nuns. In the Middle Ages, it was common for a woman to become a nun after her husband died. Nuns prayed, sewed, taught young girls, cared for the poor, and also copied and decorated books. They lived in secluded communities called convents.

Vocabulary

secluded:
to be separate or
hidden away

Two Medieval Systems

During the Middle Ages, almost all the land was owned by powerful nobles—lords, kings, and high church officials. The central government was not very strong. The nobles sometimes even controlled the king and constantly fought among themselves. To protect their lands and position, nobles developed a system known as feudalism.

The Feudal System <u>**Feudalism**</u> was a system of political ties in which the nobles, such as kings, gave out land to less powerful nobles, such as knights. In return for the land, the noble, called a vassal, made a vow to provide various services to the lord. The most important was to furnish his lord with knights, foot soldiers, and arms for battle.

The parcel of land granted to a vassal by his lord was called a fief (feef). The center of the lord's fief was the manor, which consisted of a large house or castle, surrounding farmland, villages, and a church. A fief might also include several other manors or castles belonging to the fief-owner's vassals.

Connections to History

The Bayeux Tapestry This famous work of art depicts the invasion of England by William the Conqueror in 1066. The Bayeux (by•YOO) Tapestry is a series of scenes from the point of view of the invaders, who came from Normandy. Normandy is a part of what is now France. The work is an important source of information about not only the conquest of England, but also medieval armor, clothing, and other aspects of culture.

Although called a tapestry, the work is really an embroidered strip of linen about 230 feet long. It includes captions in Latin. The Bayeux Tapestry was probably made by nuns in England about 1092.

Manorialism On the manor, peasants lived and farmed, but they usually did not own the land they lived on. In exchange for their lord's protection, the peasants contributed their labor and a certain amount of the food they raised. Some peasants, known as serfs, actually belonged to the fief on which they lived. They were not slaves, but they were not free to leave the land without the permission of the lord. This system, in which the lord received food and work in exchange for his protection, is known as **manorialism.**

Place • Although castles were large, they were built for defense. Castles were usually located on high ground with a series of walls and towers. ▲

Medieval Ways of Life

Medieval nobles had more power than the peasants. However, the difference in the standard of living between the very rich and the very poor was not as great as the difference today.

Castle Life The manor houses or castles may have been large, but they were built more for defense than for comfort. Thick stone walls and few windows made the rooms cold, damp, and dark. Fires added warmth but made the air smoky. Medieval noble families may have slept on feather mattresses, but lice and other pests were a constant annoyance. Most castles did not have indoor plumbing.

Peasant Life Peasants lived outside the castle walls in small dwellings, often with dirt floors and straw roofs. They owned little furniture and slept on straw mattresses. It was common for peasant families to keep their farm animals inside their homes.

Peasants often worked two or three days a week for their lord, harvesting crops and repairing roads and bridges. The rest of the week they farmed their own small plots. Many days were religious festivals during which no one worked.

Connections to Economics

The Middle Class In the early Middle Ages, only a small percentage of people in Western Europe were wealthy landowners. Most people worked on manor lands or at some sort of craft. However, those workers who found jobs in towns often were able to save money and build businesses. Eventually, their improved status led to the rise of a middle class.

Unlike nobles, the members of this new middle class did not live off the land they owned. They had to continuously earn money, as most people do today.

The Growth of Medieval Towns

By the middle of the 11th century, life was improving for many people in Western Europe. New farming methods increased the supply of food and shortened the time it took to harvest crops. Fewer farmers were needed, and workers began to leave the countryside in search of other opportunities. People moved back into towns or formed new ones that grew into booming centers of trade. The population increased, and more and more people owned property or started businesses.

Guilds As competition among local businesspeople grew, tradespeople and craftspeople created their own guilds, or business associations. Similar to modern trade unions, a **guild** protected workers' rights, set wages and prices, and settled disputes. Membership in a guild was also a common requirement for citizens who sought one of the few elective public offices.

Reading
Social Studies

B. Analyzing Motives Why did people create guilds?

The Late Middle Ages

Over time, the towns of the late Middle Ages grew in size, power, and wealth. The citizens of these towns began to establish local governments and to elect leaders.

Governments Challenge the Church The Pope insisted that he had supreme authority over all the Christian lands. Kings and other government leaders, however, did not agree that the Pope was more powerful than they were. This is an issue that continues to be discussed today.

The Magna Carta The rulers of Western Europe also struggled for power with members of the nobility. In England, nobles rebelled against King John. In 1215, the nobles forced the English king to sign a document called the **Magna Carta** (MAG·nuh KAHR·tuh), or Great Charter. This document limited the king's power and gave the nobles a larger role in the government.

Region • High taxes and failures on the battlefield made King John one of the most hated kings of England. ▼

Region • The Magna Carta influenced the creators of the U.S. Constitution. ▲

SECTION 4 ASSESSMENT

Terms & Names

1. Identify:
   (a) medieval
   (b) Charlemagne
   (c) feudalism
   (d) manorialism
   (e) guild
   (f) Magna Carta

Taking Notes

2. Use a flow chart like this one to show how Europe changed over four time periods: A.D. 476, the 800s, the mid-1000s, and the 1200s.

   476
   ↓
   [ ]
   ↓
   800s
   ↓

Main Ideas

3. (a) Why is this era of European history called the Middle Ages?

   (b) Describe the role of the Church in medieval society.

   (c) How did manorialism help both nobles and peasants?

Critical Thinking

4. **Contrasting**

   How did life differ for nobles and peasants under feudalism?

   Think About
   - where they lived
   - what they ate
   - how they did their work

ACTIVITY -OPTION- Review the information about serfs. Write a series of short **journal entries** describing what a week in the life of a serf might have been like during the Middle Ages.

TERMS & NAMES

Explain the significance of each of the following:

1. peninsula
2. plain
3. city-state
4. Aegean Sea
5. Athens
6. republic
7. empire
8. Constantine
9. feudalism
10. Magna Carta

REVIEW QUESTIONS

A Land of Varied Riches *(pages 273–277)*

1. What is special about Europe's physical environment?
2. Why is the Great European Plain an important region?

Ancient Greece *(pages 278–282)*

3. What helped to unite the separate city-states of ancient Greece?
4. What caused the people of Athens to join forces with their rival city-state, Sparta, in 480 B.C.?

Ancient Rome *(pages 284–289)*

5. Why did the ancient Romans call the Mediterranean Sea "our sea"?
6. Why did the Roman Senate ask Julius Caesar to resign?

Time of Change: The Middle Ages *(pages 290–295)*

7. Why did the people turn to the Roman Catholic Church for leadership and support during the Middle Ages?
8. What contributed to the growth of towns during the Middle Ages?

CRITICAL THINKING

Recognizing Effects

1. Using your completed chart from Reading Social Studies, p. 272, identify changes in art, culture, religion, and social structure from the time of ancient Rome to the Middle Ages.

Hypothesizing

2. Many myths and plays of ancient Greece have been the basis for modern films and dramas. What does this indicate about these ancient stories and characters?

Analyzing Causes

3. How did the long, peaceful reign of Augustus help to promote architecture, literature, and art in the Roman Empire?

Visual Summary

1 A Land of Varied Riches

- The rich natural resources and varied geography of Europe helped to shape its development.

England
Chunnel
English Channel
France

2 Ancient Greece

- The ancient Greeks developed a complex society and system of government.
- The achievements of the ancient Greeks in architecture, literature, and philosophy had a lasting impact on the world.

3 Ancient Rome

- Under strong leadership, ancient Rome experienced a time of great growth.
- Ancient Rome's contributions to government, engineering, and literature influenced Western culture.

4 Time of Change: The Middle Ages

- The social order and government of the Middle Ages transformed Europe into a modern society.

SOCIAL STUDIES SKILLBUILDER

"Across the Roman Empire . . . [T]here were gods to protect the house, gods of healing, in fact gods of all aspects of life."
—*Ancient Rome*

"[The ancient Greeks] believed there were many gods and that those gods controlled the universe."
—*Greek Gods and Heroes*

"Each [Roman] home had a special niche or place for the household gods. Every aspect of nature had its particular spirit too."
—*The New Book of Knowledge*

SKILLBUILDER: Making a Generalization

1. What information do these passages have in common?
2. What generalization can you make from the passages?

FOCUS ON GEOGRAPHY

1. Location • What bodies of water does the Gulf Stream flow through on the way to Europe?
2. Movement • How might the Gulf Stream help transportation by sea?
3. Location • From looking at the map, what countries in Europe do you think are most directly affected by the Gulf Stream?

Interdisciplinary Activity:
Language Arts
Writing a Newspaper Report
Research the assassination of Julius Caesar by a group of Roman senators in 44 B.C. Write a front-page news article about the event. Include a headline and answers to the *who, what, where,* and *when* questions of good reporting.

Cooperative Learning Activity
Creating a Playbill With a group of two or three students, design and create a playbill, or program for the audience, for a Greek tragedy. Assign responsibilities for the playbill.
• Design a cover illustration.
• List and identify the characters.
• Provide information about the playwright.
• Include a brief summary of the story.

INTERNET ACTIVITY

Use the Internet to research the natural resources of Europe. Focus on one region, such as the Ruhr Valley, the Mediterranean Sea, or the independent republics of Eastern Europe. Identify the major natural resources and explain how they contributed to that region's development.

Presenting Your Findings Organize your research for a class presentation. Include a map that shows the region and its resources. Prepare a short oral report about how that region has developed in modern times. List the Web sites you used to prepare your report.

For Internet links to support this activity, go to

RESEARCH LINKS
CLASSZONE.COM

CHAPTER 11

The Growth of New Ideas

How can trade spread disease?

Movement • In 1347, an epidemic of bubonic plague (boo•BAHN•ihk playg) hit Europe. This plague, also called the Black Death, started in Asia. Caravans and trading ships carried it to port cities on the Mediterranean Sea. The plague spread from Sicily to the Italian Peninsula and then to France, Spain, and England.

The Black Death was carried by fleas that infected both rats and humans. Rats did not die from the plague. Instead, they served as hosts, or carriers, for the disease. By 1349, the horrors of the epidemic reached Switzerland, Austria, and Hungary. Later, it even reached as far north and east as Scandinavia and Russia. Historians estimate that this plague killed one out of every three persons in Europe.

What do you think?

♦ Why might the plague have reached Italy before it spread to England?

♦ How do you think the Black Death might have affected the economy of Europe?

Place The Cape of Saint Vincent is at the southwest tip of Portugal, jutting into the Atlantic Ocean. This was the location of Prince Henry's School of Navigation, where Portuguese sailors learned ways to explore the oceans of the world.

READING SOCIAL STUDIES

BEFORE YOU READ

▶▶ *What Do You Know?*

Do you know who first sailed around the world? Do you know that Leonardo da Vinci drew plans for a helicopter 400 years before it was actually built? Think of other discoveries, inventions, events, and famous people. What do you think life was like for common people during this time? Think about movies you have seen, books you have read, and what you have learned in other classes about the Renaissance, the Industrial Revolution, and political revolutions in France, Russia, and the United States.

▶▶ *What Do You Want to Know?*

Decide what you know about changes in the West from the Renaissance into the 1800s. In your notebook, record what you hope to learn from this chapter.

READ AND TAKE NOTES

Reading Strategy: Categorizing One way to make sense of what you read is to categorize ideas. Categorizing means sorting information by certain traits, ideas, or characteristics. Use the chart below to categorize details about the topics covered in this chapter.

- Copy the chart into your notebook.
- As you read each section, look for information about ideas, people, and events.
- Record key details in each category.

Movement • New tools and inventions contributed to social and political changes. Some improvements include the astrolabe (above), the steam engine (left), and movable type (below). ◀

Influences	New Ideas	People/Achievements	Events/Effects
The Renaissance			
European Exploration and Conquest			
Scientific and Industrial Revolutions			
Political Revolutions			
The Russian Empire			

Renaissance Connections

TERMS & NAMES
Crusades
Renaissance
Florence
Leonardo da Vinci
William Shakespeare
Reformation
Martin Luther
Protestant

MAIN IDEA

The rebirth of art, literature, and ideas during the Renaissance changed European society.

WHY IT MATTERS NOW

Many accomplishments of the Renaissance are high points of Western culture and continue to inspire artists, writers, and thinkers of today.

DATELINE

EXTRA

PARIS, FRANCE, 1269

Paris is buzzing with activity as thousands of European soldiers assemble here. This is the starting-off point for the eighth Crusade, which has nearly a thousand miles to travel. King Louis IX of France, who is in command, is confident that his armies can restore European power over the Holy Land.

Since the Crusades began in 1096, the Christians have fought against the Muslims and founded four states in the eastern Mediterranean. European power has weakened since then. However, King Louis's army looks ready to recapture the lost territory for Christianity.

Movement • Crusaders will make their way toward the Holy Land. ▲

Europeans Encounter New Cultures

BACKGROUND

The Holy Land of the eastern Mediterranean is important to Christians, Jews, and Muslims.

The **Crusades**—a series of military expeditions in the 11th, 12th, and 13th centuries by Western European Christians to reclaim control of the Holy Lands from the Muslims—had a great influence on life in Western Europe. The long distances traveled by the Crusaders opened up trade routes, connecting Western Europeans with people of southwestern Asia and North Africa. This increased contact also helped Europeans rediscover the ideas and achievements of the ancient Greeks and Romans.

Italian City-States, c. 1350

Milan
Venice
Mantua
Genoa
Pisa
Florence
Corsica
42°N
Rome
Sardinia
Naples
Tyrrhenian
Sea
40°N
Sicily
Mediterranean Sea
38°N
12°E   14°E   16°E   18°E

0   50   100 miles
0   50   100 kilometers

I T A L Y
Adriatic Sea

Florence
Genoa
Milan
Kingdom of the Two Sicilies
Papal States
Venice

GEOGRAPHY SKILLBUILDER: Interpreting a Map

1. **Location** • Which city-state does not have access to water?
2. **Location** • Which city-state was in the best position to trade by land and sea with Asia?

Over time, this interest in the ancient world sparked a new era of creativity and learning in Western Europe. This cultural era, which lasted from the 14th to the 16th century, is called the **Renaissance**.

The Rebirth of Europe

The Renaissance began on the Italian Peninsula in the mid-14th century. During this time, many artists, architects, writers, and scholars created works of great importance. These included beautiful paintings, large sculptures, impressive buildings, and thought-provoking literature. As new ideas and achievements spread across the continent of Europe, they changed the way people viewed themselves and the world.

The Italian City-States In the 14th century, the Italian Peninsula was divided into many independent city-states. Some of these city-states, such as **Florence,** were bustling centers of banking, trade, and manufacturing.

BACKGROUND

After Rome fell, many achievements of ancient times were lost. Many books and manuscripts, however, were preserved by Muslim and Christian scholars.

Region • Florence, once a wealthy city-state, remains an important economic and cultural center. The Duomo, shown here, is a symbol of the city's Renaissance past. ▼

Region • The wealthy merchants in Italy built large palaces, called palazzos, such as Florence's Palazzo Medici shown here. ▶

The wealthy businesspeople who lived in these city-states were members of a new class of aristocrats. Unlike the nobles of the feudal system, these aristocrats lived in cities, and their wealth came from money and goods rather than from the lands they owned.

A Changing View of the World Religion was important to people's daily life during the Renaissance, but many wealthy Europeans began to turn increased attention to the material comforts of life.

New wealth allowed aristocratic families to build large homes for themselves in the city centers, decorating them with luxurious objects. They ate expensive food and dressed in fine clothes and jewels, often acquired as a result of the expanded trade routes. Aristocrats also placed increased emphasis on education and the arts.

Learning and the Arts Flourish

BACKGROUND

Some Renaissance architects, such as Filippo Brunelleschi (BROO•nuh•LEHS•kee), studied the ruins of Roman buildings and modeled their new buildings after ancient designs.

Wealthy citizens were proud of their city-states and often became generous patrons. A patron gave artists and scholars money and, sometimes, a place to live and work. They hired architects and designers to improve local churches, to design grand new buildings, and to create public sculptures and fountains. As one Italian city-state made additions and improvements, others competed to outdo it.

The Medici Family Among the most famous patrons of the Renaissance were the Medici (MEHD•uh•chee). They were a wealthy family of bankers and merchants. In fact, they were the most powerful leaders of Florence from the early 1400s until the 18th century.

Along with Lorenzo, pictured below, the Medici family included famous princes and dukes, two queens, and four popes. Throughout the 15th and 16th centuries, the Medici supported many artists, including Botticelli, Michelangelo, and Raphael. Today, Florence is still filled with important works of art made possible by the Medici.

As part of the competition to improve the appearance and status of their individual city-states, patrons wanted to attract the brightest and best-known scholars and poets of the time. Patrons believed that the contributions of these individuals would, in turn, add to the greatness of their city-states and attract more wealth.

The Visual Arts: New Subjects and Methods Most medieval art was based on religious subjects. Painters and sculptors of the early Renaissance created religious art too, but they also began to depict other subjects. Some made portraits for wealthy patrons. Others created works showing historical scenes or mythological stories.

Leonardo da Vinci One of the most famous artists and scientists of the Renaissance was **Leonardo da Vinci** (lee·uh·NAHR·doh duh VIHN·chee) (1452–1519). Among his best-known paintings are the *Mona Lisa,* a portrait of a young woman with a mysterious smile, and *The Last Supper.* Da Vinci was more than just a talented painter, however.

Throughout his life, da Vinci observed the world around him. He studied the flow of water, the flight of birds, and the workings of the human body. Da Vinci, who became a skilled engineer, scientist, and inventor, filled notebooks with thousands of sketches of his discoveries and inventions. He even drew ideas for flying machines, parachutes, and submarines—hundreds of years before they were built.

The Northern Renaissance

As the new Renaissance ideas about religion and art spread to Northern Europe, they inspired artists and writers working there. The Dutch scholar and philosopher Desiderius Erasmus (ih·RAS·muhs) (1466–1536), for example, criticized the church for its wealth and poked fun at its officials. During the late 16th and early 17th centuries, another writer—the Englishman **William Shakespeare**—wrote a series of popular stage plays. Many of his works, including *Romeo and Juliet* and *Macbeth,* are still read and performed around the world.

Culture •
Leonardo da Vinci completed the painting *La Belle Ferronnière* **in 1495.** ▲

Reading
Social Studies

A. Contrasting
How did the subject matter of Renaissance art differ from medieval art?

Connections to Math

Perspective During the Renaissance, artists began to use a technique called linear perspective. Linear perspective is a system of using lines to create the illusion of depth and distance. In the drawing below, notice how the perspective lines move toward a single point in the distance, giving the picture depth.

The Reformation

BACKGROUND

In 1516, the English writer Thomas More published a famous book called *Utopia*. It describes the author's idea of a perfect society. Today, the word "utopia" is used to describe any ideal place.

Roman Catholicism was still the most powerful religion in Western Europe. Some of the views of the northern Renaissance writers and scholars, however, were in conflict with the Roman Catholic Church. These new ideas would eventually lead to the **Reformation,** a 16th-century movement to change church practices.

Martin Luther The German monk **Martin Luther** (1483–1546) was one of the most important critics of the church. The wealth and corruption of many church officials disturbed him. Luther also spoke out against the church's policy of selling indulgences—the practice of forgiving sins in exchange for money.

In 1517, Luther wrote 95 theses, or statements of belief, attacking the sale of indulgences and other church practices. Copies were printed and handed out throughout Western Europe. After this, Luther was excommunicated, or cast out and no longer recognized as a member of a church, and went into hiding. While in hiding, he translated the Bible from Latin into German so that all literate, German-speaking people could read it. Under Luther's leadership, many Europeans began to challenge the practices of the Roman Catholic Church.

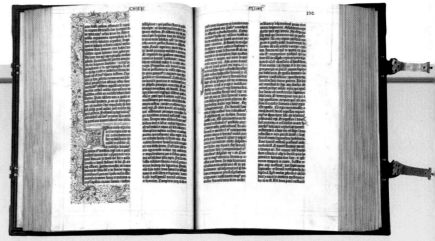

The Printing Press Until the Renaissance, each copy of a book had to be written by hand—usually by monks or nuns. A Renaissance invention, however, changed that forever. Around 1450, a German printer named Johannes Gutenberg (Yoh•HAHN•es GOO•tuhn•BERG) began to use a method of printing with movable type. This meant that multiple copies of books, such as this Bible, could be printed quickly and less expensively.

Although many Renaissance books dealt with religious subjects, printers also published plays, poetry, works of philosophy and science, and tales of travel and adventure. As greater numbers of books were published, more and more Europeans learned to read.

THINKING CRITICALLY

1. **Recognizing Effects**
   What were three effects of the invention of Gutenberg's printing press?

2. **Synthesizing**
   Before the printing press, who produced the books?

A Conflict over Religious Beliefs

Reading Social Studies

B. Clarifying How did Protestants get their name?

Luther's followers were called **Protestants** because they protested events at an assembly that ended the church's tolerance of their beliefs. Many people in Western Europe still supported the church, however. This conflict led to religious wars that ended in 1555. At that time, the Peace of Augsburg declared that German rulers could decide the official religion of their own state.

The Spread of Protestant Ideas By 1600, Protestantism had spread to England and the Scandinavian Peninsula. Protestants pushed to expand education for more Europeans. They did this because being able to read meant being able to study the Bible. They also encouraged translation of the Bible into the native language of each country.

The Counter Reformation The Roman Catholic Church responded to Protestantism by launching its own movement in the mid-16th century. As part of this movement, called the Counter Reformation, the church stopped selling indulgences. It also created a new religious order called the Society of Jesus, or the Jesuits. Jesuit missionaries and scholars worked to spread Catholic ideas across Europe, to Asia, and to the lands of the "new world" across the Atlantic Ocean.

Region •
Martin Luther's writings and actions changed Christianity forever. ▲

SECTION 1 ASSESSMENT

Terms & Names

1. **Identify:**
   (a) Crusades
   (b) Renaissance
   (c) Florence
   (d) Leonardo da Vinci
   (e) William Shakespeare
   (f) Reformation
   (g) Martin Luther
   (h) Protestant

Taking Notes

2. Use a spider map like this one to chart the characteristics and accomplishments of the Renaissance.

Renaissance Accomplishments

Main Ideas

3. (a) Where and when did the Renaissance begin?

   (b) In what ways were the wealthy Europeans of the Renaissance different from the wealthy Europeans of feudal times?

   (c) What was the Counter Reformation?

Critical Thinking

4. **Hypothesizing**

   Why do you think Protestantism spread so quickly in Northern Europe?

   Think About

   • new methods of printing
   • the ideas of the northern Renaissance
   • the work of Martin Luther

ACTIVITY -OPTION-

Write a **letter** to an imagined patron asking for support to create a project—such as a public sculpture, park, fountain, or building—to beautify your community.

Traders, Explorers, and Colonists

TERMS & NAMES

Prince Henry the Navigator

Christopher Columbus

Ferdinand Magellan

circumnavigate

imperialism

MAIN IDEA

European trade and exploration changed the lives of many people on both sides of the Atlantic.

WHY IT MATTERS NOW

Today, citizens of the Americas continue to feel the effects of European exploration and colonization.

DATELINE

SAGRES, PORTUGAL, 1421—
Portugal's Prince Henry may not have journeyed to sea, but he has earned a well-deserved nickname: "The Navigator." He has organized expeditions of sailors to explore the west coast of Africa. Five years ago, Henry also founded a School of Navigation. It is here in Sagres, at Portugal's southwestern tip, which juts into the Atlantic Ocean.

Astronomers, geographers, and mathematicians gather here to study and teach new methods of traveling across the seas. They plan expeditions using the latest maps, tools, and information about the winds and currents of the Atlantic Ocean. Sometimes the scholars add to their knowledge by talking with sea captains about their voyages.

Movement • Prince Henry of Portugal founded the School of Navigation. ▲

Trade Between Europe and Asia

For centuries before the Renaissance, European traders traveled back and forth across the Mediterranean. Merchants commonly journeyed from southern Europe to North Africa and to the eastern Mediterranean. Spices were one of the most important items traded at this time.

The Spice Trade Spices were in great demand by Europeans. Before refrigeration, meat and fish spoiled quickly. To help preserve food and to improve its flavor, people used spices such as pepper, cinnamon, nutmeg, and cloves. These spices came from Asia.

For centuries, Italian merchants from Genoa and Venice controlled the spice trade. They sailed to ports in the eastern Mediterranean, where they would purchase spices and other goods from traders who had traveled across Asia. The Italian merchants would then bring these goods back to Europe.

The Possibility of Great Wealth Transporting goods across these great distances was costly. Everyone along the way had to be paid and wanted to earn a profit. By the time the spices reached Europe, they had to be sold at extremely high prices.

European merchants knew that if they could trade directly with people in Asia, they could make enormous profits. In the 15th century, Europeans began to search for a new route to Asia.

BACKGROUND

In addition to spices, European countries traded for precious metals, which they used to make coins. Metals such as gold and silver were scarce in Europe.

Leaders in Exploration

The small country of Portugal is at the westernmost part of the European continent. Portuguese sailors had navigated the waters of the Atlantic Ocean for centuries. As shown on the map below, they traveled down the west coast of Africa and as far west into the Atlantic as Madeira, the Azores, and the Canary Islands.

Exploring the African Coast In the early 1400s, Portugal's **Prince Henry the Navigator** decided to send explorers farther down the coast of Africa. He believed that if explorers could find a way around Africa, it might be a shortcut to Asia. Portuguese explorers returned home from these expeditions with gold dust, ivory, and more knowledge of navigation. By the time Henry died in 1460, the Portuguese had ventured around the great bulge of western Africa to present-day Sierra Leone.

Portuguese Explorers, 1400s

Dias 1487–1488
da Gama 1497–1498

GEOGRAPHY SKILLBUILDER:
Interpreting a Map
1. **Movement** • Which explorer reached Asia?
2. **Location** • Which continent was most explored by the Portuguese?

The Race Around Africa Bold Portuguese explorers continued to push farther down the African coast. Finally, in 1488, Bartolomeu Dias (BAHR·too·loo·MAY·oo DEE·uhsh) rounded the southern tip of Africa. The Portuguese named the tip the Cape of Good Hope.

Less than ten years later, Vasco da Gama (vas· KOH deh GAH·muh) led a sea expedition all the way to Asia. Da Gama and his crew traveled for 317 days and 13,500 miles before reaching the coast of India. They were the first Europeans to discover a sea route to Asia. Now, the riches of Asia could be brought directly to Europe. After setting up trading posts along the coast of the Indian Ocean, Portugal ruled these waterways.

Europe Enters a New Age

Portugal was not the only European country to understand that whoever controlled trade with Asia would have great power and wealth. Spain and England quickly entered the race to find a direct sea route of their own.

Christopher Columbus Some explorers believed that the shortest way to Asia was to sail west across the Atlantic Ocean. Queen Isabella of Spain agreed to fund an expedition across the Atlantic.

In August 1492, an Italian named **Christopher Columbus** and 90 crew members left Spain aboard three ships—the *Santa Maria,* the *Pinta,* and the *Niña.* The Atlantic Ocean proved to be wider than maps of the time suggested. On October 12, after weeks at sea, the crew spotted land. Although Columbus thought he had found Asia, they were off the coast of an island in the Caribbean. This was still a great distance from their spice-rich destination.

Ferdinand Magellan In 1519, Spain funded an expedition for the Portuguese explorer **Ferdinand Magellan** (muh·JEHL·uhn). Magellan left Spain with five ships and more than 200 sailors. As they traveled west, the crew battled violent storms and rough seas. Food was in short supply, and starving sailors ate rats and sawdust. Some died of disease.

Connections to Science

New Ships In the early 15th century, Portuguese shipbuilders designed a sturdy ship called a caravel, pictured below. Built for exploration and trade, the caravel was small and had a narrow body. This helped the ship to cut through waves and to travel in shallow water.

The caravel also used a combination of square and triangular sails. These made sailing easier against strong, shifting winds.

Reading
Social Studies

A. Recognizing Important Details What continent did Columbus reach, and where did he think he was?

Reading
Social Studies

B. Identifying Problems What were the main problems faced by Magellan and his crew?

Movement • Sailors figured their ship's position with the astrolabe. It measured the position of the sun and stars in relation to the horizon. ▼

By the time Magellan and his ships reached the Philippines in Asia, the sailors had spent 18 long months at sea. Then, during a battle there, Magellan and several crew members were killed. The expedition returned to Spain after a three-year journey. Only one boat and 18 crew members succeeded. They had to **circumnavigate,** or sail completely around, the world.

John Cabot King Henry VII of England did not want Portugal and Spain to claim all the riches of Asia. He funded a voyage by Italian-born Giovanni Caboto, called John Cabot by the English, who believed that a northern route across the Atlantic Ocean might be a shortcut to Asia.

Aboard one small ship, Cabot and 18 crew members sailed west from England in May 1497. When they reached land the following month, Cabot thought they had found Asia. Most likely, they landed in present-day Newfoundland in Canada.

The Outcomes of Exploration

The kings and queens of Europe sent explorers in search of a direct trade route to Asia. These expeditions, however, turned out to have unexpected results.

A Clash of Cultures European countries founded many new colonies along the coastal areas of Africa and North and South America. This practice of one country controlling the government and economy of another country or territory is called **imperialism.** These conquered lands were already home to large, self-ruling populations. They had their own cultural traditions. After the arrival of the Europeans, the lives of these indigenous peoples would never be the same.

Religious Conversion The European monarchs were Christians. They had strong religious beliefs, and they sent missionaries and other religious officials to help convert conquered peoples to Christianity. The European rulers also hoped that these new converts would help Christianity overcome other powerful religions, especially Islam.

The Spread of Diseases Without knowing it, the European explorers and colonists carried diseases with them, including small-pox, malaria, and measles. These diseases were unknown in the Americas, and killed tens of thousands of people there.

Vocabulary

indigenous: born and living in a place, rather than having come from somewhere else

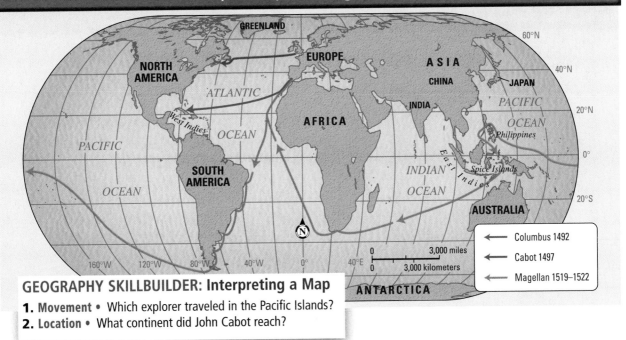

Columbus, Cabot, and Magellan, 1492–1522

GREENLAND
60°N
EUROPE
ASIA
40°N
NORTH
AMERICA
CHINA
JAPAN
ATLANTIC
INDIA
PACIFIC
20°N
West Indies
OCEAN
AFRICA
OCEAN
Philippines
PACIFIC
0°
Spice Islands
SOUTH
AMERICA
INDIAN
East Indies
OCEAN
OCEAN
20°S
AUSTRALIA

⟵ Columbus 1492
⟵ Cabot 1497
⟵ Magellan 1519–1522

ANTARCTICA

0   3,000 miles
0   3,000 kilometers

GEOGRAPHY SKILLBUILDER: Interpreting a Map

1. **Movement** • Which explorer traveled in the Pacific Islands?
2. **Location** • What continent did John Cabot reach?

Slavery European explorations also led to an expanding slave trade. The Portuguese purchased West Coast African people to work as slaves back in Portugal, where the work force had been reduced by plague. In other colonized areas, such as Mexico and parts of South America, Europeans forced conquered peoples to work the land where they lived. For hundreds of years, Africans and conquered peoples of the Americas would be forced to work under horrible conditions.

SECTION 2 ASSESSMENT

Terms & Names

1. **Identify:**
   (a) Prince Henry the Navigator
   (b) Christopher Columbus
   (c) Ferdinand Magellan
   (d) circumnavigate
   (e) imperialism

Taking Notes

2. Use a chart like this one to compare characteristics of the voyages of Christopher Columbus and Vasco da Gama.

Columbus's Voyage	Da Gama's Voyage

Main Ideas

3. (a) Why were spices so important to Europeans?

   (b) Why did Europeans want to find a new route to Asia?

   (c) Name three ways in which European exploration affected the indigenous peoples of North and South America.

Critical Thinking

4. **Making Inferences**

   Why do you think the Portuguese became leaders of European exploration?

   Think About

   • the location of Portugal
   • early Portuguese voyages
   • Prince Henry and his School of Navigation

ACTIVITY
-OPTION-
Reread the information about Magellan's voyage around the world. Write a **journal entry** describing the events of the voyage from the point of view of a crew member.

Researching Topics on the Internet

▶▶ Defining the Skill

The Internet is a computer network that connects libraries, museums, universities, government agencies, businesses, news organizations, and private individuals all over the world. Each location on the Internet has a home page with its own address, or URL (universal resource locator). With a computer connected to the Internet, you can reach the home pages of many organizations and services. The international collection of home pages, known as the World Wide Web, is an excellent source of up-to-date information about the regions and countries of the world.

▶▶ Applying the Skill

The Web page shown below is the European Reading Room at the Library of Congress Web site. Use the strategies listed below to help you understand how to research topics on the Internet.

How to Research Topics on the Internet

Strategy ① Once on the Internet, go directly to the Web page. For example, type http://www.loc.gov/rr/european/extlinks.html in the box at the top of the Web browser and press ENTER. The Web page will appear on your screen.

Strategy ② Explore the European Reading Room links. Click any of the links to find more information about a subject. These links take you to other Web sites.

Strategy ③ Always confirm information you have found on the Internet. The Web sites of universities, government agencies, museums, and trustworthy news organizations are more reliable than others. You can often find information about a site's creator by looking for copyright information or reviewing the home page.

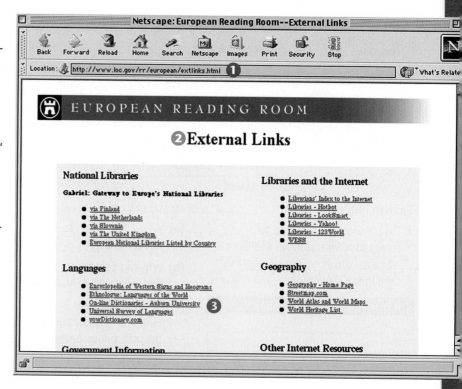

▶▶ Practicing the Skill

Turn to Chapter 11, Section 1, "Renaissance Connections." Reread the section and make a list of topics you would like to research.

For Internet links to support this activity, go to

RESEARCH LINKS
CLASSZONE.COM

The Age of Revolution

TERMS & NAMES
Scientific Revolution
Industrial Revolution
labor force
capitalism
French Revolution
Reign of Terror
Napoleon Bonaparte

MAIN IDEA

Scientific, industrial, and political revolutions transformed European society.

WHY IT MATTERS NOW

European revolutions in science, technology, and politics helped to create modern societies throughout the world.

EXTRA

DATELINE

LEIPZIG, GERMANY, APRIL 1839

A new era in German history has begun. The Leipzig-Dresden railway is open for business. Although short rail lines have been in service for a few years, this is the first long-distance railway in this part of Europe.

The steam locomotive that powers the German train was made in England. It is the latest improvement to George Stephenson's "Rocket" train, which set a speed record of 30 mph in 1829. Already, this new form of transportation is changing Europe. The railroads are attracting many passengers and are also ideal for hauling goods. It seems that wherever new train stations are built, growth and prosperity soon follow.

Region • Leipzig's railway will now take passengers all the way to Dresden. ▲

Changes in Science and Industry

The steam-powered locomotive was only one in a long line of technological improvements made in Europe since the 1600s. In fact, scientists and inventors made so many discoveries during these years that Europe experienced both a scientific and an industrial revolution. These periods of great change would help to create modern societies.

Vocabulary

revolution: a period of great change

The Scientific Revolution In the 16th and 17th centuries, scientific discoveries changed the way Europeans looked at the world. This led to the **Scientific Revolution**.

In Italy, Galileo Galilei (GAL·uh·LEE·oh GAL·uh·LAY) (1564–1642) studied the stars and planets using a new invention called the telescope. Later in Holland, Antoni van Leeuwenhoek (LAY·vuhn·huk) (1632–1723) used a microscope to explore an unknown world found in a drop of water. The Swedish botanist Carolus Linnaeus (lih·NEE·uhs) (1707–1778) even developed a system to name and classify all living things on Earth.

Culture •
In 1610, Galileo used his telescope to observe that Jupiter had moons. ▲

The Industrial Revolution Many inventions of the Scientific Revolution began to change the way people worked all across Europe. Machines performed jobs that once had been done by humans and animals. This brought about such great change that it led to a revolution in the way goods were produced: the **Industrial Revolution**.

Machines were grouped together to make products in large factories. Early factories were built in the countryside near streams and rivers so that they could be powered by water. By the late 1700s, however, new steam engines were used to power the machinery. More and more factories could now be built in cities. People, in turn, moved from the countryside to the cities in search of work.

Reading
Social Studies

A. Finding Causes How did the Scientific Revolution lead to the Industrial Revolution?

The Scientific Method During the Scientific Revolution, scientists began doing research in a new way, called the scientific method. This scientific method is still used by scientists today.

First, scientists identify a problem. Next, they collect data about the problem. Using this data, they develop an explanation for the problem and test the explanation by performing experiments. Finally, they reach a conclusion.

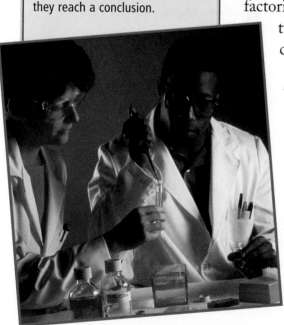

The Workshop of the World

The Industrial Revolution began in England in the late 1700s. The first English factories made textiles, or cloth. The steam-powered machines of the textile industry produced large amounts of goods quickly and cheaply. So many factories were built in England that the country earned the nickname "The Workshop of the World."

BACKGROUND

In the 1850s, laws were finally passed to help protect women and children from long hours and harsh working conditions.

Hard Work for Low Pay The Industrial Revolution created a need for workers, or a **labor force,** in cities. The workers who ran the textile machines made up part of this labor force. Most workers could earn more income in cities than on farms, but life could be hard. Factory laborers worked long hours and received low pay. In fact, many families often sent their children to work to help create more income.

In 1838, women and children made up more than 75 percent of all textile factory workers. Children as young as seven were forced to work 12 hours a day, six days a week.

The Spread of Industrialization

The textile industry in 18th-century England was one step in the development of an economic system called **capitalism.** In this system, factories and other businesses that make and sell goods are privately owned. Private business owners make decisions about what goods to produce. They sell these goods at a price that will earn a profit.

Industrialization spread from England to other countries, including Germany, France, Belgium, and the United States. Cities in these countries grew rapidly and became more crowded and dirtier. Diseases, such as cholera (KAHL·uhr·uh) and typhoid (TY·foyd) fever, spread. Smoke from factories blackened city skies, and pollution fouled the rivers.

Population Growth in European Cities

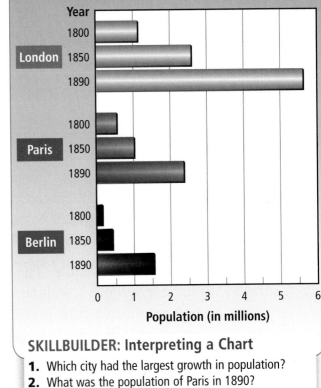

Population (in millions)

SKILLBUILDER: Interpreting a Chart

1. Which city had the largest growth in population?
2. What was the population of Paris in 1890?

Place •
Factories, like this one in Sheffield, England, were found throughout Western Europe by the mid-19th century. ▶

The Growth of New Ideas **315**

The French Revolution

Along with changes in science, technology, and the economy came new ideas about government. In the late 18th century, many ordinary citizens began to fight for more political rights.

Ripe for Political Change

By the 1780s, the French government was deeply in debt because of bad investments and the costs of waging wars. Life was miserable for the common working people. Poor harvests combined with increased population had led to food shortages and hunger. People were forced to pay heavy taxes. At the same time, the French king, Louis XVI, and his queen, Marie Antoinette, continued to enjoy an expensive life at court, entertaining themselves and the French nobility.

Reading Social Studies

B. Analyzing Motives Why did the French citizens demand a new government?

Storming the Bastille

The citizens of France demanded changes in the government, without success. Then, on July 14, 1789, angry mobs stormed a Paris prison called the Bastille (ba•STEEL). The attack on this prison, which reflected the royal family's power, became symbolic of the **French Revolution.**

Revolts spread from Paris to the countryside, and poor and angry workers burned the homes of the nobility. By 1791, France had a new constitution that made all French citizens equal under the law.

Region • The storming of the Bastille remains a symbol of the French Revolution. ▼

BACKGROUND
Until the French Revolution, the guillotine was only used to execute nobles. It was considered the most humane type of execution.

The French Republic In 1792, France became a republic. King Louis XVI was found guilty of treason, or betraying one's country. In 1793, he and Marie Antoinette were sentenced to death. They were beheaded on the guillotine (GIHL·uh·teen).

Still, France was not at peace. The new revolutionary leaders refused to tolerate any disagreement. Between 1793 and 1794, these new leaders executed 17,000 people. This period of bloodshed became known as the **Reign of Terror.**

Napoleon French leaders continued to struggle for power until 1799, when General **Napoleon Bonaparte** (nuh·POH·lee·uhn BOH·nuh·PAHRT) took control. The French Revolution and the disorder that followed were finally over.

However, the new sense of equality brought about by the Revolution stirred feelings of nationalism among the French. Nationalism is pride in and loyalty to one's nation. Soon, the citizens of other European nations began to fight for more political power. Slowly, they, too, won more rights.

Region • Napoleon Bonaparte crowned himself emperor of France in 1804. He led France to victory in what became known as the Napoleonic Wars. ▲

SECTION 3 ASSESSMENT

Terms & Names

1. Identify:
   (a) Scientific Revolution
   (b) Industrial Revolution
   (c) labor force
   (d) capitalism
   (e) French Revolution
   (f) Reign of Terror
   (g) Napoleon Bonaparte

Taking Notes

2. Use a chart like this one to list some of the scientific, industrial, and political changes that occurred during the Age of Revolution.

Scientific Changes	Industrial Changes	Political Changes

Main Ideas

3. (a) Describe at least three inventions or discoveries of the Scientific Revolution.

   (b) How did the Industrial Revolution change the way people in Europe worked?

   (c) What changes occurred in France after the French Revolution?

Critical Thinking

4. **Recognizing Effects**

   How did industrialization change the cities to which it spread?

   Think About
   • population
   • diseases
   • the environment

ACTIVITY -OPTION- Reread the section about the French Revolution. Write a **poem** or **lyrics** for a folk song that describe the events from the point of view of a common citizen or a member of the royal family.

SECTION 4

The Russian Empire

TERMS & NAMES
czar
Ivan the Terrible
Peter the Great
Catherine the Great
Russian Revolution

MAIN IDEA

Strong leaders built Russia into a large empire, but the country's citizens had few rights and struggled with poverty.

WHY IT MATTERS NOW

Russia has had a great influence on world politics and is experiencing a period of great change.

DATELINE

MOSCOW, RUSSIA, 1560—Today, the most magnificent church in Moscow opened with a grand celebration. The Cathedral of St. Basil has ten domes—each one unique. The massive structure, built of bricks and white stone, is decorated with brilliant colors.

Ivan IV built this cathedral to celebrate his victory eight years ago over the Tatars (TAH•tuhrz). These Turkish people who live in Central Asia have long threatened Russia's security.

The victory also added the lands of the Tatars, including their capital at Kazan, to our growing empire. Russians everywhere should be proud of Moscow's new church and of the victory it symbolizes.

Place • Ivan IV has honored a Russian victory over the Tatars with the construction of St. Basil's Cathedral. ▲

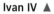

Ivan IV ▲

Russia Rules Itself

Russia, geographically the world's largest nation, is located in both Europe and Asia. It takes up large parts of both continents, and both continents have helped shape its history.

Mongols from eastern Asia conquered Russia in the 13th century and ruled it for about 200 years. During the 15th century, Russia broke free of Mongol rule. At this time, the most important Russian city was Moscow, located in the west.

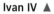

318   CHAPTER 11

Reading
Social Studies

A. Clarifying Why did the Russian people give Ivan IV the nickname Ivan the Terrible?

The First Czars of Russia In 1547, a 16-year-old leader in Moscow was crowned the first **czar** (zahr), or emperor, of modern Russia. His official title was Ivan IV, but the people nicknamed him **Ivan the Terrible.** Ivan was known for his cruelty, especially toward those he viewed as Russia's enemies. During his rule of 37 years, the country was constantly at war.

During the reigns of Ivan the Terrible and the czars who followed him, Russia had an unlimited government. This is a form of government in which a single ruler holds all the power. The people have no say in how the country is run.

Conflicts at Home The first Russian czars were often in conflict with the Russian nobles, who possessed much land and wealth. The czars viewed the nobles as a threat to their control over the people. Ivan the Terrible ordered his soldiers to murder Russian nobles and church leaders who opposed him.

The poor farmers, or peasants, of Russia also suffered under the first czars. New laws forced the peasants to become serfs, who had to remain on the farms where they worked.

Region • Ivan the Terrible is said to have worn this fur-trimmed crown at his coronation in 1547. ▲

The Expansion of Russia

In addition to strengthening their control over the Russian people, the czars wanted to gain new territory. Throughout the 17th and 18th centuries, rulers such as Peter the Great and Catherine the Great conquered neighboring lands.

A Window on the West An intelligent man with big ideas for his country, **Peter the Great** ruled Russia from 1682 to 1725. After defeating Sweden in war and winning land along the Baltic Sea, Peter built a port city called St. Petersburg. This city, which Peter saw as Russia's "window on the west," became the new capital.

BACKGROUND

In 1721, Peter the Great changed his title from *czar* to *emperor,* a title that he thought sounded more European.

One of Peter's goals was to have closer ties with Western Europe. He hoped to use the ideas and inventions of the Scientific Revolution to modernize and strengthen Russia. During his rule, Peter reformed the army and the government and built new schools. He even ordered Russians to dress like Europeans and to shave off their beards. Peter's reforms made Russia stronger, but they did not improve life for Russian peasants.

Movement • Peter the Great brought to Russia many of the improvements of the Scientific and Industrial Revolutions. ▲

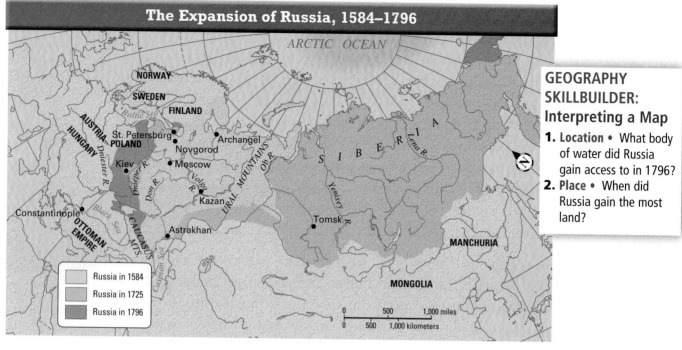

The Expansion of Russia, 1584–1796

Russia in 1584
Russia in 1725
Russia in 1796

GEOGRAPHY SKILLBUILDER: Interpreting a Map

1. **Location** • What body of water did Russia gain access to in 1796?
2. **Place** • When did Russia gain the most land?

A Great Empress **Catherine the Great** took control of Russia in 1762 and ruled until her death in 1796. Catherine added vast new lands to the empire, including the present-day countries of Ukraine (yoo•KRAYN) and Belarus (behl•uh•ROOS). Like Peter the Great, Catherine borrowed many ideas from Western Europe. She started new schools and encouraged art, science, and literature. Catherine also built new towns and expanded trade.

During Catherine's reign, Russia became one of Europe's most powerful nations. The lives of the peasants, however, remained miserable. Catherine thought about freeing them, but she knew the nobles would oppose her. When the peasants rebelled in the 1770s, Catherine crushed their uprising.

Movement • Catherine the Great continued Peter the Great's practice of bringing the ideas of Western Europe to Russia. ▼

A Divided Russia

In the 19th century, Russia remained a divided nation. Most people were poor peasants, and most of the wealth belonged to the nobles. This division would lead to conflict and eventually to a political revolution.

The Nobles Many Russian nobles sent their children to be educated in Germany and France. In fact, many noble families spoke French at home, speaking Russian only to their servants. The Western Europeans introduced many new ideas to the Russian nobles, among them the idea that a nation's government should reflect the wishes of its citizens.

BACKGROUND

Catherine the Great was born in Germany. She came to Russia at 15 to marry the heir to the throne, Peter III. He was a weak ruler, however, and Catherine, supported by the army and the people, overthrew him.

Many Russian nobles were army officers or government officials. Most supported the czar and were proud of Russia's growing power. In 1825, one group of nobles tried to replace the government. Their attempt to gain more power failed.

The Serfs In the 19th century, the Russian serfs still had no land or money of their own. They worked on farms owned by others and received little help from the Russian government.

In 1861, Alexander II decided to end serfdom in Russia. He hoped that freeing the serfs would help his country compete with Western Europe. The serfs had to pay a heavy tax, though, and the land they were given was often not good for farming. Most former serfs felt that they had gained very little.

Bloody Sunday The serfs were not the only unhappy Russians. Many university students, artists, and writers believed that the government's treatment of the serfs was unfair. Some joined groups that tried to overthrow the government. In addition, workers in Russia's cities complained about low pay and poor working conditions.

In 1905, a group of workers marched to the royal palace in St. Petersburg with a list of demands. Government troops shot many of them. News of the events of this "Bloody Sunday" spread across Russia, making people even angrier with the government and czar.

BACKGROUND

In the 1850s, Russia fought the Crimean War against Turkey. Two of Turkey's allies were Britain and France. When Russia lost, Alexander II thought this proved that his country was still far less advanced than Western European nations.

Spotlight on CULTURE

The Hermitage Museum One of the world's greatest and largest art museums is the Hermitage in St. Petersburg. It contains many famous works of art, including French, Spanish, and British paintings. Part of the collection is displayed in the former royal residence, the Winter Palace.

Both Peter the Great and Catherine the Great were collectors of European art. On a trip to Amsterdam in 1716, Peter bought paintings by the famous Dutch artist Rembrandt. Approximately 50 years later, Catherine purchased more than 200 works of art when she visited Germany. These priceless royal collections became part of the Hermitage when it opened as a public museum in 1852.

THINKING CRITICALLY

1. **Analyzing Motives**
   Why did Peter the Great and Catherine the Great collect art from Western Europe?

2. **Making Inferences**
   Why do you think the works of art were displayed to the public in a museum?

The End of the Russian Empire

In 1914, World War I began. Nicholas II—a quiet, shy man who did not want war—ruled Russia, but he failed to keep his country out of the battle. Russia, whose allies included the United Kingdom and France, suffered terrible losses fighting Germany and its allies.

During World War I, there were food shortages in the cities and workers went on strike. Russian revolutionaries organized the workers against the czar. Even the Russian army turned against their ruler, and in 1917, Nicholas was forced to give up power. This overturning of the Russian monarchy is known as the **Russian Revolution**.

Nicholas II and the royal family (the Romanovs) were imprisoned by the revolutionaries. On July 17, 1918, they were all shot to death. This execution ended more than 300 years of rule by the Romanov family and nearly 400 years of czarist rule.

Reading
Social Studies

B. Analyzing Motives Why did Russian workers strike?

Strange but TRUE

Rasputin One of the most influential people at the court of Czar Nicholas II was Rasputin. He came from Siberia in eastern Russia and was a self-styled holy man. Crown prince Alexis suffered from the disease hemophilia, and no doctor in Russia could cure him. Rasputin seemed to mysteriously heal the boy, gaining favor with Nicholas's wife, Czarina Alexandra. However, in 1916, Russian nobles killed Rasputin out of fear of the considerable power and influence the monk had.

SECTION 4 ASSESSMENT

Terms & Names

1. **Identify:**
   (a) czar
   (b) Ivan the Terrible
   (c) Peter the Great
   (d) Catherine the Great
   (e) Russian Revolution

Taking Notes

2. Use a chart like this one to describe three characteristics of czars of Russia.

Ivan the Terrible	Peter the Great	Catherine the Great	Nicholas II

Main Ideas

3. (a) What effects did an unlimited government have on Russian peasants?

   (b) How did Peter the Great help reform Russia?

   (c) Alexander II ended serfdom in 1861, but this did little to help the serfs. Why?

Critical Thinking

4. **Finding Causes**

   What events led to the Russian Revolution?

   Think About
   - the life of the serfs
   - Bloody Sunday
   - the events of World War I

ACTIVITY -OPTION- Look at the map on page 320 that shows the expansion of Russia. Write a brief **summary** to describe how the Russian nation grew from the 1500s to 1800.

James Watt's Double-Action Steam Engine

Amid the excitement of the Industrial Revolution, James Watt (1736–1819), a Scottish inventor, patented a new steam engine. Steam power had been used for many years, but Watt's invention was an improved, double-action steam engine. This system, in which the steam pushes from both sides of the piston rather than from just one, enhanced efficiency and increased power. Watt's invention helped to advance manufacturing and transportation and influenced later inventions. Watt's double-action steam engine was one of the most important inventions of the Industrial Revolution.

How the Engine Works

Steam from the **boiler** enters the **piston cylinder**. The pressure of the steam pushes the **piston** to one side, moving the **piston rod**. When the piston reaches the end of the stroke, the **slide valve** shifts the steam to the other side of the piston, forcing it back and releasing the steam it compresses as exhaust.

❶ As water is converted to steam, its volume increases 1,600 percent.

❷ When the steam enters the piston cylinder, it forces the piston rod to one side.

❸ As the piston reaches the end of its stroke, the slide valve channels steam to the other side of the piston.

❹ The piston rod is pushed back, forcing the "old" steam out as exhaust.

Action 1

Slide valve • Boiler • Piston rod • Piston • Piston cylinder • ❶ • ❷

Action 2

Slide valve • ❸ • ❹

| Key: | Steam | Exhaust |

THINKING *Critically*

1. Drawing Conclusions
How did the steam engine help power the Industrial Revolution?

2. Recognizing Effects
How did Watt's steam engine change the lives of working people?

TERMS & NAMES

Explain the significance of each of the following:

1. Renaissance
2. Leonardo da Vinci
3. Reformation
4. Ferdinand Magellan
5. circumnavigate
6. imperialism
7. Industrial Revolution
8. Napoleon Bonaparte
9. Peter the Great
10. Russian Revolution

REVIEW QUESTIONS

Renaissance Connections *(pages 301–306)*

1. How did the subjects chosen by artists change during the Renaissance?
2. Why were the followers of Martin Luther called Protestants?

Traders, Explorers, and Colonists *(pages 307–311)*

3. Why were spices from Asia so expensive when sold in Europe?
4. What did Portuguese explorers bring back from their expeditions to western Africa?

The Age of Revolutions *(pages 313–317)*

5. When and where did the Industrial Revolution begin?
6. What conditions in France during the 1780s led to the French Revolution?

The Russian Empire *(pages 318–322)*

7. How did Ivan the Terrible earn his nickname?
8. What ideas did Catherine the Great borrow from Western Europe?

CRITICAL THINKING

Finding Causes

1. Using your completed chart from Reading Social Studies, p. 300, list the events that led to the growth of cities during the Industrial Revolution.

Recognizing Effects

2. What were the effects of the Crusades on life in Western Europe?

Analyzing Causes

3. In 19th-century Russia, the lives of poor citizens were very different from those of wealthy citizens. How do you think this division led to political revolution?

Visual Summary

 1 Renaissance Connections

- European society was transformed by the art, literature, and ideas of the Renaissance.
- The accomplishments of this period are an important part of Western culture.

 2 Traders, Explorers, and Colonists

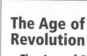

- People on both sides of the Atlantic were changed by the voyages of the European explorers.
- European exploration led to colonization and to the slave trade.

The Age of Revolution

- The Age of Revolution resulted in great changes in European society, industry, and politics.
- These changes were felt around the world.

 3

4 The Russian Empire

- Many citizens of the Russian Empire were deprived of their rights.
- Today, Russia is a large nation experiencing great change.

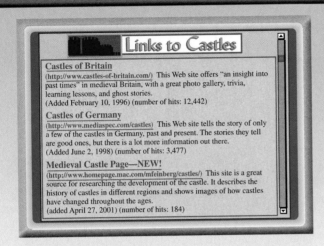

Links to Castles

Castles of Britain
(http://www.castles-of-britain.com/) This Web site offers "an insight into past times" in medieval Britain, with a great photo gallery, trivia, learning lessons, and ghost stories.
(Added February 10, 1996) (number of hits: 12,442)

Castles of Germany
(http://www.mediaspec.com/castles) This Web site tells the story of only a few of the castles in Germany, past and present. The stories they tell are good ones, but there is a lot more information out there.
(Added June 2, 1998) (number of hits: 3,477)

Medieval Castle Page—NEW!
(http://www.homepage.mac.com/mfeinberg/castles/) This site is a great source for researching the development of the castle. It describes the history of castles in different regions and shows images of how castles have changed throughout the ages.
(added April 27, 2001) (number of hits: 184)

SKILLBUILDER: Researching Topics on the Internet
1. What is the subject of this Web site?
2. Which site would you visit to learn about the history of castles?

FOCUS ON GEOGRAPHY

1. **Movement** • How might the path of the plague be related to trade routes?
2. **Place** • Why might the plague have reached Russia later than it reached the other countries in Europe?

- Spread of Black Death
- Extent of Black Death

| 0 | 250 | 500 miles |
| 0 | 250 | 500 kilometers |

60°N
Arctic Circle
0° 10°E
N
50°N
North Sea
ATLANTIC OCEAN
40°N
Adriatic Sea
Black Sea

Interdisciplinary Activity: Science
Explaining an Invention Research one of the many scientific inventions of Leonardo da Vinci. Write a paragraph that explains how da Vinci came up with his idea and how it works. Find a copy of one of da Vinci's sketches or a photograph of a model, or make your own sketch to illustrate your paragraph.

Cooperative Learning Activity
Tracing a Voyage Work with three or four students to research and make a presentation about the voyage of Ferdinand Magellan, the first explorer to sail around the world.
- How many ships and sailors set out? Who helped finance the trip?
- Create a map of Magellan's route.
- Find details about the hardships the crew faced.
- Include information about what happened to Magellan.

INTERNET ACTIVITY

Use the Internet to research the Scientific Revolution. Focus on the discovery or invention of one great European scientist of the time, such as Galileo Galilei. How did the discovery help change daily life or add to people's knowledge of the world?

Presenting Your Findings Design a poster to explain your findings. Include a diagram or illustration that visually presents information about the scientific discovery. If appropriate, explain how the discovery or invention affects life today.

For Internet links to support this activity, go to

RESEARCH LINKS
CLASSZONE.COM

The Growth of New Ideas **325**

Europe: War and Change

EUROPE AND THE FORMER SOVIET UNION

PACIFIC OCEAN

PACIFIC OCEAN

ATLANTIC OCEAN

INDIAN OCEAN

N

Place Berlin's Kaiser Wilhelm Memorial Church remains semi-destroyed as a monument to World War II. Germany has since rebuilt its cities. It is once again an important part of Europe's economy, politics, and culture.

P
←
2 Stunden
9–18 h

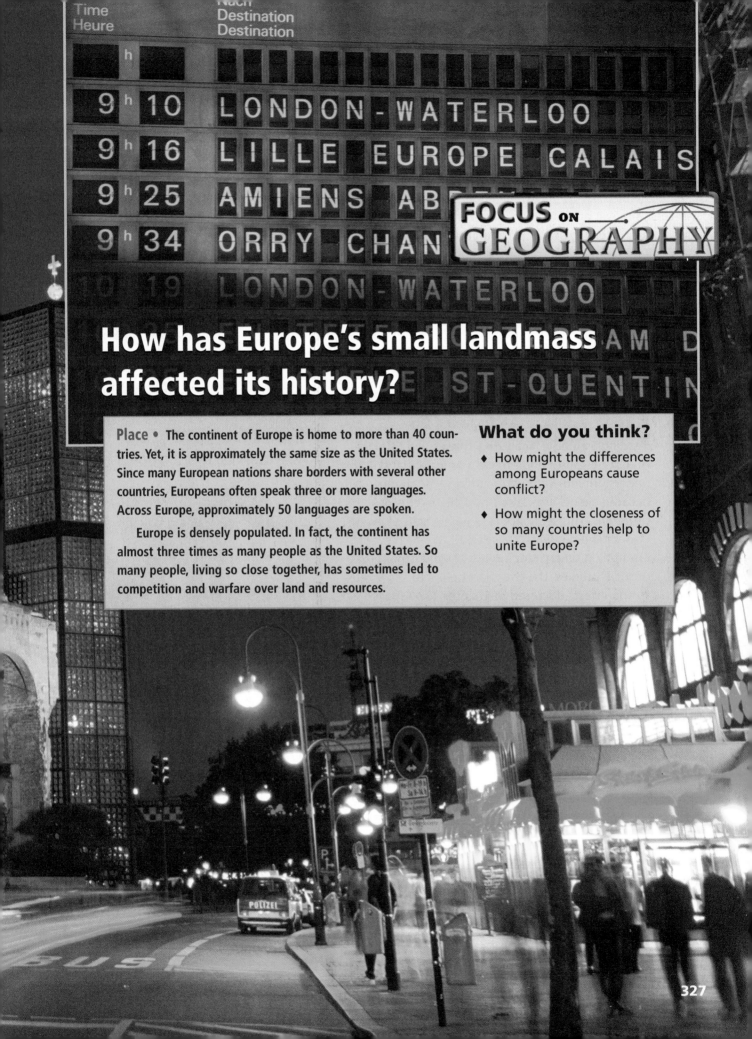

FOCUS ON GEOGRAPHY

How has Europe's small landmass affected its history?

Place • The continent of Europe is home to more than 40 countries. Yet, it is approximately the same size as the United States. Since many European nations share borders with several other countries, Europeans often speak three or more languages. Across Europe, approximately 50 languages are spoken.

Europe is densely populated. In fact, the continent has almost three times as many people as the United States. So many people, living so close together, has sometimes led to competition and warfare over land and resources.

What do you think?

♦ How might the differences among Europeans cause conflict?

♦ How might the closeness of so many countries help to unite Europe?

BEFORE YOU READ

▶▶ *What Do You Know?*

Do you know that during World War I, armies trained dogs to guard supplies and assist soldiers? What do you know about World War I and World War II? Have you ever seen a movie or read a book about either conflict? What do you hear in the news about current events in Europe? Think about how events in Europe in the past century might have contributed to life there today.

▶▶ *What Do You Want to Know?*

Decide what you know about Europe's history in the 1900s and what it is like there today. In your notebook, record what you hope to learn from this chapter.

Region • The image of the hammer and sickle became the symbol of the Soviet Union. ▲

READ AND TAKE NOTES

Reading Strategy: Analyzing Causes and Effects
Analyzing causes and effects is an essential skill for understanding what you read in social studies, because events are caused by other events or situations. This sequence is called a chain of events. Understanding which causes lead to which events is essential in understanding history and other areas of social studies. Use the chart below to show causes and effects discussed in Chapter 12.

- Copy the chart into your notebook.
- As you read, record causes and effects for each event.

Region • During World War I, armies trained dogs to assist them. ▲

Causes	Event	Effects
	World War I	
	World War II	
	Growth of Soviet Union	

European Empires

TERMS & NAMES
nationalism
colonialism
Austria-Hungary
dual monarchy

MAIN IDEA

The beginning of the 20th century was a time of change in Europe, as feelings of nationalism began to take hold.

WHY IT MATTERS NOW

Feelings of nationalism continue to lead to conflicts that change the map of Europe.

DATELINE

EXTRA

NORWAY, SEPTEMBER 1905

It could have been war in the Scandinavian Peninsula. The armies of Norway and Sweden had begun preparations.

Instead, Sweden ended the crisis peacefully by granting Norway independence. Norway had been under Swedish control since 1814. Although Norway ran its own affairs within the country, Sweden set foreign policy and controlled

Norway's international shipping and trade.

Prince Charles of Denmark has been invited to become king of Norway. The Norwegians will vote to approve their new leader. If chosen, he will become King Haakon VII.

The king's role will be largely ceremonial. His chief task will be to help unite the newly independent people of Norway.

Region • Prince Charles of Denmark, pictured here with his family, hopes to become King Haakon VII of Norway.

The Spread of Nationalism

Norway's independence from Sweden was a sign of new ideas that were sweeping across Europe at the time. During the late 19th and early 20th centuries, **nationalism,** or strong pride in one's nation or ethnic group, influenced the feelings of many Europeans. An ethnic group includes people with similar languages and traditions, but who are not necessarily ruled by a common government.

Constitutional Monarchies In part, the spread of nationalism was fueled by the fact that more Europeans than ever before could vote. For centuries, many monarchs had unlimited power. In country after country, however, citizens demanded the right to elect lawmakers who would limit their monarch's authority. This kind of government is called a constitutional monarchy. A constitutional monarchy not only has a king or queen, but also a ruling body of elected officials. The United Kingdom is one example of a constitutional monarchy.

By 1900, many countries in Western Europe had become constitutional monarchies. Citizens of these countries strongly supported the governments that they helped to elect. When one country threatened another, most citizens were willing to go to war to defend their homeland.

The Defense of Colonial Empires At the beginning of the 20th century, many Western European countries—including France, Italy, the United Kingdom, Germany, and even tiny Belgium—had colonies in Asia and Africa. Colonies supplied the raw materials that the ruling countries needed to produce goods in their factories back home. Asian and African colonies, sometimes larger than the ruling country, were also important markets for manufactured goods.

Reading Social Studies

A. Contrasting How does a constitutional monarchy differ from a democracy?

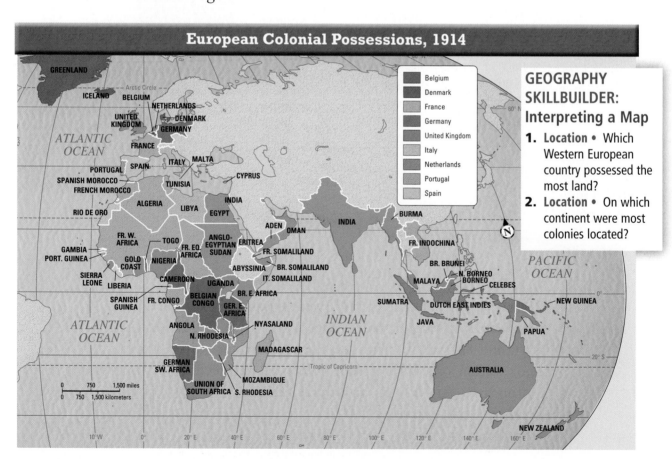

European Colonial Possessions, 1914

Legend:
- Belgium
- Denmark
- France
- Germany
- United Kingdom
- Italy
- Netherlands
- Portugal
- Spain

GEOGRAPHY SKILLBUILDER: Interpreting a Map

1. **Location** • Which Western European country possessed the most land?
2. **Location** • On which continent were most colonies located?

Location • In 1914, the United Kingdom could truthfully state that the sun never set on the British Empire. ◄

During this period of **colonialism,** Western European nations spent much of their wealth on building strong armies and navies. Their military forces helped to defend borders at home as well as colonies in other parts of the world. Colonies were so important that the ruling countries sometimes fought one another for control of them. They also struggled to extend their territories.

Spotlight on CULTURE

The Ballets Russes Begun in Paris, France, in 1909, the Ballets Russes (ba•LAY ROOS) brought together artists from all across Europe. Under the direction of the famous Russian producer Sergey Diaghilev (dee•AH•guh•LEHF), this dance company became both a critical and a commercial success.

Many talented dancers and choreographers, such as Nijinsky, worked for Diaghilev. In addition, famous composers—including Claude Debussy (duh•BYOO•see) and Igor Stravinsky—wrote music for performances. The Ballets Russes also attracted Pablo Picasso, Marc Chagall, and other great artists to design its sets. It continued until Diaghilev's death in 1929.

THINKING CRITICALLY

1. Synthesizing
How did the Ballets Russes benefit the European art and theater communities?

2. Clarifying
How did the Ballets Russes represent more than a collection of dancers, musicians, and artists?

Europe: War and Change **331**

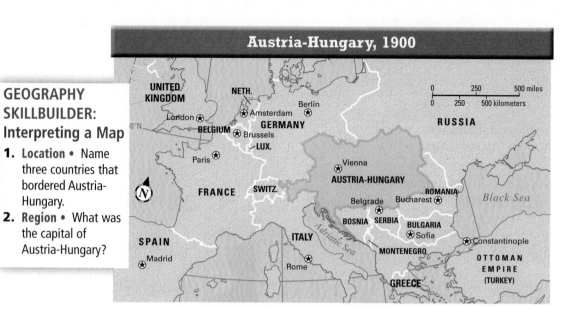

Austria-Hungary, 1900

GEOGRAPHY SKILLBUILDER: Interpreting a Map

1. **Location** • Name three countries that bordered Austria-Hungary.
2. **Region** • What was the capital of Austria-Hungary?

Austria-Hungary By the end of the 19th century, most nations of Western and Northern Europe had become industrialized. The majority of Eastern Europe, including Russia, remained agricultural. These Eastern European countries imported most of their manufactured goods from Western and Northern Europe.

The largest empire in Eastern Europe in 1900 was **Austria-Hungary**. The empire was a **dual monarchy**, in which one ruler governs two nations. As you can see in the map above, Austria-Hungary also included parts of many other present-day countries, including Romania, the Czech Republic, and portions of Poland.

Reading
Social Studies

B. Making Inferences Why do you think governing a dual monarchy was difficult?

SECTION 1 ASSESSMENT

Terms & Names

1. **Identify:**
   (a) nationalism
   (b) colonialism
   (c) Austria-Hungary
   (d) dual monarchy

Taking Notes

2. Look at the map on page 330 that shows European colonial territories. Use a chart like the one below to list the major colonial powers and their colonies.

Nation	Locations of Colonies

Main Ideas

3. (a) Identify one reason for the spread of nationalism in Europe.

   (b) Why did Western European nations spend much of their wealth on armies and navies?

   (c) How did the nations of Eastern Europe differ from those of Western and Northern Europe at the end of the 19th century?

Critical Thinking

4. **Drawing Conclusions**

   Why were their colonies so important to European nations?

   Think About
   * land and people
   * competition among nations
   * the production and sale of goods

ACTIVITY -OPTION-

Reread the information about the Ballets Russes. Write an **outline** of a story or book that might be a good choice for a ballet. Explain your choice.

Europe at War

TERMS & NAMES
World War I
alliance
Adolf Hitler
fascism
Holocaust
World War II
NATO

MAIN IDEA	WHY IT MATTERS NOW
During the first half of the 20th century, European countries fought each other over land, wealth, and ideals.	The changes brought about by the two world wars continue to affect Europe today.

DATELINE

SARAJEVO, BOSNIA-HERZEGOVINA, JUNE 28, 1914—Today, Archduke of Austria-Hungary Franz Ferdinand and his wife, Duchess Sophie, were murdered as they drove through Sarajevo. A nineteen-year-old Serb, Gavrilo Princip, jumped on the Archduke's automobile and fired two shots. The first killed the Duchess. The second killed the Archduke, who was next in line to be emperor of Austria-Hungary.

The Serbians have protested against Austria-Hungary since 1908, when the empire took over Bosnia and Herzegovina (BAHZ•nee•uh HEHRT•suh•GOH•VEE•nuh). Princip has been arrested.

Region • Archduke Franz Ferdinand and his wife, Duchess Sophie, were fatally shot in Sarajevo. ▲

Region • Gavrilo Princip assassinated the future emperor of Austria-Hungary and his wife. ▲

The World at War

Because of the murder of Archduke Franz Ferdinand in 1914, the emperor of Austria-Hungary declared war on Serbia. When Russia sent troops to defend Serbia, Germany declared war on Russia. Russia supported Serbia because both Russians and Serbians share a similar ethnic background—they are both Slavic peoples. This was the beginning of **World War I.**

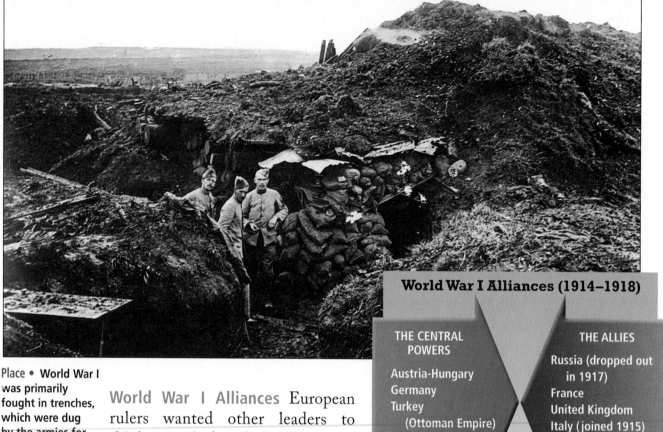

Place • **World War I was primarily fought in trenches, which were dug by the armies for better defense.** ▲

World War I Alliances (1914–1918)

THE CENTRAL POWERS	THE ALLIES
Austria-Hungary Germany Turkey (Ottoman Empire) Bulgaria	Russia (dropped out in 1917) France United Kingdom Italy (joined 1915) United States (joined 1917)

World War I Alliances European rulers wanted other leaders to think twice before declaring war on their countries. To help defend themselves, several countries joined alliances (uh•LY•uhn•sez). An **alliance** is an agreement among people or nations to unite for a common cause. Each member of an alliance agrees to help the other members in case one of them is attacked.

When Germany joined the war to support Austria-Hungary, France came in on the side of Russia. Germany then invaded Belgium, which was neutral, to attack France. Because Great Britain had promised to protect Belgium, it, too, declared war on Germany. After German submarines sank four American merchant ships, the United States joined the side of Russia, France, and Great Britain.

The chart above shows the major powers on both sides of World War I. Italy had originally been allied with Germany and Austria-Hungary but joined the Allies after the war began. Russia dropped out of the war completely after the revolution in that country in 1917.

Reading **Social Studies**

A. Recognizing Important Details Why did Great Britain enter World War I?

SKILLBUILDER:

Interpreting a Political Cartoon

1. What does the artist mean by naming the figure "Progress"?
2. Why is the man wearing a gas mask?

World War I was costly in terms of human life. When it was over, nearly 22 million civilians and soldiers on both sides were dead. The Allies had won, and Europe had been devastated.

Europe After World War I

More people were killed during World War I than during all the wars of the 19th century combined. Afterward, people in many countries on both sides of the costly war—and even those not directly involved—were poor, homeless, and without work.

The Allies blamed Germany for much of the killing and damage during the war. In 1919, Germany and the Allies signed the Treaty of Versailles (vuhr•SY).

Strange but TRUE

War Dogs During World War I, dogs were trained to guard ammunition, to detect mines, and to carry messages. Dogs even helped to search for the wounded.

War dogs saved many lives. They were especially helpful in forested areas and at night. These dogs are wearing protective masks to keep them safe from poison gas attacks.

GEOGRAPHY SKILLBUILDER:
Interpreting a Map

1. **Location** • What body of water does the coast of Yugoslavia reach?
2. **Location** • Name three countries that border Czechoslovakia.

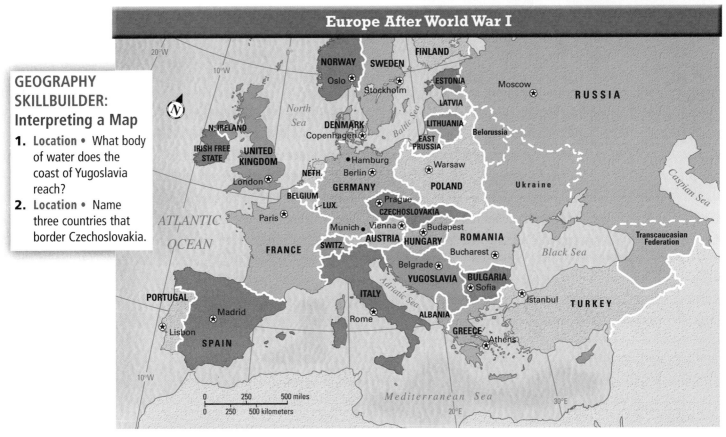

Europe After World War I

The Treaty of Versailles demanded that Germany be punished by being forced to pay for the damage done to the Allied countries. Germany was also made to give up valuable territory.

A New Map of Europe Additional treaties during the following year also altered the political boundaries of many European countries. As the map on page 335 shows, Austria-Hungary was divided as a result of the war, becoming two separate countries. This allowed several Eastern European ethnic groups that had been part of Austria-Hungary to gain their independence.

World War II

By the 1930s, Germany was still paying for the damage done to the Allied countries during World War I. The German economy was in ruins, and the Germans greatly wished to rebuild their own country. In 1933, citizens elected **Adolf Hitler** and the National Socialist, or Nazi, Party. The Nazi Party believed in fascism. **Fascism** (FASH·IHZ·uhm) is a philosophy that supports a strong, central government controlled by the military and led by a powerful dictator. People believed that this new leader would help Germany recover.

World War II Alliances (1939–1945)

THE AXIS POWERS
Germany
Italy
Japan

THE ALLIES
United Kingdom
France
(until June 1940)
Soviet Union
(formerly "Russia")
United States
(joined in 1941)

Reading
Social Studies

B. Finding Causes
What conditions led Germans to find hope in Adolf Hitler?

BACKGROUND

Like Germany, Italy was also ruled by a fascist dictator after World War I: Benito Mussolini (1883–1945).

Hitler and the Nazi Party Fascists practiced an extreme form of patriotism and nationalism. Fascists also had racist beliefs.

In the 1930s, Hitler unjustly blamed the Jewish citizens of Germany, among other specific groups, for the country's problems. His Nazi followers seized Jewish property and began to send Jews, along with disabled people, political opponents, and others, to concentration camps. During this **Holocaust,** millions of people were deliberately killed, and others starved or died from disease.

In 1934, Hitler took command of the armed forces. Then, in 1939, Hitler's army invaded Poland. **World War II** had begun. By June 1940, Hitler's army had swept through Western Europe, conquering Belgium, the Netherlands, Luxembourg, France, Denmark, and Norway. A year later, Germany invaded the Soviet Union.

WWII Alliances The chart on page 336 shows the major powers on both sides of World War II. As in World War I, the United States at first tried to stay out of the conflict but entered the war after Japan bombed U.S. military bases at Pearl Harbor in Hawaii on December 7, 1941.

Europe After World War II

World War II turned much of Europe into a battleground. By the end of the war, the United States, France, and the United Kingdom occupied Western Europe. The Soviet Union occupied Eastern Europe, including the eastern part of Germany.

Once peace was established, the western allies helped to set up free governments in Western Europe. In 1949, the countries of Western Europe joined Canada and the United States to form a defense alliance called **NATO** (NAY·toh). The members of this alliance, whose name stands for North Atlantic Treaty Organization, agreed to defend one another if they were attacked by the Soviet Union or any other country. Without a common enemy, political differences quickly separated the Soviet Union from Western Europe and the United States.

Place • The Kaiser Wilhelm Memorial Church in Berlin was nearly destroyed by Allied bombs. The ruins still stand today as a World War II monument. See pages 326–327. ▲

Anne Frank In July 1942, during World War II, Anne Frank and her family went into hiding in Amsterdam—a city in the Netherlands. The Frank family were Jewish and were afraid they would be sent to a concentration camp. Anne was only thirteen.

For two years, Anne, her father, mother, sister, and four other people lived in rooms in an attic. Their rooms were sealed off from the rest of the building. While in hiding, Anne kept a diary. Although the family was discovered and Anne died in a concentration camp, her diary was eventually published. Today, this famous book—translated into many languages and the basis for a play and a film—lives on.

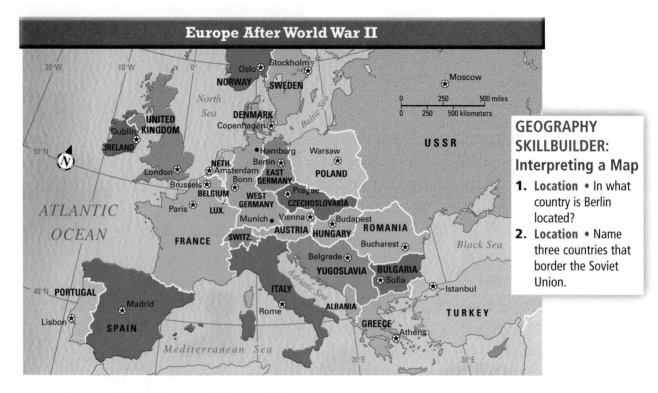

Europe After World War II

GEOGRAPHY SKILLBUILDER: Interpreting a Map

1. **Location** • In what country is Berlin located?
2. **Location** • Name three countries that border the Soviet Union.

The Marshall Plan United States Secretary of State George C. Marshall created the Economic Cooperation Act of 1948, also known as the Marshall Plan. This plan provided U.S. aid—agricultural, industrial, and financial—to countries of Western Europe. The Marshall Plan greatly benefited war-torn Europe. It may also have prevented economic depression or political instability.

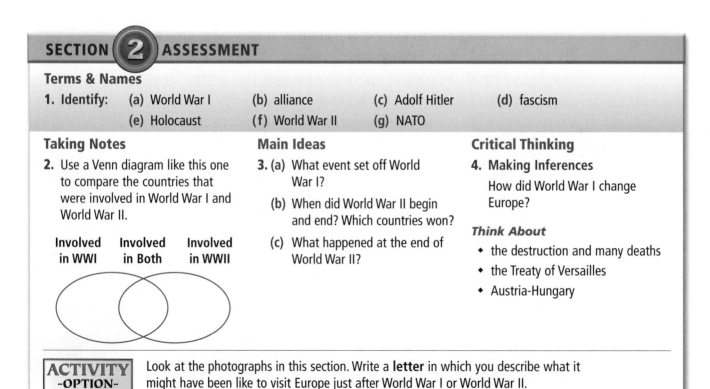

SECTION 2 ASSESSMENT

Terms & Names

1. **Identify:**
   (a) World War I
   (b) alliance
   (c) Adolf Hitler
   (d) fascism
   (e) Holocaust
   (f) World War II
   (g) NATO

Taking Notes

2. Use a Venn diagram like this one to compare the countries that were involved in World War I and World War II.

   Involved in WWI   Involved in Both   Involved in WWII

Main Ideas

3. (a) What event set off World War I?

   (b) When did World War II begin and end? Which countries won?

   (c) What happened at the end of World War II?

Critical Thinking

4. **Making Inferences**

   How did World War I change Europe?

   Think About

   • the destruction and many deaths
   • the Treaty of Versailles
   • Austria-Hungary

ACTIVITY -OPTION- Look at the photographs in this section. Write a **letter** in which you describe what it might have been like to visit Europe just after World War I or World War II.

Reading a Political Cartoon

▶▶ Defining the Skill

Political cartoons—also known as editorial cartoons—express an opinion about a serious subject. A political cartoonist uses symbols, familiar objects, and people to make his or her point quickly and visually. Sometimes the caption and words in the cartoon help to clarify the meaning. Although a cartoonist may use humor to make a point, political cartoons are not always funny.

▶▶ Applying the Skill

This political cartoon was created in the period between World War I and World War II. However, Europeans were already concerned about developments in Germany.

How to Read a Political Cartoon

Strategy ❶ Read the cartoon's title and any other words. For example, some cartoons have labels, captions, and thought balloons. Then study the cartoon as a whole.

Strategy ❷ If the cartoon has people in it, are they famous? Sometimes the cartoonist wants to comment on a famous person, such as a world leader. Look for symbols or details in the cartoon. For example, in this cartoon a German soldier is climbing out of the Versailles Treaty. Think about the relationships between the words and the images.

Strategy ❸ Summarize the cartoonist's message. What is the cartoonist's point of view about the subject? What does this cartoonist think was the cause of Hitler's rise to power?

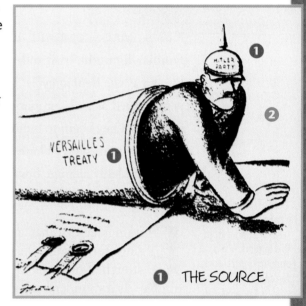

Make a Chart

A chart can help you to analyze the information in a political cartoon. Once you understand the cartoon's elements, you can summarize its meaning. Use a chart such as this one to help you organize the information.

Important Words	Hitler Party; Versailles Treaty
Important Symbols/Images	German soldier with "Hitler Party" on his helmet crawling out of the Versailles Treaty that officially ended World War I.
Summary ❸	The terms of the Versailles Treaty led to the rise of Hitler's party in Germany; Hitler's party, symbolized by a soldier, is war-like and threatens Europe.

▶▶ Practicing the Skill

Study the political cartoon in Chapter 12, Section 2, on page 334. Make a chart similar to the one above in which you list the important parts of the cartoon and write a summary of the cartoon's message.

Fionn Mac Cumhail and the Giant's Causeway[1]

FIONN MAC CUMHAIL, more commonly known as Finn MacCool, is a familiar figure in Irish folk tales. He first appears in the ancient Celtic tales known as the Fenian cycle. In the following story, retold by Una Leavy, Fionn is portrayed as a clever giant, hard at work with the Fianna, his band of Irish warriors. They begin to build a bridge from Ireland to Scotland, because, as the boastful Fionn says, "There are giants over there that I'm longing to conquer." Plans suddenly change, however, and Fionn must go home.

1. The Giant's Causeway, which takes its name from this legend, is a striking natural rock formation on the coast of Ireland.

2. The region of Ireland where Fionn and the Fianna are building their bridge to Scotland. It is the location of the actual Giant's Causeway.

Fionn Mac Cumhail and the Fianna worked quickly on the bridge, splitting stones into splendid pillars and columns. Further and further they stretched out into the ocean. From time to time, there came a distant rumble. "Is it thunder?" asked the Fianna, but they went on working. Then one of their spies came ashore. "I've just been to Scotland!" he said. "There's a huge giant there called Fathach Mór. He's doing long jumps—you can hear the thumping. He has a magic little finger with the strength of ten men! He's in training for the long jump to Antrim."[2]

Fionn's face paled. "The strength of ten men!" he thought. "I'll never fight him. He'll squash me into a pancake." But he could not admit that he was nervous, so he said to the Fianna, "I've just had a message from Bláithín, my wife. I must go home at once—you can all take a holiday."

He set off by himself and never did a man travel faster. Bláithín was surprised to see him. "And is the great causeway finished already?" she asked.

"No indeed," replied Fionn.

"What's the matter?" Bláithín asked. So Fionn told her.

"What will I do, Bláithín?" he asked. "There's the strength of ten men in his magic little finger. He'll squish me into a jelly!"

Bláithín laughed. "Just leave him to me. Stoke up the fire and fetch me the sack of flour. Then go outside and find nine flat stones." Fionn did as he was told. Bláithín worked all night making ten oatcakes. In each she put a large flat stone, all except the last. This one she marked with her thumbprint. "Go and cut down some wood," she said. "You must make an enormous cradle."

Fionn worked all morning. The cradle was just finished when there was a mighty rumble and the dishes shook.

"It's him," squealed Fionn.

"Don't worry!" said Bláithín. "Put on this bonnet. Now into the cradle and leave me to do the talking."

"Does Fionn Mac Cumhail live here?" boomed a great voice above her.

"He does," said Bláithín, "though he's away at the moment. He's gone to capture the giant, Fathach Mór."

"I'm Fathach Mór!" bellowed the giant. "I've been searching for Fionn everywhere."

"Did you ever see Fionn?" she asked. "Sure you're only a baby compared with him. He'll be home shortly and you can see for yourself. But now that you're here, would you do me a favor? The well has run dry and Fionn was supposed to lift up the mountain this morning. There's spring water underneath it. Do you think you could get me some?"

"Of course," shouted the giant as he scooped out a hole in the mountain, the size of a crater.

Fionn shook with fear in the cradle and even Bláithín turned pale. But she thanked the giant and invited him in. "Though you and Fionn are enemies, you are still a guest," she said. "Have some fresh bread." And she put the oatcakes before him. Fathach Mór began to eat. Almost at once he gave a piercing yell and spat out two teeth.

"What kind of bread is this?" he screeched. "I've broken my teeth on it."

"How can you say such a thing?" asked Bláithín. "Even the child in the cradle eats them!" And she gave Fionn the cake with the thumbprint. Fathach looked at the cradle. "Whose child is that?" he asked in wonder.

"That's Fionn's son," said Bláithín.

"And how old is he?" he asked then.

"Just ten months," replied Bláithín.

"Can he talk?" asked the giant.

"Not yet, but you should hear him roar!" At once, Fionn began to yell.

"Quick, quick," cried Bláithín. "Let him suck your little finger. If Fionn comes home and hears him, he'll be in such a temper. With an anxious glance at the door, the giant gave Fionn his finger. Fionn bit off the giant's magic little finger. Screeching, the giant bolted from the house. Fionn leaped from the cradle in bib and bonnet and danced his Bláithín round the kitchen.

Reading
THE LITERATURE

Before reading this story, how did you expect Fionn Mac Cumhail to act? Did you expect him to be the hero of the story? Who is? How does the character solve the problem in the story? What skills are used to solve it?

Thinking About
THE LITERATURE

In many European myths and legends, the heroes are powerful and fearless. How does Fionn act in this story? What words does the author use to make clear Fionn's attitude toward the danger he faces? How does he differ from other legendary figures that you have read about?

Writing About
THE LITERATURE

Often, myths are created in order to answer questions about or explain mysteries in the world. This legend explains why the causeway was never finished. How might the story about Fionn be different if the causeway had been finished?

About the Author

Una Leavy, the author of *Irish Fairy Tales & Legends,* is an Irish writer who lives with her husband and children in County Mayo, Ireland.

Further Reading *The Names upon the Harp* by Marie Heaney recounts myths and legends of early Irish literature, including the stories about Fionn Mac Cumhail that make up the Fenian cycle.

SECTION 3

The Soviet Union

TERMS & NAMES
Iron Curtain
puppet government
one-party system
Joseph Stalin
collective farm
Warsaw Pact
Cold War

MAIN IDEA

After World War II, the Soviet Union was the most powerful country in Europe, but life for most Soviet citizens was difficult.

WHY IT MATTERS NOW

Russia, the former Soviet Union, remains powerful and is currently experiencing great change.

DATELINE

EXTRA

WARSAW, POLAND, MAY 14, 1955

Today, the Soviet Union and most Eastern European countries announced that they have signed the Warsaw Treaty of Friendship, Cooperation, and Mutual Assistance. The members of this alliance agree to offer military defense to one another for a period of 20 years.

Yugoslavia is the only country in Eastern Europe that did not sign the agreement.

The new treaty, also called the Warsaw Pact, allows the Soviet Union to keep troops in the countries that are located between the Soviet Union and Western Europe. The Warsaw Pact is a response to the formation of NATO, an alliance that Western European countries joined six years ago.

Region • Warsaw hosted Eastern European officials who signed a military alliance here in the Palace of Culture. ▲

East Against West

After World War II, political differences divided the Soviet-controlled countries of Eastern Europe from those of Western Europe. These differences gave rise to an invisible wall known as the **Iron Curtain.** While there was no actual curtain, people of the East were restricted from traveling outside of their countries. Westerners who wished to visit the East also faced restrictions.

The Strongest Nation in Europe The Union of Soviet Socialist Republics, or USSR, was the official name of the Soviet Union. It included 15 republics, of which Russia was the largest. The Soviet Union entered World War II in 1941, when Germany invaded its borders. German troops destroyed much of the western Soviet Union and killed millions of people. This invasion brought the Soviet Union close to collapse. However, with the defeat of Germany, the Soviet Union rose to become the strongest nation in Europe.

Region • The hammer and sickle became the symbol of Soviet Communism. The tools represent the unity of the peasants (sickle) with the workers (hammer). ▲

Vocabulary

establish: set up; create

Communism After World War II, the Soviet Union established Communist governments in Eastern Europe. The Soviets made sure—either by politics or by force—that these new Eastern European governments were loyal to the Soviet Union.

Soviet Control of Eastern Europe The Soviet Union controlled the countries of Eastern Europe through puppet governments. A **puppet government** is one that does what it is told by an outside force. In this case, the Eastern European governments followed orders from Soviet leaders in Moscow.

Reading Social Studies

A. Making Inferences How do you think the Soviet Union enforced a one-party system in Eastern Europe?

Most Eastern Europeans did have the chance to vote, but they had only one political party to choose from: the Communist Party. All other parties were outlawed. This meant that there was only one candidate to choose from for each government position. This is an example of a **one-party system.** Soviet citizens could not complain about the government. In fact, they could be jailed for expressing any view that the Soviet leaders did not like.

Movement • The government-controlled factories in the Soviet Union did not produce enough of certain items. When goods that were often in short supply—such as bread and shoes—finally became available, people had to wait in long lines to buy them. ◄

Joseph Stalin

Joseph Stalin (STAH·lihn) (1879–1953) ruled the Soviet Union during World War II. Stalin took power after the death of Vladimir Lenin. Lenin was a Communist leader who had helped overthrow the czar and ruled the Soviet Union from 1917 until his death in 1924. The name Stalin is related to the Russian word for "steel." Stalin was greatly feared, and his rule was indeed as tough as steel. He controlled the government until his death.

Region • Joseph Stalin ruled the Soviet Union from 1928 to 1953. ▲

The Five-Year Plans Under Stalin, the government controlled every aspect of Soviet life. Stalin hoped to strengthen the country with his five-year plans, which were sets of economic goals. For example, Stalin ordered many new factories to be built. The Soviet government decided where and what types of factories to build, how many goods to produce, and how to distribute them. These decisions were based on the Communist theory that this would benefit the most people.

ARCTIC OCEAN

FINLAND
SWEDEN
NORWAY
60°N
North Sea
W. GERMANY
UNITED KINGDOM
IRELAND
NETH.
BELG.
FRANCE
SWITZ.
PORTUGAL
ITALY
SPAIN
DEN.
E. GERMANY
POLAND
CZECH.
AUS. HUNG.
YUGO.
ALB.
GREECE
ROMANIA
BULG.
TURKEY
Baltic Sea
Black Sea
Mediterranean Sea

AFRICA

GEOGRAPHY SKILLBUILDER: Interpreting a Map

1. **Region** • Which countries were behind the Iron Curtain but not in the Soviet Union?
2. **Location** • What was the western-most country in the Warsaw Pact?

Region • The Soviet government managed the factories while citizens provided the actual labor. ◄

The Iron Curtain and the Warsaw Pact Nations, 1955

ARCTIC OCEAN

N

Yenisey R.

Lena R.

SIBERIA

UNION OF SOVIET SOCIALIST REPUBLICS

Ob R.

Volga R.

Caspian Sea

PACIFIC OCEAN

ASIA

ARABIA

	Soviet Union
	Warsaw Pact members
	Western European Nations
——	Iron Curtain

0   1,000   2,000 miles
0   1,000   2,000 kilometers

140°E

Soviet Agriculture Stalin also hoped to strengthen the Soviet Union by controlling the country's agriculture. During the 1930s, peasants were forced to move to collective farms. A **collective farm** was government-owned and employed large numbers of workers. All the crops produced by the collective farms were distributed by the government. Sometimes farm workers did not receive enough food to feed themselves and their families.

Region • Similar to urban factory workers, Russian peasants labored on government-controlled collective farms. ▼

The Secret Police Stalin used his secret police to get rid of citizens he did not trust. The secret police arrested those who did not support the Soviet government. Suspects were transported to slave-labor camps in Siberia. Millions of men and women were sent to this remote and bitterly cold region of northeastern Russia. Many never returned home.

The Cold War

From 1941 to 1945, the United Kingdom, the United States, and the Soviet Union shared a goal: to defeat the Axis Powers. They became allies to make that happen. Once the war ended, however, these countries no longer had a common enemy—and had little reason to work together. Most Western European countries were constitutional monarchies or democracies, and most Eastern European countries had Communist, largely Soviet-controlled, governments.

Spotlight on CULTURE

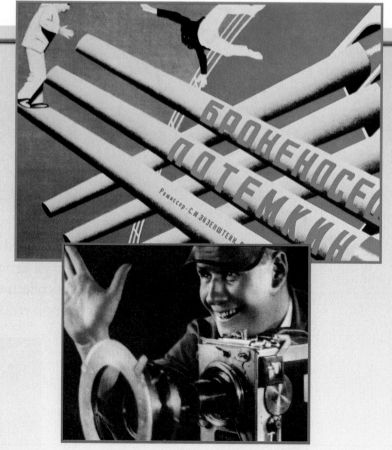

Soviet Film The Russian director Sergey Eisenstein (EYE•zen•stine) (1898–1948), bottom right, made only six movies, but they are among the most important works in film history. The silent film *Battleship Potemkin* (1925), whose poster is to the right, is one of Eisenstein's most famous. It is about a mutiny at sea. The director's use of close-ups and his method of combining short scenes changed the way films were made all over the world.

Just before the start of World War II, Eisenstein made the film *Alexander Nevsky* (1938). It tells the story of a historic battle that the Russians won against German-speaking invaders in the 1200s. This film became very popular during World War II, which it seemed to foreshadow.

THINKING CRITICALLY

1. Clarifying
What influenced Eisenstein to direct war films?

2. Synthesizing
What did Eisenstein want to show about the relationship between Russians and Germans?

Region • The Brandenberg Gate was a part of the Berlin Wall that separated East Berlin from West Berlin. ◄

Reading
Social Studies

B. Comparing Compare the Soviet Union's fears in the Cold War with those of the United States and Western Europe.

The members of NATO and the nations in the **Warsaw Pact**—the alliance of Eastern European countries behind the Iron Curtain—refused to trade or cooperate with each other. The countries never actually fought, so this period of political noncooperation is called the **Cold War.** Both sides in the Cold War were hesitant to start a war that would involve the use of newly developed nuclear weapons, which could cause destruction on a global scale.

The United States and Western Europe feared that the Soviet Union would influence other countries to become Communist. At the same time, the Soviet Union wanted to protect itself against invasion. This led the countries on either side of the Iron Curtain to view and treat each other as possible threats. The tense international situation caused by the Cold War would continue for almost 40 years.

SECTION 3 ASSESSMENT

Terms & Names
1. **Identify:**
   (a) Iron Curtain
   (b) puppet government
   (c) one-party system
   (d) Joseph Stalin
   (e) collective farm
   (f) Warsaw Pact
   (g) Cold War

Taking Notes
2. Use a chart like this one to describe three elements of Joseph Stalin's rule of the Soviet Union.

Five-Year Plans	Agriculture	Secret Police

Main Ideas
3. (a) What happened to the Soviet Union during World War II?

   (b) How did the governments of most Western and Eastern European countries differ?

   (c) How did Joseph Stalin rule the Soviet Union?

Critical Thinking
4. **Analyzing Motives**

   Why do you think the Soviet Union wanted to control the countries of Eastern Europe?

   Think About
   - the events of World War II
   - the location of the Eastern European countries
   - the governments of the Soviet Union and Western Europe

ACTIVITY **-OPTION-**

Reread the information about the secret police. Write a dramatic **scene** in which the main character is sent to a labor camp in Siberia.

TERMS & NAMES

Explain the significance of each of the following:

1. nationalism
2. colonialism
3. World War I
4. alliance
5. World War II
6. NATO
7. Adolf Hitler
8. Warsaw Pact
9. Iron Curtain
10. Cold War

REVIEW QUESTIONS

European Empires *(pages 329–332)*

1. What was the largest empire in Eastern Europe in 1900?
2. What is one reason why European nations built up their military?

Europe at War *(pages 333–338)*

3. Why did European countries join alliances?
4. What did the Treaty of Versailles require Germany to do?
5. What country did Germany invade to begin World War II?

The Soviet Union *(pages 342–347)*

6. Why did most Eastern European voters have only one political party to choose from?
7. How did the Iron Curtain affect the lives of Eastern Europeans?
8. Why were both sides in the Cold War hesitant to start a war?

CRITICAL THINKING

Identifying Problems

1. Using your completed chart from Reading Social Studies, p. 328, list some of the causes and effects of World Wars I and II.

Making Inferences

2. Why might a citizen who has helped elect a government be more willing to fight to defend it?

Hypothesizing

3. How do you think Soviet peasants felt about collective farms? Why?

Visual Summary

European Empires *1*

- In early-20th-century Europe, feelings of nationalism arose.
- Western European nations ruled colonial empires.

Europe at War *2*

- Due to a complex set of alliances, most of Europe was drawn into World War I.
- The Treaty of Versailles set the stage for an even more widespread conflict—World War II.

The Soviet Union *3*

- After World War II, the Soviet Union was very powerful.
- However, life was difficult for many Soviet citizens.

SOCIAL STUDIES SKILLBUILDER

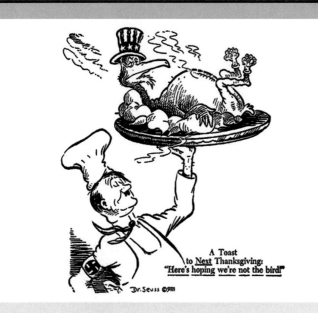

SKILLBUILDER: Reading a Political Cartoon

1. Who is the subject of this cartoon?
2. What do you think the cartoonist, Dr. Seuss, was worried about?

FOCUS ON GEOGRAPHY

1. **Place** • Which areas of Europe are most densely populated?
2. **Place** • Which areas of Europe are least densely populated?
3. **Place** • Why do you think some areas are much more populated than others?

CHAPTER PROJECTS

Interdisciplinary Activity: Language Arts

Presenting an Oral Report
Research one of the European colonies in Asia or Africa. What was life like around 1900? Present your findings to the class in an oral report. Be sure to show the location of the colony on a map.

Cooperative Learning Activity

Designing a Monument In a group of three or four students, design a monument to commemorate an event in 20th-century Europe, such as a particular battle from World War I, the Holocaust, or World War II.

• Present background information about the event to the class.

• Display a drawing or a model of the monument.

• Show your suggested location for the memorial on a map.

INTERNET ACTIVITY

Use the Internet to research a European country that was not directly involved in World War I or World War II. Examples include Spain and Switzerland. What can you find out about that country's government and economy? What was life like there during the first half of the 20th century? How was the country affected by the wars?

Presenting Your Findings Write your findings in a report and include illustrations. List the Web sites that you used to prepare your report.

For Internet links to support this activity, go to

RESEARCH LINKS
CLASSZONE.COM

CHAPTER 13

Modern Europe

SECTION 1   Eastern Europe Under Communism

SECTION 2   Eastern Europe and Russia

SECTION 3   The European Union

EUROPE AND RUSSIA

ATLANTIC
OCEAN

PACIFIC
OCEAN

PACIFIC
OCEAN

INDIAN
OCEAN

OCEAN

Movement High-speed trains, like this one in France, make travel in Europe very convenient.

118

SNCF

FOCUS ON GEOGRAPHY

How are the new republics of Eastern Europe using natural resources to build their economies?

Human-Environment Interaction • Natural resources are often an important part of a nation's economy. When the Soviet Union broke up in 1991, the newly independent nations of Eastern Europe chose to develop market economies.

In Ukraine, which is rich in coal and iron, mining and manufacturing are major industries. (Ukraine once had vast petroleum and natural gas resources, but heavy production used up much of them.) Estonia, Latvia, and Lithuania have large forests and good farmland. Estonia is also rich in oil shale, which it uses to make electricity.

What do you think?

♦ How do natural resources affect the types of goods a country produces?

♦ Why is it important for countries to use natural resources carefully?

READING SOCIAL STUDIES

BEFORE YOU READ

▶▶ *What Do You Know?*

Before you read the chapter, think about what you already know about Europe. Do you have family, friends, or neighbors who were born in Europe? Have you read books, such as the Harry Potter series, that take place in Europe? Think about what you have seen or heard about Italy, England, France, or Germany in the news, during sporting events, and in your other classes.

▶▶ *What Do You Want to Know?*

Decide what you know about Europe today. Then, in your notebook, record what you hope to learn from this chapter.

Region • Euros are the most visible symbol of economic unity in Europe. ▲

READ AND TAKE NOTES

Reading Strategy: Comparing Comparing is a useful strategy for understanding how events change societies. As you read this chapter, compare Eastern Europe under Communism with Eastern Europe after Communism. Use the chart below to take notes.

- Copy the chart into your notebook.
- As you read, notice how government, economics, and culture differ under the old and new systems.
- After you read each section, record key ideas on your chart.

Place • Some Christians in Ukraine dye Easter eggs brilliant colors. ▲

Aspect	Under Communism	After Communism
Government		
Economy		
Culture		

Eastern Europe Under Communism

TERMS & NAMES
propaganda
private property rights
Nikita Khrushchev
deposed
détente

MAIN IDEA

The Communist government of the Soviet Union controlled the lives of its citizens.

WHY IT MATTERS NOW

Today, many republics of the former Soviet Union have become independent nations.

DATELINE

EXTRA

THE KREMLIN, MOSCOW, APRIL 12, 1961

A 27-year-old Soviet pilot has become the first person to travel into space. Soviet officials proudly announced today that cosmonaut Yuri Gagarin had orbited Earth in 1 hour and 29 minutes.

His 4.75-ton spacecraft, *Vostok I*, flew at a maximum altitude of 187 miles above the planet. Its top speed was 18,000 miles per hour.

Gagarin graduated from the Soviet Air Force cadet school just four years ago. He is the son of a carpenter and began to study flying while in college. Gagarin's space flight puts the Soviet Union a giant step ahead of the United States in the space race.

Movement • Yuri Gagarin becomes the first human in space. ▶

Soviet Culture

The Soviet space program of the 1950s and 1960s brought international attention to that country. Daily life for citizens of the Soviet Union and of the Eastern European countries under its control, however, was difficult. Most people were poor and had little, if any, say in their government.

Strange but TRUE

Space Dogs Four years before Yuri Gagarin blasted into space, a Russian dog orbited the planet. Her name was Laika (LY•kuh), which means "Barker." Laika, pictured below, was launched into space on *Sputnik 2* in November 1957. The Soviets did not then have the ability to bring a spacecraft down safely, and Laika lived in space for only a few days.

In August 1960, however, the Russians sent two other dogs into space. Named Belka and Strelka, they were the first living creatures to go into space and return safely to Earth.

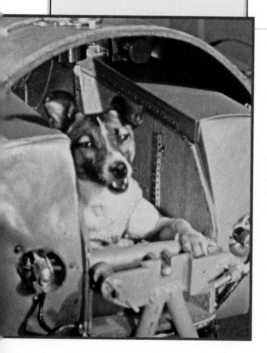

Creating a National Identity The Soviet government was fearful that some ethnic groups might want to break away from the Soviet Union. To keep this from happening, Soviet leaders tried to create a strong national identity. They wanted people in the republic of Latvia, for example, to think of themselves as Soviets, not as Latvians.

To help achieve its goals, the Soviet government created and distributed **propaganda** (PRAHP•uh•GAN•duh), or material designed to spread certain beliefs. Soviet propaganda included pamphlets, posters, artwork, statues, songs, and films. It praised the Soviet Union, its leaders, and Communism.

Soviet Control of Daily Life To prevent different ethnic groups from identifying with their individual cultures rather than with the Soviet Union, the Soviet government outlawed many cultural celebrations. It destroyed churches and other religious buildings and killed thousands of religious leaders. The members of many ethnic groups were not allowed to speak their native languages or celebrate certain holidays.

The Soviet government also controlled communications media, such as newspapers, books, and radio. This meant that most Soviet citizens could not learn much about other nations around the world.

Literature and the Arts The works of many writers, poets, and other artists who lived during the Soviet era often were banned or censored. Soviet artists were forced to join government-run unions. These unions told artists what kinds of works they could create. Artists who disobeyed were punished. Some were imprisoned or even killed.

Region • This statue, a form of propaganda, displays the Soviet belief in the unity of the worker (hammer) and the farmer (sickle). ▼

Ethnic and Cultural Groups of the Soviet Union, c. 1950

ARCTIC OCEAN

Bering Sea

RUSSIA
ESTONIA
LITHUANIA
LATVIA
BYELORUSSIA
MOLDAVIA
UKRAINE
RUSSIA
GEORGIA
ARMENIA
AZERBAIJAN
KAZAKHSTAN
UZBEKISTAN
TURKMENIA
KIRGHIZIA
TAJIKISTAN

Baltic Sea
Black Sea
Caspian Sea

0   250   500 miles
0   250   500 kilometers

- Caucasian peoples
- Indo-European peoples
- Uralic and Altaic peoples
- Sparsely populated

GEOGRAPHY SKILLBUILDER: Interpreting a Map

1. **Place** • Where in the Soviet Union do most Uralic and Altaic people live?
2. **Region** • What is the most common ethnicity of the Soviet Union?

Sports The leaders of the Soviet Union wanted their country to be seen as equal to, if not better than, other powerful nations. One way to achieve this goal was to become a strong competitor in the Olympics and in other international sports competitions.

The Soviet government supported its top athletes and provided for all their basic needs. It even hired and paid for the coaches and paid for all training. The hockey teams and gymnasts of the Soviet Union were among the best in the world.

The Soviet Economy

In addition to controlling the governments of the Soviet Union and of those Eastern European countries under its influence, Soviet leaders also ran the economy. When the Soviets installed Communist governments in Eastern Europe after World War II, they promised to improve industry and to bring new wealth to be shared among all citizens. This did not happen.

Government Control Communism in the Soviet Union did not support **private property rights,** or the right of individuals to own land or an industry. The Soviets wanted all major industries to be owned by the government rather than by private citizens. So the government took over factories, railroads, and businesses.

Region • Romanian gymnasts, like Nadia Comaneci, won medals at the Olympics. ▼

Modern Europe **355**

The Soviet government decided what would be produced, how it would be produced, and who would get what was produced. These choices were made based on Soviet interests, not on the interests of the republics or of individuals. Communist countries of Eastern Europe were often unable to meet the needs—including bread, meat, and clothing—of their citizens.

Reading **Social Studies**

A. Clarifying Who benefited most from Soviet industry?

Attempts at Change

Starting in the 1950s, Eastern Europeans began to demand more goods of better quality. They also wanted changes in the government. In 1956, Hungary and Poland tried to free their governments and economies from Soviet control. But the Communist army put an end to these attempts at change.

Khrushchev From 1958 until 1964, **Nikita Khrushchev** (KRUSH·chehf) ruled the Soviet Union. During this period, called "The Thaw," writers and other citizens began to have greater freedoms. Khrushchev even visited the United States in 1959, but the thaw in the Cold War did not last. In 1964, with the Soviet economy growing weaker, Khrushchev was **deposed,** or removed from power.

Spotlight on CULTURE

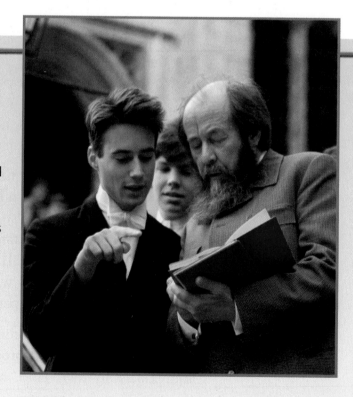

Solzhenitsyn In 1945, army officer Aleksandr Solzhenitsyn (SOHL·zhuh·NEET·sihn), far right, called the Soviet leader Joseph Stalin "the boss." For this, he was sentenced to eight years in slave-labor camps. Later, Solzhenitsyn wrote books about his experiences in those camps. He also wrote a letter against censorship. The government called him a traitor, and in 1969 it forced Solzhenitsyn to leave the writers' union. Five years later, Solzhenitsyn left the country.

Although Solzhenitsyn's works were banned, many Soviet citizens read them in secret. Copies of his and other banned books were passed from person to person across the nation. Through such writings, Soviet citizens learned many things that the government had tried to hide from them.

THINKING CRITICALLY

1. **Analyzing Motives** Why would the Soviet government stop people from reading Solzhenitsyn's books?

2. **Comparing** Compare the censorship of literature in the Soviet Union with censorship in the United States.

Reading Social Studies

B. Recognizing Important Details How did the Soviet Union maintain control over other Eastern European nations?

The Prague Spring In January 1968 in Czechoslovakia, Alexander Dubček (DOOB·chek) became the First Secretary of the Czechoslovak Communist Party. His attempts to lessen the Soviet Union's control over Czechoslovakia led to a period of improvement called the "Prague Spring." Czech citizens enjoyed greater freedoms, including more contact with Western Europe. In August of that year, however, the Soviet Union sent troops to force a return to strict Communist control. Dubček was later replaced, and Soviet controls were back in place.

Place • Nikita Khrushchev, the son of a miner and grandson of a peasant, lessened government control of Soviet citizens. ▲

Détente The member nations of NATO, which were concerned about starting an all-out war with the Soviet Union, were unable to stop the Soviet control of Eastern Europe. In the 1970s, however, leaders of the Soviet Union and the United States began to have more contact with each other. This led to a period of **détente** (day·TAHNT), or lessening tension, between the members of NATO and the Warsaw Pact nations.

Region • Citizens of Czechoslovakia protested Soviet control in 1968. ◄

357

Place • The old city of Dubrovnik is in Croatia, a part of the former Yugoslavia, which was a Communist country in Eastern Europe. ▶

Economic Crisis By the 1980s, economic conditions in the Soviet Union and in those countries under its control had still not improved. Even after détente, the Soviet government continued to spend most of its money on the armed forces and nuclear weapons. In addition, people who lived in the non-Russian republics of the Soviet Union now wanted more control over their own affairs. Many citizens began to reject the Soviet economic system, but the Soviet leaders refused to give up any of their power or control.

SECTION 1 ASSESSMENT

Terms & Names

1. Identify: (a) propaganda (b) private property rights (c) Nikita Khrushchev
(d) deposed (e) détente

Taking Notes

2. Use a chart like this one to list and describe major aspects of Soviet culture.

Aspects of Soviet Culture

Main Ideas

3. (a) Why did Soviet leaders try to create a strong national identity?

(b) What began to happen in Eastern Europe in the 1950s?

(c) Describe the significance of the "Prague Spring."

Critical Thinking

4. Analyzing Motives

Why do you think the works of many writers, poets, and artists were banned or censored during the Soviet era?

Think About

• what Soviet citizens learned from Solzhenitsyn's works

• the government's use of propaganda

• what life was like for most Soviet citizens

ACTIVITY -OPTION- Reread the information under "Literature and the Arts" and the Spotlight on Culture feature. Write a **speech** for or against censorship in the arts.

Using an Electronic Card Catalog

▶▶ Defining the Skill

To find books, magazines, or other sources of information in a library, you may use an electronic card catalog. This catalog is a computerized search program on the Internet that lists every book, periodical, or other resource found in the library. You can search for resources in the catalog in four ways: by title, by author, by subject, and by keyword. Once you have typed in your search information, the catalog will give you a list of every resource that matches it. This is called bibliographic information. You can use an electronic card catalog to build a bibliography, or a list of books, on the topic you are researching.

▶▶ Applying the Skill

The screen below shows the results of an electronic search for information about the Danube River. To use the information on the screen, follow the strategies listed below.

How to Use an Electronic Card Catalog

Strategy ❶ To begin your search, choose Subject, Title, Author, or Keyword. The student doing this search chose "Subject" and then typed in "Danube River."

Strategy ❷ Based on your search, the catalog will give you a list of records that match that subject. You must then select one of the records to view the details about the resource. The catalog will then give you a screen like the one to the right. This detailed record lists the author, title, and information about where and when the resource was published, and by whom.

Strategy ❸ Locate the call number for the book. The call number indicates the section in the library where you will find the book. You can also find out if the book is available in the library you are using. If not, it may be available in another library in the network.

SEARCH REQUEST: Danube River

❶ Subject   Title   Author   Keyword

Find   Options   Locations   Backup   Startover   Help

❷ Lessner, Erwin Christian. The Danube; the dramatic history of the great river and the people touched by its flow. Westport, Conn.: Greenwood Press, 1961.

AUTHOR: Lessner, Erwin Christian

❷ TITLE: The Danube; the dramatic history of the great river and the people touched by its flow

❷ PUBLISHED: Westport, Conn., Greenwood Press, 1961

PAGING: 529 p.

NOTES: Includes maps, bibliography

❸ CALL NO: 914.9603 L   Book Available

▶▶ Practicing the Skill

Review the text in Chapter 13, Section 1 to find a topic that interests you, such as Yuri Gagarin. Use the Subject search on an electronic card catalog to find information about your topic. Make a bibliography about the subject. Organize your bibliography alphabetically by author. For each book you list, also include the title, city, publisher, and date of publication.

Eastern Europe and Russia

TERMS & NAMES
Mikhail Gorbachev
parliamentary republic
coalition government
ethnic cleansing
Duma

MAIN IDEA

After the breakup of the Soviet Union, many former Soviet republics and countries of Eastern Europe became independent.

WHY IT MATTERS NOW

Nations once under Soviet rule are taking steps toward new economies and democratic governments.

DATELINE

THE KREMLIN, MOSCOW, 1988—To reduce military spending, the Soviet Union has begun removing large numbers of troops and arms from Eastern Europe. This latest news is just one of many changes in the Soviet government since Mikhail Gorbachev (GAWR•buh•chawf) came to power three years ago.

Although Gorbachev believes in the ideals of the Soviet system, he thinks that change is necessary to help solve the country's economic and political problems. Since 1985 Gorbachev has reduced Cold War tensions with the United States. At home in the Soviet Union, he has allowed more political and economic freedom.

Region • Mikhail Gorbachev leads the Soviet Union toward a freer society. ▲

The Breakup of the Soviet Union

<u>**Mikhail Gorbachev**</u>'s reforms did not solve the problems of the Soviet Union. The economy continued to get worse. When Gorbachev did not force the countries of Eastern Europe to remain Communist, this further displeased many Communists.

Vocabulary

coup d'état: the overthrow of a government, usually by a small group in a position of power; often shortened to "coup"

In 1991, a group of more traditional Soviet leaders tried to take over the Soviet government. Thousands of people opposed this coup d'état (KOO•day•TAH), and the coup failed. Then, one by one, the Soviet republics declared independence. The Warsaw Pact was dissolved. By the end of 1991, the Soviet Union no longer existed. The huge country had become 15 different nations.

Modern Eastern Europe

Each former Soviet republic set up its own non-Communist government. The countries of Eastern Europe that had been under Soviet control held democratic elections, and many wrote or revised their constitutions.

BACKGROUND

The Central Asian Soviet republics were mostly Muslim. These republics are now the countries of Kazakhstan, Turkmenistan, Uzbekistan, Kyrgyzstan, and Tajikistan.

In some countries, such as the Czech Republic, former Communists were banned from important government posts. In other countries, such as Bulgaria, the former Communists reorganized themselves into a new political party and have won elections. Many different ethnic groups also tried to create new states within a nation or to reestablish old states that had not existed in many years.

Parliamentary Republics Today, most of the countries of Eastern Europe are parliamentary republics. A **parliamentary republic** is a form of government led by the head of the political party with the most members in parliament. The head of government, usually a prime minister, proposes the programs that the government will undertake. Most of these countries also have a president who has ceremonial, rather than political, duties.

Former Soviet Republics and Warsaw Pact Members, 2001

GEOGRAPHY SKILLBUILDER: Interpreting a Map

1. **Location** • Which former Soviet republics and Warsaw Pact members border Russia?
2. **Region** • On which continent are most of these countries located?

In some countries, small political parties have joined forces to work together to form a government. This is called a **coalition government.**

New Economies Under Soviet rule, Eastern Europe struggled economically and its people's freedoms were severely restricted. Although Eastern Europeans gained their freedom, they also faced problems such as inflation and unemployment.

Eastern Europe's countries are changing from command economies to free-market economies. Some countries, such as Slovakia, made this change slowly. Others, such as Poland, reformed their economic system and achieved economic success.

Many former Soviet republics, which did not quickly reform their economic systems, are in bad economic shape. Some of these nations are terribly poor. Struggles for power have led to violence and sometimes civil war. Pollution from the Soviet era threatens people's health. Still, some republics, including Ukraine, Latvia, Lithuania, and Estonia, are making progress as independent nations.

Defense After the breakup of the Soviet Union, Eastern European nations no longer looked to the Soviet government to defend them. Many wanted to become members of NATO. Belonging to NATO would help assure them of protection in case of invasion.

Reading
Social Studies

A. Comparing
Compare a command economy with a free-market economy.

Spotlight on CULTURE

Easter in Ukraine In Ukraine, most Christians belong to the Orthodox Church. These Ukrainians are known for the special way in which they celebrate the Easter holiday. They create beautiful Easter eggs, which are dyed bright colors and covered with intricate designs. These eggs are so beautiful that people around the world collect them.

Ukrainian families also bake a special bread for Easter. They decorate this bread with designs made from pieces of dough. Families bring the bread and other foods to church to be blessed on Easter. These foods then make up the family's holiday feast.

THINKING CRITICALLY

1. Analyzing Issues
Why were Ukrainian Easter eggs not common during the Soviet era?

2. Comparing
Compare how your family prepares for holidays with preparations made by Ukrainians in the Orthodox Church.

In 1999 three new members joined NATO: Poland, Hungary, and the Czech Republic. In 2001 Bulgaria, Romania, Slovakia, Slovenia, and the Baltic states were also working to become NATO members.

Vocabulary

Baltic states: Estonia, Latvia, and Lithuania—former Soviet republics that are on the Baltic Sea

War in the Balkan Peninsula

Since the late 1980s, much of Eastern Europe has been a place of turmoil and struggle. Yugoslavia, one of the countries located on Europe's Balkan Peninsula, has experienced terrible wars, extreme hardships, and great change.

Under Tito After World War II, Yugoslavia came under Marshal Tito's (TEE·toh) dictatorship. Tito controlled all the country's many different ethnic groups, which included Serbs, Croats, and Muslims. His rule continued until his death in 1980. Slobodan Milošević (sloh·boh·DON muh·LAW·shuh·vich) became Yugoslavia's president in 1989, after years of political turmoil.

BACKGROUND

By 1991 Croatia, Slovenia, Macedonia, and Bosnia-Herzegovina had gained independence from Yugoslavia. Only Serbia and Montenegro were still part of the Yugoslavian federation.

Milosevic Slobodan Milošević, a Serb, wanted the Serbs to rule Yugoslavia. The Serbs in Bosnia began fighting the Croats and Muslims living there. The Bosnian Serbs murdered many Muslims so that Serbs would be in the majority. The Serbs called these killings of members of minority ethnic groups **ethnic cleansing**. Finally, NATO attacked the Bosnian Serbs and ended the war.

Connections to Science

Pollution Soviet leaders thought that industry would improve life for everyone. Developing industry was so important that the Soviet government did not worry about pollution. Few laws were passed to protect the environment.

In the 1970s and 1980s there was not enough money to modernize industry or to reduce pollution. Some areas also could not afford proper sewage systems or recycling plants. Today, Eastern Europe has some of the worst pollution problems on the continent.

The Balkan States, 1991 and 2001

▨	National boundaries, 2001
▨	Yugoslavia, 1991
▨	Autonomous province boundaries, 2001
★	National capital

AUSTRIA
HUNGARY
Slovenia
Croatia
Vojvodina
YUGOSLAVIA
Belgrade
ROMANIA
Bosnia and Herzegovina
Serbia
SAN MARINO
Adriatic Sea
Montenegro
Kosovo
BULGARIA
ITALY
Macedonia
ALBANIA
GREECE

0   100   200 miles
0   100   200 kilometers
12°E   18°E

GEOGRAPHY SKILLBUILDER: Interpreting a Map

1. **Location** • Which Balkan state borders Greece?
2. **Region** • How many countries developed from Yugoslavia?

In 1995 the Serbs, Croats, and Muslims of Bosnia signed a peace treaty. In 1999 Milošević began using ethnic cleansing against the Albanians in Kosovo, a region of Serbia. NATO launched an air war against Yugoslavia that ended with the defeat of the Serbs. In 2000, public protests led to Milošević's removal. He was subsequently arrested and tried for war crimes by the United Nations.

Modern Russia

Life in Russia has improved since the breakup of the Soviet Union. Russian citizens can elect their own leaders. They enjoy more freedom of speech. New businesses have sprung up, and some Russians have become wealthy.

Reading
Social Studies

B. Identifying Problems What are the main problems that face Russia today?

Unfortunately, Russia still faces serious problems. Many leaders are dishonest. The nation has been slow to reform its economic system. Most of the nation's new wealth has gone to a small number of people, so that many Russians remain poor. The crime rate has grown tremendously. The government has also fought a war against Chechnya (CHECH•nee•yah), a region of Russia that wants to become independent.

Russian Culture The fall of communism helped most Russians to follow their cultural practices more freely. Russians gained the freedom to practice the religion of their choice. They can also buy and read the great works of Russian literature that once were banned. At the beginning of the 21st century, writers and other artists also have far more freedom to express themselves.

New magazines and newspapers are being published. Even new history books are being written. For the first time in decades, these publications are telling more of the truth about the Soviet Union.

Russia's Government Russia has a democratic form of government. The president is elected by the people. The people also elect members of the **Duma** (DOO•muh), which is part of the legislature.

Russian Icons A special feature of Russian Orthodox churches is their beautiful religious paintings called icons (EYE•kahns). Russian icons usually depict biblical figures and scenes. They often decorate every corner of a church.

The greatest Russian icon painter was Andrei Rublev (AHN•dray ruhb•LYAWF). He worked in the late 1300s and early 1400s. Rublev's paintings, one of which is shown below, are brightly colored and highlighted in gold. His work influenced many later painters, and today he is considered one of the world's great religious artists.

BACKGROUND

One of the most popular pastimes in Russia is the game of chess. In fact, many of the world's greatest chess players, such as Boris Spassky, have been Russian.

Russia's Natural Resources Today

Legend:
- Forest
- Grassland
- Desert
- Tundra
- Farmland
- Fishing
- Natural gas
- Coal
- Oil
- Iron
- Gold
- Lead

ARCTIC OCEAN

Bering Sea

Sea of Okhotsk

R U S S I A

80°N   60°N   180°   160°E   140°E   40°N

0   250   500 miles
0   250   500 kilometers

GEOGRAPHY SKILLBUILDER: Interpreting a Map

1. **Human-Environment Interaction** • Name three of Russia's more common natural resources.
2. **Place** • What is the most common type of land in Russia?

Democracy is still new to the Russian people. Some citizens are working to improve the system to reduce corruption and to ensure that everyone receives fair treatment. Even the thought of changing the government is new to most Russians. Under the Soviets, people had to accept things the way they were.

Resources and Industry The map above shows Russia's major natural resources. The country is one of the world's largest producers of oil. Russia also contains the world's largest forests. Its trees are made into lumber, paper, and other wood products.

Russian factories produce steel from iron ore. Other factories use that steel to make tractors and other large machines. Since Russian ships can reach both the Pacific and Atlantic oceans, Russia also has a large fishing industry.

Economics Following the lead of Eastern European countries, Russia has been moving toward a free-market economy. Citizens can own land, and foreign companies are encouraged to do business in Russia. These changes have given many Russians more opportunities, but they have also brought difficulties.

BACKGROUND

Russian highways are in poor condition. Also, many rivers and major ports are closed by ice in the winter. As a result, most Russian goods are transported by railroad.

Connections to Language

The Russian Language More than 150 million people speak Russian. It is related to other Slavic languages of Eastern Europe, including Polish, Serbian, and Bulgarian.

Russian is written using the Cyrillic (suh•RIHL•ihk) alphabet, which has 33 characters.

Many of the newly independent republics are now returning to the Latin alphabet, used to write English and most other languages of the Western world. The major powers in the world economy base their languages on the Latin alphabet, making communication easier with other countries.

Hello
Привет

Place • Forestry is a major industry in Russia. These harvested logs are being floated downriver to be processed. ▶

Prices are no longer controlled by the government. This means that companies can charge a price that is high enough for them to make a profit. At the beginning of the 21st century, however, people's wages have not risen as fast as prices. Many people cannot afford to buy new products.

Some Russians have done well in the new economy. On the other hand, people with less education and less access to power have not done as well. Also, today most new businesses and jobs are in the cities, which means that people in small towns have fewer job opportunities.

BACKGROUND

The Russian government is unable to enforce tax laws. Many people don't pay their taxes. Without that money, the government cannot provide basic services, such as health care.

SECTION 2 ASSESSMENT

Terms & Names

1. Identify:
(a) Mikhail Gorbachev
(b) parliamentary republic
(c) coalition government
(d) ethnic cleansing
(e) Duma

Taking Notes

2. Use a flow chart like this one to outline the changes in Eastern Europe and Russia from 1988 through 2000.

1988:

↓

↓

Main Ideas

3. (a) What happened to the governments of the former Soviet republics after independence?

(b) How have the economies of Eastern European countries changed now that those countries are free?

(c) In what ways has life in Russia improved since the breakup of the Soviet Union?

Critical Thinking

4. Making Inferences

Why do you think many Eastern European countries would like to join NATO?

Think About

- what happened to the Warsaw Pact
- the economies of Eastern Europe
- the relationship between Eastern Europe and Russia

ACTIVITY -OPTION- Reread the information in the Spotlight on Culture feature. Write a short, personal **essay** that describes a special family, school, neighborhood, or holiday celebration in which you participated.

The European Union

TERMS & NAMES
European Union
currency
euro
tariff
standard of living
Court of Human Rights

MAIN IDEA

Europeans want to maintain a high quality of life for all citizens while preserving their unique cultures.

WHY IT MATTERS NOW

A prosperous and culturally diverse Europe provides goods and markets for the rest of the world.

DATELINE

WESTERN EUROPE, DECEMBER 2001—Starting next month, people in many Western European nations will begin trading their old bills and coins for euros—the new money of the European Union (EU). The design of the bills, below, is the same for all EU members.

The design of the euro coins, however, will be different. Individual countries are minting their own. As shown here, one side has a standard euro design. The other side has national symbols that relate to each country. In 1996, artists and sculptors from all over Europe entered a contest to design the coins. The winner was Luc Luycx (lewk lowx) from Belgium.

Region • Euros reached the European market in January 2002. ▲

Western Europe Today

Today, in Western Europe, all national leaders share their power with elected lawmakers. Citizens take part in government by voting and through membership in a variety of political parties. The Unit Atlas on pages 260–269 shows modern Europe.

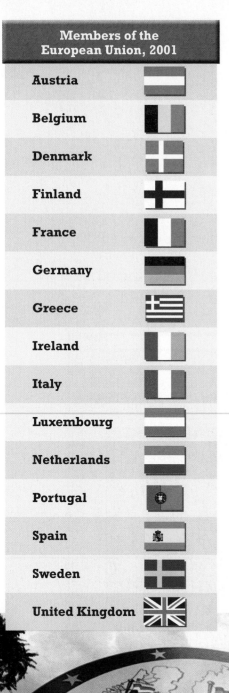

Members of the European Union, 2001

Country	Flag
Austria	
Belgium	
Denmark	
Finland	
France	
Germany	
Greece	
Ireland	
Italy	
Luxembourg	
Netherlands	
Portugal	
Spain	
Sweden	
United Kingdom	

The European Union Many countries of Western Europe belong to a group called the **European Union** (EU). At first, countries joined the EU to encourage trade. This economic group, however, is becoming a loose political union.

Many former Communist countries of Eastern Europe want to join the Union too. They know that membership will help them economically and politically. Eastern European countries, however, cannot automatically join the EU. Many must first make legal, economic, and environmental improvements. The EU has agreed to include them over time. With a possible membership of more than 20 nations by 2003, the EU may be the best hope for European peace and prosperity.

Regional Governments In Western Europe, each nation also has regional governments, similar to those of individual states in the United States. Regional governments are demanding—and receiving—greater power. As a result, many people in Western Europe enjoy increased self-rule and participation in the political process.

BACKGROUND

In 2001, the EU gave initial approval to the Czech Republic, Estonia, Hungary, Poland, and Slovenia to join in the near future.

Region • The headquarters of the European Central Bank is located in Frankfurt, Germany. ◄

EU Economies

BACKGROUND

Some EU nations, including the United Kingdom and Denmark, have not agreed to give up their existing currency.

Traditionally, each European nation has had its own **currency,** or system of money. The EU is meant to make international trade much simpler. With more Europeans using the **euro,** the currency of the EU, currency no longer has to be exchanged every time a payment crosses a border.

Improved Trade To encourage trade, members have also done away with tariffs on the goods they trade with one another. A **tariff** is a duty or fee that must be paid on imported or exported goods, making them more expensive. EU members have lifted border controls as well. This means that goods, services, and people flow freely among these member nations.

Another goal of the EU is to achieve economic equality among its members. To reach this goal, EU members are sharing their wealth. Poorer countries such as Ireland receive money to help them build businesses.

Reading
Social Studies

A. Clarifying
How would improved trade raise the standard of living?

A Higher Standard of Living Member nations hope that increased trade and shared wealth will help give all citizens of the EU a high standard of living. A person's **standard of living,** or quality of life, is based on the availability of goods and services.

People who have a high standard of living have enough food and housing, good transportation and communications, and access to schools and health care. They also have a high rate of literacy, meaning that most adults are able to read.

Additional Benefits The members of the EU are helping the countries of Eastern Europe to raise their environmental standards. They are willing to pay up to 75 percent of the cost for a new waste treatment system in Romania, for example. The program includes recycling centers for paper, glass, and plastics. It will clean up and close old dumping grounds, which were leaking pollution into the ground water.

Connections to Economics

Tourism For many European nations, tourism is an important part of the economy. In fact, the continent represents about 60 percent of the world's tourist market. Visitors come to enjoy Europe's climate, historic sites, museums, and food.

Popular destinations include Spain, Italy, Austria, and the United Kingdom. France, below, is the most visited country in the world. In 1999 it hosted more than 73 million tourists.

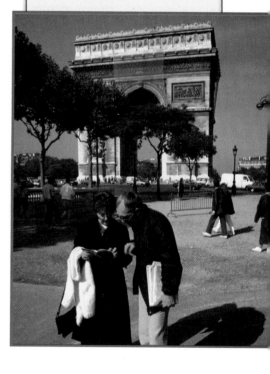

The EU also runs programs that train people for jobs. As citizens of a member nation, people are not limited to a job in their own country. They may work in any part of the EU. They can even vote in local elections wherever they live. In addition, the Council of Europe's **Court of Human Rights** protects the rights of all its citizens in whichever member country they live.

Cultural Diversity

Although many European nations are part of the EU, they still have their own distinct cultural traditions. These traditions may include different languages, unique foods, certain ways of doing business, and even special games and celebrations. Many of these traditions developed over hundreds of years.

Some nations are a mix of several cultures. In Belgium, for example, Flemings live in the north and speak Dutch. Another major group, the Walloons, lives in the south. They speak French. A third group of German-speaking Belgians lives in the eastern part of the country. Many Belgian cities include people from all three groups.

City Life Many of the world's famous and exciting cities are located in Western Europe. London, Madrid, Paris, Amsterdam, and Rome are just a few of the major centers for the arts, business, and learning. These cities are centuries old, and Europeans work hard to preserve them.

Europeans also take pride in the conveniences that their cities offer. Most major urban areas have excellent public transportation, including subways, buses, and trains. Sidewalk cafés are also popular, where people come to meet friends, eat, and relax.

Reading
Social Studies

B. Identifying Problems What are the main problems facing the European Union?

Region • Many Europeans center their social lives around urban sidewalk cafés, such as this one in Italy. ▼

Region • Quaint small European villages are popular tourist attractions. ▶

BACKGROUND

Many European families cannot make a living on a small farm. The government may offer support to such families, to help preserve the nation's rural culture.

Country Life European cities have much to offer, but the countryside is also popular—especially for vacationers. The Italian region of Tuscany (TUHS·kuh·nee) and the French region of Provence (pruh·VAHNS) are two of the best-known examples of the many beautiful rural areas.

Small European villages may have only a café, a grocery store, a post office, a town square, and a collection of houses. Many families who live in such areas have been farming or raising animals on the same land for generations. Some even live in houses that their families have owned for hundreds of years.

SECTION 3 ASSESSMENT

Terms & Names
1. Identify:
- (a) European Union (EU)
- (b) currency
- (c) euro
- (d) tariff
- (e) standard of living
- (f) Court of Human Rights

Taking Notes
2. Use a chart like this one to compare aspects of city life and country life in Europe.

City Life	Country Life

Main Ideas
3. (a) Describe the importance of the new shared currency that is based on the euro.

(b) Can any European country automatically join the EU? Why or why not?

(c) List at least two benefits, other than a shared currency, for countries that are members of the EU.

Critical Thinking
4. Synthesizing

Why may the EU be the best hope for European peace and prosperity?

Think About
- the number of member countries
- the goals of the EU
- modern European conflicts

ACTIVITY -OPTION- Choose one photograph from this section that shows a place in Europe. Write a **postcard** or **e-mail** to a friend or family member as if you were there. What sights and sounds will you describe?

90 1910 1920 1930 1940 1950 1960 1970
1700 1710 1720 1730 1740 1750 1760 1780 179
0 2020
1800 1810 1820 1830 1840 1850 1860 1870 188
890 1900 1910 1920 1930 1940 1950 1960 19
1980 1990 2000

Linking Past and Present

The Legacy of Europe

Movable Type

Before Johann Gutenberg (1400–1468) invented the printing press in Germany, European monks copied books by hand. Movable type made it possible to print multiple copies of books quickly, allowing people access to them. The printing process advanced greatly in the 1930s. By the mid-1940s, printed works included complex illustrations and color. Today, people create text and images and print them directly from their computers.

Early printing press ▲

Nitroglycerin

For almost 20 years, Alfred Nobel (1833–1896), shown at left, worked on developing a way to safely contain and ignite nitroglycerin, a powerful explosive. Eventually, chemists and doctors realized that nitroglycerin widens blood vessels and can be used to treat patients with heart conditions. Given in tablet, patch, or oral-spray form, nitroglycerin has saved countless lives.

Architecture

The White House in Washington, D.C., is one of many buildings in the United States that has been influenced by Roman architecture. Roman buildings often featured vaulted domes, columns, and large interior spaces. This type of architecture has influenced other buildings in the United States, including many banks and courthouses.

Democracy

Around 500 B.C., several Greek city-states established democracies, replacing their single-ruler governments. The word *democracy* derives from two Greek words: *demos,* meaning "people," and *kratos,* meaning "power." Today, the idea of rule by the people is found around the world, from the United States to France to India.

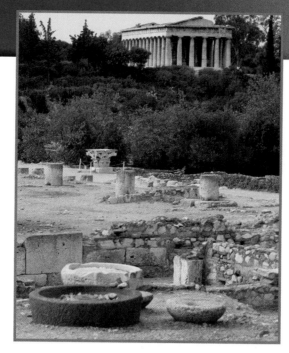

The agora, or marketplace, of ancient Athens was often the scene of political activities. ▲

Find Out More About It!

Study the text and photos on these pages to learn about inventions, creations, and contributions that have come from Europe. Then choose the item that interests you the most and use the library or the Internet to learn more about it. Use the information you gather to create a poster celebrating the contribution.

RESEARCH LINKS
CLASSZONE.COM

Yacht ▼

Robot ▶

Flamingo ▶

European Languages

Many words of different European languages have made their way into English. For example, the word *dinner* is actually French in origin. As English people traveled and settled around the world, they borrowed words from such European languages as German, Spanish, and Norwegian to use in their everyday communication. Examples of some of these words we use today are *kindergarten* (German), *dinner* (French), *yacht* (Dutch), *corridor* (Italian), *vanilla* (Spanish), *flamingo* (Portuguese), *robot* (Czech), and *ski* (Norwegian).

ASSESSMENT

CHAPTER 13

TERMS & NAMES

Explain the significance of each of the following:

1. propaganda
2. Nikita Khrushchev
3. détente
4. Mikhail Gorbachev
5. ethnic cleansing
6. Duma
7. currency
8. euro
9. tariff
10. standard of living

REVIEW QUESTIONS

Eastern Europe Under Communism *(pages 353–358)*

1. Why did the Soviet government outlaw many cultural celebrations?
2. Explain why most Soviet citizens learned little about other nations around the world.
3. How did the Soviet Union maintain control over Eastern European countries?

Eastern Europe and Russia *(pages 360–366)*

4. How did the Soviet Union change during 1991?
5. List at least three of Russia's major natural resources.

The European Union *(pages 367–371)*

6. What is the importance of the European Union (EU)?
7. Name one benefit of being a member of the EU.
8. Identify at least three of Europe's major centers of the arts, business, and learning.

CRITICAL THINKING

Comparing

1. Using your completed chart from Reading Social Studies, p. 352, compare Eastern Europe under Communism with Eastern Europe after Communism.

Summarizing

2. Outline the changes to the Russian economy since the breakup of the Soviet Union.

Recognizing Important Details

3. What types of changes must Eastern European countries make in order to join the EU?

Visual Summary

1

Eastern Europe Under Communism

- The Soviet Union's communist government controlled the lives of its citizens.
- Under Nikita Khrushchev, citizens began to have greater freedom.

2

Eastern Europe and Russia

- Today, independent nations once under Soviet rule are taking steps toward new economies and greater freedom.

3

The European Union

- Many European countries are members of an economic and political alliance called the European Union (EU).

SOCIAL STUDIES SKILLBUILDER

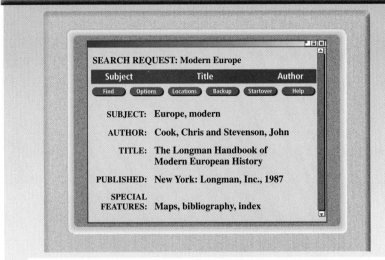

SEARCH REQUEST: Modern Europe

| Subject | Title | Author |

Find   Options   Locations   Backup   Startover   Help

SUBJECT: Europe, modern

AUTHOR: Cook, Chris and Stevenson, John

TITLE: The Longman Handbook of Modern European History

PUBLISHED: New York: Longman, Inc., 1987

SPECIAL FEATURES: Maps, bibliography, index

SKILLBUILDER: Using an Electronic Card Catalog

1. Who wrote this book, and when was it published?
2. Will this book help you find other books related to the subject you researched?

FOCUS ON GEOGRAPHY

1. Human-Environment Interaction • Which nation or nations appear to have the largest amounts of farmland?
2. Place • Which nation or nations do not have coastal fishing resources?
3. Place • Which nation or nations appear to have the smallest amounts of forests?

Barley
Coal
Corn
Dairy
Fish
Hydroelectric power
Iron ore
Petroleum
Agricultural
Livestock and herding
Forests
Nonagricultural

ESTONIA
LATVIA
LITHUANIA
RUSSIA
BELARUS
UKRAINE
Baltic Sea

0   150   300 miles
0   150   300 kilometers

CHAPTER PROJECTS

Interdisciplinary Activity: Math

Making an Inflation Chart This activity will help you to understand the effects of inflation on the economy. Look at a flier from a local grocery store. Write the names and prices of five food items in the first column of a chart. Then figure out and record what the prices would be for each item for the next two years.

- To find next year's price: multiply the original price by .03 (the rate of inflation). Add this to the original price.
- To find the following year's price: multiply next year's price by .03 (the rate of inflation). Add that to next year's price.

Cooperative Learning Activity

Creating a New Government Work in a group of three to five students to create a new class government and constitution.

- Assign each student a role in the new government, such as congressperson or president.
- Be sure to outline the responsibilities of each member.
- Write a brief constitution for your government. Include sections outlining basic rights, freedoms, and responsibilities of citizens.

INTERNET ACTIVITY

Use the Internet to do research about the economy in Slovenia. Specifically look for information about the types of industries in Slovenia. What are its major imports and exports?
Writing About Economics Write a short report of your findings. Be sure to list the Web sites that you used to prepare your report.

For Internet links to support this activity, go to

RESEARCH LINKS
CLASSZONE.COM

Europe Today

Place London's Piccadilly Circus is an intersection of major roads, with an Underground, or subway, stop at the center. Piccadilly Circus is a popular tourist attraction and shopping district.

UNDERGROUND

SWEDEN
POLAND
UNITED KINGDOM
GERMANY
ATLANTIC
FRANCE
PACIFIC
PACIFIC
OCEAN
OCEAN
OCEAN
INDIAN
OCEAN
OCEAN

Why is it important for Europeans to protect their seas?

FOCUS ON GEOGRAPHY

Human-Environment Interaction • The United Kingdom, Sweden, France, Germany, and Poland have borders along the North Sea or the Baltic Sea. These European seas are major transportation corridors. The North Sea contains one of the world's most important oil deposits. The Baltic Sea has some oil and is heavily used for transporting oil.

Accidents sometimes happen at sea. About three oil spills occur every year in the Baltic Sea. The North Sea has also had major spills. One occurred in November 1998, killing thousands of sea birds. Today, nations are working on ways to prevent spills and to clean up those that occur.

What do you think?

♦ Why is it important for countries to protect the seas?

♦ What effect might oil spills and other pollution have on the seas?

♦ What economic purposes do oceans and seas serve?

BEFORE YOU READ

▶▶ *What Do You Know?*

Did you know that from the end of WW II until 1990, Germany was two separate countries and Poland was controlled by the Soviet Union? Do you have relatives or friends who come from the United Kingdom, Sweden, France, Germany, or Poland? Have you ever seen the Queen of England or the Pope, who is from Poland, on television? Have you heard of the Nobel Prize, which is awarded in Sweden? Think about what you have learned in other classes, what you have read, and what you have heard or seen in the news about these countries.

Region • Sweden's Nobel Prize honors great achievements worldwide. ▲

▶▶ *What Do You Want to Know?*

Consider what you know about the countries covered in Chapter 14. In your notebook, record what you hope to learn from this chapter.

READ AND TAKE NOTES

Reading Strategy: Comparing Comparing is a useful strategy for evaluating two or more similar subjects. Making comparisons also helps you to better understand what you have learned. Use the chart below to compare information about the United Kingdom, Sweden, France, Germany, and Poland.

- Copy the chart into your notebook.
- As you read, look for information for each category.
- Record details under the appropriate headings.

Movement • The German-made Volkswagen Beetle is the best-selling car ever. ▲

Country	Physical Geography	Government	Economy	Culture	Interesting Facts
United Kingdom					
Sweden					
France					
Germany					
Poland					

The United Kingdom

MAIN IDEA

The United Kingdom is a small nation in Western Europe with a history of colonization.

WHY IT MATTERS NOW

British economic, political, and cultural traditions have influenced nations around the world.

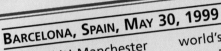

DATELINE

EXTRA

BARCELONA, SPAIN, MAY 30, 1999

They did it! Manchester United won the triple crown of soccer. The British fans here are going wild, and their excitement is easy to understand. Manchester United is only the third soccer team to win its league championship, cup titles, and the Champions League final.

Football, or "soccer" as Americans call it, is the world's most popular sport. The British invented a form of the game, called "mob football," in the 1300s. Back then, the playing field was the size of a small town, and there might have been as many as 500 players. A set of rules for the game was developed in 1863. Today, football is the national pastime in the United Kingdom.

Region • Manchester United celebrates after winning soccer's triple crown. ▲

A Kingdom of Four Political Regions

The United Kingdom is a small island nation of Western Europe. Its culture has had an enormous impact on the world. The nation's official name is the United Kingdom of Great Britain and Northern Ireland. **London**, located in southeastern England, is the capital.

Vocabulary

Great Britain: the name for the island that contains Scotland, England, and Wales

United Kingdom

England

Scotland

Wales

Northern Ireland

Four different political regions make up the United Kingdom: Scotland, England, Wales, and Northern Ireland (see the map below). The British monarchy has ruled over the four regions for hundreds of years.

National Government Today, the government of the United Kingdom is a constitutional monarchy. The British monarch is a symbol of power rather than an actual ruler. The power to govern belongs to Parliament, which is the national lawmaking body.

The British Parliament has two parts. The House of Lords is made up of nobles. Elected representatives make up the House of Commons. The House of Commons is the more powerful of the two houses.

The prime minister leads the government. He or she is usually the leader of the political party that wins the most seats in the House of Commons. The other political parties go into "opposition," which means their role is to question government policies.

Regional Government in Great Britain Recently, the national government of the United Kingdom has returned some self-rule to some regions of Great Britain. In the late 1990s, voters in Wales approved plans for their own assembly, or body of lawmakers. Also at this time, the Scots voted to create their own parliament. Both Wales's assembly and Scotland's parliament met for the first time in 1999.

Vocabulary

monarchy: government by king or queen

Reading Social Studies

A. Clarifying Who is the head of government in the United Kingdom?

The United Kingdom Today

Map labels: NORTH ATLANTIC OCEAN, 12°W, 8°W, 4°W, 0°, 4°E, Shetland Islands, NORWAY, 59°N, Orkney Islands, Hebrides, Moray Firth, Highlands, Inverness, SCOTLAND, Dee, Aberdeen, Grampian Mts., Dundee, Firth of Forth, Edinburgh, Glasgow, Clyde, Tweed, North Sea, Cheviot Hills, Londonderry, Carlisle, NORTHERN IRELAND, Belfast, Isle of Man, Cumbrian Mts., Durham, THE PENNINES, Swale, Irish Sea, Bradford, Leeds, Humber River, Dublin, Shannon, Manchester, Liverpool, Dee, Sheffield, NETH., IRELAND, Cardigan Bay, Cambrian Mts., ENGLAND, Birmingham, GERMANY, Cork, Wye, Severn, Cambridge, St. George's Channel, WALES, Oxford, Cotswold Hills, London, Canterbury, Cardiff, Thames, Strait of Dover, Dover, BELGIUM, Celtic Sea, Southampton, Plymouth, Isle of Wight, English Channel, FRANCE, LUX.

Map legend:
0   50   100 miles
0   50   100 kilometers

National boundary
Regional boundary
★ National capital
• Other city

GEOGRAPHY SKILLBUILDER: Interpreting a Map

1. **Location** • Which region of the United Kingdom is on a different island?
2. **Location** • Which body of water separates the United Kingdom from France?

BACKGROUND

The roots of division in Northern Ireland go back to at least the 1600s, when English and Scottish colonists settled there. These Protestant settlers took over the lands of Irish Catholics.

Governing Northern Ireland Throughout the 20th century, there were conflicts in Northern Ireland between Irish Catholic nationalists and Irish Protestants who supported the government of the United Kingdom. In fact, during the 1960s, many Irish Catholics wanted Northern Ireland to **secede,** or withdraw from, the United Kingdom. They hoped to unite Northern Ireland with the Republic of Ireland. Irish Protestants—a majority in the region—generally wanted to remain part of the United Kingdom.

In 1969, riots broke out, and the British government sent in troops to stop them. Violence between groups of Protestants and Catholics continued for almost 30 years. In 1998, representatives from both sides signed the **Good Friday Accord**. This agreement set up the Northern Ireland Assembly, which represents both Catholic and Protestant voters. For this government to succeed in Northern Ireland, however, the former enemies will need to work together.

The WORLD'S HERITAGE

Parliament The Houses of Parliament have been used by the British government since 1547. The buildings are located in London, alongside the River Thames (tehmz). They include the House of Commons, the House of Lords, and Westminster Hall. One of the most famous parts of this complex is the clock tower. Commonly called "Big Ben," this is actually the name of the 13-ton bell inside the tower, not the tower itself.

In 1834, a fire destroyed much of the original buildings. The reconstruction by architect Sir Charles Barry was completed in 1860. The Houses of Parliament are visited and photographed by tourists from around the world.

When Parliament is in session, the Union Jack flies from Victoria Tower.

House of Lords Chamber

Westminster Hall is more than 900 years old.

The clock tower that holds Big Ben is 316 feet high.

House of Commons Chamber

Region • London's New Globe Theater is a replica of the 17th-century playhouse that originally hosted William Shakespeare's works. ◄

Cultural Heritage

The United Kingdom has a rich cultural heritage that includes the great Renaissance playwright William Shakespeare. With a long history as an imperial power, the nation has been exporting its culture around the world for hundreds of years. For example, India, Canada, and other former British colonies modeled their governments on the British parliamentary system. British culture has also set trends in sports, music, and literature.

Music British music influenced the early music of Canada and the United States, both former British colonies. One British tune long familiar to people in the United States is "God Save the Queen." You probably know it as "My Country, 'Tis of Thee." Several countries have put the words of their national anthems to this traditional British melody.

During the 1960s, many British musical groups—including the Beatles and the Rolling Stones—dominated music charts around the world. In later decades, other British singers, including Elton John, Sting, and Dido, became popular favorites.

Literature The best-known cultural export of the United Kingdom, aside from the English language itself, may be literature. In the 19th century, Mary Shelley dreamed up Frankenstein's monster, and Sir Arthur Conan Doyle first wrote about Sherlock Holmes. Another popular author of the time was **Charles Dickens** (1812–1870), who wrote *Oliver Twist* and *A Christmas Carol*.

Region • In the early 1960s, the Beatles became wildly popular, not only in the United Kingdom, but also around the world. ▼

Reading
Social Studies

B. Recognizing Important Details Why was the United Kingdom able to spread British culture across the world?

Two gifted British writers of the 20th century are Virginia Woolf and George Orwell. Modern British authors have also given the world many popular stories for young people. They include C. S. Lewis, who wrote *The Chronicles of Narnia*, and J. K. Rowling, who created the Harry Potter books.

The British Economy

The United Kingdom is an important trading and financial center. Many British citizens also make their living in mining and manufacturing. Factories in the United Kingdom turn out a variety of products ranging from china to sports cars. The nation has plenty of coal, natural gas, and oil to fuel its factories, but it has few other natural resources.

The need for imported goods makes trade another major industry of the United Kingdom. The nation imports many raw materials used in manufacturing. It also imports food, because the farms of this nation produce only enough to feed about two-thirds of its large population.

Region • J. K. Rowling's Harry Potter books have captured the imaginations of children worldwide. ▲

SECTION 1 ASSESSMENT

Terms & Names

1. **Identify:**
   (a) London
   (b) secede
   (c) Good Friday Accord
   (d) Charles Dickens

Taking Notes

2. Use a chart like this one to describe the major aspects of the United Kingdom's modern government, economy, and culture.

Modern United Kingdom	
Government	
Economy	
Culture	

Main Ideas

3. (a) Identify the four regions that make up the United Kingdom.

   (b) What role does the British monarch play in the government of the modern United Kingdom?

   (c) What impact has the culture of the United Kingdom had on its colonies and on other parts of the world?

Critical Thinking

4. **Analyzing Issues**

   Why do you think the conflict in Northern Ireland is so difficult to resolve?

   Think About
   - differences in religious beliefs
   - recent changes in British regional governments
   - the long period of continued violence

ACTIVITY -OPTION- Reread the information about British football from the "Dateline" feature that opens the section. Write a **description** of a sport that interests you.

Sweden

TERMS & NAMES
Riksdag
ombudsman
armed neutrality
hydroelectricity
acid rain
skerry

MAIN IDEA

Sweden offers its people a high standard of living, although it also faces environmental problems.

WHY IT MATTERS NOW

Modern Sweden is dealing with environmental issues that affect many countries around the world.

DATELINE

STOCKHOLM, SWEDEN, DECEMBER 4, 2001—This week in Stockholm, Sweden's capital, hundreds of past winners of the Nobel Prize gather to celebrate the centennial, or 100th anniversary, of this award. Concerts, lectures, and banquets lead up to the award ceremony in Stockholm City Hall on December 10.

The first Nobel Prize ceremony was held in Stockholm in 1901. Since then, awards in physics, chemistry, economics, medicine, literature, and peace have gone to more than 700 people, representing every inhabited continent. Besides achieving worldwide honor and fame, the winners receive a medal and a cash prize. The award was established at the request of Alfred Nobel (1833–1896), a Swedish chemist and millionaire who invented dynamite.

Place • Stockholm, Sweden, hosts events celebrating the 100th anniversary of the Nobel Prize. ▲

Sweden's Government

Sweden is famous for the Nobel Prize, but it is also one of the most prosperous and beautiful countries in Europe. The Kingdom of Sweden shares the Scandinavian Peninsula with Norway in Northern Europe (see the map on page 385). The country is a constitutional monarchy, meaning that the Swedish monarch has only ceremonial powers. He or she cannot make laws. Instead, the people elect representatives to four-year terms in the Swedish parliament, called the **Riksdag** (REEKS·DAHG).

The Riksdag The 349 members of the Riksdag nominate Sweden's prime minister. They also appoint ombudsmen. **Ombudsmen** are officials who protect citizens' rights and make sure that the Swedish courts and civil service follow the law.

Swedish citizens vote to determine how many members of each political party serve in the Riksdag. Before 1976, the Social Democratic Labour Party had been in power for nearly 44 years. Today, the Swedish government includes four other parties.

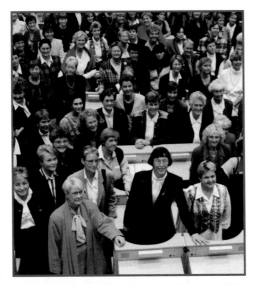

Region •
Women are active in Swedish government. ▶

Foreign Policy Since World War I, Sweden's foreign policy has been one of **armed neutrality**. This means that in times of war, the country has its own military forces but does not take sides in other nations' conflicts.

Even during peacetime, the Swedish government tries not to form military alliances. Unless Sweden is directly attacked, it will not become involved in war. The country is a strong supporter of the United Nations.

Reading
Social Studies

A. Synthesizing How does Sweden's neutrality affect its foreign relations?

The Economy and the Environment

Privately owned businesses and international trade are important to Sweden's economy. It exports many goods, including metals, minerals, and wood. Engineering and communications are major industries. The automobile industry also provides many jobs.

GEOGRAPHY SKILLBUILDER: Interpreting a Map

1. **Location** • Which country shares the Scandinavian Peninsula with Sweden?
2. **Region** • What is the national capital of Sweden?

The Swedish Labor Force After World War II, many Swedes left their towns and villages to find work in the large cities in the south. Today, more than 80 percent of the population lives in these urban areas. Much of Sweden's labor force is highly educated and enjoys a high standard of living.

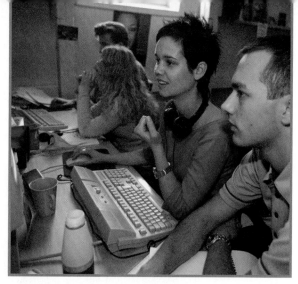

Place • Many in Sweden's highly educated labor force work in the high-tech and engineering industries. ▲

Power Sources **Hydroelectricity,** or power generated by water, is the main source of electrical power in Sweden. Nuclear power is also widely used. The Swedish government is looking into other, safer sources of energy, which include solar- and wind-powered energy.

Acid Rain Sweden and its neighboring countries share similar environmental problems. One of the most severe problems is **acid rain.** Acid rain occurs when air pollutants come back to Earth in the form of precipitation. These pollutants may soon poison many trees throughout the region. Sweden and neighboring countries are working to clean up the environment by trying to control air pollutants produced by cars and factories.

Region •
December 13 is
St. Lucia's Day,
one of Sweden's
most important
Christian
holidays. ▼

Reading
Social Studies

B. Clarifying
What causes
acid rain?

Daily Life and Culture

Culturally and ethnically, Sweden is primarily a homogeneous country. Ninety percent of the population are native to Sweden and are members of the Lutheran Church of Sweden. The majority of people speak Swedish.

Since World War II, immigrants from Turkey, Greece, and other countries have brought some cultural diversity to Sweden's population. Today, about one in nine people living in Sweden is an immigrant or the child of an immigrant.

Recreation Workers in Sweden have many benefits, including long vacations. The Swedes love taking time to enjoy both winter and summer sports. Sweden, with its cold weather and many hills and mountains, is a great place for cross-country and downhill skiing. Skating, hockey, and ice fishing are also popular.

Vocabulary

homogeneous:
the same
throughout

Place • Sweden's cold winters have made downhill and cross-country skiing popular. ▶

Many small islands, called **skerries,** dot the Swedish coast. In the summer, many people visit these islands to hike, camp, and fish. Tennis, soccer, and outdoor performances such as concerts are popular as well.

Contributions to World Culture Sweden is well-known for its contributions to drama, literature, and film. The late 19th-century and early 20th-century plays of August Strindberg are produced all over the world. Astrid Lindgren's children's books, including *Pippi Longstocking* (1945), still delight readers everywhere. Ingmar Bergman is famous for the many great films he directed.

SECTION 2 ASSESSMENT

Terms & Names

1. Identify:
   - (a) Riksdag
   - (b) ombudsman
   - (c) armed neutrality
   - (d) hydroelectricity
   - (e) acid rain
   - (f) skerry

Taking Notes

2. Use a spider map like this one to outline the major aspects of Sweden's government, economy, and culture.

Main Ideas

3. (a) On which European peninsula is Sweden located? What other country shares this peninsula?

   (b) What happened to the Swedish labor force after World War II?

   (c) How has immigration since World War II changed the population of Sweden?

Critical Thinking

4. **Evaluating Decisions**

   What do you think might be the advantages and disadvantages of armed neutrality for Sweden?

   Think About
   - Sweden's location
   - the damage and expense of war
   - the benefits of alliances

ACTIVITY -OPTION- Reread the "Dateline" feature at the beginning of this section. Write a short **description** of which category you would like to earn a Nobel Prize in and why.

Interdisciplinary Challenge

Spend a Day in Renaissance Florence

You are a traveler visiting Florence, Italy, in the year 1505. It is exciting to be here now. All over Europe, people have heard about the Renaissance, or cultural rebirth, that is taking place in this beautiful city. Artists, architects, writers, and scientists are turning out brilliant work. In the day you spend here, you want to learn about this new cultural movement. You want to be able to tell people at home about Renaissance Florence.

COOPERATIVE LEARNING On these pages are challenges you will encounter as you tour Renaissance Florence. Working with a small group, choose one of these challenges to solve. Divide the work among group members. Look for helpful information in the Data File. Keep in mind that you will present your solution to the class.

LANGUAGE ARTS CHALLENGE

"Florence is home to brilliant artists and writers."

Why did the Renaissance start here? Florence is home to brilliant artists and writers. Successful merchants and craftworkers, along with several powerful families, have made the city rich. Many wealthy people are patrons, or sponsors, of artists' work. You are curious about the people of Florence. Who are the leading figures? What is life like here? Choose one of these options to discover the answers. Use the Data File for help.

ACTIVITIES

1. Choose one major figure who lived in Florence during the Renaissance and research his or her life. Then write a short first-person monologue in which, speaking as that person, you describe your life and work.
2. Imagine you are an ordinary young Florentine living in 1505—for example, a goldsmith's apprentice. Write journal entries for a week in your life.

LANDMARKS OF RENAISSANCE FLORENCE

- Florence is built on both sides of the **Arno River**. Its population during the Renaissance was about 100,000. Most of the famous buildings are on the right bank. Besides its artists, Renaissance Florence was known for its craftworkers, such as goldsmiths and leatherworkers.

- The **Duomo** stands on the Piazza del Duomo, an open square. In 1418, Filippo Brunelleschi won a contest to build a dome over the unfinished church. He invented new methods and machines to build it. As in earlier domes, vaults or pointed arches support the dome. Brunelleschi added a circular support wall, called a drum, to build it higher.

- The **Ponte Vecchio** ("Old Bridge"), built in 1345, is one of several bridges across the Arno River. Shops, especially those of goldsmiths, line both sides of the bridge.

- The **Pitti Palace**, built in 1458, is on the left bank of the river.

MAJOR FIGURES OF THE RENAISSANCE

- **Filippo Brunelleschi** (1377–1446), architect of the Duomo and the Pitti Palace.

- **Dante** (1265–1321), poet, author of *Divine Comedy.* Dante pioneered the usage of everyday language, instead of Latin, in literature.

- **Isabella d'Este** (1474–1539), noblewoman and patron of many artists.

- **Leonardo da Vinci** (1452–1519), painter, sculptor, engineer, scientist.

- **Michelangelo** (1475–1564), sculptor, painter, architect; sculptor of *David* (1504).

- **Raphael** (1483–1520), painter and architect.

To learn more about Renaissance Florence, go to

RESEARCH LINKS
CLASSZONE.COM

SCIENCE CHALLENGE

"Its red-tiled dome soars above most other buildings."

The people of Florence are proud of their cathedral, known as the Duomo ("dome" in Italian). Its red-tiled dome soars above most other buildings. People say that its architect used new techniques to build the dome. What discoveries have Renaissance scientists made? How important is science in this cultural movement? Use one of these options to present information. Look in the Data File for help.

ACTIVITIES

1. Draw a cross-section diagram of the dome of the Duomo, designed by Filippo Brunelleschi. Be able to demonstrate how a dome like this is supported.
2. Prepare to interview Brunelleschi about his ideas and inventions. Research his life and work, and create a list of questions to ask him.

Activity Wrap-Up

As a group, review your solution to the challenge you selected. Then present your solution to the class.

France

TERMS & NAMES
Charles de Gaulle
French Resistance
Jean Monnet
socialism
European Community
impressionism

MAIN IDEA	**WHY IT MATTERS NOW**
France was ruined politically and economically by World War II but has since made a full recovery.	France is an important member of the European Union and continues to influence the world's economy and cultures.

DATELINE

EXTRA

PARIS, FRANCE, AUGUST 26, 1944

Paris is free! The church bells are still ringing from yesterday's celebrations. After four long years of German control, Paris finally has been liberated. General Charles de Gaulle returned from the United Kingdom yesterday and celebrated the liberation by leading a parade from the Arc de Triomphe to Notre Dame Cathedral.

The liberation of Paris is the result of a two-and-a-half-month advance of Allied forces from the beaches of Normandy in northern France. The French Resistance in Paris began disrupting the German occupiers on August 19, and yesterday, the French army entered Paris.

Region • The liberation of Paris is a significant symbolic victory for the Allies. ▲

The Fifth Republic

During World War II, **Charles de Gaulle** (1890–1970) was a general in the French army. After Germany conquered France in 1940, de Gaulle fled to the United Kingdom. There, he became the leader of the French in exile and stayed in contact with the French Resistance. The **French Resistance** established communications for the Allied war effort, spied on German activity, and sometimes assassinated high-ranking German officers.

Region • Charles de Gaulle is a hero to the French. ▲

France Today

UNITED KINGDOM

Calais • Dunkerque
Lille •
BELGIUM
English Channel
Cherbourg
Amiens • Arras
— LUXEMBOURG
Le Havre
Rouen • Reims
Caen *Seine* • Paris • Nancy • Metz
GERMANY
Brest
Chartres Troyes
Strasbourg
Rennes Le Mans
Orléans
Loire
Mulhouse •
Nantes Tours
Dijon • Besançon
SWITZERLAND
Bay of Biscay
La Rochelle
Bourges
Clermont- Vichy
Ferrand Lyon
45°N
Limoges
Dordogne
St.-Étienne *Rhône* • Grenoble
ITALY
Bordeaux FRANCE
Garonne
Avignon
Bayonne
Nîmes Nice
— MONACO
Lourdes
Montpellier
Cannes
Toulouse
Carcassonne
Narbonne Tóulon Calvi
Perpignan Marseille
Ajaccio Bastia
SPAIN
ANDORRA
Mediterranean Sea

0   100   200 miles
0 100 200 kilometers
3°E   6°E

⊛ National capital
• Other city

GEOGRAPHY SKILLBUILDER:
Interpreting a Map

1. Location • Name three countries that border France.
2. Location • Which bodies of water does France have access to?

On December 21, 1958, Charles de Gaulle was elected president of France. He reorganized the French constitution and instituted the Fifth Republic of France.

The Government of the Fifth Republic France is a parliamentary republic. Governmental power is split between the president and parliament. The president is elected by the public to a seven-year term; beginning in 2002, the president will serve a five-year term. The president's primary responsibilities are to act as guardian of the constitution and to ensure proper functioning of other authorities.

Parliament has two parts: the Senate and the National Assembly. The president chooses a prime minister, who heads parliament and is largely responsible for the internal workings of the government. The French government is very active in the country's economy.

A Centralized Economy

World War II left France poor and in need of rebuilding. The National Planning Board, established by **Jean Monnet** (moh•NAY) in 1946, launched a series of five-year plans to modernize France and set economic goals for the country.

Reading
Social Studies

A. Comparing
Compare the term and role of the president of France with the president of the United States.

Connections to History

Lascaux Cave Paintings On September 12, 1940, while hiking in the hills of Lascaux (lah•SKOH) near the town of Montignac in southern France, four teenage boys discovered ancient cave paintings. They found the caves after their dog fell in a hole in the ground.

Henri Breuil (broy), one of the first archaeologists on the scene, counted more than 600 images of horses (shown here), deer, and bison. The cave paintings are about 17,000 years old, making them some of the oldest works of art yet discovered.

The result of these plans was a mixed economy, with both public and private sectors. The French government nationalized, or took over, major banks; insurance companies; the electric, coal, and steel industries; schools; universities; hospitals; railroads; airlines; and even an automobile company.

This nationalization of industry is a form of socialism. **Socialism** is an economic system in which some businesses and industries are controlled by the government. The government also provides many health and welfare benefits, such as health care, housing, and unemployment insurance. However, today the French government is slowly placing more of the economy under the control of private companies.

Energy The French economy grew rapidly after 1946, and the country's industry was powered mainly by coal, oil, and gas. When worldwide oil prices rose in the 1970s, the French economy suffered. In the 1980s, France turned to nuclear power so that its economy would be less dependent on oil. Today France draws 75 percent of its power from nuclear energy, a higher percentage than any other nation in the world.

Most famous for its wines, France also exports grains, automobiles, electrical machinery, and chemicals. Although only about 7 percent of the labor force works on farms, France exports more agricultural products than any other nation in the European Community.

The **European Community** is an association developed after World War II to promote economic unity among the countries of Western Europe. Its success gave rise to greater unity, both politically and economically, in the European Union.

Reading
Social Studies

B. Analyzing Motives Why does France produce a large amount of nuclear energy?

BACKGROUND

Tourism is a major industry in France. The country hosts more than 70 million visitors annually, making it the most visited country in the world.

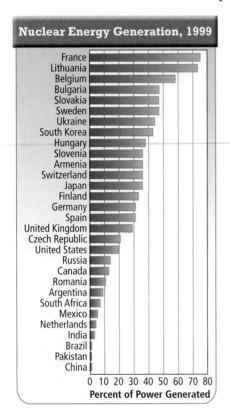

Nuclear Energy Generation, 1999

Country	
France	
Lithuania	
Belgium	
Bulgaria	
Slovakia	
Sweden	
Ukraine	
South Korea	
Hungary	
Slovenia	
Armenia	
Switzerland	
Japan	
Finland	
Germany	
Spain	
United Kingdom	
Czech Republic	
United States	
Russia	
Canada	
Romania	
Argentina	
South Africa	
Mexico	
Netherlands	
India	
Brazil	
Pakistan	
China	

0 10 20 30 40 50 60 70 80
Percent of Power Generated

Region • Nuclear power plants are a common sight in the French countryside. ▼

The Culture of Paris

Paris, the capital city of France, is famous for its contributions to world culture, most especially in the arts. Nicknamed "City of Light," Paris has long been an intellectual and artistic center.

Edouard Manet (muh·NAY) (1832–1883) helped influence one of the most important art movements of modern times, impressionism. **Impressionism** is an art style that uses light to create an impression of a scene rather than a strictly realistic picture. Manet inspired such artists as Claude Monet (moh·NAY), Pierre Renoir (ruhn·WAHR), and Paul Cézanne (say·ZAHN). This group of artists worked together in Paris and shared their thoughts and opinions of art.

Region • Monet and his family often modeled for Manet, as in this 1874 painting, *Monet Working on His Boat in Argenteuil.* ▲

Paris's Musée d'Orsay and the Louvre (loove) house two of the greatest collections of fine art in the world. The School of Fine Arts leads a tradition of education and art instruction that has produced artists such as Pierre Bonnard (baw·NAHR) (1867–1947) and Balthus (1908–2001).

Literature France has a rich tradition of literature as well. Marcel Proust, who wrote *Remembrance of Things Past,* was an influential writer in the early 20th century. Other significant writers include Albert Camus (kah·MOO), who wrote *The Stranger,* and Simone de Beauvoir (boh·VWAHR), author of *The Mandarins.*

SECTION 3 ASSESSMENT

Terms & Names

1. Identify: (a) Charles de Gaulle (b) French Resistance (c) Jean Monnet
             (d) socialism (e) European Community (f) impressionism

Taking Notes

2. Use a chart like this one to list the major aspects of French government, economy, and culture.

	Major Aspects
Government	
Economy	
Culture	

Main Ideas

3. (a) What role does the French government play in the country's economy?

   (b) What is France's primary source of power?

   (c) Name three contributions of French culture to the world.

Critical Thinking

4. **Clarifying**

   How was the liberation of Paris a symbolic victory?

   Think About

   ◆ the actions of the French Resistance

   ◆ the cultural life of Paris

ACTIVITY -OPTION- Reread the text on Manet. Draw an impressionist **portrait** of a classmate, friend, or family member.

Germany

TERMS & NAMES
Berlin Wall
reunification
Ludwig van Beethoven
Rainer Maria Rilke

MAIN IDEA

Germany has overcome many obstacles to become both a unified and a modern nation.

WHY IT MATTERS NOW

Germany has helped to shape recent European history and contemporary Western culture.

DATELINE

BERLIN, GERMANY, OCTOBER 3, 1990— It is just past midnight. Church bells are ringing, fireworks are exploding, bands are playing, and the streets are filled with celebrating Germans. At midnight, the treaty to reunite East and West Germany became official. Germany is whole once more!

Just a year ago, the Berlin Wall—a 103-mile-long barrier of concrete and barbed wire—still separated East and West Berlin. Constructed in 1961, the Wall kept East Germans from escaping from their Communist government to democratic West Germany. Then, in 1989, as the Communist government weakened, the Wall came down.

Location • Germans celebrate unification in front of the Reichstag, the seat of the federal government. ▲

Location • The largest remaining sections of the Berlin Wall, which stand up to 15 feet high, are covered with paintings and signatures. ▲

A Divided Germany

Today, the reunified nation of Germany is one of the largest countries in Europe. When World War II ended in 1945, however, Germany was divided. United States, French, and British soldiers occupied the new West German nation, and Soviet soldiers occupied the new East Germany.

West Germany The United States helped West Germany set up a democratic government. In part, the United States supported the new nation because it was located between the Communist countries of Eastern Europe and the rest of Western Europe.

With the help of U.S. loans, West Germany experienced a so-called economic miracle. In 20 years, it rebuilt its factories and became one of the world's richest nations. Its economy later became the driving force behind the European Union.

East Germany In contrast to West Germany, East Germany remained poor. Most East Germans saw West Germany, and Western Europe in general, as a place where people had better lives. East Germany's Communist government, however, discouraged contact between east and west.

By 1989, the Soviet Union's control of Eastern Europe was weakening. Hungary, a Soviet ally, relaxed control over its borders with Western Europe. East Germans began crossing the Hungarian border into Austria and eventually made their way into West Germany. After the **Berlin Wall** came down in 1989, more East Germans fled to West Germany.

BACKGROUND

Although Berlin was inside East Germany, it had a large free zone defended by the Allies. The Berlin Wall separated the two parts of the city: East Berlin and West Berlin.

Germany Today

GEOGRAPHY SKILLBUILDER: Interpreting a Map

1. **Location** • Which country is nearest to Germany's national capital?
2. **Place** • Which was larger, East or West Germany?

Region • The new Volkswagen Beetle is typical of German car design, known for its simplicity and style. The first Volkswagen was designed by Ferdinand Porsche (POOR•sheh) in 1934. ▲

Reunified Germany

Since the 1990 **reunification,** or the reuniting of East and West Germany, the German government has spent billions of dollars rebuilding the eastern part of the country. The effort has included roads, factories, housing, and hospitals. The city of Berlin, once again the nation's capital, was also rebuilt. The newly reunified nation also restored the Reichstag (RYK•shtahg), where the Federal Assembly meets.

However, reunification has also caused tensions between "Ossies" (OSS•eez) and "Wessies" (VEHSS•eez). Many Ossies complain about the lack of jobs and the cost of housing. Many Wessies complain about paying taxes to rebuild the nation and to help support the former East Germans.

Reading
Social Studies

Clarifying Why did East Germany need to be rebuilt and not West Germany?

Vocabulary

Ossies: former East Germans

Wessies: former West Germans

German Culture

Germany's rich cultural traditions may help to unite its people, who are especially proud of their music and literature. Germans are also famous for designing high-quality products, such as cars, electronic appliances, and other complex machinery.

Music Three of Germany's best-known composers are Johann Sebastian Bach (bahck) (1685–1750), George Frederick Handel (HAHN•duhl) (1685–1759), and **Ludwig van Beethoven** (LOOD•vig vahn BAY•TOH•vuhn) (1770–1827). Their music is still performed and recorded all over the world. German composer Richard Wagner (VAHG•nuhr) (1813–1883) wrote many operas, including a series based on German myths and legends known as the Ring Cycle.

Beethoven Perhaps the best-loved German composer is Ludwig van Beethoven. Beethoven began to lose his hearing when he was in his 20s. By the time he was 50, he was almost deaf.

Beethoven refused to let his deafness stop him from creating music, however. "I will grapple with Fate, it shall not overcome me," he wrote. In 1824, he finished his Ninth Symphony, which ends with a section containing the well-known "Ode to Joy." An orchestra played this same symphony at an open-air concert during the destruction of the Berlin Wall.

Literature One of the greatest writers in the German language was **Rainer Maria Rilke** (RIHL·kuh) (1875–1926). His poems, which are still admired and studied today, were a way for Rilke to communicate his feelings and experiences.

Other important 20th-century German authors include Günter Grass (grahs) (b. 1927) and Thomas Mann (man) (1875–1955). Grass has written about the horrors of World War II, the setting for his novel *The Tin Drum.* Both writers were awarded the Nobel Prize in Literature—Mann in 1929 and Grass in 1999.

BACKGROUND

More than 100 million people around the world speak German.

Place •
Half-timber architecture, shown here, is common throughout Germany. ▲

SECTION 4 ASSESSMENT

Terms & Names

1. **Identify:**
   (a) Berlin Wall
   (b) reunification
   (c) Ludwig van Beethoven
   (d) Rainer Maria Rilke

Taking Notes

2. Use a chart like this one to compare aspects of Germany before and after reunification.

Before Reunification	After Reunification

Main Ideas

3. (a) Describe the economic miracle that occurred in West Germany.

   (b) Why has there been tension between the Ossies and the Wessies?

   (c) On what projects has Germany spent billions of dollars since 1990?

Critical Thinking

4. **Synthesizing**

   What makes Germany an important European country?

   Think About

   ◆ its location
   ◆ its size
   ◆ its role in modern history

ACTIVITY -OPTION- Reread the "Dateline" feature at the beginning of the section. Write a **short story** describing what it might have been like to celebrate the reunification of Germany in 1990.

Making an Outline

▶▶ Defining the Skill

Before writing a research report, you must decide on your topic and then gather information about it. When you have all of the information you need, then you begin to organize it. One way of organizing your information before writing the report is to make an outline. An outline lists the main ideas in the order in which they will appear in the report. It also organizes the main ideas and supporting details according to their importance. The form of every outline is the same. Main ideas are listed on the left and labeled with capital Roman numerals. Supporting ideas are indented and labeled with capital letters. Supporting details are indented farther and labeled with numerals.

▶▶ Applying the Skill

The outline to the right is for a biography of Marie Curie, one of the great physicists of all time. Use the strategies listed below to help you learn how to make an outline.

How to Make an Outline

Strategy ❶ Read the main ideas of this report. They are labeled with capital Roman numerals. Each main idea will need at least one paragraph.

Strategy ❷ Read the supporting ideas for each main idea. These are labeled with capital letters. Notice that some of the main ideas require more supporting ideas than others.

Strategy ❸ Read the supporting details that are included in this outline. These are labeled with numerals. The writer of this outline did not include the supporting details for some of the supporting ideas. It is not necessary to include every piece of information that you have. An outline is intended merely as a guide for you to follow as you write the report.

Strategy ❹ A report can be organized in different ways. This biography is organized chronologically, that is, according to time. It starts with Curie's birth and ends with her legacy after death. The outline follows the order of events in her life. A report can be organized in other ways, such as comparing and contrasting or according to advantages and disadvantages. The outline should clearly reflect the way the report is organized.

❶ I. Who Was She?
    A. Polish-born physicist
❷   B. Birth and early life
    C. Schooling
        1. In secret in Poland (women were not allowed to enter
❸   higher education)
        2. In France at the Sorbonne
❹   a. license of physical sciences, 1893
          b. license of mathematical sciences, 1894
II. The Physicist
    A. Life and work with husband, Pierre Curie
        1. Discoveries
          a. polonium, summer 1898
          b. radium, fall 1898
        2. Nobel Prize in Physics, 1903
          a. shared with Henri Becquerel
          b. Marie was the first woman to ever be awarded
           a Nobel Prize
    B. Her own accomplishments
        1. Became the first female professor at the Sorbonne
          a. took over Pierre's position after his death, 1906
        2. Her research on radioactivity was published, 1910
        3. Nobel Prize in Chemistry, 1911

▶▶ Practicing the Skill

Look through Chapter 14 and find a topic that interests you. Gather information about that topic, and then write an outline for a report about that topic. Be sure to use the correct outline form.

Poland

TERMS & NAMES
Solidarity
Lech Walesa
Czeslaw Milosz
censorship
dissident

MAIN IDEA

Poland has gone through the difficulties of establishing a new democratic government and a new economic system.

WHY IT MATTERS NOW

Poland is an excellent example of the success that has been achieved by the newly independent Eastern European nations.

DATELINE

EXTRA

GDAŃSK, POLAND, 1980

In response to recent increases in food prices, many strikes have broken out across Poland. Today's strikes are much larger than the strikes that occurred in 1976. The shipyards in Gdańsk have 17,000 striking workers. One of the strikers' demands is the right to form labor unions. The recent strikes are yet another sign of the country's weakening economy, which has continued to decline over the past decade. Poland's attempts to improve its economic health by borrowing money from other nations have not helped, as the government is unable to repay those loans.

Place • Polish workers protest poor conditions under the Communist government. ▲

Political and Economic Struggles

The strikes and riots of the 1970s and 1980s were not the first actions Polish citizens took against their government. In 1956, Polish workers had rioted to protest their low wages.

In fact, there have been political and economic struggles in Poland since World War II ended in 1945. At that time, Communists took over the government and set strict wage and price controls.

Poland Today

GEOGRAPHY SKILLBUILDER:
Interpreting a Map

1. **Location** • Name a port city in Poland.
2. **Location** • How many different countries border Poland?

Solidarity In 1980, labor unions throughout Poland joined an organization called **Solidarity**. This trade union was led by **Lech Walesa** (LEK wah·LEHN·suh), an electrical worker from the shipyards of Gdańsk (guh·DAHNSK).

In the beginning, Solidarity's goals were to increase pay and improve working conditions. Before long, however, the organization set its sights on bigger goals. In late 1981, members of Solidarity were calling for free elections and an end to Communist rule. Even though Solidarity had about 10 million members, the government fought back. It suspended the organization, cracked down on protesters, and arrested thousands of members, including Walesa.

BACKGROUND

Poland's capital and largest city is Warsaw. The nation's citizens are called Poles.

Region • In 1980, Solidarity leader Lech Walesa gained the support of labor unions. Ten years later, he became Poland's president. ◀

Region • **Poland's senate helps ensure that all the country's citizens have representation.** ◀

A Free Poland

In the late 1980s, economic conditions continued to worsen in Poland. The government asked Solidarity leaders to help them solve the country's economic difficulties. Finally, the Communists agreed to Solidarity's demand for free elections.

When the elections were held in 1989, many Solidarity candidates were elected, and the Communists lost power. In 1990, Lech Walesa became the president of a free Poland.

A New Constitution Today, Poland is a parliamentary republic. The country approved a new constitution in 1997. This constitution guarantees civil rights such as free speech. It also helps to balance the powers held by the president, the prime minister, and parliament.

Parliament Poland's parliament is made up of two houses. The upper house, or senate, has 100 members. The lower house, which has 460 members, chooses the prime minister. Usually, as in the United Kingdom, the prime minister is a member of the largest party or alliance of parties within parliament.

A number of seats in parliament are reserved for representatives of the small German and Ukrainian ethnic groups in Poland. In this way, all Polish citizens are ensured a voice in their government.

A Changing Economy

Besides a new government, the Poles have also had to deal with a changing economy. In 1990, Poland's new democratic government quickly switched from a command economy to a free market economy. Prices were no longer controlled by the government, and trade suddenly faced international competition.

Reading
Social Studies

A. Recognizing Important Details What led to free elections in Poland?

BACKGROUND

The Polish president, who is elected every five years, is the head of state.

Inflation Although Polish shops were able to sell goods that had not been available before, prices rose quickly—by almost 80 percent. With this inflation, or a continual rise in prices, people's wages could not keep up with the cost of goods.

Many Polish companies, which could not compete with high-quality foreign goods, went out of business. This, in turn, resulted in high unemployment. As more and more people lost their jobs, Poland's overall standard of living fell.

An Improving Economy In time, new Polish businesses found success, giving more people work. Inflation started to drop. By 1999, inflation was down to around 7 percent. By 2000, Poland no longer needed the economic aid it had been receiving from the United States.

One way to measure the strength of a country's economy is to look at consumer spending. Between 1995 and 2000, Poles bought new cars at a high rate of half a million each year. Today, Poland has 2 million small and medium-sized businesses. The success of these small businesses is another sign of Poland's healthy economy.

Region • With Poland's economy on the rise, unemployment has decreased. ▲

Poland's Culture

The history of Poland has been one of ups and downs. In the 1500s and 1600s, Poland was a large and powerful kingdom. By 1795, Russia, Prussia, and Austria had taken control of its land, and Poland ceased to exist as an independent country. Poland did not become a republic until 1918, after World War I. Throughout the centuries, however, Poland has had a rich culture.

Literature Polish literature is full of accounts of struggles for national independence and stories about glorious kingdoms won and lost by heroic patriots.

One of Poland's best-known writers of recent times is **Czeslaw Milosz** (CHEH•slawv MEE•lawsh) (b. 1911). Milosz published his first book of poems in the 1930s. After World War II, he worked as a diplomat in the United States and then France.

BACKGROUND

A famous Polish general and patriot, Thaddeus Kosciusko (KAHS•ee•UHS•koh), fought on the side of the colonists during the American Revolution.

Milosz, who became a professor at the University of California at Berkeley, won the Nobel Prize in Literature in 1980.

Reading
Social Studies

B. Analyzing Motives Why did the Communist government control the media?

Censorship Under Communist rule, the Polish media were controlled by the government. The government decided what the media could and could not say. It outlawed any information that did not support and praise the accomplishments of Communism. As a result of this **censorship,** many writers could not publish their works. Some of them became dissidents. A **dissident** is a person who openly disagrees with a government's policies.

Supporting the Arts In order to help Polish writers, the government now allows publications printed in Poland to be sold tax-free. To help Polish actors, screenwriters, and directors, movie theaters are repaid their costs for showing Polish movies. Public-sponsored television stations are supported not only by free-market advertising but also by fees the public pays to own television sets.

Place • In 1978, Poland's pride was greatly boosted when Polish-born John Paul II was elected pope. He was the first non-Italian to be elected pope in 456 years. ▲

SECTION 5 ASSESSMENT

Terms & Names

1. **Identify:**
   (a) Solidarity
   (b) Lech Walesa
   (c) Czeslaw Milosz
   (d) censorship
   (e) dissident

Taking Notes

2. Use a chart like this one to compare and contrast one aspect of Poland with the same aspect of the United Kingdom, Sweden, France, or Germany.

Poland	Other Country

Main Ideas

3. (a) How did the Polish government respond to Solidarity's goals?

   (b) What was the outcome of Poland's free election in the late 1980s?

   (c) Describe the recent changes in the economy of Poland.

Critical Thinking

4. **Summarizing**

   How would you describe what life was like in Poland before the changes of 1990?

   Think About
   ◆ strikes and riots
   ◆ the Communist government
   ◆ censorship

ACTIVITY -OPTION- Reread the information about Solidarity. Write a short **speech** that might have been given to gain support for the organization in the 1980s.

TERMS & NAMES

Explain the significance of each of the following:

1. London
2. Good Friday Accord
3. armed neutrality
4. hydroelectricity
5. Charles de Gaulle
6. socialism
7. Berlin Wall
8. reunification
9. censorship
10. dissident

REVIEW QUESTIONS

The United Kingdom *(pages 379–383)*

1. What are the two houses that form the British Parliament? Which is more powerful?
2. Why is it necessary for the United Kingdom to import foods and other goods?

Sweden *(pages 384–387)*

3. What role do ombudsmen play in the Swedish government?
4. Why is Sweden an excellent place for skiing?

France *(pages 390–393)*

5. What is France's main source of energy?
6. Identify at least three Impressionist painters.

Germany *(pages 394–397)*

7. What role did the United States government play in West Germany after World War II?
8. Identify at least three famous German composers.

Poland *(pages 399–403)*

9. Why is Lech Walesa important to modern Poland?
10. Describe the new constitution that Poland approved in 1997.

CRITICAL THINKING

Comparing

1. Using your completed chart from Reading Social Studies, p. 378, compare the governments and economies of the United Kingdom, Sweden, France, Germany, and Poland.

Hypothesizing

2. One of Sweden's severe environmental problems is acid rain. Why might it be difficult for a country to solve this problem?

Making Inferences

3. Why do you think it was important to the United States that West Germany have a democratic government?

Visual Summary

The United Kingdom *1*

- British economic, political, and cultural traditions have influenced nations around the world.

2 **Sweden**

- Sweden offers its people a high standard of living.
- Sweden is dealing with environmental issues such as nuclear power and acid rain.

France

- France has made a speedy recovery from World War II.

3

Germany *4*

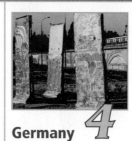

- Germany has overcome many obstacles to become a unified and modern nation.

Poland *5*

- Poland is an example of the success made possible by the recent independence of Eastern European nations.

SOCIAL STUDIES SKILLBUILDER

Jacques Cousteau (koo•STOH) (1910–1997) was the most famous undersea explorer of the 20th century. While serving in the French navy in 1943, Cousteau invented the Aqua-Lung, also known as scuba gear. *Scuba* stands for "self-contained underwater-breathing apparatus." Scuba gear allowed divers to more freely explore the depths of the oceans, which cover more than three-fifths of Earth's surface. Cousteau became a household name after he popularized underwater exploration through books, films, and a television series.

SKILLBUILDER: Making an Outline

Outline the text above.

FOCUS ON GEOGRAPHY

1. **Place** • How many airports does the map show in Germany? What cities are they located in or near?
2. **Movement** • Describe at least two possible routes that connect London and Stockholm.
3. **Place** • Which cities in Poland are located along major rail lines?

CHAPTER PROJECTS

Interdisciplinary Activity: Art

Preparing a Written Report Research the life and work of a well-known painter, sculptor, or other artist from the United Kingdom, Sweden, France, Germany, or Poland. Use your findings to write a short report. Be sure to include a description or a copy of at least one important work of art.

Cooperative Learning Activity

Researching a Festival In a group of three students, organize a classroom presentation about a festival or holiday that is celebrated in the United Kingdom, Sweden, France, Germany, or Poland. What is the importance of the festival? When is it celebrated? What kinds of activities or foods are associated with it?

- Research information about different festivals or holidays and select one that interests your group.
- Decide what form your presentation will take.
- Discuss how the festival compares with others that are familiar to you.

INTERNET ACTIVITY

Use the Internet to research a major tourist site in the United Kingdom, Sweden, France, Germany, or Poland. Focus on one location, such as Edinburgh, Stockholm, Paris, Munich, or Warsaw. What special attractions or activities does that location offer to visitors?

Presenting Your Findings Write up your findings and include illustrations of the location. Be sure to list the Web sites you used to help you prepare your report.

For Internet links to support this activity, go to

Europe Today **405**

The War on Terrorism

Reporter's Notes
By Kevin McCoy

NEW YORK—First came a deep rumble. Then a roar like a giant speeding train. But the sound came crashing from the sky, not along steel tracks. In an instant, a warm, sunny September morning at the World Trade Center in Lower Manhattan became a darkened moonscape of choking cement dust and swirling paper, wailing sirens and screaming victims.

"I heard the rumbling and I looked up, and one of the towers was coming down," said Sergeant Moises Cruz, a New York City police officer who ran for his life with other survivors of the most horrible terrorist attack in U.S. history. Lower Broadway, normally a bustling checkerboard of financial traders, government officials, businessmen and tourists, lay silenced under a three-inch carpet of gritty gray dust.

"I can't even describe it, it was so awful," said Wilbert, a 50-year-old elevator maintenance worker. "All I could do was run."

News reporters who covered the attacks knew instinctively this was the most significant story of a lifetime.

The twin towers of the World Trade Center in New York City, before (inset) and after the terrorist attacks of September 11, 2001

The Attack on America

Flight Path of the Hijacked Airliners, September 11, 2001

L. Michigan

MICHIGAN

L. Ontario

NEW YORK

NEW HAMPSHIRE

Boston

MASSACHUSETTS

ATLANTIC OCEAN

L. Erie

Cleveland

New York City

INDIANA

OHIO

PENNSYLVANIA

Pittsburgh

Shanksville

RHODE ISLAND
CONNECTICUT

NEW JERSEY

0   50   100 miles
0   50   100 kilometers
Azimuthal Equal–Area Projection

Dulles   Pentagon   DELAWARE

return path undetermined

MARYLAND

WASHINGTON, D.C.

American Flight 11
American Flight 77
United Flight 93
United Flight 175

KENTUCKY

WEST VIRGINIA

VIRGINIA

McCoy's reporter's instincts were right. Before the day was over, there would be more than 3,000 victims of the most destructive act of terrorism in modern history. **Terrorism** is the calculated use of, or threatened use of, violence against individuals or property for the purpose of intimidating or causing fear for political or social ends.

The terrorist attacks on September 11 were aimed at well-known symbols of the economic and military power of the United States. But what they mainly destroyed was something Americans value much more—the lives of thousands of individual citizens.

UNIMAGINABLE HORROR

On the morning of September 11, 2001, many New Yorkers were heading for work or school when 19 Arab terrorists hijacked four airliners from East Coast airports. The first plane crashed into the upper floors of the north tower of the World Trade Center and exploded into flames. About 20 minutes later, the second plane sliced into the south tower.

Desks, chairs, paper—and people—blew out of the windows of the twin towers. People on the streets below watched in horror as more than a dozen workers on the upper floors jumped from the blazing buildings to their deaths. Other workers poured out of the towers to escape the fire.

Less than an hour after the twin towers were hit, the third hijacked plane rammed into the west side of the Pentagon in Arlington, Virginia. It tore a 75-foot gash in the five-sided, five-story building. That crash

site, too, immediately became engulfed in flames. Meanwhile, passengers on the fourth hijacked plane had used their cell phones and had heard about the other plane crashes. Some of the passengers rushed the hijackers and prevented them from striking their intended target, thought to be either the White House or the Capitol.

Because of these heroic efforts, the plane crashed not into a crowded building but into an empty field in Pennsylvania. No one will ever know how many lives the passengers saved as they gave up their own.

Recovery efforts continue on the collapsed section of the Pentagon's southwest side two days after the attack.

The Destruction The planes were loaded with fuel. They became destructive missiles when they crashed into the World Trade Center and the Pentagon. As one investigator noted, the hijackers "couldn't carry anything—other than an atom bomb—that could be as bad as what they were flying."

The explosions and fires so weakened the damaged skyscrapers that they crumbled to the ground less than two hours after impact. The fire and raining debris caused nearby buildings to collapse as well. Nine buildings in New York City's financial district completely or partially collapsed. Six others suffered major damage. The disaster area covered 16 acres. The damage at the Pentagon, though extensive, was confined to one wing of the building.

But it was the toll in human lives that most grieved Americans and others around the world. About 3,000 people died in the attacks. All passengers on the four planes were killed, as well as workers and visitors in the World Trade Center and the Pentagon. The dead included more than 300 New York City firefighters and 40 police officers who rushed to the scene and were buried in the rubble when the skyscrapers collapsed.

Grieving Families and Companies "Please tell the children I love them," said a father of three from the World Trade Center before the phone line went dead. From the burning towers and the hijacked planes, men and women used their last moments to call and to speak with their families for the last time.

In the first hours and days after the September 11 attacks, family members and friends of people in the World Trade Center frantically tried to find their loved ones. They checked hospitals and posted pictures of the missing on lampposts and walls. The thousands of people who escaped before the towers collapsed were reunited with their families. But only a few survivors were pulled from the wreckage of the buildings. For thousands of people, loved ones never returned home. Also, several businesses with offices in the towers lost large numbers of employees.

The horror of September 11 has haunted more than just the survivors and witnesses of the attacks, although they were the hardest hit. Millions of Americans watched the events on television shortly after they occurred. They, too, would have difficulty forgetting those horrifying images.

RESCUE EFFORTS

Amidst the brutal destruction at the World Trade Center, the courage, selflessness, and noble actions of New York City's firefighters, police officers, and rescue workers stood as a testament. Many of the first

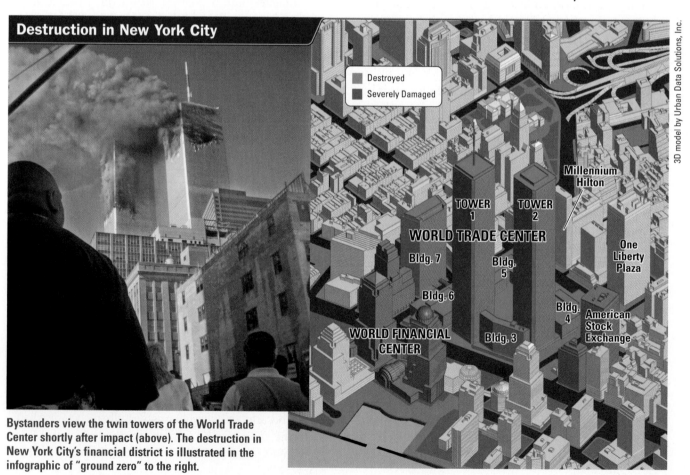

Destruction in New York City

Destroyed
Severely Damaged

Millennium Hilton
TOWER 1   TOWER 2
WORLD TRADE CENTER
Bldg. 7   Bldg. 5
One Liberty Plaza
Bldg. 6
Bldg. 4   American Stock Exchange
WORLD FINANCIAL CENTER   Bldg. 3

3D model by Urban Data Solutions, Inc.

Bystanders view the twin towers of the World Trade Center shortly after impact (above). The destruction in New York City's financial district is illustrated in the infographic of "ground zero" to the right.

How the debris is removed

Truck staging area
Fifty-four city sanitation trucks, parked at 55th and West Side Highway, are dispatched along secure routes to the site to pick up any debris considered still sensitive by the FBI. Separate, privately owned trucks are picking up debris from ConEd and the Transit Authority.

Truck capacity:
6 tons or more

Total debris moved in one day:
6,000 to 10,000 tons

Hudson River

MANHATTAN

55th Street

Broadway

30th Street

14th Street

West Street

Warren Street

Hot Zone

First Avenue

E. Houston Street

Broadway

Rector Street

East River

Makeshift morgue where medical examiners inventory and catalog human remains for identification

Sources: City of New York; Federal Emergency Management Agency; Caterpillar; Mueser Rutledge Consulting Engineers

Reporting by Debbie Howlett and Martha Moore, USA TODAY ®; graphic by Frank Pompa, Robert Ahrens, Adrienne Lewis and Dave Merrill, USA TODAY ®

① Trucks are loaded at the site and driven to marine transfer stations, where debris is loaded onto barges.

② The barges carry 600 tons of debris on each trip.

③ Trucks carrying the heaviest debris, such as steel beams, make the trip by flatbed trucks via the Battery Tunnel and across the Verrazano Narrows Bridge.

Staten Island

At the landfill site

④ Two piles are created. one that is considered debris...

⑤ ...and the other, which may yield more evidence. The workers have created a grid system on the ground; these truckloads are dumped into a checkerboard that is then sifted through in large, table-like trays with mesh-screen bottoms. FBI investigators are searching for clues, such as those that led to the cracking of the Oklahoma City bombing case when they found the Ryder truck axle with the vehicle identification number on it.

Debris
Screen
Dirt filtered out
Tray

---

firefighters at the scene disappeared into the burning buildings to help those inside and never came out again. Entire squads were lost. New York City Fire Department chaplain, Father Mychal Judge, was killed by falling debris just after giving the last rites of the Catholic Church to a firefighter at the scene.

Firefighters worked around the clock trying to find survivors in the wreckage. They had to contend with shifting rubble and smoky, ash-filled air. Medical workers from the area rushed to staff the city's trauma centers. But after the first wave of injured, there were few survivors to treat. One emergency medical technician said, "We were set up for any emergency. It was a great site, full of surgeons. But we were treating firemen and police who needed their eyes washed."

A flood of volunteers assisted rescue workers. Ironworkers helped cut through steel beams, while high school students helped provide water and food for the rescue workers. From around the country, people sent donations of blood, food, and money to New York City. The city kept functioning in the hours and days that followed the attack under the direction of its mayor, Rudy Giuliani.

The Cleanup After the first few days, the work at "ground zero," the World Trade Center disaster site, shifted to recovering bodies and removing the massive amount of debris. The twin towers alone contained more than 200,000 tons of steel, 425,000 cubic yards of concrete, and 14 acres of glass—an estimated 2 billion pounds.

SEARCH FOR TERRORISTS BEGINS
In the weeks that followed, the U.S. government organized a massive effort to identify those responsible for the attacks. Officials concluded that Osama bin Laden, a Saudi Arabian millionaire, directed the terrorists. He had been exiled from his native country because of suspected terrorist activities. Bin Laden was hiding in Afghanistan, protected there by the strict Islamic government known as the Taliban. The effort to bring him to justice would lead the United States to begin military action against Afghanistan in October, as the next section explains.

Thinking Critically

CURRENT EVENTS
CLASSZONE.COM

- Why were the specific targets of the September attacks selected by the terrorists?
- What might cause individuals to use terrorist tactics to attempt to change situations they think are a problem?

Reporter's Notes
By Tim Friend

AFGHANISTAN— I entered Afghanistan from the north on an aging ferry boat at dusk on October 22. All I could see in the encroaching darkness were silhouettes of Northern Alliance fighters with Kalishnikov weapons slung loosely on their shoulders. My passport was stamped in a small mud hut under a dim lantern, then I was off to the village of Hoja Baddahuin, where the Northern Alliance had set up headquarters after the Taliban had taken over most of the country.

The United States had entered the war in Afghanistan after the terrorist attacks on September 11, 2001. Covering the war in Afghanistan has been the single most challenging experience of my career as a reporter at USA TODAY.

The most dangerous part of the experience was traveling through the front lines as I made my way to Kabul. My jeep had to cross minefields and the most narrow mountain roads imaginable. At Taloqan, the first city to be restored to the Northern Alliance, I wrote my stories while gunfire erupted outside my walled compound. I paid two men to stay inside with their machine guns and to answer the door should someone come knocking. Taliban fighters were still hiding out in houses just down the street. Through it all, I learned to stay calm by doing the best I could to ensure both my safety and the safety of my team, and to leave the rest to a healthy dose of faith.

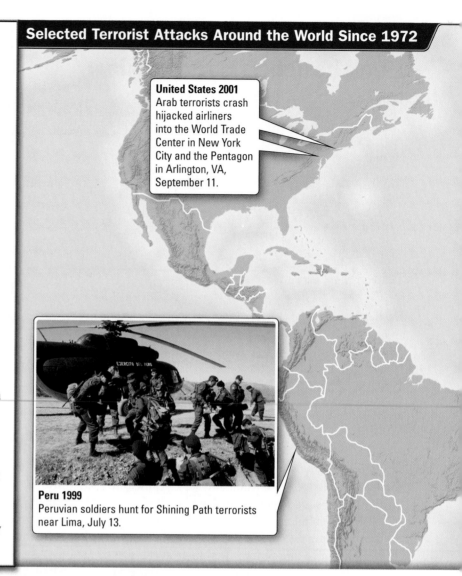

Selected Terrorist Attacks Around the World Since 1972

United States 2001
Arab terrorists crash hijacked airliners into the World Trade Center in New York City and the Pentagon in Arlington, VA, September 11.

Peru 1999
Peruvian soldiers hunt for Shining Path terrorists near Lima, July 13.

Hunting for the Terrorists

Terrorism is not new. Reporters like Tim Friend have been covering terrorist attacks across the globe for the last three decades. Throughout history, individuals, small groups, and governments have used terror tactics to try to achieve political or social goals— whether it be to bring down a government, eliminate opponents, or promote a cause.

In recent times, however, terrorism has become an international problem. Since the late 1960s, more than 14,000 terrorist attacks have occurred worldwide. International terrorist groups have carried out increasingly destructive, high-profile attacks to attract global attention. Many countries also face domestic terrorists who oppose their governments' policies or have special interests to promote.

The reasons for modern terrorism are many. The traditional motives, such as gaining independence, expelling foreigners, or changing society, still drive various terrorist groups around the world. These terrorists use violence to force concessions from their enemies, usually the governments in power. But other kinds of terrorists, driven by radical religious motives, began to emerge in the late 20th century.

The goal of these terrorists is the destruction of what they consider the forces of evil. This evil might be located in their own countries or in other parts of the world. These terrorists often threaten to use weapons of mass destruction, such as chemical, biological, or nuclear weapons, to kill their enemies.

West Germany 1972
Israeli athletes are killed after being taken hostage by Arab terrorists at the Summer Olympics in Munich, September 5.

Japan 1995
The Tokyo subway system is attacked with deadly nerve gas by the Aum Shinrikyo cult, March 20.

Northern Ireland 1979
Irish Republican Army assassinates Lord Mountbatten, a member of the British royal family, by blowing up his boat off the Irish coast, August 30.

Israel 2001
Suicide bombings by Hamas terrorists in Jerusalem and Haifa kill and wound many civilians, December.

India 2001
Kashmiri terrorists attack the Indian Parliament Building in New Delhi, with guns and grenades, December 13.

Kenya 1998
U.S. Embassy personnel in Nairobi, Kenya, evacuate area after Arab terrorists detonate truck bombs at embassy buildings there, and in Tanzania, August 7.

TERRORISM AROUND THE WORLD

The problem of international terrorism first came to world attention in a shocking way during the 1972 Summer Olympic Games in Munich, Germany (then West Germany). Eight members of a Palestinian terrorist group called Black September killed two Israeli athletes and took nine others hostage. Five of the terrorists, all the hostages, and a police officer were later killed in a bloody gun battle. The attack became known as the Munich Massacre. Since then, few regions of the world have been spared from terrorist attacks.

The Middle East Like Black September, many terrorist organizations have their roots in the Israeli-Palestinian conflict over land in the Middle East.

(*Middle East* is the political term for the geographic region of Southwest Asia.) Arab terrorist groups such as the Palestine Islamic Jihad, Hamas, and Hizballah have sought to prevent a peace settlement between Israel and the Palestinians. They want a homeland for the Palestinians on their own terms, with the most extreme among them denying Israel's right to exist. In a continual cycle of violence, the Israelis retaliate after each terrorist attack, and the terrorists attack again.

Among Muslims in the Middle East, the Israeli-Palestinian violence has bred widespread Arab anger at Israel—and at the United States for supporting Israel. For example, the Lebanese-based group Hizballah seeks to eliminate all non-Islamic influences in Muslim countries. It is thought to have been responsible for bombing the U.S. embassy and marine barracks in Beirut in 1983 and the U.S. embassy annex in Beirut in 1984.

In December 2001, terrorist attacks on Israeli civilians in Jerusalem and Haifa killed 27 people and wounded more than 200. Hamas claimed responsibility, and the Israelis responded with military strikes against Palestinian targets.

Israel then declared a "war on terrorism," patterned after the U.S. response to the September 11 attacks. Moderates in the region believe that the only long-term solution is a compromise between Israel and the Palestinians over the issue of land.

Europe Many countries in Europe—including Great Britain, Germany, and Italy—have been targets of domestic terrorists who oppose government policies. For example, for decades the Irish Republican Army engaged in terrorist attacks against Britain because it opposed British control of Northern Ireland. By 2001, however, the British and the IRA were peacefully negotiating for greater autonomy for Northern Ireland.

Both Germany and Italy have suffered terrorist attacks by extreme left-wing and right-wing domestic groups. In general, left-wing groups oppose capitalism, and right-wing groups support capitalism and oppose government regulation.

These groups sometimes join forces with other terrorist organizations when it suits their purposes. In 1975, for example, West Germany's Red Army Faction and Italy's Red Brigades cooperated with the Palestine Liberation Organization to kidnap officials at a meeting of the Organization of Petroleum Exporting Countries (OPEC) in Vienna, Austria.

South Asia and East Asia South Asia has become another hotbed of terrorism in recent years. Afghanistan became a haven for international terrorists after the extremist Muslim Taliban came to power in 1996. In that year, Osama bin Laden moved to Afghanistan and began using mountain hideouts in that country as a base of operations for his global network of Muslim terrorists known as al-Qaeda.

Muslim extremists from all over the world came to al-Qaeda training camps. Bin Laden and these other extremists were opposed to American influence in Muslim lands. Bin Laden called for terrorist attacks against Americans and U.S. allies.

Terrorist groups have arisen in East Asia, as well. Japanese terrorist groups include the Aum Shinrikyo (Supreme Truth Sect) and the Japanese Red Army. The Aum Shinrikyo (called Aleph since 2000) is a religious cult that wants to control Japan. In 1995, it released sarin, a deadly nerve gas, in subway stations in Tokyo. Twelve people were killed and more than 5,700 injured. This attack brought global attention to the threat of biological and chemical agents as terrorist weapons.

Africa Civil unrest and regional wars were the root causes of most terrorist activity in Africa at the end of the 20th century. But al-Qaeda cells operated in

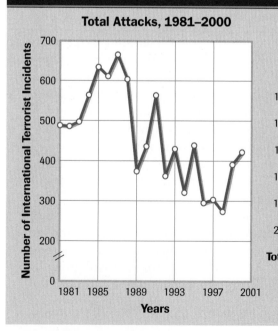

International Terrorist Attacks

Total Attacks, 1981–2000

International Casualties of Terrorism, 1995–2000

	Africa	Asia	Euroasia	Latin America	Middle East	North America	Western Europe
1995	8	5369	29	46	445	0	287
1996	80	1507	20	18	1097	0	503
1997	28	344	27	11	480	7	17
1998	5379	635	12	195	68	0	405
1999	185	690	8	9	31	0	16
2000	102	898	103	20	69	0	4
Totals	5782	9713	199	299	2190	7	1232

Source: U.S. Department of State

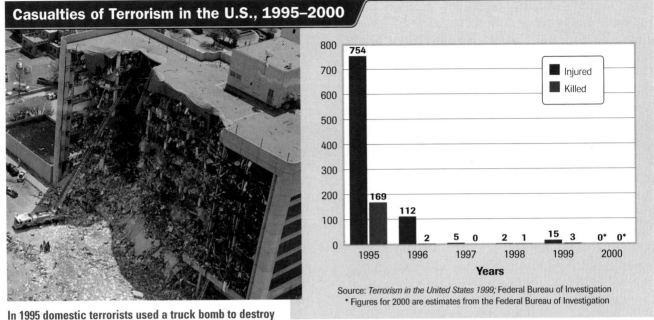

Casualties of Terrorism in the U.S., 1995–2000

Years	Injured	Killed
1995	754	169
1996	112	2
1997	5	0
1998	2	1
1999	15	3
2000	0*	0*

Source: *Terrorism in the United States 1999;* Federal Bureau of Investigation
* Figures for 2000 are estimates from the Federal Bureau of Investigation

In 1995 domestic terrorists used a truck bomb to destroy the Murrah Federal Building in Oklahoma City, Oklahoma.

many African countries, and several major attacks against U.S. personnel and facilities in Africa were linked to al-Qaeda.

For example, a 1993 attack on U.S. soldiers in Somalia killed 18. In 1998, bombings at the U.S. embassies in Kenya and Tanzania left 301 dead and more than 5,000 people injured. The United States responded to these attacks with missile strikes on suspected terrorist facilities in Afghanistan, and in Sudan where bin Laden was based from 1991 to 1996.

Latin America In 2000, more terrorist attacks occurred in Latin America than in any other region of the world. Terrorist activity was particularly heavy in Colombia, a country where powerful narcotics organizations have frequently turned to violence. The Revolutionary Armed Forces of Colombia (FARC) is a left-wing guerrilla group responsible for numerous bombings, hijackings, and kidnappings of Colombians and foreign citizens. It has attacked Colombian political, military, and economic targets, as well as those with American ties. FARC is linked to narcotics traffickers.

The region where the borders of Argentina, Brazil, and Paraguay meet has become a center of Islamic extremism and terrorist financing. The Israeli embassy in Buenos Aires, Argentina, was bombed in 1992, and another Israeli target was hit in 1994.

The United States Before September 11, the most destructive act of terrorism on American soil had been the 1995 truck bombing of the Murrah Federal Building in Oklahoma City, Oklahoma. That attack killed 168 people, but it was an act of domestic terrorism. It was carried out by an antigovernment extremist named Timothy McVeigh. Such domestic terrorists are motivated by the belief that the government has too much power to regulate people's lives.

The longest-lasting terrorist campaign by an individual in U.S. history was conducted by Theodore Kaczynski, who was known as the Unabomber. From 1978 to 1995, Kaczynski mailed bombs to business executives and scientists because he opposed the effects of modern technology on society. He killed 3 people and injured 23 others.

The attack on the World Trade Center on September 11 was not the first to have occurred there. A previous attack took place in 1993, when a van filled with explosives was detonated in the center's parking garage. Six people died and more than 1,000 were injured. The person responsible, Ramzi Yousef, was captured and imprisoned, but Osama bin Laden was suspected of being part of the plot. Another bin Laden-linked attack was the bombing of the destroyer USS *Cole* in Yemen in October 2000.

FINDING THOSE RESPONSIBLE
Immediately after the September 11 attacks, the Bush administration launched the largest criminal investigation in U.S. history. The FBI searched across the country—and the world—for clues to the identities of the suicide hijackers and those who aided them.

In an address to Congress and the nation, President George W. Bush pledged, "Whether we bring our enemies to justice or bring justice to our enemies, justice will be done." He called the terrorist attacks "acts of war" and declared that the United States would wage a war to end global terrorism. He vowed that as a part of that war, "We will pursue nations that provide aid or safe haven to terrorism. Every nation in every region now has a decision to make. Either you are with us, or you are with the terrorists."

Seven nations were on a U.S. government list of state sponsors of terrorism in 2001—Iran, Iraq, Syria, Libya, Cuba, North Korea, and Sudan. In addition, Afghanistan, Pakistan, Lebanon, and Yemen were considered major centers of terrorist activity. After the September 11 attacks, however, some of these countries, including Pakistan and Sudan, began to cooperate with the United States in hunting down those responsible.

The investigation into the September 11 attacks soon showed that top leaders in the al-Qaeda network were responsible for planning the attacks. The U.S. government then undertook a worldwide hunt for terrorists linked to al-Qaeda.

The United States built an international coalition, or alliance, to fight the war on terrorism. Canada, China, Great Britain, Pakistan, Russia, and many other nations joined the coalition. They agreed to share intelligence information, to arrest terrorists operating within their borders, and to seize the financial assets of terrorist groups. The coalition also gave support to U.S. military action in Afghanistan.

Great Britain took an especially active role in the coalition. One Londoner left a card at the U.S. embassy that reflected the surge of support that the United States received immediately after the devastating attacks: "Dear America, You supported us in two world wars. We stand with you now."

The War in Afghanistan

The U.S. government first focused its military response on Afghanistan, because that country was the home base of Osama bin Laden's al-Qaeda network. The strict Islamic regime that controlled most of Afghanistan—the Taliban—had harbored bin Laden and al-Qaeda since 1996. In return, bin Laden helped keep the Taliban in power by providing fighters in their civil war against the Northern Alliance, a coalition of anti-Taliban Afghan groups.

The United States demanded that the Taliban turn over bin Laden. After they refused, the United States began military action. The U.S. goals were to find bin Laden, to destroy al-Qaeda, and to end Taliban rule.

USA TODAY first appeared in print 10/16/2001

The corporate structure of Terror Inc.

Osama bin Laden's terrorist organization, al-Qaeda, is organized like a business. Here is a flow chart of its structure, as of the terrorist attacks on September 11, 2001:

Emir
Osama bin Laden

A key member of the military committee is Muhammad Atef, also known as Abu Hafs el Masry. The second-ranking person in al-Qaeda, he was indicted in the U.S. embassy bombings in Kenya and Tanzania in 1998. Atef was killed during the bombing of Afghanistan.

Shura council
A policymaking council of about 30 top aides, business associates and religious scholars.

Ayman al-Zawahri

A key member of the shura council is Ayman al-Zawahri, bin Laden's top aide. The Egyptian-born surgeon, sentenced to death for terrorism in his native country, reportedly slipped into the United States in 1995 as Abdel Moez for a fundraising tour. He supplied $250,000 in 1991 for the purchase of a farm for al-Qaeda in Sudan.

Military committee   **Atef**
Responsible for training, weapons acquisition and planning attacks.

Money/business committee
Runs al-Qaeda business operations. Key members include Abu Fadhl al Makkee and Abu Hammam al Saudi.

Media committee
Ran now-defunct al-Qaeda newspaper, *Newscast*, and did public relations.

Islamic study/ fatwah committee
Issues *fatwahs*, or religious edicts, such as an edict in 1998 telling Muslims to kill Americans.

Travel office
Provides plane tickets and fake passports.

Payroll office
Pays al-Qaeda members.

Management office
Oversees money-making businesses (banks, farms).

Abu Fadhl and Abu Hammam managed the business operations and deployed assets and al-Qaeda members. Abu Fadhl was identified in court papers as "the man who bought bin Laden a salt farm in Sudan." Abu Hammam did advance work on the move to Sudan.

Source: Reported by Dennis Cauchon, USA TODAY®   By Dave Merrill, USA TODAY®

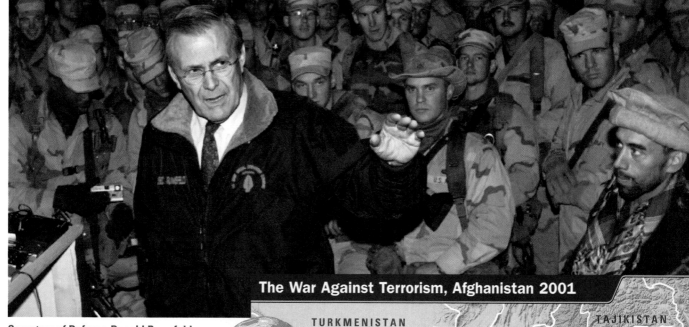

Secretary of Defense Donald Rumsfeld addresses U.S. troops in Afghanistan.

The War Against Terrorism, Afghanistan 2001

(Map of Afghanistan showing locations including TURKMENISTAN, TAJIKISTAN, Mazar-e Sharif, KONDOZ, TAKHAR, Feyzabad, JOWZJAN, BALKH, Konduz, BADAKHSHAN, Meymaneh, SAR-E-POL, Baghlan, Taloqan, BAGHLAN, LAGHMAN, FARYAB, SAMANGAN, KAPISA, KONAR, BADGHIS, PARVAN, KABUL, Herat, Bamian, BAMIAN, VARDAK, Kabul, Jalalabad, INDIA, HERAT, GHOWR, LOWGAR, NANGARHAR, Islamabad, Shindand, AFGHANISTAN, PAKTIA, Farah, FARAH, ORUZGAN, GHAZNI, Khowst, ZABOL, PAKTIKA, Qandahar, HELMAND, PAKISTAN, IRAN, NIMRUZ, QANDAHAR)

Legend:
- Estimated area of Northern Alliance control
- ■ Suspected training camps/militia bases
- ◆ Taliban army bases
- ✈ Military and/or civilian airfields
- Province boundaries

0   100   200 miles
0   100   200 kilometers
Conformal Conic Projection

In October 2001, the United States began bombing Taliban air defenses, airfields, and command centers, as well as al-Qaeda training camps. On the ground, the United States relied on anti-Taliban groups—first, the Northern Alliance and later, the Eastern Alliance—to do most of the fighting against the Taliban. These Afghan groups were assisted by U.S. air strikes against Taliban military positions and by a small number of U.S. special-forces troops and marines.

In December, the Taliban were driven from power, but the fight to destroy al-Qaeda continued. Meanwhile, the United Nations worked with the Northern Alliance and other Afghan groups to establish an interim government to replace the Taliban.

A number of nations in the antiterrorism coalition actively assisted the United States in Afghanistan, including Pakistan. The Pakistanis shared intelligence information and allowed the United States to stage military operations from their country.

Pakistan, a Muslim country, took a political risk by giving support to the United States. The Pakistani government's actions were opposed by groups within Pakistan who believed the antiterrorism campaign to be anti-Islamic.

The United States tried to make it clear to Muslim nations that the antiterrorism campaign was *not* anti-Islamic and that Americans respected the religion of Islam. For the United States, maintaining the support of moderate Muslim leaders was important to the long-term success of the war against terrorism—a war that in its next phase would target other nations that supported international terrorism.

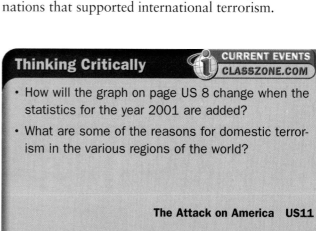

Thinking Critically

CURRENT EVENTS
CLASSZONE.COM

- How will the graph on page US 8 change when the statistics for the year 2001 are added?

- What are some of the reasons for domestic terrorism in the various regions of the world?

WASHINGTON, D.C.—A month after the September 11 terrorist hijackings, the pilot of US Airways Flight 62 stepped from the cockpit just before takeoff, an ax in his hand. "These are extraordinary times," he told passengers over the jet's public address system. The cabin quieted. Then he rattled off three scenarios in the event of a terrorist attack aboard the San Francisco-to-Charlotte flight.

"One, someone stands up and says 'bomb,' " the pilot said. "If they tell you that, it's a lie." Second, someone pretends to be an air marshal. "We don't have an armed marshal on this flight," he said, still holding the ax. Third, someone might threaten to release some sort of biological agent. Don't be afraid, he told passengers. Pilots would land the plane before any lasting harm could be done.

In any case, the pilot advised, passengers should not back down. "Throw your shoes at them. A couple of you get up and tackle him. Beat him. I don't care." As for the ax he was holding, standard on jets in case of emergency? It's kept in the cockpit, he said. "It's very sharp. I can shave with it. For anyone to try to break into this cockpit would be a very bad idea." Then the pilot paused. "Having said all this, I'd like you all to sit back, relax, and enjoy the trip." Some passengers chuckled. Almost everyone clapped.

The stunning announcement illustrates just how much flying changed in the wake of the September 11 terrorist attacks—and how quickly Americans have grown to accept the new reality.

The Impact on American Life

first appeared in print 9/18/2001

Airport security tightens up

As the nation's 400 airports get back to business, passengers around the country are finding tighter security. Since the Sept. 11 hijacking of four U.S. airliners, the procedures from ticket counter to gate are stiffer. Airlines are recommending that passengers arrive between two and four hours early for flights. Security measures and wait times varied widely, according to USA TODAY® reporters.

Security
Passengers, and their families and friends, could all go to the gate. Keys, cell phones and change could be dropped into plastic dishes or cups to one side of the metal detectors. Hand-held sensors were used if metal still detected, or sometimes a manual pat-down.

Check in
Photo ID required. Ticket agent asks "Have your bags been in your possession since you packed them?"

Curb-side luggage check-in permitted

No curb-side luggage check permitted.

Before the Sept. 11 attack

After the attack

Carry-on
Bags are placed on a conveyor belt and contents displayed on a screen. Security employees are trained to spot suspicious objects.

Increased use of bomb-sniffing dogs. Dogs and police officers were highly visible at Newark International.

Security
Only passengers beyond this point. Cell phones, keys, pagers and other loose objects have to be put on the conveyor belts, where they are screened, according to passengers at San Francisco and Chicago airports Monday. Knives and cutting tools prohibited. Overhead metal detectors are being used in addition to hand-held units. In Baltimore, some bags were checked for bomb dust.

Before security checkpoint
Passengers asked to show tickets and photo IDs again.

Check in
Baggage checked randomly. Photo ID required. In some cases, passengers had to exchange e-tickets for paper tickets. Passengers still asked if they have had their bags in their possession since packing.

Sources: FAA; reporting by Jack Gruber, Debbie Howlett, Martin Kasindorf, USA TODAY®; and Reed Stacey

By Frank Pompa, USA TODAY®

After the September 11 attacks, many Americans reported feeling that everything had changed—that life would never be the same. Before, Americans had viewed war as something that happened in other countries. Now they felt vulnerable, and the threat of terrorism began to affect many aspects of American life—as the experience of those on Flight 62 showed.

THE AIRLINES AND THE ECONOMY

In the wake of the terrorist attacks, the Federal Aviation Administration (FAA) shut down all airports in the United States for the first time in the nation's history. They did so to prevent any other hijackings. When the airports reopened and flights resumed a few days later, the airlines had few passengers. Some people did not feel safe flying, and others did not want to face the delays caused by tighter airport security.

The number of passengers dropped 43 percent in the days after flights resumed. The airline industry lost an estimated $5 billion in September and cut more than 100,000 jobs to reduce their costs. Congress quickly passed a $15-billion-aid package to help the industry get through the crisis. After September, airline business partially recovered. But even months later, the passenger airfleet was still flying well below capacity.

Industries related to the airlines also suffered. Travel agents, hotels, resorts, and theme parks all lost business. Also hard hit was the insurance industry, which would have to pay billions in death and property loss claims due to the attacks.

The New York Stock Exchange and other stock markets closed after the attacks and did not reopen until the following Monday. The last time the New York exchange had shut down for more than three days was in 1914, at the start of World War I. After the stock markets reopened, the Dow Jones Industrial Average suffered its biggest weekly drop since the Great Depression—14.3 percent.

Over the next few weeks, the markets began to rebound, but the economy continued to decline. Consumers spent less, and unemployment rose. Experts believed that the attacks had only worsened an economic slowdown that had begun early in 2001. They agreed that the nation was in a recession.

THE ANTHRAX THREAT

Not long after September 11th, terrorism struck America again, but in a different form. Letters containing spores of a bacterium that causes the disease anthrax were sent to persons in the news media and to members of Congress in Washington, D.C.

Anthrax bacteria can cause illness when they come in contact with skin or when inhaled. The skin form of anthrax is usually not fatal. But if anthrax bacteria are inhaled, the poisons they produce can damage body tissues. If not treated quickly, inhalation anthrax can cause death.

The threat of biological warfare became real when letters containing the anthrax bacterium (right) were sent to some members of the U.S. Congress in Washington D.C. (below) and persons in the news media after the September 11 attacks.

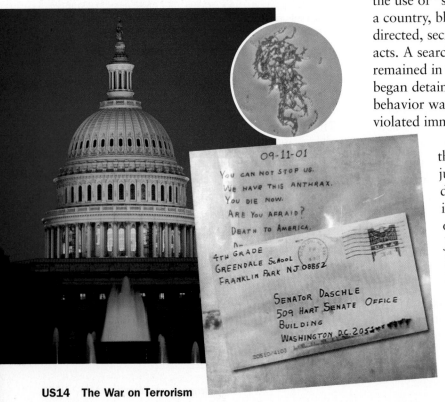

Five people who came in contact with spores from the tainted letters died of inhalation anthrax. Two were postal workers. Many others contracted the skin form of the disease. Thousands who were exposed to anthrax were treated with antibiotics.

The anthrax scare frightened many Americans. The U.S. Postal Service warned Americans to be suspicious of mail without return addresses or in strange packages and to wash their hands after handling mail. Many businesses began taking precautions.

Investigators did not immediately find a link between the anthrax letters and the September 11 attacks. Some experts believed that the anthrax letters might be the work of a lone terrorist rather than an organized group. The anthrax scare not only made Americans fearful of the mail but also of the threat of other biological or chemical weapons, such as the smallpox virus or the nerve gas sarin.

ANTITERRORISM MEASURES

The federal government warned Americans that additional terrorist attacks were likely. It then took actions to prevent such attacks. The Office of Homeland Security was created to coordinate national efforts against terrorism. Antiterrorism measures included a search for terrorists in the United States, the passage of an antiterrorism law, and the adoption of new aviation security regulations.

Searching for Terrorists The al-Qaeda network was able to carry out its terrorist attacks partly through the use of "sleepers." These are agents who move to a country, blend into a community, and then, when directed, secretly prepare for and carry out terrorist acts. A search to find any al-Qaeda terrorists who remained in the United States was started. Officials began detaining and questioning Arabs whose behavior was considered suspicious or who had violated immigration regulations.

Because the hijackers had been Arabs, the government held that the actions were justified. But some critics charged that detaining these men was unfair to the innocent and violated their civil rights. In one incident, Mohammed Irshaid, a Jordanian-born civil engineer who had lived in the United States for more than 20 years, was jailed for three weeks without being charged. His three children were American citizens. Although the incident humiliated him, he said that it "doesn't change my love of America."

President George W. Bush discusses the war against terrorism with advisers, including Vice President Dick Cheney (left) and Secretary of State Colin Powell (right).

More than three million Arab Americans live in the United States, and many were viewed with distrust by other Americans after the September 11 attacks. In one incident, three Arab Americans were taken off a plane when other passengers refused to fly with them. After questioning the men, officials allowed them to take a later flight.

Such incidents sparked debate about the need to respect civil rights while conducting searches for terrorists. The government argued that it was not unusual to curtail civil liberties during wartime in order to protect national security. This argument was also used to justify a proposal to try some terrorist suspects in military tribunals rather than in criminal courts.

Antiterrorism Law On October 26, 2001, President Bush signed into law an antiterrorism bill. The law allowed the government to

- detain foreigners suspected of terrorism for seven days without charging them with a crime
- tap all phones used by suspects and monitor their e-mail and Internet use
- make search warrants valid across states
- order U.S. banks to investigate sources of large foreign accounts
- prosecute terrorist crimes without any time restrictions or limitations

Again, critics warned that these measures would let the government infringe on people's civil rights.

Aviation Security The federal government also increased its involvement in aviation security. The Federal Aviation Administration ordered airlines to install bars on cockpit doors to prevent passengers from gaining control of planes, as the hijackers had done. Sky marshals were assigned to fly on planes; National Guard troops began patrolling airports.

In November 2001, a new aviation-security law made airport security the responsibility of the federal government. Previously, individual airports had been responsible. The law provided for a federal security force that would inspect passengers and carryon bags. It also required the screening of checked baggage.

Airline and government officials debated these and other measures for making air travel more secure. Major concerns were long delays at airports and respect for passengers' privacy. It also became clear that public debate over security measures would continue as long as the United States fights terrorism and tries to balance national security with civil rights.

Thinking Critically CURRENT EVENTS CLASSZONE.COM

- Is it important for the U.S. government to respect people's civil rights as it wages a war against terrorism? Why or why not?
- What has been the greatest impact of terrorism on American life, aside from the tragic deaths caused by the September 11 attacks?

Glossary

A

absolute location *n.* the exact spot on Earth where a place is found. (p. 36)

acid rain *n.* rain or snow that carries air pollutants to Earth. (p. 386)

Aegean (ih•JEE•uhn) **Sea** *n.* a branch of the Mediterranean Sea that is located between Greece and Turkey. (p. 279)

alliance (uh•LY•uhns) *n.* an agreement among people or nations to unite for a common cause and to help any alliance member that is attacked. (p. 334)

Anasazi *n.* a group of Native Americans who developed a complex civilization in the U.S. Southwest. (p. 88)

armed neutrality *n.* a policy by which a country maintains military forces but does not take sides in the conflicts of other nations. (p. 385)

Athens *n.* the capital of Greece and once one of the most important ancient Greek city-states. (p. 280)

Austria-Hungary *n.* in the 1900s, a dual monarchy in which the Hapsburg emperor ruled both Austria and Hungary. (p. 332)

B

Berlin Wall *n.* a wire-and-concrete wall that divided Germany's East Berlin and West Berlin from 1961 to 1989. (p. 395)

bilingual *adj.* able to speak two languages. (p. 133)

Bill of Rights *n.* ten amendments to the U.S. Constitution that list specific freedoms guaranteed to every U.S. citizen. (p. 96)

Brasília *n.* the capital of Brazil. (p. 246)

C

capitalism *n.* an economic system in which the factories and businesses that make and sell goods are privately owned and the owners make the decisions about what goods to produce. (p. 315)

Carnival *n.* a Cuban holiday that celebrates the end of the harvest each year in July. (p. 220); *n.* a Brazilian holiday that occurs during the four days before Lent. (p. 247)

cartographer *n.* a person who makes maps. (p. 45)

censorship *n.* the outlawing of materials that contain certain information. (p. 403)

chinampa (chee•NAHM•pah) *n.* a floating garden on which the Aztec grew crops. (p. 162)

circumnavigate *v.* to sail completely around. (p. 310)

citizen *n.* a legal member of a country. (p. 20)

citizenship *n.* the status of a citizen, which includes certain duties and rights. (p. 91)

city-state *n.* a central city and its surrounding villages, which together follow the same law, have one form of government, and share language, religious beliefs, and ways of life. (p. 279)

climate *n.* the typical weather of a region over a long time. (p. 75)

coalition government *n.* a government formed by political parties joining together. (p. 362)

Cold War *n.* after World War II, a period of political noncooperation between the members of NATO and the Warsaw Pact nations, during which these countries refused to trade or cooperate with each other. (p. 347)

collective farm *n.* a government-owned farm that employs large numbers of workers, often in Communist countries. (p. 345)

colonialism *n.* a system by which a country maintains colonies outside its borders. (p. 331)

Columbian Exchange *n.* the exchange of goods between Europe and its colonies in North and South America. (p. 166)

Communism *n.* an economic and political system in which property is owned collectively and labor is organized in a way that is supposed to benefit all people. (p. 217)

competition *n.* the rivalry among businesses to sell the most goods to consumers and make the greatest profit. (p. 106)

constitutional amendment *n.* a formal change or addition to the U.S. Constitution. (p. 96)

constitutional monarchy *n.* a government ruled by a king or queen whose power is determined by the nation's constitution and laws. (p. 125)

consumer *n.* a person who uses goods or services. (p. 105)

continent *n.* a landmass above water on earth. (p. 35)

Court of Human Rights *n.* the Council of Europe's court that protects the rights of all citizens in whichever of its member countries they live. (p. 370)

criollo (kree•AW•yaw) *n.* a person born in Mexico whose parents were born in Spain. (p. 175)

Crusades *n.* a series of military expeditions led by Western European Christians in the 11th, 12th, and 13th centuries to reclaim control of the Holy Lands from the Muslims. (p. 301)

culture *n.* the beliefs, customs, laws, art, and ways of living that a group of people share. (p. 21)

culture region *n.* an area of the world in which many people share similar beliefs, history, and languages. (p. 24)

culture trait *n.* the food, clothing, technology, beliefs, language, and tools that the people of a culture share. (p. 21)

currency *n.* money used as a form of exchange. (p. 369)

czar (zahr) *n.* in Russia, an emperor. (p. 319)

D

Day of the Dead *n.* a Mexican holiday, on November 1 and 2, for honoring loved ones who have died. (p. 194)

deforestation *n.* the process of cutting and clearing away trees from a forest. (p. 157)

democracy *n.* a government that receives its power from the people. (p. 91)

departamento (deh•pahr•tah•MEHN•taw) *n.* a Guatemalan state. (p. 223)

dependency *n.* a place governed by or closely connected with a country that it is not officially part of. (p. 203)

deposed *v.* removed from power. (p. 356)

détente (day•TAHNT) *n.* a relaxing of tensions between nations. (p. 357)

dictator *n.* a person who has complete control over a country's government. (p. 207)

dissident *n.* a person who openly disagrees with a government's policies. (p. 403)

distribution *n.* the process of moving products to their markets. (p. 187)

diversify *v.* to conduct business activities in a variety of industries. (p. 209)

dual monarchy *n.* a form of government in which one ruler governs two nations. (p. 332)

Duma (DOO•muh) *n.* one of the two houses of the Russian legislature. (p. 364)

E

economic indicator *n.* a measure that shows how a country's economy is doing. (p. 241)

economics *n.* the study of how resources are managed in the production, exchange, and use of goods and services. (p. 20)

economy *n.* the system by which business owners in a region use productive resources to provide goods and services that satisfy people's wants. (p. 79)

ejido (eh•HEE•daw) *n.* in Mexico, a community farm owned by the people of a village together. (p. 182)

El Niño (ehl NEE•nyaw) *n.* a current in the Pacific Ocean that results from changes in air pressure and that causes changes in weather patterns. (p. 159)

empire *n.* a nation or group of territories ruled by an emperor. (p. 287)

encomienda (ehn•kaw•MYEHN•dah) *n.* a system that the rulers of Spain established in Mexico, under which Spanish men received a Native American village to oversee and gain tribute from. (p. 176)

equal opportunity *n.* a guarantee that government and private institutions will not discriminate against people on the basis of factors such as race, religion, age, gender, or disability. (p. 90)

erosion *n.* the process by which environmental factors, such as wind, rivers, and rain, wear away soil and stone. (p. 74)

ethnic cleansing *n.* the organized killing of members of an ethnic group or groups. (p. 363)

euro *n.* the common unit of currency used by European Union countries. (p. 369)

European Community *n.* an association developed after World War II to promote economic unity among the countries of Western Europe. (p. 392)

European Union (EU) *n.* an economic and political grouping of countries in Western Europe. (p. 368)

export *n.* a product traded with or sold to another country. (p. 129)

F

factor of production *n.* one of the elements needed for production of goods or services to occur. (p. 103)

fascism (FASH•IHZ•uhm) *n.* a political philosophy that promotes a strong, central government controlled by the military and led by a powerful dictator. (p. 336)

federal government *n.* a national government. (p. 96)

feudalism *n.* in medieval Europe, a political and economic system in which lords gave land to less powerful nobles, called vassals, in return for which the vassals agreed to provide various services to the lords. (p. 292)

fiesta *n.* a holiday celebrated by a village or town, with events such as parades, games, and feasts. (p. 194)

First Nations *n.* in Canada, a group of descendants of the first settlers of North America, who came from Asia. (p. 120)

fjord (fyawrd) *n.* a long, narrow, deep inlet of the sea located between steep cliffs. (p. 274)

Florence *n.* a city in Italy that was a bustling center of banking, trade, and manufacturing during the 14th century. (p. 302)

Francophone *n.* a French-speaking person. (p. 133)

free enterprise/market economy *n.* an economy that allows business owners to compete in the market with little government interference. (p. 105)

free-trade zone *n.* an area in which goods can move across borders without being taxed. (p. 241)

French Resistance *n.* an anti-German movement in France during World War II. (p. 390)

French Revolution *n.* a revolution that began on July 14, 1789, and that led to France's becoming a republic. (p. 316)

G

Gadsden Purchase *n.* the 1853 purchase by the United States of a piece of land from northern Mexico. (p. 178)

GDP *n.* gross domestic product, or the total value of the goods and services produced in a country during a given time period. (p. 104)

geography *n.* the study of people, places, and the environment. (p. 18)

glacier *n.* a thick sheet of ice that moves slowly across land. (p. 73)

globalization *n.* the spreading of an idea, product, or technology around the world. (p. 111)

Good Friday Accord *n.* an agreement signed in 1998 by Ireland's Protestants and Catholics that established the Northern Ireland Assembly to represent voters from both groups. (p. 381)

government *n.* the people and groups within a society that have the authority to make laws, to make sure they are carried out, and to settle disagreements about them. (p. 19)

guerrilla warfare *n.* nontraditional military tactics by small groups involving surprise attacks. (p. 253)

guild *n.* a business association created by people working in the same industry to protect their common interests and maintain standards within the industry. (p. 294)

H

hacienda *n.* in Spanish-speaking countries, a big farm or ranch. (p. 181)

hieroglyph *n.* a picture or symbol used in hieroglyphics. (p. 161)

history *n.* a record of the past. (p. 18)

Holocaust *n.* the organized killing of European Jews and others by the Nazis during World War II. (p. 336)

hydroelectricity *n.* electrical power generated by water. (p. 386)

I

immigrant *n.* a person who comes to a country to take up residence. (p. 88)

imperialism *n.* the practice of one country's controlling the government and economy of another country or territory. (p. 310)

import *n.* a product brought into a country through trade or sale. (p. 130)

impressionism *n.* a style of art that creates an impression of a scene rather than a strictly realistic picture. (p. 393)

Industrial Revolution *n.* a period of change beginning in the late 18th century, during which goods began to be manufactured by power-driven machines. (p. 314)

industry *n.* any area of economic activity. (p. 129)

inflation *n.* a continuing increase in the price of goods and services, or a continuing decrease in the capability of money to buy goods and services. (p. 245)

Institutional Revolutionary Party *n.* the most powerful political party in Mexico from the 1920s to 2000, which won every presidential election during that time. (p. 183)

interdependence *n.* the economic, political, and social dependence of culture regions on one another. (p. 26)

Iron Curtain *n.* a political barrier that isolated the peoples of Eastern Europe after World War II, restricting their ability to travel outside the region. (p. 342)

L

labor force *n.* a pool of available workers. (p. 315)

ladino (lah•DEE•noh) *n.* a person of mixed European and Native American ancestry. (p. 205)

landform *n.* a feature of Earth's surface, such as a mountain, valley, or plateau. (p. 73)

latitude *n.* a measure of distance north or south of the equator. (p. 36)

limited government *n.* government in which the powers of the leaders are limited. (p. 95)

London *n.* the capital of England. (p. 379)

longitude *n.* a measure of distance east or west of a line called the prime meridian. (p. 36)

M

Machu Picchu (MAH•choo PEEK•choo) *n.* an ancient stone city built by the Inca. (p. 165)

Magna Carta (MAG•nuh KAHR•tuh) *n.* a document signed by England's King John in 1215 that guaranteed English people basic rights. (p. 295)

malnutrition *n.* poor nutrition, usually from not eating the right foods, which can result in poor health. (p. 220)

manorialism *n.* a social system in which peasants worked on a lord's land and supplied him with food in exchange for his protection of them. (p. 293)

map projection *n.* one of the different ways of showing Earth's curved surface on a flat map. (p. 47)

maquiladora (mah•kee•lah•DAW•rah) *n.* in Mexico, a factory that imports duty-free parts from the United States to make products that it then exports back across the border. (p. 187)

market economy See **free enterprise/ market economy.**

medieval (MEE•dee•EE•vuhl) *adj.* relating to the period of history between the fall of the Roman Empire and the beginning of the modern world, often dated from 476 to 1453. (p. 291)

Mediterranean Sea *n.* an inland sea that borders Europe, Southwest Asia, and Africa. (p. 274)

mestizo (mehs•TEE•saw) *n.* a person of mixed European and Native American ancestry. (p. 175)

migrate *v.* to move from one area in order to settle in another. (p. 38)

mulatto (mu•LAT•oh) *n.* a person of mixed African and European ancestry. (p. 204)

multiculturalism *n.* an acceptance of many cultures instead of just one. (p. 121)

N

national identity *n.* a sense of belonging to a nation. (p. 132)

nationalism *n.* strong pride in one's nation or ethnic group. (p. 329)

nationalize *v.* to establish government control of a service or industry. (p. 188)

NATO (NAY•toh) *n.* the North Atlantic Treaty Organization, a defense alliance formed in 1949, with the countries of Western Europe, Canada, and the United States agreeing to defend one another if attacked. (p. 337)

O

oasis *n.* a region in a desert that is fertile because it is near a river or spring. (p. 251)

oligarchy (AHL•ih•GAHR•kee) *n.* a government in which a few powerful individuals rule. (p. 280)

ombudsman *n.* a Swedish official who protects citizens' rights and ensures that the courts and civil service follow the law. (p. 385)

one-party system *n.* a system in which there is only one political party and only one candidate to choose from for each government position. (p. 343)

Organization of American States (OAS) *n.* an organization of the nations of the Americas that encourages democracy and promotes economic cooperation, social justice, and the equality of all people. (p. 234)

P

Pan-American *adj.* relating to all of the Americas. (p. 234)

Parliament *n.* Canada's national lawmaking body. (p. 125)

parliamentary republic *n.* a republic whose head of government, usually a prime minister, is the leader of the political party that has the most members in the parliament. (p. 361)

patrician (puh•TRIHSH•uhn) *n.* in ancient Rome, a member of a wealthy, landowning family that claimed to be able to trace its roots back to the founding of Rome. (p. 285)

patriotism *n.* love for one's country. (p. 91)

PEMEX *n. Petróleos Mexicanos,* or "Mexican Petroleum," a government agency that runs the oil industry in Mexico. (p. 188)

peninsula *n.* a body of land surrounded by water on three sides. (p. 274)

peninsular (peh•neen•soo•LAHR) *n.* a person who was born in Spain but who lived in Mexico after the Spanish took control. (p. 175)

philosopher *n.* a person who studies and thinks about why the world is the way it is. (p. 281)

plain *n.* a large flat area of land that usually does not have many trees. (p. 275)

plebeian (plih•BEE•uhn) *n.* a common citizen of ancient Rome. (p. 285)

polis *n.* the central city of a city-state. (p. 279)

political process *n.* legal activities through which a citizen influences public policy. (p. 91)

precipitation *n.* moisture that falls to Earth, such as rain or snow. (p. 75)

prime minister *n.* in a parliamentary democracy, the leader of the cabinet and often also of the executive branch. (p. 125)

private property rights *n.* the right of individuals to own land or industry. (p. 355)

privatization *n.* the process of replacing community ownership with individual, or private, ownership. (p. 186)

profit *n.* the money that remains after the costs of producing a product are paid. (p. 105)

propaganda (PRAHP•uh•GAN•duh) *n.* material designed to spread certain beliefs. (p. 354)

Protestant *n.* a member of a Christian church based on the principles of the Reformation. (p. 306)

puppet government *n.* a government that is controlled by an outside force. (p. 343)

Q

Quechua (KEHCH•wuh) *n.* people who live in the Andes highlands and speak the Inca language Quechua. (p. 253)

R

Reformation *n.* a 16th-century movement to change practices within the Roman Catholic Church. (p. 305)

refugee *n.* a person who flees a country because of war, disaster, or persecution. (p. 122)

Reign of Terror *n.* the period between 1793 and 1794 during which France's new leaders executed thousands of its citizens. (p. 317)

relative location *n.* the location of one place in relation to other places. (p. 37)

Renaissance *n.* an era of creativity and learning in Western Europe from the 14th century to the 16th century. (p. 302)

republic *n.* a form of government in which people rule through elected representatives. (p. 285)

reunification *n.* the uniting again of parts. (p. 396)

Riksdag (RIHKS•DAHG) *n.* Sweden's parliament. (p. 384)

Rio de Janeiro *n.* a city in Brazil. (p. 246)

river system *n.* a network that includes a major river and its tributaries. (p. 74)

rural *adj.* of the countryside. (p. 193)

Russian Revolution *n.* the 1917 revolution that removed the Russian monarchy from power after it had ruled for 400 years. (p. 322)

S

São Paulo *n.* a city in Brazil. (p. 246)

scarcity *n.* a word economists use to describe the conflict between people's desires and limited resources. (p. 20)

Scientific Revolution *n.* a period of great scientific change and discovery during the 16th and 17th centuries. (p. 314)

secede *v.* to withdraw from a political union, such as a nation. (p. 381)

Senate *n.* the assembly of elected representatives that was the most powerful ruling body of the Roman Republic. (p. 285)

separatist *n.* a person who wants to separate from a body to which he or she belongs, such as a church or nation. (p. 127)

single-product economy *n.* an economy that depends on just one product for the majority of its income. (p. 209)

skerry *n.* a small island. (p. 387)

socialism *n.* an economic system in which businesses and industries are owned collectively or by the government. (p. 392)

Solidarity *n.* a trade union in Poland that originally aimed to increase pay and improve working conditions and that later opposed Communism. (p. 400)

standard of living *n.* a measure of quality of life. (p. 369)

sugar cane *n.* a plant from which sugar is made. (p. 209)

T

tariff *n.* a fee imposed by a government on imported or exported goods. (p. 369)

technology *n.* tools and equipment made through scientific discoveries. (p. 112)

thematic map *n.* a map that focuses on a specific idea or theme. (p. 46)

tourism *n.* the business of helping people travel on vacations. (p. 189)

transportation barrier *n.* a geographic feature that prevents or slows transportation. (p. 131)

transportation corridor *n.* a path that makes transportation easier. (p. 131)

Treaty of Guadalupe Hidalgo *n.* a treaty that the United States forced Mexico to sign in 1848, giving Mexico's northern lands to the United States. (p. 177)

tributary *n.* a stream or river that flows into a larger river. (p. 157)

Tropical Zone *n.* the region of the world that lies between the latitudes 23°27' north and 23°27' south. (p. 158)

U

United States Constitution *n.* the document that is the foundation for all U.S. laws and the framework for the U.S. government. (p. 94)

unlimited government *n.* a government in which the leaders have almost absolute power. (p. 95)

Ural (YUR•uhl) Mountains *n.* a mountain range that divides Europe from Asia. (p. 275)

urban *adj.* of the city. (p. 193)

urbanization *n.* the movement of people from the countryside to cities. (p. 241)

V

value *n.* a principle or ideal by which people live. (p. 110)

vegetation *n.* plant life, such as trees, plants, and grasses. (p. 75)

W

Warsaw Pact *n.* a treaty signed in 1955 that established an alliance among the Soviet Union, Albania, Bulgaria, Czechoslovakia, East Germany, Hungary, Poland, and Romania. (p. 347)

weather *n.* the state of Earth's atmosphere at a given time and place. (p. 75)

West Indies *n.* the Caribbean Islands. (p. 203)

World War I *n.* a war fought from 1914 to 1918 between the Allies (Russia, France, the United Kingdom, Italy, and the United States) and the Central Powers (Austria-Hungary, Germany, Turkey, and Bulgaria). (p. 333)

World War II *n.* a war fought from 1939 to 1945 between the Axis powers (Germany Italy, and Japan) and the Allies (the United Kingdom, France, the Soviet Union, and the United States). (p. 336)

Spanish Glossary

A

absolute location [ubicación absoluta] *s.* lugar exacto donde se halla un lugar en la Tierra. (pág. 36)

acid rain [lluvia ácida] *s.* lluvia o nieve que lleva sustancias contaminantes a la Tierra. (pág. 386)

Aegean (ih•JEE•uhn) **Sea** [mar Egeo] *s.* parte del Mar Mediterráneo ubicada entre Grecia y Turquía. (pág. 279)

alliance (uh•LY•uhns) [alianza] *s.* acuerdo de unión entre pueblos o naciones por una causa común y de ayuda mutua en caso de que uno sea atacado. (pág. 334)

Anasazi [anasazi] *s.* grupo de indígenas que desarrollaron una cultura compleja en el sudoeste de Estados Unidos. (pág. 88)

armed neutrality [neutralidad armada] *s.* política mediante la cual un país mantiene fuerzas armadas pero no participa en conflictos de otras naciones. (pág. 385)

Athens [Atenas] *s.* capital de Grecia y una de las ciudades-estado más importantes de la antigua Grecia. (pág. 280)

Austria-Hungary [Austria-Hungría] *s.* monarquía dual mediante la cual a comienzos del siglo XX el emperador de la dinastía de los Hasburgo gobernó Austria y Hungría. (pág. 332)

B

Berlin Wall [Muro de Berlín] *s.* pared de cemento y alambre que desde 1961 a 1989 dividía la parte este de Berlín de la parte oeste. (pág. 395)

bilingual [bilingüe] *adj.* que puede hablar dos idiomas. (pág. 133)

Bill of Rights [Declaración de Derechos] *s.* las diez enmiendas a la Constitución de los Estados Unidos que enumeran libertades específicas garantizadas a todos los ciudadanos estadounidenses. (pág. 96)

C

capitalism [capitalismo] *s.* sistema económico en el cual las empresas y comercios que fabrican y venden productos y mercancías son de propiedad privada; los dueños de dichas empresas y comercios deciden lo que desean producir y vender. (pág. 315)

Carnival [carnaval] *s.* feriado cubano que celebra cada año el fin de la cosecha en el mes de julio. (pág. 220); *s.* feriado brasileño de cuatro días anterior al comienzo de la cuaresma. (pág. 247)

cartographer [cartógrafo] *s.* persona que hace mapas. (pág. 45)

censorship [censura] *s.* prohibición de materiales que contienen cierta información. (pág. 403)

chinampa (chee•NAHM•pah) *s.* huerta flotante en la que los aztecas sembraban sus cultivos. (pág. 162)

circumnavigate [circunnavegar] *v.* dar la vuelta alrededor de algo en una nave. (pág. 310)

citizen [ciudadano] *s.* habitante legal de un país. (pág. 20)

citizenship [ciudadanía] *s.* estado de un ciudadano que incluye derechos y obligaciones. (pág. 91)

city-state [ciudad estado] *s.* ciudad central y sus aldeas aledañas que acatan las mismas leyes, tienen una sola forma de gobierno y comparten una lengua, creencias religiosas y estilos de vida. (pág. 279)

climate [clima] *s.* condición típica de la atmósfera en determinada región. (pág. 75)

coalition government [gobierno de coalición] s. gobierno formado por la unión de partidos políticos. (pág. 362)

Cold War [Guerra Fría] s. período político posterior a la Segunda Guerra Mundial, caracterizado por la falta de cooperación y relaciones comerciales entre los países miembros de la OTAN y las naciones del Pacto de Varsovia. (pág. 347)

collective farm [granja colectiva] s. granja que pertenece al gobierno, que emplea a gran número de trabajadores generalmente en países comunistas. (pág. 345)

colonialism [colonialismo] s. sistema mediante el cual un país mantiene colonias en otras partes del mundo. (pág. 331)

Columbian Exchange [intercambio colombino] s. intercambio de mercancías entre Europa y sus colonias en América. (pág. 166)

Communism [comunismo] s. sistema político y económico en el cual la propiedad es colectiva y la actividad laboral es organizada de manera de beneficiar a todos los individuos. (pág. 217)

competition [competencia] s. rivalidad entre empresas por vender la mayor cantidad de productos y mercaderías a los consumidores y por obtener el mayor beneficio. (pág. 106)

constitutional amendment [enmienda constitucional] s. cambio formal a la constitución de los Estados Unidos. (pág. 96)

constitutional monarchy [monarquía constitucional] s. gobierno encabezado por un rey o reina, cuyo poder está determinado por la constitución y leyes de la nación. (pág. 125)

consumer [consumidor] s. persona que usa productos o servicios. (pág. 105)

continent [continente] s. masa continental sobre agua en la Tierra. (pág. 35)

Court of Human Rights [Corte de Derechos Humanos] s. corte que protege los derechos de ciudadanos que habiten en países miembros. (pág. 370)

criollo (kree•AW•yaw) s. persona nacida en México cuyos padres provienen de España. (pág. 175)

Crusades [las cruzadas] s. serie de expediciones militares dirigidas por cristianos de Europa occidental en los siglos XI, XII y XIII, para apoderarse de nuevo de las Tierras Santas, en poder de los musulmanes. (pág. 301)

culture [cultura] s. conjunto de creencias, costumbres, leyes, formas artísticas y de vida compartidas por un grupo de personas. (pág. 21)

culture region [región cultural] s. territorio donde muchas personas comparten creencias, historia y lenguas similares. (pág. 24)

culture trait [característica cultural] s. alimento, vestimenta, tecnología, creencia, lengua u otro elemento compartido por un pueblo o cultura. (pág. 21)

currency [moneda] s. sistema que sirve para medir el valor de las cosas que se intercambian. (pág. 369)

czar (zahr) [zar] s. emperador ruso. (pág. 319)

D

Day of the Dead [Día de los Muertos] s. feriado mexicano del 1 al 2 de noviembre en honor a los seres queridos que han muerto. (pág. 194)

deforestation [deforestación] s. proceso mediante el cual se cortan árboles y se van eliminando bosques. (pág. 157)

democracy [democracia] s. sistema de gobierno mediante el cual los gobernantes reciben el poder del pueblo. (pág. 91)

departamento (deh•pahr•tah•MEHN•taw) s. nombre que reciben los estados en Guatemala. (pág. 223)

dependency [territorio dependiente] s. lugar gobernado o que está estrechamente conectado con un país del cual no forma parte. (pág. 203)

deposed [depuesto] v. removido del poder. (pág. 356)

détente (day•TAHNT) [distensión] s. disminución de la tensión entre países. (pág. 357)

dictator [dictador] s. persona que tiene el control absoluto del gobierno de un país. (pág. 207)

dissident [disidente] *s.* persona que abiertamente muestra desacuerdo con la política de un gobierno. (pág. 403)

distribution [distribución] *s.* proceso mediante el cual se transporta la mercancía a los mercados. (pág. 187)

diversify [diversificar] *v.* llevar a cabo actividades comerciales en una variedad de industrias. (pág. 209)

dual monarchy [monarquía dual] *s.* gobierno en que un solo jefe gobierna dos naciones. (pág. 332)

Duma (DOO•muh) [Duma] *s.* una de las dos cámaras de la legislatura rusa. (pág. 364)

E

economic indicator [indicador económico] *s.* medida que muestra el estado de la economía de un país. (pág. 241)

economics [economía] *s.* estudio del uso de los recursos naturales y del modo de producción, intercambio y utilización de los productos, mercaderías y servicios. (pág. 20)

economy [economía] *s.* sistema de administrar recursos de producción en una región con el fin de proveer productos y servicios que satisfagan las necesidades humanas. (pág. 79)

ejido s. granja comunitaria en México que pertenece colectivamente a los habitantes de un pueblo o localidad. (pág. 182)

El Niño s. corriente del océano Pacífico que surge de los cambios en la presión atmosférica y que causa cambios meteorológicos. (pág. 159)

empire [imperio] *s.* nación o conjunto de territorios gobernados por un emperador. (pág. 287)

encomienda s. sistema establecido en México por los gobernantes españoles mediante el cual los españoles controlaban comunidades indígenas y recaudaban tributo. (pág. 176)

equal opportunity [igualdad de oportunidades] *s.* garantía de que el gobierno e instituciones privadas no discriminarán en contra de ciertas personas por motivos de raza, religión, edad o sexo. (pág. 90)

erosion [erosión] *s.* desgaste del terreno y suelo producido por factores ambientales tales como el viento, la lluvia y los ríos. (pág. 74)

ethnic cleansing [limpieza étnica] *s.* matanza sistemática (genocidio) de uno o varios grupos étnicos que conforman una minoría. (pág. 363)

euro [euro] *s.* unidad monetaria de los países miembros de la Unión Europea. (pág. 369)

European Community [Comunidad Europea] *s.* asociación creada después de la Segunda Guerra Mundial para promover la unidad económica entre los países de Europa occidental. (pág. 392)

European Union [Unión Europea] *s.* asociación económica y política de países de Europa occidental. (pág. 368)

export [exportación] *s.* mercadería que se vende a otro país. (pág. 129)

F

factor of production [factor de producción] *s.* elemento necesario para producir mercaderías y ofrecer servicios. (pág. 103)

fascism (FASH•IHZ•uhm) [fascismo] *s.* filosofía que promueve un gobierno centralista fuerte, controlado por el ejército y dirigido por un dictador poderoso. (pág. 336)

federal government [gobierno federal] *s.* gobierno nacional. (pág. 96)

feudalism [feudalismo] *s.* sistema político y económico de la Europa medieval en el que los señores feudales repartían tierras a miembros de la nobleza menos poderosos, llamados vasallos, quienes, a cambio de éstas, se comprometían a brindar varios servicios a los señores feudales. (pág. 292)

fiesta *s.* feriado celebrado por una comunidad o pueblo, con desfiles, juegos y banquetes. (pág. 194)

First Nation [Primera Nación] *s.* nombre que reciben en Canadá los descendientes de los primeros pobladores en Norteamérica que provenían de Asia. (pág. 120)

fjord (fyawrd) [fiordo] *s.* entrada larga y estrecha del mar formada entre acantilados abruptos. (pág. 274)

Florence [Florencia] *s.* ciudad italiana que durante el siglo XIV mantuvo una dinámica actividad bancaria, comercial y manufacturera. (pág. 302)

Francophone [francófono] *s.* persona que habla francés. (pág. 133)

free enterprise/market economy [librecambismo/economía de libre mercado] *s.* economía que permite a empresarios y comerciantes competir en el mercado con poca interferencia del gobierno. (pág. 105)

free-trade zone [zona de libre comercio] *s.* área en la que tanto personas como mercaderías pueden circular más allá de las fronteras sin que esta actividad sea gravada con impuestos. (pág. 241)

French Resistance [Resistencia francesa] *s.* en Francia, un movimiento antialemán durante la Segunda Guerra Mundial. (pág. 390)

French Revolution [Revolución francesa] *s.* revolución que comenzó el 14 de julio de 1789 y tuvo como resultado la conversión de Francia en una república. (pág. 316)

G

Gadsden Purchase [Compra de Gadsden] *s.* compra mediante la cual los Estados Unidos adquirieron en 1853 parte del territorio del norte de México. (pág. 178)

GDP [PIB, Producto Interno Bruto] *s.* valor total de los productos y servicios producidos en un país durante un período determinado. (pág. 104)

geography [geografía] *s.* estudio de los pueblos, lugares y el medio ambiente. (pág. 18)

glacier [glaciar] *s.* espesas formaciones de hielo que se mueven lentamente por la tierra. (pág. 73)

globalization [globalización] *s.* difusión de una idea, producto o tecnología por todo el mundo. (pág. 111)

Good Friday Accord [Acuerdo del Viernes Santo] *s.* acuerdo firmado por los protestantes y católicos de Irlanda del Norte que estableció la Asamblea de Irlanda del Norte, asamblea esta que representa a los votantes de ambos grupos. (pág. 381)

government [gobierno] *s.* los individuos y grupos en una sociedad que tienen la autoridad de crear leyes y hacerlas cumplir, y de resolver desacuerdos que puedan surgir con respecto a ellas. (pág. 19)

guerrilla warfare [guerrilla] *s.* tácticas militares no tradicionales llevadas a cabo por grupos pequeños que realizan ataques sorpresivos. (pág. 253)

guild [gremio] *s.* asociación creada por personas que trabajan en una misma industria, con el fin de proteger sus intereses comunes y mantener ciertos criterios y principios aplicables a la industria. (pág. 294)

H

hacienda *s.* en países hispanos, finca o granja de gran tamaño. (pág. 181)

hieroglyph [jeroglífico] *s.* dibujo y símbolo de la escritura jeroglífica. (pág. 161)

history [historia] *s.* un registro de los acontecimientos del pasado. (pág. 18)

Holocuast [Holocausto] *s.* matanza sistemática (genocidio) de los judíos europeos y otros por el partido nazi durante la Segunda Guerra Mundial. (pág. 336)

hydroelectricity [electricidad hidráulica] *s.* energía eléctrica producida por el agua. (pág. 386)

market economy Ver **free enterprise**.

medieval (MEE•dee•EE•vuhl) [medieval] *adj.* que pertenece al período de la historia comprendido entre la caída del Imperio romano y el comienzo del mundo moderno, aproximadamente desde 476 a 1453. (pág. 291)

Mediterranean Sea [mar Mediterráneo] *s.* mar interno que bordea Europa, el sudoeste de Asia y África. (pág. 274)

mestizo s. persona de descendencia mixta, con sangre europea e indígena. (pág. 175)

migrate [migrar] *v.* irse de un área para establecerse en otra. (pág. 38)

mulatto [mulato] *s.* persona con descendencia mixta, de sangre europea y africana. (pág. 204)

multiculturalism [multiculturalismo] *s.* la aceptación de muchas culturas en vez de una solamente. (pág. 121)

N

national identity [identidad nacional] *s.* sentimiento de pertenencia a una nación. (pág. 132)

nationalism [nacionalismo] *s.* intenso orgullo por el país o grupo étnico propio. (pág. 329)

nationalize [nacionalizar] *v.* pasar al control gubernamental un servicio o industria. (pág. 188)

NATO (NAY•toh) [OTAN, Organización del Tratado del Atlántico Norte] *s.* alianza de defensa que agrupa a los países de Europa occidental, Canadá y Estados Unidos, que acuerdan la defensa común en caso de ataque. (pág. 337)

O

oasis [oasis] *s.* región fértil en un desierto que se formó alrededor de un río o manantial. (pág. 251)

oligarchy (AHL•ih•GAHR•kee) [oligarquía] *s.* gobierno de sólo unos pocos individuos poderosos. (pág. 280)

ombudsman [defensor del pueblo] *s.* funcionario del gobierno sueco que protege los derechos de los ciudadanos y asegura que los tribunales y la administración pública cumplan con la ley. (pág. 385)

one-party system [sistema monopartidista] *s.* sistema donde sólo se puede votar por un partido político y por un candidato para cada puesto de gobierno. (pág. 343)

Organization of American States (OAS) [OEA, Organización de los Estados Americanos] *s.* organización de todas las naciones americanas, que promueve la democracia y la cooperación económica, la justicia social y la igualdad entre los pueblos. (pág. 234)

P

Pan-American [panamericano] *adj.* relativo a todas las Américas. (pág. 234)

Parliament [Parlamento] *s.* cuerpo legislativo nacional de Canadá. (pág. 125)

parliamentary republic [república parlamentaria] *s.* república cuyo jefe de estado, en general un primer ministro, es el líder del partido político que tiene la mayoría de representantes en el parlamento. (pág. 361)

patrician (puh•TRIHSH•uhn) [patricio] *s.* miembro de familia adinerada y hacendada en la antigua Roma, que afirmaba que sus orígenes se remontan a la época de la fundación de Roma. (pág. 285)

patriotism [patriotismo] *s.* amor por el país propio. (pág. 91)

PEMEX *s.* Petróleos Mexicanos, agencia gubernamental que administra la industria petrolera en México. (pág. 188)

peninsula [península] *s.* territorio rodeado de agua en tres de sus lados. (pág. 274)

peninsular s. persona que nació en España pero vivió en México luego de la conquista de los españoles. (pág. 175)

philosopher [filósofo] *s.* persona que estudia y piensa sobre el mundo y su naturaleza. (pág. 281)

plain [llanura] *s.* superficie extensa y plana que suele no tener muchos árboles. (pág. 275)

plebeian (plih•BEE•uhn) [plebeyo] *s.* ciudadano corriente (sin título de nobleza) en la antigua Roma. (pág. 285)

polis [polis] *s.* ciudad central de una ciudad estado. (pág. 279)

political process [proceso político] *s.* actividades permitidas por la ley mediante las cuales el ciudadano influye en las políticas públicas. (pág. 91)

precipitation [precipitación] *s.* humedad como la lluvia o la nieve que cae a la Tierra. (pág. 75)

prime minister [primer ministro] *s.* en una democracia parlamentaria, líder del gabinete y frecuentemente de la administración ejecutiva. (pág. 125)

private property rights [derechos de propiedad privada] *s.* derechos individuales de ser propietario de bienes raíces, campos o industrias. (pág. 355)

privatization [privatización] *s.* proceso mediante el cual la propiedad que pertenece a la comunidad se convierte en propiedad privada o individual. (pág. 186)

profit [ganancia] *s.* dinero que sobra luego de pagar el costo de producir un producto. (pág. 105)

propaganda (PRAHP•uh•GAN•duh) [propaganda] *s.* material cuyo objetivo es difundir ciertas creencias. (pág. 354)

Protestant [protestante] *s.* miembro de una iglesia cristiana fundada de acuerdo a los principis de la Reforma. (pág. 306)

puppet government [gobierno títere] *s.* gobierno que hace lo que le indica un poder exterior. (pág. 343)

Q

Quechua (KEHCH•wuh) *s.* habitante de los Andes que habla una lengua inca del mismo nombre. (pág. 253)

R

Reformation [Reforma] *s.* movimiento del siglo XVI que se propuso cambiar las prácticas de la Iglesia Católica. (pág. 305)

refugee [refugiado] *s.* persona que huye de un país a raíz de una guerra, catástrofe, o porque es objeto de persecuciones. (pág. 122)

Reign of Terror [reino del Terror] *s.* período comprendido entre 1793 y 1794 durante el cual las nuevas autoridades en Francia ejecutaron miles de ciudadanos. (pág. 317)

relative location [ubicación relativa] *s.* ubicación de un lugar en relación con otros. (pág. 37)

Renaissance *s.* período de creatividad y de aprendizaje en Europa occidental entre los siglos XIV y XVI. (pág. 302)

republic [república] *s.* forma de gobierno controlado por sus cuidadanos a través de representates elegidos por los cuidadanos. (pág. 285)

reunification [reunificación] *s.* acción de unificar nuevamente las partes. (pág. 396)

Riksdag (RIHKS•DAHG) *s.* parlamento sueco. (pág. 384)

Rio de Janeiro *s.* ciudad brasileña. (pág. 246)

river system [sistema fluvial] *s.* que incluye ríos principales y sus tributarios. (pág. 74)

rural [rural] *adj.* que pertenece al campo. (pág. 193)

Russian Revolution [Revolución rusa] *s.* revolución de 1917 que eliminó la monarquía rusa del poder luego de 400 años de vigencia. (pág. 322)

S

São Paulo [San Pablo] *s.* ciudad brasileña. (pág. 246)

scarcity [escasez] *s.* palabra usada por los economistas para describir el conflicto que existe entre el deseo de los seres humanos y los recursos limitados para satisfacerlo. (pág. 20)

Scientific Revolution [Revolución científica] *s.* período de grandes cambios científicos y descubrimientos durante los siglos XVI a XVII. (pág. 314)

secede [separarse] *v.* independizarse de una unidad política, como una nación. (pág. 381)

Senate [Senado] *s.* asamblea más poderosa de la República romana, cuyos representantes eran elegidos. (pág. 285)

separatist [separatista] *s.* persona que desea separarse del cuerpo al que pertenece, como la iglesia o la nación. (pág. 127)

single-product economy [economía de un solo producto] *s.* economía cuya mayor parte de los ingresos depende de un solo producto. (pág. 209)

skerry [arrecife] *s.* islote. (pág. 387)

socialism [socialismo] *s.* sistema económico en donde algunos negocios e industrias le pertenecen a una cooperativa o al gobierno. (pág. 392)

Solidarity [Solidaridad] *s.* sindicato polaco cuya finalidad inicial fue aumentar el salario, mejorar las condiciones laborales de los trabajadores y luego oponerse al Comunismo. (pág. 400)

standard of living [nivel de vida] *s.* forma de medir la calidad de vida. (pág. 369)

sugar cane [caña de azúcar] *s.* planta de la que se extrae el azúcar. (pág. 209)

T

tariff [arancel aduanero] *s.* tarifa o suma de dinero impuesto por el gobierno en productos que se importan o exportan. (pág. 369)

technology [tecnología] *s.* herramientas o equipos que se crean a partir de ciertos descubrimientos. (pág. 112)

thematic map [mapa temático] *s.* mapa que se centra en una idea o tema particular. (pág. 46)

tourism [turismo] *s.* industria que estimula a la gente a viajar por placer. (pág. 189)

transportation barrier [barrera al transporte] *s.* obstáculo que impide el transporte o lo disminuye. (pág. 131)

transportation corridor [vía de transporte] *s.* camino que facilita el transporte. (pág. 131)

Treaty of Guadalupe Hidalgo [Tratado de Guadalupe Hidalgo] *s.* tratado que Estados Unidos exigió a México que firmara en 1848, mediante el cual México cedió a Estados Unidos su territorio en el norte. (pág. 177)

tributary [tributario] *s.* arroyo o río que confluye en otro río de mayor caudal. (pág. 157)

Tropical Zone [Zona Tropical] *s.* región del mundo comprendida entre las latitudes 23°27' al norte y 23°27' al sur. (pág. 158)

U

United States Constitution [Constitución de Estados Unidos] *s.* documento que fundamenta todas las leyes del gobierno de Estados Unidos y constituye su marco jurídico. (pág. 94)

unlimited government [gobierno ilimitado] *s.* gobierno en el que las autoridades ejercen la mayor parte del poder. (pág. 95)

Ural (YUR•uhl) Mountains [Montes Urales] *s.* cadena montañosa que divide Europa de Asia. (pág. 275)

urban [urbano] *adj.* que pertenece a la ciudad. (pág. 193)

urbanization [urbanización] *s.* movimiento de personas del campo a la ciudad. (pág. 241)

V

value [valor] *s.* principio e ideal básico de las personas. (pág. 110)

vegetation [vegetación] *s.* conjunto de plantas, arbustos, árboles y hierbas. (pág. 75)

R17

W

Warsaw Pact [Pacto de Varsovia] *s.* tratado firmado en 1955 que estableció una alianza entre la Unión Soviética, Albania, Bulgaria, Checoslovaquia, Alemania Oriental, Hungría, Polonia y Rumania. (pág. 347)

weather [tiempo] *s.* estado atmosférico cercano a la Tierra en un momento y lugar determinados. (pág. 75)

West Indies [Indias Occidentales/las Antillas] *s.* islas del Caribe. (pág. 203)

World War I [Primera Guerra Mundial] *s.* guerra de 1914 a 1918 entre los aliados (Rusia, Francia, el Reino Unido, Italia y los Estados Unidos) y las potencias centrales (Imperio autro-húngaro, Alemania, Turquía y Bulgaria). (pág. 333)

World War II [Segunda Guerra Mundial] *s.* guerra de 1939 a 1945 entre las potencias del Eje (Alemania, Italia y Japón) y los aliados (el Reino Unido, Francia, la Unión Soviética y los Estados Unidos). (pág. 336)

Index

An *i* preceding a page reference in italics indicates that there is an illustration, and usually text information as well, on that page. An *m* or a *c* preceding an italic page reference indicates a map or a chart, as well as text information on that page.

Acknowledgments

Text Credits

Chapter 4, page 100: "Coney" from *Subway Swinger* by Virginia Schonborg, copyright © 1970 by Virginia Schonborg. Used by permission of HarperCollins Publishers.

Chapter 4, page 100: "Knoxville, Tennessee" from *Black Feeling, Black Talk, Black Judgment* by Nikki Giovanni. Copyright 1968, 1970 by Nikki Giovanni. Reprinted by permission of HarperCollins Publishers Inc.

page 101: "Scenic" from *Collected Poems, 1953–1993* by John Updike, copyright © 1993 by John Updike. Used by permission of Alfred A. Knopf, a division of Random House, Inc.

Chapter 9, page 239: "Chilean Earth" from *A Gabriela Mistral Reader,* translation copyright 1993 by Maria Giachetti. Reprinted by permission of White Pine Press.

page 249: Copyright © 2000 by Houghton Mifflin Company, Reproduced by permission from *The American Heritage Dictionary of the English Language, Fourth Edition.*

Chapter 10, page 281: Quote by Herakleitos, translated by Guy Davenport, from *7 Greeks,* copyright © 1995 by Guy Davenport. Reprinted by Sales Territory: U.S./Canadian rights only.

Chapter 12, page 340: "The Giant's Causeway" from *Irish Fairy Tales and Legends* retold by Una Leavy. Copyright © 1996 by The Watts Publishing Group Ltd.

Art Credits

Beverly Doyle 28; John Edwards Studio 81; Ken Goldammer 12; Nenad Jakesevic 163, 164, 168, 381, 404; Rich McMahon 44, 323; Gary Overacre 340–341; Matthew Pippin xiv, 236–237. All other artwork created by Publicom, Inc.

Map Credits

This product contains proprietary property of MAPQUEST.COM Unauthorized use, including copying, of this product is expressly prohibited.

Photography Credits

Cover *Clockwise from top left* Copyright © Michael J. P. Scott/Stone/GettyImages Copyright © Panoramic Images; Copyright © Dave Bartruff/Corbis; NASA; **ii–iii** NASA; **ii** *top left* Copyright © Michael J. P. Scott/Stone/GettyImages; *top right* Copyright © Panoramic Images; **iii** *top* Copyright © Dave Bartruff/Corbis; **vi** *bottom* NASA; *children* (See page 14 for full credits.); **vii** *left* Terry Wild Studio; *bottom* Copyright © Panoramic Images; *top* D. Robert and Lorri Franz/Corbis; *right* Copyright © SuperStock; **viii** *top* Michel Zabe/Art Resource, New York; *center* AFP/Corbis; *bottom* Staffan Widstrand/Corbis; **ix** *top left* Erich Lessing/Art Resource, New York; *bottom left* Dave Bartruff/Corbis; *bottom right* Hulton|Archive/Getty Images; *top* Erich Lessing/Art Resource, New York; *top right* Reunion des Musées Nationaux/Art Resource, New York; *center right* Scott Gilchrist/Archivision.com; **x** *top left* S. Bavister/Robert Harding Picture Library; *bottom left* John Noble/Corbis; *bottom* John Launois/Black Star Publishing/PictureQuest; *bottom right* AFP/Corbis; *top* Copyright © Brannhage/Premium/Panoramic Images; **S12** Reprinted with the permission of the *St. Louis Post Dispatch,* 2002; **S13** The Granger Collection, New York; **S26** Kevin Schafer/Corbis; **S29** The Granger Collection, New York; **S30–31** Stephanie Maze/Corbis; **S32** Mary Evans Picture Library.

UNIT ONE

2–3 NASA; **4** *bottom right* NOAA; *left* Copyright © Owen Franken/Stock Boston/PictureQuest; *top right* Science Museum/ Science and Society Picture Library, London.

Chapter 1

14 *top left* Brian A. Vikander/Corbis; *top center* Owen Franken/Corbis; *bottom left* Tim Thompson/Corbis; *center left* Kevin Schafer/Corbis; *bottom center* Maria Taglienti/The Image Bank/GettyImages; *center right* James A. Sugar/Corbis; *bottom right* Nicholas deVore III/Photographers Aspen/PictureQuest; *top right* Dean Conger/Corbis; **15** *top* John Callahan/Stone/GettyImages; *bottom left* The Purcell Team/Corbis; *center left* Helen Norman/Corbis; *center* Nik Wheeler/Corbis; *bottom center* Dennis Degnan/Corbis; *center right* Neil Rabinowitz/Corbis; *bottom right* Martin Rogers/Corbis; **16** *top* Copyright © Jim West; *bottom* K. Gilham/Robert Harding Picture Library; **17** *top* Picture Finders/eStock Photography/PictureQuest; *bottom* The Military Picture Library/Corbis; **18** *bottom* Thomas Hoepker/Magnum/PictureQuest; *top* Copyright © Ellen Senisi/The Image Works; **19** *left* Oliver Benn/Stone/GettyImages; *right* Copyright © Alon Reininger/Contact Press Images; *center* Copyright © Alex

Farnsworth/The Image Works; **20** *top right* Copyright © Jim West; *bottom left* Richard Drew/AP/ Wide World Photos; **21** NASA/Roger Ressmeyer/Corbis; **22** Joseph Sohm/Visions of America, LLC/PictureQuest; **23** *bottom* Joe Sohm, Chromosohm/Stock Connection/PictureQuest; *top* Scott Teven/Stock Connection/ PictureQuest; **24** *right* Hulton|Archive/Getty Images; *left* Lindsay Hebberd/Corbis; **26** *left* Dean Conger/Corbis; *right* K. Gilham/Robert Harding Picture Library; *center* Chris Andrews Publications/Corbis; **30** *bottom left* Picture Finders/eStock Photography/PictureQuest.

Chapter 2

32–33 Copyright © SuperStock; **33** *top* NASA; **34** *top* Christopher Morris/Black Star Publishing/PictureQuest; *bottom* David Muench/Stone/GettyImages; **35** *left* The Granger Collection, New York; **36** Schafer and Hill/Stone/ GettyImages; **37** *top* Christopher Morris/Black Star Publishing/PictureQuest; *bottom* World Perspectives/Stone/ GettyImages; **38** Copyright © Eastcott-Momatiuk/The Image Works; **39** David Muench/Stone/GettyImages; **42** *top left* Ethnic Art Institute of Micronesia; *top right* National Maritime Museum Picture Library, London; *bottom right* Royalty Free/Corbis; **43** *bottom* Austrian Archives/Corbis; *center right, top* National Maritime Museum Picture Library, London; *center left* Reproduced with permission of Garmin Corporation; **45** *right* The Granger Collection, New York; **47** The Newberry Library/The Granger Collection, New York; **50** David Muench/ Stone/GettyImages; **51** NASA.

UNIT TWO

52–53 Copyright © Panoramic Images.

Chapter 3

66–67 Paul A. Souders/Corbis; **67** *top* James Randklev/Corbis; **68** *bottom* Michael Melford/The Image Bank/ GettyImages; *top* Raymond Gehman/Corbis; **69** *right* Corbis; *left* Pat O'Hara/Corbis; **70** Michael Melford/ The Image Bank/GettyImages; **71** *top* D. Robert and Lorri Franz/Corbis; *center* Bettmann/Corbis; *bottom* Bettmann/Corbis; **72** *right* Paul A. Souders/Corbis; *left* Copyright © Didier Dorval/Masterfile; **73** M. L. Fuller and the U.S. Geological Society; **74** Paul A. Souders/Corbis; **75** Copyright © F. Hoffman/The Image Works; **76** Bettmann/Corbis; **78** *top* Raymond Gehman/Corbis; *bottom* Phillip Gould/Corbis; **79** David Reed/AP/ Wide World Photos; **82** *right* David Reed/AP/Wide World Photos; *left* Corbis.

Chapter 4

84–85 Copyright © Tom Jelen/Panoramic Images; **85** *bottom right* Dennis Brack/Black Star Publishing/ PictureQuest; *top left* Reuters NewMedia Inc./Corbis; *bottom left* Ed Kashi/Corbis; *top center* Copyright © Marianne Barcellona/Time Pix; *center* Reuters NewMedia Inc./Corbis; *bottom center* Copyright © David Lassman/The Image Works; *top right* AFP/Corbis; **86** *top* The Granger Collection, New York; *bottom* Reuters NewMedia Inc./Corbis; **87** The Granger Collection, New York; **88** *bottom* Copyright © Nancy Richmond/ The Image Works; *top* The Granger Collection, New York; **89** The Granger Collection, New York; **90** Reuters NewMedia Inc./Corbis; **92** *top left* NASA; *bottom right* European Space Agency; **93** *bottom right* European Space Agency; **93–94** NASA The Everett Collection; **94** The Everett Collection; **95** Art Resource, New York; **96** *bottom* Copyright © Topham/The Image Works; *top* The Granger Collection, New York; **100** *top* Tony Freeman; *bottom* Copyright © Rafael Macia/Photo Researchers; **101** *bottom* Copyright © Jim Corwin/Photo Researchers; **102** Copyright © Norbert Schwerine/The Image Works; **103** Teri Bloom; **104** *bottom* U.S. Treasury Department; **105** Kevin R. Morris/Bohemian Nomad PictureMakers/Corbis; **106** Copyright © Monika Graff/ The Image Works; **108** *top* Corbis; *center* Spencer Grant III/Stock Boston/PictureQuest; *bottom* Paul A. Souders/Corbis; **109** *bottom right* Culver Pictures; *top* Archive Photos/PictureQuest; *bottom left* Farrell Greham/Corbis; *center* Michael S. Yamashita/Corbis; **110** Tom Vano/Index Stock Imagery/PictureQuest; **111** *right* Terry Wild Studio; *left* William Folsom/Words and Pictures/PictureQuest; **114** *left* The Granger Collection, New York; *right* Terry Wild Studio; *center* The Everett Collection.

Chapter 5

116–117 Copyright © First Light/Panoramic Images; **117** *top* Canadian Museum of Civilization, image number S93–2826; **118** *top* Kevin R. Morris/Corbis; *bottom* Hockey Hall of Fame; **119** *all* The Granger Collection, New York; **120** Kevin R. Morris/Corbis; **121** Private Collection/Phillips, Fine Art Auctioneers, New York/The Bridgeman Art Library; **123** *top* Copyright © James Schwabel/Panoramic Images; **124** Copyright © SuperStock; **125** Copyright © Bill Brooks/Masterfile; **126** Ron Poling/Canadian Press/AP/Wide World Photos; **127** Yves Marcoux/Stone/GettyImages; **128** Bettmann/ Corbis; **131** The Granger Collection, New York; **132** Hockey Hall of Fame; **133** Copyright © J. A. Kraulis/Masterfile; **134** Lee Snider/Corbis; **135** Archivision.com; **138** *top left* Copyright © James Schwabel/Panoramic Images; *bottom left* Copyright © Bill Brooks/Masterfile; *top right* The Granger Collection, New York; *bottom right* Copyright © J. A. Kraulis/Masterfile.

UNIT THREE

140–141 Bill Pogue/Stone/GettyImages.

Chapter 6

150–151 Cosmo Condina/Stone/GettyImages; 151 *top* Kevin Schafer/Corbis; 152 *right* Richard A. Cooke/Corbis; *left* Archivo Iconografico, S. A./Corbis; 153 AFP/Corbis; 154 Danny Lehman/Corbis; 156 *top* Guido A. Rossi/The Image Bank/GettyImages; *bottom* Stephen Frink/Corbis; 157 Galen Rowell/Corbis; 160 *left* Lara Fox; *right* After Hansen 1990: II. Drawn by TW Rutledge. Used by permission; 161 *top* Richard A. Cooke/Corbis; *bottom* Copyright © Craig Lovell/Painet; 162 *top* Mireille Vautier/ Woodfin Camp/PictureQuest; *bottom* Michel Zabe/Art Resource, New York; 165 *bottom* Edwin Sulca Lagos; *top* Werner Forman Archive/Art Resource, New York; 166 Archivo Iconografico, S. A./Corbis; 168 *center left* Kevin Schafer/Corbis; *top left* Guido A. Rossi/The Image Bank/GettyImages; *bottom right* Werner Forman Archive/Art Resource, New York.

Chapter 7

170–171 Robert Frerck/Stone/GettyImages; 171 *top* R.G.K. Photography/Stone/GettyImages; 172 *top* Erich Lessing/Art Resource, New York; *center Cabacete* [Helmet] (c. 1480). Private collection. Photograph courtesy of the Cleveland (Ohio) Museum of Art; *bottom* Danny Lehman/Corbis; 173 *right* The Granger Collection, New York; *left* Richard T. Nowitz/Corbis; 174 *bottom center* Copyright © SPL/Custom Medical Stock Photography; *bottom left* The Granger Collection, New York; *top left* Erich Lessing/Art Resource, New York; *top right Cabacete* [Helmet] (c. 1480). Private collection. Photograph courtesy of the Cleveland (Ohio) Museum of Art; 175 David Hiser/Stone/GettyImages; 177 *top* Schalkwijk/Art Resource, New York; *bottom* Greg Probst/Corbis; 179 *left* PhotoDisc/GettyImages; *right* Bettmann/Corbis; 180 *top* Bettmann/Corbis; *bottom* The Granger Collection, New York; 181 *center* Bettmann/ Corbis; *bottom* Tom Bean/Corbis; 184 Latin Focus.com; 185 J. P. Courau/D. Donne Bryant Stock Photography; 186 *left* Annie GriffithsBelt/Corbis; *right* Robert Frerck/Stone/GettyImages; 187 *top* Danny Lehman; *bottom* Jose Welbers/Latin Focus.com; 189 ZSSD/ Latin Focus.com; 190 *right* Kal Muller/Woodfin Camp/PictureQuest; *left* Copyright © Erwin Nielsen/Painet; 191 Peter Menzel/Stock Boston/PictureQuest; 192 Schalkwijk/Art Resource, New York; 193 Danny Lehman/Corbis; 194 Charles and Josette Lenars/Corbis; 196 *top* Cosmo Condina/Stone/ GettyImages; *bottom* Copyright © Bernard Neuwirtch/Painet; 197 Gary S. Withey/Bruce Coleman/Picture Quest; 198 *top right* Annie Griffiths Belt/Corbis; *bottom right* Danny Lehman/Corbis; *bottom left* Schalkwijk/Art Resource, New York.

Chapter 8

200–201 Copyright © Michel Frigan/Film Works Inc.; 201 *top* Dave G. Houser/Corbis; 202 *bottom* Reuters NewMedia Inc./Corbis; *top right* Copyright © Topham/The Image Works; 203 Copyright © The Image Works; 204 James Strachan/Stone/GettyImages; 205 *center Ladino* Reuters NewMedia Inc./Corbis; *bottom Ladino* Reuters NewMedia Inc./Corbis; *top Ladino* Martin Rogers/Corbis; *bottom right* Archive Photos/PictureQuest; 206 Jeff Greenberg/eStock Photography/PictureQuest; 207 Bill Gentile/Corbis; 208 AFP/Corbis; 209 Copyright © Topham/ The Image Works; 210 AFP/Corbis; 211 *top* Bill Ross/Corbis; *bottom* Copyright © Rob Crandall/StockBoston; 212 Suzanne Murphy-Larronde; 213 Nik Wheeler/Corbis; 215 Sovfoto/Eastfoto/PictureQuest; 216 *center left* Bettmann/Corbis; *bottom left* Richard Bickel/Corbis; *bottom right* Latin Focus.com; 217 Latin Focus.com; 218 AFP/ Corbis; 219 Copyright © Marge George/Spectrum Stock; 220 Reuters NewMedia Inc./Corbis; 221 Scott Sandy/ AP/Wide World Photos; 222 *top* Latin Focus.com; *bottom* Cindy Karp/Black Star Publishing/PictureQuest; 223 Jan Butchofsky-Houser/Corbis; 224 *top* Martin Rogers/Corbis; *bottom* World Pictures/eStock Photography/PictureQuest; 225 Jan Butchofsky-Houser/Corbis; 226 *bottom left* Copyright © The Image Works; *top* Suzanne Murphy-Larronde; *bottom center* Sovfoto/Eastfoto/PictureQuest; *bottom right* Jan Butchofsky-Houser/Corbis.

Chapter 9

228–229 Layne Kennedy/Corbis; 229 *top* Eye Ubiquitous/Corbis; 230 *bottom* David Wolf; *top* Steve Vidler/eStock Photography/PictureQuest; 231 *all* The Granger Collection, New York; 233 Christie's Images/ Corbis; 234 *top* AFP/Corbis; *bottom* Bettmann/Corbis; 235 *bottom* Latin Focus.com; *top* Richard Hamilton Smith/Corbis; 238 Reuters NewMedia Inc./Corbis; 239 *top* Victor Englebert; *bottom* Corbis; 242 Steve Vidler/ eStock Photography/PictureQuest; 243 Copyright © Larry Luxner/Luxner News; 245 *bottom* Tim Page/Corbis; *top* Copyright © Les Stone/The Image Works; 246 David Wolf; 247 *top* Reuters NewMedia Inc./Corbis; *bottom* Bettmann/Corbis; 248 *top* Macduff Everton/Corbis; *bottom* AFP/Corbis; 249 *top* Dagli Orti/National History Museum Mexico City/The Art Archive; *bottom* Garden Picture Library; 250 Latin Focus.com; 251 Cory Langley; 252 *right* Richard Hamilton Smith/Corbis; *left* Victor Engelbert; *center* Charles and Josette Lenars/ Corbis; 253 Victor Engelbert; 254 Staffan Widstrand/Corbis; 256 *bottom left* Christie's Images/Corbis; *bottom center* Victor Engelbert; *top* David Wolf; *bottom right* Staffan Widstrand/Corbis.

UNIT FOUR

258–259 Stuart Dee/The Image Bank/GettyImages.

Chapter 10

270–271 Copyright © James L. Stanfield/National Geographic Society Image Collection; 271 *top* Robert Harding Picture Library; 272 *top* Sef/Art Resource, New York; *bottom left, bottom right* Erich Lessing/Art Resource, New York; 273 Bill Ross/Corbis; 274 Arnulf Husmo/Stone/GettyImages; 275 Walter Bibikow/Index Stock Imagery/PictureQuest; 276 *top left* Jonathan Blair/Corbis; *top right* Eye Ubiquitous/Corbis; *bottom* Johan Elzenga/Stone/GettyImages; 278 *all* Greek Culture Ministry/AP/Wide World Photos; 279 HorreeZirkzee Produk/Corbis; 280 Foto Marburg/ Art Resource, New York; 281 Sef/Art Resource, New York; 282 *left* Nimatallah/Art Resource, New York; *right* Scala/Art Resource, New York; 284 Copyright © Macduff Everton/The Image Works; 285 Erich Lessing/Art Resource, New York; 286 Giraudon/Art Resource, New York; 287 Erich Lessing/Art Resource, New York; 288 *top left* Jeff Rotman; *center* Scala/Art Resource, New York; *bottom right* O. Alamany and E. Vicens/Corbis; *bottom center* Bettmann/Corbis; 289 Erich Lessing/Art Resource, New York; 290 Art Resource, New York; 291 Reunion des Musées Nationaux/Art Resource, New York; 292 Catherine Karnow/Corbis; *spread* Musée de la Tapisserre, Bayoux, France/The Bridgeman Art Library; 293 *top* Jose Fuste Raga/eStockPhotography/PictureQuest; 294 Erich Lessing/Art Resource, New York; 295 *right* Dept. of the Environment, London/The Bridgeman Art Library; *left* The Granger Collection, New York; 296 *top left* Sef/Art Resource, New York; *bottom* Erich Lessing/Art Resource, New York; *top right* Jose Fuste Raga/eStockPhotography/PictureQuest.

Chapter 11

298–299 Bruno Barbey/Magnum/PictureQuest; 299 *top* The Granger Collection, New York; *center* Leonard L. T. Phodes/Animals Animals; 300 *center* Mary Evans Picture Library; *top* Reunion des Musées Nationaux/Art Resource, New York; *bottom* The Pierpont Morgan Library/Art Resource, New York; 301 The Granger Collection, New York; 302 Alinari/Art Resource, New York; 303 *top* Scott Gilchrist/Archivision.com; *bottom* Palazzo Medici-Riccardi, Florence, Italy/The Bridgeman Art Library; 304 *bottom* Scala/Art Resource, New York; *top* Reunion des Musées Nationaux/Art Resource, New York; 305 The Pierpont Morgan Library/Art Resource, New York; 306 Corbis; 307 Giraudon/Art Resource, New York; 309 North Wind Pictures; 310 Reunion des Musées Nationaux/Art Resource, New York; 313 AKG London; 314 *center* Scala/Art Resource, New York; *top* NASA; *bottom* Copyright © Will & Deni McIntyre/Photo Researchers; 315 The Granger Collection, New York; 316 Hulton-Deutsch Collection/Corbis; 317 Victoria & Albert Museum, London/Art Resource, New York; 318 *right* © Courtesy of the Estate of Ruskin Spear/Private Collection/Phillips, Fine Art Auctioneers, New York/The Bridgeman Art Library; *left* Giraudon/Art Resource, New York; 319 *top* Scala/Art Resource, New York; *bottom* Roger Tidman/Corbis; 320 Erich Lessing/Art Resource, New York; 321 Chuck Nacke/Woodfin Camp/PictureQuest; 322 Hulton-Deutsch Collection/Corbis; 324 *top left* North Wind Pictures; *bottom left* Alinari/Art Resource, New York; *bottom right* Hulton-Deutsch Collection/Corbis; *top right* © Courtesy of the Estate of Ruskin Spear/Private Collection/Phillips, Fine Art Auctioneers, New York/The Bridgeman Art Library; 325 The Library of Congress Website.

Chapter 12

326–327 Michael S. Yamashita/Corbis; 327 *top* Owen Franken/Corbis; 328 *top* Ralph White/Corbis; *bottom* Hulton|Archive/Getty Images; 329 Hulton|Archive/Getty Images; 331 *bottom* Hulton|Archive/Getty Images; *center* Gianni Dagli Orti/Corbis; *top* Mark Rykoff/Rykoff Collection/Corbis; 333 *right* Bettmann/Corbis; *left* Hulton|Archive/Getty Images; 334 *top* Hulton|Archive/Getty Images; *bottom* Art Young; 335 Hulton|Archive/Getty Images; 337 *bottom* Hulton|Archive/Getty Images; *top* Hulton-Deutsch Collection/Corbis; 339 Reprinted with the permission of the *St. Louis Post Dispatch,* 2002; 342 Paul Almasy/Corbis; 343 *bottom* Sovfoto/Eastfoto/PictureQuest; *top* Ralph White/ Corbis; 344 *bottom* Hulton|Archive/Getty Images; *top* Sovfoto/Eastfoto/PictureQuest; 345 Culver Pictures; 346 *bottom* Hulton|Archive/Getty Images; *center* The Kobal Collection; 347 Dave Bartruff/Corbis; 348 *right* Sovfoto/Eastfoto/PictureQuest; *left* Hulton|Archive/Getty Images; *center* Hulton-Deutsch Collection/Corbis; 349 Mandeville Special Collections at UCSD.

Chapter 13

350–351 Copyright © Brannhage/Premium/Panoramic Images; 351 *top* Sovfoto/Eastfoto; 352 *top* Premium Stock/Corbis; *bottom* Craig Aurness/Corbis; 353 Mark Rykoff/Corbis; 354 *left* NASA/AP/Wide World Photos; *right* Sovfoto/Eastfoto; 355 Copyright © Giuliano Bevilacqua/TimePix; 356 Bryn Colton/Corbis; 357 *top* Bettmann/Corbis; *bottom* AP/Wide World Photos; 358 Bojan Brecelj/Corbis; 360 David and Peter Turnley/Corbis; 362 Craig Aurness/Corbis; 363 Copyright © Bios (F. Gilson)/Peter Arnold; 364 Scala/Art Resource, New York; 366 Sovfoto/Eastfoto/PictureQuest; 367 *bottom* Hoa Qui/Index Stock Imagery/PictureQuest; *top* Premium Stock/Corbis; 368 AFP/Corbis; 369 Mike Mazzaschi/Stock Boston/PictureQuest; 370 S. Bavister/Robert Harding Picture Library; 371 Copyright © Malcolm S. Kirk/Peter Arnold; 372 *bottom* John Neubauer/Photo Edit/PictureQuest; *top right* Underwood & Underwood/Corbis; *top left* Bettmann/Corbis; 373 *top* Wolfgang Kaehler/Corbis; *left* Paul A. Souders/Corbis; *center* Roger Ressmeyer/Corbis; *bottom right* Academy of Natural Sciences of Philadelphia/Corbis; 374 *left* Bettmann/Corbis; *right* Premium Stock/Corbis; *center* David and Peter Turnley/Corbis.

Chapter 14

376–377 Alan Thornton/Stone/GettyImages; **377** *top* Mark A. Leman/Stone/GettyImages; **378** *top* Ted Spiegel/Corbis; *bottom* www.carpix.net; **379** *bottom right* Michael Neveux/Corbis; *center* AFP/Corbis; **382** *bottom* John Launois/Black Star Publishing/PictureQuest; *top* Copyright © Julian Nieman/Collections; **383** AFP/Corbis; **384** *right* Nik Wheeler/Corbis; *left* Ted Spiegel/Corbis; **385** Hans T. Dahlskog/Pressens Bild; **386** *bottom* AFP/Corbis; *top* Alex Farnsworth/The Image Works; **387** John Noble/Corbis; **388–389** Museo de Firenze Com'era, Florence, Italy/The Bridgeman Art Library; **390** *right* Bettmann/Corbis; *left* Corbis; **391** Bettmann/Corbis; **392** Robert Estall/Corbis; **393** Art Resource, New York; **394** *right* AFP/Corbis; *left* Thomas Hoepker/Magnum/PictureQuest; **396** *bottom center* Erich Lessing/Art Resource, New York; *top* www.carpix.net; *bottom right* Josef Karl Stieler/Archivo Iconografico, S. A./Corbis; **397** Carmen Redondo/Corbis; **399** Chuck Fishman/Contact Press Images/PictureQuest; **400** Bettmann/Corbis; **401** Dennis Chamberlain/Black Star Publishing/PictureQuest; **402** Steven Weinberg/Stone/GettyImages; **403** Vittoriano Rastelli/Corbis; **404** *top left* Copyright © Alex Farnsworth/The Image Works; *top right* Thomas Hoepker/Magnum/PictureQuest; *bottom right* Bettmann/Corbis; *center* Corbis.

The War on Terrorism

US2 Copyright © AFP/Corbis; *inset* Copyright © John Annerino/TimePix; **US3** *top* MapQuest.com; *bottom* Susan Walsh/AP/Wide World Photos; **US4** *left* AP/Wide World Photos; *right* MapQuest.com; **US5** USA TODAY®; **US6–US7** MapQuest.com; **US6** *inset* Copyright © Reuters NewMedia Inc./Corbis; **US7** *top inset* Katsumi Ksashara/AP/Wide World Photos; *bottom inset* Sayyid Azim/AP/Wide World Photos; **US9** *left* AP/Wide World Photos; **US10** USA TODAY®; *top inset* AP/Wide World Photos; *middle inset* Al-Jazeera/AP/Wide World Photos; *bottom inset* AP/Wide World Photos; **US11** *top* Copyright © David Hume Kennerly/Corbis Sygma; *bottom* MapQuest.com; **US12** Copyright © Jeff Christensen/Reuters/TimePix; *inset* Copyright © Greg Mathieson/MAI/ TimePix; **US13** USA TODAY®; **US14** *left* Copyright © Digital Stock/Corbis; *top inset* Copyright © Kent Wood/Photo Researchers; *bottom* FBI/AP/Wide World Photos; *bottom inset* Justice Department/AP/Wide World Photos; **US15** Copyright © Eric Draper/The White House/TimePix.

McDougal Littell Inc. has made every effort to locate the copyright holders for the images used in this book and to make full acknowledgment for their use. Omissions brought to our attention will be corrected in subsequent editions.